DEVIL'S REACH TRILOGY

Books 1-3

J. L. Drake

DEVIL'S REACH TRILOGY

First Print Edition: March 2019

Limitless Publishing, LLC
Kailua, HI 96734
www.limitlesspublishing.com

Formatting: Limitless Publishing

ISBN-13: 978-1-64034-553-9
ISBN-10: 1-64034-553-1

This is a work of fiction. Names, characters, places, and incidents either are the product of the author's imagination or are used fictitiously, and any resemblance to locales, events, business establishments, or actual persons—living or dead—is entirely coincidental.

TABLE OF CONTENTS

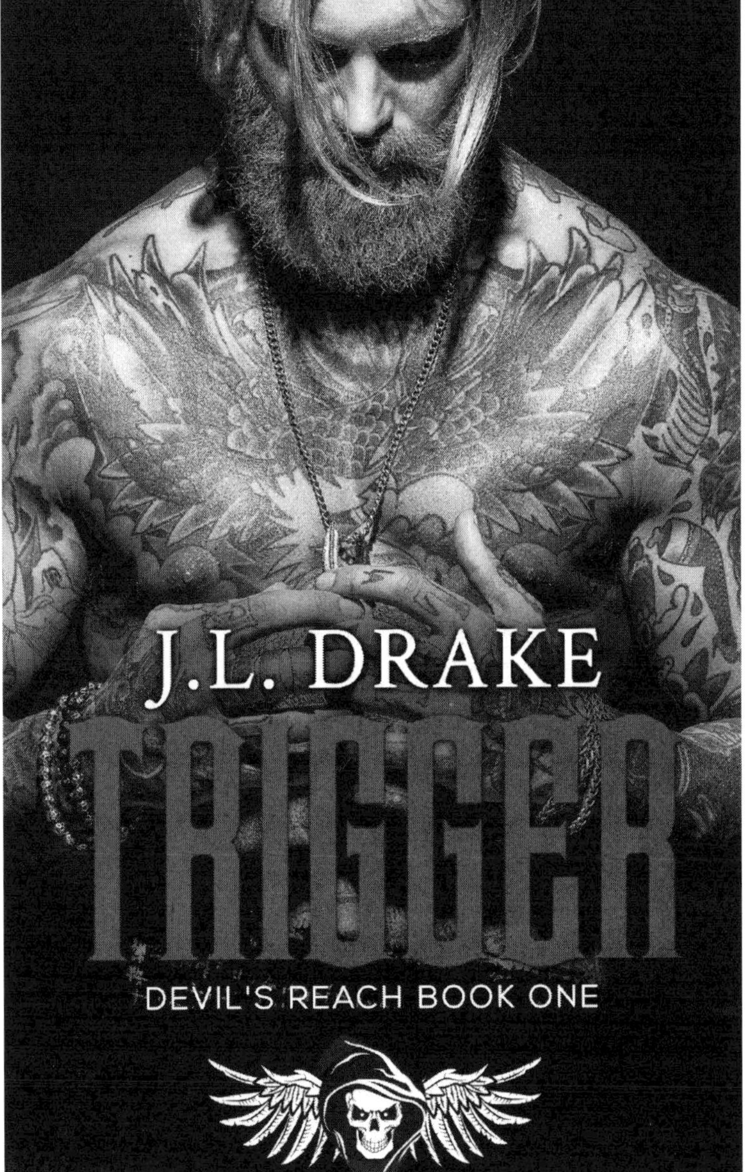

J.L. DRAKE
TRIGGER
DEVIL'S REACH BOOK ONE

PROLOGUE

I used to watch them play in the streets, kick the ball between the cones, and toss their hands in the air. They'd high five, laugh, and stop for ice cream when the truck came around the corner at the same time every Saturday.

They'd sit in the shade, pick at the grass, and tell made-up stories. Sometimes on summer break they'd stay out after dark and play *ghost in the graveyard, head for the hills*. That was, until they spotted me.

Then they'd scatter. Head for their bikes. Disappear.

Why?

Because I was weird…and weird was scary.

CHAPTER ONE

Trigger

Click! Click! Click!

"Shit!" I turned back around, barely missing the bumper of a semi-truck. His horn blew as we drew up along both sides. Two more bullets skimmed by my head and took out the mirror above me. The trucker screamed at us as he tried to keep his vehicle straight.

Jamming my empty clip into my boot, I reached to grab my spare as another truck flashed his lights and hit the horn to alert us we were in his lane. The cliffs were too close to the edge of the road to spare us any room, and the others were gaining on us.

I pointed my empty gun at the trucker to my left. "Slow down!" When he didn't react right away, I moved the gun to his tire. His hand went up and he nodded repeatedly.

He eased off the gas and allowed Cooper and me to slip in front. Cooper's wheel bumped off mine, and I reached out and used my momentum to grab his shoulder to stabilize him. The roar of our bikes ripped through the mountains, alerting my men we were coming.

"Brick!" I held up my hand, and he tossed me a clip. I quickly clicked it in place with my thigh.

The minute I saw them appear in my mirror, I signaled for my men to get ready. With one quick movement, our black van skidded to the shoulder of the road in front of us. The back doors swung open, and the four of us spread apart as my two prospects popped out with their semi- automatics. It was a beautiful sight. Orange lit the dawn sky while bullets flew into their chests, blood shot across the pavement, and three more Stripe Backs lay mangled for their crew to clean up.

They had taken our bait, and our plan worked perfectly. Though we wouldn't go down for the kill, we still made our point. *Don't fuck with my club.*

I smirked at Brick as we each tossed our Cabo Wabo Anejo tequila bottles off to the side.

We picked up speed and made good time well before any cops would be called.

Once we hit the city limits, my phone buzzed. The phone's screen attached to my handlebars popped into view.

Cray: Ready in the morning.

Good. Better to let the fear of what's to come marinate. Than to end it quickly.

I signaled to the men it was time. I decided to take the side streets so we'd be more visible and, as hard as it was, I slowed our speed to show we were in no rush.

It worked. A few local shop owners gave us a wave before they pulled their steel doors down for the night. Mud, the local surf shop owner, was out for his nightly ride and gave us a nod.

Rail and Cooper split off, while Brick and I rounded the back of our clubhouse and got to work.

***

"Ahhhh." Spit jumped from his lips, but most of it pooled in the corners of his mouth. He looked like a wild dog. His pupils dilated when they focused on the tiny eyedropper that hovered above. "Please, no! I'll do anything!"

Brick glanced at me and shook his head. I agreed; it was tiring. As much as I'd have liked to slap that comment right out of his head, I couldn't fault human reactions. It was in their DNA to beg for their lives. I always promised myself that when my day came, I would take it like a man. Silently.

The heat from the hanging lamps plastered my hair to my neck like a second layer of skin. We really needed to turn on the AC.

The slaughter room, as I named it, had tiled walls up to the ceiling, easy for cleaning, and a huge industrial drain in the middle for the larger pieces we needed to wash away in a hurry. No windows, no cameras, just lots of *equipment* to work with.

Brick brushed the hair out of the bastard's sweaty face so he could see me better. I licked my lips as I lowered myself to his level, and my men stiffened at this action. I never lowered myself to anyone's level unless I was about to make a point. His eyes met mine, searching for some trace of a soul. Unfortunately, I was not born with one.

I leaned down so he could see for himself the emptiness that lived inside me. Once he focused in and got a glimpse behind the curtain and I saw this realization, I spoke quietly. "Everyone dies sometime. We all have choices, and you made yours." I motioned for Brick to move into position and spread his eyelid open. The bright pink flesh fought to go back in its place, but it was no match for Brick's fingers. The man shook and kicked, but my expression told him to remain quiet.

Holding the dropper above his eye, I squeezed the rubber and let the tiny drop of bleach fall and coat the pupil. His screams deafened me momentarily, but I welcomed the sound. That was fate's way of thanking me for doing the devil's work.

He kicked and bucked as the minute drop burned its way through his cornea, blinding and eating as it traveled into his brain. His chest heaved and sweat pooled along his collarbone as his neck strained against the pain.

The high I got off his terror made me hard, and my heartbeat raced. I swallowed hard in an attempt to lubricate my parched throat as I continued to blind his left eye. This was what I was made for. It was what separated me from other motorcycle gangs around me. I showed no mercy and punished those who needed it through their greatest fears. I knew it was only when you had nothing that you couldn't be touched.

"Brick." I held out my hand, and he passed me a hunting knife. Walking around the steel table, I took a deep breath.

"You saw too much," I whispered as he fought to see where I was with his clouded eyes. "You heard too much." I grabbed his right ear, pulled it out, and sliced the outer part off. His face twitched, his mouth opened, and his wound quickly drained of blood, but he still stayed mute. "You stole from me." Holding his hand down, I sliced his finger off at the second knuckle. Tossing it out of the way, I pressed on his open palm and stopped the flow of blood, just to fuck with his body.

He jerked to the side and vomited in a silent cry. His mind must be spinning. Too much pain coming from too many directions could throw you off.

"You were part of this family and chose to defy me. Never again will you disobey me." I raised the blade above my head and drove it straight into his shoulder, hoping this would be the last tip to his sanity. "Just in case you think revenge is the answer..." Brick tossed me a switchblade, while Rail grabbed his head and yanked out his tongue. The blade drove through the center.

Silence. Nothing but the hum of the lights.

"See you below."

The voice in my head returned, so I waved at Brick, grabbed my shit, and left.

I waved at Morgan, who was on the phone on a smoke break, then fastened my helmet and wiped my hands clean. Revving the engine, I turned into the sun and drove out onto the smoldering road. The guys could handle the rest.

The engine was hot, and without realizing, I let my mind go there...

The burning poker skimmed my calf, and I jolted back with a scream. Tears streamed down my dirty cheeks as I hugged my knees to my chest. The heat burned the surface then traveled down to the muscle where it spread in a blanket of pure pain.

"Stop!" I cried out, desperate for him to get bored and move on to something else. I was four years old, and this was the fifth time he had done this.

"Come here, boy!" His huge hand swiped at me, but I pressed my back flat to the wall under the table, becoming as small I could.

His brown eyes squinted as he drew back the poker. Dropping it on the floor, he cursed, grabbed a fresh beer from the fridge, banged it loudly on the table, and left.

My heart pounded until it hurt my chest.

If he had wanted to, he could easily have climbed under there. Allen was a fit man, muscles that attracted all the wrong kinds of women, a strong jaw, and defined, broad shoulders with a lean waist.

I tucked the fear away and turned into the cool wall with my cheek pressed to it, seeking some relief from the terrible heat in my leg. Closing my eyes, I stayed under the table until morning, where I knew it could all begin again.

Blinking to clear my head, I pulled off onto a dusty path and headed up into the hills.

The yellow trailer sat on cement bricks; the wheels had been removed years ago. The slider-style windows were open, and broken blinds bounced around in the breeze. The place was a dump, and I wasn't sure why he insisted on keeping it, but that was his decision. He had earned that right many years ago.

Backing under a shady tree, I turned the engine off and unclipped my helmet, hanging it off the handle of my matte black Kawasaki Vulcan 900.

I turned and found a beer can flying in my direction. I caught it and opened it slowly so as not to get sprayed.

"Day?" his raspy voice croaked.

I settled into an old folding chair that dug into my legs. "Three Stripe Backs down, and one of my prospects gone."

"Anyone hurt?"

"Nope."

"Prospect stole? Or leaked?"

"Stole."

"What you remove?"

"Fingers. Eyes. Shoulder. Ear. A little tongue." I shifted so the bar didn't cut into my hip. "This shit is old, Gus."

"I'm old." He passed off my comment, like always. "How much?"

Removing my hat, I swiped my long hair out of my face.

"A little over forty thousand."

Gus shook his head and rubbed his knee. Three stab wounds to the same spot would screw anyone up. "Reason?"

"Does it matter?" I tossed my empty can in the trash before I reached for another. My dusty boots landed heavily on his wooden table.

"Where is he?"

"Thought the guys could have some fun."

He nodded.

We sat in silence. I might not talk much, but I hated the quiet. My knee started to thump, and Gus took the cue. He leaned over and tapped his phone, and a moment later the band Disturbed filled the silence, and I let out a long breath as the guitar hit my ears and calmed me.

"Hungry?" he asked awkwardly as he got out of his chair. His battered body tilted to one side as he stood straighter. His head always hung to the right because of a bullet wound to the spine. Gus was sixty, but his soul was thirty.

"No." I downed my beer and rose. "I should get back."

He followed me to my bike. "Meeting tomorrow?"

"Yeah, eleven." I buckled my helmet.

"New shipment?"

"Yeah."

"Tomorrow," he repeated with a small nod.

Raising two fingers, I waved a goodbye and kicked the engine over.

I weaved in between traffic. The bike was a part of me, and I'd been riding for as long as I could remember. Gus always joked that I drove before I learned how to walk. It was the closest thing I ever felt to freedom.

Two headlights flashed in my mirrors, a signal for me to pull over. I waited until I was sure who it was, but he always flashed lights to me the same way. One short, one long. Easing over to the other lane, I exited at the gas station and parked on the shoulder.

The Mustang came to a stop behind me, and Officer Doyle hauled himself out of the car. I chuckled as I sat on my bike and watched him take his sweet-ass time to get to me.

"Trigger, I thought that was you." His voice was raised to give a show to the people watching. Everyone knew my bike, and everyone loved to see me lose my shit on punk cops like Doyle.

"You found me," I said, playing along. "Now that you have, what can I do for you?"

Doyle kept his back to the spectators as he removed his sunglasses and cleaned them with the side of his oversized shirt. "I heard your boys got into a little trouble last night."

"Not sure what you're talking about." I shrugged. "What happened?"

"Eli's boys got hit."

Huh. "Alive?"

"Two dead, one hanging on."

"Wasn't mine."

He smirked and leaned closer. He smelled like cherry chew. "And if it was?"

I laughed at his act. I'd bet Doyle had never fired his gun other than training. "You got something to say, Doyle?"

He bent my mirror to straighten his tie, and my fingers twitched to break his. "Known you a long time, Trigger. I also know when you're lying."

Looking into the crowd who had nothing better to do than watch, I spoke very carefully, because I knew my switch was about to flick. "You have no idea who I really am. If you have a problem with my guys, you come to me with proof."

"Your boys better have some strong alibis."

"Do me a favor, Doyle. Give your sister a kiss for me." Just as he went to flip me off, I skidded my bike, kicking up a dust storm before I raced down the ramp and onto the freeway.

Letting the engine sooth my nerves as I wove through the cars, it wasn't long until I was back in my own territory and making my way down the street and into the abandoned movie theater I owned where I parked my bike. I took the elevator up to my place.

I needed some time to think.

"We are all moving forward, and my past's catching up. Time's a-running out, and my days are numbered. Too strong to run, too proud to hide, for this I'll pay, for this I'll die," I sang, watching the lights flicker below me. I leaned my weight into the hot stone wall that overlooked Santa Monica, my guitar propped on my thigh, and plucked the strings to one of my own songs.

I could see for miles. This was my town, and this was my spot. Everyone knew when I was here to leave me the fuck alone. I stroked flint against metal and held the flickering flame to the end of the joint. With a deep drag, the smooth smoke traveled to the bottom of my lungs. I could feel it dancing around inside me. I squinted, tipped my head back, and made an O with my lips, letting a trail of white float up toward the stars.

The joint slipped further between my fingers, and I brushed the strings, sending blues rock into the warmth of the night.

My mind raced back to this morning when everything had changed. The possibility that the club may have more rats was making my neck tick. I would need to flush them out with whatever means possible. Then I'd deal with them personally.

I put my guitar down and ran my hands through my hair, letting it drop back down over my shoulders. I needed an outlet, so I stripped off my vest and hung it over an old chair so the devil could stare at me. Pulling my phone free, I swiped to hear *The White Buffalo*, turning the volume up and letting it cut through the silence. I hated silence; it brought too many memories. *Of him*.

I removed my t-shirt, flexing my neck back and forth, then pulled my arms over my head and leaned back. My fingers cracked as I laced them together and gave a good tug. I stared at the punching bag for a second then let loose.

My lips curled from the impact that pounded my muscles like a hammer. Pain was good. Pain was easy to control. Every other emotion was just a waste of time.

Twisting my torso, I did a roundhouse and kicked the black bag high in the air.

Punch, punch, punch, punch. I couldn't get enough until my arms locked and my throat begged for water. I wiped my face clean and brushed my hair out of my face, holding it in place with my ball hat. Kicking open the cooler, I popped open a cold beer and leaned against the rail.

Finally, the voice was muted, but I knew it wouldn't last long.

My phone vibrated next to me.

Brick: Prospect has been dropped off.

***

Tess

I poured myself another glass of wine from the bottle that sat on my night stand. With the lights down low, I looked around my room and was thankful I was alone tonight.

Picking up the heavy book, I settled back and pulled the duvet up to my chin. My eyes scanned for the place where I left off a moment ago.

"Please stay and let me protect you." His face is inches from hers. He gently lifts the sheet and dries the corners of her eyes. "You have to trust me."

I let the book fall forward onto my lap, my eyes closed. Damn, I had to keep reading. Where was I? Oh, right. *"Did you spend the whole night with me?"*

I let the book fall again. I'd never get this book read if I kept allowing myself to become *her*, but should I? I reached for my bag and dumped it out in front of me and grinned at the purple lipstick that just so happened to have a fresh new battery inside. Why the hell not?

Later, before turning out the light and settling in for the night, I got out from under the sheets and looked out the window. I loved the night sky; something about it was peaceful. A flash of movement caught my attention, and I turned the lamp off so I could see better. Oh, my. "*Hello,* Remington Tate." I opened my window. I was totally creepin', but come on…

It was about ninety degrees in Santa Monica, yet this guy was wearing a hoodie. He moved about like a dancer, his fists hitting the bag. I heard the *bang, bang, bang* as his fists made contact with it. It was fascinating to watch. The rooftop he was on was only slightly higher than my window and gave me a good view of him, backlit by the moon. It was quite a beautiful sight.

I grew tired in spite of myself and knew tomorrow would be a busy day, including more unpacking stuff that wasn't even mine. I dragged my gaze away from the rooftop boxer and glanced around the room. It was much better than my old place. Well, anything was better than my old place. Closing my eyes to the memory, I tried to push his scent out of my mind, although I still felt the deep ache. Tears prickled my eyes, but I kept them away. I channeled the hurt into anger—something I was a pro at. Sadness never healed anyone.

I was to start a new job tomorrow at Helmond's Bar. It might be only temporary until I found something else. I didn't want to be serving drinks forever, but damn, it was money, and I needed that right now.

My phone lit up, and I smiled at the text.

Matt: T-minus eight hours.

Tess: You better be there when I arrive.

Matt: Have I ever let you down?

My heart warmed a little.

Tess: Never.

Holding up my beloved camera, I snapped a picture of my rooftop boxer, hoping I had captured the light just right. I knew it would be an image I would wouldn't easily forget.

"Night," I whispered before I crawled into bed and slipped the book under my pillow. I hoped it would bring me good dreams.

***

Nearly falling into one of the boxes, I dug for the black leather skirt and red tank that Matt told me to wear. Once dressed, I wiggled into my high heeled boots and glanced at myself in the mirror propped up against the wall. I leaned upside down and ran my fingers through my long blonde hair to give it a little more volume. Five bike chains wrapped my left wrist halfway up to my elbow, and my silver hoop earrings swung as I moved, giving me an extra pop of color.

I was never a girl who could wear cute sundresses and carry Prada bags. There was too much shit going on inside to ever wear something so cheerful.

Grabbing my bag, I downed a glass of OJ I'd bought from the gas station across the road, and then locked the door and ran downstairs and out to the sidewalk. I wasn't far from the address of my new job, but Matt had made some comment about how I should be careful which streets I used. Trouble was, he never said which ones. He told me to use a cab, but that was ridiculous. I'd Googled the location and saw it was only a fifteen-minute walk. *Sorry, Matt, but I will not call a cab for that.* Money was not something I had a lot of at the moment.

Holding the scrap of paper, I headed east and let the warm morning air wake me. That was, until I felt my bag vibrate. Not recognizing the number, I answered it, tucking the Post-it in my boot.

"Hello."

"You want to tell me where you are this time?"

My blood pressure dropped.

"What do you want?" I held up my hand to a car to let him know I was about to jaywalk. The driver whistled, and I flipped him the bird.

"Just want to know where you are. I have that right, Tessa."

"No, you don't."

There was such a long pause I looked down at the phone to see if it was still connected. After a moment, the screen indicated the call had ended. So much drama was laced up with that woman. I hurried as fast as I could. I really should have done a practice run, but moving your life from one state to another was exhausting. A few more blocks and two turns, and I shielded my eyes to read the number on the wall.

Wait. I must have taken a wrong turn. *Dammit.*

Turning back around and getting completely confused, I saw a few guys staring me down. I felt a bit uncomfortable but tried to act normal. With my head up, attempting to show confidence, I hurried but tripped in my stupid boots and tumbled to my knees. My phone went flying, leaving me to wince as pain shot through my legs.

"Yeah, right where she should be," one guy called out, making me blush from head to toe.

I scrambled to stand, when one of them reached for my arm and hauled me up like a child.

"As much as you looked good on your knees, that fall looked like it hurt. You okay?" My eyes met an elderly man, maybe in his sixties, a scary-ass lookin' dude. A deep scar ran from his right eye down to the corner of his mouth. He reeked of beer, which literally took my breath away.

"I'm fine." I pulled my arm out of his grip and somehow plastered on a smile to be nice. I caught sight of his biker vest. In fact, they all were wearing them. A skull with a devil and a snake coming out of its eye was patched on the back of them. ***Satan's Serpents.***

I should have been terrified, but all that ran through my head was I was going to be late on my first day. *I can't let my best friend down.*

One of the guys handed me my phone, but when I reached for it, he pulled it away. He clicked on the screen and grinned at the picture of me and my friend Mags.

"Pretty dress." He winked and handed it back to me. "Wear it on our date next week." My face dropped further…if that was even possible. I'd lived with men like this, and it was tiring behavior.

He started to say something else, but a loud rumble from a pack of motorcycles deafened me as they drove by a cross street. A stillness spread through all the men.

Four guys on choppers slowed as they caught sight of us. Traffic didn't seem to mind. Sunglasses covered their eyes, but I knew they saw us. I was frozen, waiting for something bad to happen. The tension was so thick it made it hard to breathe.

A few pulled their guns, but the old man with the scar shook his head, and they stood down.

Seriously, where the hell am I?

Again, the devil made its way into my vison, only their jackets had a skull resting in the Grim Reaper's outstretched hand. *Devil's Reach* was patched across their shoulders. I noticed both jackets had Santa Monica on them.

Sensing the men were preoccupied, I took advantage of the moment and darted down the street.

I fished around in my boot for the stupid Post-it that I had written Matt's address on.

Fifteen minutes later, and I was finally there—5627 Dustin Street.

I stared up at the rundown building with painted black windows. It was huge and wide, but the few buildings around it were abandoned and had some broken windows. I really hoped I had the address wrong.

I tugged on the handle, and to my disappointment, it opened, letting out a cloud of smoke. I coughed to catch my breath, and when my eyes stopped stinging, I took in my surroundings.

Holy fuck…

"You want somethin'?" a husky voice barked at me from behind the bar. I blinked to clear the haze and observed a tall man with a long beard that stopped at his belt. Tattoos ran around his shaved head like the rings on Saturn.

I shook my head and realized it might be wise to leave. "I think I might be in the wrong place."

He poured a shot and slid it my way, nodding for me to take it. I stepped up to the bar and thought *why the hell not?* At that point, I was sure I'd lost the job anyway. I tossed it back while he watched. "Where are you supposed to be?"

I waited for the burn of the whiskey to leave before I answered. "I'm looking for my friend Matt Montgomery. I think I wrote the address down wrong."

He studied me a moment then his eyebrow ring twitched as his eyes narrowed in on me.

"Brick! Company!" he shouted over my head.

Seriously?

"No, I'm looking for a Matt."

"Not anymore."

Huh?

A moment later, a door flew open and out came my best friend, who I hadn't seen in six years, wearing a Devil's Reach vest.

Okay…

He flew toward me, scooped me up, and greeted me with a big bear hug.

Hold up!

"Tess!" He smiled down at me through a mass of long brown hair that touched the bottom of his ears. "You look amazing!"

"You expected less?" I joked to give me an extra moment to process the situation. "Um, not sure where to start here, so…what's with the name *Brick*?"

His eyes flickered with something before he spoke. "Nickname."

"Okay." I noticed the words Vice President patched above his new name. What had I missed?

As bizarre as the situation was, I couldn't deny how good it was to see him. It was like hugging your blanket when you were a child.

Instant comfort.

I hugged him even tighter. “You look completely different.” I tugged on his long hair. “I love it!”

He rested me back on the ground, and I swatted his arm, nodding at the fucking motorcycle bar. “Thanks for the warning.”

A guilty grin spread across his face. “I didn’t want to run the risk of you not coming.”

“How well do you know me?” I shook my head, feeling better already. “Anything is better than the house.”

He reached for my hand and slid my bracelets up to check my wrists. His lips pressed together as his finger ran over the vertical scar on my left wrist.

“I know you better than anyone.”

I pulled my hand free and pushed the bracelets back in place.

“How are you?” Before I could answer, he gave me his look. “Without the bullshit, Tess.”

Stepping back, I noticed the bartender was listening to us with no shame.

“Fine. Like I said, happy to be away. You going to show me around?”

His shoulders sagged, but he didn’t push it. Instead, he looked over my shoulder at something.

“Yeah, I can do that.” He waved around the bar. “Helmond’s Bar. Which is the club’s bar.”

“Okay.” I saw their cut picture was painted onto the wall in black and gray, and there were three women who were high on something. Two of them were draped over a chair and a bench, and the other was butt naked, spread-eagle on the pool table.

“Nothing you haven’t seen before.” Brick shrugged.

A little boy, maybe six years old, came running out from behind the bar with what I hoped was a water gun and started to shoot the woman on the chair in the face. She squinted at him before she snatched it away and tossed it across the room.

“Go get ready for school.”

I shook my head before I saw Brick point. “That’s Gus’s old lady, and his son. You’ll meet him later.” I nodded, and he went on. “Through those double doors,” he pointed to the wall underneath the Devil’s Reach logo, “is the president’s office and the meeting room. Most of the time, the doors are open, but when there’s a meeting, they stay closed and the bar shuts down.” He beckoned for me to follow him past the bar and out through another set of huge, heavy doors. My guess was they would be bulletproof.

We headed to our left first. The hallways were wide and the floors were tile. The walls were painted a dark beige, and to my surprise, it didn't look too rundown, not like the front of the building. After a few quick glances out the windows, I saw the building was formed into a horseshoe with a party place in the middle.

"These are the bedrooms for us main guys. Pres, Vice Pres, Sergeant-at-Arms, Treasurer, and so on. This is mine." He pointed quickly before he turned me around and started back up the hallway again. Once we passed the huge doors, he opened another and let me step inside. Two women who looked to be my mother's age, and one guy who was about the size of a house, glared at me.

"Kitchen. No need to tell you their names. They have zero personality, and even if they did, they never leave this room, so it's pointless."

"Hi." I waved, and the guy snickered something in Spanish, so I shrugged. "Never knew an MC could live so well."

"We are not like most MCs." Brick laughed as he opened the door for me to leave the kitchen. "Down there are more bedrooms."

"What about that door at the end?" I noticed the same type of doors we went through to get into the living corridors were also at the end of the hallway.

"Ah, that's to go outdoors. They're normally locked, so just use this one." He tapped the door in front of me. "Okay, so, for the rules." He led me outside, maybe away from ears. I didn't know.

The courtyard was mostly concrete, with a lot of trees that shaded the actual building. There was a huge rectangular pool with a little changing house next to it that matched the look of the stone barbecue. Tables and lounge chairs were scattered around, and an old pickup truck was off to the side, hidden between some trees against the stone wall that ran along the perimeter. The place did give you the sense of safety, that was for sure.

"I get it, it's a lot to take in." Brick looked up at me with one eye closed. I sat so he didn't have to squint.

"Not that bad."

"When you're not working, you can be out here. We normally are. The guys will have their families over for Friday night dinners. You'll be working with Morgan. He's good, doesn't talk much, but he'll teach you lots. You got a problem, talk to him."

"Morgan have a family?"

"Nope. You saw Gus's old lady on the chair. Her name is Vib. She's a junkie, but she shouldn't be too much of a problem. They have two kids, Den and Fin. They are little dicks, but they're family, so we love them."

Awesome. I wasn't a huge kid person.

"Rail and Cooper are two more main guys who live here. Rail only thinks with his dick, so stay away. Cooper is…well, you can be friends with him. I'll allow that."

I smacked his arm.

"Don't touch the drugs. There's a lot kickin' around. Us higher-up guys don't touch it. Trigger, the president, wants us to stay clean. You can do pot, but not coke, okay?"

"Have you ever known me to stick a tube up my nose?"

"Been six years, Tess. A lot has changed."

"Like your name."

He laughed darkly. "Yeah, a few of us adopted a nickname after our first kill."

"Thanks for that image."

"Think about Rail's." He laughed then stood and offered me a hand. "Come on." He held my hand tightly as we walked back inside. "You have any problems, you come to me. Promise?"

"I will." I waited for him to close the door behind me, and I noticed the bar had gotten a lot busier. At least the naked chick on the pool table had closed her legs. "So, where am I working, exactly?"

He tipped his head toward the bar. "Morgan," he called out to the bartender as we joined him. "This is Tess. She's the new bartender." Morgan didn't blink an eye at me as he opened the wooden latch to let me in behind the bar top. "Hey." Matt tugged me closer. "It's Brick now, okay?"

"Yeah, that's been burned into my head nicely."

"We only deal in cash." Morgan started right in. "The guys with the skull patches on their collars drink for free. No one else, no exceptions." I failed to mention that he just gave me a free drink. "We only serve beer and hard liquor." He pointed to the bottles. "You clean?"

I glanced up at him, puzzled.

When I didn't respond, he flipped my arms over and checked my skin for tracks. "Take off your shoes."

"Pardon?"

"She's clean," Brick barked out as a warning. Morgan nodded once then went back to explaining things like he didn't just ask if I shot heroin.

"You can drink, but don't get drunk," he mumbled and stroked his thin beard and twisted it around his finger as he thought. "Don't call him Matt. His name is Brick. It's disrespectful to the club. He earned that name."

So I've heard, although Brick never used the word earned.

"Don't ask questions you don't want to know the answer to," Morgan muttered, and *Brick* seemed to agree.

Shouting from a room off to the side drew my attention, followed by a loud crash. I looked at Brick, who just shook his head as if to ignore it.

Morgan handed me another shot. "Have you ever bartended before?"

"I have."

"All you need to know is how to read the labels, pour a shot, and count." He tapped his glass to mine and tossed the shot back, and I followed suit.

"Any tips you make are yours. As long as the till is even, you're good. Make sure you wear something hot, give the guys a little somethin' to look at."

"Seems easy enough."

Morgan glanced at Brick with a bored expression then back to me. "I give her to the end of the shift before she fucking quits."

"Thanks." I glanced over at Brick, who gave me a playful wink.

A door burst open and out tumbled a man with a face full of blood. He stumbled to the bar with one eye open and the other swollen shut. I noticed Morgan stood back to see how I'd handle the situation. It didn't rattle me; not much did anymore. Brick's comfort with the situation made it obvious the guy was on their shit list. I slammed a shot glass down, poured some whiskey, and when he reached for it, I slid it aside.

"Seven fifty."

His watery, bloodshot eye stared at me. It took a second, but he realized I wasn't screwing around, and his face scrunched up.

"Bitch, give me the drink."

"Seven fifty." My hip cocked out as I raised my chin to hold my own.

He reached for it again, but I moved it further away. He didn't have the skull patch Morgan mentioned, and I wasn't going to give it to him for free. The guy leaned forward, grabbed my arm hard, and pulled me close to his face. I had to choke back the smell of blood and sweat.

"Listen, you little cuntface. You want to know what it feels like to get a fist to the—" One moment he was threating, and the next his head was slammed onto the bar top by a very battered hand.

I jumped back to see a massive man with his nose just inches from the asshole's face. His eyes were murderous as "Get the fuck out," hissed from his lips. He then picked him up and dropped him to the floor like he hardly weighed anything. Moments later, the asshole was gone, and I was left staring at the big, lean man with one hell of a set of deep green eyes. I forgot how to breathe when they locked onto mine. His white shirt was stained with blood, his knuckles were raw, and his bottom lip was cracked. His dark hair curled slightly under around his collarbone.

I rubbed my arm, the pain slowly easing.

"He's out," the man grunted to Brick. Even though he continued to stare at me. "Take care of it."

"Will do," Brick answered from somewhere close. His fingers brushed over my shoulder. "You all right, Tess?"

"Yeah."

"Trigger, this is Tessa." Brick cleared his throat. "She's the one I was tellin' you about."

Trigger? Oh, yes, the pres.

"Tess," I corrected him.

Trigger didn't say a word but held my gaze then looked down my front and back up again. His tattooed hand tugged on the bottom of his short beard. My skin heated, my chest burned, and my throat went dry. Mother of hell, his gaze was intense. Though I knew men like this and they were all the same, I was surprised by my reaction.

Trigger leaned forward to reach behind the bar, his eyes still locked with mine. He removed the whiskey bottle and tossed the cap next to me. He downed about a quarter of it then finally broke his hold to focus on Brick.

"They're gonna eat her alive." His voice had a little rasp to it, but my annoyance got the better of me.

"Gotta love the encouragement here, boys." I snickered and ignored his expression. Brick sucked in a sharp breath, and I guessed people didn't talk to him like I just did, but I really didn't care.

I worked a long shift and met everyone as they trickled in and out of the bar. I turned a deaf ear to all conversation that didn't include me. I felt like everyone was testing me to try to trip me up. So I kept my mouth shut and did my job to make sure everyone paid. Brick stayed true to his word to hang around and make sure I was okay.

Morgan helped me a few times, but for the most part, I got it. At the end of my shift, I took a seat in a booth with Brick, and he ordered us a late dinner.

The place was busy, the smoke got thicker, and the music pounded.

"When did you join?" I asked right before I bit into my burger.

I was surprised it was good. Most bar food sucked. I wasn't picky. I even ate from a stranger's plate once, but I did know good food, and this was pretty damn good.

"Six years ago." I looked up at him. "Right after you went back. I followed a lead that my father was part of the Devil's Reach. He's dead now, but I got accepted in and quickly climbed the ladder in the family."

I examined his vest and saw the skull on the front and VP patch.

"Trigger is the president, I'm vice, and Rail, who I advise you stay away from, is below me. You'll meet him tomorrow."

I rolled my eyes. "Do you like this life?"

He stuffed in a handful of fries and chased it with his beer. "Yup, best life so far." He eyed me as he thought. "Did they let you leave easily?"

"What's the bloody guy's story from this morning?"

Brick tapped his ring against his bottle. I could tell he was getting annoyed with me dodging his questions. "Stole from the club. Does your mom know you're here?" I was about to change the subject again, but he gave me a warning by crossing his arms.

"She knows I'm not in Vegas." I shook my head, remembering that morning. "I need to change my number."

"I'll get you a new one," he added quickly. "Are you all right in that apartment? Sorry it's not closer, but I'm working on that now."

"No, don't. It's perfect. Thank you. As soon as I get some cash coming in, I'll pay—"

"No, you won't." He cut me off and glanced across the bar at someone. "Just don't leave this time. If you need anything, you come to me, and I'll help you." He looked back at me then down to my stomach. "When did you get the tat?"

I closed my eyes briefly and hated that he went there. Inching down my shirt, I shifted.

"Tess."

"Two months…after you left."

"How was the funeral?"

I huffed loudly and pressed the pain down. "No money, no funeral."

His jaw locked in place before he spoke. "They never helped out?"

"You're forgetting she broke a house rule, Brick," I muttered darkly.

"Where is she?"

"With a friend."

"She okay?"

I finally looked at him full in the eyes. "Would you be?"

I saw his chest rise and fall while he thought about it. "No. I wish you didn't leave me when you did."

"You know why I did. No sense looking back. It doesn't—"

"Brick!" a larger man with thin gold glasses and a kind smile shouted in our direction.

"Shit, I gotta go." He moved out from behind the table. "That's Big Joe, Trigger's muscle. If he calls on you, go. His bark isn't nearly as big as his bite." He winked as my stomach turned. "Stay. If you want my room, it's the second door on the right. Take the bed. I have a sofa. If you're going to leave, Morgan will walk you home." He leaned over and gave me a quick kiss on the cheek and left.

After I polished off my burger and stole the rest of Brick's fries, I grabbed my bag and headed out into the quiet street. I would rather get comfortable walking home than spend any more time within those walls.

I needed fresh air.

About a dozen bikes were parked out front, and I wondered which one was Brick's. One was blacked out completely and looked like it cost more than a house. It was interesting, with thin gold lines that raced along the edges of the bike. If you looked closely, you could see faint drawings that faded as you walked by it. It was a bad-ass bike, for sure.

My heels pounded the pavement, and I enjoyed the cool breeze on my hot, sticky skin. I couldn't wait for a shower.

Three blocks, then a right, six more blocks, then a…*hmm…*

I heard laughing up ahead and saw the guy from earlier who had my cell phone. Damn! I really *needed* to use my phone so I wouldn't get lost anymore.

I slipped into an alley and hurried around the buildings. It was dark, but it was better than having to deal with those guys. I wished I knew where the border for the club's territory was. I wasn't stupid and knew borders meant everything when it came to motorcycle clubs.

A strong smell hit my nose, and Marilyn Manson's *Beautiful People* caught my attention. Sweat, booze, and desperation swarmed in my head and brought some old comfort seeping to the surface. No windows, no sign, just the beat to the song. Pushing the heavy door open, I stepped inside. Neon purple tube lighting swirled down the hallway, escorting me deep into the Dirty Demons strip club.

The bouncer who stepped in front of me was about twice my width. He flicked his head at me to pass. No need for an ID, no weapons check, and no need for male company.

Interesting.

Three platforms had naked women in cages dancing to the beat. The main stage had two women spinning on poles, and another slid across the stage thrusting her hips in a man's face. The customer tucked a twenty into her g-string before she winked and moved on.

It is a good living.

Slipping into a booth in the corner, I rested my tired feet and ordered a rum and Coke.

I let the music wash over me, and the hairs on my arms stood at attention as the goosebumps pushed them upward. I let my mind wander back to the good old days when things were so much easier.

Mags grabbed my arm as she stepped off the platform. "You're not really going up there? She'll kill you if she finds out."

I tossed my top hat in the air and caught it on my head. "What else can she possibly take from me that she hasn't already?"

"You're asking for trouble."

"Aren't I always?" I winked and saw her devilish smile widen as she motioned for me to go on.

"There's a military party in the front. They're tippin' hot tonight."

"What about—?"

"He's at the bar."

I gave her a quick kiss on the cheek before I took a deep a breath and felt the rush as I stepped out and locked eyes with him.

"You here for amateur night?" The waitress pulled me from my memory and set my drink down on a black napkin.

I handed her a ten and shook my head when she reached out to make change.

"When is it?"

"Every Tuesday, at midnight." I nodded, but she stared at me. "You wax?"

I nodded again.

"Real?" She pointed to my boobs.

"Yeah."

"Impressive." She looked over her shoulder at her boss, who was watching us carefully. "Well, I'd be happy to see you up there."

"Thanks," I muttered into my rum and Coke, avoiding her boss's nasty stare.

Settling in, I watched the girls and how they moved. Some were better than others. A few of them asked me for a lap dance, but I wasn't in the mood. Besides, it would only make the addiction stronger.

My hips shook as I dropped to the ground in a split. I swiveled to my stomach and ever so slowly pulled myself back into a sitting position. Rolling backward, I did a somersault and hooked my leg around the pole. Using my stomach muscles, I grabbed the pole with my hand and twisted into a spin. That was, until I saw her wrap her arm around his neck and look in my direction. Her look of hate ripped right through me.

As soon as the song ended, I rushed off the stage and burst through the doors and out into the stuffy night air. I rubbed my fingers over my wrist, over the spot that nearly took me away from this hell. I needed to get away from here.

I nursed my drink until I grew tired. Waving at the waitress, I found my way back outside. I stayed in the cover of darkness until I was at the back of my building then hurried to the front and let myself in.

Pressing eight on the elevator, I sank into the corner and waited for the floor to arrive. My pillow never felt so good.

CHAPTER TWO

Trigger

I woke to find a female hand rubbing my chest. I groaned when I felt the pounding against my skull. Tossing her hand aside, I headed to the shower while she cursed at me and tugged her pants on.

Women were a dime a dozen around here. I didn't sleep with Peggy. She had been trying to get in my bed for the past three years. She was lonely and desperate, and that was a fucking turn off. Not to mention she had slept with almost the entire club.

Don't need nothing growin' down there. However, she did have a pair of lips that were stronger than a Hoover, so I'd allow her to do that. Touching, however, was off limits, and she bloody well knew that.

"No." I pointed to my t-shirt she was about to pull on.

"Trigger, I don't have a top."

I opened my bedroom door. "Not my problem."

Her mouth dropped as she ripped my shirt off and chucked it at the bed.

"Asshole," she hissed as she came up to me. She pulled back her hand and attempted to slap me, but I blocked it, grabbing her wrist, and tossed her out of my room. I slammed the door behind her.

Get the fuck out!

The shower helped with my hangover. I knew to stay away from tequila, but last night I didn't care. I needed to get the guys to keep an ear to the ground. That feeling in my gut that having a prospect and a hangaround outed for stealing in one month meant something was up.

Just as I was tying my boots, I heard a knock at the door. Opening my phone, I glanced at the camera. Brick.

"Yeah."

He leaned against the door frame with his arms folded and spoke through the door. "I need to take a few days off. I got a call from the hospital that Jilly's been using, and her boyfriend beat her face in again. Need to go pay him a visit."

"Take Maze with you."

He nodded big enough that I could see on the camera. That boyfriend needed to know what a pair of broken knees felt like. Maze was nuts enough to break them on command.

I slipped my cut over my black t-shirt and opened the door. "Do I need to find a new bartender?"

"No," he chuckled, "Tess doesn't scare that easily. She may be small, but she has a set of brass balls."

"Good."

"She's good people, Trigger."

"Time will tell." The girl wouldn't last long, which was a shame because she was sexy as shit. Brick stepped aside as I moved past him. "Check in later." His eyes went down and his face hardened. His sister was a major stress.

"Yeah."

I sat at the head of the table while the guys filed in. One by one, they took their seats, all chatting mindlessly about their days. Mostly it was Rail giving our prospect shit. The boy better be able to take it. Jace learned enough when he was a hangaround, no excuses. There were thirteen months to go before we voted him in or out.

I waited for Cooper to come in. When he did, he set the sample shipment on the table in the center.

"Brick is gone for a few days." As soon as my voice was heard, everyone shut up and listened.

"What's with the little tiger behind the bar?" Gus, my sergeant-at-arms, hobbled in late and took his seat at the corner of the table. Morgan was propped up against the wall and tried to hide his smirk.

Rail leaned out the door to take a look before he whistled. "Those legs wrapped around my head would be all right." A few of the men laughed.

"Brick brought her in," Morgan chimed in as Cooper opened the bag and set the tray out in front of the two prospects.

"She his?" Cooper directed his question to me.

"Don't know." I flicked my joint with my thumb and brushed the ash away. "Cooper, do it."

Cooper dumped the white dust on the tray and handed the pipe to the prospects. I didn't want junkies, but I needed them to check my stash. Without hesitating—because they knew better—they leaned down and snorted the blow.

I watched for their eyes to gloss over and to see their first reaction. It was normally the same with my supplies. It hit hard and smoothed you out in three seconds or so. It was a ride that lasted hours without the hard comedown. My blow was the best on the market.

"Fuck me." Ty, the skinny prospect, rubbed the side of his head then sank back and slid down in his seat. "There's six different colors of red in here."

"Good, moving on." I didn't need to hear from Jace. He was already a puddle on the floor, and that was good enough for me.

"We set for the desert?"

"Yeah." Gus nodded as he lit his cigarette. "East coasters will be arriving sometime next week. They were in Colorado, last I heard."

"Good."

"We good, boss?" Big Joe stuck his head through the door.

I nodded and noticed Tess behind a table. Her long blonde hair swung around her breasts which at the moment bounced in a member's happy face. The bar was closed during our meetings, but some of the members liked to hang around to get orders when we were done.

Tess leaned over to pick up a napkin, and her tight little ass got a slap. My heels dug into the bottom of my boots and my hand twisted the leg of the table. The need to drive my fingers through that asshole's eye sockets nearly brought me to my feet, but the carefully guarded expression that Gus cut me made my senses heighten. I tried to shake the shitty feeling, but it lingered.

I shifted my eyes to where Rail was placing one of the prospect's hands on the other's crotch. He smirked when he saw me then sat back in his chair. They knew they could fuck with them, but when we were in a meeting, they usually behaved.

"Tell the guys to move the product. I want cash in three weeks."

That shut the guys up fast, and they all looked like they didn't hear me right.

"Three weeks, Trigger?" Gus's voice finally broke the silence. "Why not six?"

Rocking back in my chair, I combed my hair with both hands before I lit another joint. Once the first wave of smoke hit my lungs and the slight burn rippled through me, I spoke.

"I want to double our sales."

"Greed only speeds up shit, son."

I snapped my head over to Gus and held his gaze. He was hovering over the line, and when he broke the stare, I knew he got it.

"New Orleans has had some trouble and needs quick cash. I'd rather pull double than tap into our resources."

"We're on it," Rail added, which made the rest agree.

"Meanwhile, find me another prospect." I slapped the table when the vison of my knife slicing the thief's tongue graced my memory. "We're done here."

I waited until they left before I locked the meeting room. A snitch was supposed to stop by, and I had an itch that needed to be scratched.

I took a seat in the back and watched Tess. Her smile was pretty, and it wasn't often we had a pretty face around here. They were mostly desperate and needy or strung out on something. Removing my phone from my pocket, I tossed it on the table and started to look for the snitch's number.

"Can I get you something?" I stopped scrolling, glanced up, and leaned back, spreading my legs so I could study her comfortably. Her breasts were about to spill out of her top, but it wasn't overly slutty. Her legs were long under the skirt that stopped about mid-thigh. She was sexy, all right, and it was hard not to show interest in what was underneath. I took my time and looked her over, keeping my expression neutral.

Her eyes narrowed before she looked over her shoulder. "Was I not supposed to come over? I'm not sure of the rules here. Morgan stepped away, and I didn't want you to wait, so—"

"Whiskey."

"Whiskey," she repeated as she turned and headed back to the bar.

She returned with the glass and the bottle, which I found amusing. Twisting the bottle in her hand, she gripped the neck like she was about jam a needle into her thigh, but she poured it smoothly.

"You've bartended before?" I threw back the drink and kept my eyes on hers.

"Yeah." She smirked bleakly. I inhaled and blew my smoke in her direction, but she didn't flinch.

"Where?"

"A bar."

"Which was…?"

She poured me another and set the bottle next to me. "I'm sure you've never heard of it. Let me know if you need anything else." With that, she left and went back behind the bar.

Normally, if someone spoke to me like that, I'd beat their ass, but there was something about her that entertained me.

"Trigger." Big Joe caught my attention and pointed at a wiry guy who looked like he had way too close a love affair with the needle.

"Hey, man, it's a real pleasure." He reached out to shake my hand, but I didn't stand. He avoided eye contact, which pissed me the fuck off.

"What do you have for me, Ray?"

He lowered his skinny ass into a chair and waved at Tess. She headed right over, but I shook my head. This prick didn't need any of my booze.

"Ray?" I didn't like to repeat myself. Anger started to burn its way to the surface, and I knew he only had a few more minutes.

"Yeah, yeah." His eyes squeezed shut while he thought. "Been talk there's another drug king workin' the west coast." He rubbed his ear like there was a tick inside. "Guess he's got the shit like you do."

"How would you know what he's sellin'?" The familiar taste of tin filled my mouth, and I knew I was close. Who the fuck would come into my territory and sell my blow?

"Well, you know, I bought some." He suddenly realized what he'd said and tried to backpedal. "You…you know, so I could come back here and tell you."

"How much did you buy?"

"Not much."

I leaned forward to make sure he knew I wasn't fucking around. "How much?"

"I only had a hundred on me."

Before the words were out of his mouth, I pulled out my gun and pointed it at his head.

"You owe me thousands, and you bought a hundred dollars from someone else, on my land?"

"It's not what you think, Trigger!" His saliva pooled at the corner of his mouth, and he raised his hands in the air.

"Tess," I called out, and she dropped her glass when she noticed the gun. "Grab a mop."

Bang!

Blood and brain matter flew over tables and splattered on the floor. Rail grinned and held up his drink then threw it back as if to say "well done."

Tess returned with a pale face, but she started to mop up the blood.

"Where's the hangaround?" I shouted, and Big Joe pointed out back.

Two minutes later, he showed up, and I stood to grab the mop by the handle and pulled it away from Tess.

"Deal with this." I tossed it at him.

"Sure thing, boss."

Tess took a couple steps back but continued to watch.

"Get used to it, sweetheart," I hissed as I headed for my office. I needed to make a goddamn call.

***

Tess

Morgan was nowhere to be found, and we were out of vodka. I asked Rail to watch the bar and headed out back to look for more. I finally found the storage room after a lengthy search. Even after Brick's tour, I still found myself taking a wrong turn.

Since I was finally alone, I took a moment to breathe deeply and let what happened come to the surface. I needed to process it. Blood was still tacky on the soles of my boots. I could handle this. Damn, I'd been around worse. Sometimes the brain just needed a moment to tuck it away properly.

"Okay." I shook the tension from my hands and snapped back to it.

"Rum, whiskey." I scanned the labels one by one. Damn, there must have been thousands of dollars' worth of booze there. "Of course, there it would be!" I stretched my fingers up, barely touching the bottom of the vodka boxes which were up so high on the shelf. I reached up again on tiptoe to run my fingers along the bottom to draw the box out.

I truly didn't think this through, because the box wobbled and started to tip forward. Just as I realized what was about to happen, my heart in my throat, someone pressed against me from behind. A pair of muscular forearms stopped the box so it didn't fall on my head. Those same arms flexed as they shoved it back into place.

"Thanks," I whispered through a long breath. He didn't move, just stood like brick wall behind me, so I slowly turned and found myself locked into that deep green gaze again. His expression was blank, unreadable.

Shit, he was strong. Not beefy strong, but *strong-strong*, lean and trim so the muscles were sharply defined.

He placed a hand on my hip and gave it a nudge then leaned up to pull the box down. I couldn't help but notice the handgun stuck in the back of his jeans. It was funny how when you saw a cop with one, it was no biggy, but when a biker had one, it sent another message altogether. The vibe was totally different. Or maybe it was because it had been used to end a man's life barely an hour ago.

"If you get nervous around guns, sweetheart, you shouldn't be working here." Trigger's tone seemed to be a bit softer than before.

"I didn't run, did I?"

Setting the vodka case on top of another box, he rested his back against the wall. His long, dark hair partially obscured his face.

"Yeah, not sure why."

"It's a job." I shrugged.

"Why do you want to work here?"

"It's a job," I repeated.

"Why would an upper-class woman from Vegas want to work here?"

I bit my lip, angry that he'd checked into my past. "It's none of your business."

He actually laughed a little, which I could tell he didn't do often. "It *is* my business. I run this place, this is my family, and I want to know why you're here."

I hesitated only for a second. "Brick is one of my oldest friends, and we've always helped one another out. I hadn't seen him in six years and needed a change, so here I am. If he trusts me, so can you."

"I trust three people, that's it." His green eyes burrowed deeper into mine. He waited for me to spill, but little did he know, I was one stubborn-ass woman. "Tell me."

I looked down at my heels then at my skin-tight dress, which had already earned me fifty bucks in tips, and shook off the unwanted feeling. I shut myself down, took a deep breath, and looked back up at him. "Well, Trigger, it was nice knowing you. I really appreciated the opportunity." His head tilted to the side as I headed for the door and down the hallway.

Damn!

Rail watched me as I collected my bag from beneath the bar. I grabbed my tips and strode for the door when Morgan stepped in my way.

"Where are you going?"

I shook my head, not needing this right now. "I quit," I muttered.

"Seriously? After I finally decided you were a tiger trapped in a kitten's body?"

"I can hold my own. I just don't like being questioned." Why was I talking to him? "Excuse me."

"Tess," Trigger called out from across the room, "my office, now."

Morgan gripped my elbow. "Do as he says, there, little tiger."

"Why?"

"He's the boss and not someone you *ever* want to piss off." Morgan stopped at the open door and nodded at Trigger.

"Shut the door," he ordered as I came inside. I folded my arms, not sure what to do. His office was big and open, with not a whole lot of furniture. Just a wooden desk, leather chair, a couch off to the side, and two metal chairs facing his desk. "How long have you and Brick been friends?" Okay, so he was testing me.

"Eighteen years."

"Where did you meet?"

I shook my head. This was pathetic. This was none of his business! "Vegas."

"Why did you go six years without seeing him?"

I tossed my hands in the air. "I'm also a size four and a 34D. Anything else?"

He came around to the front of his desk and leaned his weight on the edge. "This is my family. I protect them, and I know their history—"

"But you don't trust them," I spat out. His tongue ran along his teeth. He was pissed. My cell rang, and I quickly fished around in my purse trying to turn the friggin' thing off. I checked to see the caller ID and froze when I saw Unknown Caller. I silenced it and stared at the floor.

"Problem?" He sensed my mood change.

I pulled on a smile. "Nope. Umm…" I closed my eyes to recall the conversation. "Okay, well, I'm going to go."

"Tess." He came to stand in front of me. "I don't give two shits who the hell you're fucking. But if someone is coming to my club to cause shit, you better tell me now, or you and I will have a *major* problem later."

"Everything is fine." I clenched my bag for something to hold on to. Trigger was a lot of man and stirred up some strange emotions for me.

He stared at me for several beats then nodded.

"Then get the hell back to work."

The four steps to the door felt like an eternity.

Morgan handed me two beers as I slid in behind the bar and motioned at the two men on the far end. I headed over and tried to shake my nerves. I needed money badly. Almost losing my job wasn't something I needed right now.

I was about to give them their total but saw the skulls on their cut, so I granted them a smile and moved on to the next person.

By the end of the night, I was mentally fried. My nerves were shot, and I just wanted to get the hell back to the apartment where I could think.

I asked where Brick was, since he was not answering his phone. Morgan said something about a family emergency.

*Oh, damn...*I'd bet Jilly was using again. His sister had been on and off the wagon for the past eleven years. She'd nearly sucked the life right out of him once, and I helped bring him back. I ran my hand over my stomach, remembering that day. The day I almost lost my best friend—my other half.

"Whiskey," Trigger muttered and sat in front of me. I barely heard him as I moved to pour the shot. I handed it to him and noticed his knuckles were raw and swollen again. His hands had scars along the top. Some were hidden among the tattoos, but they were there.

He stared at me for a moment then slid the glass over for another. I refilled it and he downed it, keeping his gaze on me.

"Trigger." A man I hadn't seen before sat next to him. "We need to talk." He glanced over and smiled as he moved his attention to me. "Wow, she's even prettier up close. When did you start?"

"Yesterday," I answered, a million miles away from their conversation. "Can I get you something?"

"Yes, but not for an hour." A charming smile spread across his lips, even though he had given a sleazy line. Somehow it didn't suit him. His eyes were too kind when they looked at me. "I'm Cooper, but I'll take a fireball for now."

"Tess." I poured him the shot and tended to a few others before my shift ended. Morgan handed me a wad of tips and told me to be in tomorrow around five.

I headed out and noticed the bikes, but this time they all seemed to have their own spots neatly lined up.

"You heading home?" Cooper, the guy I met earlier, leaned against the wall with one leg up. He was slightly good looking, but what frightened me were the thick scars that raced up his neck.

"Yeah, have a good night."

He nodded, blowing a puff of smoke in the air. "Lots of strange people out there."

"Ah, yeah." I dug around my very annoying oversized purse. "I guess there are. "

"Be careful."

What? Again, his words didn't match his behavior. Almost like he was acting a certain way rather than being himself.

"That's the plan."

Damn!

I swiveled on my heel. "I forgot my phone."

"That wouldn't be safe."

I headed back inside, and Joe gave me a friendly smile when he opened the door for me.

Cooper was hot but odd. Like motel hot. Easy on the eyes, but you knew there was a level of dark going on that you couldn't connect with—and didn't want to.

CHAPTER THREE

Trigger

"I think they're gonna hit Thursday." Cray, my Arizona VP, glanced over his shoulder. "I've got a bad feeling."

I tossed my shot glass behind the bar. If Satan's Serpents planned a hit, why Thursday? How did they know that was when we were doubling our cash this quarter?

Fuck me, I'm going to kill someone.

"We move our date to Saturday. This stays here." I knew they understood me. I needed that info to stay in our core group. I watched the men drink around the bar. Did I have a mole in the mix? My crew was going to shit. But who?

"Got it." Cray hopped off the stool and made a call.

I sent a quick text to Brick to see what his ETA was. I wanted him back here. I needed my second set of eyes. Truth be told, Brick *was* the only man I trusted. His father got himself into trouble a few times, but he was loyal, and so was his son.

With a bottle of whiskey, I headed outside and hopped up on the old pickup truck. I liked the way the pool water reflected the light onto the wooden deck. It was oddly soothing.

Plugging in my phone, I let my ears be filled with Slipknot. I bit the cork free of the bottle, leaned back, and closed my eyes.

"Come here, boy." He grabbed my collar and hauled me to my feet. I shook and tried not to make eye contact. "You think you can outrun me!" He pulled his arm back, and I waited for the impact.

His knuckles met my stomach with such force my dinner came right back up. He backhanded my face and tossed me in my own vomit.

"You run, and I will find you."

I didn't cry. I learned tears got you nothing but more beatings. I needed to wait him out, take my punishment, and hope to God someone killed him before he killed me.

Kids didn't take to me at school, I thought they were scared. I was big for seven, with broad shoulders and an intense stare. I barely spoke, and when I did, kids turned away. I didn't even think they knew my name.

I was weird.

I was probably just known as that quiet kid with the bruises.

"Hey." Tammy was one of the desperate women who hung around hoping to become one of our old ladies. She hit my boot to get my attention. "Whatcha doing out here all by yourself?"

I didn't answer, although I was pleased to have been pulled out of my thoughts. I tugged my headphones from my phone and let the music spill into the open air.

She stood and waded into the water. Tammy looked over her shoulder before she started to peel out of her shirt. She didn't wear a bra or panties. There she stood, naked, water up to her waist, trying to move to the beat of "Wait and Bleed" by Slipknot. I bit back a smirk. This was *not* working.

"Come on, Trigger, water's warm." She hooked her finger and called me over. Her small breasts were perked up nicely, but they really didn't do it for me. Maybe because she was so desperate to belong to one of us. On the other hand, I could beat out some frustration.

I rolled my neck and felt the needed three snaps that relieved the tension. Pushing to my feet, I hopped off the truck.

Shrugging off my shirt, I removed my belt and stripped before I hit the water. She grinned as I approached. She was excited, but this was just ten minutes of me turning off and not on to her. I didn't care that we were surrounded by three walls that held many windows. If the guys wanted to get off, they could. They knew not to show their face unless it was an emergency.

"Hands."

She placed them on the side of the pool. She knew better than to touch me. I took her hair in my fist, flipped her around, and took her from behind.

Images from my past flickered in front of me and made my stomach turn. The smell of his sweat found my nose, and I squeezed my eyes shut. Shit, my erection was always battling my memories.

"You can eat, after you kill that boy." His finger jammed in my face, his eyes wild with anger. "Until then, you get nothing."

Tammy's scream brought me back. She was close, but I didn't care—I wasn't. My hands fought for a better grip and I slammed in. I wasn't fully hard, which made it frustrating. She didn't like it rough, but she'd take it without complaint. Repeatedly, I sought relief, but my battle with my head was all-consuming, and I grew annoyed then pissed.

Changing angles, I tipped her over the edge, and she shook and vibrated against my chest. I pushed her forward, not wanting the contact. Finally, I pulled out, solid as a rock. The only thing that made me hard was that I was rough with her. My balls begged me to finish, but it was no use. Nothing was happening tonight.

"You want some company tonight?" she panted over her shoulder.

"No." I left even more pent-up than I was before I started.

Grabbing the bottle, I stood naked by my truck and waited for the heat to dry me off. It didn't take Rail long to find Tammy naked in the pool, and he lured her into his room where I hoped she'd stay.

My head ached and swarmed with a ton of ugly thoughts. Nothing I could do to turn it off. Even my kill from earlier did dick to relieve what held me hostage. Of course, I went limp the moment my father's face appeared.

"Hey!"

I broke from my thoughts, and there was Tess across the pool, staring right at me. The truck hid me from the waist down—not that I cared. "You see Morgan?"

"Thought you left." I lit my joint and blew a large puff into the dark sky.

"Forgot my phone. Big Joe said Morgan would have it."

"Haven't seen him." My gaze raked down her long legs. "You need to call a cab?"

"No." She glanced around. "Just don't like to walk alone without it."

Smart girl.

Suddenly, like on fucking cue, Peggy walked out buck naked and called my name. Tess rubbed her neck before she turned away.

"Never mind."

"Stay in Brick's room." The moment I spoke, Peggy homed in on me.

"Ohh," Peggy purred, rubbing her breasts for show. "Someone is ready for me."

When I looked back, Tess was gone.

Tugging on my pants, I headed out to the front, but she was out of sight. Peggy, on the other hand, was on her knees when I returned.

"Whatever, let's do this."

I dropped my pants.

***

Tess

I crossed a street and waved at Mud, a friend of Brick's I had only met briefly but knew wasn't dangerous. Still, I fished out my phone, thankful I caught Morgan on the way out. He'd tucked it safely away for me until I returned.

It was funny how a tiny piece of technology held so tightly in one's hand could give a person such a sense of safety. But in fact, if I were to throw this at someone, it would bounce off their head and clatter to the ground. Useless, unless given the moment to hit dial. Then maybe your odds would be better.

On the other hand, the little device could also tap into other lives and show me what *he* was up to this very moment. I swiped my thumb to open the phone. The urge to snoop was there—it always was. I tapped the icon and waited for it to load.

My head and my hands were not listening. The last thing I needed was to see them together in bed or doing something else.

Smack!

"Watch yourself." A woman wobbled backward on her heels like a raging drunk.

"Shit, sorry." I scrambled to grab my phone which had fallen at my feet.

"Bitch, please, you hit me."

"What? Right, hence why I said sorry." My stomach sank when I looked up from my knees to see I was out in front of the Satan's Serpents clubhouse.

Two pairs of shiny legs stood to my side as she leaned down. "You see something?"

Oh, fuck. Suddenly, I was yanked roughly to my feet by a man who stared down at me.

"Nothing." *I saw nothing.* "Just going home."

The drunk girl grabbed my purse and hauled me back to her. Her nails dug into my shoulders while she held me in place. "I asked you a question, bitch."

"I thought you were someone else," I lied and tugged my purse out of her grip, but the moment I did, I lost my balance and fell into her. The guy's arms wrapped around me and grabbed my breasts hard. I elbowed him in the crotch, making him curse.

"Don't fucking touch me!"

The door swung open and a wiry man looked at me then to the guy holding his crotch.

"The blonde bitch tried to attack us!" the woman yelled, and her hands flew up in defense.

"What? No!" I screamed and backed up. "You came at me." The wiry man swiped his arm out, locked his hand around my wrist, and dragged me inside the building.

Everything happened so fast that my mind raced to catch up.

It was dark in the entryway, and smoke was thick like the other bar, only it was pot, not cigarette smoke. Three inhales and I swore I was high, but it didn't help. I was panicking and trying to wiggle loose from the wiry man.

"Please, I didn't do anything."

"Tiago! We have company!" He ignored me.

I could barely feel his grip; my body had gone to ice. Why? Why didn't I look where I was going? A devil's skull with a snake crawling through its eye was burned into the wood above the bar, along with their patchwork. ***Satan's Serpents.***

A fat Hispanic man came out of a room, wiping a rag over his sweaty head, "Oh, you brought me a white girl?" He turned away in disgust. "You know I like more meat on them. This one is way too skinny. Throw her to the *desperates*." He dismissed me to some hungry looking men around a pool table. One being the asshole who took my phone the other day.

"She was starting trouble outside, Tiago." The wiry man pushed me to my knees. Oh, no…oh, shit! My heart pounded but I kept my head up. How I still had some balls left in me at that point surprised even me. It was totally beyond my understanding. "She was after Manuel's woman, scared her real bad."

"No," I cried, only to get a crack to the back of the head. My teeth rattled with the impact, and I hope I hadn't cracked one.

Tiago stood in front of me, grabbed my hair, and forced me to look up at him.

My heart beat like a wild horse in an open field. Everything went numb right down to my fingertips.

"No one touches my family." He turned his fat ring around and slapped me across the mouth. "No one disrespects me in my own home." I cried out but didn't dare say anything; I knew better. He stopped when he got a good look at me and something ran across his face. Almost like he was turned on by how vulnerable I was. He struggled to undo his pants with one hand. Fear laced with oxygen, and in two breaths I was ready to pass out. If he thought he was getting a blow job, I would bite that shit right off at the base.

"Your lips look like velvet. Keep your pretty eyes on me while I feed you my…"

Suddenly, he let go, and I fell to the ground with relief. He looked furious as he refastened his pants, and I saw he was limp. I wondered why. Too many drugs, I guessed.

He leaned down and whispered in my ear, "We will meet again one day. And we will finish what we started here. I can promise you that." He licked my cheek and ended it with a kiss. I wanted to puke.

Sick son of a bitch.

I was dizzy as hell, but my gaze landed on a man in the corner. Once he saw me looking, he turned his face away from me. I did notice a tattoo behind his ear, but I couldn't make it out.

"Chuck her out back," was all I heard before I was lifted and carried out the back door. The wiry man tossed me down on the pavement, and I scraped my elbows as they broke my fall.

Pain shot through me, but I welcomed it. Anything was better than what had been in store for me back there.

I lay still and stared up at the phone wires for what seemed like forever. I was scared to move. Blood trickled into my mouth, but the faint sound of a chopper had me scrambling to my knees. What if they came back?

I managed to get to my feet and hobbled back toward my place. The urge to cry was a battle, but I didn't want to draw any more attention to myself than I already had. My mouth felt as big as a baseball, my hip was sore from the fall, my elbow throbbed, and I was sure it was full of rocks and dirt. It was going to be a bitch to clean.

Just a little farther.

Almost there.

A girl I recognized from the eighth floor ran to open the door for me. I'd seen her a couple times with her daughter, and she seemed nice enough.

"What the hell? Are you all right?" I nodded and headed straight for the elevator. She slipped in next to me and punched the button for our floor. "Come to my place. I have a first aid kit."

My chin started to quiver as what happened set in, but I pulled myself together. She slipped an arm around me, but it made me flinch. "You look like you might pass out. I'm just trying to keep you upright, okay?"

After a long walk to her door, she unlocked it and helped me in.

She sat me down on a chair and disappeared, leaving me alone in her child-littered living room. I removed a stuffed animal from under me and tossed it on the heap.

She returned holding a box. "I'm Heidy, and you're…" She waited.

"Tess," I whispered through my swollen lip. I winced at how much it hurt.

"I like that name." She inspected my elbow then got to work cleaning the rocks out. "Wait." She headed to the kitchen and came back with a bottle of water and three large oval pills, two red and one white. "I know." She caught my hesitation. "But you'll have to trust me."

I hurt so badly that I didn't care. I tossed them back with the water. *Ouch.* The bottle killed my mouth. I whimpered but managed to get the pills down.

"That's a nasty cut on your elbow. I'm going to clean it some more and coat it in polysporin then wrap a bandage over it. You really should see a doctor, but I assume since you came back here instead of to the ER that's not something you're going to do."

I shook my head. Insurance wasn't something I've had for a long time.

After my arm was bandaged and the pain meds started to kick in, I let the warmth take over and felt my eyelids become heavy.

"Your lip is swelling pretty bad. Hold this ice pack to your face. I'm going to lay you back on my couch. There's a pillow waiting for you, and I'm going to cover you with this blanket." She spoke calmly and moved carefully, which I appreciated since every time she touched me

I jumped. I didn't like it when my guard was down. Especially around strangers. I closed my eyes as she took over, holding the pack gently to my face.

Relax, Tess. She is only being friendly. Taking my own advice, I let go and gave in to sleep.

I wished Brick was here.

***

Sunlight burned through the blinds, which didn't help my head. Inside my skull, a beating drum persisted. It was a rude awakening. My vision was clouded, but I could make out the pills in front of me on the table, and next to them was a fresh bottle of unopened water. The pills were different, smaller this time. I took them and slipped back to into a more settled sleep.

When I woke next, the sun's rays were in a different spot in the living room. The toys were picked up and now were in a heap in the corner.

I moved to sit and felt how much my body hurt. A note was written on her daughter's chalkboard.

Had to go to work. Please lock up and leave key on table. I have a spare.

I glanced at the clock and saw it was 4:45 p.m. Dammit! I cleared the board and scribbled a message back.

Thank you. I owe you one. Apt 10G—Tess

I locked up, left the key on the table, and rushed over to my place. I tried to hurry as I showered and changed then glanced in the mirror.

Shit!

I didn't have time to cover up the bruising in the corner of my mouth. My lip was cracked and raw. I tried to conceal it the best I could with makeup, but the crack couldn't be helped. I looked horrible and felt even worse. I wanted to call in sick, but I was already on Trigger's radar. I changed into short black shorts and a red silk sleeveless shirt. It was too hot to wear a sweater. I unbuttoned the top three buttons and hoped people would stare at my cleavage and not my face or arm. My hands shook as I threaded the metal hoops through my earlobes. I slipped my black cuff over my scar and headed out. My hair would have to dry on the way.

Panic set in when I got outside. I'd have to walk by that place again. I quickly spotted a cab and flagged it down.

The cabbie glanced in the mirror and squinted sympathetically. "Where to?"

I prattled off the address and removed my sunglasses because they hurt my cheek.

"You sure?"

My anger and embarrassment got the better of me.

"Yes."

Five minutes later, I was walking through the front door. I kept my head down so my hair gave me a temporary curtain. Morgan grunted at me as a greeting. His focus was on busily counting bills. Thankfully, the place was dead other than a drunk guy in the corner.

Only eight hours to go.

A guy started to fiddle with an electric guitar, making my head pound and my stomach turn. I thought I was going to be sick, so I turned to find the ice bucket and dry heaved. Morgan made a nasty sound but handed me a glass of water.

"You all right, Tiger?" His body loomed above me. I took a sip of the cold water.

"Ouch," I hissed without thinking. "Yeah, just ate something bad." I turned to carefully wipe my mouth on a paper towel. Fuck, I should have eaten something. Those painkillers burned a hole in my stomach. "Do you mind if I grab something from the kitchen?"

Morgan's back was to me as he muttered, "Go on."

I found a piece of bread and some peanut butter. Perfect. I was cleaning up when I heard a male's voice in the bar calling out for someone named Cray.

I hurried out of the kitchen and made my way back behind the bar just as a woman took a seat and ordered a screwdriver. She looked vaguely familiar with her 1990s red nails, bleached blonde hair, and brown lipstick. It made me shudder.

"You're new." She snatched her drink from me. "Who the hell hired you?"

Friendly.

"Brick," I mumbled and moved on to the new guy next to her.

Trigger came out of his office on the phone, and I noticed the girl sat a little straighter and thrust her boobs in the air. He reached over the counter for a pen and paper. I kept my curtain of hair between us while I cleaned out the sink.

"Are you single?" She clearly was scoping out her competition. I shook my head. I didn't need to make any enemies. "So who hit your face?" Why couldn't the woman shut the hell up?

Trigger stopped talking, and I closed my eyes and hoped he hadn't heard her comment.

This was none of anyone's business.

"I fell," I whispered. Maybe she would get the hint that it was a closed topic.

Trigger moved into my line of vision with the phone still to his ear. He peered down at me, and his eyes flickered with something. His large hand reached out to cup the bottom of my chin.

"I gotta go," he muttered into the phone. He didn't wait for a response before he shoved it into his back pocket. I stepped back out of his grasp and poured him his usual whiskey. He set it aside as the female scooted closer.

"Trigger, take me to dinner," she whined and ran her nasty red nails down his colorful arm. He immediately moved it away.

He ignored her and studied my face. "What the fuck happened?"

The girl laughed, which made my desire to hit her even stronger. "She fell," she answered for me.

"Peggy, shut the fuck up," he warned, but she didn't seem to care.

So, she had a name. Then it hit me she was the pathetic nude from last night. I wondered if they had sex. A picture of her nails on his back popped into my head. *Yuck.*

"What happened, Tess?"

"I fell wearing those heels yesterday. It was rather embarrassing, and I'd prefer not to relive it, if it's okay with you." I forced a smile but squinted when my lip stung.

Peggy's hand slid over and under his shirt. He reacted quickly and slammed her hand down on the bar top. She flinched and brought her hand to her lap. However, that quick glimpse of his stomach was enough for me to read the word ***Demons*** which ran along his lower belly in big, scrolling letters. What I'd seen didn't surprise me; his body was perfect. I dropped my gaze when he caught me staring.

"Take the night off."

"No, it doesn't hurt that bad. I can work fine," I lied. Of course, my face and head were killing me, but I was not about to go home.

"Morgan!" he yelled and made me jump. "Take over." Than he came behind the bar, grabbed my bag, and hauled me out the door, leaving Peggy wide-eyed.

He tossed me a helmet while buckling his own. I stood, completely shocked with what was about to happen. Not to mention it was Trigger who owned the matte black bike with the golden swirls.

I looked back at the bar as I heard him start the bike, and he stared at me, waiting. I couldn't lie. I was a little nervous to get on that beast of a thing, but the way Trigger looked on it had my hormones kicking into gear.

Of course, this turns me on. I nearly rolled my eyes at myself. I was hopeless.

"Now." He said to me over his shoulder.

Okay.

I buckled my helmet, rested my hand on his huge shoulder, and swung my leg over the bike. Shifting to get into place, he pointed where to put my feet.

"Hold on," he commanded.

I felt his muscles twitch as I gingerly placed my hands on his waist. Oh, fuck. Trigger between my legs and a vibrating bike were not a good combo for keeping my dirty thoughts at bay.

I hesitated to wrap my arms around him, so instead I dropped them down to rest on his hips.

"No." He reached back and pulled them around his waist again then gave them a pat to indicate *they stay here*. With a flick of his wrist, we started to move backward out of the parking spot, and his feet guided us onto the road.

He moved, and we jolted forward, not overly fast, but enough that my legs squeezed his hips. There was construction, so we were rerouted a different way—a longer way and one I hadn't been before.

My bladder nearly took a dive when we leapt into a turn at an intersection and it decided not to return to its rightful place. Honestly, I didn't blame it.

"Ah!" I buried my head in his shoulder blades as we split two trucks.

This was it—this was going to be my death. Yup, right here, I was going to tumble awkwardly off his bike, roll under a car, and get hit by a moped or something equally embarrassing. Just flop, no bounce and roll. Oh, sweet mother wrapped around something holy, this was it.

Finally, he slowed, and I was able to see straight. I was used to cars, enclosed in metal that protected my flesh and bones. No wind to remind me of the speed we were traveling.

And breathe. In and frickin' out.

At the third stoplight, I finally took a moment to relax. I sat back and flexed my stiff fingers. I didn't enjoy taking the turns—*at all.* It scared me and felt like death was waiting. He turned his head so I could hear him.

"When I lean, you lean," he ordered.

Sure, yeah, of course.

Dick.

I didn't nod because I was wound tight. I saw him flash a smirk in the mirror, one that made my breath catch in my throat. Lord, he was fucking sexy. His short beard called my fingers, but I behaved. I didn't even know the man.

The light was about to change, and I leaned forward and wrapped my arms around him like he showed me. We moved forward, and I shut my eyes when he slipped us in between the cars. We took a corner, and I leaned a little with him but had to admit it didn't feel natural, and my thighs were getting one hell of a workout.

He reached back and ran his hand under the back of my leg and gave me a nod. I guessed I did well, but my attention was immediately on his warm hand running over my skin.

More of that would really help calm me.

We pulled into my apartment building. It didn't surprise me he knew where I lived. No doubt Brick told him.

He stood and helped me off, and I removed the helmet and handed it to him. He reached for my arm then walked me to the door and waited for me to go first.

Umm.

Once inside the elevator, he pushed my floor number. He turned to look at me like he wanted to say something, but he didn't. Trigger was the kind of man power just seemed to ooze from, like Christian Grey, but different. Trigger's was more raw and unpredictable. He screamed danger and sexy all at once. Frankly, it was fucking with my head, and I needed some space. I started to move, but his grip on my arm told me to stay put.

I felt his gaze burning into me. I tried to ignore it, but failed.

"What?" I couldn't handle the silence anymore. I swore I saw him smirk.

The doors opened, and he released my arm and fell into step behind me. I wasn't sure what he was doing, but at the same time, I wasn't about to complain. I liked having him near, even if he was scary as hell.

Unlocking my apartment door, I walked in, then turned when I didn't feel him follow. He stood in the doorway.

"Ice your lip and get some sleep."

I dropped my bag on the table. "I could have worked tonight, Trigger. Really, I'm all right."

"That's not for you to decide," he rumbled.

I leaned against the table, my hands gripping the edge as I looked down at my feet.

I heard him come inside, but he didn't shut the door. "You wanna tell me what really happened? Don't fucking lie to me, Tess."

I sighed. He was like Brick but harsher, so I didn't lie. I just withheld some of the truth. The last thing I needed to do was start a war. I wasn't an idiot; biker families were very protective and territorial.

"Wrong place, wrong time."

"God, woman, you infuriate me!" He puffed out a long breath, and his hands flew to his hair and down the back of his head. "Do you try to piss me off?"

"No!" What the hell? "You have a bit of a temper, don't you?"

He dropped his hands as he snapped his neck to the side. His eyes locked on mine, and I swallowed back a small gasp. The man was positively frightening.

With one stride toward me, his neck was at my eye level. He was massive and radiated with anger.

"Do I scare you?" His voice was low.

"A little," I panted. My body tugged me in his direction. What the hell was wrong with me?

Snap out of it, Tess.

His strong hand slid around my neck, resting there as he studied my face, looking for something. "You like it, don't you?"

Again, I nodded.

"Stupid girl," he muttered, but before I could snap back, he turned and spoke over his shoulder. "Don't come back until Saturday night."

Four days! Christ, I need that money.

***

The next day, I unpacked everything but two suitcases, which I kept in my closet.

I propped up my laptop and watched a few episodes of *Weeds.* I loved how Nancy always survived the shit storms she got into. I guessed if she could, I could. My gaze flicked over to the bookshelf which held a collection of my favorites. I wasn't the girl who read *Jane Eyre* or *Romeo and Juliet.* Nope, I liked my dirty books with the alpha males and jacked-up situations. There wasn't a romantic bone in my body, but those books spoke to me. I flicked off the TV and reached under my pillow. I could use a little Logan right now.

By Thursday, I was feeling better. I was able to fully cover the yellow bruise, and the cracked lip was healing. I took my favorite spot by the window and hoped I would see the rooftop boxer, but he hadn't been around much.

Problem with being alone was temptation rested heavily on your shoulders. It stared at me all day, and I finally gave in. I balanced my laptop on my knees and signed into the security feed to the house in Las Vegas. No surprise, the password hadn't been changed. I didn't think they even knew it.

I moved the camera around until I found her. She answered the door to Doug. I hated all things that had to do with Doug. Her body language was the same, slutty and looking for money. She was a waste of a human being. She opened the door wider and let him in. I switched cameras and watched out back. The pool was filled and there were bodies draped everywhere over the chairs and tables. Every cabana was full. Everything was normal.

Just as I was about to log out, I saw *him*. He was in his swim trunks, hair styled as usual. His walk was that of a man who knew exactly what he brought to the table. My stomach coiled into an acid ball as my finger hovered over the mouse.

"Clark!" someone yelled.

He smiled in their direction, and I felt my walls crumble.

Logout. The screen went black. *Why do I do it?*

I face planted into the pillow and let my emotions take over. He hurt me, and I left. *Move on, Tess. He wasn't good for you. He never was.*

I spent Friday under my covers with Mark and his love of food. With a heap of Chinese boxes piled in front of me, I cracked open the book and wondered how much trouble Mark got her in for joining the Green Team.

A vibration buzzed my leg, and I pulled the phone free from under my thigh.

Oh, I had an email—junk mail, of course. I barely used this account anymore. It was mainly for my old job. However, I forgot I had set it up on my phone. Tapping away on the screen, I went into my saved messages and found the recording I couldn't bear to part with. Many times I wanted to delete it, but I couldn't. I was a sucker for punishment.

"Tess?" Her voice broke through my walls once again. It was old, but her voice brought me comfort and then pain. "Where are you? You were supposed to be here, and you're not. Are you with Matt?" Pause. "Of course, you are." There was another pause followed by a sob. It broke loose from deep inside me. *Oh, it's my sob.* "Something's not right here, Tess. I think someone might be here. I need your help. Please call. I'm really scared this time."

Dragging my heavy body across the living room, I found the bathroom and emptied my stomach into the toilet. I twisted the tap and turned on the shower, and sitting on the floor, I cried until the water hurt my skin.

Buzz, buzz, pause, *buzz, buzz.*

I peeled my dry eyes open to look at my phone. Three missed calls from Brick. Dammit. I smacked my clock to turn it toward me. Two a.m.

Buzz, buzz.

"Yeah?"

"Where have you been?" He went silent for a moment, then asked, "What's wrong?"

"Nothing."

"I'm sending someone to pick you up. We're having dinner together."

"Brick, it's two a.m."

"Night is the best time, baby. Now get some clothes on and be downstairs in ten."

"I hate you."

CHAPTER FOUR

Trigger

I jumped back and forth, kicking and punching to try to clear my damned head. I had to make a drop and seal a deal with the Reaper, and all I could do was think about who the hell hit Tess. I watched the tapes from my club, but it showed nothing. My thoughts weren't clear. This was not how I operated. I was a machine. I wasn't meant to be clouded by a fucking woman who got herself into trouble on day three of her job.

If my father were here, he'd beat the shit out of me. I was only meant to make money. I was his cash cow, a way to form the Devil's Reach. I was the reason this place existed. When he left, I was eighteen and had more life experience killing people than most of the seniors here. I had the respect of the club, but I had their fear more. Bottom line—fear was more effective.

I sent a hard blow to the bag before stopping for some water. I didn't use gloves when I fought. I never had, and my knuckles were torn up from years of fighting. My father always said you needed to be able to feel their bones break to know you were winning. He was a sick son of a bitch. He tossed his first punch at me when I was seven, and I didn't know what was going on until I started to fight back. He had grinned and given me a pat on the back. A month later, I was pulled from public school to be homeschooled and trained. I was taught to fight clean but deadly. Losing wasn't an option, so it was a good thing I was a quick study.

"Hey, shit." Allen hit my head as he came into the kitchen for another beer. "You didn't take the trash out."

Oh, no! My eyes squeezed shut as my pencil shook in my hands. My math was due, and since Allen didn't care about school, I was falling behind.

I slid off the chair and headed for the trashcan, but he stepped in front of me.

"Too late now, boy." I heard the action rather than saw it. For whatever reason, I ducked and missed the blow. He looked surprised as he tried to swing at me again. I ducked and dipped to the right. "You think you're clever?"

He swung again, and I dodged and kicked his knee, which made him lose his balance. He fell to the floor and gazed up at me with a baffled look.

I was stunned at what I had done but also felt a sense of strength. I was seven and had just made the devil fall to his knees.

"So, you can fight," he said more to himself.

That was when things took an unexpected turn.

My phone rang and pulled my attention to my pocket. I shifted my erection and answered the call.

"I've got someone here who wants to see you." Gus cleared his throat, which never helped with his raspy voice. It was only a matter of time before he kicked the bucket. Poor bastard had almost every kind of cancer you could get.

"Who?"

"A mole."

My skin tightened and I reached for my vest.

"Be right there."

Big Joe met me at the door and grabbed the keys I tossed at him. I wanted my bike to be hidden. Plowing through a group of guys, I stopped at the counter and caught Gus where he was propped up against the wall.

He nodded out back but also behind me. I found Tess and Brick having dinner, although she looked upset rather than happy.

Fuck.

"Tie him up and get the fire ready."

"Yeah." Gus disappeared out back while I walked over to the table.

"What's wrong?" Tess jumped at my tone. "I told you not to come back until tomorrow."

She glanced at Brick then back to me. When she opened her mouth to speak, Brick stepped in.

"I asked her out to dinner. I didn't know she wasn't supposed to be back."

"This isn't a hangout for people like you." My frustration with the mole was getting to me.

She raised her chin. "And what am I, exactly?"

Brick kicked her leg, but she didn't seem to get that she was disrespecting me.

"You're a rich little girl who is lashing out at her mommy and daddy. Don't use my club as a way to rebel."

"Trigger—" Brick tried to step in but shut up when I shot him a look.

Tess stood and stuck a finger in my face. "You haven't given me a chance since the moment I stepped into this club. What the fuck have I done to you? Other than show up when you needed a bartender."

"Don't forget stirring up shit with the Serpents. Not one of the chicks have had that happen." I vibrated with anger. She had a mouth on her. I grabbed her purse and jammed it into her chest. "Get out."

Brick stood but remained quiet. Tess shook her head and muttered something.

"You got something to say?"

She licked her split lip before she huffed, "I don't know what I did, but you are way more fucked up than I thought."

"Better you learn that now than later."

"Whatever." She turned to leave but stopped Brick when he started to follow. "Don't. Brotherhood, remember?"

Brick stepped back, to my surprise, and let her leave. Once she was out of sight, he turned to me.

"She doesn't belong here, Brick." I spoke before he could. "Living in hell's basement isn't a life she needs."

"Trust me, Trigger." His arms were locked at his sides, but instead of showing fear, he looked sad. "You just pushed her back into hers."

I could hear the chains rattle from down the hall. My body was jacked up, and I needed an outlet. Tess needed to leave. Whether she could handle this life or not, she fucked with my head, and I didn't need that.

Gus tossed me the metal rod, and I flicked my mental switch and watched as one of my hangarounds screamed in fear.

"Please, Trigger, it's not what you think." Saliva sprayed from his lips. They always looked the same way when fear took over. "I was trying to think outside the box. You…you needed information on the

Serpents, and I wanted to be the one to get it for you."

"And?" I twisted the side of the rod and made the flame shoot out in a fireball.

"And!" he shouted but closed his eyes to think. "And I know they have an eye on that girl."

"Girl?"

"Yeah the one behind the bar. The one Rail wants to hit."

"How exactly do they know her?"

He stopped to catch his breath, and I watched him carefully as I lit a joint. Fire poured from the device that was now resting in a sling. I kicked it and it shot out toward him.

"She has to walk by them every day to and from work. The *desperates* have already claimed her. It's just a matter of time."

I pulled over a stool and sat inches from his face.

"When were you going to share this?"

He shrugged, not following. "She's a chick, didn't think that was important. I wanted to come to you when I had something about your drugs."

"Do you?"

"Yeah." His face twisted as he thought. "The pres mentioned something about your contract. He was on the phone with someone telling them to lay low for a bit."

"Who?" I hated back stories. Just give me the fucking details.

"I don't know."

I lunged forward, holding his eye open and pressing the tip of my joint into his pupil. He screamed and bucked. I fought to hold on as he was lathered in sweat.

"I don't!" He hissed in pain. "They just used a nickname, Father something."

I wanted to kill him slowly, remove layers of his skin, break each bone one at a time for playing in their yard, but I could use him.

Grabbing his chin, I towered over his shaky body. "You listen to me. You hear anything about any one of us, you come tell me, no one else. This is your last chance." I pointed to a Serpent who we killed three nights ago and had left his body to rot a while longer before we got rid of it. "Or that will be you."

"Yes! Okay!" he almost cried.

Turning to find Gus and Brick by the door, I stormed up. "He's made his way into their clubhouse. Keep him there until he figures out what the fuck is going on."

"Yeah," Gus agreed.

"Deal with him."

Brick followed me out, and I wanted to lash out at him too. He brought Tess into my club, and now I needed to babysit her.

"Where's Tess?" I grunted.

"I don't know. Home, maybe?"

"Find her, and tell her not to walk by that fucking club anymore."

"Does she still have a job here?" He sounded confused. I didn't answer because I didn't know what the fuck to do with her anymore.

I slammed the door to my room in his face and hit my bed hard. I needed to sleep this shit off.

***

It had been four days, and Brick couldn't locate Tess. Or at least he was choosing not to. My mole was now reporting in every day, and Peggy was working the bar. That was a clusterfuck all on its own. Fuck forbid she counted over twelve.

"What the hell!" Cray jumped off his seat and shook his vest. "You got brandy on my cut, Peggy!"

"That will be seven fifty."

She grabbed a calculator and started to work out the math. *Seriously?*

"Here." Morgan handed Cray a rag and poured him a new one before he turned to Peggy with a scowl. "Skulls mean they drink for free. How many times do I have to tell you? And every shot is seven fifty. It's not going to change."

Fuck!

I spotted Vib in the corner with Den. She was trying to do his homework, and the little dick wasn't listening. Den had zero interest when it came to schoolwork. He tried, but he didn't have the patience to sit that long. I made my way over and eased into the seat across from him. Den stopped fighting with his mother and slowly looked up at me from below his long black hair.

"Sorry, Trigger. You want us to move?" Vib started to pack up her stuff.

I shook my head, and she relaxed. I moved my attention over to Den, who was picking the label off a blue crayon.

"Why you fightin' with your mom?"

He shrugged. "I'm not good at counting."

"How do you get good at things if you don't try?"

He shrugged again.

"You think I just became good at fighting? No, I trained every day."

"Now you can kill someone with one punch." His eyes lit up.

"Right." I leaned over. "So?"

"If I get a good grade, will you teach me a right hook?"

I glanced at Vib, who just laughed.

"You get all of them right, and I'll show you."

"Deal." He held out his hand and I hesitated to shake it, but I did.

"Ah, Trigger?" Ty, one of the prospects, stood nervously by the table. "A word?"

"Yeah." I stood and moved them away from the family.

"Me and Jace were at the club the other night, and…ah…we think you should see something."

"What?"

He rubbed his neck as he looked around and stepped closer. "I think you should see for yourself."

I squinted at the kid and wondered what the hell he wanted me to do. "Now?"

"Yeah, now, boss."

"This better be something big."

"It is. Promise." He rushed out ahead of me, and I signaled for Brick and Rail to follow.

Stepping outside, I followed their lead, which was hard to do.

"We need to drive?" I grew annoyed.

"I would." Jace shrugged.

Whatever. I started my bike and followed.

This better be fucking good.

***

Tess

I couldn't spend any more time looking for bartending jobs. There was nothing left in this city. I even tried to work at Walmart, but they had a long list of kids who were more qualified than I was. That was sad, and hit hard.

I had Brick's bank card, but the night Trigger kicked me out, I promised I'd never touch it. Brick had been my other half for so long that I refuse to become what his sister was. A mooch.

Rain started to fall on my way back home, and the temperature dropped, which was odd, considering it was October in southern California, but on the other hand, it would come hand in hand with my luck lately.

I stopped in my tracks when I caught wind of the music. I ran toward the only place I felt comfortable since I arrived in this city. Avoiding the puddles, I pushed the big door open and was waved in by the bouncer.

"Hey, you!" The waitress from the other night smiled down at me but quickly changed her tone. "You okay?"

"I need to make some fast cash."

She checked the time then motioned for me to follow. Once out back, she held up a two-piece country bikini.

"My girl got sick. You can have her slot."

I snatched the scrap of fabric from her hand and peeled out of my dress, kicking it aside. I was comfortable being naked, so when she was talking to me and people were walking in and out, I didn't think twice about it.

"When you hear Kid Rock "Cowboy," that's your cue." She studied me with a smile. "Here." She opened a box and pulled out a pair of boots that came above my knee. "You nervous?"

The boots were a half a size too big, but I'd manage.

"No."

"Good, you're up in ten. Anything you make up there is yours."

The mirror reflected back at me—only it wasn't me. It was someone else.

Holding the curtain back, I watched the girl slink around the stage. She was good, but she sucked on the pole. She was awkward and didn't know how to slip it through her hands. My guess was she was new, because she had only made about sixty bucks.

She hurried past me, but not before she glared. I got it. New meat meant less money for the others.

My attention went back to the stage when the lights dimmed. I stepped onto the platform and took a deep breath.

Just like old times.

The music started, and I walked out, one foot in front of the other. Nothing was planned; it was all about the feel of the music.

The steel was cool and clean, and I gripped the pole and slowly walked around in a circle. Tossing my head back, I let my long hair trail down my naked back. My breasts hiked up in a skimpy white bikini top, and my ass pretty much hung out of my jean shorts.

With my back to the audience, I slid down the pole while my right leg lifted perfectly straight. Twisting to the side, I swung, hooked my leg, and spun, holding my cowboy hat in place. That gained me some cheers, and I noticed a few men from the back took the empty seats in the front. I moved to the open floor and started to dance. Shaking my hips down to the ground, I thrust my breasts in a guy's face. He hooted and stuck a ten in my bottoms. Backing up, I sent a wave through my stomach and shook my ass.

Once the music turned into heavy metal, I jumped up high on the pole and tossed my head so my hair was everywhere. One thing I learned was men liked hair. Bills started to pour onto the stage, and the crowd went wild. I forgot what quick cash was like. Quick cash by dancing…was like a high. You dove in with excitement, you partied like a rock star, then you surfaced to reality. You felt cheap after, but at least you could eat.

I caught the waitress grinning at the manager, who had his phone up like he was recording me. Knowing that was my audition, I made eye contact with him. I slid down the pole, spread my legs, and bent forward, rolling my body back up again. I skipped before I jumped into a sexy flip and landed in a split. *Huh, nice to know I still got it.*

I was held in the high. That was until I slid across the floor on my knees and came face to face with Trigger.

Holy shit…

Brick stood beside him with his arm flexed against his chest. *Disappointed.* Rail just kept shaking his head in disbelief.

A few of the men moved over to make room for them next to the stage.

Trigger had a murderous expression, and his arms flexed at his sides as he made it clear he was staying put.

So, I did what any other person would do. I rolled with it. Slowly, I hooked my fingers into my bottoms and seductively danced back to my feet. The whole place went wild. The waitress screamed, "Shake it, baby!" from the bar top. Clearly, they hadn't had any new dancers in here for a while, because I was rusty as hell and there was no way on earth my moves looked that good.

Once in the center stage, I turned my back and dropped low, turning on my shoe in a sexy spin. The men called out all kinds of promises, and I liked it, but this was all lust, nothing more than men with dicks in the crowd.

Spinning onto my knees, I crawled over to one of them like a panther. Each hand peeled off the floor, one in front of the other, just like the way I walked in. Smooth and sturdy.

My hair was big and wild; it fit the crawl well.

He held a fifty to show me the amount and waited for me to lean back on my knees. His cold finger pulled my bottoms away from my skin and tucked the fifty against my pelvic bone.

Just as the song ended, I spun once more before the lights shut off. The tube lighting lit my way out back.

"You hear that?" The waitress screamed over the chant for me to return. "That means you have a spot here whenever you want."

"Thanks." I removed my top and hung it on the hanger.

"Where did you learn your moves?" She sat on the stool while I wiggled into my bra.

"A different life."

"Well, you, my friend, just found your ticket to a better life."

I almost laughed. Little did she know I had been running from *that* life for years now.

"Tess!" Trigger barked out as he pushed the curtain aside. His eyes dropped to my bare breasts as I clipped my bra in the front.

"Nice to see you again, Trigger." The waitress swooned over him. Of course, they'd slept together. Who hadn't? Well, me.

"Dammit, Tess." Brick popped his head in then turned around to block his eyes. "What the fuck are you doing here?"

"Since I got fired from my last job," I hissed at Trigger, "with no warning, I was left to pick back up where I started a few weeks ago." My dress was still wet, but it was better than the cowgirl outfit.

"I need a drink and some acid for that memory to burn away." Brick disappeared from Trigger's side.

Always so dramatic.

"Not me," Rail chimed in from somewhere.

Trigger made a face, and I heard footsteps.

"Ivy, could you give us a moment?"

She rose and gave me a hug. "You were amazing. The way you moved your body did fine things to my lady bits. You ever want to have a fun night, you know where to find me." She leaned in for a kiss. Her lips pressed softly onto mine, and for a show, I played back. She tasted good, like a fruity drink. Although I could only taste her for a moment before Trigger pushed her toward the door.

He stepped up and loomed over me.

"I have never wanted to hurt you before right now."

I held my ground and stepped a little closer to show him I wasn't scared.

"Well, that's too bad for you."

He smirked, but it was laced with something else. I spun to face the mirror and counted my tips. I had at least six hundred. Trigger's front pressed into my back, and I caught his eyes in the mirror. He leaned forward, trapping me in with his arms, and his lips brushed by my ear before he spoke.

"You will never dance here again."

"Is that so?"

"Ummhmm," he hummed, and I felt my body tune in to his.

"Why is that?"

"Because I own the place."

Fuck.

He chuckled as he watched my new job be suddenly sucked away.

"Whatever. I have enough for a bus ticket. I can move on."

"You'd do that to Brick?"

Fuck, he plays dirty.

I tucked my cash in my bra and turned to face him. He stood but didn't step back. He held his ground so my breasts pushed into his solid chest.

"Why was I fired?"

His face twisted, and I couldn't understand why.

"Take a ride with me."

"If I say no?"

"You won't."

CHAPTER FIVE

Trigger

The manager, Billy, had his phone out on the counter. When I walked by, I smashed it into the wall. He didn't dare say a word, but he got it. He would never video her again. I pushed Tess to move forward, keeping my hand on her hip to guide her.

Once outside, she stopped by Brick, who was already on his bike.

"You promised me, Tess."

She shook her head and shifted her purse on her shoulder. "Rough night, that's all."

"Don't slip back. You know—"

"Got it, Brick," she snapped. I looked at the two of them. I hated this shit. I didn't do this shit.

"Get on." I pointed to my bike and tossed a helmet at her.

"I'll walk."

"Tess," Brick warned and shook his head. Smart man. She had pushed me to a dangerous point.

She licked her lips and reluctantly put the helmet on and swung her bare leg over the wet seat.

The guys went on ahead by my command, and I waited for her to get settled. Of course, she sat way up on the seat. I reached back, grabbed her legs, and hauled her to me.

"Hey!" Her hands hit my shoulders to stabilize herself. "Trigger, you don't—"

I started the engine to cut her off. Her hands gripped my sides as I moved out of the driveway.

"You're such an asshole."

I smirked at her comment; I was an asshole.

Instead of driving her home, I drove to the pier. It was late—or early, depending how you thought about it—around 3:30 a.m., and I didn't feel like I could let her out of my sight yet. We had some things to discuss.

When we pulled onto the PC Highway, she tapped my shoulder.

"Where are you taking me?"

I ignored her, which only pissed her off further.

"Hey!" I felt her chest press into my back. When I didn't react, her hand slipped up my thigh, palmed my erection, and squeezed it with a tight grip. "Answer me."

Her head dropped down when I reached between her open legs. Her soft skin greeted me as I stroked along her opening. The pad of my finger broke the seal, exposing her arousal. It coated the tip and allowed me easy access. We were heading down a straight stretch, so I could really feel her. She rocked slightly, stroking me to the rhythm. Speed, weed, and sex were what I craved. I purposely slowed to circle her swollen bud.

Her grip on my erection tightened. Heat pulsed over my slick skin.

We were alone, and it was dark, and the rain was a light mist. The bike vibrated under my hand, which only made her climb faster. She started to rock in a wave while I watched the red light. Her moan had my dick begging for a dip.

Just as I felt her breathing pick up, I pulled my fingers free and drove forward.

She smacked my arm in frustration. I loved the fact she let me do that. Some girls would have been mortified.

"I'll do it myself then," she muttered. I shifted to hold her hands in place around my stomach. Her legs flexed then her head hit my back. "I hate you."

She was sexually frustrated, which meant she should listen for five fucking seconds.

Pulling into the empty lot, I carefully parked my bike behind the information center inside the gate. I knew the bright light of the street lamp would provide a contrasting heavy darkness to protect my bike from view, and I turned off the engine. I waited for her to join me, but she was even more pissed off at me now. It was a learning tool. She needed to know who was in charge.

"Take off your boots."

Her eyes narrowed in on me as she pulled her purse further up her arm. "Why? You gonna kill me?" She unzipped them and placed them by the bike.

"Don't tempt me." I freed a bottle of whiskey from my saddlebag and put her boots and purse inside.

The corner of her mouth lifted. "You're not as scary as you think you are." She smiled over her shoulder and headed for the sand.

I scratched my beard as I walked behind her. How could something so small and sexy have such a reckless personality?

She stopped at the waterline and looked back at me. "I've waited a long-ass time to dip my toes in the Pacific. Will you allow me to do so?" Her pissy face make me smirk, and she rolled her eyes before she carefully waded into the dark water.

I sat under the pier and leaned against a pillar. I lit a joint and unscrewed the bottle to take a drink.

I had a lot to think about, and she was fucking with my head. I needed to get my fill and toss her off to one of the other guys.

"Arms up, feet shoulder width apart, weight on your back heel," Langley, a small Asian man Allen hired to be my coach, barked at me. "Now, when I come at you like this..." He lunged, but I hopped to the side. He smiled and gave me a little nod. "Good."

"Boy can fight. Skip the basics and try him out."

Langley looked back at me, and I could see he was torn. I gave him a little nod to let him know I was all right with it. I didn't have a choice. And since this was my third coach in a month, I was tired of having to train from the start every time.

He raised his hands in the fighting position and came at me with a roundhouse. I ducked and slammed his ankle. He narrowed his eyes and brought his hands up again.

"You sure you're ten?"

"Yes, sir." I rarely spoke much, but I knew there was something a little different about Langley, and I tried not to let my father see I liked it.

Four more hours in the ring, and Langley gave Allen the green light to let me fight with one of his other clients. We would do one more month of training, then I was free to fight. Free. Interesting choice of words in my situation.

***

I should have been terrified of my opponent. He had at least eight pounds on me, but he was my age. There were at least some rules that they followed in order to keep the bets coming in. Bets meant money, and money was everything. However, what scared me the most was the tall man standing on the sidelines cursing my life if I lost this fight.

"Got two grand on you, boy. You lose, and you'll get more than a sleep in the basement."

Langley stepped in my view and leaned down. "Quick hands, quick feet." He pointed to his head. "Quick mind."

The bell rang, and I stepped into the middle and slapped the kid's hand.

"Let's do this!" the announcer screamed into the microphone.

Everything around me went dark and silent. All I focused on was my wild heartbeat. This wasn't right. We were kids. We were supposed to be running around in the mud and playing cops and robbers, not standing inside a ring fighting to near death for a few grand.

"Fight, boy!" Allen screamed as the big kid's fist hit my head so hard my ears rang. That shot a wave of darkness through me, and all I saw was Allen standing in front of me with the fire poker. Suddenly, a switch flipped, and I went somewhere else.

The next thing I knew, my knuckles were raw, blood splattered my chest, and the boy was on the ground, barely breathing. The crowd was wild, and the announcer was holding my arm in the air.

"You won!" Allen screamed inches from my face. "You will fight tomorrow too."

"Ahh, the boy should rest, and we need to get his head checked." Langley stiffened when Allen whirled around and stuck a finger in his face.

"You're a dime a dozen. Remember that, Chang!"

Langley stopped me from following Allen into the little room.

"You will see a doctor tonight. If you're well enough to fight, then fine. But," he turned to Allen, "we have a contract. I will make the call if the boy fights, not you."

Allen's neck flexed, but he didn't say anything.

I fought every week for the next six months.

I became a robot. Fight, train, fight.

Langley became more of a mentor than a coach. He was the one who made sure I had money in a private bank account so if anything were to happen, I would be okay.

The thunderous noise smacked me back to the present. I knew that muffler. Fuck!

Tess stared in the direction of the noise. I whistled and waved her over, and mother of hell, she actually came. She slowly waded in the water to not draw attention to herself. Thankfully, it was still dark, and we couldn't be seen that easily. I met her under the pier and tugged her up onto the dry sand.

"Who are they?"

"Not someone I want you to meet."

Keeping within the shadows, we moved to a better location under the pier so I could see them more clearly. They scanned the beach, obviously looking for a place to party. They were laughing about something. They drove their bikes down to a grassy patch near the edge of the water, but between us and the parking lot. *Shit.*

"Will you let me see?" she asked and tried to move around me. I stopped her and pushed her back behind me. "I'm not a child."

"I'm aware."

"Well?"

I turned to face her. She was so close, and I could smell her perfume. "I have six bullets to my name right now. There's ten of them. Odds aren't great."

She grabbed my arm and edged closer as the guys came down onto the beach. I backed us up to a cement wall. Tess curled into me, her face buried in my shoulder.

"Tell me what to do," she whispered.

"Don't move, and stay quiet." She nodded but peeked out as one the guys came under the pier for a piss while the others walked back down the beach.

He hummed a drinkin' tune as he pissed about twelve feet away. He could hardly stand and bumped into the pillar. His mouth was open as he face planted, eating a heap of sand. A deep curse was muffled before he coughed it out. He looked up and saw us. He squinted, his mouth still open, wet sand around his lips.

"Wait, now. I know you…" he slurred at Tess then swiped out for her leg.

"No!" she hissed. "Trigger."

"I could do such nasty things to you."

Her fingers dug into my arm as I lifted her up behind me.

He moved to his knees, not at all registering me in front of him, his eyes glued as they were on her.

"I'll use every hole—"

I lost sense of everything around me. One moment he was grabbing for her, and the next he was in a bloody pool of water, unconscious. My fist throbbed and blood made my neck pulse with adrenaline. Killing for disloyalty within my club was part of the job, but when my switch got flipped, it was a different feeling. Like going from one to one hundred in a blink, a sudden rush without being ready for it. I forgot how much I loved that feeling.

Panting in short breaths, Tess had her hands over her mouth as she stared at me.

"You scared of me now?" I muttered as I filled his shirt with rocks and tucked it into his jeans. She didn't respond. She just sat there.

Tugging his body farther into the ocean under the pier, I waded above my knees and let him sink to the bottom. I knew it was the best I could do under the circumstances. Normally, I'd toss him off the end of the pier, but the rest of his members had made a fire and were already heavy into the booze.

Fuck me.

I snatched Tess's arm and hurried her toward the lifeguard hut. My jeans were heavy, so it made it harder to move, but we needed a place to wait them out. The Serpents had a reputation, and two against nine wasn't something I wanted to deal with right now.

"Come on." I lifted her onto the platform and jumped up behind her. Once inside the little hut, I made her sit while I watched the men for a while. One did shout out a name, probably the guy I had whacked, but he eventually sat down and continued to party with the rest of them. The light rain didn't seem to have any effect on their party, but I hoped it would eventually make them move on.

"Are you sure he's dead?" she whispered. It was too dark to see her expression, but I could imagine what was going through her head.

"Well, yeah."

"Good," she huffed, to my surprise. "He's nuts."

Hold up. "You know who he is?"

"No…I…" she stumbled, which made me turn. "He just seemed nuts."

The sound of the rain on the roof helped buffer our movements inside.

"What will they do if they find us here?"

With another glance over my shoulder at the Serpents' party off in the distance, I sank to the floor and pulled out a joint and felt the paper. It was still dry, surprisingly. There was an offshore breeze this evening, so I knew they wouldn't smell it. I wet one tip and lit the other.

I caught a glimpse of her worried face.

"Not me I'm worried about." Smoke poured from my lips.

"Oh." She paused. "What will they do to me?"

"You ever see that movie, *Black Snake Moan*?"

She cleared her throat quietly. "Yes."

I didn't say anything else; she got it. They would destroy her.

Tess didn't move after that, and I wasn't sure where her thoughts went.

The silence killed my head, and I needed something to distract me.

"Come here," I commanded, but when she didn't move, I reached for her hand and tugged her to me.

She crawled in between my bent legs in that sexy way from the strip joint. Flowers filled my head; her perfume was strong tonight. She was frozen, and her touch was like ice on my arms.

"You're frozen."

"I'm fine," she whispered in a shaky voice and moved closer.

Her lips hovered above mine, her breath hot on my face. Her breasts just below my chin were a fucking tease. Her slender fingers cupped my jaw. When I breathed out, she leaned in and inhaled what I exhaled. My hands moved to slide down the backs of her cold thighs. The joint hung between my fingers as she moved to straddle my waist.

She started to touch me, but I grabbed her wrists and held them in place.

"Why don't you let people touch you?"

I flinched at her question. I didn't do personal information. I pulled her mouth to mine, and she came willingly. Her mouth parted and let me control the kiss. Delicious pain drove into my shoulders as her nails clawed through my shirt, hungry for more.

"Trigger." She pulled back and lifted herself off my lap.

Gripping her hips, I slammed her back down. Her weight was perfect and helped ease the pain of my erection, which was constant when she was near.

"I can't help myself around you." She started to grind my lap with a little moan.

I started to ask what she was doing when she pulled at my belt. This girl was reckless at the worst of times.

Grasping her hands again, I held them up. "Not here." I closed my eyes to control myself. My adrenaline was still lingering. "It's not safe."

She slipped her hands out of my grip. "I'm not scared of them."

"I'm not talking about them."

For a split second, she froze before she shuffled backward. "Lipstick it is, then."

I dismissed her strange comment and watched as she sat across from me, her legs out straight, touching mine. I lit the joint that had gone out and took a long drag before I handed it to her.

"So?" She blew out a puff of smoke. "Why don't you let people touch you?"

Really?

"You're sexy as shit, Tess, but let's not get the lines blurred."

"Wow." She laughed then handed me back the joint. "I'm not sure what you think I'm looking for, Trigger. I have zero interest in locking *you* into a relationship. I don't date, don't want kids, don't want to answer to anyone."

I chuckled. "You'll answer to me."

"Because you are my employer." She added, "For now."

That's what you think.

We sat for a while, sharing the joint, and listened for company. After a bit, I heard her breathing even out. She curled herself into a ball in the corner. Finally, I let my guard down slightly. With one more glance out the window at the men on the other side of the pier, I knew they weren't going anywhere anytime soon. I closed my eyes. The sun should be up soon. I tried to tune in to everything around me, but it wasn't long before I was fighting sleep.

"You fight for me, no one else. You want to live another day, you win. No one wants a loser, and the moment you lose, it's over. Remember that."

"No!" Her voice shot me back. To sunlight…

I scanned the room, and there was Tess holding my gun on me, but her eyes looked past me, and I felt cold steel press into my temple. *Oh, shit.* We'd been found.

Her hands shook as she clutched the gun. "Only a coward would kill a man in his sleep."

"Tess." I caught her attention, but only until he spoke.

"I'll teach that mouth a lesson when I'm through with him."

Her face flushed as her anger rose. The gun pulled to the side as she squeezed the trigger, her eyes tightly shut.

Bang!

The wall above me blew up, and wood went everywhere. I took that moment and elbowed him in the crotch. He yelped as he fell backward and tumbled to the sand.

"No!" Tess lowered the gun, trying to fire it again, but it jammed.

I jumped and raced out after him. The guy tripped on the rocks as he tried to climb the wall below the parking lot.

At that moment, I saw it was a Serpent. His crap was next to the pillar. He must have passed out and was looking for a place to sleep off the rest of his hangover when he found us.

My boots filled with sand as I closed the distance between us. Just as he looked over his shoulder, he tumbled and hit his chest, knocking the wind out of him.

I grabbed a hefty rock, held it above my head, and smashed it into his head. His skull crushed, and blood sprayed everywhere.

I should have been more careful, but the fucker was about to kill me and Tess. I glanced about but didn't see any of the other members. I dragged him toward the water and hoped he would join his buddy on the sea floor.

When I looked up at the shore, Tess was flipping all the bloodied rocks over.

Who the hell is this girl?

I let my irritation surface as I hurried back up to the beach. We had to get the hell out of here in case any of the others were still here and sober enough to look for their men.

"Let's go." My fingers locked around her arm and rushed her up the rocks to my bike. Goosebumps lined her skin, so I tossed her my hoodie and handed her the boots from the saddlebag. Oddly, it was a turn-on seeing her in my clothes. Her shaky hands fumbled with the helmet strap. Pushing them aside, I helped her then started the bike. She awkwardly climbed on behind and rested her hands on my hips. With a sigh, I pulled her arms further around me. When would she learn?

With a twist of my wrist, I pulled out onto the highway. The Serpents might be on our ass soon. Weaving through morning traffic, I caught her expression in the mirror. It was empty, just as I predicted it would be. My life wasn't meant to be shared by two.

I pulled up to her apartment and parked. Before my boots hit the ground, she jumped off with her purse and hung her helmet off the seat.

"Hey." I grabbed her wrist. "You okay?"

"Are you?"

"That would imply I feel things."

"Right." She nearly laughed.

Fuck. "I just need to know you can handle what you saw." Her back straightened and her jaw locked in place. "Brick may have gotten you in over your head coming here."

"I might be smaller than you, Trigger, but I don't break that easily."

I laughed, surprised, and she got pissed. Her arms crossed as she shook her head.

"Demons find all kinds of people." Her eyes darkened. "Just because I don't share them doesn't mean they aren't running right alongside my life."

"I'm listening." I smiled, but it fell when her face twisted into a no-go warning.

"We don't share, remember, Trigger? Stories lead to feelings, and feelings lead to pain. No one wants pain."

"I guess everyone has their own *version* of pain." I couldn't help my sarcasm at this little chick, who most likely got dumped by a high school sweetheart and thought she knew how the world could dish out pain. Cute.

"You know what?" Her gaze fell to the ground and a small smile appeared. "Forget it."

She started to walk to the door.

"Tess!" She ignored me. Hopping off my bike, I snagged her arm so she'd look at me. "Don't walk away from me when I'm talking to you."

"You're a bit of an asshole, aren't you?"

"Yeah." I shrugged, not giving a shit. It was the truth. "Just tell me if you're okay or not."

Her eyes crinkled, but I caught a glimpse of exhaustion before she stepped forward and gently slid her hand over my erection, giving it a good tug. I fought the image of her mouth down there. I had to hold back my reaction. I didn't care we were outside. I would take this woman now.

"I have balls of steel too, Trigger." She backed into the building. "I'm not yours, so why do you care?"

"Be at the club at six." With that, I left.

***

Tess

I felt a little better after my five-hour nap, hot shower, and a salmon stir-fry. It was amazing how eating right could make you feel decent after so much drama. It was a huge step up from when Brick and I used to steal McDonald's creamers and sugars.

I tucked away what happened with Trigger. For whatever reason, the dead bodies didn't bother me. Maybe because when I was eleven I saw a girl overdose in our living room and watched as they hid her in a trashcan like she was a roll of carpet. Disposable. I reminded myself to check in with my past every once in a while because it was a wise thing to do. It helped keep my guard up.

I grabbed my bag and headed down toward the waiting cab. The roar of a bike made me look up, and Rail beamed at me.

"Want a ride?"

I eyed the beast of a bike and decided it beat some dirty cab. I stepped away as the cab drove off.

What am I doing?

"Here." He handed me a helmet and waited for me to climb on. I placed my hands on his waist, and it felt strange. "You good?"

No, my nerves kicked in.

I nodded once, and we sped away. He took the corners tight, and I felt the heat from the pavement on my legs. He ran reds, and when he did stop, he jolted instead of braking smoothly. He drove differently than Trigger, more recklessly, or maybe Trigger had just been kinder to me, but either way, I wouldn't be riding with Rail again for a while. By the time we got to the club, my fingers ached and my feet had never been happier to hit solid ground.

Land!

"Thanks," I muttered, rubbing my ass as I handed him back the helmet.

"Anytime." He grinned at me.

"You're back," Brick called out, coming over for a hug, but instead he spun me around. "Damn, girl! I can see the bottom of your ass. Where are the rest of your shorts?"

I rolled my eyes and gave him a kiss on the cheek. "It's more than the other chicks wear."

"That's different!" He came up behind me. "You're not supposed to be sexy. There're too many men here who want a piece of you already. Don't get me started on last night either."

"Since when is there a dress code in this club?" I smacked his arm. "I can handle myself, Bricky." I smirked at the nickname. I walked backward toward the bar. "Big girl, remember?" I turned, dropped my bag, and bent over at the waist to make him more uncomfortable. This was why we were best friends. We were assholes with big hearts…but assholes first.

"Such a dick."

I scooped up my bag. "Why, thank you."

"But, really, the strip joint?" He leaned on the bar and watched me unpack. "Seriously, Tess, what were you thinking?"

I saw Trigger walk by the bar. He had changed into jeans, biker boots, and a dark t-shirt—and, of course, his cut. That was his normal attire.

"I was thinking I was fired and had no money."

"Yes, you do."

"No, Brick." I rubbed his hand lovingly. "I don't."

His mouth twisted as he thought. "How much you need?"

"No." I pointed the whiskey bottle at him.

"I might have a second job you could do to make some extra cash."

"Really? Where?" Now, this idea, I liked. Money brought pride, and I really needed some of that right now.

"Rail owns a garage. Maybe you can do the paperwork or something?"

I thought for a moment then grinned. Other than his driving skills, he was fun to be around. "Would I get to wear those cute little coveralls with the zipper down the front?"

"I hate you."

"Maybe I could roll it down and tie it at the waist, and have a cute little belly top."

Brick tried to smack my arm, but I hopped out of the way. "Come here, Tess!"

I ducked under the bar and held my hands up as he got closer. "Or maybe no top at all!" I held up my hands like I was about to fight.

"That's cute."

"Come on, Brick." I slapped his shoulder as I hopped back and forth. "Don't hold back on me now. I saw how you were on the streets."

"All right, Tess, show me your best."

Morgan leaned over the counter and watched. Brick punched, but I jumped back with a yelp. I knew he'd never hurt me, but I wanted to win.

"Come on, Tiger," Morgan hooted. "Use your assets."

"Dude." Brick dropped his arms and glared at him. "She's my fucking sister."

I tapped his cheek and laughed. "That's, what? Two for me now? Yeah, two."

"Oh." Jace, the newer prospect, slipped in near Morgan. "I get winner!"

Brick started to scowl but stopped himself when he saw me move in closer.

"Nice try, but that won't—"

"Brick!" Gus rounded the corner. "We have a problem."

"Damn." He stopped, and I knew we were done. "Give me a few. I want to talk to you more."

Jace hopped over a seat when I went to wipe down the tables. His boyish grin made me smile. He was a bit infectious sometimes, and sweet in a dorky way.

"So, you and Brick lived on the streets?"

He was a cute kid, but he was a kid. I was almost thirty-two and had witnessed too much to date down. I did enjoy Jace, though. He seemed genuine.

"Yeah," I admitted.

"What was it like?"

I folded my arms and sat on the table. "Great at first, then fucking horrible."

"What happened?"

"I was fourteen, young, and had no money. I was what they called prime meat."

He moved closer and sat on a chair backward. His arms leaned over the back. "So, a pimp?"

I laughed, but it stopped short when I recalled the horror of it. "Worse."

"What's worse than a pimp?"

"What brought you here, Jace?"

He shook his head. "I heard you dodge personal questions."

"It's one of my many talents."

"Like dancing?"

I snapped my head around to look at him. Shame and a deep craving tore through me. One battled to take over, but I never let the other win. I wouldn't let either define me.

"I heard you rocked the place."

I nodded as I pulled the rag through my fingers, deep in thought.

"Sometimes humans slip back into old habits. Sometimes the craving is so intense you can't think of anything else." I stepped over to him.

"How did it make you feel, being up there?" I began to use my *assets* on him and he swallowed hard as he tried not to react.

"You ever have someone take over your body, mind, everything?" He nodded. "It's like that, but for…" I felt Trigger's eyes on me from across the room, but I ignored him. "But imagine that times thirty."

"Thirty?"

"Thirty pairs of eyes were on me, thinking whatever they wanted."

He shifted as I stood directly in front of him. His gaze fell on my breasts. "What d-did you want?"

I leaned down and whispered, "I wanted to be their fantasy, their best of the night. In return, I'd use them as my escape."

"Escape from what?"

I pulled back and stared him right in the eye. His throat contracted and his cheeks flushed. For once I went with the cold, bare honesty. "From this."

"Tess," Trigger called out.

"Excuse me." Tossing the rag on the table, I made my way over. "Yeah?" I stepped into his office and found him next to his desk staring at a photo.

"You showed."

"Well, you fired me from my other gig, sooo…" I shrugged.

"How'd you get here this morning?"

I shook my head at his sudden change of direction. "Um, Rail."

"He spent the night?"

"What the hell are you talking about?"

He rubbed above his eyes. "Did you fuck Rail?"

"No. I came downstairs and he was there, and he offered me a ride."

He dropped the photo and sat in his chair with a heavy thud. Something weighed on him.

"You okay?"

My eyebrows drew together. "Why do you keep asking me that?"

"Because you won't answer me."

I opened my mouth to snap back, but I stopped myself. He was right. I rubbed my arm and then my wrist.

"I'm fine. There was a point last night where I was scared, but I was with you, so I knew we'd be all right."

His stare became intense. "Okay. So, you trust me?"

"I trust parts of you, yes."

"Parts?" He seemed amused by that.

"I think you genuinely care if I get hurt. Brick is your best friend, and I'm his, so I can see how that would go hand-in-hand. I appreciate what you did for me last night, but not other things."

"Other things."

"I don't think you have a right to stop me from dancing."

"My club."

"Right, a club where I can make *us* a good living. What you did was a bad business move."

He chuckled and fiddled with his pen. "Now you're giving me business advice?"

I groaned internally and went back to my original argument. We were not going to agree on this.

"I think I'm a little confused about why you called me in here."

Trigger tossed me a photo. I picked it up and swallowed hard. There was me walking by the clubhouse, my face stuck in my phone.

"Turns out you made an impression on the Serpents."

"Not sure how I did that." Son of a bitch, how did he find out about that night?

"I have a mole who said the Serpents have been watching you go to and from work. You might want to think of taking over one of the free rooms we have here."

"You want me to move in here?" I wanted to laugh.

"Something wrong with my clubhouse? It's not the Hilton, but it's safer than where you are now."

My temper rose. That was my problem with Trigger. He assumed he knew me. "Whatever gave you the idea I was from money?"

"No one walks through that door and becomes part of my family without me knowing who they are."

"Why am I here, Trigger?" I was tired already.

"I told you, the Serpents have their eye on you. It's only matter of time. I need to know you're okay and that you won't tell a soul what happened yesterday."

Seriously?

"First, I would never. And second, why am I here?"

"I just told you why."

I closed my eyes and tried to find the right words. "All I do is drive you insane. Why on earth would you want that?"

He didn't answer. He just stared at the floor as I stood and headed for the door. "I don't know why," he whispered, bringing me to a standstill. "I just do, so fucking deal with it."

I opened the door and stopped. "Besides liking my alone time, there is one other reason why I love my apartment." He remained quiet. "Let me think about it, okay?"

I heard his chair squeak.

"Stay off my men's bikes."

I turned to glare at him. "Why?"

"Because it means something."

"I rode on yours. What does that mean?"

"It means stay the hell off their bikes."

"Uncle T?" Den popped his head in the door. His big, dark eyes beamed up at me. "Hey, Tess."

"Hey, kid."

"Look!" He held up a paper to Trigger. "Got them all right."

Trigger flashed him a smile that nearly had me mesmerized. Christ, he had sexy moments.

"So, you can count, you little shit." Trigger lit a joint, and I laughed, catching his attention.

"Good job, Den," I chimed in, feeling like the boy could use a female touch.

Den looked at my shorts then over at Trigger. "Nice."

"She's too old for you," he huffed.

I shot him a look then glanced down at the seven-year-old perv. "I don't date, sweetheart, but you'd be the first on my list." I winked.

"So, now will you teach me to toss a right hook?" I heard him ask as I shut the door behind them.

Brick stared me down from across the table. Morgan came over twice to bring us a drink, but Brick sent him away each time. Which sucked because I was thirsty.

"Details, now." He nodded at Trigger's hoodie that was stuffed in my bag.

I rolled my eyes and granted him a side smile. "He offered me his hoodie last night. I was going to return it." Morgan was at my side. He froze, and they both stared at me. "What?"

"Trigger *offered* you his hoodie?" Brick repeated.

"Yes." I shrugged. "I don't get what you are thinking here, guys."

Morgan ran his hand down his long beard. "You had Trig's

hoodie?"

I dropped my glass down on the hard wood with a deep sigh. "No matter how many ways you ask me, guys, the answer is still the same. Please tell me what you want to hear."

"Says anything without a care, wears his hoodie…" Brick turned to me like he was counting. "Have you ridden on his chopper?"

Oh, Christ…

"You have, haven't you? I'm honestly lost for words."

"That's a first," I joked.

"It's like a fucked up blind date with the devil," Morgan muttered in amazement.

"Pardon?"

He glanced over my head at Brick. "Make this right."

"Make what right? Seriously, guys, feel free to include me in this conversation." I shoved Brick, who looked stunned. Finally, he snapped out of it and moved as I stood. He grabbed my shoulders and bent down to my eye level.

"Tess, you're walking a thin line. Trigger is not someone you fall in love with. I don't even think he would know how to. Since he was a boy, he's been surrounded by nothing but hate. He's been killing since you were on the school playground."

"Easy," Morgan warned.

Brick squeezed his eyes shut briefly before he reined himself in. "Nothing positive will come from it."

I shook free from his grip, beyond pissed my best friend was giving me a pep talk. "And you think I am capable of such feelings?" I suddenly felt uncomfortable in my own skin.

"I know you are."

"Stop, Brick," I warned in a tone I didn't like to use. "Move on."

Morgan stepped in between us. "All right, Tess, take a break. Go for a walk."

CHAPTER SIX

Trigger

"What's wrong?" Brick was a million miles away, and I needed him here with me.

He glanced outside the meeting room. "Can I ask you something with the risk of stepping over the line?"

No.

"Depends."

"Are you interested in Tess?"

I chuckled and lit my joint. After a long exhale, I spoke. "She is quite a woman, isn't she?"

"But that wasn't my question."

Clearing my throat, I swallowed my annoyance. "She intrigues me."

"Tess is good at that." He played with the clip of his gun, and I knew there was more to come. "Look, there is so much you don't know about her. I can't tell you not to do anything, but I'm saying please be careful. She's fragile, and her past is still hot on her heels."

"Care to explain some of it?"

"No." He looked at me right in the eye. "I'd tell you my deepest secret, but I won't ever risk losing her again. I would never break her confidence, and she is a very private person. She's the closest thing I've ever had to family, and I would die for her."

"You sure you're not in love with her yourself?" My own words bothered me. Who was I to ask that?

"Oh, I love her, but not in that way. We've had lots of chances to have something happen, but that's not what we need from each other."

"All right."

"All right?" he questioned.

"I'll take all of that into consideration."

He wasn't happy with that, but he let it go, as he should. I didn't do personal, but I would bend a little for Brick.

"We done with this?" I pulled out a spreadsheet.

"What you got?"

I tossed the sheet at him and folded my arms. "Why hasn't the second half of the money come through?"

"I thought Cray and Rail were looking into it."

"Well, now I need you to. New Orleans will be arriving in a few days, and I want to be able to clear their debt. The last thing we need is more Stripe Backs here."

The Stripe Backs attempted to run the northeast. They formed a few years back and had been encroaching on my territory for a while now. Our New Orleans VP saw an opportunity to buy some guns and turned around and sold them to a buyer working with the Stripe Backs. Needless to say, the deal went bad, and now they owed thirty grand. Normally, I'd deal directly with them myself, but I didn't need another enemy on my shoulders. I was still cleaning up the mess from Keith's little situation with the Almas Perdidas. Although I did have a detective friend who was handling it. Also, Cole stayed true to his word and had helped me get back one of my Arizona crew who had managed to get tangled up with the cartels.

Fuck.

"Anything else?" Brick opened his phone and sent off a quick text. When I didn't answer, he looked up. "What?"

I rubbed my beard before I glanced out into the bar. "Keep your ear to the ground about a priest."

"Priest, as in stale bread and holy water?"

"Our hangaround took the liberty to embed himself into the Serpents' club."

Brick sighed. "So, he's dead."

"Normally, yeah, but he heard there's a priest poking around our route."

Brick leaned forward. "You think he's dippin'?"

"Don't know, but I'm going to find out."

"Shit."

"Mm-hm," I agreed.

Brick stood and grabbed the file I had on the table. "I'll do some digging."

I followed him out and frowned at Morgan, who now worked the bar solo.

"She needed a moment—think she's out back."

I grabbed an apple and a small carton of milk and slipped out back, trying to clear my head. Kneeling, I made a kissing sound and waited. Her little black head popped out from under my truck's wheel well and made the tiniest cry.

"Come here, girl." I poured the milk in her dish and watched as she dropped to the ground and hurried over. Her pink tongue stuck out and slurped up the puddle. I sat and leaned against the hot steel. I could really use some sleep, but my head was set on spin.

What the hell was up with my crew?

As soon as the little cat was finished, she clawed her way up my jeans, dug into my arm, and settled in on my shoulder. She batted at my hair and purred happily.

"Don't mind me," I whispered sarcastically but scratched under her chin.

"Mew." She pawed my face for more attention. Her big yellow eyes blinked, wondering what I waited for.

"Maybe I want to be rubbed. Hmm?" She sneezed and fell from the force of it, landing in my lap. "That's what you get for demanding something from me." She burrowed her head in my hand and purred.

The roar of an engine caught my attention, mainly because I heard Tess laugh.

"Back to your bed, kitty." I lifted her up into the wheel well and helped her into the spot I made for her when I first found her.

Tossing my apple over the fence, I hurried around back and slipped through the fence. When I rounded the corner, I was shocked at what I saw.

Tess was on Jace's bike as he showed her where everything was.

"Just ease it forward."

"I can't." She looked nervous and small on the bike. "It'll fall."

"Nah," he grinned, "just ease out."

"Then what? Ease into traffic and take it for a spin?"

I couldn't help but smile at her comment. She was right—then what?

"Here, shift back and I'll show you."

She hesitated and squared her shoulders. "Just give me second."

Jace caught sight of me and looked terrified. I didn't blame him. As a prospect, he hadn't yet earned his place here. I shook my head to let him know it was fine. She wasn't going anywhere. She was too nervous.

I tried not to think about her ass hanging out of her jean shorts as I slid in behind her. Her body froze stiff as a board.

"Let go of the brake and ease onto the gas." She sagged into me when my hands moved to cover hers. "Go on."

The bike jumped forward, and she yelped.

"Never mind. This was a bad idea."

My lips moved to her ear. "I disagree." Pressing down, I held her hands in place and gently moved the bike forward and out onto the road.

Jace rode a chopper with ape hanger handlebars, which meant our arms were extended up high and I could really study her toned figure. She felt good between my legs, where I had her all to myself.

When we came to the light, both my feet hit the ground, and she did the same. Her body shook, her nerves getting the best of her.

"You're fine."

I pointed to the exit and flicked on the blinker to jump on the PCH. Traffic was light heading north, the water was calm, and the sunset spread along the ocean's horizon.

Tess seemed to ease up a little, and her legs released their death grip on the sides of the seat.

We hit a patch of traffic, and she pulled back on the gas, but I sped us up. She shook her head, but I pushed on.

"Trigger," she looked panicked, "it doesn't feel right."

"Hey." I squeezed her hand. "Have I ever let anything happen to you?"

Her head turned, and her mouth opened, but instead she just gave me a little nod. She didn't complain, but she did keep her eyes squeezed shut until I finally had to tap her arm.

When she opened them, I saw her relax in the mirror.

We were now on the open road, cruising through the mountains with only one other car which faded quickly behind us.

She slipped her hands from under mine and spread them out at her sides, arching her back, and rested her head on my shoulder.

I smiled and knew what she was feeling. There was nothing like a ride at night all alone with nothing but the moon to keep you company.

We weren't far from where I wanted to stop. It was a huge field that overlooked the ocean from high up on a towering cliff.

"Hands back down," I ordered, and she placed them back on the handlebars. I leaned into the turn, and we rushed onto the long, grassy path that led us to a favorite spot. Parking behind the protection of some bushes, I turned the engine off.

Tess dropped her arms and shook them. "How do you guys do that for long trips?"

I swung my leg and offered her a hand. "You get used to it."

"Your bike is different, not so high up."

"Just a preference." I took her hand and tugged her behind me. "Come."

She dug her heels into the dirt, and I stopped and looked at her. "We are miles from the club. I sure as shit won't be riding that beast solo." She shrugged. "I'm not looking for a gentleman, but for once you could say '*Would you come with me?*'"

I wanted to snap back with something, but I thought about what she was saying. As much as it was foreign to me, I gave it a try.

"Tess, I want to show you something. Would you like to see it?"

She bit down on her bottom lip, but it broke free as her grin spread across her sexy face.

"Yes, I would."

"Good." Because that wouldn't happen again.

I helped her up the path and over the rocks to the lookout. Once she got her footing, she gasped.

"Wow," she sighed at the view. "It's beautiful."

I lit a joint and sat on a rock a few feet from her. I liked to stand back and watch Tess. Besides her perfect body, she was easy to be around. She rubbed her shoulders as the breeze picked up. It was cooler up here than down in the city. Which was why I loved it here so much.

She glanced back at me. "You seem to have an endless supply of those." She pointed at my joint.

I tapped my head. "Helps with the shit inside."

Her eyebrows rose when she smirked. "I get that."

"Yeah?" I wanted to laugh, but her expression told me not to. So I went in a different direction, one that bothered me. "Where did you learn how to dance like that?"

Her hand went to her wrist and fiddled with her stack of bracelets. "Not that difficult."

"No." I cut her off. "More than half those girls don't know how to use the pole right. But you—"

"Me, what?" She stepped in between my legs, removed the joint, placed between her pink lips, and inhaled.

"But you know how."

She leaned down and hovered over my lips. "Beginner's luck. "

"Don't," I warned, but she pressed her body against mine, and I lost it. Grabbing her waist, I hiked her up as I stood and slammed her against the trunk of a tree. "Don't start something you can't handle, Tess."

Her chest heaved, but her eyes were wild.

"I'll break you."

"Can't break something that is already broken, Trigger." Her hands slipped into my hair, and I fought to flip my switch.

"Don't use sex as a weapon on me," I growled while my body vibrated with the need to tear into her.

"Stop fighting this, Trigger, and do it!" She squeezed her legs hard around me, and I felt myself slip closer to the edge.

"Stop!"

"Flip your fucking switch!" she taunted me before she slapped my cheek. "Flip it."

Flick.

I grabbed her head and smashed my lips to hers. Once I knew she wouldn't pull away, I used my leg to hold her in place as I grabbed her arms and pinned them above her head. She wiggled them free, and they landed heavily on my shoulders. To my surprise, it didn't throw me into a memory. They slid up my neck and into my hair, while our mouths were attacking each other. I hiked up her shirt and rubbed her nipple through her bra.

Her lips moved to my neck, and I shuddered at the sensation. I couldn't remember a time when I allowed a woman to be there. She drew in my skin and sucked with a hum.

"If you want to keep these shorts, get rid of them now." I bit at her earlobe and pushed back when she tried to move. My jeans were off, and as she kicked off her shorts I had her in my arms again, back in position. "You on the pill?"

She cringed. "Yeah." I didn't wait to warm her up; she wanted it as bad as I did. Lining up, I slid her down on me until I was fully in. "Goddamn!" She struggled to adjust to my size, clawing at my arms with a moan.

"I don't do slow, Tess, so—"

"So, shut up and fuck me." She grabbed my face and kissed me.

Shit…this woman.

Holding her hips steady, I thrust rapidly, harder than normal to make my point. The entire time, she kissed and panted but didn't seem to mind that I used her body like a goddamn blow-up doll.

"Harder, Trigger!" she shouted as I lost my head in the moment. She felt tight, warm, and wet, and the combination was overwhelming. My mind went fuzzy and my skin broke out in a wildfire that shot down to my fingertips.

*Pound, pound, pound…*The sound only made it that much better. Her breasts swung and bounced at my assault, and her grip around my waist cut into my skin. The pain was perfect. Careful to make sure she wasn't hurt by the tree, I protected her skin with my arm. My head couldn't focus on anything but the fact I was deep inside this fucking woman.

Just when I thought my knees were going to give out, she broke the kiss to scream and shake. Her head flopped back, and I dove into her neck, nipping at the skin as I followed. My stomach coiled and released with a bang as I shot myself deep inside of her.

"Shit." I shook out a little more before I felt the effects of what she just did to me. I always knew sex with Tess would be different, but that was something else. Pulling free, I lowered her to her feet and waited until she was steady.

She held on to the tree as she scooped up her shorts and pulled them on. I had to turn my back while I got dressed, wanting more. Just as I fastened my belt, I felt my phone ring.

"Yeah?"

"Fuck, Trigger, I have been trying to get hold of you for a week now."

I glanced at the number. "Donny?"

"Yeah, we need to talk." His voice broke in and out.

"I can't hear what you're saying." I moved about to get better reception. Fucking mountains.

"Not…guns…Backs…Priest." My blood went cold when I caught the last word.

"Donny! Have you made it to California yet?"

No answer. Fuck! I looked at the screen, and the call had dropped.

"Fuck!" I whirled around and hopped on the bike. "Get on."

***

Tess

The ride back was hard. Trigger was silent as he stewed about his phone call, and I couldn't get the feeling of him being inside of me out of my head. I would have gone six rounds with him if that stupid Donny hadn't called. Who the hell was he, anyway?

Trigger picked up speed as we approached the city limits. Four times I had to duck my head into his shoulder because he weaved in between huge trucks. I thought I was going to be sick. Finally, at a stoplight, I unlatched my fingers from their death grip and shook the blood back through my poor limbs.

I wished I knew what was going through his head; his face was so serious. The streetlights only made him look more intense in the mirror.

Just as the bike took off again, my mind slipped away from me.

"What's wrong?" I sat next to him on the bed.

"I need to tell you something, something that is going to hurt you, but you need to hear me out before you freak out, okay?" I heard him, but his face scared the shit out of me.

"I don't know if I can take any more hurt."

His mouth opened and the words came out, but I soon felt like I was falling down a black hole. My stomach dropped. How could this happen? He just kept going, and the last words that ripped me apart were...

"I'm still here, just in a different way now."

I jolted forward as Trigger slammed the bike to a halt and hopped off. He stopped and looked at me, and I saw what appeared to be regret wash across his face.

"Don't think that what happened back there means anything—"

It took me a moment to realize what he saw; my eyes were watering.

Oh, for God's sake!

"Save it, Trigger. I want nothing from anyone." I chucked my helmet at him and headed inside.

"Well, then, why the hell are you crying?"

I whirled around, ignoring Big Joe's offer to hold the door open for me. "You don't do relationships, but you're consistently asking me what's wrong, which would imply you care. So, why don't we just call this what it is. We had fun. That's it."

"You didn't answer my question."

I looked up at the sky and closed my eyes before I turned. "Thanks,

Joe."

"Sure thing, sweetheart."

When will that man realize I want nothing more than some fun? Why do men always think women are scamming them? I get I'm not most women, but damn, dude, relax.

"Please tell me you didn't wreck my bike." Jace hopped to his feet and rushed by me, knocking over a stool. Morgan tossed me a rag and gestured for me to come wipe down the place.

"Sorry, Morgan."

"Nope. You were with the boss, no need to apologize." He glanced over his shoulder. "You good?"

I couldn't help but smile a little.

"What?"

"Nothing." I tried to control my grin.

"Spit it out, Tiger."

"You care about me, don't you?"

He rolled his eyes and went back to counting the money.

"Aw, Morgan." I held out my arms. "Come on, give me a little lovin'. You know you wanna."

"Don't do contact."

"Is that the club motto?" I laughed humorlessly before I wrapped my arms around his shoulders and, just to piss him off more, I kissed his cheek. He stiffened but didn't pull away. "I'm fine, but thank you for caring."

"I don't."

"Okay." I winked, and he broke his tough act and smiled.

"You *are* trouble."

"So I've been told."

I made sure I pulled more than my share of the weight the rest of the night. I felt bad that Morgan couldn't depend on if I was coming or going.

Brick sat across the table. He was upset with me for riding a bike, even though Trigger was there.

"I don't like it," he huffed, pushing the dinner plate away. "I think it might have been a mistake bringing you here."

"Ouch."

"I'm nervous for you, Tess. You're reckless."

"I am, but I'm aware of it, and I've managed to stay alive for thirty-two years, so I'd say I'm not terrible at being reckless."

"It's not a joke."

I took his hand and drew a square over the top with my finger until he finally let the topic go. When we were on the streets, Brick had nightmares about his brother. Nick disappeared when Brick was eight, and he always thought the worst about what might have happened to him. Brick's night terrors would sometimes get us thrown out of the safe homes, so I'd tell him a story about how we lived in a box where no one could touch us. I'd trace over his hand, and it would calm him. I wanted him to know I was okay. I really was.

"How's Jilly?" I had to know. I didn't trust his sister wasn't after him for money again.

He rubbed his forehead, a telltale sign it wasn't good. "She's bad again. I found her with a needle sticking out of her arm, passed out in the bathroom." *Yikes*. "She's in trouble. She wanted money, but I dealt with it my own way."

"Meaning?"

"Meaning I found out her debt and took care of it."

I rolled my eyes, finishing off my rum and Coke. Morgan came by with a fresh one. That was how it worked here. You kept the drinks coming until they passed out. I thanked him and looked back over at my friend, deciding to drop the deadbeat junkie sister topic.

"You seeing anyone?"

He smiled over the lip of his glass. "If I was and you met her, would you be kind?"

"Probably not," I half joked. His laugh made a few people look over at us.

"Speaking of getting some…" He pointed as my face burned. "When was the last time you got any?"

I pressed my lips together for a moment, curious if he could tell. Images of Trigger clawed their way to the surface, and I had to hide my blush. I could really use another go.

"By a man or a toy?"

His eyes lit up, and I saw him remember something. "Holy shit, do you still buy those?" He grabbed my purse and rooted around inside.

"Brick, I swear to Lucifer, if you pull it out, I'll sell Jilly on the black market."

"Ahh." He held up my purple lipstick with a laugh. "I see Pleasure Pace is still around."

I snatched it from his grip along with my purse and attempted to change the topic away from me.

"You gonna tell me who you are dating? And, I swear, if it's Peggy, our friendship is over."

Brick made a face, clearly disgusted with my comment. "You think that low of me?"

"No, I just witnessed her nasty red nails on more than one person's lap since I've been here." Well, actually, just Trigger's, but I wanted to hear what he had to say about her.

"Really?" He shook his head. "She's been after Trigger for three years."

"He's not interested?"

"Nah, you have to be able to touch someone to screw them. Trigger *hates* to be touched."

This, I knew, but I wanted to know why from Brick.

"Why is that?"

"Not sure. There's been talk it has something to do with his childhood."

"Was he molested?" That would explain it.

"Nah, more like physical abuse." He leaned in a little closer since the place was getting louder. "He and his father started the Devil's Reach. They say Trigger was always covered in blood, black eyes, jacked up hands. My guess is he fought a lot, and some say he was involved in some underground fighting thing."

"Oh." I nodded, but I really didn't know much about it.

"Oh…is right. He was only ten, although I think it was earlier than that. But that's a little fucked up, if you ask me." *Screw off, ten!* "They put you in a ring, and you fight with no protection till basically you or your opponent are beaten to a pulp."

"Bullshit, Brick, no way! Ten years old in a ring, fighting."

"I know." The lines between his eyes deepened. "There's no other word for it but fucked up. His father was a bastard and needed money. Trigger wasn't a small boy, from what Gus said the few times that he shared a story." He sighed and sipped his drink to take a moment to think. "Have you heard anything from—"

"Brick!" a female shrieked from somewhere behind, almost deafening me. "You're back!"

His face dropped, giving me a *you better be nice* look. "Be good," he warned.

A redhead came bouncing over, hopped on his lap, and stuck her tongue down his throat. What did I do? I laughed. I laughed hysterically, because I knew my best friend was freaking the fuck out inside that I got to witness this.

Brick was not someone who liked PDA, so being the asshole best friend, I pulled out my phone and snapped a lovely picture and took a five second recording to play back later for pure enjoyment. He gave me the finger as he pried the redhead from his lips.

"Minnie," he eyed me as I threw my head back and laughed harder, "this is my asshole best friend, Tess."

"Hi!" She swiveled on his lap and granted me a rather crooked but sweet smile. "Nice to meet you."

"Oh, no, the pleasure is *all* mine." I smirked into my cup. Minnie—who had huge eyes like Minnie Mouse—started talking a mile a minute to Brick about her manicure that went horribly wrong.

While I tuned her out, I caught sight of Trigger heading out to the back.

I didn't bother to tell Brick where I was going. He wouldn't have been able to hear me over the mouse's chatter. Blowing him a kiss, I eased out into the midnight air, called a cab, and went home.

Sitting in my window, I watched for the rooftop boxer, but once again, he didn't show. I dumped out my purse and found my lipstick. Inching down, I turned it on and lost myself in the memories of Trigger deep inside me.

The next morning, I Google Mapped a different route to the clubhouse. It was an extra thirty minutes, but anything was better than walking by that building. The beach could be seen on the main road, and I couldn't wait until I had a day off to enjoy it. The Vegas desert made the ocean seem like a dream.

By the time I hit the bar, I was fully awake and ready to start my shift. Morgan eyed me as I got closer. He blocked my path and stared down at me.

"Morning."

"Good morning, Morgan."

"The sink needs to be cleaned out."

"I guess you should let me pass so I can do it."

He nodded, but I saw a smile when he turned. As I headed for the kitchen, I thought I might have someone who cared about me here besides Brick. Speaking of which, I was curious to know if he was around today.

My phone vibrated inside my pocket, and with wet hands, I pulled it free and read the ID.

Unknown Caller.

I started to answer, but I felt someone sit down in front of me. I tossed it on the bar top and looked up.

Fuck, he was intense.

"Whiskey?" I reached for the bottle, but he shook his head.

"I want to know why you were crying last night."

Turning to place the whiskey label to face forward on the shelf, I answered. "You guys failed to mention to keep an extra pair of sunglasses on hand for riding. The wind whipped my face and made my eyes water."

When he didn't answer, I found his reflection in the little mirror.

"Try again."

"Not sure what you want to hear."

"I want the goddamn truth."

"Funny," I stuck my hip out and folded my arms, "I could demand the same thing."

He made a noise before he rubbed his face angrily. "I don't want to hurt you, Tess. If I made you cry, then I have the right to know."

Wow, not what I expected.

"You didn't make me cry, Trigger." Once again, I gave him the truth, but I could tell it wasn't enough. "And if you did?" I challenged.

"Then I wouldn't touch you again."

"So now you know." I couldn't help but drag my eyes down his front, stopping to gawk at his lean muscles. Where just a night ago my nails dug into each groove.

He opened his mouth to argue, but my phone went off with the same unknown caller.

Trigger picked it up and read the screen before he passed it over.

An uneasy vibe burst across my skin. *Damn.* "It's fine. Let it go to voicemail."

"Answer it."

I shook my head. Before I could react, he hit answer, and the blood felt like it dropped from my head to my toes.

"Hello?" His eyes stayed locked onto mine. "Who is this?"

This isn't happening.

His hand lowered, and I saw the call end.

"Who was that?" His tone sent my nerves a jolt.

"Wrong—"

"You sure you want to lie right now, Tess?" Leaning in, he was inches from my face.

My mind was ping-ponging all over the place. Old life and new life were never supposed to collide. I needed a new number immediately.

"I'm not sure." I cleared my throat but couldn't seem to produce any more than a whisper. "I'm not sure who it was."

"But you have a guess."

I closed my eyes and nodded.

"Don't fucking lie to me!" he barked, and my chin quivered. "I better not find out there's a shit storm coming my way." He left, slamming the bar stool to the ground.

Morgan approached me from the other side, his eyebrow cocked with confusion.

"My advice—"

"I didn't ask for it."

"Maybe not, but you're gonna hear it anyway. Don't piss off Trigger. You want him on your side when shit goes down."

"He doesn't need to know everything about me."

"Yeah, he does." Morgan moved to face me head on. "You are a part of this club, therefore you are a target. Trigger employed you, therefore he looks out for you. This is a family, Tess, and if you're bringing a shitty element into the house, we need to be prepared. This is not Walmart or the 7-Eleven. This is our house, and we don't listen to outside rules. If something bad is coming, you better tell us, or…" His head shook. "If you can't hang with that, you're not made for this life."

I tried to push the chip off my shoulder, my *protect yourself or die* motto. Where the hell was Brick? I could really use some backup right now.

"Fine." I ducked under the bar top and over to his office door. I knocked twice before I looked back at Morgan.

He said, "Look up to the left corner."

Sure enough, there was a camera, and a moment later I heard a click.

"Yeah," he yelled as a command to enter.

Pushing the door open, I found Trigger at his desk, a joint dangling from his fingers. The smell made me take a step inside.

"Can I come in?"

"You already are. What do you want?" He turned some papers over so I couldn't see. Little did he know, I didn't give a rat's ass what he was up to. I just needed a paycheck.

"You're right. We are a family, and I should be honest."

He didn't look up. He really was dicky sometimes.

I ran a hand through my hair as I went on. "The unknown caller is most likely my ex. He wasn't happy with me moving." I shrugged.

Trigger leaned back and watched me. He seemed to do that a lot.

"Is this ex going to pay you a visit anytime soon?"

"He would have to know where I am, and only Brick knows that, so my guess would be no."

"Don't need problems, Tess. We've been through this before."

"I know."

"Do you?"

I bit back my sassy comment and nodded.

He sucked back his joint and exhaled slowly, which made his eyes cloud over momentarily. There was something about this man that screamed sex. He made even a little movement like puffing out smoke hot.

His gaze dropped down my body, stopping at my jean skirt.

"You sore?"

His question threw me.

"No." I hated that my thighs flexed as hunger traveled right to my core. Then I saw him smirk, which in turn made me push back. "I finished myself a few more times when I got home."

His eyes darkened and his tongue brushed over his bottom lip. I wanted to lie down on his desk and let him do whatever he pleased, but I liked to fuck with him too.

"Pace steps in when I need him to." I was headed for the door when I hear the lock click.

CHAPTER SEVEN

Trigger

Her back stayed to me as I came up behind her and brushed her messy blonde hair off her slender shoulder. "Never," I whispered, sinking my teeth into her neck gently the way I knew she loved, "use Pace while we are actively fucking."

"You weren't there."

"Then move in here." My hand traveled down her leg and up under her skirt, where I found her wet. My mind shut off and all I wanted was to be in her. I pushed two fingers in, and she moaned. I circled her bud and spread her arousal around. Her arms came up and pressed my lips back to her neck. I sucked hard and twisted my tongue in the same pattern my fingers were moving.

My dick pressed into her back and beat to the blood pumping through it.

"Trigger, I'm too close. I was riled up from before." She ground into my painful erection.

"Good." I pulled my fingers free, whirled her around, and caught her chin. Her wild eyes flashed with anger. "We have company coming, and I need you to serve us in the meeting room."

"What?" She tried to catch up. Her cheeks were flushed, and I wanted to sink balls-deep in her, but I also needed her to stop fucking lying to me about shit.

I moved to unlock the door and sat on the edge of my desk.

"Screw you."

"Yes, you will be."

Just when I thought she was going to go off, she turned on her heel and marched out to the bar.

I didn't yell at her to close the door, mainly because I wanted to watch her walk away. Her tight little ass made my mouth water. I cringed when Brick's crotch blocked my view.

"What?"

"Can we talk?" He held up a hand to show me his camera.

I nodded for him to sit, and he did, but not before glancing once at Tess.

"She in trouble?" he asked without thinking.

I hated to be questioned. "You tell me."

His face twisted in confusion. "I don't think so."

"Is her ex someone I need to be concerned about showing up here causing problems?"

"Ah…" he stumbled and looked over his shoulder. His fingers flicked the camera on and off. "Look, you know I will never lie to you. But her history is something else. Not my place to tell it. I will say he's unstable, but from what I understand, he doesn't know where she is. So…"

I didn't like his answer. I could force it out of him, but Brick and Tess went way back, and I didn't want to take that from him.

"But I'll talk to her and see what's up."

"What's on the camera?" I nodded at him to close the door.

"Seems our bottle drop did the trick. I took this around four this morning. The Stripe Backs had three of the Serpents' men nailed to the back of their clubhouse wall. Blood drained from their necks, wrists, and ankles." The video was exactly what I wanted. My plan was to move the heat off my club's contract and over to the Stripe Backs.

When the video shut off, I saw myself. There was a time where my own reflection appeared unrecognizable. It was haunting, and now I saw myself for what I truly was. The son of the devil.

A knock sounded at the door, and I moved over to my computer and tapped a button to see the camera feed. There was Tess holding a lipstick in the air, and then she gave me the middle finger. I couldn't help but smirk. The chick flirted with my switch, and I liked it.

Suddenly, Morgan was in view and I buzzed it open.

"Hey, Trigger?" Morgan knocked at my door. "Prospects are on the way with the cash. Rail called it in."

"The other half?"

"Yes."

I nodded then pushed to my feet when I heard a commotion outside. Morgan turned but stepped back when I approached him.

"Seems we have some strays." Morgan laughed under his breath.

My tongue ran along my teeth in search of that tin taste that came when I was about to kill.

"Indeed."

I saw it in Morgan's eyes. He recognized the beast that was about to show itself. "You're going to frighten Tiger." He nodded toward Tess, who looked hesitant to serve them.

"Better she learns now."

Morgan smiled darkly before he stepped away.

I sat next to the preppy looking one and waved at Tess for some whiskey. She placed it in front of me, not looking in my direction. I took a deep breath. It'd been a while, and I needed this kill.

"Who sent you?"

The kid's eyes bulged and his neck contracted when he took me in.

"I-I…" he stammered. "It was just a dare, man. Part of the whole freshman thing."

"Who," I repeated and downed my shot, "sent you?"

"Nah, man," the other little prick cut in. "School thing."

Both my elbows fell heavily to the bar as I pulled myself in. Rubbing my chin with the back of my thumb, I weighed out their options. Tess started to wipe down the bar.

"So, can we get a drink?" The guy interrupted my thoughts again. "Just need a quick photo of it and we'll be on our way. Maybe with the girl?"

Brick stepped into view, his gun out, waiting for my command.

"You guys are insane," Tess hissed under her breath. "Just leave."

The kid next to me stood and hit his friend on the shoulder. "Come on, dude. Let's go."

"Look," the guy moved over one seat, "I'll make you a deal. One picture, and we leave. I'll tell all my friends about this place, and your business will triple."

"Stop." Tess tossed her rag on the counter and ducked under the door, rounding on us. She snatched the asshole kid's phone, fumbled with the screen, then held it up. "One, two, three." She snapped the phone and slammed it to his chest. "Now get the fuck out before he kills you."

"Thanks, doll!" The guy had a death wish. He went to kiss her on the cheek, but in one movement, she kneed him in the crotch, dropping him to the ground.

I hardly realized I had moved, but I felt his arm break in more than one place. My foot crushed down on his knee, rotating it out of its socket. Tess turned on me as I expected, but to my surprise, she grabbed the guy's phone and snapped another picture then tossed it at his stunned friend.

"Get him out of here, or you're next."

She stood between him and me. Her chest heaved, but she held her ground well. Somehow his friend dragged his broken ass out of my bar.

I broke the silence. "Who the fuck is watching the door?"

Tess turned around and tossed her hair out of her face with a huff.

"This place always this eventful?" she muttered, going back behind the bar.

"It's you, little Tiger." Morgan laughed from behind me. "Seems like your reputation might be out."

"Reputation?"

"Prime meat," he joked.

"Whatever."

The door burst open, and in walked Rail and the prospects. "Boss, we come with a gift."

"Good. Count it, bag it, and get it ready for our trip."

"Done and done." Rail grinned, but then something hit him. "Don't we have company tonight?"

"We do, indeed," Brick purred.

"Oh, please, let me play with one of them?" Rail whined, and I knew he and Brick were out to start another bicker match.

"One," I muttered and turned to face Tess then saw Peggy slide into a seat.

"You good?"

"Yeah, I took care of myself." She shrugged.

"Whose lipstick?" Peggy picked up a tube of purple lipstick off the counter, and I heard Brick roar behind me as Tess's face went about six shades of red. Peggy pulled off the top. "It's plastic?" She turned to look at us. "Who owns this?" She jumped when it started to vibrate. My eyes flickered back to Tess, who gave me a smirk.

"Why don't you try it on, Peggy?" Tess laughed as Peggy dropped it, confused.

"Is that yours?"

"Women have needs—needs that are not always fulfilled."

I lunged forward and snatched it up before Tess could.

"Think I'll hang onto this for a while."

"Didn't really think you were into that kind thing." Tess snickered.

"But, sure, I have plenty more."

Peggy looked back and forth between the two of us before her hand landed on mine and squeezed hard. I moved it out of her reach, but as usual, she didn't get the hint.

"Trigger, let's go for a swim."

"No."

"You did with Tammy the other night."

Tess's hand hesitated just long enough for me to catch it, but that was the only emotion I saw.

I searched her face, almost wanting a sign so I could end things with her. Tess as a fuck buddy seemed too good to be true, and I kept waiting for the shoe to drop. Again, she showed nothing.

Good.

"Jace!" I barked. "Close the bar down."

***

Tess

"Listen up!" Trigger's voice boomed across the room, silencing everyone. "We have some company arriving in twenty. Make sure you're carrying, and those of you in the meeting, you know the rules. Tess." He glanced at me, and I couldn't help but drop my gaze to his mouth. "You'll be serving."

"Okay," I whispered, completely shocked at how quickly the mood had changed in the room.

"Do as he says, Tiger," Morgan warned.

"I will, but damn, you are all so intense," I muttered to Morgan once Trigger barked out a few more orders and left. "And who is coming? Why is it such a secret?"

Morgan's hands landed on my shoulders as he stared at me straight in the eye. "You don't get to ask questions. Your job is to look sexy and serve them. When are you gonna learn women don't have much say around here? So, shut up and do your job."

"Inspiring pep talk, Morgan."

"Here." He jammed a tray in my hands. "You always serve from the top down." I gave him a confused look. "Trigger first, Brick, Gus, Rail, then the company. The booze is in there, only thing missing is you." He stepped back and looked at my outfit. Jean skirt and black top with a zipper down the front to expose as much cleavage as I wanted. "Shit, he'll love you."

"Who?" My mouth went dry. "Who will?"

"We need to win them over. I'm sure that's why Trigger is using your body on this one."

Most women would have taken offense to that, but not me. Respect was never part of my life. I knew my assets, and I used them to my advantage.

Morgan looked over my head. "They're here. Look, Tess." He rubbed his hand over his beard and seemed as if he were deciding something. "This needs to go smoothly. The club's future could ride on the outcome of this meeting. You need to keep your head down, listen, and do as you're told. Can you do this for me?"

"Yeah, of course." Sweet lord, the whole thing was frightening.

"Good, now go." He turned me around and pushed me toward the double doors.

"Don't fuck up." Peggy giggled from the corner of the room where she was giving someone a lap dance.

"I'd say the same to you, but…" I looked at the sweaty dude she was riding. She gave me the finger, and the guy spoke up to get her attention.

Opening the doors, I walked in and saw the bar off to my left. With my head down, I hurried over and started to pour the guys a double, being careful to follow Morgan's instructions as to who to serve first, second, and next. As I turned around, I froze like a deer caught in headlights, and I stood stock still as the blood drained to my fingertips.

Holy mother of Christ.

Trigger caught my expression and body language, and his eyes narrowed in on me, but as usual, he kept his composure.

I forced myself to move with shaky hands and legs. I made my way over and set Trigger's drink in front of him. It spilled a bit over my hand, and I was ready for him to make a comment, but he only nodded at me.

"Who wants a drink?" he asked the table as I handed Brick his.

"A drink or something else, perhaps," Mateo, the president of the Satan's Serpents, hissed at me like the snake he was. The skin on the back of my neck prickled as his gaze dragged up my front then turned pointedly over to another member. I followed his line of sight, and my stomach dropped. I tripped in my nervous state and stumbled toward the table. I managed to catch myself, but my heart was in my throat. Tiago, the fat man who had hit me in the face and tossed me in the trash, smirked back at me. He was obviously delighted with my predicament.

"Something else?" I managed to get out.

"Tequila." Trigger directed the order to me but kept his gaze on Tiago.

Tequila. Okay, I just needed to get one, two, three…I looked up and counted. Twelve shots. The pres spoke to Trigger about something, but Tiago had his eyes locked on my ass.

Shit, shit, shit, you can't mess this up! Morgan's words bounced around inside my head. I felt the whole outcome of this meeting might already be ruined simply because of my presence.

One, two, three. My breathing was rapid, and it took a great deal of concentration to fill the shots.

My tray was full when I turned back around. The guys were talking, but not one word got through my terror. I began to hand them out. I moved fast, hoping it would help make the shakes less noticeable.

When I got to Tiago, I flinched. He noticed, and his mouth turned upward. He loved my reaction. He was thoroughly enjoying this, the son of a bitch.

Suddenly, his hand latched onto my wrist and held me in place. I wanted to punch his balls, but Morgan's words were still inside my head. "What's your name, girl?"

"Tess."

"Tess," he repeated slowly. "Why don't you be a doll and give me a peek at what I'm working with, here."

I heard Brick's chair slide out, but Trigger's voice stole my attention.

"No." The word made me break out in a cold sweat. "Tess."

I tried to pull away, but he held onto me for an extra beat. As soon as I was free, I bolted for Trigger. I wasn't sure what to do, so I stood with the tray in my hands to hide the fact that I was vibrating. I felt a familiar burn in the pit of my stomach and knew my fear was beginning to change to anger, which it often did, and I was working hard to get myself under control. I knew how much this could mean to Trigger, so I stayed quiet.

"Mateo." He gestured for him to continue, but Tiago interrupted.

"How much for the girl?"

Trigger tilted his head and sat a little straighter. His broad shoulders stretched out and his muscles contracted. The sound of the leather vest flexing over his back was oddly comforting.

"No," he answered simply.

"I'll give you three of my finest for her. One night, bruises optional." He laughed. My feistiness kicked in, and I almost spoke, but Trigger's hand landed heavily on my hip. He pulled me to his lap where he held me in place. "I don't share."

Tiago's fat thumb rubbed his brow. "Why? She taken?"

Brick shook his head, warning me to stay silent. Gus calmly ran his finger along his lips too.

Okay, I'll stay quiet.

Trigger spoke impatiently. "Are we here to discuss old ladies or the contract?"

Mateo waved his hand. "Fine, contract. Go on."

Trigger's hand held me tightly in place, and I knew when not to move. "There are six more months until this agreement is finished, then we're done."

"Actually…" Mateo leaned back and didn't bother to hide his smirk. "…you might think that, *but* your father agreed that if anything were to happen to *him* before the entire contract was fulfilled, the club would step in for an additional twenty years, starting the day after his death."

"Where is this stated, exactly?

"In the contract." He held up a bunch of papers.

"Not in mine, the one Allen and *you* signed." Trigger used his free hand and mimicked Mateo.

Mateo rubbed his chin and glanced at Tiago, who stared at me. "Perhaps we can come to some kind of an agreement. Yes?"

"Which is?"

My heart leapt into my throat. Trigger must have felt me flinch, and his grip tightened.

"We draw the map, work out the streets, and set it in stone."

Trigger's grip loosened, and I felt him relax a fraction. He took his time before answering. "Yeah, I think it's about time."

"Good, maybe we can come to some understanding." Mateo smiled.

"On?"

"Things." He smiled wider. Damn, that smile shook me to the core.

"I need you to be a little more specific."

Mateo glanced at Tiago before he leaned back, puffing out his huge stomach. "Seems we have a little problem with the Stripe Backs."

"Oh?"

"They took out three of my men, claiming we did the same to

them."

"Did you?"

"No."

Trigger nodded and motioned for him to go on. This was not something I should be hearing. I didn't want to be a part of this. I knew none of the other women were allowed to be in on these discussions. I felt like I was going to be sick. I tried to keep my eyes on Trigger's face to ground myself.

"You help me retaliate, and I'll think about this contact."

Trigger's eyes were cold. "We sign here and now that if we help you, you drop the entire contract. Clean slate."

Mateo shifted in his chair before he lit a fat cigar, taking a moment to think. God, he was a disgusting man. When I glanced up, his gaze caught mine then burned into my chest. *Do they remember me? Or are they just fucking with me?*

Then he spoke. "Fine. But I would like to add that this little one comes to our meetings from now on."

Brick didn't blink. He just placed the paperwork in front of Mateo and waited for him and Tiago to sign. Then Trigger and Brick did the same.

Trigger's fingers strummed the table before he spoke. "Let the VPs work out the rest, and we'll meet back up in a few days to discuss how we move forward."

"Good." Mateo slapped the table, and I jumped.

Trigger rubbed my leg, comforting me. Although, knowing Trigger, he probably thought I was going to run. "Until then."

One of the club members who wasn't allowed inside opened the door and showed them out a different way, a way they must have entered.

Brick, Rail, and Gus all stared at me. Well, at Trigger, but also at me. After the door shut, the silence was painful. I started to move when Brick spoke up.

"What happened, Tess?"

"Huh?" I swallowed hard.

"Everyone but Brick, leave," Trigger ordered the guys. Their eyes widened, but they didn't hesitate. After they left, Trigger stood, bringing me to my feet. His huge body towered over mine, making me aware of my own small size.

"How do you know Mateo?"

"I don't."

"Don't lie to me, Tess."

"I'm not, I promise, Trigger. It's the other one I know." It was the truth.

His finger rubbed his scruffy but manicured beard as his gray eyes studied mine. *Shit, they were gray, not green right now.*

"You need to tell the truth, Tess," Brick said as he paced the room. "I'll only cover for you on certain things. If something happened, now is the time."

Fuck, Morgan had said this was important, and here I was fucking it up for everyone.

Sinking my weight onto the table, I crossed my legs and gripped the edge to support myself.

"I was walking home. I think it was my third or fourth shift, and I had to pass the Serpents' clubhouse."

"No, I texted you the way to go," Brick interrupted.

"No, you didn't, but I am fine." I hated that he was wrong.

"I did." He held his phone up. "Dammit, to the old number. I guess I was a little late sending it to you. Sorry, Tess."

"Don't be." I loved Brick, and he could do no wrong in my eyes.

"And…" Trigger held up his hand with no emotion.

"And I accidentally ran into a girl whose boyfriend went and told Tiago that I was causing trouble." I breathed deeply through my nose then glanced at Trigger, whose fist rested against his lips.

"What did he—" Brick stopped mid-sentence when it hit him. "Holy shit."

"I'm sorry I didn't say anything. I didn't want to be starting trouble on my first week. I thought it was better swept under the rug. Who am I to cause all of this?"

"What exactly happened?" Trigger watched me closely.

"I was pulled inside the clubhouse, pushed to my knees, where Tiago was. They brought—"

"Then what?" Trigger interrupted.

I glanced at Brick, who was now staring at me as well.

"He hit me and chucked me out back in the trash and left." A blush heated my face. "May I go?" I directed my question to Trigger.

"Stay here tonight. I'll find you a room."

"I'd rather go home, after my shift."

"No." Trigger glared at me.

I turned to my best friend and said weakly, "I'm sorry."

"I know," he whispered, grabbing my hand with a quick squeeze.

CHAPTER EIGHT

Trigger

I vibrated with anger. I knew when she fed me that bullshit lie about her tripping over her shoe something had happened, but I never imagined it was connected to the Serpents.

"What do you think we should do?" Brick asked.

"Nothing, please do nothing," Tess snapped at me from the door way.

I tried to think, but that chick had some nerve telling me what we should and shouldn't do.

"Tess." Brick shook his head.

"No, don't warn me to shut up. This happened to me, not Trigger. I'm the one he forced on my knees and called me too skinny to rape. Slapped the hell out of my face and chucked me in the trash to die." Her voice creaked. "We do nothing, because I said so."

"You lied," I growled, making her jump.

"No, I just didn't tell you all of the truth."

My vison clouded over when I glanced at Brick, who looked nervous at what I might do. I didn't blame him. I wasn't sure what I was about to do either.

"Trigger?" Morgan knocked on the door. "Sorry, man, but I could use her help out here."

Tess gave me a pointed look before she followed him.

Brick sank into the seat across the table from me and rubbed his head. "I never meant to cause any trouble bringing her on with us."

I thought for a moment. As much as I despised lying, this could be used to our advantage.

"They like her, maybe we can use her to gain some information."

"Ah..." Brick cleared his throat, visibly uncomfortable. "I'm not sure how I feel about this. I mean, what if she got hurt?"

Never will happen.

"She won't be alone, and she won't be stepping inside that clubhouse without me. But they have a contract with Allen's signature, and I want to see it. I think they're full of it, and if Tess can get something on them, maybe we can flip the tables. Gain back all of our territory."

"Why would Allen do something like that? What does he gain by an additional twenty years when he's not even here for it?"

"Because revenge from the grave is the best kind of revenge there is."

"Sick shit."

"Mmm," I muttered, moving to my feet and opening the door. Tess stood in the doorway. Her expression appeared upset, but she swallowed it back.

"Rail wants you." She spun on her heel and headed back to the bar where some more members were crawling in for a drink. Morgan must have opened the bar back up early. I didn't blame him. We were all on edge from having our enemy in our house.

"Brick," I ordered over my shoulder.

"Yeah, I'll find out if she heard anything." He started to leave but turned around. "Be careful with Tess. She's *damaged* when it comes to men."

"That directed at me or them?"

He looked around to make sure she was out of earshot. "Sometimes I think she was born damaged. She can be reckless, but will fight to the death if she thinks it's for the right cause." Brick tucked his hands into his pockets before he left to meet Tess at the bar.

I needed a break, so I headed out back with my bottle.

The breeze was hot and my shirt stuck to my body. The pool reflected light onto the walls. It entertained me while the pot coursed through my lungs. I still remembered when my father bought this property twenty-seven years ago. The pool was stained brown and hadn't been updated since the early 70s. The house itself was huge. It was previously owned by a porn director, so every room was grand and flashy. It took thirteen months to gut the place and rebuild so it was sealed up from the street. High walls ran to the back where we had a hidden gated driveway. My club was a fortress, with only one door in front and one out back. Both were watched by cameras and men.

Then one night six years later, my father took a run at me with a knife right after a meeting. He said I wasn't man enough to take over such an empire. He managed to stab me twice before I flipped the blade and rammed it into his intestines. I was sixteen and was left with a crew of four who had witnessed the fight. We were vulnerable, and a few crews tried to clean us out, but Gus took my father's place and ran the club until I turned twenty. That was the day I hoped I'd finally be free, only to realize I still had to do the dirty work of the Reaper.

A movement off to the right caught my attention. I pulled out my gun and rested it on my knee. My joint hung from between my lips as I focused on the intruder.

My skin flickered with excitement. A good kill might be exactly what I needed. I hadn't felt right since this afternoon.

Easing the safety, I cleared my head of everything but this moment. I raised it and pointed in the direction of the movement, then the wind went out of my lungs and I took my finger from the trigger. *Damn*.

Tess kicked off her shoes, shimmied out of her skirt, and unzipped her top with only a quick glance around. I lowered my gun and tucked it away.

Fucking girl had almost had herself splattered against the concrete wall. Brick needed to remind her she shouldn't sneak around.

My phone buzzed.

Cooper: I gotta go deal with Dad. Okay if I step out?

Trigger: Do what you gotta do. You need anyone?

Fucking Bruce and his booze.

Cooper: Nah, just wanna see how bad Mom is.

Trigger: If you need another room, use my account.

Cooper: Okay.

His mother wouldn't be around much longer. I went back to watching Tess.

In a bra and panties, she walked out to the end of the diving board and dove in cleanly. She swam to my end of the pool. I was hidden in the shadows in the back of the old pickup bed.

Her head popped up and she glanced around again before she flipped over and floated on her back. Her skin was flawless, and I could see her tan lines. Her body glowed under the water from the lights, and I watched as she duck-dived back under to the bottom. She could hold her breath a long time.

As I started to get up, I heard the door open. Brick walked right by me and sat on the chair only a few feet away and waited for her to surface.

"Hey," he whispered loudly.

She whirled around then smiled happily. "Is this okay?"

"Yeah." He held up a towel to show her. "I might suggest wearing a bathing suit."

"It's hot as hell in there. I didn't care."

"You will when the guys come out."

She looked back to the door. "Are they coming?"

Brick checked his watch. "Not yet. Another thirty, and they'll come."

She pushed off backward from the side and treaded water in the middle. "How much trouble am I in?"

Brick rubbed his face and breathed a long sigh. "I think if you were anyone else, you'd be gone. Trigger's loyal to me, so I think you're okay. I wish you had told me the truth."

"I know." His posture made her expression change. "Out with it."

"Trigger was asking about your past."

She stopped treading and swam closer to him.

"I didn't say anything." His hands rose. "But I need to know, are you still talking to them?"

Them?

"No," she shot back, annoyed. "I left, Brick. They know I'm not in Vegas, and that's it."

"Are you sure?"

"Why?"

Brick rubbed his face; he was stressed out by something. "Because if they come here and start something, it's on me."

"They won't. No one knows I'm here. I left in the middle of the day, and I took three cabs before I got to the airport. I did everything you told me to do. Christ, I even hitchhiked from John Wayne to my place."

"They can track your cards."

"I'm only using cash."

"Your phone?"

"I used the phone you got me. I have no idea how she got that number. I've changed it since then." She ducked under the water and popped back up to smooth her hair out of her face.

"Do you like it here?" he asked, and I listened harder. "I can try to move you to Arizona if you'd like to keep moving."

"No." She stopped him. "I like it here. I'm fine. Please stop worrying about me."

He stood and tucked his hands in his pockets. "Then tell Trigger what's up in case something does happen."

"Matt." She used his real name, and this piqued my interest. She lifted herself out of the pool and stood in front of him. I stayed very still, as she was facing me. She started to speak then stopped herself. She looked like she might cry, but she maintained control. Then Brick grabbed her wrist and pushed up her bracelets. She ripped her arm from his and looked away.

"People who love you don't drive you to do *that*."

"Stop," she warned.

"You'll be protected here, Tess. Let him in a little."

"What am I supposed to say, Matt? 'Hey, Trigger, I was young and stupid. I wanted a way out, tried, and failed?' Now I live with that reminder, see it every day. I have enough reminders of how much I was not *wanted,* so to have that cross over into this new life isn't something I want to do." A sob caught in her throat, but she pushed it back. She was strong; I'd give her that.

"He's not a bad guy, Tess. I know I've warned you about falling for him, but Trigger is a good man. He'll get it, *all* of it."

"Somehow I doubt that. There's dark, then there's my story."

I held very still, not sure I wanted to hear the next thing out of her mouth.

"I really wish you'd stop worrying about me falling in love, Brick." She snagged the towel and wiped her face.

"I see how you look at him."

"Yeah, the man is fine as hell. Jesus, I might be damaged, but my lady bits still work fine."

I couldn't help but smirk at Brick's reaction.

"Don't…don't refer to that…" his hand waved in front of her, "…area of your body as your lady bits. The mental image is doing things to my head." He pretended to shudder.

She rolled her eyes. "Shall I remind you of the little video clip of you and the mouse?"

"And we're done here." He clapped his hands once for emphasis. "Look, Trigger might ask you to help him out. It's your call if you want to do it or not."

"Such as?"

"I'll let him talk to you about it. But for now, if you hear from them, promise me you'll at least let me know."

"I promise."

He leaned over and kissed her cheek. "Love you, Tessa."

"Love ya, Matt."

He rubbed her shoulder before he left her standing with her arms wrapped around her middle. Her hand rubbed under her bracelets. So, there was a scar there, and I planned on finding out what the hell that was about.

I waited for the door to close before I took a swig from my whiskey. The glass must have caught the reflection of the light, because she looked right over in my direction and squinted.

She stepped back and grabbed her clothes as I lit my joint. Then she caught my face and sighed.

"You always creep in the dark?" she muttered, drying herself off.

"My house," I grunted back, but my eyes followed her hands. She had a tight little body and an impressive chest, and the memory of me deep inside her was hard to push aside. My dick grew hard against my pants, and I shifted to ease the pressure.

She bent over at the waist to grab her clothes, and I stroked myself once, needing something to tame my need.

I hopped down off the truck and made my way over to her. She set her clothes on the chair and rested her hands on her hips.

"Yes?"

"Who are *they*?"

"They, who?" She played dumb.

"Don't fuck with me, Tess."

She closed her eyes with a sigh before she sucked in her bottom lip and spoke. "You wouldn't understand."

"Try me."

"No." Her eyes were full of fight, and instead of wanting to drown it out of her, I wanted to fuck it out of her. She stepped closer and pushed up on her toes, and her eyes flicked to my lips. "You might scare me, Trigger, but not enough to share that."

Slamming her back against the wall, I hovered over her with a growl. I saw red and wanted to prove my point. My hands ached to punish her, but I managed to hold it back.

"Be careful, Tess," I huffed in her face, making her chin rise. "You have no idea how far you're pushing me."

"I do, and I remember what happened the last time you flipped your switch." Her finger hooked my belt and pushed the button free. I hated that Brick was just inside. Fuck, they all were. Normally, I wouldn't care who I was doing out here, but Tess…

I homed in on a drop of water that fell from her hair and raced down her neck. Fuck it. My tongue dragged from between her breasts up her collarbone to the nape of her neck. She sucked in a sharp breath but held still. My lips ran over her skin and sucked.

Jesus, she tasted good, and when I increased the pressure, her hands clutched my shoulders. I allowed it. A million different thoughts ran through me at once, and they all included Tess naked. I could take her here, flip her over, rip those tiny scraps of fabric off her, and make her tell me what I wanted to know.

Voices off in the distance had her pushing me away, but I only sucked harder. My hands held her bare hips in place.

"Trigger." She tried to sound in control, but she wasn't. "I don't have any clothes on."

I released my lips and hovered over my work. She sagged back with a frustrated sigh before she moved around me and grabbed her clothes.

"No." I hooked her by the waist and dragged her over to the truck where we were hidden. I sat her down on the tailgate and held her head in my hands. "Tell me who *they* are."

"Please, Trigger." Her hand fell to the center of my chest and her head dropped forward. It was the first time in my life I didn't snap back with a demand. I was actually lost for words. When her head rose, I saw it. I knew that look. Real pain deep in the soul. "Please don't make me talk to you about something that took a part of me away. I will, I promise, just not yet."

Instead, I leaned down and gently kissed her lips. I thought we were both shocked by the moment. Her hands moved up my shoulders and around my neck. A different emotion ran through me, and I wasn't sure how to navigate it. To my surprise, the demons in my head stayed away, like they often did when I was around her. It was great, but it also scared the hell out of me. She kept me off balance, and I didn't like the feeling.

I pulled away, unsure what to do next, so I let my mouth run.

"I'm not your Prince Charming, Tess. I wasn't made that way."

She grabbed the hem of my shirt to get my attention. "Prince Charming is overrated, Trigger. People like us need people equally as fucked up. It evens shit out." She pushed me aside as she pulled her clothes on. I wanted to take her there and then, but she was upset, and the moment was gone.

I snapped my hand around her arm. She tried to move it free, not in a rough manner, but I could tell her emotions were on edge. I pressed her closer to me, and she struggled against it.

"I'm going to kill Tiago." She shivered at my words. "Not today, but it will happen. He will pay."

"I know."

I let her go, and as she put her last shoe on, Gus and the two prospects came out, and several others followed.

"Hey, Tess." One of my more promising prospects, Ty, offered her a hand. She smiled at him, and I admired how she could channel her emotions and act like nothing was wrong.

"What are you guys up to tonight?"

Gus caught my eye before he tossed a bag at my feet behind her. A severed hand and an ear bounced out, and a few other human remains were still inside the gory bag.

"Serpents got to him first. This was all that we could grab. Not sure what they know yet, but I have someone digging now."

Tess made a noise and her hand covered her nose as she looked down at the bloody bag and its spilled contents. When I looked over, she seemed interested.

"Sit," I ordered, but she ignored me.

"Is that one of your members" She tried to scrape a piece of, quite possibly, brain matter from her shoe.

"Was," Rail answered to my surprise as she came up to join us. "They sawed his limbs off while he was still alive. Probably started with the ears then worked their way down. Makes for a slower, more painful death." He smiled at her. "You okay, sweetheart?"

"It's not how I would have done it." She shrugged, taking a second to pretend to think.

"Oh, yeah?"

"Mmm." She bent down to examine the hand. "I would have started with the nails, then maybe some oil and fire." Her gaze moved to mine then lowered to my twitching erection. "Watched as the layers burned one by one down to the bone."

"I've never found a woman hotter than you are right now." Rail laughed and broke her eye contact with me. She stood and glanced over her shoulder. "I should go."

"Cops will be there tomorrow," Gus whispered. "Not sure who is out tonight."

"Tess." I stopped her before she got to the door. "Sleep here tonight."

"Minnie's here."

"I have a couch," Rail offered.

"Take my room." Everyone went silent, and even Tess's eyes widened in surprise. "I won't be sleeping tonight."

"I don't have a change of clothes."

"I said take my room."

"Okay," she whispered before she headed inside.

***

Tess

Music followed me down the long hallway. Leaning my shoulder on the wall, I glanced around at my new home, at everyone who had now become my family. I smiled at Brick, who had Minnie dancing around him, clearly enjoying her drink.

"What do you think?" a rough voice asked from behind me. I turned to Gus, who popped a cap off a beer with the palm of his hand. He tossed it in the trash before he chugged more than half of it.

"It's different, but I like it."

"It's not for everyone, but you seem to fit in nicely."

I looked over at the smoke-infested bar, getting higher as each moment passed. "Good."

"My boy seems different with you around too."

"Boy?" When he didn't answer, I looked back, curious who he was referring to.

"My nephew."

"Trigger?" He nodded. "I didn't know you were his uncle."

"Have been now for thirty-six years." His laugh was followed by a heavy cough. "Hasn't always been easy, but he's a good kid. Despite how he comes across."

Unsure how to respond, I went back to people watching.

"Well," he gently touched my shoulder, "I'm glad you're here."

"Thanks, Gus."

"You should get some sleep."

"Oh, um, if I wanted to take a shower?"

"Trigger's got a real nice one. He won't mind."

An uneasy feeling spread through me. I didn't want to overstep my boundaries.

"He won't bite too hard, Tess, and if he does, I have no doubt you can handle yourself." He winked before he shoved the young prospect Jace out of a chair and settled in.

With a glance at my best friend, who was giving Rail shit, I decided to leave. The whole meeting today had mentally fried me, and I could use some alone time.

To my surprise, Trigger's room was clean. Everything was in place, and it smelled almost like fresh laundry. Not sure what I expected, but it wasn't that. His bathroom was impressive. Not much décor, but that seemed to suit him. It was large and had a huge tub, although my guess was he never used it. The shower had gray etching that swirled down the glass, French doors, and matching gray tiles offset by white.

Listening outside, I stripped down and turned the water on. It took a few moments to warm up, but then I sank into it. The steam quickly filled the space, engulfing me in cloud-like heaven. I searched for his body soap and lathered myself in his scent. The urge to stay there and relieve some tension was strong, but I didn't want to be too long. I made quick work of my hair and laughed when I found he had very expensive conditioner. I guessed it to be about seventy-odd dollars a bottle. *Hmm.*

The scent was strong, and Trigger's face kept appearing in front of me. My fingers inched downward, and I found my spot and gave it a little circle. I closed my eyes and let my imagination run, his strong hands on me, his lips to my neck on that certain place, his look—oh, his look, the one that held me in place and made me instantly wet.

My free hand pressed to the glass as I tipped myself over the edge, nearly tumbling to the floor. I moaned and let the internal warmth flush through me.

I dragged myself out of the shower and wrapped myself in his oversized towel. Searching through his drawers, I found a whole basket full of brand new toothbrushes. I questioned if he had a lot of women over, but that wasn't any of my business. I left the bathroom as it was when I arrived and slipped into his bed and into the softest sheets known to man.

If I hadn't just had my shower, these sheets would have been the next best thing. Sliding my hands all around, I nearly lost it again.

It wasn't long until I my eyelids grew heavy. I welcomed it, as today had been exhausting.

I woke with a start when I heard the door shut. The clock screamed 4:00 a.m., and I tried to see in the room, but it was too dark.

Finally, the bathroom light clicked on, and I saw Trigger's massive body fill the doorway before the light disappeared as the door closed.

My heart raced then my mind kicked in. I should move. My head did loops.

Just as I was going to get up, the door opened, and I stayed still. He removed his cut and draped it off over the back of a chair. His jeans were tossed in the hamper, and his shirt followed. In only his boxer briefs, he turned toward me. There was only a dim light from the bathroom, but I felt him get closer.

A rush of cold found me as he pulled back the covers and slipped inside. I felt his arm move to tuck under his head, and his feet kicked the sheets free of its hold.

"You smell like me," he grunted.

Again. I froze. He knew I was awake. "Is that okay?"

"Yeah, just different."

Different. Okay.

I rolled my back to him and hugged my pillow. My hair was finally dry, so I was a bit more comfortable. Minus the two hundred pound, six-foot-three beast of a man lying next to me. He twitched, and I wasn't sure if it was me or something else bothering him. After about ten minutes, I couldn't take it anymore. I attempted to sit up, but his hand latched on my arm.

"Where are you going?"

"The couch."

"Why?"

"To give you your bed."

"No."

No again. Not much to key off.

"You're twitching, and I wasn't sure if it was because of me."

He yawned. "It is."

"Oh, well, in that case…" I dripped with sarcasm.

"My dick and my head want two different things," he muttered through another yawn. "My head won, so go to sleep."

"Lucky for me your shower gave me what I needed." I snickered before I tucked myself back down into the blankets. He chuckled, but I heard him whisper something.

His hand swiped over, grabbed my midsection, and tugged me to him in one quick motion. I thought he was going to attack me, but instead he curled around me, and his hand tucked in between my legs. His erection pushed into my lower back, but he controlled himself.

It was amazing how we as humans could control our minds when we really tried. All I wanted to do was wiggle my body and have him lose himself on me, but on the other hand, he admitted he needed sleep. So, I controlled my head to think of other things. Finally, I allowed myself a little giggle.

"Mm?"

"Nothing."

He fell silent, and I found it even harder to control my laughter.

Trigger's hand fell to my hip and pressed lightly.

I jumped and rolled into him. "Hey!"

"What's funny?" He pushed my hair off my face.

"I was just thinking for such an ass, you sure have the softest sheets I've ever felt."

He huffed, almost a laugh, but he controlled it. "You done?"

I shoved his shoulder, but I heard the lightness in his voice, and it was damn sexy. "If I wasn't?"

His arm scooped around me and yanked me to his chest. I rolled around so I could feel more of him. I couldn't help but think how nice it felt to be held again as I slipped back to sleep.

***

Black-out curtains could really throw a person off. The clock read nine, and I wanted to go back to sleep, but I was cold and realized I was alone again. I searched for my clothes, but they were gone.

Shit!

I saw a yellow dress on the chair next to my heels.

Who the hell does this belong to? One of his weekend sluts? No, thank you. Besides, I have never worn yellow. Ever.

I tossed it aside and rooted for something else, anything else. I found a hunter green t-shirt of his and a pair of scissors. Living on the streets, you became very handy when you needed to be. He had a bag of safety pins under his sink, so I dumped them on the bed and went to work.

After twenty minutes, I wiggled into the new *dress* and admired it in the mirror.

I used some of the extra material I had cut from the sides to thread through the holes I made. It was closed to just above mid-thigh. Four safety pins held the rest and added flair to the bottom. The neckline swooped low and looked like a bear had ripped it across the chest.

"Not too bad." I grinned at the sexy little number I made before I hurried out front.

I should have known something was off when I walked in and Morgan gave me a quick nod. He then looked off to the corner where Trigger and three cops were sitting. I tossed my bag under the counter and grabbed a tray and headed over to the table. My shift didn't start for another six hours, but that didn't matter anymore. If I was here, I was working.

Morgan hissed at me to stay put, but I didn't listen.

"Can I get you something?" I directed my question to Trigger, who eyed his shirt…well, what was left of his shirt.

"Gentlemen?" he asked calmly. "A drink?"

"No." The man closest to me looked up, and his face smoothed out into a warm smile. "You're new."

"I am."

"I'm Detective Aaron, and this is my partner Detective Rich. And you are?"

"Tess."

"You have a last name?" He pulled out a pen and paper.

"I do."

"May I have it?"

"Why?"

Trigger huffed out a small laugh as he played with a joint between his fingers.

"Because one of your club members was found dismembered this morning, and we need to know who did it."

"And that requires you to know my last name?"

"Everyone is a suspect, miss."

I played this part well. My hands went to my chest, and I watched their eyes land there and lowered my voice with concern.

"Surely you don't think someone like me could do a thing like that?"

The detective cleared his throat before he eyed his partner. "We're not pointing fingers. We just need to know where you all were last night."

"Like I told you, we were here." Trigger's tone was smooth. I didn't think anything rattled him.

The detective turned his attention to me again. "You two were together last night?"

"Yes, with Brick, Gus, Rail, Morgan, all of us."

"The whole night?" He tried to cut me off.

"Yes."

"You have proof?"

I leaned over the table to make my point. Detective Rich shifted back, but Detective Aaron stayed put, nearly in my cleavage. "I do, but it would be a little inappropriate to show you here." My hand moved to my shoulder, giving them a little glimpse of Trigger's mark.

Trigger stood but didn't leave my side. "We're done here, guys. Until you have something, there is the door. I did my part, now do yours."

"Have a good day, boys." I winked before I moved back, waiting for them to leave. "They were nice," I joked to Trigger, who was staring at my handiwork. He was hungry; I could feel it.

"Didn't like the dress?"

"Not interested in wearing one of your one night stand's leftovers." I looked down. "I liked this better."

"I'd have to agree," he purred in my ear.

"Oh, great, you're back." Peggy snickered from the bar. The guy on her arm looked to be way past his ability to drink. "Thought maybe you were the one chopped up."

"Hey." Trigger grabbed my arm so I'd look at him. "You're moving in here."

"Trigger…" I liked my freedom, my space, my rooftop. I could see the battle wouldn't even happen. He was set on it. Didn't mean I couldn't make him work for it. "Ask nicely."

His face twisted. "No."

"Fine." I turned to Ty. "Could you drive me home tonight?"

His face dropped and his eyes shifted nervously to Trigger. "Ah, Tess, I don't think that's a smart idea."

"Tess," Trigger growled. He squeezed his eyes shut, and when they opened, I saw he was struggling with his temper. He stepped closer, took my arm, and angled himself away from the others. "It would be wise if you considered moving in here."

"Okay."

He blinked a few times. "I'm not fucking around, Tess."

"I didn't think you were. Just nice when you ask rather than order." His grip eased up, but his eyes were content with staring me down.

"Bitch, a drink now," the drunk guy snapped at me. Trigger's gaze shifted over my head.

"It's fine." I slid my arm out from his grasp, but he didn't hear me. With a cheery voice, I sauntered over and tried to smooth Trigger's nerves from afar. I was pleased with the little progress I had made with him.

"Vodka, double," Peggy barked.

Shoving it in her hand, I ignored her whispers and went back to working.

It wasn't until much later when I heard Brick's voice that I tuned in to the time. Shit, it was almost midnight. I barely noticed.

"Hey, Tess—what the hell is that?" He leaned over the bar, pushing my hair off my neck.

Morgan stepped closer to get a look as well.

"Don't tell me you gave up your lipstick for a Hoover?"

I smacked Brick on the arm while I rolled my eyes. "How's Mouse?" I referred to his girlfriend.

"No, no, no. No. No."

"No," Morgan chimed in, pointing at me. "We want to know about that."

Trigger passed by on the phone, sounding upset over something, and the guys' mood instantly changed.

He signaled to them, and before I knew it, ten guys were checking their gun clips and pulling hoodies up over their heads.

"Gotta go." Brick kissed me on the cheek as he rushed by.

"What's going on?"

I jumped when Morgan pumped his shotgun behind me. "Nothing you need to worry about, Tiger. Just stay here and don't leave."

"Yes, thank you, that's incredibly comforting, Morgan."

"Hey." Trigger pulled me aside. "I gotta go for a few days."

Days!

"Where?"

"You'll move your stuff in tomorrow."

"I will."

His lips moved into a straight line as he thought. "Take Big Joe with you. Don't walk by the Serpents' clubhouse. Promise me that."

"Am I in some kind of troublc?"

"No." He looked over my shoulder and nodded at someone. "But I am."

My stomach sank and my hands went cold. Peggy caught my eye, and I felt her hate from way across the room.

"Are you going to be okay?"

He smirked. "I live for this." He grabbed the back of my head and slammed his lips to mine. I was shocked that he kissed me in public, but I fell into step with equal intensity. As quick as the kiss happened, he was gone.

At least eleven of the guys left before the place went quiet. Big Joe was the only one who stood off by the blacked-out window with a gun dangling from his fingers.

Den and Fin came running in dressed as cowboys, shooting cap guns at one another. Vib was nowhere. My guess was she found another line to blow.

"You boys eat?" I howled over their screams. They both stopped in their tracks and looked at me. Typical boys, whenever food was mentioned, their attention was found.

"No. Why? You got some?" Den jumped up on the stool and hauled his brother up to join him.

"What do you like?"

"Pizza. Burgers. Fries." He started to number the foods off on his fingers.

I studied the little bugger. He was cute for his age and had real potential to be a little hottie.

"What's Trigger trading you for good grades?"

"Gonna teach me how to fight."

"Ah." I nodded. "You know why Trigger is so good, right?"

"Because he's the king!" Fin yelled.

"Besides that." I laughed at his little voice.

"No," Den interrupted. "Because he practiced."

"Yes, that, and because he ate well. Can't be quick on your feet with pizza and burgers in your tummy all the time."

"I'm seven. Mom won't let me drink whiskey."

I rolled my eyes at Den, but the kid had a point. Trigger did drink a shit-ton of whiskey.

"How about turkey, fries, and carrots?"

They both made a face, but Den's mischievous eyes let me know I was in for a bargain. "Burger, fries, and carrots."

"You think Ali ate a burger before a fight?" I was making this crap up, but, Christ, this kid could stand to eat something that wasn't smothered in grease. "Besides, the ladies don't want to see that. Yuck."

"Whatever." Den waved his hand, but I could tell he was hooked.

I ordered the food, and thirty minutes later it was sitting in front of them. I didn't act like I cared. I just buzzed around them doing my own thing.

"Not that bad." Den shrugged, finishing the last piece of turkey on the plate. "Tastes like chicken."

"Tess?" Fin grinned at me when I turned around. "Try this." He held up a piece of turkey that had been dipped in peanut butter.

"That's one of my faves." I snatched it out of his grubby little hand and swallowed it back.

"Oh, my God, she actually ate it!" He made a nasty face to his older brother. "You're so gross!"

"You're kidding me." I leaned over the counter, stealing a fry. "Anything tastes better smothered in peanut butter."

"Protein," Vib huffed as she rounded the bar. "Nice to see you're actually eating something that didn't come from a box."

Den shrugged but he glanced over at me. "You think you can get Uncle Trig to teach me a choke hold?"

"Maybe? Although that's a big one." I poured myself a drink. "Maybe I can pull some strings if you ace your report card."

"I'll see what I can do."

"Bed," Vib ordered, and they both hopped off the stools, waving goodbye. "Thanks, Tess. Sorry. The night got away from me."

None of my business.

"They were easy."

"No," she laughed a little, "they aren't, so…thanks."

Just as my shift was over, someone I hadn't met yet slid up to the bar.

"Whiskey." He tossed a fifty at me, which was confusing because he had the skull.

I pushed the bill aside and poured him a double.

He looked to be late thirties, although the lines around his eyes aged him a few more years.

"Rough night?" I was bored and had started to miss Morgan's company.

"Sitting in a car for five days, watching pieces of shit do random women, gets a little draining."

"Why are you doing that, exactly?"

His tired eyes looked up at me. “You’re new, right, Tess?”

“Yeah.”

“Word of advice.” He rubbed his head before he stood, passing me the fifty. “Don’t piss off your boss, no matter how close you think you are.”

Leaning forward to relieve my sore calves, I decided to get personal. “What’d you do?”

He laughed around the brim of his glass. “I’m Loose.”

“Loose?” I couldn’t help but laugh. “What, you are easy for women?”

“Not quite.” He nudged his glass for another. “So, tell me something, Tess. How do you like it here?”

I hopped up on the counter and thought for a moment. “It’s better than where I came from.”

“Which is?”

I snatched his glass and took his shot. “Which is not here.”

“Are you always this forthcoming?”

“I could ask you the same.”

He grinned and seemed to let his guard down some. “Look, this is the best crew to be a part of. The Devil’s Reach is the most feared club in the US when it comes to drug running. Just be careful. Trigger is not someone to cross or to trust. He has loyalty to only two people. Gus and Brick, whose father paved him a golden road into the club.” I started to defend my best friend, to explain that his loyalty ran deeper than stepping into someone else’s shoes, but I wanted to hear what this guy had to say.

“So, the club makes money from selling—”

“Coke,” he answered for me without realizing it. All things I knew, but interesting, nonetheless. I slid the bottle closer, now understanding his nickname. Yup, Loose had loose lips. “No one has the qualities Trigger has.” His tone was more annoyed than proud. “Everyone *loves* Trigger.”

“Seems like there might be a story with the two of you?” I poured myself a shot and cheered him. Yikes, these went straight to my head.

“Huh.” He leaned back and really looked at me. “Are you off now, Tess?”

“I am.”

“Good.” He stood on his wobbly legs. “Can I take you somewhere?”

I locked the cash and liquor cabinet and followed him and the bottle of whiskey out front.

"Where you are going?" Big Joe stepped in my way, and his grip on his gun made me uneasy.

"Out."

"Where?"

Loose grabbed my arm and hauled me past him. "She'll be fine, Joe."

"Trigger doesn't want—"

"If Trigger wanted her to stay, he should have stayed here to watch over her."

"Tess." Big Joe came closer, and I could tell I was putting him in a bad spot, and I didn't like to do it.

"I'm okay, Big Joe. You advised me otherwise, and I will make sure that is said later, but I need a break from this place, okay?"

He stepped back, shaking his head. Poor dude. I knew he was just following orders, but a little fun would be nice right now. I had not explored Santa Monica other than the pier, and maybe this was my chance. It was harmless.

"Here." Loose handed me a helmet. "Put this on."

"We are a ten-minute walk from the beach. I could use the exercise." *And you're loaded, so…pass.*

"You don't like bikes?"

"No." I could hear Trigger's words now. *Riding on someone's bike means something.*

"Please, Tess," Big Joe pleaded without any eye contact.

"Go back to your post, dude. I got her."

"You know." He pointed at Loose. "You know what you're doing right now. You'll piss him off more than you already have."

Wait, what does that mean?

"Look, Loose, if you are trying to piss off Trigger by using me, you won't get very far," I chimed in, feeling annoyed. Revenge was a bitch. "There's nothing going on between us." I lied a little, but I wanted to make sure Joe wasn't right. I would not be used again.

"I just wanted some human company tonight, Tess." He shrugged. "Sorry for welcoming the newbie, Big Joe."

"Okay, whatever. Let's go." I turned to Big Joe. "I have your back, and that's a promise. I just need a little break from here, that's all."

"Please, Tess." His big brown eyes begged me. "Loose is trouble." He slipped something into my bag, but when I tried to look, he stopped me. "Just in case."

"Okay." I respected him enough not to look while Loose watched us. However, by the weight of it, I had my suspicions. I followed Loose, who had already crossed the street. Big Joe shook his head but disappeared inside.

We headed to the beach where the salty air held a promise that I carried close to my heart. I really needed to stop coming here in the dead of night. My skin begged for some vitamin D.

"Where you from?"

I rolled my eyes. "Las Vegas. You?"

"Here. Born and raised and never left."

Once we hit the parking lot, I took a deep breath, but instead of heading to the water, he stayed up on the concrete.

"I'm not much of a water person." He patted the bench seat next to him. "Besides, I want to see who's coming. This is mutual territory."

"Oh, yes, that's right. The Serpents."

"Yeah?" He glanced at me, surprised at this knowledge. Little did he know…

"Well, then…" A shiver ran up my arms. "So, why are we here?" I felt a ping of disappointment. It might be early morning, but I would have sold my soul to have felt the Pacific on my toes again.

"The sea is relaxing for most people, but for me it's a reminder of how powerful it can be. The sea exploded an oil rig in 2010, killing eleven people on board and wounding countless others." He sounded like a newscaster as he delivered that line, then he sucked in a deep breath and took a swig of his drink. "And one man who holds too many secrets can destroy you with a single command."

I wanted to correct him that it wasn't actually the sea that exploded the oil rig, but I got what he was saying.

"Trigger?" I wanted him to confirm.

"I'm happy Brick could help you when you needed it, but, Tess, be careful. One day you're serving drinks, the next you're in his bed, and after that you're on the side of the road begging for money because even Walmart won't touch you. You know what happened to his father, right? The *actual* founder of Devil's Reach?"

"No, what?"

"Trigger never liked how his father ran the club. So he killed him, sliced him right across his throat, buried his body under the pool. Ask him sometime when the pool got re-done. He acted like he just disappeared. Sick son of a bitch."

"How exactly do you know this?"

“Because I was there.”

My heart leapt high in my throat before Loose shifted closer—a little too close. “I’m guessing that’s his handiwork.” He nodded at my hickey. “Please, Tess, don’t. Just work here with your head down until you can move on.”

I took a moment to place everything. Between warnings from Loose, Brick, and Morgan, my curiosity was getting the best of me.

“What happened with you guys?”

He downed the rest of the bottle, tossing it toward the waves but falling short by a mile. “I’m not even sure where to start on that question, but I can tell you he destroyed my sister. She fell in love with him, and he broke her like he does all his women. He makes them feel special, and once they fall, he drives a spike into their heart. Ruins them so they are permanently damaged. He’ll do it to you, Tess. He does it to all of them.”

“Lucky for me that’s something I’ve already been through.”

He bent down and groaned, resting on his toes before he shot back up into my face with a finger inches from my nose. “You can fucking lie to me about your past. I don’t care, and I won’t judge. But look the devil in the eye, and I dare you to lie to him.”

His expression was so haunting I wanted to pull away, but I couldn’t.

“He will see through all your bullshit. You better know exactly what you’re doing and the consequences for doing it.”

Christ, my body wanted to coil inward from his words, but I didn’t want to show fear. My past was my past and no one else’s.

We sat in silence for a few beats then moved our attention to the ocean. It wasn’t until the sun came up that he suggested he get me home.

CHAPTER NINE

Trigger

"That him?" I wiped my gun clean as Cray, my Arizona VP, came up next to me. His knuckles were bloody and raw.

"Yup."

The man was hunched over a rock, laughing. The Stripe Back thought he could intercept my New Orleans crew at the state line.

"I know it was you who killed our guys up north." He spat blood at the ground and ran the back of his hand across his face. "I know because you, my friend, have a mole with a big mouth."

I glanced at Brick as he brushed a finger over his lips. He too tried to remain calm. I felt my switch tip upward, and it was only a matter of time before I lost my shit on my club.

The man leaned back and squinted at me. "I've waited for this moment for so long." He started to laugh again. "The big, bad Reaper just fucked with the wrong people."

"Explain." Cray kicked him in the knee. He yelped in pain, but it was overshadowed by something else.

"You haven't made the connection yet?" He fixed his cut and pointed at his patch as he sat back up. "You killed Damon's brother."

Fuck me. I hid my reaction, but the darkness spread through my entire crew. We killed the pres and founder's brother. That, right there, meant a war. Looked like my deal with the Serpents would happen sooner rather than later. How did we not know Lou had switched coasts?

"Now imagine his reaction when he finds out it was you and not the snakes." He laughed again, and I cracked my neck to release some pressure. "You can kill me, but the mole will get to him first. Damon already has it out for you and your assets."

I slipped on a few rings and flexed my arms to warm them up. I could have shot him, sliced his throat, but with what was traveling through my veins at that moment, I needed to slip back to old faithful.

"Stand up."

He sighed before he moved off the rock and held open his arms like he was offering himself up.

"I won't fight you, Trigger. Your day is coming soon enough."

"Maybe, but it ain't today." I tossed my first punch to his head and knocked him right off his feet. He hit the ground hard, but to my surprise, he got back up. Three more blows, and blood coated his teeth. His eyes swelled quickly as he wobbled to stand. I lunged forward, ramming him into the tree trunk with all my strength.

I heard the air shoot from his lungs and his ribs snap. The impact was so intense it killed him instantly.

I stepped back and let him slump to the ground. With a turn, I pointed to the next member in Cray's arms. "Let's do this."

Seventy-three minutes later, I had killed five more members of the Stripe Backs. The two prospects dragged the bodies to a hole where they would light the men on fire and later bury them around the mountain.

"Really?" Brick pointed to the cut above my eye.

"Yeah." I sipped a beer in the shade. I liked to be hit. It was a reminder that I could be. Cocky never got anyone shit.

"Who the fuck is our mole? You think it was the hangaround?"

I sucked back on my joint and took a moment to think. The hangaround wasn't even at the club the night we came back. We had celebrated before I killed the other fucker who stole from me. Now he was chum at the bottom of the ocean. So, that made two, and now there was a possible third? What the hell was going on? "No, I don't."

Sleep didn't come easily that night, not that it ever did. The motel was damp and smelled like gasoline, or perhaps that was me. I didn't dare try the shower in fear I'd catch something. Tomorrow night we would be staying somewhere nicer, but for now I needed to be out of the sight of others. Motel 6 off the bypass meant we got to sleep with more protection. Cray's crew.

In the morning, my phone buzzed and I pulled it free. The sunlight burned through the shit brown curtains, which made my head ache.

Big Joe: Loose came back last night. He took Tess out.

I slowly rose, as did my temper.

Trigger: When did she come back?

Big Joe: She didn't.

A hiss escaped from deep inside me.

Trigger: I'll be in touch.

My shirt blocked my view as I pounded on Brick's door until he opened it. I threaded my arm through, and he squinted to see me. "Morning?"

"I need your phone."

He stepped back to let me inside. It was on the table, and I tossed it at him.

"Text Tess and find out where she is."

"Why?" His face fell and he became more awake.

"Loose came back last night and took her out. She hasn't been back at the club."

He yawned as he entered his password. "She probably went home."

"Text her."

He blinked a few times before he started to type and sank into a wicker chair. His hand hovered over the screen and he looked up. "What if it's Loose?"

"He's fucking stupid but not suicidal."

"You fucked up his sister something bad."

I licked the inside of my dry mouth. I didn't like his tone. "She knew how it was."

He shook his head as his phone buzzed. He held it up and showed me. "She's at breakfast, on her way back soon."

I slammed the door behind me.

Trigger: Let me know when she arrives.

Big Joe: Sure thing, boss.

Just as I was about to round up the guys, it buzzed one more time.

Big Joe: She wouldn't ride on his bike.

It wasn't until that night that we met back up with the New Orleans crew. Cray's club had us over for a party to celebrate the bloodshed. Rock music poured from two large speakers that had been pulled outside next to the barbecue. Endless rows of ribs lined the grill, along with steak and tri-tips. Three Rottweilers guarded the entrance of the club, as well as eight prospects.

Brick, Rail, and Cooper sat around the fire with me, all silent and wondering who the fucker was who dared cross us.

"Gentlemen, please help yourselves to anything." Cray nearly tripped over his feet as he signaled for some women to join us. Such a drunk.

A young girl, maybe seventeen, tried to settle on my lap. I pushed her aside as another moved in.

"Why so pissed?" She eased down on the stone ledge in front of me. Her brown hair brushed her legs as she crossed them. Her breasts were overinflated, but she was sexy in a fake way. "Not a talker…okay." She nodded while she thought. "Well, you don't seem like you want company, so why don't I stay right here until the girls find someone?"

I nodded, liking that idea.

"What, are you gay?" a chick yelled at Brick, who flipped her the finger as she stormed off.

"There was this one time," Rail chimed in before Brick's beer bottle smacked him in the chest. "I just wanted to come clean," he whispered in a fake cry.

That seemed to break the tension for the rest of us, and we got in on the joke.

"I couldn't sit for a week." Morgan snickered. "Best I've ever had."

"Blow me," Brick hissed.

"It's your turn, and you weren't very good last time," Morgan reminded him, deadpan. "You need less teeth. Curl the lip, curl the lip." His hands mimicked the action.

Brick's head flopped back with a sigh, but it soon turned to laughter. "I hate you all."

The girl across the way eyed me as she sipped from her beer bottle.

I tossed my empty into the trash and made my way to the bikes to take a leak. I found the Stripe Backs' bikes off behind the bar and decided it was the perfect pissing hole.

I felt the demons sneakin' up on me. They were never far away.

On my way back, the girl pushed off the side of the building. "Why don't you come over here and show me why they call you Trigger."

I smirked and followed her back into the shadows. She leaned against the wall and grabbed my belt, tugging it free. I grabbed her waist and held her place as I dove down to meet her lips. Her hands fell on my chest, and I pushed them away. They moved to my hips, and I fought to shove them back. She huffed and moved them to my hair, and I cursed but kept kissing her. She tasted off, and my head started to slip.

"Look at me, boy. Look deep inside and see that you are a part of me and a part of this. We are meant to do this, so quit being a pussy and taste the shit you will be selling." He stuck the straw on the table and shoved my head to it.

I turned off the hate and sucked in deep, removing the entire line of cocaine. It hit me like a hammer to the head. A billion shades of blue flickered across my pupils as my entire body turned into liquid sand. I became one with the room and could feel the air travel from the bottom of my lungs to the tip of my tongue before it leapt off and went somewhere.

"That's grade-A shit, boy." He leaned over and took a hit himself. When he looked back at me, his face morphed into a skull, and a scorpion came out of the roof of his mouth. "Time for one more."

I was eleven.

When her lips moved to my neck, I couldn't take it. I pushed her away and chased the memory out. Fuck, I was limp. I needed him out of my friggin' head!

"What, you want something else?" She started to get on her knees, but when her hands touched my thighs, I nearly jumped at the burn.

"Go."

"What?"

"Go!" I shouted, and she fell back and scrambled to her feet. "Ah!" I needed to hurt something fast. I spun and everything tilted. The memories tried to surface. They clawed at my eyes and turned up the volume in my ears.

I knew Cray kept a punching bag in the barn, so I headed there and fought my demons well into the morning hours.

***

TRIGGER

Tess

My new room was a little hard to get used to, even though the big window that looked over the courtyard was pretty, and a huge tree provided shade. The window was open, and a hot breeze fluttered the crisp, white curtains. My bed was big and grand and didn't fit the whole bad ass biker theme on the outside, but whatever.

I had to check. I pulled the gray duvet back and ran my hand along the white sheets. My eyes closed and a blissful smile raced across my lips. They were like butter.

Thank you, Trigger.

The prospects had moved my boxes in, and now it was up to me to unpack for the second time in just over a month. My shower wasn't fixed, but at least I had a toilet and sink to myself. And Brick didn't have to pay rent for me. Or maybe he did; I wasn't sure who paid for what around here.

After a few hours, I had everything unpacked and sorted. My books were my main concern, but they had a place on the shelf next to my bed. I flopped on my bed, exhausted. I remembered my phone was plugged in, so I pulled it free and saw the annoying icon that glared at me. Had been for several days now. Many times, I almost deleted it, but I couldn't.

I tapped the play button and held it to my ear.

The first six seconds were silence, then I heard it, and everything around me stopped.

"Are you sleeping with the guy who answered your phone? I don't know what you are up to, but you best get home now. Enough of this bull. You promised me that you'd be good. You made me a lot of promises, and I hope you intend to keep them. I know I hurt you, but you have to see why I did what I did. I love—" There was a scuffling noise before I heard him speak to someone.

Then she was there. She was always there. She must have taken the phone because she *shh'd* him. "Who the fuck is this?"

The message ended.

I hated what that did to me, and my hand brushed over the little bumps on my wrist while I tried to push the horrible thoughts away. God, I missed Mags so much it hurt.

Pushing off the bed, I headed off to find the guys.

Peggy had been up my ass all morning long, looking for her drinks. How her liver hadn't shriveled up yet was beyond me. Every hour she would have some member pull her into a room and bang her senseless. It was amazing a person could have that much sex and still be able to walk. She was pathetic.

Cooper worked the day shift, and I burrowed down with my face buried in my book. Twenty minutes in, and it was just getting to a good part when someone stopped in front of me.

"Well, look at that." A man covered head to toe in tattoos pulled out a chair and sat across the table from me. If Cooper wasn't at the bar, I might have shouted for help. He was a very big, scary guy. "Did you know most of that story is true?"

"What is?" Somehow, I found my voice.

He reached over and tapped my book. "Their story. The author did a good job of keeping to the truth."

"You know them?" I couldn't help but wonder who the hell I was sitting across from.

"I do." He leaned back and held my gaze. "I worked under Cole for years. He's a great guy. He and Savannah are very happy."

Gah! I have a million questions, but I need to stay calm. "Worked?"

"That's right. I later moved to another house."

"Where?"

He smiled, and I saw a softer side of him that I would guess not many saw. "Don't stress over the ending, okay?" He nodded at my book again, avoiding my question.

"Why would I stress?"

He laughed softly. "Let's just say the author is known for her asshole cliffhangers."

"Good to know. So, are you in here?"

"A bit."

"Why only a bit?"

"I guess my story hasn't been written yet."

Fair enough.

"I'm Tess."

"Mike." He glanced over my shoulder and he moved his head as if to greet someone. He stood and looked down at me. "Nice to meet you, Tess."

"You too." I turned to find Gus coming up behind me. The urge to ask the questions that were on the tip of my tongue was strong, but I knew better.

"Been a while. How are you, Mike?" Gus shook his hand and motioned for him to sit at the bar.

I hopped up and hurried over to Cooper, who tucked the broom away. The last thing I wanted was to look like I was getting special treatment because the boss kissed me the other night.

"Don't slip, Tess." He pointed to the puddle of soap. "I need to get a towel. Damn thing won't drain. You got them?"

"Yeah." I started to pour Gus a drink when Mike asked for a beer.

"How's the house?" Gus asked the giant man.

Mike rubbed his bald head before he glanced at me. "We're good."

"Keith?"

"He's good too."

I tried not to listen, I really did. But, Christ, it was like watching *TMZ Live.*

"All right, what's going on?" Gus downed his drink and slid his glass over for another.

Mike ran his fingers over his wrist while he thought, and I noticed he had a troll tattoo. Not wanting to laugh at the huge man with a child's toy slapped on his skin, I turned and started to dry the damp mugs.

"Where's Trigger?"

"Business."

When his head moved, it caught the light's reflection, and I saw more of his artwork. Scales of a koi fish almost glittered. It was beautiful.

"Look, Keith wanted to repay Trigger for everything he did with Lexi."

"That's been squared away."

"I know, but," he glanced over his shoulder, "we have respect for your club, and we heard something and wanted to bring it to your attention." Gus leaned in closer. "There's been some talk of, ahh…" Mike cleared his throat loudly, "…of your shipment being zig-zagged."

When Gus didn't respond, I looked up and saw he wasn't moving at all. He stood like a stone. His eyes were on the bar top and his fists were clenched.

Carefully, I poured his drink, which seemed to pull him from his daze.

"We picked up a package last week, and we overheard some of them talking," the big guy continued.

"About?" His voice was haunting. He sounded much like Trigger would sound.

Mike pulled out a piece of paper. "I'm just handing over what I know. You handle the rest yourself." He stood as he downed his beer. "Enjoy their story, Tess."

"I will." I waited for him to leave and touched Gus's arm. "Everything okay?"

"What time is it?"

I leaned back and checked the clock. "Five."

"I need to think."

Stiffly, he moved between the stools and hobbled outside. What the hell was a zig-zag?

I found my purse and jumped up on the bar, emptying the contents in front of me. *There you are.* I snatched up my phone and saw three missed calls from the same unknown number, only this time there was a voicemail.

"You wanna know a secret?" Cooper beamed over at me.

I tucked my phone away. "Always."

"When the guys are away, I like to listen to my kind of music."

"If you say Miley, I owe Brick twenty bucks."

"What? What the hell is Brick feeding you?"

"It gets a little intense around here, so we bet a lot." I shrugged unapologetically.

He moved over to the stereo and connected his phone to it. Using his thumb, he scrolled through his music and waited.

"Promise you won't tell?"

"Promise." Mainly because I would use this against Brick and make a quick fifty.

He turned it up, and I squinted as I heard the singer.

"Ohh, turn that shit up!" Big Joe popped his head in the door and started to rock out.

Hang on here a moment.

"Chris Stapleton!" Cooper yelled in between verses. "You know him?"

I laughed and wondered what world I just dropped into. It sure wasn't Led Zeppelin or Black Sabbath.

"Yeah, I know Stapleton." I joined in the chorus of "Nobody To Blame."

Cooper clutched his chest, closed his eyes, and smiled the sweetest smile I'd seen on him yet. "I think I died and went to heaven."

"Sing it, girl!" Big Joe appeared again and belted the words.

Cooper pointed to the burned-out light above me and handed me a bulb. I swiveled to my feet and carefully balanced on my six-inch heels.

"I was going to say take your shoes off, but I forget you know how to work it in those," he shouted just as the song changed to "Might As Well Get Stoned."

I held the long pipe and unscrewed the bulb, handing it to him. "You'd be surprised what I'm capable of."

My shirt rose above my skirt, and I was aware that I was showing a tad more than I wanted to.

"Damn, girl, be careful," Loose hooted from the pool table before he tossed his cue and headed over. "You let her up there?"

"She's fine, dude, relax." Cooper rolled his eyes at me.

Suddenly, the door opened, and a flash of light blinded me momentarily.

"Who the hell touched my speakers?" Morgan carried his shotgun against his shoulder. "Country? Fuck, no!"

Cooper closed his eyes and cursed.

"You got a problem with my choice of music, Morgan?" I crossed my arms and towered down at him from the bar top.

His famous smile broke out. "Hey, there, Tiger. Didn't picture ya for a country girl."

"I like to indulge a little here and there. Spice things up a bit."

Trigger dropped a bag at the end of the bar. Damn, I didn't even see him come in. He looked tired and pissed.

"Jesus, warn a person, Tess. I can practically see your—" Brick held his stomach. "I need a drink."

"Always with the dramatics," I muttered and took Morgan's hand. Once I was on the floor, the music switched back, and the guys moved about, ordering drinks.

"Hey." I leaned against the bar, curious as to what mood I was going to find Trigger in. "How was the trip?"

"Long."

"Looks like you had fun." I pointed to his bloody knuckles.

He cleared his throat and tossed down a shot Cooper handed him. "Mom?" he asked him, which threw me as to what that had to do with anything.

"Okay at the moment." Cooper shrugged, his playful demeanor lost. "Moved her somewhere safe."

Trigger nodded once. "Bottle," he ordered and started to walk by me. "Sounds like you had a good time here."

I tried to follow his random conversations.

"What does that mean?" I grabbed the bottle out of Trigger's reach. He glared at me while his thumb ran along his bottom lip. When I thought he was going to speak, he leaned over the bar and grabbed another bottle before he headed to his office.

"Jesus, you have balls." Cooper let go a breath of air. "Or a death wish."

"Hey!" I called out after him, stopping the door before it shut. "What did that mean?"

"You screw Loose?"

My head snapped back. "What?"

He moved right in front of me, inches from my nose. "Did you fuck Loose?"

Without thinking, I slapped him right across the face. His eyes flickered as he stood taller.

Oh no.

One minute he was in front of me, and the next he was out the door about to swing at Loose.

Brick tried to intercept but got tossed to the side. Peggy, who of course was here again, smiled as she hopped up on a bar stool, and Morgan shrugged like it was an everyday event.

I ran up behind them and saw blood spray in the air. "Trigger!" Once I was close enough, I yanked on his arm, only to be thrown forward by his swing. I scrambled to my knees between the two of them. "Trigger! Stop!" He suddenly backed off, shaking his head as if to clear it. His eyes looked black as the night.

My chest heaved as I struggled to stand on shaky legs. I stepped toward him to take a moment to allow my head to catch up. "Nothing happened," I whispered harshly. "If you've got something to say, Trigger, say it, but Loose did nothing but be a friend." I blinked a few times when I realized what I had said. Was I a fucking pawn being used by Loose? Was that his plan all along?

His darkness held me captive as he thought. No one moved or said a word. The tension was so thick I couldn't think straight.

Just when I thought he was going to say something, he turned and marched back into his office.

"Get this place cleaned up," he grunted.

What the hell! My nerves were shot!

"What did you do, Tess?" Brick headed over to Loose, who surely had a broken nose. "He needs a clear head tonight. He can't be trigger-happy right now. He has too much shit on his plate."

"What happened?"

"Doesn't matter," Morgan muttered. "What matters is that you just stirred up the beast."

Mother of hell!

I grabbed a bottle of whiskey from the bar and headed back to his office.

"Not smart, Tess," Brick warned.

"I know."

I didn't knock. I just went in to find him pacing the room. He was literally vibrating, and his arms were up like he was about to fight.

"Get out, Tess."

I ignored him and took a long swig of the whiskey. I sat on the edge of his desk and watched his chest move heavily, his eyes shut as his fists opened and clenched. He suddenly picked up a chair and sent it flying across the room. I swallowed back my nerves.

"You shouldn't be here."

I waited for him to get closer before I reached for his hand and tugged him toward me. To my surprise, he came. His jacked-up body towered over me.

"I have no idea what you thought happened, but I did not get on Loose's bike. We just walked to the pier and chatted. He walked me home, and that was it." And just to drive the truth home, I added, "You have my word."

His eyes were glued to mine. I couldn't read his expression, so I decided to show him where my head was. I moved my hand up and slid my fingers to the button of his jeans. Again, with slow movements, I opened his pants and freed his erection. It fell heavy in my hands. He was long and thick, everything I would expect in a man like Trigger. I ran my fingers downward and gave him a little tug.

A hiss of air escaped through his teeth, and he shifted to twine his hands roughly in my hair.

I licked my lips and leaned in without waiting for his command. I pumped it twice and licked the slit. His hips flexed forward as he held my head in place.

"Mm." I took him to the base without hesitation. I loved the look of pure pleasure on his face.

I sucked deep, twirling my tongue all around. My hand pumped with the rhythm my mouth set. His salty taste smothered my taste buds, and his primal scent made me clench my legs together.

"Fuck."

My nails drove into his hips, only making him more turned on.

"Harder."

I did, and turned off all my thoughts. He needed this, because I had done this to him. Whatever his reason was for getting pissed right now didn't matter. What mattered was making it right between us.

His grip tightened as a warning he was about to come.

"You started this, you better finish it."

I cupped his balls and relished his groans as he came. I milked every last drop he had for me.

When I pulled back, he was a little calmer. His jaw didn't tick like it had, and his eye color lightened. He was back to himself, though I knew *Trigger* wasn't far beneath the surface.

His fingers slipped up my thigh and cupped my opening. They rubbed my nub and felt how wet I was. It was true blow jobs normally turned me on, but with Trigger I was almost soaked.

Stepping back, he tucked himself back into his pants and handed me the bottle of whiskey. I shook my head. I didn't want to rinse my mouth out. I swore I saw a tiny smile before he took a swig and watched me intently.

I hopped off the desk, pulled my dress down, and headed for the door, but his voice stopped me. "Stay away from Loose."

"Why?"

"Because I said so."

I rolled my eyes and made sure he saw my reaction then headed back to the bar where Peggy tried to whore herself out to Morgan. He ignored her while he loaded ammo into his shotgun.

"Thanks for your help back there, Morgan," My sarcasm was thick.

"No one gets in between Trigger and his next mark. You notice Loose didn't swing back?"

"Not that Trigger would even feel it," Peggy chimed in. "The man's a beast. He feels nothing."

I didn't like how her comment made me feel. I was the queen of turning off my "humanity switch," but everyone felt something at some point. It was a sad, sick truth in life.

Morgan zipped the duffle bag next to him. "How you didn't get torn a new asshole for jumping in is a surprise. You gotta be careful, Tiger. Trigger is not someone you fuck with."

I thought back to my past and allowed myself a moment to feel the pain. It helped me fuel my drive to move on.

"I've dealt with worse."

Morgan stopped what he was doing to face me. "That man in there," he pointed to Trigger's office, "was raised by the devil himself." He ran a hand through his beard. "Don't play with fire, Tess—"

I sighed. "—'cause I'll get burned."

"You'll get fried."

I found Brick nursing a beer by the pool. I kicked off my heels and dipped my feet into the cool water. My phone lit up my purse, and I saw another call come through. My stomach turned, but a part of me wanted to know what was on the voicemail.

"Hey," I kicked my legs under the water and watched the ripples flutter across to the other side. "What's a zig-zag mean?"

He shifted in the chair. "It's when someone fucks with your drug route. Steals it or tampers with it in some way. Why?"

Well, fuck, no wonder Gus went white. I decided not to start anything right now. I wasn't supposed to be eavesdropping in the first place.

"Just something I heard. So, who's Mike?"

He rolled his head on the lounge chair to face me. "Bald, tattoos head to toe?"

"Add in terrifying, and that be him. How the hell do you know him?"

Brick leaned back and thought. His leg started to thump, and I knew he knew something.

"Who is he?"

"Believe it or not, but Trigger once tried to join the Army."

"Seriously?"

"They strung him along for a bit, but before boot camp, they denied him. His record was something else. That's where he met Mike, but Mike had a clean record. They became close, but, well, you can see they divided them quickly. I know they always kept in contact, helping one another out here and there. Trigger and Cole have some weird understanding-bond thing that I don't know much about, and, frankly, it's none of my business. He never talks about it…surprising, I know." He laughed.

I could barely keep up, but Trigger in the Army completely threw me for a loop.

"Wow, how old was Trigger at the time?"

His lips stretched into a grim line. "Eighteen."

"He had that bad of a rap sheet at eighteen?"

No way.

"All Trigger was brought up to do was kill." Brick held my eyes and watched as I absorbed what he had said. "You have no idea how dark his roots actually run, Tess. It's not like when we were on the streets, dealing with wanna-bes and *juvies*. This is all real. So, when you get hauled into clubs and beaten or summoned by detectives, it's a big fucking deal. We run cocaine from Mexico to Seattle constantly. We have the best quality and the best trails. Problem is sixty percent of the money goes to the Serpents."

"Sixty percent?" I didn't want him to stop talking. Brick stood, and I joined him. I blocked his path and tried to get him to go on. "Goes to the Serpents? You mean all of that contract stuff with his father."

"His father made the deal and left Trigger to clean up his mess."

Loose's words came flooding back to me. "Brick, can I ask you something?"

"Yeah."

"Loose mentioned that Trigger cut his father up and buried him under the pool. You believe that? You really think Trigger would kill his own father?"

He leaned in close to my ear. "Would you kill your mother?"

I jerked away and forced that thought out of my head. Because I had thought of it, and he knew it. It wasn't lost on me that Brick didn't give me a straight answer.

"Sorry," he muttered, trying to grab my arm.

"Don't."

We stood a few feet away from each other. I tried to fight the horrible feeling that crept over me, and Brick dealt with his own demons.

"Whatever you do, Tess, *never* bring up his father."

I nodded, fully expecting to keep that promise. I started to chuckle. The more I thought about Trigger in the Army, the more I couldn't see it.

"What?" Brick came closer.

"Could you imagine someone in army fatigues barking orders at that man in there?"

Brick chuckled, shaking his head. "No, I really can't." He left me by the pool, my reflection mirroring my thoughts of her. I hated that people thought we were sisters. We were nothing alike, nowhere near. She was black, and I was white.

I knew he was in there. I knew she was too. The door was left open a crack, and I pressed my chest to the doorframe and peeked inside. Her long, silky nightgown fluttered in the breeze of the open window. Her blonde hair was styled in her normal fifties 'do, pinned up on one side. She liked to play up the prim and proper look, which was such a joke, considering she screwed more men than a whore with a pimp.

Her hand ran up his arm, along his shoulder, and around his chest from behind. I fought the urge to scream, kick, and cry. I wanted to rip her apart. Why? Why him? Why not anyone else?

Suddenly, as if she knew I was there, she looked directly at me and smirked.

I hated her.

***

Trigger

"You look like death." Brick set his beer and Cheerios in front of me. "Tammy is here somewhere. You want me to grab her?"

"No." I rubbed my scratchy eyes and fell forward on my elbows. My head was set in a loop of shit, and nothing could unjam it. Something gnawed at my guts like a tick slowly burrowing into my flesh.

"Too late." He stole my attention and flashed a forced smile over my head.

Two hands blocked my view, but she didn't touch me. She knew better.

"Guess who?"

My hand snapped over her wrists, and I pulled her around to the chair. She looked good today. Her fakes were still hanging out, but whatever.

"You look like you could blow off some steam." She played with a piece of hair before she lifted her leg and placed it on the side of the chair. Pink panties peeked out, but she reached down and pulled them aside and gave me a clear shot of her interest. "No prep work needed."

Brick snorted some beer and tried to hold it in, but he couldn't.

"Yuck." He wiped his face and laughed before he leaned over and asked, "Do you go home and practice the lines, or do they just come naturally?"

"Fuck you."

"Nah." He downed his beer. "Thanks, I'm good."

"Whatever." She looked back to me. "So, what do you say?"

Brick quivered through a laugh, which made Tammy start up again. My head pounded and muscles ached from the intense workout I had put myself through last night. I couldn't take any more of their shit banter, so I shoved Tammy's leg and stood.

"Ready?" Her eyes lit up.

"No," was all I said before I left for my bedroom. I needed something strong, fast. When I rounded the corner, my pace slowed when I saw my door wasn't latched. I pulled my gun and pushed it open to hear water running.

What the fuck?

I rushed across the room and carefully turned the knob to a steam-filled room. Kaleo played from a phone on the counter. Then I caught wind of her voice. Tess sang softly into the spray of the water. I kicked off my shoes and moved farther into the bathroom. It was the first time I hated the drawings on the shower doors. They hid her curves.

The heavy weight that had held me immediately lessened when she was near. I opened the door and stared at her long, wet hair that clung to her. The side of her breasts bounced as she rubbed her face. She was still oblivious to my presence, which I rather enjoyed. Her voice rose when the song hit the chorus, and I smiled. She had a sexy rasp that hit right to my painful erection.

"Goddamn!" She jumped when she finally felt my eyes on her. "Are you trying to kill me?" Her chest heaved and glistened under the water.

"My bathroom." I shrugged, not at all caring.

She didn't try to cover herself. She just stared right back at me.

"My shower is broken, and Gus caught me on my way to Brick's room. Minnie was using his, so he told me to use yours. I wanted to ask, but you were busy." *Tammy.* Her eyes shifted downward. "Sorry if I overstepped."

I barely heard what she said because my eyes were glued to the faint hickey on her neck. Fuck, that was sexy.

"I'm almost done, so—" She stopped when I stepped inside and tore my t-shirt off. My jeans instantly stuck to my legs, but her hands were on my belt, freeing me.

My hands slid up her stomach to her perky breasts and cupped them. Her skin was soft and warm, and I couldn't keep myself off her. I kicked my jeans in the corner and walked her back to the wall. Both arms moved to the wall next to her head as I stared down at her hungry eyes.

Her head tilted to the side, and I could tell she was thinking by the way she squinted. Slowly, her hands rose to show me her intentions. I pushed away my natural urge to flinch and didn't say no, to my own surprise.

The tips of her fingers moved to mine, and very cautiously moved to my battered knuckles, wrist, forearm, bicep, shoulders. Her eyes followed her movements, and mine drifted closed. It didn't hurt, didn't burn, or make my mind snap back to any haunted memories. No, it felt different, like a warmth that lingered wherever she went. She skimmed past my jaw and brushed my wet hair back from my face.

I heard her whisper something, but I couldn't make it out. She started to trace the tattoo across my heart before both hands flattened on my chest. She pushed upward and gently kissed underneath my jaw just once before she lowered back down and turned into the spray.

I jerked as I exploded unexpectedly. With a groan, I reached around her middle and hauled her to me. I huffed in her ear and rode out the moment. She ground her hips and reached back for my head. Her lips found mine, and she threw herself into the kiss. Pumping myself to get hard again, I spread her open and slipped in. I moved her hands to the wall to tell her to stay there as I gripped her sides and eased back and forth. The way I disappeared inside her to the root was mesmerizing. Her body bowed into a sexy shape as she climbed her way to a climax. She was beautiful. There was no other word to describe Tess.

"Trigger!" she cried and beat her fist on the wall. "Please!"

I stepped forward to haul her back to me so we were chest to back and held her tightly as I pumped harder. Her arms wrapped around mine as she fell apart screaming. Four more thrusts, and I followed. My teeth sank into her shoulder, and I nearly lifted her off the floor with the force.

With a twist, I sagged against the cold tile and struggled to catch my breath. Tess tried to move, but I wasn't ready yet.

My head was fuzzy and my body hummed. Tess jerked when I twitched inside her.

"I'm going to be late," she whispered.

My arms locked around her. "Late?"

"It's my day off."

"I don't remember this."

She rolled her head to look at me, her eyes lit up, and I saw her feistiness was right there. "Morgan gave it to me."

"Morgan doesn't have that authority," I grunted.

She wiggled out of my hold only because we were both wet. I groaned when I fell out of her with a heavy thud. Her hands slipped over my shoulders into my hair.

"You taking my day away from me?" Her teeth grabbed my bottom lip as her smile spread. "Surely you're not that mean."

I am.

"Please." Her lips were at my neck, and my hands were on her ass. "Please," she repeated between kisses. "Just one day."

I growled, hating the idea of her not being here.

"Where are you going?"

"Beach." She moved up my jaw to my lips.

"With who?"

"A boy with dark brown eyes."

Both hands grabbed her hips, and I pulled her back to stare at her face.

She started to laugh. "My book. I just want a few hours to tan, read, and not have to deal with anyone."

"Take a prospect."

She won't be going alone.

"No." Her head dropped forward. "Trigger, please, women need alone time. You asked me to move in here, and I did. But now you want me to take one of them with me? I'd rather take Loose."

She jerked back when she realized what she had said. Anger burned through me; I hated that fucker.

"I just mean he looks in my eyes when he speaks to me. Jace and Ty, they…don't." She reached over and turned off the water. "He doesn't ask too many questions either. It's just easy."

Tess stepped out and wrapped a towel around her body. She handed one to me before she went out to my room.

"You going to the pier?" I asked, not wanting to fight. The hammer in my head had finally left, and my body felt back to normal.

"Yeah." Her eyes narrowed in on mine.

"Where's your phone?" She pointed to the phone on my bed, stepped over, and unlocked it. I entered my number and handed it back. "Keep it on you at all times."

"Okay." She fought a smile.

"What?" I shrugged on a t-shirt and jeans and reached for my cut from the back of the chair.

"It's just nice."

I sat on the couch to tie my boots. "What is?"

"You talking to me rather than at me."

Standing, I checked my gun clip. "You fight me less this way."

She went quiet, so I glanced over, flipping the hair out of my face. She had on ripped jean shorts and a tank with hot pink straps underneath that peeked out on the sides of her shoulders.

"You kinda like me feisty." She winked before she tucked her phone in her bag and headed for the door.

I came up behind her and slammed the door closed again. She turned and grabbed my face and kissed me hard. Before I could think, she slipped under my arm and out the door.

Well, shit...

"Where are you going?" I heard Brick yell from somewhere.

"It's my day off."

"That didn't answer my question!"

"I know."

I smiled at her sass. Damn, that chick was—

"You talk to her about the trip?" Rail's question stopped my thought.

"We ready for the meeting?" I avoided answering him. I wanted Tess to have her day off before I told her about our plan.

Gus, Rail, Brick, and Morgan sat around the table, all mulling over the information Mike dropped off. Seemed we had a zig-zag in our cocaine route. Not to mention we had a fucking mole.

It was time to change things up. I pointed my next comment to Rail.

"Send some San Diego men to travel the route with the next shipment. Have them check in at each stop. I want to know everything."

"I'll make a call." He downed his beer.

Brick looked around then glanced at me. "What's with the knee?"

I looked down and saw my knee bounced around like mad.

"You okay today?"

I hate to be questioned.

"Where's Tammy?" Rail cut in, and I shot him a look.

"You all want to talk about feelings and pussy?" Gus pulled the attention to himself. His arms were folded, and he looked like I felt. Fucking annoyed. "Or can we discuss the fact that we have a mole?"

"Truthfully, boss, I haven't heard a thing." Morgan tugged on his beard. "Not sure how I'm gonna feel when that brother gets ousted."

"Agreed." Gus nodded.

I leaned back and ran through all the men we had living here—

fifteen. But that didn't count the other ten who lived outside of the clubhouse. Then the two prospects and the hangarounds.

"Look." Rail cleared his throat. "Not trying to be a dick, but there's always our newest bartender."

The sound of my neck snapping made him glance over. I did the other side to relieve some of the tension that had instantly built in my chest.

"Are you kidding?" Brick began to stand, but I held up a hand. If anyone was about to snap, it was going to be me.

"No."

Rail let out a heavy breath, and I knew he wasn't done. "It's just that she was inside the Serpents' clubhouse."

"Yeah, and got her ass beat."

"Did she?"

"Enough." I slammed my fist on the table. "We killed the brother before Tess even started. There is no way she had a part in this."

"Then who?" Rail tossed his gun on the table, more to make a point. "'Cause it sure ain't me."

"You sure about that?" Brick hissed under his breath.

"This is what he would have wanted." I almost flinched at my own words. I never spoke about my father. Even Gus's face fell at the mere mention of him. "We watch for anything. We listen for everything."

I dismissed the guys and took a moment to calm down. This shit was unreal.

"Trig, you know where Tess is?" Brick asked with his head down in his phone.

"The pier."

He looked over. "Neutral ground."

"Jace is watching her."

His face didn't change expression when he looked out the door. "Then why is Jace right there?"

CHAPTER TEN

Tess

"Seriously?" I tossed the paperback aside. Warning or not, that was a dick cliffhanger.

I watched as people splashed around the freezing cold water. *You know you're a tourist, when?*

Curious to know what Brick was up to, I grabbed my phone and started to text him.

"What?" I shaded the screen. "No, no, no! Dammit!" I swore as I chucked my dead phone in my purse and flopped on my stomach with a huff. *First a cliffhanger, now my phone. Awesome.*

My nap was short-lived as a kid decided to build a sandcastle next to me. She was cute, but hummed the same tune for about thirty minutes, and I wished I had brought headphones. Her bright orange mermaid swimsuit was blinding, and I wondered if her parents secretly let her wear it so that no matter where the hell she was on the beach, they'd be able to find her. She was like a frickin' beacon next to me.

"What up, Tessa?" I jerked around to find Jace standing by me. "Don't get mad, but I guess there was some miscom…commui…"

"Miscommunication?" I tried to fill in the blank.

"Yeah, that. Anyway, I was supposed to stay, but I didn't, so now he's here." He pointed with his head.

Who?

There was Trigger in the parking lot next to his bike.

"He wants to talk."

"Wait, you've been here watching me?"

Oh, for fuck's sake. Seriously?

"Yeah, but, Tess." He moved closer. "I'm sorry. I didn't know.

Sometimes the orders go in and get all fuzzy. Can you try and—"

"Don't worry, Jace." I squeezed his shoulder. I knew how hard it was for him. I headed in the very large man's direction.

His sunglasses made his look that much more intense. He pushed off his bike and unfolded his arms as I got closer.

"Checking up on me?"

"Yeah." He smiled slightly. Damn, he was sexy. "Your phone is off."

"It died."

He ran a frustrated hand through his hair, and I could tell he was stressed about something.

"I'm fine, Trigger. Just been here reading. I sent Jace home because he didn't need to be here."

I knew he saw through my lie, but they were always talking about looking after their own. Well, this was me doing that.

"I thought you said I could have the day off."

He eased back down on his bike. "This is neutral territory."

"The beach is crowded today. I'm pretty hard to spot."

"No, you're not."

I rolled my eyes and moved my hands to my hips. "You do this for all the girls in the club?"

"No." He again looked unapologetic.

Then it hit me.

"Ah, right. Brick."

"Look…" He stopped for a moment, almost as if to listen for something. "We are heading out to the desert for our annual party. All the crews will be there, and I need your help on some stuff."

"Like serving drinks?" I joked.

"I need you to listen for anything strange within my club. You know, keep your eyes and ears open."

That caught my attention. "Okay, I can do that."

He rubbed his beard. "We've extended our invite to some of the Serpents."

My face dropped, and I turned away from him and looked back over to Jace, who was now on my towel. A few of the people around him shifted back. They seemed uncomfortable with him being there. *Perhaps it was the Reaper shoving a skull in their faces.*

A wave of nausea washed over me when I thought of Tiago being that close again.

"Why?" I whispered more to myself.

"He won't get close to you."

"You can't promise that."

"Hey." He tugged my wrist and pulled me between his legs. He flipped his glasses up and cupped my cheek with his huge, colorful hand. "Not gonna let shit happen to you."

"This would imply that you care, here, Trigger."

"I care enough that I don't want to see you get hurt."

I swallowed past the lump in my throat and knew he was right.

"We need them there, for a few reasons."

"Care to share some of them?"

His face twisted and his teeth sank into his lip. I could tell it went against his nature to let a woman in on anything. But, Christ, I wanted to know.

To my surprise, he answered me. "We need to see who they interact with in our club. We need them in case the Stripe Backs come. They like you, Tess. I hoped you could help me."

"I won't sleep with them," came flying out of my mouth without a thought.

His tongue swiped his teeth before he chuckled darkly. "Even if you wanted to, that would not happen."

I shook off a heavy sigh and nodded. "Fine, when do we lea—"

Trigger suddenly stood and pulled me closer as we heard the rumble of a bike. It was low and deep, and when I saw who was on the bike, I held my breath. Two Serpents rode side by side and stopped on the side of the road. Even though they had a deal with our club, I didn't trust them, and apparently, neither did Trigger.

"Trigger?" I somehow whispered. My grip on his arm tightened as he slid me behind him. "Should we leave?"

They were maybe thirty feet from me, but they might as well have been right next to us.

"No."

Awesome. Classic Trigger and his one word answers. It gave me no sense of comfort when he did that.

One of the men flicked his head before he roared off, followed by the other.

My head hit Trigger's back as I sagged with relief.

"Go get your stuff." His muscles flexed as he moved to his bike.

I didn't move because that was intense, and my heart was still pounding.

"Tess, go get your shit so I can get you back to the clubhouse."

"Were they watching you or watching me?"

"Do you ever listen?"

"Sorry," I shot back in frustration. "Believe it or not, that was a little scary. Not that I expect you to understand, given that you don't have a fear gene."

His chest fell, and I saw he understood I sometimes did get scared. That sometimes this life could be a little much for me.

"Okay," he whispered softy.

I shook off my nerves. "Your one word answers are stellar at times like this."

Trigger motioned at Jace, who had moved up when the bikes appeared and was standing not far from us.

"Head back."

A man of few words.

The clubhouse was quiet, with only a few members playing pool off in the back corner. Morgan was drying glasses and shot me a smile when he saw me.

"How was your day off?"

"Eventful. Yours?"

"I had the privilege off watching Minnie tell off Peggy." He chuckled. "Gotta love a cat fight."

I dropped my stuff at the side of the bar and took a seat.

"Drink?" he asked.

I shook my head. Too much sun and liquor would make me pass out. Besides, I was more interested in what happened.

"Why did Minnie tell her off?"

He lit a cigarette and leaned forward on the bar top. "Peggy was running her mouth about you, and she stepped in." He started to laugh. "I believe the phrase *I'm going to slap you in the vagina* was used."

"Classy," I mumbled. "What the hell did I do to Peggy, anyway?"

"It wasn't what you did to Peggy that's got her tits in a twist. It's who you're doing." His gaze shifted over my shoulder to Trigger, who was with Big Joe.

Oh.

"We're not dating."

"Don't care if you are." He raised his hands. "Don't do drama, but the fight was pretty hysterical."

Men.

I picked up my bag. "So, who won?"

"Brick got involved, but I'd say Minnie."

Oh, shit, poor Brick. I should go find him and see how he was.

"Thanks for the heads-up, Morgan. You still okay for tonight?"

"Yup." He winked and went back to what he was doing.

His room was next to Trigger's. I felt a sense of warmth when I saw he had carved a small wooden square around the handle.

That's right, Brick, you're safe here.

After I knocked a few times, I let myself in. I liked his room. I guessed because he always wanted a place that was his, but also a family. Now he had it, and the happy pictures on the wall proved that to me. I found the one of the two of us at the mall photo booth. Someone had left a credit in the machine, so we jumped inside and were total losers making funny faces. We split them in half. I forgot how goofy we looked at seventeen.

Curling up on his bed, I closed my eyes and remembered the few good times.

"Oh! I thought you were Brick." I jumped at Minnie's voice. Where the hell had she come—

Oh, my God!

I started to laugh. I laughed so hard I didn't make any noise. I fell forward on his bed, heaving as my lungs begged me for air. Tears streamed down my face and Minnie started to grin. She tossed a pillow at me, and I finally was able to take a deep breath of sweet oxygen.

"You're an ass." She totally ignored the fact that she was the one who presently wore a whipped cream bikini.

I held up a hand to try to regain my composure. "Sorry." I wiped my cheeks dry. "But you caught me in a moment, and that *outfit* is just priceless."

"Yeah, well, I didn't expect you to be on his bed either." She shrugged on a robe and took a seat next to me. "Where is Brick, anyway?"

"That's who I was looking for too. Just thought I'd wait him out. As much fun as this was, I'm actually glad you're here. I wanted to thank you."

"Thank me?" She swiped her finger along her leg and licked her finger. "For what?"

"Morgan told me about Peggy running her mouth. Thanks for having my back."

"Peggy's a dick. She's just jealous. She's wanted Trigger for years, but he's not having her. I wouldn't either. She's opened her legs so many times, I doubt they can even close anymore. They just flop around for whoever, whenever."

"Thanks for that graphic image." I moved up to lean against the headboard, and Minnie shifted so we both stared at his mirror on his dresser. "Confident place for a mirror," I joked.

"Yeah, well, Brick is a bit crazy in bed."

"Oh," I groaned, "I really didn't need to know that. He may not be blood, but he's still my brother."

She leaned over, grabbed a bottle of champagne from somewhere, and started to fill two glasses. She handed one to me. "Sometimes I just want a girly drink." She clinked my glass. The taste was refreshing, and I downed it quickly. She did the same and refilled them. "I'm glad to hear he's your brother." She gave me a small shrug. "I was worried when he told me you were coming. You know, the best friend shows up, and then they fall in love after finally realizing their feelings for one another."

I laughed. "I love Brick more than anyone in the world, but we've never been attracted to each other like that. We've been through too much at an early age. I know he likes you, though." I smiled when her eyes lit up, and went on. "He mentioned you to me. He's never been like that before. That's a good sign you're more than just some girl."

She let out a big sigh. "You have no idea how much I needed to hear that. Especially with what's coming this weekend."

She filled my glass again, and I started to relax. "What's this weekend?"

"The annual party at the camp." She made a face, and I remembered Trigger had mentioned the desert. "Hence, *why* I'm doing this." She waved her hand over her body. "Women are a dime a dozen here. Even if you think you are in the perfect relationship with your man, I promise you when you turn your back, another hoe will be on her knees offering up her mouth." She ditched her glass and took the bottle. "It sucks, plus some like to share, and you don't ever want to refuse because you'll be replaced real fast."

She handed me the bottle, and I took it. "Well, now I'm glad I'm single."

"Oh, please, Tess. The others might be dumb, but you touched Trigger's arm. No one touches him. Be ready to leave Friday afternoon. Pack a sexy bikini. Actually, pack everything sexy. This place may be in the middle of the desert, but still pack your heels," she warned as the champagne lightened my head. "It's like Vegas without the flashy hotels."

"Where do we sleep?" I started to make a mental note of everything.

"Well, we are in with the founder, so we stay in three pimped out RVs. The rest are all in tents and pop-up trailers. All that is already there waiting for us, so know you'll be riding in on the bikes. It sucks! My ass is numb on a one-hour drive, but three? Shit."

"How long have you been around the Devil's Reach?" I liked Minnie. She was really genuine.

She closed one eye as she thought. "Been with the crew for five years, been with Brick for roughly a year. And to answer your next question, no, Trigger hasn't had a steady girlfriend. In fact, I don't think he's ever had a girlfriend. He just fucks a few women, and then we never see them again. But," she held up a finger, "watch out for Tammy and Peggy. Peggy's a slippery little bitch, and now that you're on her radar, she's going to make your life a living hell. She's had her eye on Trigger, as you know. Now, Tammy," her face twisted uncomfortably, "she's different. She's normally Trigger's go-to. They are always screwing in the pool. She talks less and knows not to touch him, so he puts up with her."

"Great," I muttered while my stomach turned. "So, you're saying whipped cream bikini?" We looked at each other and burst out laughing.

"I'm so sticky." She laughed harder when she opened her robe. "Oh, shit. It's everywhere." She turned so I could see.

"Oh no!" My hands covered my face as I bucked with laughter. Everything was hysterical. Damn, I needed more bubbly drink.

"Really, now?" Brick raised an eyebrow from the doorway, but I could see he was happy. "As hot as this might seem, I don't do incest." Minnie tossed a pillow at him as I tried to stand, but it was hard.

"Night, Min." My wave was sloppy. I hugged Brick and headed back toward the bar.

I ducked under the counter and popped up next to Morgan with a happy grin.

"Hi, Morgs."

"Tiger," he studied my face, "you've been partying?"

I held my fingers up. "A little. I needed something." I suddenly tuned in to the music. "Oh, I love this song."

Morgan tossed his head back and let out a husky laugh.

I belted out the lyrics to "Cryin'" by Aerosmith very dramatically, but the music was so loud hardly anyone noticed.

"Sing it, sweetheart!" Morgan shouted and slammed down a shot.

***

Trigger

The guys were in full swing with the prospects. Brick was close to breaking down Ty, who had a bit of a chip on his shoulder. Pissed me off, but he also had balls, so I respected that.

"We all set?" Rail paused. "Someone is having fun."

I decided to check it out. Tess was singing at the top of her lungs with Morgan rocking out next to her.

"I don't think I've ever seen Morgan dance." Cooper shook his head. "I don't think I want to anymore."

Tess slapped the bar and took a shot with Loose, who it seemed to me was wherever she was. My fists clenched as I fought the urge to stab him in the neck.

"We ready for this weekend?" Rail asked, but he was cut off by a scream.

My eyes went immediately to Tess, who had thrown her arms in the air, her face a picture of fear.

It only took me a moment to see why. One of the Serpents had a gun pointed at her.

I was behind him in three strides and calmly spoke. "I'm going to ask you this only once, so think carefully."

The man turned slightly to eye me but didn't back down.

"Why the fuck do you got a gun pointing at my girl?"

"Bitch went for the piece," he spat out. "I was just here to deliver a message."

I glanced at Tess, who wasn't breathing. "Which was?"

"We are accepting your invite to the desert."

I made a show of scratching my beard while I got my guys in sight. "Well, I have a message for you." I elbowed him in the throat and grabbed his head and slammed it to the bar top. He bounced back and fell to the ground.

"Get 'im out of here," I shouted to Big Joe, who dragged him out by his feet. "Why the fuck wasn't he patted down!"

"You can put your arms down now, Tiger," Morgan whispered to Tess who looked frozen in time. The music turned back up and everyone went right back to drinking.

"You okay, Tess?" Loose tried to grab her attention.

She shook her head and dropped the rag in the sink. "I think I'll head to bed."

Morgan looked worried but returned to serving. I followed behind her.

"Hey," I called after her.

"I'm fine, Trigger." She wouldn't look back.

I caught her arm just as she was about to turn the corner. "Don't walk away from me," I barked, but the moment I saw her face, I felt like a dick. Her eyes were red and her cheeks were flushed.

"I said I'm fine."

"Really? 'Cause you're shaking."

Her eyes closed and she swallowed hard. "I swear, I didn't know there was a handgun there."

"You think I care if you did?" She was crazy. "Are you okay? Look at me in the eye, and don't you dare lie to me, Tess."

Her face flinched, almost like she remembered something.

"What?"

"Nothing," she sighed. "Don't mind guns now. Your club broke me of that. But he looked unstable, and I wasn't sure—"

"Trigger?" I turned to see Tammy in a towel, her bright green nails stroking her chest. "I was just going to go for a swim and thought you might like to join me?" She dropped the scrap of fabric and was ass naked in the hallway.

I cursed before I turned to Tess, but she was no longer in front of me.

"Is that a no?"

"That's a *fuck* no, Tammy."

"Why do you look like that all the time?" Vanessa, a local girl who seemed to think I was her personal project to fix, joined me on the steps of the movie theater.

My fight got out four hours ago, and I liked to watch the sun rise to remind me that I lived to see another day. Sometimes I wondered if it was a good thing or not. Maybe lying in the dirt would be better than walking on the grass.

"You just like to fight people?"

I spat some blood on the ground. The shit had sucker punched me in the lip. It was dirty, but I knew dirty all too well, and three hits from me and the fucker was done. "Don't really have a choice."

"Everyone has a choice."

I smirked. Spoiled brat probably had everything handed to her.

She'd never known what a hard time really was.

"You know," she moved down to my step, "if you smiled more and didn't act like you were about to snap and kill us all, maybe you'd have some friends."

"You think I want friends?" The chick was insane.

"You're what, fifteen? I have never seen you speak to another person. Gotta be lonely."

"It's not."

"You know they call you the boy with bruises?" She eyed me for a reaction. Well, she didn't get one. I learned a long time ago to mask everything. If you showed a reaction or an emotion, you became weak. Weakness was cancer for people like me. She moved forward with her keys around her fingers. "You could tell me your actual name."

"I could."

"But you won't."

"Why? What's the point?"

Why the fuck couldn't she leave me be?

Her face twisted and she looked annoyed. She stood and brushed her long black hair off her shoulder with huff.

"I know you have a different life than me, and that you think I have everything easy. Well, you know what, I do. I won't apologize or excuse what I have. I'm fortunate. But I just wanted to let you know that your bruises and ripped up knuckles don't scare me off. I just thought you could use at least one friend."

"I don't." No one would be my friend if they really knew me. I was unlovable, untouchable, and frankly, unreachable mentally.

"Such an ass."

"Pretty much."

Her face flushed and her hands flew to her hips. "Good luck being lonely."

I nodded as she rushed down the steps and into her awaiting car. Vanessa lived in a different world than I did. Even if I wanted a friend, I wouldn't drag someone who had the potential to be something good down into my hell. She might see me as an ass, but really, I was saving her.

"Boy!" He slapped my head hard.

Yikes, I didn't even know he was there.

"Who the hell was that?"

"No one."

"You lying to me, boy?" His voice sent a chill across my achy

muscles. "She's way out of your league." He chuckled while he cupped his hand around his cigarette to light the tip. "You'll never be enough for anyone. All you're good for is fighting. Don't ever forget that."

Always so inspiring with the pep talks.

"You keep that head on straight and remember where you came from and who raised you." A puff of smoke passed by and stung my nose. "You ever forget, and I'll make sure you remember."

That was a promise I knew he'd keep.

That night I sat in my dirty little excuse for a room and stared up at the poster on the wall. Most kids hung movie posters. I hung one of the ocean. I promised myself that someday I would live by the sea where I could sit and hear the waves and be alone and not have him next to me. I would find my own freedom.

The door opened, and I saw his silhouette.

"Get up. It's time."

My feet swung to the edge of the bed, and I slipped into my sneakers. Tonight, I'd fight three guys. If I won, he'd make fifty thousand. If I lost, I'd be locked in the room in the basement. I cringed at the thought. It was so quiet. I hated the quiet. I tossed my headphones aside and followed him downstairs.

That night I won all three. He was fifty grand richer, and I was left with a broken hand, three cracked ribs, and a swollen face.

Least I didn't get the room.

I jolted awake and saw him at the end of my bed. Only for a moment, but he was there with that same ugly look that haunted my nightmares.

"Fuck!" I flipped on the light and grabbed the clock. Four a.m.

I can't stay here. With my sneakers and hoodie, I headed for my rooftop.

***

"Where were you?" Brick sipped a coffee as he poured a bottle of beer in his Cheerios.

"How does that even taste good?" Rail made a face. "You make an alcoholic look sober."

I grabbed a water from the bar fridge and sank onto the stool next to them. "I needed to clear my head."

"How long did you work out?"

I glanced at the clock and did the math. "A few hours. I need a shower."

"You want some company?" Rail asked over the lip of his beer.

Brick and I both stared at him.

"Not me. Shit, I mean Tammy. She's eye fucking you from over there."

I shook my head and reminded myself to lock my door when I went to get ready for the drive to the desert.

"You sure you meant Tammy?" Morgan laughed.

"Morning, sweetheart." Brick glanced over my shoulder. "You need some help?"

"Nope." Tess struggled to roll her suitcase to the door. "The wheels are just a bitch."

I hopped off my stool and took the handle from her. "Give it to me."

"Thanks." She tossed her hair out of her eyes before she looked up at me. Her gaze dragged across my face. "You didn't sleep last night?"

How the hell could she tell?

"I barely sleep," I grunted.

She eyed the guys then looked back to me. "You slept pretty well the other night."

I stood her bag upright and whistled for Ty to take it to the van.

"Different."

"How?"

"Van." I pointed to her suitcase.

"Sure, boss."

"Trigger?" Brick had his phone to his ear. His face lit up, and my excitement heightened. "We got a treat for you."

"Bring him in."

I turned to see Tess watching us.

"Who?"

"Just kickin' off this weekend with some fun."

"That comment scares me." She half laughed, but I could tell she was uneasy.

"Nice to know you do scare."

She rolled her eyes and headed back toward her room. Her leather skirt made my erection hurt.

"Ready?" Brick grinned.

The hum of the lights, the heat of the room, and the smooth floors under my bare feet sent sparks of exhilaration through me. This was what I loved, what I craved, what I lived for. That was what I was shaped into as a man. *This is who I am.*

With one last glance in the mirror, I saw him behind me and made eye contact.

It was time.

Fernando, the Stripe Backs' newest sworn-in member, had his arms hung from chains that were attached to the wall. He was on his knees in only his jeans. The rest had been stripped away so I could see the damage I was about to inflict.

I nodded, and Brick dipped his cut into a bucket of gasoline then lit the corner and tossed it in front of him.

Fernando fought the chains as he stared at his future slowly turning to ash. It was my prologue to what was to come.

I removed my t-shirt and cut and pulled my hair back out of my face. Pointing the remote to the far corner, I turned on the music to Radiohead's "Bodysnatchers." There was something about Thom Yorke and what I was about to do that went hand-in-hand for me. It awoke the demons and rattled their cages.

The heavy spiked ball fell from my fingertips and dangled from the leather strap. A flicker of light danced crossed his face then his chest as he tried to rise above it. His eyes were locked onto the massive beast, but I could smell his fear. It stung my nose much like a drug would.

Rolling my head slowly side to side to snap and relieve the tension, I let out a long sigh.

Let's do this.

Before he could prepare himself, I twisted and swung hard. The metal barbs hit and bit deeply into his skin in one smooth, satisfying motion.

He screamed out loud, but to me it was a silent cry. The music pumped out a beat and muffled all his sounds of terror.

I hopped back and forth, jacked up on the high that raced through my veins. When the chorus came on, I quietly sang the words, feeling my adrenaline surge.

With a flick, I removed the weapon from his flesh and swung it over my head then dipped low and drove it into his kidneys. Blood sprayed everywhere and coated my chest as I dragged it around his front. His flesh tore from his bones and hung in jagged pieces.

I repeated the same action on his other side. This time I heard his screams and his pathetic cry for mercy.

All of this was his choice, not mine.

I stepped back a few feet and lined up with his stomach. Swinging the strap in a circle, I lunged forward and drove the spikes deep into his lower abdomen. Skin ripped, and I was covered with his insides.

That was when Brick caught my attention. His face fell when he glanced at his phone.

Shit.

CHAPTER ELEVEN

Tess

"Anyone see Brick?" I asked Morgan as he was locking up the liquor cabinet. His bag was on the bar, and his gun was next to it.

"Slaughter room," Loose answered for him.

"What's that?"

"Last room down in your wing of the house."

"What the fuck, Loose?" Morgan snapped so quickly I jumped.

I stared at both of them before I headed that way.

"Tess, you can't go in there!"

"Watch me."

Morgan jogged down and tried to block my path, but Big Joe came out of his room and made a block so that Morgan was stuck behind me.

"What's up, Morgan?" Big Joe asked, totally unaware of what he just did for me.

I slipped around the corner, past my room, and stopped at the big double doors which I was told by Brick led outside.

Pushing it open, I disappeared into the darkness. With both hands out, I felt the wall and followed it toward the strobe light that could be seen flickering up ahead.

Music pounded my ears, and a bad smell attacked my nose.

I stopped dead in my tracks as I saw Brick's horrified face before he looked at Trigger.

Trigger slowly turned, and my stomach plummeted. Blood dripped from the ends of his hair, rained down his face, and pooled along where his jeans hit his waist. His chest heaved and his muscles glistened in the pulsating light. He was jacked up on something.

Brick and Rail stood beside him. Their faces all wore horrified expressions, and their body language alone made me realize I had majorly transgressed.

I moved my gaze over to the man whose arms hung like Christ on the cross from his chains fastened to the wall.

"He's a Stripe Back, and he tried to fuck with Trigger's bike, messed the steering up," Morgan whispered in my ear from behind. "You and Trigger would have been killed on the way to the desert."

Somehow, in a flash of clarity, I knew that in the MC world, the term eye for an eye was being played out here. I also knew with no uncertainly that this was a make or break moment for me.

And on another sick level, I was relieved to know that the blood dripping from Trigger's chest wasn't his.

I nodded once and moved toward him. The music switched to "Jigsaw Falling into Place." I knew this song well. Once in front of Trigger, I held his gaze as my hand slipped down his strong arm and removed the weapon he held.

"This is who I am," he whispered as if it were a confession.

I turned away from him and took a few steps back before I tightened my grip on the handle and swung it with all my might toward the man who had wanted us dead.

The ball smoked him across the face, and his body jolted backward and hit the wall with a splat.

Brick's face fell, but it was more from shock and amazement than disappointment. Trigger held up a hand, and the three men left, but not before Brick placed his hand on his chest as if to tell me he understood I was okay.

It was true; I was. I now understood their world, and to prove it, I fully embedded myself in it.

Trigger stood a few feet away, his eyes dark and hard to read. His chest rose and fell, and before he could say anything, I turned to strike the man again.

Right before I swung, he grabbed my arm to stop me. He bent down from behind and whispered, "Don't do something you'll regret—something you can't come back from, Tess. There's dark, then there's that."

Slowly, his hand slid up my wrist and removed the weapon from my fingers.

He was right, but at least we knew we were both equally fucked up inside.

Reaching over, he changed the song, cracked his neck, and flexed his shoulders. I stepped back, unsure what to do.

His hand tightened over the leather handle before he started back on the crumpled man. He swung, beat, and ripped the man's body apart while the music continued to beat. As disturbing as it all was, there was a part of me that understood the level a person can sink to when they've been pushed too far.

Whack.

Whack.

Whack.

Finally, after there was hardly anything left, he dropped the weapon and grabbed his phone. He snapped two pictures before he turned back in my direction.

He moved to stand in front of me, and his hand slipped around my neck and urged me to look up at him.

"I needed you to see that, Tess. I am not someone to fall for. I am a monster."

My eyes prickled. I did fall for him, and I hated it. I mustered all that I had to make him understand and went with the truth.

"You're not a monster to *me,* Trigger." My voice was clear, which surprised me.

I saw pain flash across his face momentarily. Then his expression softened, and I knew that for once he actually believed me.

Just when I thought he was going to walk away, he moved closer and wrapped his arms around my shoulders. He hugged me hard and buried his face into my hair.

"I got you." My hands moved to his back and held on just as tightly. "Let me help."

I moved back and spotted a shower on the far wall. "Hang on."

He didn't want to let go, but he did and watched me turn the water on and remove my clothes. I felt his hand run across my stomach as he pulled me to him. He quickly dropped his pants. His erection pressed hard against my back, and he kissed my shoulder as I stepped into the spray. I tugged him under with me.

He reached over my head and grabbed the soap and a big, puffy sponge. Covering it with the blue soap, he rubbed it over my stained arm. Blood swirled in circles around our feet.

Once I was clean, I took it from him and did the same. I turned him around and started to wash his strong back. It was the first time I was able to study his tattoos.

On his shoulder blade were two boxers, one with blue shorts, and one with red. They both had their fists up ready to fight in a ring. The Grim Reaper rested its arms on the rope that sagged under his weight. The words ***Death Is Never Far*** were scrolled above.

I stretched on my toes and kissed the words. He froze but let out a sigh when I moved back to my feet and continued to wash him.

He reached behind and pulled me to his front.

"I don't do romance, Tess, or tender, or any of that shit." His eyes closed and I saw how hard it was for him to express himself intimately.

"Me either," I confessed. I was just as lost as he was as to where we were, but I wanted to try.

He dipped down and kissed my cheek, the corner of my mouth, then my lips. He tried to be tender, but I wanted him to lose it on me. Like he said, *we don't do this shit.*

"Trigger?" I fought to keep my thoughts in order.

"Tell me." He nipped at my shoulder.

"Flip your switch."

I heard his throaty laugh that nearly made my knees give out. Before I could think, he flipped me around, grabbed my shoulders, and sank himself to the root.

I screamed as he did it again and again. The way my body reacted to his was like a million orgasms going off at once. My muscles clutched around him, and I heard a deep hiss escape.

"Bend," he ordered, pushing my front down to the floor. I grabbed my ankles and held on. "Jesus!"

Water poured down my face, and I gasped to find my breath. It was an intense angle. Right before I thought I couldn't take it anymore, he moved me upright then picked me up so I was straddling his waist again.

"I want to see you come." He bit and pulled my nipple roughly. The jolt of pain traveled down to the center of my stomach. "Give it to me, Tess."

I turned my head off and let myself fall. I vaguely registered my screams as I shook and shivered from intensity of it all.

"Where did you come from?" He thrust inside one last time and rested his forehead to mine. I was far too gone to answer him.

***

"Do I even wanna know?" Brick blocked my way as I came into the bar.

“Watch out!” Rail ducked as he came by. “Chick’s got an arm.”

“Yeah, remember that the next time you piss me off,” I joked.

Brick pulled me aside and lifted my wet hair between his fingers. He looked back at Trigger, whose hair was also wet. His eyes shut for a moment as he accepted the proof. “I’m going to say this once, that’s it.”

“Okay.” I knew better than to fight him. He needed to get his big brother fix out of the way.

“Tell him.”

“Huh? Tell him what, exactly?”

He sucked his lips in while he thought. “If you really are with Trigger, fine. Just know that if he finds out your past and you haven’t told him first, he might not be able to get past it.”

“Brick, my past is my past. But you’re right. I’ll try.”

I hated this topic.

“Yours is sexual, Tess, his is violence.”

“I’ll be fine, Matt.” I touched his arm to make my point.

“Yeah?” He grabbed my arm when I turned to leave. “Then why in the fuck did *he* call your cell?”

I felt my face blush, not from embarrassment, but because my best friend went through my phone.

“First,” I whispered, “you want to tell me why you were going through my phone?”

“I wasn’t, but when you were in there, he was calling your phone, like, fifty times. I finally went to silence it and saw it was the famous unknown number.”

“So, what? You decided to answer it?” Oh, I was fucking pissed.

“Yup.”

“And?”

“And, just like always, he listened and hung up.”

I crossed my arms and tried to calm myself. The fact that my past was mixing with my present was terrifying.

“Tess,” he bent down to eye level, “do you still love him?”

“No.” *No, of course not…*

“You can lie to yourself, but you sure as hell can’t lie to me.”

Fuck!

“It’s hard to let go of something that held you so close for so long.”

“I know that, but if he tracks you down and Trigger finds out, I’m not sure what he’ll do.”

I tossed my hands in the air, which made a few look over. “He won't find me."

Brick closed his eyes then stepped back and waved his hand for me to leave.

"I love you, Tess," he whispered before I turned and dove into his arms. Brick knew I loved him too, but he also needed to back off. I didn't do well being smothered. With that, I headed to my room.

A short while later, with one last look in the mirror, I eyed my outfit. Black Jack Daniel's tank, black leather pants, and heels. Gold bracelets stacked up my arm, with matching gold on my shoes.

It was a little fancy for a bike ride, but when I glanced over at Minnie, I saw she was dressed to impress, and I knew I made the right choice.

I flipped my sunglasses down and thanked Big Joe for opening the door for me while he texted someone.

The sun was hot, but there was a slight nip, a promise that cooler weather was on the way. The guys were loading up the van the prospects would drive in ahead of us.

"Damn." Rail hit Brick's shoulder and pointed at me. "How did you not hit that?"

Brick cursed then whistled at Trigger and punched Rail in the arm. "I have no words for how much I despise you right now."

Trigger lit his joint and hopped off the wheel well. "Damn." His eyes went from my heels to my face in a long, sexy minute. His arms slid around my midsection before he leaned in and kissed me hard.

"So, she's driving with him?" I heard Peggy whine from behind me.

"Yup," Cooper said. "Get on, Peggy."

"No way."

"Prospect it is, then."

"No, wait."

I rolled my eyes at Trigger. Peggy was so irritating. He huffed with a laugh before he led me over to his bike.

I was very happy to see there was a backrest for me. Trigger handed me a different looking helmet.

"See here." He turned it over and showed me two buttons. "Top one is so we can talk, and the second is to control the music from your phone."

"Seems easy enough."

"Good. Ready?"

I couldn't help but smile at the fact he was asking me instead of ordering.

"What?"

I shook my head then leaned up and gave him a quick kiss. "Nothing. Ready." I slipped on the helmet as he reached for the straps and secured it in place.

"You look," he shook his head, "like you belong on a bike."

"A bike?" I questioned playfully.

"My bike."

He eyed my shoes but didn't say anything. With a swift movement, he climbed onto the bike and waited for me to join him.

He hooked my legs and dragged me against his back when I tried to test out the backrest.

With a pat to my thigh, he eased us out of the parking spot, we started down the street, and the rest of the bikes followed behind.

To my surprise, Big Joe and Gus rode with us, along with Cooper, Brick, and Rail. We headed down the PCH, and I breathed the salt air in deeply. I sat back and enjoyed the view.

Two hours into the drive and now following the desert road, Trigger's voice found my ears.

"You good?"

It took me two attempts to figure out how to hold the button down when I spoke.

"I am."

"Coming up to a truck stop in about five minutes."

"Okay."

When the gas station was in sight, I thought I would ask the question that had been on my mind the whole drive.

"Trigger?"

"Yeah?"

I fought to keep my voice level.

"No one on here but us, so just say it."

"When do the Serpents show up?"

"Not sure." He reached back and patted my thigh.

"Okay."

He looked over his shoulder before he took the off ramp and turned to the gas station.

We parked in front, and I felt a little bad for the few people who were there. We did look pretty intense as the whole club rolled in.

Minnie hooked an arm around my waist as she joined us.

"Your pants make me want to take you in the bathroom."

Trigger gave her a frown before he urged us into the station.

"Grab something to drink." He nodded at the huge fridge that covered the whole wall.

"So." Minnie pulled me away from the guys. "How's it going?"

"Good." I removed a bottle of water and drank about half of it before I felt a little better. Damn, I didn't miss the desert.

"I heard something strange earlier and thought since you're—"

"So close to Trigger maybe I know if it's true or not?" I finished for her.

She shrugged. "Yeah, pretty much."

"What is it?"

"That we have a mole in the club. That he's leaking information to the Stripe Backs."

"Huh." I remembered Trigger saying he needed me to keep my ears open. That was a horrible thought. I hoped it wasn't true.

"Rail thinks it's you."

My mouth dropped open then I turned to spot the little shit who was filling up a Big Gulp cup like a six-year-old.

"Honestly, Minnie, I didn't hear much about it." That was the truth.

"Figured as much."

I quickly paid for my water and pushed the doors open to see Rail at his bike. I raced across the road, nearly getting creamed by a semi, who beeped his horn at me. I flipped him the finger before I got closer to the guys.

"Rail!" I shouted as he looked over and waved.

"'Sup, Tess?"

I didn't think as I pulled my hand back and slapped him right across the face. He rose, shocked as hell at what I had done.

"You think I am the problem here?" I shouted again, so hurt that one of these guys would think I would be anything but their family.

"What?" He stood to tower over me. "What did I do?"

"You." I felt an arm lock around me and haul me back. "How could you, Rail?"

When I looked down, I saw it wasn't Trigger's arm around me. I struggled to get away, but whoever it was, he wasn't having it.

"Calm down!" he shouted in my ear. "What the fuck are you doing?"

My eyes scanned the crowd. Brick's face was horrified but not scared.

"Hey!" I heard Trigger come up behind us. "What the fuck! Moe, let her go!"

Who the hell is Moe?

"Bitch slapped your boy."

Pardon me!

"Bitch?" I hissed. *Who the hell is this guy?*

"I said let her go!" Trigger marched over and released me from his hold. "You okay?"

"Yeah," I huffed, rubbing my stomach. The ass had one hell of a hold.

"She with you?" Moe, the ass, glared down.

"Yes. What happened here?"

"My guess," Rail ran his tongue around his mouth, "would be Tess heard what I said about her inside the meeting room." He glanced at Brick, who shook his head.

"How could you think that, Rail? I love it here. I love all of you guys. I would never—"

"Rail." Trigger cut me off. "Get the guys. It's time to go."

Trigger pulled me over to his bike and handed me my water I had dropped.

"You good?"

"Yeah, sorry."

He shrugged. "You did what I wanted to, when I heard him say it." He smirked darkly. "Although I wouldn't have slapped."

"A knife to the gut?" I joked.

"Something like that."

I glanced over to the guys, who were all getting ready to move on.

"You don't think I am, right?"

He tugged me close and looked down at me. His tight hold on my hips told me the answer. "You think I'd let you in if I did?"

"Well, there is that saying, keep your friends close and your enemies closer."

His lips found mine as he kissed me hard, and his hands slid down my butt, giving it a squeeze.

"I don't only want you closer, I want you under me too." He handed me the helmet. "Come on."

***

Trigger

I pointed at the horizon where I saw the smoke rising into the air.

The guys had a fire going as a signal to the rest of us.

Tess's grip around my center tightened. I knew she was nervous, but I wouldn't let a soul touch her.

Moving my hand to hers, I drew it up to my lips and kissed her knuckles. I caught my reflection in the mirror and froze at the man staring back at me. Who would have thought I'd allow someone in or allow myself to care? It scared the shit out of me.

I rested her hand on my thigh and placed mine over it. Her touch calmed me in ways that were hard for me to understand. It was the first time in years I rode without music. I didn't need it or want it.

What the hell is happening to me?

With my blinker on, I signaled to the rest of the guys and took the turnoff. Thankfully, the path had been beaten down and the road wasn't too rough.

Three miles in, we finally rounded a mountain, and I saw her eyes grow wide in the mirror. It was a spectacular view of hundreds of tents and trailers spread across the sand in between three mountains. A huge fire pit was in the middle, but small ones were scattered around the tents as well. Music pumped through speakers, and the booze was flowing. This annual party lasted five nights and six days. It took me three weeks to recover from it last year.

I'd seen the bottom of the barrel far too many times. I did it more to mask the voices in my head than anything else.

After I parked by our RV, I helped Tess off. She bent down and stretched her back. When you weren't used to riding, these trips could be a real bitch on the muscles.

"Trigger!" Minnie wrapped her arms around Tess's waist. "I'm stealing your girl for a few."

My jaw ticked at the thought of her walking around here on her own, but Minnie knew the lay of the land. "Not too long. Sun will be down soon."

"You afraid of the monsters?" She winked.

"Something like that."

"Tess," she held onto her shoulders, "when were you going to tell me your birthday was coming up?"

"And now the position of my best friend is officially open." Tess flipped Brick the finger, but he only laughed at her. "Never. The answer is never." She looked at me with a shrug.

Huh, never cared enough to know someone's birthday. I made a mental note of it.

"Well, I think we need to celebrate!" Minnie sang the words.

"Kill me now," Tess muttered at me, but she gave a little wave as Minnie tore her away through the tents, talking a mile a minute.

"Been far too long, my friend." I heard Tristen, my North Carolina VP, come up behind me. "How are you?"

I shook his hand and pulled out a black bag. "Good. Got the final count to get New Orleans squared away."

He chuckled quietly. "Our club has more money than any other, but you won't pull it from the account?"

"I have my reasons."

"I'm sure you do." He handed me a beer and tapped the neck to mine. "I see you invited some *guests*."

I nodded. I had spotted Mateo, Tiago, and a few others earlier. They looked real comfortable as they took up the seats by the fire. They each had a beer and were ordering their chicks around.

"Heard you had your reasons for bringing them here."

"Yeah." Tristen waited for me to say more. "Think we got a mole. Need to flush him out."

"Shit, seriously?" I knew how he felt. I felt it too. We were a family, a brotherhood. To abuse that was a painful thought. "Any ideas?"

"No," I answered honestly. "But I intend to find out soon."

We both sat and let that sink in. More and more people trickled in, and soon the place was partying hard.

Tristen and my crew sat around the fire swapping stories about the kills we'd had on the Stripe Backs. The Serpents slowly started to migrate toward us, and I felt the vibe change. They acted as their name implied and slithered their way around until they were within hearing range. They kept in the shadows, but their presence could be felt.

"Huh," Tristen caught my attention, "I see we have a newbie."

"Where?" Rail practically fell out of his chair to catch a glimpse.

"By the trailer, leather pants, hot as hell blonde." He grabbed his crotch and gave it a rub.

"No." Brick shook his head, annoyed. "Completely off limits."

I noticed Tiago had already caught sight of her too, which caused my grip on my bottle to tighten. He wouldn't get three steps before one of us slammed his head in, so I knew she was good.

Tristen tossed his beer back before reaching for another. I could have stepped in, but Brick was entirely too entertaining when it came to Tess.

Rail rolled his eyes, but when he saw how much it affected Brick, he couldn't resist.

"I heard she's insane in the sack."

I cleared my throat and tried not to throat punch Rail. It never bothered me when they joked about Tammy or fucking Peggy, but Tess brought out the need to protect.

Tristen licked his lips, clearly turned on by Tess. "The crazies are always the best in bed."

"Just ask Brick." Rail leaned over and gave a wink.

"I will tie your dick around your balls if you say that again."

Rail unzipped his pants, and Brick glared.

"I could use a little tug."

"Enough." I laughed as I kicked the legs of Rail's chair and he toppled backward.

Tess glanced over at the commotion and gave me a sexy smile.

Loose appeared out of nowhere with some of his friends. They surrounded her, and Minnie laughed at something.

To my surprise, she excused herself and headed my way.

That's my girl.

"Oh," Tristen sat straighter, "watch me wrangle this one in."

"Go get her," Gus huffed through his cigarette. He winked at me.

Tess leaned down and hugged Brick from behind and gave him a quick kiss on his cheek. I admired the love they had for one another. They were all they had, they were family, and I understood. My club was my family.

Tristen stood as she pulled away from Brick. He handed her a beer, and she looked at him before she took it.

"Ah, thank you."

"Tristen." He pointed to himself and waited as she stared at him. "You have a name. You wanna tell me what it is?"

She glanced at me then smiled. "Okay, why not. Tess."

"Pleasure."

"Sure." She laughed as she noticed we all were watching to see what was going to happen next.

Shit, the way her ass moved in her pants had my hands flexing.

Tristen moved closer, and I leaned forward to rest my arms on my thighs.

"You come here with anyone?"

Tess bit down on her lip when it hit her what we were doing.

"Yeah, I did."

Tristen grabbed his chest dramatically in pain. “Well, that ass shouldn’t have let you out alone. Someone might want to steal you.”

“Ass?” She laughed at Minnie, who had now set up shop on Brick’s lap. “Yeah, that pretty much sums him up most of the time.”

The guys all tried to hide their laughter, and I couldn’t help but smirk. I was an asshole, but with good reason.

“So, you wanna come back to my trailer? I’m the VP of the North Carolina crew.”

She pushed his chest to stop him when he stepped too close. “That depends,” she purred in her sexy voice.

“Fucking shoot me now…please, anyone?” Brick buried his head in Minnie’s chest.

Tristen ignored him. “On?”

“On if Trigger will share me.”

Tristen’s face dropped and he slowly turned to face me. “Oh, come the fuck on. Really?”

“Not happening.” I grabbed Tess when she came into my reach. I lowered her to my lap and wrapped my arms around her waist. She grabbed my face and kissed me to prove possession.

It was a fuckin’ turn-on.

“You enjoyed the show,” she whispered against my lips.

“I did.”

“Mmm.” She kissed me once more before she turned to Brick, who looked ill. “I had to walk in on *Varsity Blues,* dude, so consider us even.”

“Hey,” Minnie whined, “I thought you dug it?”

“Oh, I did.”

“Yeah?” She stood and hooked her finger for Tess to come her way.

Tess bit her lip as she grabbed Minnie’s jacket. “It was pretty hot.”

“How hot?” She held Tess’s head and slammed her lips to hers.

“Fuck.” Rail rubbed his beard.

Brick twisted in his seat. “So many things wrong with this.”

“No, dude.” Rail leaned back and kicked his feet up on the rocks. “So many things good with this.”

Fuck, no.

I pulled Tess out of Minnie’s grasp and held her close. “Don’t share with anyone. Chicks or not.”

Minnie wiped her lips and winked at Tess. “Sweet dreams, doll.”

“Night, Min.” Tess pulled me toward the trailer. “Remind me what you can offer, Trigger.” She laughed as she opened the door and disappeared inside.

I didn't bother to look back.

Tess had her hands on me the moment the door slammed.

"Get her taste out of my mouth." She jumped in my arms. I wasted no time stripping her down. I tossed her on the bed and stared at her perfectly naked body.

"Fuck," I cursed as I ditched my pants and shirt. "How can someone be so…" I stopped my words as I realized I had said it out loud.

"What?" She caught my lips as I laid my body over hers. "Tell me."

I brushed her hair off her face and held her chin gently in my hands. "How can anyone so beautiful be with someone like me?"

A flinch raced across her face before her hand cupped my cheek. "How do you see yourself, Trigger?"

Dark, twisted, fucked up.

"Don't do personal, Tess."

"Try."

"Tess."

"Trigger."

Fuck me.

"That's a loaded question," I finally bit out.

She rolled me back and straddled my waist. Her hands fell to my chest, and I had to remind myself it was Tess, not anyone else touching me.

"Well, why don't I tell you what I see?"

I smirked as propped myself up higher on the headboard and rested my hands under my head.

This should be interesting.

"I see a young boy who had a horrible upbringing. One that I might never understand. You were shaped into a machine and built up walls to keep people away. I think you only know how to be hard on yourself and others around you, because that's how you were raised. Because it's easier to keep people out than to allow them in. But," she leaned down and kissed me across my chest, "I've seen you smile, and you know what?"

"Mm?" I huffed as she wiggled down further, leaving a trail of kisses.

Her head tilted as she looked up at me from my stomach. Fuck, her eyes held me hostage.

"I see past the walls, scary stuff, and guns. I see a man who has a big heart for his club, and maybe, just maybe, a little room for me." At the last part, her voice lowered, and I could tell she was nervous to even say it. "I shouldn't have said that." She started to move, but I grabbed her arms and pinned her to me.

"Thought you didn't date?"

Her mouth opened, but nothing came out. Instead, she cleared her throat and tried to move away.

"Shit." I was an asshole. "I'm not good at this. This is why I don't do personal. I don't have the right words to use."

"Okay." She tried not to frown.

"But, ah, thanks for seeing me that way. I don't think anyone has before…or would want to."

"I want to."

I twisted a piece of her hair around my finger as her hand drew a pattern over my tattoos.

"What is…" I stopped myself. "Can I ask you something?" I knew she liked it when I asked, so I felt I was really making an effort.

"Yeah," she replied, but her voice told me she knew what I wanted from her.

I stopped her hand and fingered her stack of bracelets she never took off, or at least she never did around me.

She slowly rose and rubbed her arm uncomfortably. I knew from Brick there was a huge story behind it, and I needed to know.

"I was fourteen," she whispered, to my surprise. "Life wasn't great, never met my dad. My mom is…well, that's not important. Let's just say I got pushed to a point where I thought it was the best way out."

With her body on me, I felt her muscles tense as I pulled the bracelets off her wrist. A thin white line ran straight down about four inches. "They found me before I could do the other."

"Then what?"

"They take you in and set you up for a seventy-two-hour watch. Mom took me out early with a promise to watch over me. They agreed to it because it was my first attempt." Her eyes brimmed with tears, but she let her hair fall forward as if to hide from me. "Two days later, I met Matt." She shook her head. "Brick."

"Sorry."

"Don't be. He was the best thing that could have happened to me. I mean, I went back and forth to the streets, to him, but still, he was my rock."

"I get that."

She smiled cynically, and I could see there was so much more than that. "I want to get a tattoo to cover it, just haven't gotten the nerve to do it yet."

"You know what you want?"

"I do, a vine."

"Why a vine?"

She jumped when a ton of fireworks blasted into the air, then her head fell forward with a laugh. "That just stole ten years off me."

"Kickoff."

She leaned over to pull the curtains apart. "Who pays for all this?"

"Me."

"Wow." She turned back to me. "Good to be in the drug business."

My chest tightened; she had no idea how wrong she was.

"We don't make dick with the cocaine. I was smart with my money early and invested at the right time."

She lay down on her stomach next to me. "This is all your *personal* money? I can't even imagine what the bill would be for something like this."

I shrugged. My club was my life, and didn't matter what it cost. "They deserve it."

"Well, that's pretty generous."

"Sure." I hardly heard her as my hand inched toward her hip and traced her tan lines down to her belly. "What's the lily for?" I rubbed the pad of my thumb over its petals.

"Just something I don't want to forget." Her voice lowered. "I guess like yours."

Pushing off the pillow, I rolled to the side and faced her, thinking how my body was so much larger than hers.

Tess closed her eyes as my fingers roamed. When they opened again, my dick twitched. I never understood how a man could be lost in a woman until now.

She threaded her hand through mine and pulled it up to examine my artwork. "What does this one mean?" The tip of her finger moved along the barbed wire that encircled a skeleton.

"To remind me that even after death, I will still be trapped."

"Trapped?" Her brows pinched together. "How so?"

"Don't know what free feels like. After I killed someone close to me, I thought it would get better, but it didn't."

Something ran across her face, but she remained silent.

"What?"

"Nothing."

"Tell me." I pushed down on her side, and she jerked forward with a yelp when I tickled her hip.

She laughed and shoved my shoulder. "Don't play dirty, Trigger."

"I'd never agree to that."

"You never speak about your mother."

As usual, at the mention of her, my emotions shut down. "She was a stripper, got knocked up, most likely in some alley. She raised me until I was two and a half then dropped me off at my father's. Really don't know much more than that."

"Have you ever seen her since?"

I hated this, and I needed to change the topic. Her nipples were hard from the AC, and I zeroed in on her. My fingers slid between her legs.

She caught wind of my mood. "Sorry."

"I don't like this topic, Tess, any more than you do." I fought my temper. I knew it was probably normal for people to talk about this kind of thing, but I was far from normal.

"Hey." She shifted to press her lips to mine. "Sorry." With a hand under her side, I scooped her up to straddle me again.

It took me a moment to change my head space from that to this, but the moment I felt her wetness over my erection, all demons were slammed behind closed doors.

Easing onto my growing erection, she lowered on me to the base. Her body bowed as she adjusted to my size. With both hands clamped at her sides, I started to pump into her from below. She met each thrust and palmed her breasts, granting me a show.

Just as I was about to haul her down to me, I had a new idea. I fumbled in the drawer and found what I was looking for.

"Here." I handed her the rubber ring. Her eyes moved to mine, and I saw she was intrigued. I slipped out of her and nearly moaned when she dragged the heavy ring down the length of my erection.

She wiggled back into place and started to rock. I waited until her eyes closed to push the button on the side and her body bucked forward. The ring held a vibrator on the side that stimulated her and sent vibrations through me.

"Holy shit," she moaned into my neck. "Yes!" Her breath was hot on my skin, and I dragged my nails down her back to her thighs. I thrust harder, and her gasps shot past my ear. I pulled out and waited for her to squirm then lightly pressed the vibrating bullet to her and felt her thighs tighten around me. Her breathing was erratic, her eyes were wild, and her face flushed with need. It was a sexy sight. Her breasts were soft as silk when they met my skin, and I didn't want this to end. But when she squeezed me like a glove, I knew she was close.

One moment she was climbing, the next she leapt then fell, clawing at my chest.

The pain was delicious. I rolled to be on top, changing angle and position. She grabbed my head and crashed her lips to mine as another orgasm built inside her. I could see it in her eyes; she wanted me to lose it. I loved that she liked it just as rough as I did. With a hard slap to her ass, I lifted her so she straddled my lap as she rode me, and I nipped at her breasts.

She yelped at my teeth but pushed her chest into my face. We were animals and couldn't get enough. I wanted deeper, and she wanted harder. We both fought to get our way, and it was fucking hot as hell.

Finally, I used my weight to win and pinned her face down on the bed. I gripped her hips and hauled her up and thrust back in. She pushed to lean up on her arms, but I wouldn't let her. I wanted this angle. It was submissive, and I needed it.

With my hand on her shoulder and hip, I flipped my switch and lost myself inside her. She shook and screamed, begging me for more. My legs burned and my chest heaved as I burst into her. She panted to catch her breath when I finally slowed and came back from wherever the hell I was. Easing out of her, I rolled to my side and tried to catch my own breath.

I needed a shower and so did Tess, but this was more desirable than moving.

"I love when you lose it," she whispered through a laugh.

"You have a death wish."

"Maybe, but what a way to go."

I smirked as she laughed. Her presence chased the demons back into the shadows, if only for a while.

Just when I was about drift off to sleep, I felt her take a breath.

"You weren't born a sinner, Trigger," she said softly, as if she forgot to include me in her conversation.

"Neither was the devil, but look how things turned out for him."

CHAPTER TWELVE

Tess

"Where the shit have you been?" Brick snapped at me when I returned from the other side of the camp.

"Hello, there," Rail purred as Brick slapped him upside the head. "What, dude? She ain't my family."

"Something tells me even if she was, you'd have your hands down her pants."

I rolled my eyes, but truth be told, Rail was growing on me. I personally thought it was great how much crap he gave Brick.

Brick circled me. "Why are you wet?"

"You sure you want to know?" I winked.

"Don't throw me off with your sex thing." His face scrunched up. "Why are you wet?"

"Done yet?"

"No, I could keep going."

"Spare me the big brother act. I was with Gus, and he introduced me to some other women." I pulled off my shirt, and Brick nearly punched Rail. "Jesus, relax your balls. I have a suit on."

"That doesn't explain why you're wet."

I tilted my head at my best friend and chuckled before I leaned up and kissed his cheek.

"When are you going to see that I am not that little girl you met in the alley?"

His expression softened, but I knew how he felt. I felt the same way about him. It was good to care, but care and worry were two different things, and I didn't want to be why he had a stroke at thirty-five.

Dust rising in the distance drew our conversation to a halt. Three bikes came to a stop next to Trigger's camper.

The atmosphere felt a little off, but I couldn't place my finger on it. I followed Brick and Rail over to meet them.

"Where's Trigger?" one of them asked as he looked me up and down like he hadn't seen a woman in years. He was taller than I was. He had bright blue eyes, and his face was tattooed like the skin of an alligator.

Yuck.

"Better yet, who is this?"

Rail came into view and wrapped an arm around my neck playfully. "This here is Tess."

"Your old lady?" he asked while he gave his attention to my breasts.

Rail laughed before he shook his head. "Trigger's."

"Yeah, right." He laughed, and the others did too. "Can't fuck the untouchable."

My anger sparked quickly, but I saw Trigger approach us. Rail dropped his arm, and when Trigger was close enough, I grabbed his shirt and neck and slammed my mouth to his.

He froze at first, but then I felt his hand run along my ass and the other into my hair. After a moment of him controlling the kiss, he pulled away with a look that made me wet. He squinted as he tried to read my thoughts.

"Well, fuck." The reptile on the bike looked back to a woman who had her eyes glued to Trigger. "Looks like my gift will have to be shared."

I gripped Trigger's arm, and he held me closer. I hated to be a jealous person, but she was beyond hot and had a pair of tits that made even me stare.

I was no match for that.

"Who the hell is that?" Minnie asked as she joined us.

"He's the runner," Brick whispered.

"No, I meant the bitch who's eye fucking Trig."

I love Minnie.

I jumped when the reptile tossed a bag at my feet. "We should talk."

Trigger nodded to the prospects to move the bag off to a bunch of chairs around a fire pit.

The reptile motioned for his people to follow before he offered a hand to Trigger.

"Good to see you again."

"Yeah, you too, Gator," Trigger answered then looked down at me.

"You good?"

"I am."

"You look cold. You should put on a shirt."

My hands went to my hips. He must be kidding. "It's eighty-two degrees out. I can assure you I am not cold."

He looked over my head as he thought, his lips pressed into a thin line, before he spoke. "People are drunk." He stopped himself. "I don't want to have to kill anyone—" He cursed, and I couldn't help but laugh. "You enjoy this too much."

"Kinda." I beamed, happy that he cared about me and struggled with it. I had always fought with the terror of letting my guard down with someone else, but with Trigger, it was different. "Ask me, and I might consider it."

He hissed and ran his tongue along his teeth then took my chin in his hand. His sexy green eyes were inches from mine, and I thought he was mad. "Put a damn shirt on so I don't have to kill Gator for staring at what's mine."

Air-sucked-from-lungs.

Mine.

Did he just say mine?

Holy Mother of Lucifer, where the hell did that come from?

I nodded like a moron because I couldn't speak, even if I could will the words to my tongue.

My feelings battled. I liked the sound of that, but there was the guarded part that warned me to walk away.

Brick tossed a shirt at me.

Of course, the dick would take my moment and crush it.

I flung it back at him and headed to the camper.

Ten minutes later, I had changed into a black dress and boots. I couldn't do the skinny heels tonight. My poor ankles were not able to handle the rocky ground anymore, and these heels had a bit more chunk to them.

My hair had dried with a slight wave, and I had touched up my makeup. I felt pretty good until I saw the expressions everyone around the fire pit wore. That, and the fact that two prospects were standing in the middle, their faces blank.

What the hell is going on?

Trigger leaned against a picnic table with his arms folded. His face was grim, and his body language told me something was wrong.

I pushed through and ignored the prickly comments. I popped out between two people to see Gator place a tray down on the table and hand the prospects, Jace and Ty, each a tube.

"What the hell is going on, Trigger?" someone yelled from across the circle.

Trigger held up a hand to quiet the chatter. "Someone is tampering with our shipments." The entire crowd went silent. "Normally, my prospects would test the quality. However, knowing there is a risk, I don't expect them to try it."

Horrible comments wove through the crowd, but none were from our club.

"They're prospects," a dick yelled out next to me. "There's five more to replace them."

"Screw you," I snarled. "You get up there and do it, then."

"The fuck you say, bitch?"

What was with that word? I started to say something, but Tristen blocked my path. I rolled my eyes and went back to the horror in front of me.

Jace caught my eye, and I saw how terrified he was. His hands were clenched into fists to fight the shakes that had a hold on him.

"Don't do it," I mouthed.

Ty stepped up and held out the glass tube. He took a seat, leaned forward, and took a deep inhale of the powder before anyone could speak.

Jace went white and took a step toward the table, but Trigger held out his arm to stop him.

Ty's head flopped around, and he shook and foamed at the mouth. His eyes were blood red and he started to choke.

My hands flew to my mouth as the urge to scream crept up the back of my throat.

His neck contracted, and he turned a bluish color. His nails scraped the wood so hard they broke off at the base. Blood tricked out of his ears and dripped down the little scruff that lined his jaw.

He fell backward and landed with a final shake before he stopped breathing.

Trigger snapped his head in my direction almost like he felt me there.

"Joe." He nodded at me, and I felt arms around my shoulders that guided me away from the circle.

"Come on, sweetheart. You don't need to see this."

Minnie joined me on the steps of the camper a while later. She had a bottle of champagne and handed it to me.

"How you doing, honey?" She brushed my hair off my shoulder in a loving way.

I took a long chug before I gave it back. "You want the truth or what I should say?"

She shrugged. "Can't be as bad as what I'm thinking."

I eyed her then let out a long breath. "I'm reckless, so I understand the pressure Ty felt to do what he did. Makes me think about my actions, you know?" I glanced over to see her agree with me. "But, to be honest, I'm glad it wasn't Jace."

"Well, I see we are both going to hell, because you are not alone in that thought." She giggled, but she stopped herself with a frown. "When I first got here, Ty was just a hangaround. We made out one time in Rail's garage. Moment of weakness thing." She took a sip from the bottle. "When I met Brick, I fell hard, and when Ty saw that, he told Brick what we did."

"What did Brick do?"

She smiled warmly. "He said he had done worse, and as long as I wasn't going to do it again, we were fine."

"Huh." I wiped a pesky tear, more for the fact that Trigger lost a man than for the man himself. "Matt, I mean Brick, has always been the one who could see things more clearly. He helped me figure out a lot of shit. I'm really happy you two are good."

Her eyes softened when I looked at her.

"What?"

"I like when you call him Matt."

I chuckled. "They can call him whatever they want. To me, he's Matt Montgomery, the boy in the alley who saved me from *them*." I felt the pain that followed that story.

Minnie hopped to her feet and shook like she was getting rid of her own bad feelings. "I want to do something other than sit here and bitch." An idea seemed to hit her, and she held out a hand. "Wanna see something cool?"

Why the hell not.

***

"Really, Minnie." I awkwardly grabbed a shrub and hauled myself up. Tumbling forward, I managed to stagger upright. I was covered in dirt, but my sides hurt more from laughing at the ridiculous hike she had us on. "That's more of a workout than Trigger."

"You sure about that?" She giggled as she popped the cork of the somehow unbroken bottle of champagne she had stashed in her purse.

"Where the hell are these things coming from?" I dug inside her purse. "You're like an alcoholic Mary Poppins."

"I can fly too." She handed me a joint.

"Oh, I think I just fell in love with you." I lit the tip and took a long drag. "*Oh, yes.*"

Minnie went to the edge of the cliff and dipped her head back. "This right here is my favorite spot when we come here. No men, no shit, just me and the open sky."

I joined her and took a deep breath of the desert air. "I needed this," I confessed.

We sat on the edge of the cliff and chatted about anything that wasn't personal.

"You read?" I asked after an hour's chat about the newest *Fifty Shades of Grey* movie.

"I do." She handed me a bag of peanuts.

"You will make a great mom," I joked but took them, as I had a bad case of the munchies. "What was the last book you read?"

"*Real*, by Katy Evans."

"Shut the hell the up! I'm a huge Remington Tate fan."

She laughed.

"I knew we'd hit it off. Wanna hear something?" She nodded so I went on with my confession. "When I moved here, I was in bed and heard this odd noise. When I went to my window, I saw this guy boxing on a rooftop. So fucking sexy, totally Remy. I like to take photos, you know? I loved the way he looked, but I couldn't see much. He had a hoodie and whatnot. Christ, Min, I can't get that guy out of my head."

She chuckled. "You live on 6th and Ocean, right?"

"Yeah."

How does she know…? Ah, yes, Brick.

"Your window looks across to the old movie theater."

"Yeah?"

"Yeah, your Remington Tate is Trigger."

I looked at her with delight but also disbelief.

"What are you…what? I need you to explain further, please."

She tucked the bottle between us and stretched out her legs. "Brick wanted you to be safe. Safest place besides the bar is right next to another building his boss owns. He knew Trigger goes there a lot. Ergo, you were being looked after without you even knowing it."

I wanted to be mad, but how could I, when my best friend would go to such lengths to protect me? Plus, I fell for a man twice without realizing it. It also explained how he knew where I lived.

"That actually makes me happy."

She shoved my shoulder. "Wow, Tess, you used the word happy in a sentence. Big day for you."

"Yeah." I felt myself blush, and I wasn't sure why. "I need to pee."

"Thank God, me too." She stood and offered a hand. "We should go back down. Trigger will kill me if we're gone too long."

Somehow, with my bladder screaming, we managed to get back down the mountain with the use of our cellphone flashlights.

The bubbly drink had gone to my head, so I had to latch on to her arm for support. "You know that expression, I have to pee so bad I can taste it?"

"Yes," she giggled.

"I can't go any further." The camp was just across the other path, but I knew I couldn't go on.

"Fine. I'll be over there doing the same. I'll meet you over by that rock."

"Sure." I stumbled off the path and over to a cluster of boulders. Wiggling my thong down, I so-un-lady-like rested my back against the rock and had the best pee of my life. No joke, angels were cheering me on. If that wasn't what heaven sounded like, I might change my membership card and head down south.

Rolling along the rock, I moved toward the road. Footsteps off to the right froze me mid-step. I held still, barely breathed, and waited.

"Well, who the fuck brought it to him?" a man shouted.

"Gator. Trigger had them follow the drugs up the run. When they zig-zagged, they caught it and grabbed a bag off the truck to bring here."

Why does he sound so familiar?

"And?"

"Prospect died. Shit, it was a rough one."

I know you.

"Fuck, he will not be happy with this."

"When does he release the shipment on the market for Trigger?"

Wiggling my thong back into place as they came closer, I sank deeper between the rocks. My knees shook, and I was sure they would hear my teeth clattering.

"Day after tomorrow."

"Does he have any idea where the church is?"

My brain ping-ponged through my mental files, trying to place who that voice belonged to.

"It's fifty miles from where the drop-off point is, so my guess would be no."

They both went silent for a moment then the other voice spoke up.

"Why didn't Trigger do the cocaine?"

Two more footsteps toward me, and I had to cover my mouth.

"He never does it, only prospects. He smokes pot and drinks. That's about the extent. He only has one interest at the moment, and it's the blonde."

"That so?"

My entire body went cold and I felt my blood pressure drop. Suddenly, my cell stuck in my bra started to vibrate. I could never hear the damn thing or even feel it, as a rule, but, in the dead of the night in the middle of ass-fuck nowhere, it went off, and it was loud.

I fumbled with it to send it to voicemail and covered the screen so I wouldn't be a damn beacon.

"Seems we are not alone tonight." The other voice sent a shiver through me. I started to lose my balance, so I shifted, and my heel scraped across the dirt.

Fuck!

"Go back to the camp. I'll deal with this."

"You sure?"

"Oh, yeah." I heard the click as he jacked the slide of a handgun.

A light flashed out in front of me, so I lifted my legs and pulled them back to my chest. It scanned all around me, but luckily, the way the rock bent around me covered me with its shadow.

"I can feel you," he hissed like a cat. "I will find you."

Pressing my back painfully into the boulder, my blood drummed through my ears. I found a pebble, and I thought it was the best option I had. With all my might, I hurled it over my head and off into the distance.

When the light moved down the direction I came from, I pulled out my phone, and with shaky hands texted Minnie as fast as I could, cupping the phone to keep the light down.

Tess: Make a distraction!

"Clever," he chuckled, "almost had me, there."

Oh, come on! My fists clenched at my sides, and I repeated my own version of a prayer.

"Were the hell did I lose my panties?" My savior Minnie's voice broke through, and my breath caught in my throat.

The light flickered off, and the footsteps moved away. They soon stopped, and I knew he was still close, but I didn't care.

"I really need a pair that glow in the damn dark!" As soon as she was a few yards away, I bolted off the ground and directly to her arms.

"Run!" I grabbed her hand, and we raced back toward the camp.

"Tess, what the hell?"

"Just run, Min!"

Once we hit the first trailer, I let go and ran toward where I'd seen Trigger last.

"Where is he?" I shouted at Peggy, who for once in her damn life answered without being snarky. I must have really caught her off guard.

"Last I saw, he was in his trailer."

Without thinking, I tore open the door and stepped inside.

"Trigger?" I called out and felt like I had been hit by a pile of bricks.

There were Trigger's legs hanging over the end of the bed and Tammy naked on top doing what I was doing only hours ago. His jeans were still on, but she was butt naked, and he didn't move when he heard my voice.

Fucking coward.

The trailer was dark, but I saw her face when she looked up at me. She knew what was racing through my mind. All my walls that he had torn down immediately stacked right back up.

As I leapt out of the trailer, I collided with Gus.

"Wow, sweetheart, you okay?"

"No." I started to run, but pictured Ty's face and stopped myself. Reckless was not a good thing. "I'm just going to walk the perimeter. I won't wander off."

I could tell he wanted to ask more, but didn't push. "Keep your phone on you. The reception here sucks."

"Okay." I needed to breathe, and right now this was the last place I wanted to be. Instead of heading in the direction I normally would, I headed for the far back corner. So many people were hammered and barely noticed me, and I was happy to be a wallflower. Only a few women glared at me and made sure I knew who was theirs. You couldn't pay me enough to sleep with half of these men, whose dicks double dipped over the course of one night.

I cringed when I saw an older man hold an iron poker from the fire pit to a prospect's arm. He bucked and jumped, but never made a peep. Crazy, stupid drunks.

Finally, I spotted an open area right before I hit the mountain. I hurried up the hill and collapsed in a little dug-out spot next to a ledge.

I pushed my hands to my head to relieve the pressure growing behind my eyes. Or maybe to stop the tears. I wasn't sure. Either way, I hurt.

My phone vibrated, and I saw Brick's name come up. I felt like crying more; I felt betrayed. I wasn't ready to go down the "I fell hard, and you were right" road yet. I also knew I couldn't let it go to voicemail without some kind of explanation.

Tess: Need a moment, be back in a few.

Brick: What happened?

"You know," a voice came from somewhere, "it took me a while to figure out how I would get you back, my skinny white girl." He lit a joint, and I nearly died on the spot.

Tiago.

I started to get up, but he held up a hand and blocked my path. My phone slipped from my nervous grip and fell a few feet away.

Breathe, Tess.

"Not so brave without your pres to protect you, hey?"

"I never meant to start anything with your club," I huffed and wondered where the hell that came from. "It was all a misunderstanding."

He ignored my comment.

"I'm surprised he let you out of his sight." He moved closer, and I stepped back. "You are like all the rest of his women, you know. Disposable. But right now, he wants you, and that makes you an asset."

I flinched at that. His comment tore through me. His sweaty forehead leaned to the side as if he could read my thoughts. A delighted smirk raced across his lips, and I saw he knew. He saw the truth.

"Oh, so you *are* back on the market. That's why you are up here all by yourself."

He scratched his cheek and moved another step closer. So close, in fact, I could smell the booze pouring off him.

He clapped his hands in excitement. "Well, well, tonight is shapin' up to be all right."

***

Trigger

I wiped my dirty hands on my jeans and fastened my helmet. I started the bike and eased along the bumpy path. We were six miles from camp and had just buried Ty deep in the ground. It took us four hours to get down the six feet. The damn hard desert made you work to return a body to the ground. At least this would keep the Reaper satisfied for a while.

Once we hit the main road, I started to feel better. My phone found a signal and blew up with text messages and missed calls.

10:58 p.m.
Brick: You with Tess?

11:34 p.m.
Brick: What happened to Tess? Pissed!

11:45 p.m.
Gus: May have a problem here, son. Tammy just played Tess. You will need to fix this shit.

11:56 p.m.
Brick: I am going to kill Tammy!

12:57 p.m.
Brick: I can't find Tess.

2:00 a.m.
Brick: Call me.

I hit the button on my helmet and tapped Brick's name on my phone. Three rings in, and he finally answered.

“I still can’t find her, man.”

My fingers flexed over the handlebars. “What happened?”

“Minnie told me they got split up—”

“Put Minnie on,” I interrupted. I hated a middle man.

“Here she is.” I heard him whisper to her who it was before she took it.

“Trigger?” Her voice sounded just as worried.

“What happened?”

“We were up on a mountain for a while, then we came down to pee, and that’s when we got separated. I went back to the camp to see if she passed me, when I got a text she needed help. I walked back the route we came, and suddenly she popped out of nowhere and screamed at me to run. I tried to ask what happened, but she kept saying she needed to talk to you. One moment she raced inside your trailer, and then next she took off. That was the last I’ve seen or heard from her. Brick told me—”

“Put him on.”

“The last time I heard from her,” he started right where Minnie left off, “was when I texted to see if she was all right. She said she needed a moment. That was two hours ago, and I can’t find her anywhere.”

What the hell was going on?

A darkness tightened my chest as I waved to the guys something was up.

“Where are the Serpents?”

“Ahh…” There was a pause. “I see Mateo and Tiago.”

“Have they been there the whole night?”

“No idea. I tried to avoid them as much as a possible.”

I hit my blinker and changed gears to pick up speed. “Meet me at my trailer.”

I hung up and concentrated on the road.

Should’ve killed him when I had the chance.

Once I arrived, Gus was there to greet me.

“She seemed upset when she left. She told me she was just going to walk the perimeter. She promised to keep her phone on her. My guess, she got a visitor.” He nodded at the Serpents. “Though they claim they haven’t seen her.”

My phone buzzed, and I saw it was Rail.

“Yeah?”

“I got her. I’m coming up behind your trailer.”

“Gus,” I pointed at the snakes, “watch them.”

I rounded the trailer and saw Rail with Tess in his arms.

Everything around me went quiet.

Everything went still.

I scooped her up and hurried through the back door. I didn't need an audience right now. Brick followed, and Rail closed the door behind us.

"Where was she?" I asked as I laid her on the bed and covered her with a blanket. I checked her breathing and pulse.

"North ridge. I heard something and found her whimpering. When I saw it was Tess, I tried to get her to focus and speak, but once she saw me, she passed out."

"Is she okay?" Brick hovered over my shoulder just as Gus and Cooper came in. Loose followed but stayed on the other side of the trailer when Gus waved him off.

"Some cuts and bruises on her legs and stomach, but the rest I don't know." I inspected her hands and saw she must have fought something or someone. I stepped back to show the guys.

Rail looked just as pissed off as Brick. "I didn't see anyone. Too dark to see footprints, and at this point, mine are in there too." He ran a hand through his hair before he let out a long breath. "Tell us what to do, just give the order."

"We've never had this before." Brick added. "Not until now."

"We do nothing but watch." I felt the mood change, but I held a hand up. "I would bet my club it was Tiago, but if it wasn't, we can't risk the contract." I leaned against the counter and rubbed my head, taking a moment to think. "Get our crew and Cray's to watch them tonight. As soon as she wakes, we find out what she knows."

"Shit." Morgan nearly fell over the chair as he hurried inside. "Where is she?"

"Okay, but out of it," Rail answered as I looked back at her small body under the blanket.

"This is Tammy's fault, Trigger," Minnie whispered from behind Brick. I didn't even know she was here. "She set Tess up."

"How?" My rage started to kick in again. It was a horrible mix of pain and anger, something else I hadn't felt before.

"She was giving Tristen a blow job on your bed, and she kept the lights off so it looked like you. She and Peggy have been trying to get rid of Tess since she got here."

I glanced at Gus. "Tammy's done."

"Yeah."

We all stood in silence.

"All right, let's all get the hell out," Morgan said. "Trigger, we'll keep watch, make sure our girl is okay. I'll get Sphinx over here in the morning to check her out."

I nodded at Brick's white, angry face.

"You want to stay?"

He shook his head. "No, I need to walk or something."

"Yeah, I get that. We'll set this straight, Brick. I just need to think."

Minnie put her arm around Brick as they left.

Gus rose and leaned against the table across from me. He shifted awkwardly until he found a good spot.

"Never seen your face like that before." He huffed, and I glanced up at him, feeling a massive weight on my shoulders. "You okay?"

"Yeah."

"I'm not asking Trigger, I'm asking *Nolan*."

I shut my eyes. It had been about thirty-somethin' years since my real name was used.

"I…" My voice was raw with fury. The demons sat off in the distance, curious what their next move was. "I don't just want to kill…I want someone chained-up-in-the slaughterhouse, just-us-alone. I want the Reaper to sell his soul to me."

"We'll make that happen." He sighed and looked at Tess. "Until then, get some sleep. We'll handle out there."

"I need to be there—"

Gus turned to me and stuck a finger in my face. "Don't let her wake to Jace or Big Joe. She needs you, and you need to make sure she knows what the hell really happened."

He left and locked the door behind him.

He was right; it wasn't about me anymore. It was about her too.

Fuck, the use of my name started to play on me.

"What's your name?"

I looked over at my father, who had the same expression he used whenever he was trying to win over a woman. "Nolan. He's a good kid. Just wants to be loved."

A woman reached down and cupped my cheek. She smelled good, like, clean. "I'm Misty, a friend of your daddy's."

She had a nice smile and didn't yell at me like my father, so I liked her.

"Who couldn't love a boy with such green eyes?"

Misty was around for a year, and she was the nicest woman I knew. She made me cookies and cleaned my clothes from time to time. Then, one day, she was gone...just like my mom. Just like any other woman my father brought around. He always said I was the reason they left.

What did I do wrong?

What could I do to make them stay?

Why was I so unlovable?

I sagged into the counter and spotted a bottle of whiskey on the table. Normally, I'd mask the pain with booze, but…

Her cry ripped through me as I crawled onto the bed, helpless as to what to do.

"Hey." I brushed her hair off her face. "Look at me, Tess."

Her eyes fluttered open and focused on me. Tears filled her gorgeous green eyes, and I felt my body crumble.

"Hi." I ran my shaky fingers down her face. "You scared the shit out of me."

Her chin quivered as her eyes squeezed closed. She started to shut down.

"No, Tiger." I moved closer, feeling Nolan on the outskirts of my brain. He was five, and watching. I felt his hurt and the oh-too-familiar pain of that situation. "That wasn't me you saw with Tammy on my bed, it was Tristen. They set you up. I was off burying Ty. I wouldn't do that to you."

She moved to study my face. I tried to show the truth. I had no idea how, but I tried.

"I would never hurt you like that, Tess."

She covered her face and rolled into my chest with a sob. I wrapped my arms around her and pulled her in close.

"I got you." I kissed her head softly. "I'm so sorry, Tess. I'm sorry I promised to protect you. Just tell me, was it one of the Serpents who did this to you?"

Her terrified stare held mine, confirming one had something to do with it.

It was the first time in my life I fought to hold my switch down. She needed me more.

She wouldn't answer any questions after that, she just shook and cried. She just needed to get it out and feel safe. So, that was what I was for her. Safety. However, the storm inside my head was something completely different. The Reaper would be impressed by my desire to hunt and murder Tiago bit by bit.

By 3:00 a.m., she had finally fallen asleep. I reached down and unzipped her boots and slipped them off so she'd be more comfortable.

She reached out and grabbed my t-shirt then fisted it as if I were her anchor.

"Don't leave me," she whispered.

"Not even if you wanted me to."

We fell asleep tangled around one another. Surprisingly, I slept hard, no dreams or voices, just peaceful darkness. I didn't even know there was such a place.

Sadly, once I came to, my reality came crashing down. The demons inside my head were there, gnawing at the corners of the doors and begging to be let out. The sound was haunting and irritating.

Unfolding her fingers from my shirt, I swung my feet out of bed and got dressed.

Gus handed me a cup of coffee and took a seat across the table from me. I kept what Tess confirmed quiet until I knew more. I was nervous that the guys' reactions would tip me over the edge. I glanced at the clock for the five-hundredth time that evening. Tess had been asleep all day, and I was getting anxious. Sphinx was outside, ready to look at her when she woke. He reassured me she'd be fine, and I knew he wouldn't leave camp. The fact that there wasn't a visible head injury was a good sign.

That wasn't my major concern.

"Um, Trig?" Rail was in the door, and he looked like hell. "You might wanna come here."

Gus held up a hand to tell me that he would stay with her.

Stepping outside, I saw Mateo and Tiago next to my entire crew.

Their weapons weren't drawn, so I was guessing this was the first time we heard this.

"We heard your girl got hurt last night." Mateo's thick accent was harsh, not like his normal purr. "Tiago knows something about it." He shoved Tiago's shoulder, and he shrugged forward.

I cracked my knuckles and felt my blood pump to my muscles as my body prepared to fight.

Tiago snarled. I could tell he wasn't happy about the situation, but he was here, and so was I.

"I saw your girl up on the ledge, and I followed her up there." He watched for any reaction from me, which I kept at bay. All the demons were screaming at me to kill him, a quick rip to the chest to stop the heart. My fingers flexed at the thought.

"She was upset, said you guys broke up. Said she was lonely."

I lunged and swung at his skull, and he slammed backward and crashed into the picnic table. Mateo raised a hand, and my men lifted their weapons.

"Hear him out."

Tiago stumbled to his feet and spat blood on the ground as he chuckled at me. Mateo yelled at him in Spanish, and his smiled faded.

"You can't deny she's hot. I just wanted a little taste." He winked, and I raised my arm but held it back. "When I went to kiss her, the bitch kicked me in the balls. She tried to run down the hill, but I grabbed her hair, and she slammed into the ground. She twisted and fought when I was just trying free myself from her." He held out his hands, palms up. "She owed me a blow job, after all, and besides, I can't help it if her screams turned me on…" He smiled, enjoying this.

He had a death wish.

"But in the next moment I am hit over the head." He shrugged. "I woke there by my trailer with a big headache. I had a cold beer and didn't think much more of it."

I nodded as I turned to look at Brick, who had once again turned white.

"I didn't hurt your old lady, Trigger, not that much. I don't know who else was there, but I wasn't alone." He made a show of rubbing the back of his head.

"But you did beat her up at your club a while back." Morgan chimed in just as angry as the rest of us. She was family, and you didn't fuck with family.

Tiago's throat contracted and his fingers twitched at his side.

I laughed as I pulled my gun free and pointed it at his dick. I pulled the trigger and slammed a bullet into what he would never have use for again.

Tiago's eyes bulged as he grabbed what was left of his mangled dick. Blood soaked through his jeans in seconds and pooled at his feet. Still stunned, he fell to the ground with a thud and screamed in pain. His neck contracted and his head whipped around as he tried to grasp the reality of what just happened.

"Holy shit!" Mateo cursed with his hands in the air. "He didn't have to tell you the truth!"

"No, he didn't." I pointed the gun at Mateo's head. "I brought you out here to extend our friendship, and this is how you repay me?

Trying to take what is mine!" I was vibrating with the need to jam a bullet into his skull. This would be settled. Now. "We are done with the cocaine, we are done with the forty percent, and we own Santa Monica. Do you hear me?"

He nodded, but I stepped forward, pressing the hot tip of the gun to his head. I snapped my finger and Jace was next to me with a phone, recording us. "Say it."

"*Sí*, done with the cocaine, done with the contract, the Devil's Reach owns Santa Monica."

"You have two weeks to find a new city or I will burn you—all of you—till there's nothing left."

I stepped back as two of their crew helped Tiago to his feet and into their van. Mateo was on his bike, gunning it hard toward the road and leaving the rest of his snakes to gather their shit.

Panting with the need to finish them off, I turned as Tess appeared in the doorway in nothing but my hoodie. Her teeth bit at her bottom lip, her face chalk-white.

I walked over and stopped at the bottom of the step. Her eyes brimmed with tears, but she managed to keep them under control.

"You didn't kill him?" she whispered.

"Not yet."

She nodded several times, and I could tell she was trying to process it all. Her chin quivered.

"I think we all need to talk." She turned and went inside. I motioned for the guys to join me.

She paced back and forth as she filled us in on the conversation she had overheard on her walk. The entire time, Brick kept eyeing me. I knew how he felt as we both listened to her words. It was a hard hit directly to the gut to think she could have been killed twice last night.

"Do you have any idea who it could have been?" Gus asked as he rubbed his chin.

"I know that I know that voice. I have heard it before, but I just can't place it. It was as if someone I knew was suddenly talking differently." She grew frustrated for a moment. "Like if Brick was talking with a deep southern accent. You know it's his voice, but it's altered in some way. I think it will come to me, but it's not quite there."

"Okay, go on," Gus urged.

"I texted Minnie to help create a diversion, and we ran back to the camp. I went directly to the trailer to find you, Trigger, and that's when…" She looked over at me, and I saw the damage Tammy had done.

"Trigger was gone, Tess, you have my word," Brick said. "He wouldn't do that to you, anyway."

I nodded at him. I made sure he knew I appreciated and respected him for that comment.

"I know." She rubbed her arms, but I knew the memory of what she thought she saw was burned permanently into her head. "I just needed a walk, and I wasn't trying to be reckless. Ty had put a few things in perspective for me. I wanted somewhere quiet to clear my head, without all the craziness around me."

She wrung her hands as she continued. "When you texted me, Brick, I wanted to answer and not make you worry, but I needed a minute to think first. I was almost ready to send you another text with what was happening, but that's when Tiago showed up. I guess he was there, and I came up on him. I really don't know. It wasn't hard to figure out what he wanted to do. When he grabbed me, I fought him the best I could. When he was on me, I thought I would rather die." She stopped to catch her breath. Rail handed her the bottle of whiskey and she poured some in a cup, spilling half of it.

"Here." Rail used a napkin to wipe it up.

"Thanks," she sniffed, and I could see she was nearly done in with the telling of it. She downed the glass and squeezed her eyes shut as the burn spread through her.

"When someone pulled Tiago off me and knocked him out, I had a moment of relief. I wanted to hug my hero. When he offered me a hand, I took it. But when I tried to get a look at his face…he, ah…" Her hands covered her mouth and her shoulders shook. Rail moved as I bent down in front of her and rested her head on my shoulder.

"I just wanted you," she whispered through her tears. "I was so scared."

Her words tore away another layer from the carefully built walls inside me. I felt Nolan inch closer inside my head, wanting me to let her pain in. Let myself feel it so I could experience what normal was. It was such a foreign thing for me to allow, but I tried.

I tried for her.

I peeled her hands away from her face and lifted her chin.

"I'm here, not going anywhere. But, Tess, I really need you to tell me everything." Careful with my big hand, I wiped her cheek dry. "I can't kill a faceless man." I poured her another drink and placed it in her hand. I needed details.

She pursed her lips and blew out some air then visibly shook off her nerves and tried again. “He twisted my arm behind me and slammed me into the rock wall. His free hand touched me everywhere, all around my body and up under my dress. He stopped when he heard somebody coming. I tried to yell, but he hit the back of my legs, and I fell hard. I could barely breathe. He came down close to my ear and told me I was lucky, that this time it was only a warning.”

“Warning?” Brick interrupted. “Warning for what?”

“To honor the rest of the Serpents’ contract. To continue running the drugs or there will be consequences.”

“Such as?” Morgan chimed in.

Her cold hands fell onto mine.

“Such as me.”

The entire place went quiet, and all I could hear was my heart beating in my ears. My switch was about to flip.

Gus sighed heavily. “They know she is your weakness, Trigger.”

Yeah, she is. Our eyes met, and I knew she heard what I thought.

“Any idea who he was?” Brick asked.

“I’m sorry. I didn’t recognize his voice at all, not like that other guy. I can tell you he was wearing a cut with two green eyes on the front. I know because they glowed in the dark.” I glanced at Brick then at Gus. “But that’s not Serpents, right?”

“No.” I cracked my neck, but there was no relief in it. “That was a Stripe Back.”

CHAPTER THIRTEEN

Tess

The guys had a long meeting after I told them my story, and the whole time Trigger kept an eye on me through Jace, who was ordered to stay by my side. I couldn't say I was opposed to the idea. I hated this mess happened during what was supposed to be their annual party.

Trouble always followed me, but this was the first time I'd ever allowed myself to fall for someone after the damage that had been done before. And now look what I had brought on him.

"You look like you could use this." Minnie drew close and took a chair. She handed me a mug. "Baileys and coffee."

"Thanks." I wrapped my fingers around the warmth and sipped the brew. *Yikes*, it was strong.

She winked as she settled across from me and indicated the mug. "I don't do singles. Triples are my specialty."

"So I taste."

"I can smell that from here." Jace chuckled from the trailer step.

I pushed the chair next to me with my foot. "You don't need to lurk out there in the dark, Jace. Come over here and join us." After he sat, I said, "You know it's not your fault what happened to Ty yesterday."

He nodded, but I saw he was still struggling with it. "I know." He tried to smile at me. "Just feel like a chump not going first."

"He was reckless." I sipped my liquor with its splash of coffee. "Ty's now six feet under, and chump or not, you're still standing. Consider yourself lucky."

"I guess. I don't know." He dropped his head and closed his eyes.

Minnie was on her phone and had zero interest in making him feel better, but I liked Jace and knew what he was going through.

"Believe it or not, I've been where you are." He looked over at me, his eyes tired and stressed. "You can't know what's going to happen. You might think you do, but you don't know. You can't predict shit."

"But Trigger said it could have been laced with something."

"I know, Jace, and when I said I've been there, I really meant it. We had a warning back then too, but still, one person had to step up and take one for the team. *She* did that, and so did Ty." Tears slipped down my face as the memory of her beautiful smile came to me. "So…" My breath caught in my throat and I spoke harshly. "Now, as fucking hard as it is, *we* need to live." I reached out and took his hand. "Move forward, take a few precautions, learn from your mistakes, and *live*."

He sniffed before his shoulders slumped and he broke into tears.

"Come here." I stood and pulled him into my arms. He was so sweet, like a little brother you wanted to protect. "It's okay to feel glad it wasn't you who died, Jace. That's perfectly normal. The guilt hurts like a bitch, but that means you're human."

"You guys okay?" Brick mouthed.

"Yeah," I rubbed my hand over Jace's to soothe him. A few of the guys looked over, but none of them said anything. Not even Rail. He gave me a little nod as if he understood we all needed a moment to digest all the crap we had been through this weekend.

Jace pulled back and caught his breath. His eyes were bloodshot and his cheeks were puffy, but I smiled to show I could be strong for both of us.

"Thank you, Tess." He closed his eyes. "Are they all staring at me?" I looked up and glared at everyone to make sure they turned away from Jace.

"Nope, but why don't you go inside for a bit?"

"I can't."

"I know he told you to watch me, but I'll go stand by Trigger until you get back."

He hesitated. "Ahhh."

"Go."

"Thanks." He rushed inside the trailer, and I walked over to stand next to Trigger, whose eyes were on me the minute he saw me get up. He took my hand and pulled me onto his lap.

"Where'd Jace go?"

"He needed a moment." I kissed his lips. "Ty's death is playing on him."

"It playing on you too?" Trigger studied my face, and I looked away. "I *asked* you something, Tess."

I guessed he did ask.

"A little, I guess. Just stirred up some old memories."

"Which are?"

I lifted a brow. "Just because you ask, Trigger, doesn't mean I will always answer."

He shifted me so I faced him. "I shared a lot with you."

His eyes were relentless, and I swallowed heavily. He was right; he had shared. "I lost someone kind of in the same way Ty died. I wanted Jace to know it's okay to feel relieved to be the one left standing. Doesn't mean the guilt doesn't hurt like a bitch."

"Mm," he agreed. "I'm glad you weren't the one too."

My fingers ran through his beard. "You're getting pretty good at this whole relationship thing."

"Mm."

I smiled and kissed him again. *Man of few words.*

"Anyone else still fucking thrown by this whole Trigger has a girlfriend thing?" Rail broke the silence around us and made the guys laugh. "I mean, really, most girls would have been dumped on their ass or barked at for saying shit."

Trigger lifted me so I straddled him, making a point. I was happy to help out by placing his hands on my ass.

"You like that, Brick?"

"I will tie your nuts in a bow, Rail, if you don't fuck off." Brick groaned. "Tess, you're such an ass."

I pulled away and held up my phone. "Seems to me I have a video to prove this makes us even."

"I'm sorry, come again?" Rail held up his hand, and I tossed my phone to him.

I ignored the fist fight that erupted as Trigger stood with me in his arms.

"You need to be under me," he whispered harshly.

After convincing Trigger the bruises didn't hurt, he finally let loose. Thankfully, I now knew how to flip his switch. A good feisty fight always set it off. I was sure I wouldn't be able to walk for a week.

***

I woke alone, which was not unusual. The sun was blasting through the window. Unfamiliar voices found me, and I raced to the shower and into my clothes.

I found Trigger at the table outside with two cops from Santa Monica. What the hell?

Morgan shook his head at me as I came up behind Trigger, but I was way past worrying about hearing shit that wasn't meant for my ears. I slipped my hands around his shoulders from behind and kissed his cheek. He tensed, but when he heard my voice, his muscles relaxed.

"Everything okay here, Trigger?"

His hands covered mine with a squeeze. "Seems one of the Serpents didn't make it home last night. Someone claims he was shot while he was here in the desert."

"Really?" I looked at Detective Aaron. "Aren't you a little out of your district?"

"I am, but I got authority."

"Umm…" Seemed a bit convenient, although the normal rules never seemed to apply when it came to the MC life, so I waited a beat before I went on. "Any idea who or where?"

"Well, ma'am, that's why we're here."

"Ma'am?" I laughed. "I thought by now we were on a first name basis, Aaron." He blushed slightly before he straightened his sunglasses. "I mean, you did come to my place to talk to me about club life. Surely you recall asking me to call you by your first name."

Trigger cleared his throat, and I felt his muscle tighten under my hands again.

"Yes, that's right. You are hard to forget, *Tess.*" He looked pointedly down at my chest. "I'm just here to follow up on a few leads."

"Okay, well, ask away."

He shook his head. "I need to figure out a few things first."

"Like?" Trigger's voice had changed. Yeah, he was pissed.

"Like the fact that Tiago had female blood on the clothes he had in his bag." My stomach twisted, and I felt the blood drain from my face. Detective Aaron pulled his sunglasses down and eyed the scrape on my leg. "You get into some trouble?"

Trigger stood, but I pushed my body in front of his. "Minnie and I went for a hike. I took a fall, the result of too much champagne and stupidity."

"I guess in," he rolled his wrist and checked his watch, "five hours, we'll find out just how smart you really are."

I stood my ground, but Trigger hooked his arm around me to act as silent support.

"Now, if you don't mind, I have some more people to speak to." He nodded at his partner Detective Rich before he headed off.

Trigger didn't move until I looked up and saw his jaw was locked in place. *Yikes*, that was bad.

I opened my mouth to speak, but he shook his head and took my hand and pulled me inside the trailer. He shut the windows and turned on the air conditioner.

He pulled me close and held my head in his hands. That was not what I was expecting.

"This might get messy before it gets better. Do you trust me?"

"Of course, I do."

He leaned down and kissed me hard. I wanted more, but he pulled away.

"Why did the detectives come to your place?"

"After that time they came to the club, he came to my place to warn me that club life has no place for me. That I should pack up and go back to wherever it was I came from. People seem to have a false impression of who I am and where I come from."

His eyes were on mine the whole time.

"What did you tell them?"

"That I knew what I was doing. That I loved the club."

"Anything else?"

"He asked if I was dating you."

"What did you say?"

I shrugged. "We weren't then, so I said no, but they didn't believe me."

He leaned down so we were eye level. "I'm sorry for what happened with Tiago. I broke my promise, and I will never forgive myself for that. But you have my word that from now on I will do whatever it takes to protect you."

"I never once blamed you for what happened the other night, Trigger. Please don't take that on."

"Tess," he leaned his forehead to mine, his hands on my shoulders, "I've never apologized to anyone in my life. Please take it."

"Okay." I couldn't help but feel a ping in my heart. I didn't think I had ever heard such a comment before.

"For the next two days, stay away from the detectives. No questions, no small talk, nothing. Promise me?"

"I promise." *Wait.* "How long are we staying?"

"Few more days than I planned."

"Why?" I would think he'd want to get back to the clubhouse.

"Few reasons."

"Can I know?"

"You will when I know." He kissed my head then stopped and reached in his pocket for his phone. An unexpected expression broke out on his face. His moods were all over the place today.

"What?"

He shook his head once before he answered it. "Keith, how are you?"

"Wait." I followed behind him, and everything else instantly faded away. "Trigger, is that Keith—as in Keith-Keith?"

He went to the fridge, and I tried to listen, but it was no use. Trigger was too tall for me to get close enough to the phone.

Rail came in and sat at the table nursing a beer just as Trigger stepped outside.

"Tess?"

"Mm?" My attention was not on him at the moment.

"Let's talk?"

"Ah, sure."

He motioned for me to join him on the other side of the table. I grabbed a water and did as he wanted.

"I never meant to throw you under the bus before. It was a fucked up call on my part. I want us to be good."

"Okay." I shrugged. "I could see how I would be the obvious choice. Just sucked that it happened."

"Mmm," he agreed before he downed his beer. "Lot of shit sucks right now."

"You guys have any idea who the mole is?"

He rubbed the back of his messy hair then signed heavily. "You apparently know more than we do, since you heard his voice."

"So, we know nothing." I hated that I couldn't place him. Fuck me, I felt like I was letting down the entire club.

"We'll get him, somehow. Just doesn't make the gut feel good."

"Nope."

We sat in silence for a while. I was happy we cleared the air, but the weight of the club still bothered me. Nobody knew what or who was next.

"You hungry?" Trigger asked from the doorway.

"I guess so."

That night, we said goodbye to most of the crew, who would get an early start on the road tomorrow. I had to admit I enjoyed being out in the desert away from the city life. No traffic, noise, or that horrible smog smell. Just dust, dirt, and heat here. Although I did miss the ocean; I wouldn't give that up.

When we were about to head in to bed sometime in the early morning hours, we had an unexpected visitor. Cray from the Arizona crew pulled up in front of our trailer, hopped off his bike, and raced over to the fire pit and waited.

All right…

"Go on inside. I'll be right in." Trigger kissed me quickly before he opened the door to the trailer and waited for me to step inside.

"Everything okay?"

"Not sure."

I squeezed his hand then disappeared inside.

I tried to stay awake and listen to what they were saying, but Rail was passed out in the front of the trailer, and he was about to wake the dead with his sleep talking. The dude needed to lay off *Games of Thrones*. He had a serious obsession with Jon Snow that he might not want to have leaked.

The sun sat heavy on the mountains when I woke early the next morning. I was up before the guys and was happy to have the quiet to myself. I sipped my coffee and eased onto the bench sideways so I could feel the early morning sun directly on my face. The rays pricked my skin and drew the blood to the surface. It felt wonderful.

Sometimes it hit me how much I had been through in my life, and where I was now. Maybe I should get an author to write my story? Lord knew, there was enough twisted shit there to fill at least one novel.

Warm arms wrapped around my stomach, and his chin rested on my shoulder. "Morning." His raspy voice made me wiggle closer. "I'll take it Rail cleared the air with you?"

I leaned my head back to rest on his. "Yeah. It was good."

"Good. Hey," he kissed my neck to get my attention, "I need to go deal with something, and I need you to stay here with some of the guys."

Something in his tone made me face him, straddling the seat again.

"I know that look," I pointed to his face, "and I don't like the feeling I'm getting." I ran my fingers down his temples. "I feel like the darkness is taking you over, and I'm afraid I'm about to lose you." I missed that other part he was showing me lately, like a different side of himself.

He pulled my hand to his mouth and kissed the back of it before he placed it to the center of his chest. "No matter what happens, know you got further than anyone has."

My stomach dropped. "What the hell does that mean?"

He smirked and tried to kiss me.

"No." I shoved his chest, growing angrier by the moment. "You don't make me fall for you, then tell me you're leaving and might not come back."

"I didn't say that."

"We're not in some kind of shit western, here, Trig. Where the hell are you going?"

I saw his excitement, and it scared the hell out of me. "We found where my shipment is being zig-zagged to."

"Where?" barely slipped past my lips.

His head pressed over mine. "Twelve miles north of here."

Brick, Rail, and Cray came out around the trailer and headed to their bikes. My stomach was in turmoil.

"Hey," he took my head in his hands, "I didn't mean to scare you. It'll be fine. I'll be back in a few hours, and we'll go ahead and leave for the city, okay?"

My head spun and my eyes watered. Panic rushed through me, and I wasn't sure how to process this situation, but I knew deep down he was going into danger.

"Um…" I stumbled for the right words to say then gave up and lunged into his arms. I put every bit of passion I could into that kiss. He matched it and held me with such strength that he gave me hope he would be okay.

He lifted me to my feet and pulled away, holding my hand as led me to his bike. He held his helmet under his arm and gave me his serious face. "Be careful while I'm gone. That's not me *asking,* Tess."

"I will."

"It'll be good."

I swallowed past the emotion jammed in my throat. I wanted to cry. "I'll promise you anything. Just come back in one piece, okay?"

"I'll remember that." He grinned and stared into my eyes before he eased onto his bike and left.

I didn't move until they were out of sight. A hand slipped over my shoulder and gave it a little squeeze.

"Come on, Tiger, they'll be fine. Let's get something to eat."

An hour later, I was going crazy, so I decided to pack up the trailer. I was around back when I heard Detective Aaron's voice.

Where the hell did he come from? Frantically, I looked for a place to hide. The back door to the trailer was locked, and I couldn't go around front.

Damn.

I hurried over to the prospects' van and opened the back door. Thankfully, it wasn't locked, and I scrambled inside and locked it. I tried not to fall over all the guns and ammo that were stacked about knee deep on the floor. *Shit, what are they expecting?* Clearing a spot, I settled in and hoped he hadn't heard anything. Trying to push the idea that my fingerprints were now all over the place and on sixteen or so guns, I tried to stay still.

"Hey, I tried to get her to leave many times. No offense, but she doesn't listen."

Her, who? Me?

"Yeah, I've seen them together." There was a pause. "Yeah, Tess is sleeping with Trigger. I know because I've watched. I sent photos to your email."

What the hell! I wanted to be sick. My fingers wrapped around the handle of a gun, and I raised it to the window and flipped off the safety.

What was I doing?

"Look, Clark, other than kidnap the bitch, what do you expect me to do?"

My heart stopped. I slowly lowered the gun till it rested on my lap. My body sagged into itself as his name bounced around inside my head. Fear poured through me and down to my gut like a hole in a dike.

Fuck me, he found me.

Clark.

Clark.

As in, my Clark.

He found me.

"No, we had a deal. You have something on Trigger, and in exchange I bring you Tess. I need that file. If you don't, the next photos you'll get won't be of Trigger and Tess…they'll be of me and Tess."

He stopped, and a moment later I heard why. Screams and a bottle breaking broke the silence and stole everyone's attention.

I pushed myself up to see out the window, keeping low. I watched as Detective Aaron raced off toward a car.

Jace was yelling at Morgan as they jumped in the van and fired up the engine.

I moved to my knees, about to attempt to let the guys know I was here, when Morgan spoke up again.

"I have never been more excited to meet the fucker who zig-zagged our shit than I am right now. Trigger is going to fucking lose his switch over this guy!"

What? The mood in the van was unreadable.

I sank back out of sight, intrigued.

CHAPTER FOURTEEN

Trigger

We hid our bikes a few yards away from the old church. Two cars were in the driveway of the home on the left. Even though it looked quiet, I knew chances were someone was watching the place.

I motioned for the men to get into position. We had gone over the plan three times last night, and I was confident we had it down.

The Arizona crew wasn't far away either, but since we were in the middle of ass-fuck nowhere, we needed them out of sight. If shit went down, we were on our own for at least twenty. Jace was to show up with more guns and the van in about thirty. We were covered. We had this.

"It's not lost on me it's Sunday, and we are about to enter the Lord's house with guns," Brick hissed, drawing the cross over his chest backward.

"What has the Lord ever done for you, Brick?" I checked over my shoulder as I raced to the old tractor. As soon as Brick joined me, I continued. "He took your mother and you lost your brother, took the only good man from you early. Something tells me you don't need to be worrying if it's Sunday or fucking Monday."

"Good point." He snapped his clip into place.

I signed at Rail across the driveway to cover me as I opened the wooden door and slipped inside.

The smell attacked my senses, and I covered my nose with the back of my hand until I got myself under control. Using the end of my gun, I opened the closet door and found a man hanging from hooks by his flesh. I would say he had been there for the past two weeks. Flies buzzed around, and maggots were feasting on his insides.

Cautiously, I drew my gun up and cleared both bathrooms, noticing how quiet the place was. The donation pot was cleaned out, and the last entry on the visitors' book was from 2006. Moving my attention to the actual chapel, I moved on.

The floorboard directly under the threshold was loose and squeaked loudly. I rolled back on my foot and bent down to examine it. Using the pad of my finger, I lifted the corner and saw a piece of rubber was wedged underneath. *Huh.* I grinned. It was something I would do. Every other board was nailed down tight but this one and…I lowered my head and spotted the others. The three right as you started to walk up the aisle. All markers, to let the men below know where you were in the room.

I pulled out a spare gun clip and tossed it ahead of me. Nothing. Silence.

Okay. I rose and decided to move on in.

Sunlight burst through the stained-glass windows. Christ dressed in a white gown hung in the center of the altar directly behind the pulpit. Though the place looked clean and used, the actual benches were dusty, which was another red flag. It was a front.

Rail popped up on the raised sanctuary through a back door and shrugged.

"Nothing," he whispered.

None of it felt right. My bones ached with a warning something was coming. "Nah, someone is here. Keep watch out back."

"Yeah, boss." He left.

I cleared the room and found nothing. No visible cameras, no mics, no traces of cocaine…still, something felt dark, a level of darkness I couldn't shake. Not to mention the little things. The dust, the markers, the outdated Bibles.

Sinking into a pew two rows down from the front, I hung my head and whispered to the only person I knew how to connect with—my old coach, my friend.

"Where is it, Langley? Tell me I'm not chasing a ghost."

A heavy hand dropped down on my shoulder, and every bit of horror I'd ever witnessed in my life came rushing back in one jacked up wave.

My fingers dug into my palm and drew blood.

"Can't chase a ghost, son, but they can chase you."

He stepped in front of me, and his black suit made me sick. I wasn't religious, but that was low. I slowly lifted my gaze and skimmed past his white collar to lay eyes on the one face I never thought I'd ever see again.

Impossible.

"You look a little confused, son."

Impossible.

He smirked and tugged on his collar. "Fuck, this thing is tight. You'd be surprised how much respect I get wearing this thing." He chuckled. "To think all I had to do was steal it from some dude in Palm Springs."

The lights from the airport blinded me right before my father's ugly face came into focus in front of me. His expression went from a grotesque smile to a murderous glare. He waited until the officer walked away.

"Look at me, you little shit. If you ever think you can run from me again, know that I will always find you. I raised you. I made you into who you are today. You owe me. You will always owe me. You can't kill the devil, and I am the motherfucking devil."

I was eleven, and after a weeklong stay in the room in the basement, I never tried to run away again. Sometimes it just wasn't worth the fight.

I went for my gun but noticed it was missing.

"You forget, son, when you slip into your memories, you drop your defenses." He held up my gun. "Plus, your old man has gotten a lot better at outsmarting his spawn after all these years."

He was fucking with my head. That was what he did toward the end when he found out Langley tried to help me escape.

Christ, my head hurt.

Pound, pound.

My nails drove deeper into my flesh like a saw.

"Trigger?" Her voice broke through his hold on me.

I whirled around in my dazed state to see Tess step into the room.

No! It had to be a trick.

"Trigger?" She started to walk toward me but eyed my father. "I'm sorry for interrupting, Father, but I need to speak to Trigger for a moment. It's really important."

Pure panic ripped through me when I realized this wasn't fake. This was fucking real. My two worlds were colliding in the worst way possible. My heart raced and lodged in my throat, my legs were lead, and my head screamed to form some goddamn words. Everything was jammed up. My father's eyes lit up with excitement.

Shit, they must have told him about her.

My weakness.

"Stop!" I ordered her, but of course it barely slowed her steps.

"I know I shouldn't be here, but, Trigger, I have to tell you something."

"Tess, get the fuck out of here! Go back to Jace!" My life had nothing but pain, but if he hurt her, it was over. He would destroy the one thing that gave me a reason not to give up. It would destroy the only piece of Nolan I had left inside me.

"No, please join us, my dear. My name is Father Louis." He extended his hand to her, and I dug deep and played a card I would never forgive myself for, not as long as I lived.

I would rather her hate me than be killed as a pawn in this game.

"Fuck, Tess! Why can't you ever listen?" I barked, and it echoed throughout the wooden structure. I braced myself for what I was about to do. "Brick told me your story." Her face dropped. "I can't be with someone like *you*. So get the fuck out of here." I watched her soul implode at my words. *Fuck me.* "Get out!"

Her eyes went from mine to my father's as shame and pain flashed over her gorgeous face.

I would never hate myself more than I did at that moment.

She spun on her heel and raced out the door.

"Wow." My father's wicked laughter tore through my pain. "Whoo! It's good to be back, baby!"

I whirled around to see eight of his men fill the sanctuary, and they all had guns pointed in my direction.

"As much as this has been epic," he clapped his hand together, "I must be going, but I will visit you again real soon."

"Wait." My mind raced to catch up with everything. "Why did you draw me here? Just to fuck me over and leave?"

"Oh, son, *this* was to let you know the devil does walk among the living. That I can't be killed." He stepped closer, tugging at his collar before he smoothed his hands down the lapels of his jacket. "And that I will be running this town like I was meant to many years ago." His hand landed on my shoulder and squeezed it tightly. "Before you stole it from me." His pupils dilated as my skin crawled from his touch. He ran a finger across his lips. "Officer Doyle will be paying you a visit in the next few weeks. He has some business to discuss with you."

"Doyle?" I couldn't keep up. Sure, I knew him from when we were younger, and I screwed his sister a few times, but fuck, what the hell would he have to do with any of this shit?

As quickly as the devil appeared, he left me in the dust in unbelievable pain. I still couldn't get my head straight.

I dropped my hands to my knees and tried desperately to suck in some air.

What the fuck just happened?

Where the fuck were the guys?

Where was Tess?

I burst out the front door to find Rail bleeding from a gunshot wound to the stomach.

"He's okay, just grazed." Morgan helped him to the van.

A cloud of dust off in the other direction told me we were alone.

"Where the hell is Tess?" I snapped at Jace, who must have let her come. I grabbed his cut and tightened it around his neck as I picked him off the ground and held him up to my face. "Where is she?"

"I-I don't know. At the camp?"

"Trigger!" Brick was at my side. "What the fuck happened in there?"

"Where were you guys?"

Brick pushed himself between me and Jace so I'd let the kid drop. My brain was firing off all over the place, and I knew I had to get a grip.

"We were ambushed by some assholes over by the house." Brick shook his head. "Why are you asking about Tess?"

"We got to go!" Morgan shouted.

"Go where?" I shouted at him. "She was fucking here!"

"What? When?"

I wanted to kill someone. I needed him to catch the fuck up, here.

"Jace, go with Morgan." I ordered. "Wait." He stopped, nearly falling over. "Did you let Tess come with you?"

"No, honest, I have no idea how she got here."

"Did you check the van before you left?"

His face froze, and I fucking knew.

"Go!" He needed to leave before I killed him myself.

"What the hell happened?" Brick clawed at his face as Cray joined us.

"He's not dead." The words were like acid as they flew from my lips.

"Who?"

"My father."

The two guys looked as confused as I fucking felt. Impossible. Cray and Brick's old man had seen me kill him. He was dead.

"So, wait," Brick held his hands up. "How does Tess play into this?"

The mention of her name set off the pain in my head again. Fuck my father. My hatred for him burned through me like fire.

"Shit, Tess! I had to do it, Brick." I felt my head go light at what I had done to her.

"What the hell did you do?" Brick grabbed my shoulders. Something he'd never done and I'd never allowed. "Tell me."

"I needed her to leave. He knew who she was. He was going to use her against me. I couldn't let him touch her." I held his gaze fiercely so he knew how fucking serious I was. "I told her I knew her story, that I couldn't be with someone like her."

Brick's glare burned through me, and he stepped back like he was going to throw up. "You said what?" He made a horrible, frantic noise. "You don't even know!"

"I needed her to leave, and she wouldn't."

"You tell her I told you?"

I hated it, but I nodded.

"Holy fucking hell!" He looked at Cray like he couldn't believe what he was hearing. "You have no idea what you have just done."

"Anyone care to fill me in?" Cray tried to catch up.

"Trigger." Brick grabbed my shoulders again. His eyes were bloodshot. "You just drove her back into his arms. You don't understand what that means. It took *six fucking years* to get her back. This time…the damage you did to her and to me…she's gone."

***

I knew I had to be alive, because things were moving around me. I got hungry once a day, I got drunk, but it did nothing, I got tired but couldn't sleep with my demons.

It had been two days since we had left the church. No one had seen Tess. Her phone was off, and her cards were canceled. It was like she never existed. I even told Ivy at my strip joint to let her dance if she showed up, to do anything to hold her there until I arrived. But…nothing.

Brick spent most of his time on the phone trying to figure out where she went. So far, no luck. He barely spoke to anyone, least of all me.

Morgan sat down in front of me, his face a mirror of mine. "I don't get it, man. I have so many questions. Why was she in the van? How did she get in the church? How did she get by me?" He rubbed his head, no doubt in the same thick fog I was livin' in. "But most of all, how the hell did she get from the church out to the main road? To wherever?" His head dropped down in his hands, and we were back in our silent space again.

How was I supposed to move forward when everything inside my body desperately needed to go back? I needed a chance to explain. A chance to say I how sorry I was. A chance to say I loved her.

***

Tess

The last two days gave me a chance to sort out my feelings, and it was one hell of an adventure. Someday, I would allow myself to go back and process when it didn't hurt so much.

I didn't leave out of shame and embarrassment because Trigger found out about my past, or that he couldn't love me in spite of it. I knew I was unlovable. That had been proven to me at an early age. Trigger just drove that home.

No, I left *because* I loved Trigger. I would do anything for him, including face my past to protect him and the one family I knew and loved. The Devil's Reach.

I stood in front of the metal gates, punched in the code, and walked down the long driveway toward the house that was almost out of sight from the street.

The key was not in its usual place, and I had tossed my set long ago.

Three knocks, and I heard the whir of the camera as it turned to focus on me. My face grew hot, and I could almost hear the whispers and the exchange of bets.

Yup, that's right. I'm back.

The door slowly opened, and there he stood, handsome as ever. He smiled at me and leaned against the doorframe. I never thought I'd be back in this position again.

"Welcome home, Tessa."

"Clark."

The End

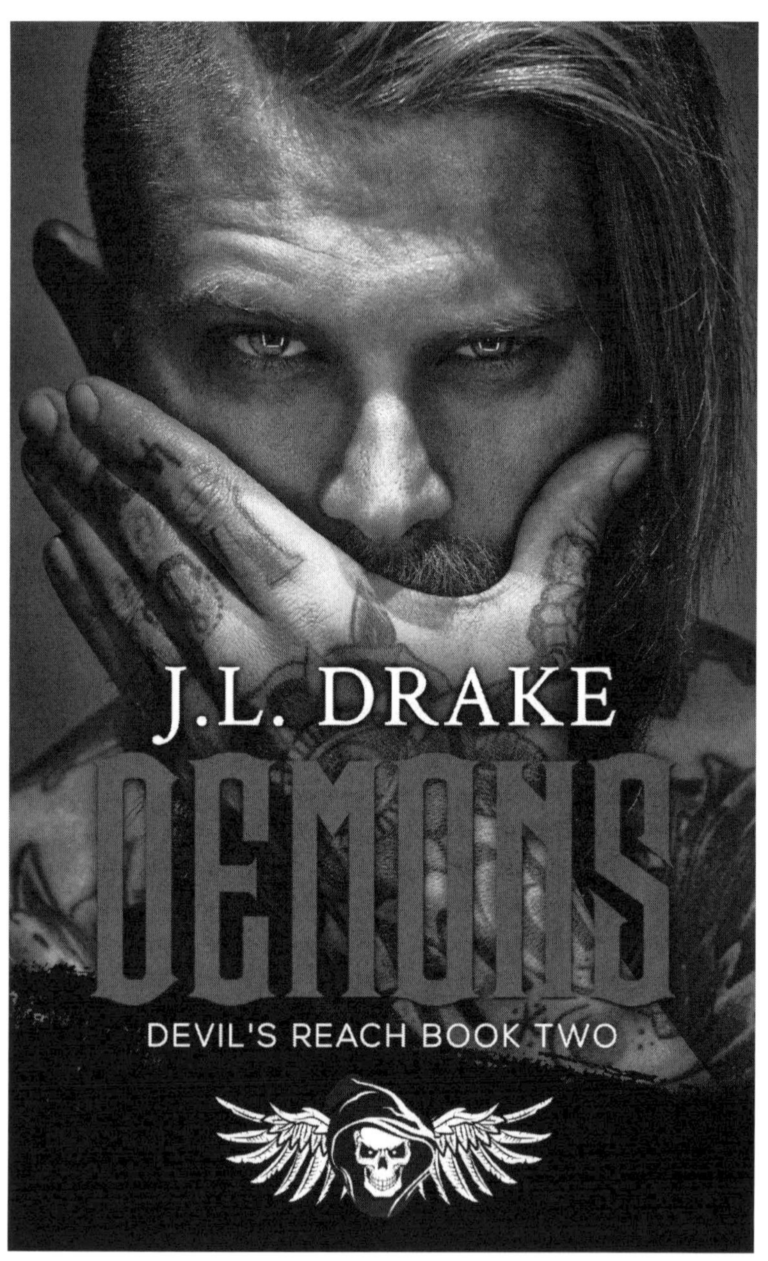
J.L. DRAKE
DEMONS
DEVIL'S REACH BOOK TWO

PROLOGUE

I squeezed the clutch, rolled the throttle toward me, and switched into fifth gear. The wheels screamed as they tore at the pavement, blurring the colors around me.

I was pissed. They knew better than to pull this shit on my territory.

Traffic was heavy for midnight, but I managed to take the back roads and alleys most of the way.

The fire was high, which meant the match would soon be over, and my blood burned through my ears when I came up over the dusty hill. I'd been more than fair with these guys, but since they disobeyed a direct order, blood would be shed.

As soon as my engine was heard over the screams, the massive crowd jumped out of the way and let me swing my bike into the center of the commotion.

Both men pulled the savage dogs apart and dropped them at their feet.

I rested my bike on the kickstand and removed my helmet. A few people ran away, and others tried to see who I was.

I pointed right at the local drug runner, who mostly sold shitty weed, and waited for him to sweat it out.

"Trigger, man, I know what you said, but…"

I tuned him out and looked down at the pit bull. His throat was mangled, and he struggled to breathe and let out the tiniest whimper. A plea to end this shit.

He never asked for this life, never asked to fight to his death for a few hundred bucks.

I couldn't help but see my own reflection in his eyes. See the hate rooted deep, entangled to his core. No peace, only darkness.

"I needed the cash, man. My sister is in trouble, and my ma is strung out." The drug dealer tried a different angle.

I raised my gun and pointed it at the junkie while I whistled for Brick and Rail to remove the dog to a safer place. At least he could die somewhere peaceful, if only for a moment.

"What the fuck, man? He had another fight left in him."

I swung around and punched him so hard he blew back off his feet and landed next to the winning dog, who was foaming at the mouth.

The owner looked around while he fought to hold back the hungry dog.

"I said no dog fights." My voice boomed over the crowd. "Not on my territory."

No one said a word as I took the rope and pushed the owner next to the drug dealer. I leaned down and stroked the dog's back. He started to bark and whip around at my touch. Something I understood all too well.

"Go," I said simply and let the rope race through my fingers.

The crowd went still as the dog ripped apart the two men limb by limb. Blood covered his head, and screams flooded into the night.

CHAPTER ONE

Tess

"What's your name, sweetheart?"

I glanced up from my book and saw the man again. I had noticed him at least a couple of times over the last few days. He moved closer. He wore a suit and tie, but he pulled at his collar as if he were uncomfortable in it.

He sat forward on his stool and shifted it closer, and his Hershey-brown gaze held mine. He pushed up the spine of the book, and his brows rose.

"Nora Roberts? Isn't that a little old for a...?" He waited for me to answer.

"Ten, and no." I glanced around the room. "When you grow up here, mister, nothing is left to the imagination."

He smiled, and his mouth rose higher on one side. His hair was a little longer than most of the men in here, but it was styled as if each strand had its own place. "Fair enough."

I waited for him to leave, but he unbuttoned his jacket and made himself comfortable. I went back to reading then felt his eyes on me again. I looked up to find him smiling, as if waiting for me to answer something I missed.

"What?"

"You never answered my question."

Huh?

"What's your name?"

I studied him for a beat before I finally let my guard down. "Tess."

"Nice to meet you, Tess. I'm Clark."

"You wearin' Spandex under your suit?"

He paused before he broke into a husky laugh, which immediately put me more at ease. "Yes. Is it showing?"

"You may want to fix your collar."

He tugged at it dramatically. "Better?"

"It'll do."

"Clark Anderson?" Rachel, the receptionist, called in our direction. "We're ready for you."

My stomach sank and reality came crashing down when I remembered he had an appointment at the house. He must have picked up on my mood, because he frowned before he rose and fastened his coat.

"Have a nice day, Tess."

"Yeah." I broke open my book and sank back into a fantasy world where everything was okay.

The door opened, and there he stood, handsome as ever. He smiled at me and leaned against the doorframe. I never thought I'd be back in this position again.

"Clark."

"Welcome home, Tessa."

His smirk rose on the one side as his gaze dragged down my front then snapped back up to my face. He looked smug, as always.

"Guess I won the bet." He opened the door for me to walk through. His chest was a little smaller than I remembered, and his arms had lost a little of their sexy curve. "About time you finally listened to me."

I rolled my eyes and shifted the heavy bag over my shoulder. "I'm not staying for long."

"You're not leaving again." He grabbed my wrist and turned me to face him. His expression darkened. "I'll make this work."

My insides twisted. There was a time when I would have sold my soul for him to utter those words to me, but now…

"I've heard your empty promises before." I eyed his hand, and after a beat, he let go. "You made your choice."

"It's not like that…" His voice trailed off when he saw a woman move forward to block me. "Felicia, look who came home."

My mother's face contorted with hate, as it did whenever we were in the same room. Her hands landed on her slim waist wrapped in a velvet corset and a gray silk robe that flowed about her with feather-like softness as she walked. This was the expected dress in the house—lingerie and heels. My mother was stunning and knew it. Everyone said we were sisters, and she'd reply, "She's older."

"You need money?"

There's my loving mother.

"Felicia." Clark cleared his throat and nodded at two men who stood within earshot.

I saw her pull her mask down, and her tone came out a little less harsh.

"If you're back, you work as one of the girls. I already have a shitty receptionist, and I don't need another."

I hid my sudden nerves. I once worked the front desk but was soon pulled onto the stage. Whenever there was talk about me working as "one of the girls," I nearly flipped the fuck out. I promised I'd never lower myself to my mother's level. No one was allowed to touch me on stage, and I felt safe, so now…my hand flew to my stomach as it took a dive.

When I started to speak, she shot me a look, and I swallowed my words. Now wasn't the time for this. Besides, the men were approaching us.

"Work or leave. Your choice, Tessa."

I cringed whenever she used my full name, but at this point, I had thirty-five cents and maybe some lint in my pocket. What was I supposed to do? Plus, I needed to know what Clark had on Trigger.

"Fine," I hissed, and Clark flinched. "I'm going to shower."

My mother dismissed me when she greeted the men, linking her arms with theirs to steer them away from me. Clark made a move to get in front of me, but I dodged and left him to deal with his new clients.

I was shocked to find my room was the same as I had left it, empty and over the top like the rest of the house. The walls were swathed in red velvet that matched the drapes and canopy. The black bedspread was satin and had fancy buttons that dimpled the fabric to give it a pillow-like effect. A shag rug lay at the foot of the bed where I stood feeling unbelievably lonely.

I dropped my bag and sat on the edge of the mattress. The idea of going backward in my life scared the shit out of me, but there I was, standing in the very spot I promised I wouldn't be again. This place had broken me more than once. I could only imagine what it would do this time around.

Laughter drew me out to the balcony. I saw Clark with his arm around my mother's waist as they showed the guests the pool, and then they moved off to where I knew there were underground personal hot tubs reserved for the VIPs.

I rested my arms on the marble rail and let my mind wander.

It all started out with warm smiles and conversations that made me incredibly happy and sometimes made me blush. He often came into my room after dark. He would close the door and sit on the edge of my bed and pay me compliments. He was such a gentleman then.

"You have such pretty eyes, Tessa. They're like little gumdrops with a sugar coating." His hand would gently brush over mine. He would talk to me about TV shows or music. He would ask questions and listen to my replies like he was really interested in what I had to say. He usually stayed about an hour, and as he left, he would always turn and repeat the same words as he went out the door. "I love that we have secrets, Tessa. Secrets mean we're close, and I want to stay close to you."

I craved attention from him, and maybe I knew deep down inside that it wasn't right to have a much older man as a friend, but I didn't care. The world I lived in was all about sex, and had been from day one. I knew a lot for my age, and I wasn't stupid, but he wasn't like the rest of the people here.

I wasn't wrong at the beginning. I never thought how it might look. All I cared about was that this man was paying attention to me. Finally, for once in my life, someone cared about me.

When I focused on my surroundings again, I caught Clark staring at me. I shook my head to clear my thoughts and turned to leave when I heard my mother snicker at him to focus on her.

He made his choice a long time ago. I was just too stupid to see it.

The hot water pounded against my skin as I washed away the grime from the Greyhound bus. Desert dirt swirled around my feet before it flowed into the drain, leaving me behind. I moved my fingers around my ribs and felt how sore they were, then probed my lower stomach, which hurt like crazy too. Blue and yellow still marred my flesh, and I wondered how long it would take for it to go away. Everything was so fucked up…what the hell happened? My throat constricted, and my eyes prickled.

"No." I pressed my hands against the cool tile and forced my head anywhere but there. Trigger's wild eyes flashed in front of me, and my guts twisted.

"Stop." I breathed through the tears to control my emotions.

Just as I was about to open the door to my bedroom, I heard another door shut.

"Hello?" I tightened the towel around my chest. "Mom? Rachel?"

Nothing.

I stepped into the room and glanced around. It appeared to be empty. I needed to remember the number one rule of the house. If you weren't entertaining, you locked the door to your bedroom.

With the remote in my hand, I turned on some music to help drown out my thoughts. Chris Stapleton's "Fire Away" softly flowed throughout the room, easing the nerves that had attacked my stomach.

Suddenly, I honed in on a dark blue corset with black ribbon and lace that was laid out on my bed along with a pair of heels. So, I *had* heard an intruder.

"Shit." I ran my hand along the garter clips then noticed my jeans and tank top were missing. I whirled around to see my Chuck Taylors were gone too. "No!" I swiped my bare foot under my bed and caught the strap to my bag that I had slipped under there earlier. Tugging it free, I clung to it as I searched for a safe place to keep it. My hand cupped the heavy grip through the fabric, and I hoped to God the safety was on. I pulled on the armoire and freed it from the wall and peeled back the paneling. My secret place. When I was younger, I found this little space when the painters were working on my room. I used to hide all my books and cash there. My bag fit perfectly inside, along with my beloved camera.

I hated this place.

I glanced in the mirror one last time and recognized my worst nightmare. I had become my mother. I cringed and closed my eyes. This was only temporary. I tried to use my fingers to soothe the achy spots, but the bone inlay of the corset didn't help.

Draping the cool silk robe along my arms, it rested around mid-thigh and flowed around me like a cape. I knew it was only a matter of time before someone came looking for me. Better to save face now than look like I was hiding.

I shook off my nerves and headed downstairs.

***

Trigger

Two weeks later

Radiohead pounded through the slaughter room. The beat vibrated through the bottoms of my feet, up my legs, and filled the dark space inside my chest.

The three men who sat across from me had been stripped of their clothes and sat naked in a line. Sweat dripped from their foreheads and settled along their brows.

"Choose." The word eased off my lips.

The first man shook as he glanced at his options. His skinny fingers skimmed over the lineup of weapons.

In front of them were a hunting knife, pliers, bleach, a gun, and a pair of brass knuckles.

He tapped the gun and closed his eyes.

I raised the pistol and blew a hole in the center of his face.

One down.

The second started to cry. His chest pumped in fear, and his hand rubbed the side of his head.

"You had your chance to leave, but you didn't." I placed the gun back in the lineup and sat back, waiting to see what he wanted. I couldn't care less. I was bored and wanted to feel something, but like the last few weeks, I felt nothing. "Choose."

"And if I don't?" he challenged as his bloodshot eyes searched the room for a way out.

"Then I do."

He knew better and looked over at his friend, who was in total shock.

"Fuck! Gun, the gun!"

I rolled my eyes and wished Brick hadn't suggested it at the last minute. I slid the weapon over in front of him. He looked up at me, confused.

"You do it."

"Me?"

"Five, four…" I started to count.

"This shit for real?" He looked at Brick, then Morgan, who both were behind me.

"Three, two, one." I snatched the gun away. "Now I choose."

With a flick of my wrist, I flung the gun off the table and rammed the knife into his neck. I turned and used my momentum to kick the last guy's hand away from the brass knuckles. He screamed but stayed put as Brick held his gun to his cheek.

I twisted the blade into his jugular and felt it tear. He slumped in his seat, and I released him and turned back to the last pathetic excuse for a man.

I shoved the table out from between us and leaned down with my hands on the armrests. Hovering just above his shaky head, I waited for him to look me in the eye.

"Where's Mateo?"

His eyes closed as he mumbled a prayer.

Enough of this shit!

I snatched Brick's gun and shot the asshole in the thigh. He screamed, and I grabbed his sweaty head and yanked it back to look at me.

"Where's Mateo?"

"Ah!" he shouted, but I saw he was close to the edge.

"Matching set it is, then." I shot the other thigh.

He bucked and tried to slide off his seat, but my fingers found the gaping hole and dug deep.

"You like to fuck with me? Allow me to repay the favor." I fished around and felt bone fragments.

"Him and Tiago!" He huffed between screams. "They are hiding up north somewhere."

"Where?"

"I don't know!" He stared up at me, the skin around his mouth growing paler as the seconds ticked by. His eyes became dull, and I saw his soul packing up its shit to leave.

Fuck.

"Why did you stay behind?"

He squinted as he tried to form a thought. "They're not done with her yet."

I heard Brick shift his weight at the mention of *her*.

"Fine." I rose to my feet then pointed the gun at his head and shot him in the mouth. Blood drained from another hole in his body.

Silence fell. The only things screaming were the demons inside my head. My anger rose rapidly.

"Jace!" I barked. "Clean this shit up."

He and the newest prospect, Rich, started to push the human waste down the industrial drain with a shovel.

Blood dripped from the tips of my hair and ran down my face. I grabbed the razor we used to skin the heads and moved over to the mirror. I gathered the hair in the center of my head and lifted it up then buzzed the sides. I left the mohawk long.

Better.

I flipped my hair out of my face and spun around to face my men. They seemed unsure what to think.

"Like the new look." Rail said, trying to break the tension.

Gus nodded in agreement, but I caught him glance to where Morgan stood off to his side.

"Fuck, I would give my left nut to have Tess back," Rail muttered to Brick.

Brick remained silent, which was good, as I was moments from flipping my fuck switch.

I grabbed a bottle of whiskey on my way out and stuck it in my saddlebag before I kicked my bike to start the engine. The air was cold and whipped through my hoodie as the smell of the rain to come made memories come thick and fast about the last time it poured.

Her lips shivered, but her eyes told me she had a lot more fight in her.

"You're cold.

"I'm fine." She pulled the joint from my lips.

I shook that thought from my head and turned down a side street. I cut the engine and found Mud outside his surf shop.

"Evening." He grinned when he saw the bottle dangling from my fingers. "You want to keep going?"

I nodded and removed my hoodie and tossed it on the table, but carefully laid my cut on the leather couch away from the mess.

He motioned for me to take the chair. I flopped back and looked up at the naked posters that littered the ceiling.

Mud lit a joint before he spoke. "This new?" He pointed at his head.

I nodded.

"You want a glass?"

I wiggled the cap off with one hand and drank the neck before I set it aside. Mud huffed with a grin, and smoke poured out of the corners of his mouth. He tapped his phone, and The Black Keys' "Lonely Boy" played through shitty speakers. I eyed him, curious if it was meant for me, but he just clicked the machine on and went to work on my pec.

I focused all my energy on the needle that drilled tiny pinpricks into my flesh, but sadly, it didn't last long. The pain subsided, and I was left with my demons gnawing on my memories.

Nolan was nowhere to be found.

CHAPTER TWO

Tess

"Sorry, Tess." Venna, the only trustworthy friend I had left in this house, gave me a grim frown. She turned the computer around and showed me I had a four p.m. client this afternoon. I broke out in a sweat.

Somehow, I had managed to avoid being booked by complaining about the pain I was in from my stomach, and threw in being on that time of the month. Plus, Rachel still worked the front desk, and when I showed her my bruises, she felt bad for me. Of course, I kept the truth of what really happened quiet and only gave a vague story, which seemed to work better. Everyone loved a little mystery.

"You see who booked it?" She tapped the screen, her expression pissed off. "Seems kinda fucked up, if you ask me."

I glared at my mother's name. "She never thought of me as her daughter, anyway, so this doesn't shock me. All I am to her is someone she can pimp out to make money."

Venna's hand landed on mine. "Least you're getting booked. Felicia has me on probation for leaving."

"This is my punishment for coming back."

She bit the inside of her lip, thinking about something. Before she could say it, she stood a little straighter and tapped the keyboard to make the schedule disappear.

"Clark," she greeted him before she checked her phone.

"Ven, you look lovely today."

She blushed.

"That's right, you're a fan of red." Her fingers brushed down the front of her red corset. "I really need a new one. This is getting old."

"I'm sure that can be arranged." He glanced over at me. "I see you picked the blue one. Nice choice."

Internally, I rolled my eyes, but decided to treat him as I would any other man here. "Well, let's hope my four p.m. agrees."

His brows pinched together as he swung the computer screen to face him and hit the keyboard.

"Felicia booked it." I pushed away from the desk. "Time to pop the house cherry." I snickered as I left the two of them alone.

I heard him whisper, "That's not entirely true."

It took everything in me not to waver my step.

Wow.

Back in my room, my hands shook, and my heart beat to an unknown rhythm as I watched the time tick by. I didn't think I could do this. My stomach ached, and my ribs were on fire.

"Tess?" Venna slipped in and closed the door behind her. "How hard would it be to convince you to let me take your spot, and you can dance tonight?"

I nearly fell forward as I grabbed the post at the end of my bed.

Someone is looking out for me somewhere.

She came closer and noticed my pale face. "You okay?"

"Ven, I'll take any spot you want to trade with me."

"I need the money, Tess. I need to get the fuck out of here."

I so wanted to repeat her words back at her, but I would rather take a little more time making the money dancing than have someone stick their pencil dick in me.

"The appointment is all yours."

Her face lit up, and a sense of relief spread through me. "Just keep it quiet, okay?"

"Trust me." I waved her off and eased back on the mattress. "If my mother thinks I'm working here the way she wants, she'll leave me alone. My lips are sealed."

A knock at the door brought us both to our feet. Venna grabbed my hand and pulled me closer. "Get him set up, and once he's ready, I'll step in."

I nodded, and she disappeared into my bathroom. I walked on shaky legs to meet my client.

My fingers brushed my bracelets to remind myself to stay strong, and I took a deep breath and opened the door.

"You have no idea how long I have been waiting for this moment, Tessa." Bret flashed his million-dollar smile at me then reached out and fingered the lace between my breasts. It was difficult to hold my tongue, but somehow, I managed. "Let's see if you're anything like your mother."

I want to puke.

Bret had been a member of the house for seven years, and had his eye on me for the last five. Of course, his wife and three children had no clue their daddy wasn't at the office. Bret loved the chase, and he continued to chase me because I sure as hell would not let that man poke me with anything.

I stepped back and motioned for him to enter. He slapped my ass as he strolled in and removed his jacket and tie.

"Top or bottom?"

My mouth went dry, but I managed to speak as I moved to my dresser and pulled out a blindfold. "I had something else in mind."

He reached out and hooked my waist, pulling me to him.

Don't slap him, don't slap him.

His long, bony fingers dug into my hips, bordering on painful rather than sexy.

"The kinkier the better."

I pushed out of his hold and patted the mattress. He complied willingly and obeyed my instructions.

Yuck. I hated a man who wanted to be told what to do. I wanted to be thrown up against the wall for passionate, animal sex. Trigger's face flashed in front of me, and I tried to shake the memory away.

He doesn't want you, Tess.

The cuffs snapped over his wrists, and satin ties held his ankles in place. I straddled his waist while I slipped the blindfold over his hungry gaze. Turning up the music, I whispered, "Let me grab the oil."

He thrust his hips to grind his erection into my leg. I hopped off and hurried into the bathroom where Venna was prepping herself. Thankfully, we had the same length hair and were pretty much the same body shape.

"He's all yours."

"Is he big or small?"

I shrugged. "Depends on what you call big. Just be sure if he's in or not before you fake anything."

She laughed then headed out to the room, and I sank to the cool floor with a disgusted huff. It wouldn't always be that easy to avoid clients. I inched toward the counter and grabbed the phone Brick had given me. It was turned to airplane mode so it couldn't be tracked. My finger hovered over the photo app, and after a moment, I tapped the screen, and a ton of pictures flashed in front of me. I scrolled through and stopped at my favorite, Trigger standing next to his bike, reading something off his phone. I took it one morning as I rounded the corner to the clubhouse. He looked so real at that moment. The darkness that normally surrounded him wasn't there. He was just a man leaning against his bike before he started the day. Hell, I missed him. I closed my eyes as the pain lashed at my raw memories.

After I got Bret out of my room and had wiped his long kiss goodbye off my mouth, I hurried down to the back yard. I raced through the maze of high shrubs, down the little hill to the building where the strip club was nestled in a sea of greenery.

Dirty Promises was built twenty years ago and was one of the most prestigious strip clubs in Vegas. The membership alone cost more than most homes there.

I wiggled a pebble out of my shoe as I knocked twice on the big industrial door. Music, cigar smoke, and booze blasted me like a gust of wind as it opened in a hurry.

"Oh, shit, look who came back." Jarmon, the doorman, laughed and gave me a hug. "They always come back to the pole."

"Thanks, Jarmon," I muttered but surrendered to his hug. He was a good guy and always had our backs.

"Are you filling in for someone?"

"Yup, Venna."

He didn't ask any questions, simply pointed to her locker and told me to help myself.

The perks of having Mommy own the place.

I opened the door to her locker and sighed. "Really, Ven?" I grabbed the outfit and reached for the hook in the back of my corset when I felt someone bat my fingers away.

My gaze flashed to the mirror, and I yelped.

"You look like you saw a ghost, sweetheart."

Squinting to be sure I was right, I slowly lowered my arms. "Sean?"

"It's Shantee now." He—or rather, *she*—made duck lips in the mirror, admiring herself. She was stuffed into a shiny gold dress with a rack that would make Pamela Anderson self-conscious. A straight brown bob lined her jaw and made her silicone-plumped lips pop. Sean was never small as a man, and now that she had transitioned, she had lost some weight. I had to say she was now quite stunning. "Turns out Felicia has quite the homosexual client list. So, naturally, I stepped up and took one for the team."

"I'm impressed."

"Not shocked. You always were good with weird." She pulled my zipper down, freeing my ribs. I heaved forward with a wince.

"You okay, sweetheart?"

"Yeah." I felt around, curious to know if I did any more damage to them.

She pushed my hands away again and leaned down to examine the injury. Her drawn-on eyebrows rose in speculation.

Just when I thought I was going to be drilled with questions, she leaned back, grabbed her designer purse, and handed me a pill bottle.

"Take two now, two at bedtime."

"What are they?"

We both went quiet when I was paged that I was up next.

"Does it matter?" She snatched them out of my hold, dropped two in my hand, and gave me the glass of gin and tonic she had been nursing.

"Thanks." I tossed them back and pulled on the ridiculous outfit.

"Tess," she called out when I hit the first step to the stage. "I hope whoever did that to you got his ass handed to him."

I tried to force a smile. I pictured those green eyes staring at me from his cut. "He will."

"Glad you're back."

That comment had my stomach in knots. I didn't want to be back.

Dressed in a skimpy business suit and tie, I stood behind the curtain and waited for Justin Timberlake's "Drink You Away" to pound through the curtains.

I couldn't help but scan the crowd for his face, but he wasn't there. Of course, he wasn't. Trigger didn't even know where I was.

***

Trigger

I flipped the joint back and forth through my fingers like a drummer would his stick. My skin ached, and it aggravated my nerves. The smallest thing would set me off. I needed a reason to hurt someone.

Brick finally joined us in the meeting room. He mumbled something about not getting enough sleep. Gus glanced at me, and I knew what he was thinking. We needed to get past this shit if the club was going to continue to run smoothly.

"Anything?" I barked out at the guys. They all leaned back in their seats and looked around the room.

"My guess would be back in Vegas," Brick finally said, but he wouldn't look at me.

"I was referring to the asshole who rose from the grave," I shot back.

His head came up, and he held up his phone. "I need to make a call."

I nodded for him to leave, but it was a shit excuse.

"It's like he dropped right off the grid again." Morgan tugged at his beard as he thought. "You think you can get some help from Blackstone?"

I was debt clean with the Blackstone guys, but given the situation, I might consider the idea.

"Gus," I turned my attention to him, "spread the word to the VPs. I want all the eyes I can get."

"Okay." He left with the phone to his ear.

"What about Fox? Are we all still lookin' for him too?" Jace spun his paper cup between his fingers.

I wanted Fox's head mounted above my office door for what he did to Tess in the desert. It took some digging, but the jackass was runnin' his mouth at a bar about how he beat up Tess. Once the word was out, I knew he'd disappear. Coward.

"Yeah, but I better be the last fucking face he sees."

"Got it."

Twenty minutes later, I shut down the meeting, not wanting to hear petty shit about Tammy being back. I'd deal with her myself when I saw her.

"Trigger," Jace stayed behind as the rest filtered out, "can I steal you for a moment?"

I lit my joint and swiveled my chair to face him. The smoke hugged my lungs while the THC absorbed into my system. I welcomed the hit as it momentarily tamed the demons. My mind played with the image of them as they hunkered down at the door of their cages, eyes wary.

"I know I'm overstepping here, but I want to look for Tess."

I sucked in a tight breath that came with the mention of her name.

He lifted his hands when he sensed my mood change. "Look, that girl was there for me when others didn't see me slippin'. Let me do the same for her."

Fuck. I rubbed my brow, more out of sexual frustration than anything else. I would give my left nut to have that chick back, but with my father back in the picture, it was a whole new level of dark.

"Trigger," he stepped closer, but I could tell he was scared shitless, "just let me make sure she's all right until you decide whatever it is you're doing or not doing with her." His gaze moved away from mine. "She's my friend too. I just wanna know she's okay."

I closed my eyes and inhaled deeply to take a moment to think this shit through. I wanted her here, next to me, safe. However, history had proved itself to be a bitch, and when I was near anyone I remotely cared for, they became a target.

"Jace—"

"Please." His shoulders tensed when he realized he blurted that out, but he went on. "Just let me see if she's okay."

I swallowed back the lash of words for interrupting me. I could see he was genuinely concerned for her.

I gave a slight nod, and that was all he needed before he broke out in a boyish grin and bolted from the meeting room.

Fuck me. I hoped that didn't backfire. I would be annoyed if I had to kill Jace too.

***

Sweat poured down my face, my hands ached, and my knees were like rubber by the time I finished my workout on the rooftop. I popped off the cap and downed my third beer and leaned over the edge to where Tess's old apartment was.

"Hey, man." Brick stopped me at my bike. "You know how Tess is coming in next week?"

I shrugged and clipped the buckle to my shell cap helmet.

"Look, I think she should have her own place. I wanted to rent out the room across from your building. You know, more eyes on her and shit."

"Yeah, fine." I started my bike, not thinking more of it.

"I think you'll like her."

"I don't really like anyone." I tossed the bike into gear and roared down the open road.

I dropped my bottle and watched how it shook from the wind and exploded in the garbage bin below. I wanted to know what she was up to, but at the same time, I didn't.

During the ride home, I couldn't get Tess off my mind. Jace's absence didn't help me keep my head on straight. I noticed his bike was gone when I arrived at the club. Just as I backed in, Big Joe was at my side with his phone out. He handed it to me and stepped back.

I hated that my body jerked with amusement when I scanned the encrypted email. To anyone else, it would look like a jumbled mess of codes, but to me, it was a second language.

First prize—a hundred grand
Second prize—fifty grand
First and second place winners will move on to the semifinals. Location revealed when winners are announced.

I was intrigued, but fucking irritated he would hand me the one thing I promised I'd never do again.

"What, you think we need the money?"

"Nah, boss, I think you need the outlet."

Fuck!

I jammed the phone in his hand and went inside. Morgan had a full bar, and it was only eight p.m. Nice to see the business was picking up.

"Brick?" I shouted when I came behind the bar for a water.

"Out back in the gym."

Minnie blocked my path.

"What?" She had fire, but not the kind I liked.

Her arms folded over her chest, and she cocked out her hip. "When are you going to fix whatever the shit is between you and B?"

"Not now, Minnie."

"Yes, now. And go get Tess so you can get laid again, because honestly, you're a huge asshole without her. And why the fuck is Tammy back? She could be the damn mole, for shit's sake."

Closing my eyes, I tried to calm my temper, which proved harder than I thought. When I opened them, I saw she had walked away.

Good.

The gym was stuffy and hot. We hated to use the AC when we worked out. Living in the desert, you needed to have stamina when it came to the heat. Couldn't fight if you went lightheaded. Shit happened, and you died.

Brick was bouncing around in the ring with Rail, who looked to have gotten hit in the face a few times. It wasn't a fair fight. Brick was stronger and leaner.

"Rail," I called out. He dropped his arms and ducked under the ropes.

I hopped in and raised my fists to spar.

"No." Brick sighed.

"Didn't ask." I smacked his shoulder and then his cheek.

"Why?" He flinched when I punched his arm.

"Fight back."

He rolled his eyes and took a punch at my face, but I ducked and kicked his knee. He yelped, but it fed his fire.

About fucking time.

He swung again, and I let him smoke my face. He saw through me and cursed. Physical pain was my drug.

"I hate that you made her leave."

"Wasn't my intention," I grunted. Dodging his hit, I sent a blow to his chest.

"You tossed me under the bus." He kicked my ribs hard.

"I did, but it was either that or have my father sink his claws into her." It was hard to hold back when I nailed him in the jaw with my foot.

He stepped back and spat blood from his split lip. He pointed his taped-up hand at me. "You know she loved you, and you fed her to the wolves like just another pussy that got too close."

I lunged and grabbed him around the neck, slamming him into the corner of the ring. A few of the guys rose, but Rail raised his hand to tell them to back the fuck off.

My fingers curled into stone as I drew my hand back. My heart pumped at a dangerous rate, and my vison clouded. My switch begged to be flipped, but I held it down. What he said sank in, and he closed his eyes with a frustrated sigh. I waited a beat before I let go and dropped my arms heavily to my sides. The demons screamed at me to rip his head off. Fucking animals wouldn't let up.

"She *is* at the house," Brick muttered, which made me whip around. "I just got a call from a friend who still lives there. You were out, and I needed to process it." He waved around the ring.

Jesus Christ.

"Tell Jace."

"He knows. He was there when he called."

I turned to leave when Brick stopped me.

"It's not as easy as going in there and getting her back. If she went home, it means she went back to *him*."

"You ready to tell me who *him* is now?"

***

Allen

My hands flexed over the sides of the pulpit as I felt the connection with those below me. Power traveled through the soles of my feet. I envisioned myself like a tree, absorbing it through my roots, and the heat of it flooded through my soul. I inhaled deeply with my eyes closed.

Slowly, my eyes opened, and I gazed down at the twenty pairs of ears waiting for me to speak.

"Today, we talk about sacrifice and how the Lord wants you to do him justice."

Two hours later, I packed up my things and shook many hands before I loosened my collar and downed a bottle of Jack from under the dusty organ. This gig was pretty damn good. I could really get off on this whole preacher in the pulpit thing. It suited me.

"Alle—" Zay, one of the oldest members of my *family,* cleared his throat when I glared at him. "Father, we have a new development."

"Which is?" I cleaned the dried blood off the ridges of my knife with my jacket. The edge of excitement I had experienced earlier after disposing of a local was only now beginning to dull.

"We found the girl."

That piqued my interest. Trigger had never given a shit about anyone before, but for whatever reason, he cared enough to make that blonde woman leave. I couldn't get my head around it. Far as I could see, broads like her were a dime a dozen, nothing more than a warm, wet hole. Love was a conspiracy that was beaten into our brains by society, like we needed an old lady to make us feel complete. I snorted out loud at the thought. All you would be left with was a bitch to nag you and suck away all your money. If the common man could step back and look at our history, they would see that feelings like love were nothing more than lust. A few hip thrusts and a spent dick, and that was it.

Like that old saying goes, fuck and chuck.

"Where is she?" He looked over his shoulder and handed me a folded piece of paper. That was why I kept Zay around. He was loyal, discreet, and could find anyone. He was, after all, the one who came up with the idea to win over the Stripe Backs.

I glanced at the address and smiled. "Put fifty on blackjack for me."

He nodded. "I'll report in tonight." With that, he left.

The rest of the men started to bring in the shipment of guns that arrived last night. I moved to the table and relished the smell.

"What do we have here, Father?" My potential buyer was practically salivating.

I pointed to the far end of the table. "AK-47, ML 18 inch 5.56, and this." I picked up the sexy, sleek weapon and looked through the scope. "This is the Black Mamba."

"Which is what, exactly?" He eyed the rifle and ran his tongue over his lips. I slipped it back into the soft velvet case.

"Custom made. It's a cross between both of those weapons. Sniper approved."

His eyebrows rose and he shook his head, clearly not interested in my specialty. "I won't lie. I was surprised to hear you were dealing weapons."

I flipped a bullet between my fingers. "Actually, I'm not looking to sell. I'm looking to build an army."

His face fell, and he flexed his jaw. "Army? Who exactly are you fighting?"

"Devil's Reach," I said bluntly as I eased into a chair.

He stepped back and held his hands in the air. "Fuck, man, I don't know why you'd go up against someone as crazy as Trigger, but I want no part in it."

"Scared?" I taunted.

His fingers ran along the Black Mamba before his gaze flickered over to mine. "I watched him screw up my nephew's eyeballs with a fork because he caught him skimmin'. Then he tore out my uncle's fuckin' kidneys because he defended him. I lived, but those images are burned in my brain." He rubbed his head. "I don't know what was worse, watching that or living with it." He closed the lid on the gun. "I was fine with buying guns from you, Father, but if you're looking for an army, my men would rather off themselves than go up against Trigger."

I hated that my son had such a reputation. If I hadn't gone into hiding, I'd be more feared than he was by now.

"Suit yourself."

He looked away, his face growing paler by the moment. Fucking pussy. "When are you planning to move on him?"

I tilted my head as I studied his face. I wondered what his motive was. "Why?"

He shoved his hands into his pockets. "Because I want to be as far away from you as possible when it happens."

I grinned, excited to know the war would be epic.

CHAPTER THREE

Tess

For three days, Venna and I played every client. All it took was some acting, a blindfold, and some music to drown the voices. I hated every moment of it. I felt dirty and used, more by my mother than by the clients. I may not have been sleeping with the men, but more than half the time they would stick their tongues down my throat or slip their fingers into my panties every chance they got, but at least they weren't hiding who they were.

The only time I felt all right was when I was dancing. They weren't allowed to touch me then. Venna was making a fortune, and I wasn't too far behind. Half my money was going somewhere else, so it would take me a little longer to get out of here. It was a hard pill to swallow, but I still needed to find out what Clark had on Trigger and the club.

I spun once more on the pole then started to feel ill. My ribs were on fire, and my stomach rolled. Feeling like the world was about to fly off its rocker, I danced around and waited until the lights flickered off.

I nearly fell down the stairs as I descended and crashed heavily into someone who broke my fall.

"What's wrong, Tess?" Clark bent down to my eye level.

"Nothing." I pushed him away, but he wouldn't have it. He half carried me to the private dressing room and sat me on a chair before he handed me a bottle of water.

"You're white as a ghost. Have you eaten today?" He felt my forehead, but I pushed his hand away.

"Yes, and stop touching me." Even the water made me want to vomit.

"You're not fucking pregnant, are you?"

My eyes stung as I glared at the asshole in front of me. "If I was?"

He rubbed his face, then his neck. His expression darkened, and I could see where his head went. *He thought it was Trigger's.*

I slowly rose out of the chair and turned toward the door before he jammed himself between me and it.

"Are you?"

"Move." I breathed through my nose to try to calm the storm inside.

He bit his lip but lost the asshole behavior. He brushed my hair away like he used to, and he carefully lifted my chin so I'd look at him. "Despite your anger toward me, sweetheart, I really care about you and your wellbeing." His fingers dragged across my bottom lip, and for a moment, I gave in to it. It felt good, like I was home again. He leaned in and brushed his lips across mine, and I nearly broke. "I missed this." When I started to speak, he sealed his mouth over mine and kissed me sweetly. His kisses had always seemed tender and caring, but really, they were a mind fuck. "Tess," he whispered against my wet skin. "I just want to know if you're okay."

It was as if someone sucker punched my heart. I stepped back, wiping my lips dry.

"Don't." I wanted to cry with how much his words made me miss Trigger.

"Don't what?" He moved closer. "Don't do this?" He again pushed himself on me, but in a gentle manner. It felt wrong. I was so fucked up and twisted inside, any sweetness during intimacy made me feel gross.

He did that to me.

His arms wrapped around my back and pulled at the string holding my top on. "Remind me of how sweet your breasts are."

Jesus.

Tears prickled my eyes, and that annoying lump returned to the center of my throat. I ripped the string out of his hold and wiggled away with my hand over my breasts.

"Clark, *enough*," I bit out and tried to make sense of my million and one mixed emotions.

"Sorry." He held up his hands. "Just hard when I haven't seen you in a while. You know what you do to me."

"I need to go."

"Okay." He got the hint but still waited a beat before he opened the door for me.

Once I was alone in the hallway in the back corridor of the house, I slid to the floor and held on to my knees for something to stabilize me.

Clark stirred up so many dormant feelings that I'd finally managed to chase away. He wasn't good for me, but shit, that kiss clouded my head.

Later that night, my ribs got worse. Or was it my stomach? I couldn't really tell. Taking the pills Sean—or *Shantee*—had given me, I slipped off to a very uncomfortable sleep.

The next day I spent in my room trying to take it easy. My mother was pissed she had to reschedule my appointments, but Clark helped convince her. I stayed in bed, hoping time and rest would help. Sadly, by three p.m. the next day, that wasn't the case.

***

The lady behind the desk kept her eye on me while I waited for the doctor, who was running behind. I could have seen the house doctor, but the last time I did, it had severely scarred me. Literally.

"Tessa Marin, come on back." The doctor smiled at me from behind her red-framed glasses. Her office was just as funky as her outfit that peeked out from her white coat. She had taken a sponge to her walls and had made a neat mural of the park across the street.

"So, you're new to me." She grinned at me as she propped up her laptop. "Why are you here today? Tell me a little bit about yourself."

Where to begin?

"To make a long story short, I was in the wrong place at the wrong time and got jumped. My ribs took the majority of the beating."

"Okay." Her tone immediately changed to a more serious one. "Did you see a doctor when it happened?"

"Kind of." I made a face that told her my story had some holes. "He didn't see any problems that would lead me to think I should go to the hospital."

She squinted before she typed something in her laptop.

"I'm having some pain here." I pointed to my lower abdomen, and her eyes followed my hands. "Not really sure if it's connected to what happened, but it doesn't seem to be getting any better."

She placed her laptop on the desk and started to warm her hands by rubbing them together.

"Lean back and let me take a look."

Easing back on the bed, I lifted my shirt and watched her facial expressions. Her cool hands felt around, and I nearly hit the roof when she applied pressure to my left side.

"Your bruises are yellow, so to be having that kind of pain, I would think there may be more going on. Maybe a cracked rib as well." She glanced at my file before adjusting her glasses as she looked me over. "I would feel more comfortable if we did some x-rays."

"Now?" I needed to get back.

"Yes."

"I can't. I have to get back to work."

"I'll squeeze you in."

Fuck.

"Okay."

She sank back in her seat and scrolled through her laptop. "Okay, let's go."

Twenty minutes later, I quickly dressed and promised the doctor I'd come back for the results.

I gathered my things and plastered a smile on face. "I'll be waiting for your call."

She stood as I handed her the very lengthy questionnaire she made me fill out. She immediately flipped to the third page and frowned. "Here." She handed me a prescription. "I have a theory on what's going on, but until I'm sure, please take these. If they don't help, come back, and I'll try something else. In the meantime, take it easy, okay?"

"I'll try."

"Tess?"

I opened the door and stood in the doorway as if to ask, *what*?

"Whoever did that to you, were they caught?"

Trigger's face broke through my walls and made me smile. "One did, and the other will get his day."

She nodded then reminded me once again to keep my word to return for the results.

I didn't even get outside before my phone lit up. I tossed back two of the pills she gave me and opened my messages.

Ven: I'm stuck at the club and your mother is on a rampage. Call Rachel asap!

Tess: Not a good time.

Not even ten seconds later, I felt her reply.

Ven: Call her NOW!

Shit.

"Where the hell are you?" Rachel, the house admin, screamed at me.

"I had an appointment."

"Not from what I see. You know the rules better than anyone here, Tessa. You always block out the times you're not here."

"Sorry. I wasn't thinking."

"Yeah, well, you better, because there's a new client here insisting he has an appointment with you."

Come on, not today!

"Can you rebook him?"

"Girl, he's sitting in the waiting area saying he'll wait until you arrive. When your mother stepped in to try to get him to take someone else, he said no, but that he'd triple the normal rate for you."

Who the hell was this guy?

"I'm fifteen minutes away."

"Make it five." She hung up.

I quickly called Ven and told her what was going on. She told me she'd wait in the lobby, and we'd go from there.

I skipped on the Uber and nearly ran all the way back. I managed to get there in under ten. Thankfully, the sidewalk was clear, and the atmosphere was heavy with upcoming rain. Autumn in Vegas was the best.

"You look like shit," Rachel muttered as she tried to smooth my wild hair. "Go over there and get changed." She pointed me toward a small changing room we rarely used, but it was good for times like this. "I'll get him to your room."

"Wait." I caught the door before she left. "Where's Ven?"

"Felicia needed her for something. She just rushed her away about three minutes ago."

What?

I pulled my phone free, and sure as shit, there was a text.

Ven: Your f'ing mother needed me to take care of her client. Not sure if she is on to us.

The blood drained from my face and pounded in my chest.

No.

I can't.

I won't.

My hands shook as I did up the zipper on my corset. I flinched at the pain but quickly masked it as I tried to figure out what was about to happen.

"Tess!" my mother barked from the other side of the door. "Move it!"

I opened the door, and her cruel expression lashed through me.

"You look like shit. This man has a ton of money. You better not screw this up for me." She pinched my cheeks painfully and rolled her eyes at the rest of me. "Why he wants you is beyond me. Go!"

"Your encouragement always does wonders, Mother."

She snickered at my sass before she walked away.

Each step took a tremendous amount of energy and willpower. I shook like a leaf as I opened the door. He was standing in front of the window looking out at the pool area.

Kill me now.

He turned to look at me, and I nearly fell over.

***

Trigger

Brick downed the neck of the whiskey before he clinked my bottle. We were in the back of my pickup truck by the pool. We had just gotten back from dealing with my North Carolina crew and needed a breather.

"You have to understand that you come after Tess. You know I'm all about loyalty, and I have always had your back. But Tess always comes first."

"Okay." I understood that. Loyalty was earned over time and proven in the worst situations. Based on what I did know about Brick and Tess's past, they had a tight bond. Still, it was time to hear the truth.

He sighed and tossed a beer bottle into the trash bin a few feet away. "Clark weaseled himself into her life when she was ten, and not the way a father would."

My grip tightened around the neck of the bottle as his words burned my stomach lining.

"Clark is eleven years older. He saw an opportunity and took it."

Fuck. He was only twenty-one when he met her. To be so twisted at that age was something else.

"Why?" My throat quickly became dry.

He chuckled darkly then rubbed his free hand over his jeans. "Because Tess was vulnerable and needy, but mostly because she comes from a lot of money, not that she's seen a dime of it."

My chest ached when I remembered all the times I'd given her shit over being a spoiled princess running from Mommy.

"Did they ever…" I cracked my neck to relieve some tension.

Brick stuck his thumb over the mouth of the bottle then looked at me with the most haunted look I'd ever seen on his face.

"Don't make me answer questions that will flip that switch of yours, dude."

I hated to be denied an answer to something I wanted to know, and my dark expression made it clear to him he should go on.

"Come on, Trigger."

"Brick," I warned.

He huffed through a sigh. "They didn't have sex until she was eighteen."

"Least he waited until she was legal."

"Yeah, for sex." My head whipped over to find his jaw locked in place. "I'm telling you, Clark sank his claws into her at an early age."

"Then, what?" I needed to know everything now, so I could deal with it.

"It's not a matter of *what*. It's that he won over her trust, messed around with her, made her fall in love with him, then saw an opportunity to secure himself in the house and married her mother. He ripped her world out from underneath her and betrayed her."

Wait, what?

"How old was she when he married her mother?"

Brick nodded. "Eleven."

That's when she tried to kill herself.

"I know Clark loves Tess in his own sick way, but he loves money just as much. That way, he got both. Only took him a few years to brainwash Tess back into submission after the wedding. Hence them sleeping together on her eighteenth birthday."

Jesus Christ.

"Clark is the only man who paid any attention to her. Her father wasn't around, and her mother looks right through her like she doesn't exist. Clark stole any innocence she had. You can see why she was his target. She's pretty, smart-mouthed, and underneath her armor, she has the biggest heart, and he fucking destroyed her."

"So, why did she come here then run back to him?"

Brick lowered his voice when Rail brought a girl to the edge of the pool and dove in.

"Something changed six years ago, and she decided she wanted to go back to the house when I wanted to leave town. No matter how many times I begged her to come, she wouldn't budge. Whatever it was, it was important enough to keep her there, so whatever happened after that to make her leave to come to me must have been big. She lived on the streets before we met, and I know she must be lost if she went back there. Tess has a lot of demons she keeps locked up because of that house."

The girl with Rail screamed when he grabbed her from behind and tossed her in. I spotted Peggy watching us from across the property, and when I caught her eye, she licked her fingers and motioned for me to come over. I looked away then downed my whiskey.

"What was Tess like on the streets?"

Brick chuckled then leaned back, clearly at ease with this topic.

"She was guarded and sassy, but I earned her trust. Doesn't take long for a girl who looks like Tess to find trouble on the streets. Every guy wanted a piece of her, and every girl wanted to hate her. You can imagine how much sleep she got."

I shuddered at the thought.

"Did she ever take you to the house?"

He folded his arms and sighed.

"Once, she tried, but we never got through the gates. She had a full-blown panic attack, and I told her it wasn't worth it." He glanced at me. "I'm telling you, that is not the place for her to be."

"Trigger?" Morgan suddenly appeared next to me. "We should talk."

Once inside, I closed the door behind Morgan and sank into my seat at the head of the table. Morgan pulled out his phone.

"You remember Harmos?"

I thought for a moment until I placed the memory.

"Yeah, nephew skimmed off the Vegas drop, and the uncle had a hand in it?"

"Yup. Well, you remember how we let the other uncle go?"

I nodded, wondering where the fuck he was going with this.

"Well, that uncle just ran his mouth to Cray. Turns out he crossed paths with your father."

My hands drew into fists, and I steadied myself for what was next.

"Seems your father is looking to build an army and wanted him to join."

"That so?" I bit out. "And did he?"

"Nope, said he wasn't going up against you. Not worth it."

"Smart man," I muttered and thought about what my next move would be. "Any lead on his location?"

"He wouldn't say anything much, but that he was still posing as a priest, seems to like being called Father." He looked at me for a reaction to that, but as ironic as it was, I let it pass. "Puts up like he's all about selling guns, but really he's drawing in men to recruit."

I let the information absorb without comment then drew a heavy breath.

"Who do we have right now?"

Morgan pulled out a seat and thought for a moment. "I mean, we got Ty's replacement."

"I want Rich here, especially while Jace is gone. Send Cooper."

"Your father knows our men. Why not send in Peggy?"

"For what, a handy? She's useless. Send Moe."

"On it."

I leaned back and tried to piece together what the fuck my father was up to. Was he building a club? Or was it a trap?

"The first key to succeeding, boy, is making others think you're doing one thing when really you're doing another," he barked at me from the corner of the ring. "People are expendable, and the sooner you realize that, the better off you'll be."

Langley stepped in front of me and rested his hand on my shoulder. I jerked back, but his hand stayed in place.

"Clear your mind, Trigger. The longer you keep him inside your head, the harder the fight will be. Focus on me, and me only."

I nodded but eyed my father, who watched us. He was threatened by Langley, but needed him more. He was, after all, the only one who kept me in line when Gus couldn't.

"Like I said," my father slammed Langley hard on the back, "everyone is expendable."

CHAPTER FOUR

Tess

My hands flew to my mouth as the tears flowed from my eyes.

"Hey there, Tess." Jace beamed at me in a three-piece suit. He opened his jacket like he was impressed at how he cleaned up. "I look fucking fetchin', right?"

I laughed at his words. How he got in here was beyond me.

"I know I'm not Brick, but can I still get a hug?"

I hurried over and wrapped my arms around his midsection. He smelled like the club, and the walls I had been carefully building started to buckle under the pressure.

I flinched when his arms tightened.

"Oh, you okay?"

I nodded while I stepped back and willed the tears away. "Just still a little sore from—" I shook off the memory. "How did you get here? They run a detailed background check on everyone. You'd have to have at least a hundred grand in your account, or they wouldn't even consider you."

He smiled as he sat on the edge of my dresser. He looked so different and so much more grown up. Well, until he opened his mouth.

"You're forgetting Trigger's rich, and he knows a lot of people."

The very mention of Trigger's name in such a casual way nearly tore me down. I reached behind me for the mattress and eased back to help with the heaviness.

"I suppose that's true." My mouth became dry.

"This room is bomb, Tess, and that bathroom! Shit, your tub is the size of my bed." I welcomed Jace's lack of attention to my emotional state. "No wonder Brick got you an apartment and didn't make you slum it at the clubhouse right away."

Trigger.

Brick.

Clubhouse.

All the words I hadn't dared to utter since I left three and a half weeks ago. Damn, it felt so much longer, but with Jace here, it felt like yesterday. I rubbed my chest where my heart was determined to make an imprint.

I yelped when he jumped onto my bed like a seven-year-old, landing on his back. His arms went behind his head as he sighed. "I slept in Rail's garage for a month before I got a spot in the clubhouse. I thought that was nice." He chuckled as he wiggled into the comforter. "Now I can see why you came back here."

I hated that he didn't see how dark this place was for me. How much I'd died inside the past few weeks. My insides coiled, and I wanted to scream. I closed my eyes and tried to calm down, but it was hard because he kept rambling. "Why are you here?" I blurted, harsher than I intended.

He sat up and tugged at his tie, and his mood changed.

"Trigger needed to know where you were."

My body tingled in an alarming way. There was more to this.

"Why?"

"Someone showed up and caused problems." He wouldn't look at me, and I wanted to question why. "Trigger just needed to know you were all right."

Oh.

"Well," I cleared my throat and rubbed my wrist, "as you can see, I'm fine."

"Yeah, I can see that." He grinned, but it fell when I didn't match it. "You sure you are Tess?"

My phone vibrated, and I pulled it from my purse.

Ven: The Wicked Witch is finally busy. You need me?

Tess: I got this one.

Ven: Okay…just text me when you're done, okay?

Tess: K.

"How's Brick?" I diverted the attention off me.

"Pissy."

I felt my lips go up without thinking. Brick could be wicked at shutting people out when he was digesting something heavy.

"Give him a chocolate milk drink box."

Jace looked at me oddly. He folded his arms and nodded for me to elaborate.

"Just something from when we were younger."

"I'll stop on my way home."

Home. Ugh.

"Any tricks for Trigger?"

His words were like a physical punch to the gut.

"You should see the slaughter room. It's permanently stained red."

Shit.

He stood and straightened his tie in the mirror. "Even Tammy can't get near him." He grinned at me and missed my mood change yet again. "Well, I've seen you, and you look fucking sexy. I'll report back you're great."

"Jace." I huffed in disbelief that this was happening.

A knock at the door sent a jolt through me.

Oh, no!

"Jace, lose the jacket and look like you're buttoning up your shirt."

"What?"

"Play along, okay?" I tugged off his jacket and pushed him on the bed. Just as I settled in on his lap, the door slowly opened.

"Tessa—oh, forgive me." Clark's eyes narrowed in on Jace's shocked expression. "I didn't realize you were working."

Like hell. The blood pumped to my face, and I hid behind my hair. My hands trembled as I pressed them into Jace's chest.

"Close the damn door, asshole." Jace covered my hands to hide my nerves and glared at Clark.

Clark ran his tongue across his lips as he stared at Jace, and then he looked back at me.

"Tessa, please find me when you're finished here."

I gave a slight nod and waited for the click of the door. I let out a long, deep breath to calm my nerves.

"Thanks for that, Jace." I couldn't look him in the eye.

"Shit, so you *are* a—an escort."

No wonder Trigger sent him. To confirm his ex was a tramp.

My eyes welled up. This wasn't something I chose, it was

something I was born into. I had never slept with any of the men here except Clark, but that was different.

"No wonder Trigger flipped the fuck out after you left the church."

I shifted back and covered myself up with my pathetic excuse for a robe. I shoved hard against his chest. "How dare you judge me? It's none of your fucking business, or Trigger's. Get the hell out, Jace, and tell him I'm just fine."

Jace shifted on the bed and pulled his phone free.

"I gotta go." He shrugged on his jacket and mumbled about missing his bike. "I miss having you around, Tess. I wish you hadn't left."

"Well, I did, so…"

"Okay, well, I gotta run."

I tucked my hair behind my ear and nodded. I wished it was Morgan who came instead of Jace. He would have heard me.

I barely registered his hug and turned away as he left. I felt raw and exposed, and I had to get a grip on my emotions.

I locked the door, turned off the lights, closed the curtains, and curled up in a tiny ball on the blanket in the center of my bed.

Maybe I wasn't a whore, but I sure felt like one now.

***

The next morning, Clark paced his office like a panther, while I stood like stone, curious what he had to say. I was *sure* it was something important.

"Are you enjoying working here?"

I felt my back go up. Seriously?

"If I did?"

"Clients are asking for you specifically now?"

"Clark," my voice carried a warning, "I never asked to work in the house. I wanted to go back to the stage. If you want to change that, I welcome it. You made your choice, so keep your jealousy out of it."

He thought for a moment before he came around the desk and towered over me, just like Trigger used to. His soap was different, though, and it brought back so many memories of feeling loved and cherished by him. I had to shake myself and remember the truth, that there had been an undertone of deceit the whole time, and I would do well to not forget. I took a step back. He clouded my head and confused me.

"Tessa," he whispered and brushed my hair off my shoulder. "God,

I have missed the heat from your skin."

I closed my eyes and tried to concentrate, and I pulled hard from a deep place. His lips brushed my earlobe, and I turned my chin away.

"Don't."

"You used to love it when I kissed you here." He pressed on the side of my neck, and Trigger flashed before my eyes.

"Stop."

"Your body doesn't agree with your words, sweet girl."

I pushed at his shoulders and shoved him away before I turned on my heel and hurried to the door. It opened as I touched the handle.

My mother's evil glance tore a hole through me. Her eyes honed in on my neck, and I felt she could see his kiss.

"Clark, honey," she said over my head, "come to bed."

I sighed as I moved around her. My mother's hand snapped to my upper arm. She glared inches from my face. "Give me a reason to kick you out *again,* Tess. Just one."

"Felicia." Clark's tone told me he knew what she was referring to. "Enough."

Her words lashed at the deep wound. Just as she was about to let go, her hand slid down and fingered my scar.

"Sometimes you *do* have good ideas. Shame you can't follow through with them."

The air was sucked from my lungs as she slammed his door in my face.

***

Trigger

"Where?" I rolled out the map in front of Cray, the VP of the Arizona crew. Morgan leaned over the table with Gus. Brick closed the door behind him after he sidetracked Peggy, who wouldn't take *get lost* for an answer.

"Here and here." Morgan pointed to two spots that ran over Twenty-Third and Ocean Park Boulevard.

I glanced at Gus. He knew southern California like the back of his hand.

"Just an old drive-in theater. There's a building in the back. Maybe he's squatting there?"

I popped my neck, weighing the odds of whether this was a trap.

"Look, I have eyes everywhere. If they said they saw him, I believe them." Morgan stood while we all sat. I knew he trusted his men, but I didn't. I caught Brick's eye, and he shrugged, but I could tell he wanted to follow this lead.

"Vote," I ordered.

"Aye." Morgan started us off and raised his hand.

"Aye." Cray nodded.

Gus started to cough from his joint but managed to squeak out, "Aye."

"Aye. This shit needs to end." Brick checked his phone before he tucked it away.

My eyes hurt as the demons within weighed in their vote.

"Just us, and bring the rifles. We leave at dark."

Morgan waited until the rest of the guys left before he rolled the map and put it away.

"I need Peggy out from behind the bar," he muttered as he turned to look at me. "She can't pour for shit, she's leaving to fuck whoever during her shift, and God forbid she counts to twenty."

I leaned back, not needing that right now, but I knew his frustrations were legit. Peggy was a fucking train wreck.

"Who do you want?"

"Tess," he blurted and sucked his lips inward.

A burn ripped over my skin, and I relished it. Pain was good for the body, kept you sharp. What her name did to my head was a different story.

"I have someone I can bring in for a while," he said, not fazed by my look. "My friend's cousin used to work in that shithole by the beach. If he could work there, he could work here."

"Fuck Tess. She's gone. No outsiders. Speak to Cray, see who he can send over." I was pissed. I had never needed a damn bitch to care about, and now look what the hell it was doing to my head. Just the sound of her name set me on fire.

He nodded, but I could tell he wasn't happy about it.

The nights were cooler, and the days were shorter now that it was November. Our hoodies covered our skin, the rags hid our faces, and the reaper rode bitch on our backs.

I tapped the button on my helmet and filled the dead night with "Psychosocial" by Slipknot. I needed something to calm the chatter.

A thick thrill seemed to hover in the air. It sent tiny shocks into my skin that absorbed into my bloodstream and set my senses to overdrive.

I pointed to the turnoff, and our headlights lit the driveway as we swung in off the main road. We stopped a few yards back behind an old bus.

We moved swiftly in pairs across the property to the only door on our side.

"This feels a little too familiar." Next to me, Brick checked the clip of his 9mm. "Ready?"

I scanned the guys to make sure we were good to go. Big Joe was further back and would stay outside to text if we got company. I opened the door with my flashlight and stepped into the blacked-out warehouse.

The moment my boot landed and I felt the texture, I didn't need to look down to know what it was. The smell hit second. Rotting flesh was something you only needed to experience once to have it permanently burned into your memory.

Rail gagged behind me but kept it together. Brick snickered something, and he shut up.

"What's the noise?" Morgan whispered as he came up to my side. "Pipe leaking?"

I tuned out the guys and moved forward, my light scanning at waist height so as not to miss anything. There was a door ahead, partly open. I nodded to the guys that I was heading over, and they followed. I turned back once to count to make sure they were all with me. I didn't trust this place, and the mole was playin' hard on my mind. If one was going to show themselves, now would be the time.

The slime grew thicker as we approached. Our boots squashed with each step, alerting anyone around that we were there. All things my father would think of.

I pushed the door open, and my light played over the walls. I felt a deep chill enter the room.

"No," Gus hissed when he saw one of his oldest friends hanging from the ceiling with barbed wire wrapped several times around his neck. The blood had drained from his body in sticky puddles. His hands were torn up, and a bone from his thumb was sticking out—all signs of a fight to the death.

A heavy wave of grief ran over us when we saw more of our San Diego crew strung up across the room like holiday lights. One, two, three, four, five, six, seven. I stopped when I saw the seventh was different than the rest. I stepped closer and saw the tattoos.

Gator.

His lips were sewn shut with wire in an X, meaning he ran his mouth. Gator had brought the drugs to Palm Springs to test the zig-zagged product, and the result was Ty, my prospect, meeting the same fate. A brutal death. I shook my head, and rage started to take over my body.

"Seven," I hissed at the men when they joined me.

"Eight," Gus corrected. "They got the other runner too."

My fingers were buzzing. The blood pumped to my arms, and the veins grew big and thick with it as the pressure increased under my skin.

He touched my family.

My phone lit up my pocket just as a door in the far corner opened and slammed shut.

Holy shit, we're not alone.

Rail was the first to step forward when we heard three shots from outside.

"What the hell?" Morgan quickly raised his weapon to scan above us.

I turned my phone over to read what I thought was Big Joe's warning.

Jace: I found Tess.

Suddenly, the lights flickered on, and there were at least thirty cops with laser beams pointed at our chests.

"Drop your weapons!"

Fuck me!

***

Everyone was separated and taken to the station in handcuffs. Big Joe had fled the scene before anyone saw him. He called our lawyer, who was now next to me and had just given me the same old speech about keeping my mouth shut. I had been through this enough times to know what to do—and what not to.

We sat in a room for four hours before we saw anyone else. The loss of my men sat heavy on me, but that three-word text from Jace hounded me the most. Was she okay?

"Sam." I kept my head down. I knew we were being recorded. "I need my…" I made a gesture for my phone under the table.

That he was nervous around me had been made clear a few times before. I punched him in a bar once for mentioning information in front of a prospect. Sam was good, which was why he was still employed. "I can't. They have it."

"Get hold of Jace for me."

He nodded and pulled out his phone and started to text. Just then, the door swung open, and in walked one of the biggest dicks I knew.

"Officer Doyle." I leaned back in my chair and examined the douche-bag kid I grew up with. His sister was decent in bed, but she wanted more, and I didn't. I thought Doyle was more upset about that than we were. "I hear you've been working a side job."

His smile confirmed what I'd hoped was a lie.

"Well, now," he pulled the chair out and held his tie back as he eased into the seat, "always fun seeing you with bracelets on."

"Not for long."

"We'll see." He opened the file in front of him and ran his finger along my rap sheet.

"My client didn't do this," Sam started. "There was no evidence that would suggest they were there during the actual murders, and let's be frank, this is his crew. No reason to kill his own."

"There's always a reason when Trigger's involved," Doyle answered while still reading.

The door opened, and there was Sam's hot assistant. She gave me a shy glance before she handed him an envelope.

Sam smiled as he pulled the photo out and slid it across the table. "As you can see, my clients were caught on camera coming out of the bike shop at the time of the murders." He tapped the time stamp. "Now," he stood and motioned for me to do the same, "we are done here."

"Actually," Doyle squinted, "there is still a little problem with the shooting that happened only two minutes before we turned the lights on. Sit back down, Trigger. You're in for a long night."

"You don't think my client shot that guy and raced back inside in time."

"I don't know anything at this point." Doyle's tone dropped. "So, sit back down until we do."

I folded my arms. "Must feel good to finally have a little power in your life."

"Trigger," Sam warned as he settled into his seat again.

"You know what? It kind of does." He smirked.

I calmed myself then glanced at the clock and wondered if Jace made it home yet.

"I want my phone call."

CHAPTER FIVE

Tess

There were pros and cons to living in a house that never slept. There were always enough people to blend in with, but there were always people around. I waited for Rachel to be pulled away by my mother before I tapped on the keyboard to bring up my schedule. I was curious to know if Jace had booked any more sessions with me. I hit the arrow to slide through the month, only to find I was booked at least five times a week, but not with Jace. Disappointment rippled through me, but it only proved I needed to get the hell out of here fast. At least Venna was still booked for the stage, which meant I was.

I heard my mother's voice and had just enough time to click out and turn down the hallway. I pressed my back against the valet wall and listened to learn if they noticed I was there.

"Take her off the books," my mother snapped. "She's a train wreck. We don't need another Mags."

My heart sped up. I hadn't heard my best friend's name mentioned in this house for so long. I inched closer to the corner.

"Do I pay her for the week?"

"She almost cost me our biggest client. I should be taking her pay." She slammed her hand down on the desk. "Clear out her room, toss her shit in a cab, and get her off my property within the next six hours, or you'll be looking for another job."

"Yes, ma'am." Rachel started to type away on the keyboard.

"Where's Clark?" I turned myself carefully so I could just barely peek around the corner.

"Um," Rachel clicked on the cameras and studied each one, "he's in the pool with Summer and Angela."

"Of course he is." She snickered and stormed off.

Damn, I hate that woman.

"Girl, are you asking for trouble?" Rachel was typing again, but I knew she was speaking to me.

I shamefully came around the corner with a shrug.

"You're lucky I saw you on the feed before your mother did. Why are you creepin' around?"

I ran my hand through my hair and wondered how safe it was to share with Rachel. I'd known her almost my whole life, but that wouldn't mean much in this house.

"Just wanted to know who was being canned."

"Dezzy. She took too much coke before her client came and nearly overdosed during a BJ. Dude almost lost his twig."

Shit.

Her dark eyes narrowed in on me. "Why are you really here? Don't lie to me. No one would have come back after what happened to you last time."

"Money." That was a fucking lie, but I wasn't going to go there.

"Umm hmm," she muttered. "I heard you were tangled up in some biker gang. That true?"

"What do you know about it?"

"I know Clark had some real shit-looking cops here dressed in plain clothes. They flashed their badges to get in. Once they got inside, Clark nearly took their heads off for coming to the house. Something about you and a biker gang. Once they talked to him for a bit, though, he cooled off, and they went into the bar. Right as they were leaving, they handed him something that looked like a computer stick, you know, one of those USB thingies. Then he went right into his office."

"You hear a lot for working the desk, Rach."

"You be surprised what goes down in this house, Tessa." She gave me a strange look and went back to typing.

"Good to know," I whispered then headed upstairs, but instead of going to my room, I went to Clark's office. Now that I knew he was given something, I needed to find it and deal with this shit. I wouldn't last much longer.

His office was locked, but I had picked up a few tricks while living on the streets. I used my keycard that allowed access to the viewing rooms and wiggled it past his sorry excuse for a lock. It only took a couple tries to get it open. With a look over my shoulder, I slipped inside and gently closed the door behind me.

I never liked his office. It had white walls with white furniture. How fucking bland could you get? I headed for the file cabinet first and thumbed through the tabs, but nothing really stood out. I did pull my file and placed it aside while I opened the next drawer.

"Come on!" I flipped through everyone who ever worked here since the nineties. For someone who had such a modern office, he certainly had an old-school filing system.

My stomach jerked when I saw her name written in red pen across the tab.

Mags Hurtle.

I flipped it open and leafed through her paperwork. Her family's info, her health report, details of her pregnancy with Lily, the asshole baby-daddy's info. I stopped when I came to the police report. A lot of it was blacked out, which was odd but not surprising. I shifted to lean against the desk when a DVD dropped to the floor and slid under his bookshelf.

Fuck.

Just as I bent to grab it, Clark's phone rang. I jumped, shoving the file back into place.

"Jesus." I tried to calm my nerves as I fingered the DVD out from underneath the bookshelf. I jammed it into the back of my corset.

With a frustrated sigh, I moved to his desk again. It was a simple desk with no drawers, just a table with four legs. I clicked on the keyboard, and his Mac screen flickered on. I closed my eyes, wondering how the shit I was going to navigate through this. I was used to Microsoft technology.

After four failed attempts at the password, I turned off the screen and looked elsewhere. If they handed him something, the proof should be here. I checked inside the few little containers on the desktop for a small USB, but had no luck.

Dumb yourself down, Tess, and think like Clark.

Think.

Think.

Think.

I saw his Monet panting on the wall and wondered if maybe he was that much of a cliché to hide a safe behind it. The frame was about an inch from the wall. My fingers moved along the bottom and tugged, but nothing.

Hmm.

Then I spotted a display box for his beloved rocks on the table under his bar shelf. I was five feet from it when I heard the familiar footsteps. I scanned the room, desperate to find a place to hide. His shit furniture provided zero cover, so I slipped into house mode.

"Tess?" Clark stopped when he saw me sitting in his chair in front of his desk. "What?" He looked over his shoulder then closed the door behind him. "What are you doing here? How the hell did you get in?"

I crossed my legs, which typically drew his gaze to my upper thigh. I dragged my fingers from my stomach, lingered at my chest, across my collarbone, and up to my ear to play with my earring. Clark was incredibly predictable when it came to the female body, so I used what I had.

"I want to ask you to talk to my mother about my schedule."

He pulled the chair next to me around so he could face me head on. *Crap*. I noticed I hadn't moved my own folder that I had pulled.

Mother of fucking Christ, Tess!

"You know that would be easier said than done with our history." His hand fell on mine, and I felt like my skin was on fire. The urge to pull away was overwhelming. "Have you spoken to her about it at all?"

I saw my opportunity and used it.

"Yes, I just tried, which is why I was in here." I waved my hand around but made sure to stop at the file. "Why I ever thought she'd listen is beyond me." I slowed my breathing to make my point. My free hand landed on his. "Clark, I can't do this. It's not who I am. I'll dance, but to be a madam…I just can't. Please."

"Tessa," he leaned closer, and I responded and leaned into him, "just let me have a taste, and I'll see what I can do."

Trigger's face popped up in front of me, and I had to force myself not to pull away.

As Clark's lips pressed to mine, so much resentment filled me I wondered at my ability to control myself. I thought hard about why I was here, forcing away the belief that it felt like cheating. God, I didn't even know if I was really with Trigger.

"Clark," I whispered and dropped my head.

"What?" He trapped my legs between his. "Just give in to me, Tessa."

I jerked back and felt the fire lick through my veins. I shoved him away, jumped up, and darted to the door, but before I opened it, I turned to him as he stood.

"If you ever loved me at all, you will get me back on the stage, Clark."

"I do love you, Tessa."

"No." I cut him off. "If you did, you would have let me go years ago, not played mind games with me, not hunted me down, and not destroyed lives along the way."

His face dropped, and I could see he was conflicted but didn't really get what I was saying.

"Tessa! What the hell?"

I slammed the door. Clark was so embedded under my skin it was hard on my emotions. He twisted them up and confused me. It was no wonder I was such a mess.

I heard footsteps and wondered if Rachel saw me on the camera and let my mother know I was here. I tried the door across the hall, but it was locked. *Shit*, I didn't have time to pick it. I moved to the other, and thankfully, it opened. Closing the door to a small slit, I saw my mother swing open his door.

"Where is she?" she hissed at him. "Rachel said she saw her up here."

"Calm down, calm down. She was here. She just wanted to discuss being put back on stage, and you know what, Felicia, I have to agree. It's strange you'd even allow her to be a call girl. She's your own daughter."

"Please spare me your concern for little miss perfect. She's been a pain in my ass since the day she was born. I'm just making her work in the house so she'll leave. She's like an alley cat. You feed it once, and you can't get rid of it."

"Wow," Clark muttered. I wanted to take her head off but stayed where I was.

"Don't make me remind you, Clark, I know your secrets too." I heard her heels click on the wooden floor before she spoke again. "Ones that could destroy her."

"We had a deal."

"Yes, we did, and a deal works both ways, so keep your dick in your pants."

***

Trigger

After sixteen hours, I slipped into off mode on the outside but gave in to the chaos happening inside. That was what they wanted, after all—for me to sweat. Thing was, there was no way they could pin that murder on me. There wasn't enough time for one of us to have done it. It was just a waiting game on their turf.

The mirror that faced me rattled slightly, more than likely from a door being shut. I waited for a moment and slowly let my lips part into a smile. The same smile I used whenever Doyle brought up his sister. It rattled again before the door opened, and there stood Doyle and Sam.

Sam tapped his side, which signaled me they had to let me go since there was no evidence.

Doyle's pissed-off face was the icing on the fucked-up cake. I stood and reached for my phone Sam held out before I towered over Doyle.

"The next time you think about arresting me and my men, you better have some goddamn good evidence. Now, move."

His face twitched, and he cleared his throat and stepped aside so I could pass.

"Where are the guys?" I grunted at Sam as he raced to catch up.

"Waiting in the car. You were harder to get released." He raised a hand and scrambled to get in front of me. I stopped and looked up from my phone. "Trigger, I need you to know this looks like a setup."

"I know."

He fixed his glasses and shifted his files from one hand to the other. Sam was a plump little man who looked like an inmate's bitch. His clothes were wrinkled, and his face was always beet red. But he was smart and had my back, even at the times I didn't think he had. Besides, he wouldn't fuck me over. He knew what I was capable of, and he had a family to lose. I had made it a point to meet the wife and kids when we first hooked up.

"You want to share anything with me? I need to be kept in the loop."

I rubbed my head. "My father is still alive." I let that sink in. "And, apparently, he is determined to get me six feet under, or behind bars, at least."

"Jesus Christ."

"Not even close." I stepped around him and scanned my text messages. Nothing else from Jace.

"Trigger, we need to discuss this."

I tapped Jace's contact info to start a call and turned to Sam. "We just did."

Cooper was at the curb in his 1966 Lincoln Continental convertible. Way flashy for my taste, but the guys had picked up our bikes, so it would have to do.

I slipped into the front seat and motioned for him to leave.

Jace finally answered on the sixth ring. "You're out?"

"You found Tess."

"I did. She's in Vegas."

I glanced away from the side mirror and closed my eyes. At least she was okay.

"Trigger, you need to know something."

"What?" *Fucking spit it out.*

"She is working as a prostitute."

I glanced back at Brick, who apparently heard Jace. He muttered something and looked out the window.

"You sure?"

"Yeah, and that Clark guy is a real dick."

"You met him?"

"He came in her room. He thought we were done." I pushed away the murderous thought of the two of them in bed together. "He wasn't happy. He wanted to see her after."

"And besides that?"

He took a moment to answer, and I wasn't sure why.

"Sad, man. She seemed just…sad. But you know Tess. She turned it to mad."

I rested my elbow on the open window and covered my eyes with my free hand.

"I don't wanna overstep here, but—"

I hung up and tossed my phone on the dash.

We all remained silent as I mulled over Jace's words.

What the fuck is she doing? And who *the fuck is she doing?*

"Hey, Trigger." Morgan stopped me before I went inside. He was visibly rocked by what went down. "I swear, man, I didn't—"

"I know." I moved around him and headed for my room. I needed a hot shower.

Cray and a few of his men stayed for dinner. Seven tables were pushed together, and Rail filled the guys in on what happened to the San Diego crew.

"I'll pay for the family to stay at the Hilton," Cray chimed in. He glanced at Moe, who shrugged. Moe barely felt much inside. I understood that and made sure he was directly under Cray in ranks. Unemotional people tended to screw up less.

"Yeah," Moe said. "I'll send someone to get them."

"Did you find anything?" I knew the answer was no. I would have heard if Moe had gotten his hands on the Harmos family.

"Nah, skipped town."

I nodded and nursed my beer. Morgan finally joined us but remained quiet. The whole situation played on him, and he needed to get over it.

This was all my father—what he did best. Fuck with people's heads.

"Trigger?" Big Joe stood in the doorway with a box. "This just came for you."

I flicked my head at Jace, and he jumped to get it. He set it in front of me and cut the tape along the top before he stepped back. Rising from my chair, I slowly opened it and pulled out Gator's leather cut. I slammed it on the table and lifted out the rest of the cuts piece by piece.

Anger surged. The guys were waiting for me to explode, and I was about to let fly when I saw there was an envelope taped to the bottom of the box.

What the fuck was this?

I glanced at Gus before I ripped the paper and freed the note.

Eight down. Who is next?

You want this to stop?

Step into the ring.

"It's a trap," Brick hissed from behind me. "He knows you can't resist the ring."

Gus made a strange noise, and I looked over.

"What?"

He shook his head, but he still cleared his throat, which meant he was going to give me his two cents anyway. "It's just what he wants."

"Did I say I was going to?"

"No, but addicts slip, and he's playin' you."

Fuck. I needed to be alone to work off some of the tension that was building. My fists were clenched tight, and I couldn't relax my fingers.

"Get these cuts cleaned up, and we'll give them to the families," I barked at Jace, and he quickly gathered them up without a word.

The door swung open, and my newest prospect, Rich, looked around the room, his excitement obvious.

"Excuse me." He blinked to find the right words for interrupting my fucking meeting. "Trigger, I saw some of them."

"Who?" My entire body immediately came to high alert.

"Five men from your father's army."

With a quick glance at Brick, we all stood and grabbed our weapons and followed Rich out back to where we had parked our bikes.

We didn't need a plan. We'd make one once we arrived and checked the place out.

"There." Rich pointed at a group of men who looked like they were part of a kid's birthday party being held at a park just outside the border of my territory on the Stripe Backs' land.

"How many kids?" Brick checked his phone.

"Ah," Rich craned his neck and looked around, "seven, no, ten. Ten kids in total. Including the baby on that chick's tit."

"You and Rail go around and draw them out. Brick and I will meet up behind."

I motioned for Cooper to go and headed around the cars to the other side.

"Ready?" Brick and I stood on either side of the line of Stripe Back bikes and tipped them in toward each other, so it was harder to stand them up in a rush. It would buy us an extra ten seconds or so.

We rushed in the opposite direction to create a distraction that would pull the Stripe Backs away from us.

Just as we rounded the area near the restrooms, we saw Cooper nail one of my father's men in the head with a rock. They jumped to their feet and started to chase them through the garden area and up to the road.

"What the fuck, Samuel!" One of the Stripe Back members had a kid by the collar. "I told you not to touch the bikes."

"Poppy, I didn't!"

I signaled for Brick to follow me. We stayed low and made our way through the path and up the hill where Cooper was getting his ass kicked, and Rail had one in a neck hold.

My knuckles were curled tight as stone, and my heart jump-started into high as I ran in and swung with all my might. One man flew into another, and they both went down, which gave me a few seconds to take out the fucker on Cooper's back. I felt a blow to my shoulder and whirled to cave in the face of the first guy I could reach.

Pound.

Pound.

Pound.

My muscles screamed me on, and I reveled in each bone I broke. One by one, we took out each man, and every hit I took amped up my desire to kill.

"Where is Allen?" I heard Cooper shout at one of the men. "Where is he?"

The bastard laughed as blood drained from his mouth. "The Father is too protected, his army too big." His heavy accent made his words hard to follow. "You don't find him, he finds you."

"You're dead, anyway."

"*Sí*, but I die knowing where Father is. You," he poked Cooper's chest, "do not."

I stepped over and snapped his neck.

"He won't talk."

Cooper grabbed his legs and dragged the body to a nearby car. We had found it unlocked earlier and decided to fill the trunk with our gift.

I jumped back into the fight. Fuck, I needed this.

Rail's guy was huge, so I took over. I got lost in the fight. He was almost my size, but his swing was shit. He lasted at least a few minutes on his feet before he went down like a fucking tree.

My chest heaved with a cocktail of thirst and fuel. I needed more, but they were dead. I glanced back at the party and saw the Stripe Backs were aware of our visit, so it was time to go.

"Snap a photo, cut their fingers, and send them to the church. No note, just leave a bag of coke with our symbol. Whether he's still there or not, it'll get back to him."

"Wish I could see your old man's face when he opens it." Brick huffed and pulled out his phone. "Tess?" His tone was off. "Tess, hon, is that you?"

My legs were moving before my mind kicked in. He turned and caught my expression, and his face twisted with worry.

"You need to tell me what's going on."

CHAPTER SIX

Tess

The DVD was on a seven-second loop. I watched my beautiful friend Mags as she came into the viewing room at the house to meet her baby's father, and what happened next made me go cold with shock and throw up my dinner.

My legs went out from under me as I slid down the wall in the far corner of my room. My cell phone was still on airplane mode as it shook in my hands. I watched the little plane disappear and change to the cell reception icon. My knuckles were white, and I didn't know what else to do, so I gave in.

I swiped my thumb over his number and pressed call. Heavy, hot tears raced down my face, each one reminding me of my new truth.

"Hello?" His voice made my stomach hurt.

"Brick?" I whispered. I needed him so much right now.

"Tess." There was a pause. "Tess, hon, is that you?" I pictured his face and how much he must hate me for leaving. "Are you okay? Where are you?" He stopped his chatter and waited a beat before he spoke again. "You need to tell me what's going on."

I tried to get my head to work, but the words came out jumbled. "He strangled her." I sobbed and rolled to my side. Everything hurt.

"Who strangled who, Tess?"

"Clark," I choked out. "He killed Mags! George was there and helped get rid of her. Mom ordered them around. I can't breathe. I always thought it was George, not…" My heart fought for room in my chest. Air was trapped half way up, and everything was tangled up inside.

"Shit." He covered the phone and said something. "Tess, are you there now?"

"Matt," I sobbed out his real name, and it felt good to say it, "I'm so sorry—"

"No," he shouted. "I don't know what black shit is going through your head right now, Tess. But you have nothing to be sorry for. I'm going to fly out to you tonight. I'm going to take you home, okay?"

"I can't." I felt so tired. My body needed sleep. It always shut down when things became too much. "I don't know everything yet."

"I think you got your answers."

Before I could explain that wasn't what I meant, he hung up. I needed to lie down for a while. I didn't bother changing, I just slipped on a robe and climbed on top of the covers.

I raced up the slippery steps of the old wheat mill. You had to be so careful where you stepped. It had been abandoned about fifteen years ago. Rusty nails, broken windows, or trash could take you down in a flash.

I reached for the metal rail for support as my heart beat out of my chest and vibrated up my throat. The three guys were only two floors below and were gaining on me fast. It had been a stupid move, me trying to get the blanket back. They had grabbed it the night before last, and I'd nearly frozen to death without it. I thought they were out of it drunk when I pulled it free, but I had underestimated their street smarts, and they were on me pretty fast.

I hit the top floor and frantically glanced for a place to hide or for a weapon to use.

Nothing.

I raced for the stairs on the other side of the room. Just as I flew through the open the door, I heard them yell.

I dodged all the weak-looking patches on the steps and leapt down three, nearly falling on my ass.

My mind raced to figure out a game plan once outside. This exit led to an alleyway, and if they beat me down there, I would have no way of getting out.

I knew I could kick and knee hard, so I focused all my energy on that as I burst through the door and fell at a hit to the back of my legs.

Shit.

"Wow." One guy grinned down at me, and it took a moment for my brain to clear.

"I get first dip." Another groaned as he held his dick with his dirty

fingers. "Let's see what we're dealing with."

Two hands clamped down on my ankles. I kicked and twisted, but another grabbed my wrists.

"No!" I screamed and bucked with all my might, but they were too strong. I wasn't sure how many there were, but I could tell who the ringleader was. He bent over me and tried to wiggle off my pants while the others held me tight. My head jerked, and I tried to bite at the closest arm.

"Stop! Get off me!" My lungs nearly burst when I sucked in and screamed again, hoping to scare them off.

The man above me started to cut my jeans off with a blade while yelling at the others to hold me still. In hindsight, I should have been more scared of the pocketknife skimming past my flesh, but better to get a wild infection than be poked by this sick son of a bitch with his whore of a dick.

"Damn, no panties!" He licked his lips.

"You touch me, and I promise I'll bend your dick like a goddamned balloon animal." I hissed and thrashed again and was able to knee his friend in the face.

"Fuckin' bitch!" The guy held his bloody nose. "Do it, already, Glen!"

"Mm, I love how soft a girl's thighs are."

I wanted to puke, but instead I focused my energy on where I was going to head butt next.

His hands moved higher up, and I prepared for when he bent down. Tears gushed, but I hardly felt them. My muscles were locked in place when his fingers reached my upper thigh.

"No! Help!" I screamed and bucked, but he was ready for it, and a heavy roar from an exhaust drowned out my cries.

"Relax, darling. You're going to love this."

Oh, my God, this was going to happen, right here, in this alley below a bright green neon sign that advertised the show girls next door. It would be the day I died inside. I thought the house was rough, but this…this was something else.

I felt him move into position, and I squeezed my eyes shut and waited for him to make any kind of move.

Someone will make a mistake.

Just when I thought his dick would tear into me, I felt him jerk off me. My eyes flew open, and there was a guy I'd never seen before beating the shit out of him. One by one, he fought them all off, plowing one guy's head into a wall. His hand rose and fell with a sickening sound. I wasted no time getting out of there and ran back into the mill where my stuff was hidden in one of the corners. Somehow, I managed to put a pair of shorts on and got my stuff swung over my back.

I raced to the window and looked down. My attackers were all on the ground, knocked out cold or dead. I didn't care which. Then I heard a noise and whirled around as the guy found me. He had short, messy hair, wore a hoodie, and had a backpack of his own.

I was trying to decide on an escape route when he held up his hands. "I'm just making sure you're okay."

I held my stuff closer to my body. "I'm fine." I stepped back and wondered why he helped me. In my experience on the streets, no one ever helped, fearing they'd become a target too.

"Okay, good." He looked around then back at me again. "Are you here by yourself?"

"You care, because...?"

"Because you'll only get jumped again if you are."

I shrugged, and my defenses went up. "Been doing pretty well on my own so far."

He smirked. "Bet you have to keep moving."

"Yeah." He was right about that, and I didn't need to lie. Truth was, I didn't have a spot that was my own. "So?"

"You always this friendly after someone helps you out?"

I couldn't help myself and responded to his warm smile. I sighed and dropped my pack to the floor, exhausted. I followed suit and sat back against the cool wall. "Sorry." I tried to relax, but the memory of what almost happened began to surface. "That was fucking scary."

He slowly approached and sat warily but at a respectable distance, which I appreciated. "It was."

We sat in silence for a few moments before he moved in a bit and held out a hand. "Matt."

"Tess."

Sirens filled the room, and we jumped to our feet.

"Shit." He rushed to the window. "I dropped the brick I was using on them down there. We need to go. Can you run?"

"Yeah."

"Good. Hold my hand." We disappeared down the stairs.

***

Trigger

We stopped for gas and something to drink at the M Resort Casino just off the Fifteen Freeway. It had been pouring all night, so our drive took much longer than normal. Even on a bike, splitting traffic was a bitch. Every driver in any vehicle would be so intent on keeping themselves from hydroplaning they sure as hell wouldn't see us on the road.

"That semi drenched me." Brick wrung out his pant leg. "I wanted to blow out his tires."

I grunted out an agreement and poured a shitty cup of coffee from the corner store tucked into the side of the entryway. I eyed the creamer and saw a layer of curdled dairy on the top. I tossed it in the trash and grabbed a fresh one from the fridge.

"Sir, you can't—" The young clerk's sentence trailed off when she took in my annoyed face. "Never mind."

I grabbed a protein bar and held out a twenty to the girl then wiped my hair out of my eyes. Her cheeks were pink as she slid it away from me and proceeded to make change.

"You guys staying at the resort?" She glanced at me again.

"No." I left a five and headed out with Brick behind me. I stopped under a dry spot and lit a joint. The rain was still heavy and showed no sign of letting up.

"How far?"

Brick lit his and blew out before he answered me. "Fifteen. I've never been past the gates, but if Jace got in, you know you will. It all comes down to the money."

I eyed the pack on the side of my bike and hoped Eli had come through with what I asked.

"Jesus." Brick shuddered like he had just had a nasty thought. "That house has some crazy shit darkness inside."

I tilted my head back to stare up at the clouds and hoped she was alone right now. I knew I would kill someone if she wasn't.

"What happened that made her go back to that house the last time you guys split up?"

Brick closed his eyes. "Well, I want to know why she stayed away for six years more."

I didn't point out he avoided my question. He'd told me a lot, and I respected that. For now.

"Come on." I tossed my joint into the dirt and started my bike. As I eased out, I caught sight of a man in a truck staring at us.

Do I know you? His face tugged a recent memory, but I couldn't place him.

Once we hit the road, I clicked the button on my helmet.

"You see the tan truck as we left?"

"No."

"Tan, Chevy, two-door. Keep an eye out."

"Copy that." He gave me a thumbs up.

Lightning shot across the sky as we turned into the Wynn parking lot around three-thirty in the morning. We pulled up to the valet and handed the kid our keys. One glance at my cut, and he handed me my ticket. I hated the idea of someone else riding my bike, but I knew the kid would probably roll it into place by how scared he looked.

"You good?" He nodded at me. "Look after it."

"Of course."

Inside, Eli was in the lobby waiting for us, dressed like he owned the place. Well, maybe that was because he was the owner's stepson.

"Nice to see you again," he greeted us but took note that I wasn't in the mood to gamble or drink. "Please follow me."

We headed to the elevators where we joined an older couple. The guy had a tiny poodle thing stuck in his arms that whined when we came closer.

Don't blame it. The couple shifted closer to the far wall and turned the dog to face away from us.

Once on the thirty-ninth floor, Eli took us to our room. He opened the door and pointed to the table. The place had glass floor to ceiling windows.

"Everything you will need is here." He pointed to my ID, bank account number, and car keys. "And, of course," he motioned for me to look, "your pick of clothing." There was a garment rack thick with outfits for me to try.

I glared at Brick, who had already broken into the fully stocked bar. "Suck it up, Trigger. If you want to get in, you need to play the part."

"Fuck." The last time I wore a suit was when I won my last fight. My asshole father scammed a gambler, and I had to play a part in that shit too. *Hated every minute of it.*

Eli waved around. "The kitchen is stocked, bar is too. You have the room for however long you need." He stepped closer and rubbed above his lip. "You need help, you know my number. All I ask is keep it out of my hotel."

"Like you did my club?"

Eli had enemies too and brought them right to the steps of my club. He owed me, and he knew it.

He pressed his hands down his suit uneasily, but before he left, he plastered on a smile and said, "Enjoy."

Brick set a bottle of whiskey on the counter. "You'll need this before you go."

I downed about a quarter before I moved to look out over the Strip. An unexpected memory of Tess drew my head elsewhere.

"Does the name Lily mean anything to you?"

I watched Brick's reflection in the window, and he went still and hesitated before he answered.

"Tess didn't have many friends in the house until a girl named Mags arrived. She was from North Carolina and had dreams of being a showgirl. Of course, she got tangled up in some shit and ended up at the house looking for fast cash. Mags and Tess hit it off right away. A few years later, Mags got involved with a client who got her pregnant and then proceeded to beat Mags whenever she didn't do as she was told. Lily was four when her mother was killed. They said it was a pill overdose in the living room, but now we know it wasn't." He sank into a chair. "I hate that Tess had to see that video."

"Where's Lily now?" I downed some more whiskey.

"Parents. They're here now."

"The boyfriend?"

"He's around, draining her parents dry. I'm assuming that's why Tess cuts her paychecks in half, to help them out."

"Not her problem." I shrugged.

"It kinda is. Mags left Lily to Tess."

I turned around as I absorbed that.

"Yeah, but Tess doesn't want kids. She's got too much going on inside to raise a child. Besides, Mags's parents are good people. They wanted to raise her, so Tess agreed. Trouble is they don't have much money, especially after hiring shitty investigators to look into Mags's death. Their lawyer was bought off and ran off with their money."

"Shit luck."

"Hmm." He opened a beer and made a nasty face at the taste. "You should see Tess with Lily. They have a bond."

"I'll take your word on it." I didn't want kids. Never had.

Brick nodded. "You better get ready."

CHAPTER SEVEN

Tess

I started to wake, hating that feeling of being emotionally exhausted, but my body begged me to move. I stretched then felt like someone was watching me. I jolted upright and glanced around through dry, scratchy eyes.

Empty. The room was empty. Just like me.

With all my willpower, I peeled off the bed, showered, and changed into another house uniform.

I glanced at my phone to see if the doctor had emailed or called, but there was nothing. I pushed that dark cloud aside. Couldn't worry about something that hadn't happened yet.

I squeezed my eyes shut and held onto the counter for support.

Don't cry, Tess. You're stronger than this. That terrible video played over and over in my mind. How could I face them? I wanted to scream and tear them all apart with my bare hands. How could they do that to Mags? This place had taken so much from me. How I fucking hated it.

I had to pull myself together, as I had to in the past. I forced all grief from my mind and allowed the anger to flow through me and used it to steady myself. I moved purposefully to my bedside table and slipped a cuff over my wrist, dried the tears, and eyed my knife and envisioned it slicing through his skin and into his black heart.

Fuck. I shook off the craving and headed downstairs. It wasn't time. Soon, but not yet.

The main floor was busy, as usual. The bar was in full swing. That was Vegas for you. No sleep, just sex, booze, and endless amounts of money. I spotted Clark at a table with a young girl. I assumed it was the cocaine junkie's new replacement. He spotted me and nodded for me to come over.

I want to carve your heart out and jam it on a stick, so everyone can see your lies.

I loathe you.

I turned away and headed in the opposite direction. I wasn't ready to face him yet, and the odds of me losing it were high. Again, I pictured myself snapping off his balls and jamming them down his throat, and it made me feel a little better.

I noticed my mother flirting with a client in the living room, right about where she helped kill Mags, and my stomach rolled, but I reminded myself I was here for a reason. I hadn't felt this emotional in a long time, and frankly, I despised it. Nowhere was safe. Everywhere I looked, there were liars and murderers. How was I going to do this? How could I be here?

I could slice them both up and bury them under the house. Lord knew how many bodies were already there.

I can't do this. I can't be here.

"Tessa?" Rachel called out, slapping me back to the present. "Can you come here, please?"

Shit. No!

"Wow, rough night?" She narrowed in on my face. I wondered if she knew the truth, and if she saw the video too. "Jesus, Tessa, what happened?"

"That's a loaded question." *I wish I had my loaded gun.*

She waved off my sarcasm, and her whole face lit up. "Well, snap out of it 'cause you have a client who requested you. Damn, you must be a freak in bed, girl."

Jace is here? The vise around my chest loosened a notch.

"Same guy as last time, right?"

"Nope." She pointed behind me, and I felt the vise tighten again.

Then, who?

My heart jumped into my throat when I saw him. Trigger sat in a chair, relaxed like he belonged there. His intense green eyes locked onto mine, and I felt the unforgettable hold he had on me. He slowly rose and buttoned his jacket with ease.

Jacket?

Wow. He was dressed in a dark gray three-piece suit. A navy-blue dress shirt peeked out from under his gray and black tie.

Wait…his hair was different. Shit, he looked more intense than ever.

My clit strummed to my wild heartbeat.

He strolled toward me, his broad shoulders a reminder of how large he was. He extended his hand and waited.

Breathe, Tess.

I hesitated, unsure if my body would work. Cautiously, I slipped my hand into his.

If it was possible to orgasm from a simple touch, it would be from his.

"Tess." He nodded and squeezed my hand, but didn't let go. "I've been waiting patiently for you."

Oh, my God, what was he doing here? I started to freak the fuck out inside. I hoped to God Clark hadn't spotted him, but he was deep in conversation with another man.

I battled with wanting to kill everyone and the fact that Trigger stood in front of me.

So many things fired off inside my head at once, I couldn't seem to find my voice.

He leaned toward my ear, still holding my hand, and I couldn't help but turn into him. Heat poured off his neck, and my head went light.

"Take me somewhere, Tess."

The fog lifted.

It was like his words brought me back to a sudden clarity. I dropped his hand, stepped out of his space, and glanced at the time on the desk.

"Well, I know I'm booked today, sir, but if you can wait, I'm sure we can work something out."

He clicked his tongue as he absorbed what I said, and then he glanced around. "I have all the time in the world to wait for you, darling. I could use a drink."

"Tessa, dear, who is this?"

Fuck. My mother shot a fresh dose of panic through my veins. *This cannot be happening.*

Trigger studied her and made the connection quickly, as we are basically twins. He muttered something, but I couldn't make it out.

My mother extended her hand limply and gave him a slutty smile. "Felicia. I'm the owner of this house."

Trigger didn't acknowledge her hand, just stared at her.

Oh, shit. I hope he doesn't lose it. Well, actually…

My mother looked at me, confused, but kept her smile plastered on her Botoxed face.

Yes, mother, it's hard to believe, but you can't use sex as a weapon on all men.

"So," she came behind the desk, "who are you scheduled to see today?"

"He's here to see Tessa," Rachel answered for him. "He won't see anyone else."

"Tessa seems to be fully booked today, sir."

Rachel pointed to the screen, and my mother's face changed.

"My, my. Well, let me see what I can do."

Yeah, she saw his bank account.

"I'll just move Bret to your lunch break. Lord knows you could skip a meal here and there," she muttered, and I felt my face flush. She cleared her throat when she realized what she had said in front of a potential customer and tried to backpedal.

"Tessa knows I joke."

Bitch.

"Actually, we were just going to have a drink. Come this way, sir." I pushed by her, and Trigger reached out to take my elbow. He kept a good pace as he steered us into the bar area but away from the other girls who were busy entertaining their own clients.

Clark glanced in our direction, but he didn't seem to recognize Trigger, or at least he didn't let on that he did. Many men like Trigger had come through our doors. As long as they had the money, they were allowed in.

Jesus. My nerves were shot. Once we were out of earshot, I forced a big smile at Trigger to keep up the facade.

"What the hell are you doing here, Trigger?" I was moments from losing my shit. My two worlds were colliding in the worst possible way. I should have known he might come after Jace filled him in. I was angry with myself as well as him.

"I needed to talk—"

"So, you thought coming here was the best idea?"

He brushed his tongue over his teeth and tugged on his tie. "What was I supposed to do? Call? Email? You're unreachable."

"You *told* me to leave, if I remember correctly." I didn't want to toss it in his face, but come on.

"I had to say that to you, Tess. I had my reasons. It's part of what I need to talk to you about."

"Hey, Tessa." Bret popped out of fucking nowhere holding a glass of scotch. Damn, he stank.

"Get lost, man." Trigger stood straighter.

"You can't claim the women here." Bret laughed. "Gotta pay for a spot." He reached out and fingered the corset between my breasts, like always.

Die, Bret. Just die.

Trigger reached out slowly and took Bret's hand and squeezed it so hard he had to let go, all the while holding Bret's gaze with his cold, green eyes. "Let's not make a scene here, but if you touch her again, I will kill you."

"Jesus, man. I pay a lot of money for this chick to ride me, and I've booked her right now."

I was about to blow. "I'm so sorry, Bret, but there was a conflict. Felicia wants to see you."

"Mm, I just might work out a mother-daughter combo." He sneered at Trigger.

I closed my eyes and moved the hair out of my face. I guessed my secret was out anyway. Trigger had made it quite clear he wasn't okay with who I was back at the church, so why should I care?

"Did you sleep with him?" Trigger didn't hide his disgust.

Oh, hell no!

"If I did?"

"Did you?"

"Un-fucking-believable." I covered my face to take a moment to think. I needed him out of here. "What do you want, Trigger? I really don't have a whole lot left inside me right now."

"I told you I want to talk."

"Now isn't a good time."

"When?" He crossed his arms. I tried hard to figure out something.

I looked around to see who was watching. "Look, there's a café down the street called Brew. Meet me there at four p.m."

"Fine."

I waited for him to leave, but he didn't. "Why aren't you leaving?"

He waved the bartender over. "I think I might stay, check the place out."

"No."

"Whiskey, top shelf."

"Of course." The bartender acted quickly.

"No, Trigger, you can't stay here."

"Watch me."

Fuck! Stubborn ass.

My hand landed on his arm, and he stared at it then closed his eyes. I almost forgot what it was like to be close to him. To touch him. To be the only one who could.

"There were reasons why I left, and one of those reasons is over there." I tilted my head. "You want to talk, and so do I. Please," I whispered. "Please don't start anything. I don't know how much more I can take right now."

He followed my line of sight then turned back to me. His gaze fell to my neck, and warmth spread between my legs. My skin heated, and I knew I wanted him to do something about it, but that would have to wait.

"I have to go." I was about to step back when his arm locked around my waist.

He leaned in and brushed his lips over my earlobe. "I'll make you a deal."

I could barely handle how close he was again.

"If you're not wet, I'll behave. If you are, it's fair game. After all, look where we are."

"Trigger." I nearly panted as his free hand slid down my side, over my hip, and curled around the edge of my panties. Before I could stop him, he stroked my folds with the pads of his fingers. He chuckled and slipped his fingers inside me with ease.

"You lose." His voice vibrated through me.

I reached out and held his shoulder for support. The fact we were in public failed to matter. Trigger knew exactly how to stroke to build me up.

"D to the N," Shantee chimed in behind me. I pulled quickly out of his hold and pushed his hand away. Trigger looked like he might murder her. "I heard there was some new meat in the house, but no one prepared me for this." Shantee reached out to touch Trigger, and I grabbed her hand and pulled her closer.

"Shantee, meet…" I stumbled to come up with a name.

"Don't need a name, sweetheart." She bit her finger in an attempt to be sexy. "I just want to know what side of the road he drives on."

Trigger downed his drink as I asked for another. "Straight, but flattered."

I was pleasantly shocked by Trigger's manners.

"Well, give me time." She turned to me. "Venna is looking for you. Said you took her shift, and you need to be there now."

"Shit, that's right. Okay, thanks."

Trigger eyed me sideways. "Shift?"

***

Trigger

I sat in my car outside the gate and sent off a few emails and touched base with the guys. Cooper told me my father got the package. We were waiting for what would come next. Eye for an eye, bitch. I never started this war.

Truth be told, I couldn't watch Tess dance. I'd kill someone, and she didn't need that right now. She had agreed to talk later, and that was enough for me.

Brick: You kill anyone yet?

Trigger: Night's still early.

Brick: How is she?

Trigger: Guarded.

Brick: Clark's got his claws in her, then?

Trigger: Yeah.

A flash of purple raced by the window, and it took me a moment to squint through the rain to see it was Tess. She looked to be in a hurry in her high heels and house outfit.

What the hell?

I slammed the car into drive and eased up beside her. She stopped, closed her eyes, and muttered something before she opened the door and slipped in.

I blasted the warm air and moved my bag to the back seat before I headed out into the flow of the traffic.

"What happened to your shift?" I eyed her outfit, and she covered herself with the soaking wet robe.

"Couldn't do it."

"Why?"

"Trigger—" She stopped herself and looked out the window. "Just forget it."

She stayed quiet but wiped her cheeks a few times. Her damp hair made it hard to read her face, but she needed time to get over her pissed off feelings.

I pulled up to the Wynn and tossed the keys at the kid who jumped when I parked.

"Good evening, sir. Do you need any help this evening?"

"No." I pulled the bag from the back seat and wrapped my jacket around her shoulders. I placed my hand on her back to steer her to the elevators. Once inside, she put distance between us, so I closed the gap, and again my hand was on her hip.

I pulled the key free and opened the door and waited for her to come in. She hesitated until she heard the TV. She peered inside and saw Brick as he poured a beer into his Cheerios. He looked her over as if to see if she was okay before he went back to his show.

"You look like shit, Tess."

She rolled her eyes and came further into the room.

"Yeah, hell will wear you out."

"How was the bitch?"

Her shaky fingers tucked a piece of hair behind her ear. "She booked me solid."

"To dance?"

"No."

Brick flicked off the TV and turned to face her. All fun was gone. He started to approach her but thought better of it and stood back. "Tess, you didn't." He rubbed his head. "Please tell me you—"

"Venna is back. We made a deal that she'd take my clients, and I'd dance. She needed the money more." She glanced at me then quickly looked away. "It wasn't easy and took me to a dark place, but it was only temporary."

"Temporary? Why did you even go back?"

I slammed a glass on the bar and filled it to the top with whiskey.

"He's just pissy he had to wear a suit." Brick waved me off. "Tess, did Clark…I mean, did he do anything?"

Her silence pulled my attention in their direction. Tess shook her head and moved over to the bar. "Pour me one of those. I've things to tell you, but I need a shower first."

Brick pointed to my room. "Towels are under the sink."

"Thanks." She pulled my jacket off her shoulders and hung it on the back of the chair.

Brick waited for the water to start running before he joined me at the bar.

"Well?" I grew impatient.

"I'm glad we got to her when we did. It's obvious she knows something she's not ready to talk about."

"Any idea?"

"My guess would be the million-dollar question why Tess stayed at the house for six years."

I tugged the tie off and tossed it on the table and unbuttoned the shirt. I wanted to change into my cut and jeans, but Eli had advised me to dress the part of a businessman so as not to draw too much attention to the fact that we were here.

I ordered room service, and when the bellman arrived, he glanced over my shoulder and smiled. I followed his line of sight and found Tess in one of my t-shirts. A part of me was glad she didn't choose one of the dress shirts. I liked her in my clothes.

"You like your dick?" I snapped at the bellman, who couldn't seem to keep his eyes off her.

"Sorry." He straightened and handed me the slip. "If you could sign here."

I signed and shoved it back at him.

He pointed to one of the covered plates. "Here is your steak with sweet potatoes and—"

"I ordered it," I reminded him.

"Right." He peeked at Tess again, and my temper rose. "Is there anything I can get you, miss?"

Tess came to my side and shook her head. "Thank you."

"Of course." He didn't leave.

I pulled out my gun and checked the clip. It was full. The man cleared his throat then turned and left quickly.

She sighed. "That was rude."

"He was staring at you."

"So do you," she challenged.

"That's different."

"How?" She propped her hands on her hips and lifted her chin.

"You're mine."

For a split second, I saw her flinch, but she kept it together.

"Was," she corrected before she turned back to the bedroom.

"Where the hell are you going?"

"Bed."

"You need to eat, and we need to talk."

She glanced back at me from the doorway. "I do appreciate you ordering it, but I'm not hungry. I'm also super tired, Trigger. I need to sleep."

Fine.

Later that night, the rain turned into a storm and lit up the entire place. Tess took Brick's room, and he slept on the couch in the other room.

My head was chaos. The demons wouldn't sleep, so I drank to keep them quiet. I lit a joint and kicked my feet up on the rail of the balcony. Whenever the rain blew, I got sprayed, but the cold felt good on my throbbing head.

It was a habit to sit in the far corner of a space, so no one could sneak up behind me. Plus, fewer people would interact with the lurker in the shadows.

I wasn't a fan of Vegas. Too many fights held here, too many desperate women looking to trap a man into marriage.

My dick twitched when I saw Tess step out onto the balcony with her phone to her ear. I strained to listen over the storm.

"I'm sorry, Ven. I just needed to step back for the night." She sounded exhausted. She paused to listen then dropped her head. "Yeah, he's just someone from my past."

Just? I didn't like that word.

"Clark will be fine. No, I don't want to talk to him. Tell him I'll be back tomorrow." She rubbed her head. "Thanks, girl. I'll make it up to you somehow." She hung up and ran her hand through her hair before she caught me out of the corner of her eye. I drew back the smoke and let it coat my lungs, taking in her body under my shirt.

"Jesus, Trigger." She held her chest. "Miss your pickup much?"

I smiled at her comment; she had a point. I did. I liked how I could blend in the shadows in the back of my truck.

The wind blew her shirt back, outlining her body. Her nipples grew hard, and so did my erection.

"What are you doing out here?"

I flicked the joint then handed it to her. She thought for a moment before she stepped up and was careful not to make skin to skin contact.

She sat on the footstool and crossed her legs, hiking the shirt up further.

"Couldn't sleep."

She blew out the smoke and nodded. "Understand that one." She jumped when a clap of thunder burst above us. "I like your hair."

I was pleased she liked it and took that moment to lean over and pull her stool between my legs. Her hands landed on my shoulders to stabilize herself.

"You need to be closer."

"Why?"

I pointed to my head. "The only time they're quiet is when you're near me."

"It's all mental, Trigger. You can override that shit."

I leaned closer, using my size to prove my point. "No, Tess, only you can." My lips were close to hers, and I smelled her arousal lingering in the heavy mist around us. I wanted to attack her, dominate her, but I didn't yet. The Clark thing hung between us. He was too close and had sunk his claws in too deep.

She dipped her head to block my access. "We should talk first."

"Then, talk." I moved her legs apart and slid my hands up her smooth, cool thighs. It was as if someone draped a cloak over my demons' cages, granting me a moment of sanity. I suddenly became thirsty for her taste, my tongue begging to lap at her skin.

Her hands landed on mine, but it didn't stop me. She moved out of my hold and stood at the balcony. I covered her back with my front and slipped my hand into her wet panties. I parted her smooth folds and slipped two fingers inside.

Her head flopped back onto my shoulder, but I felt her desire to fight me. My mouth latched onto her neck and drew in her intoxicating taste. My erection was painful, so with a free hand, I let it out and lined up with her. Before she could protest, I dove in until I hit my base.

She screamed and arched her back. I held her tightly and sucked harder.

I could barely think as her walls adjusted to my size. I hiked her leg up on the chair and leaned back to get a different angle. I drew out to my tip and slammed back in. She screamed my name and clawed at my arm around her stomach.

"Harder." She reached back inside my pants and cupped my balls. My switch was dangerously close to flipping. She drove me wild as her nails dug my flesh.

"Tess," I warned through a locked jaw, "careful."

"Careful?" she bit out and pulled away so I'd slip out. The loss of contact made me instantly angry. "Careful of what? Because you've lost your shit on me before? Or are you saying careful, like you might throw it in my face that I'm a whore?"

What the fuck?

"I never called you a whore, Tess."

"You may not have said the word." She stepped back when I came near her.

"Don't walk away from me." I saw red, and my dick grew hot.

"You screw anyone while I was gone, Trigger?"

I hated the head games, but I hated to be questioned more.

"I can fuck whoever I want." I marched up and backed her into the corner. "When I want."

Her hand rested on my chest, and her head dropped, but not before I saw the sadness in her eyes. "Then you don't need me."

That stopped me in my tracks and held me in place, and she slipped around me and disappeared inside.

I hated my fucking ego.

CHAPTER EIGHT

Tess

The next morning, I woke to a pounding headache. I showered and put my house clothes back on. Careful not to wake Brick, I searched for my shoes, but they weren't in the room.

Damn. I must have kicked them off in the living room.

Thankfully, the place was quiet, and I found my shoes by the coffee table. Just as I slipped the second one on, I heard the couch squeak.

"Tess?" Brick rubbed his eyes. "Where are you going?"

I stood and headed for the door. "I need to go to work."

"What?"

"I'll call you later."

"Hang on—"

I opened the door to Trigger holding a tray of coffee cups.

He used his bulk as he moved forward and forced me to back up. He shot me the most pissed off look and handed me a Starbucks coffee.

"Brick." He held my gaze, and Brick headed for the bedroom, leaving us alone.

"I'm late. I need to go." I held up the coffee. "Thank you."

He beat me to the door and slammed it shut. His arms folded over his chest, and I got hit with the scent of his body soap. I flinched, and I knew he caught it.

"I didn't drive four and half hours, dress in a fuckin' monkey suit, and be in the same room with your goddamned ex just for you to sneak out on me."

"I never asked you to do that." I felt like a child with my response, but if he was going to use that excuse, I was going to remind him of mine.

He took a step closer, and I held my ground. "Do you want to be there?"

"No."

He threw his hands in the air with an exasperated sigh. "Then why the fuck are you going back?"

"Because of you!" I shouted, and his face twisted in confusion. "You may think I'm a whore, and that I'm beyond fixable, and you know what? I am. I don't wanna be fixed." I pointed to my head. "I deal with my fucking demons too. My past is way more fucked than even Brick knows." Tears streamed down my cheeks.

"Then share! You said you wanted to talk, that you had something to tell me." His voice made my ribcage rattle.

"Why? So you can throw that in my face too?"

"No, so I can understand!"

Oh. Well, he asked for it.

"I fell in love with a man at ten years old. He made me feel like I had a place in this world." My throat burned with the words. "That I wasn't just a fuck-up in the back of a dingy strip joint. He loved me. He talked to me and bought me shiny things. We had secrets. It was wrong, I see that now, but it felt so good. I was happy and felt loved." I angrily brushed my tears away. "My mother was and is a jealous bitch and saw he wanted her money. She hated what I had, so she used him and got him to marry her. I'm not stupid, and I know he saw an equal opportunity and went along with it." I yanked up my bracelets to show my scar. "Just another reminder of my failure as a woman. You wanna know what happened after my mother brought me back from the psych ward? She made sure I would see them having sex, or kissing. She wanted me to try this again," I held up my wrist, "and she still does."

I stopped to catch my breath, and he stared.

"Clark tried everything to get me to understand why he married my mom. Said he had to for us to be together. Didn't take that long for me to fall for him again. Love is like that, especially when you're young. My eighteenth birthday, he took me to on a weekend trip where we had sex for the first time."

I hoped that stung him as much as it did me telling this story.

"He stole my heart and my virginity. I thought things would be different then, but every time my mother won, and every time my world would crash around me. There's so many broken pieces of me floating around inside, I don't know what fits where, and what doesn't."

I couldn't go on. I couldn't go that one step further and utter the horror that might tip the scale too far. I was permanently scarred.

"The last six years after I left Brick at the warehouse…" My shame got hold of me, and I stopped. "Look…"

I took a deep breath, but it was no use. I was too vulnerable to be rational.

"I made a promise that I wouldn't step foot inside that house after I left, after he stole the very last piece of me." I started to cry harder.

"Why did you? What did you mean, you did it for me?" he asked softly as he kept a safe distance away. I didn't blame him. I was a mess.

I eased into the chair, too tired to stand. "It's what I wanted to tell you, why I came to you in the church. That day, I heard Detective Aaron on the phone, talking to Clark about how he had something that could destroy your club. Clark was pissed because Aaron didn't keep his end of the bargain."

"Which was?"

"Me for the information."

Trigger popped his neck.

"I hid in the van. Jace and Morgan had no idea. I just wanted to tell you, and I didn't know when you'd be back. But you…" I closed my eyes for a moment before I stood on shaky legs. "I need to go back before Clark sends someone else to find me or leaks whatever information he has on you."

"Tess…" He rubbed his face.

"Please don't. I don't want to hear an apology."

"I'm not sorry."

I huffed out a laugh. "Of course, you're not." I headed for the door, but he hooked my arm and swung me around to face him.

"I'm not sorry for lying. Brick never told me. I just knew you were hiding something, so I played dirty. You never listen to me, so I had to hurt you so you would. I know you're still lying about it. Maybe not lying, but you're holding something back. But," he moved closer, "that man dressed as a Father of the Church…is actually my own father."

What?

"But…"

"I would have said anything to get you as far away from that man as possible. You think I scare you, times that by ten."

"But I heard you killed him."

He broke eye contact and shook his head. "I'm still trying to figure that out."

Wow, I wasn't expecting that.

He cursed and looked back at me; his eyes held so much emotion. "You've seen many sides of me, Tess, and accepted me in spite of it all. But the hole that opened in me when I saw my father standing there, still with a heartbeat, did something to me I can't explain. When you showed up, I had to get you away from him. He may have looked like a man of the Church, but believe me, he is wicked fuckin' Satan underneath. We might share demons, darlin', but mine would seriously hurt you."

I stepped into him, unable to stop myself. Trigger, raw with words, was indescribable. I reached up to show my intent and ran my hand over his cheek. His eyes bore through me. I knew we were both shitty at the intimacy part, but I wanted to show I heard him. I wanted to show him I was trying.

"You…" He stumbled and tried again with a harsher tone. "You are the last person I would want to hurt."

"Okay."

He nodded once but kept his hand locked around my arm as if I grounded him.

"Do you still love him?" he blurted, and my hand dropped away.

I fought with the wall that wanted to shoot up.

"We have a history, Trigger."

"That's not what I asked."

"I know." I took a sip of my coffee and backed up. Surprisingly, he let me go.

"He killed your best friend. How are you going to tell me you still love him?"

He was right. I was sure I didn't, but for whatever reason, I couldn't say the words.

"I need to go."

He blocked my path just as Brick, who no doubt was eavesdropping, came into the room.

"Tess," he said, "I really don't think you should go back. Let us figure out what Clark has on the club, and we'll deal with it."

"How?" I felt wrung out.

"We know people."

"I need my stuff." It was true; I did. I wanted my camera more than anything else.

Trigger's annoyance was evident. "Stuff can be replaced."

"*Stuff* has memories for me, Trigger. I don't have many things, and the few I have, I want to keep." I rubbed my head, not sure where to go from here. "Give me the weekend, at least, to get my stuff."

Trigger glanced at Brick, and they exchanged some kind of thought.

"Guys, I can't leave Venna there, not without an explanation. She was, after all, the one who saved me from working the house. She kept me from having to sleep with countless men." That wasn't entirely true. I was sure I would have left before that happened, but I knew it would hit Trigger hardest.

"No," Trigger ordered, and when I began to protest, he cut me off. "I'll drive you there, so you can get your stuff and talk to your friend, then we'll meet Brick here and leave for Santa Monica tonight."

"Tess," Brick took my hand in his, "do this for me."

Fuck.

"You play dirty."

He beamed when he knew he had me.

"First, I need to buy some new clothes."

Brick went behind the bar and handed me a bag. "Something from home."

I peeked inside and smiled.

***

Although I slept well at the hotel, it did nothing for my head space. In fact, it tossed me right back to street survival mode. I peeled my tired body off the leather seat of the Lexus and stood on heavy feet. Trigger eyed me cautiously as he rounded the car and steered me inside.

"You okay?"

I nodded, but I was nowhere close.

He came up next to me, and I whirled around, confused.

"You can't come inside. Clark knows your face."

"Don't worry about it."

"No." I cringed. "They'll kill you, or they might release the information."

He shrugged and nodded toward the house, urging me forward.

"Hey," I grabbed his arm and felt the warmth that came with my touch, "you may not care, but I do."

He licked his lips. I knew it was hard for him to put himself in another's shoes. That was the problem with giving a fuck, but I was serious.

"I may not care about myself, but I..." He rubbed the back of his head as if he were annoyed.

"Fine," I huffed and headed up the stairs. "Stubborn ass."

He chuckled behind me, which only made me more pissed off. Just to add fuel to the fire, he reached forward and opened the door and waved me on.

Oh, sure, now you're a gentleman.

Gilbert stepped in front of Trigger and asked him to spread his arms.

"Gilbert, let him pass."

"You know the rules, Tessa."

I glanced at him, worried, as he felt Trigger's jacket, waistband, legs, and ankles. The entire time, I witnessed the battle in his head. I wanted to help, but I didn't want to draw attention to us either.

"All clear. Have a good day, sir."

I pointed to the bar. "Give me twenty, and I'll meet you here."

He shook his head, but when he realized I wasn't going to budge, he backed down.

"You have ten before I come find you myself."

Each step up the stairs ignited my anger further. Flashes of Mags made their way into my head, and as I glanced over my shoulder at the living room, something snapped inside. I unlocked my bedroom door and grabbed my stuff then landed on my bed in a heap of confusion.

Nothing was making sense. All I could focus on was Mags. Her body—her limp body—being tossed around by people I once thought I knew and cared about.

I cringed away from the mirror and hated what looked back at me.

Emptiness.

I fingered the handle on the night table and pushed the papers aside. I felt the smooth blade and drew it free, looked at it, then held it tightly by my side.

Hatred consumed me from my very core, and I rose in a weightless stance.

I made my way cautiously out of my bedroom. My steps never wavered as my subconscious pointed me in the right direction. I felt like I had been drugged; my body operated on its own.

I had lost control.

I turned a corner and heard footsteps but didn't care. I pushed on. Someone raced across the hall but didn't notice me. It was, after all, a house that never slept. Just sex, booze, and endless amounts of money.

My feet barely lifted off the carpet as one moved in front of the other. I was numb all over.

The dark cherry-wood door was locked, but I knew just how to wiggle the handle to get it to open. Once I heard the release of the pin, I took a deep breath, and with an internal kick to the gut, I gave it a turn and stepped out of the light and into the dark.

Little lights that shone no brighter than the moon lit the crisp, white sheets of their bed and *his* outline. The smell of sex was still in the air, and I searched for her clothes but couldn't spot them.

Hmm.

I knew my mother well enough to know that whenever she got some, she'd have her smoke in her office and finish up her paperwork for the day. She wouldn't be interrupting us.

The blade tapped my bare leg, a reminder of why I was there.

At the foot of the bed, I came to a stop, pulled up my sleeves, and like a cat, crawled over his body. Using my knees to support my weight, I lifted the knife, but he must have felt me, and his erection bumped my thigh. The cool sheet brushed over my legs and made my skin heat with lust and rage.

Stab.

Stab.

Stab.

Mags's lifeless face appeared in front of me and turned to look at me right before they rolled her up in the carpet. Disposable, just like he was.

I stabbed again and twisted the blade roughly through his flesh to tear it at the roots. There was barely any struggle as I sliced at his soul the way he did mine.

Stab.

Stab.

Stab.

I couldn't see where he began, there was so much blood. My legs slipped around as I attacked more of him. Years of pent-up rage poured out of me in my blind state of mind.

It felt so good. So right.

I swore I felt Mags by my side, fueling me on.

Stab.

Stab.

With the knife in the air, I froze and jolted back and stumbled to my feet. It was as if someone suddenly pressed pause on a movie. I slapped my free hand over my mouth as I focused on the bed.

It was Bret.

Then it hit me. My mother suspected Clark was sleeping with someone else. I just never thought it was Bret!

Oh, fuck.

His naked body drained of blood quickly, and I was stuck in a fucking loop. What the fuck just happened?

I heard a sound and headed for the other door. I slipped and slammed into the dresser but managed to pull myself up and out of sight.

My ankle throbbed as I jolted out the door and down the hallway, holding the bloody knife with flesh still stuck to the blade.

My heart and lungs fought for room, and my stomach crept into my throat.

Slam!

I heard a stifled scream as someone pulled me upright and practically pushed me into my room and shut the door behind us.

"What the hell, Tess?" Venna jumped away from my bloody form. "Oh, my God. What did you do?"

"I-I…" I couldn't think quickly enough. "I killed."

"Killed who?" She grabbed the sheet off my bed and covered my shaking body while I stood like a zombie.

I couldn't seem to make myself answer, so she pushed me aside and frantically looked around. She spotted my phone on the side table and scrolled through it.

A flicker of light pulled my attention, and I caught the mirror again, only this time I stood straighter and stared directly into my own eyes. The knife still dangled from my fingertips, and I saw someone else looking back at me. A stronger me, not the me who always seemed to go dormant when I was here.

"Shit, Tess, where is Matt's number?"

Boom! The door burst open, and there was Trigger, lookin' fit to kill. He ran his eyes down my bloody body and quickly locked the door behind him.

He looked at Venna. "Tell me what you know."

"Nothing. She just slammed into me in the hallway, and I pulled her in here."

"Tess," he shook my shoulders, and I slowly met his eyes, "whose blood is this?"

"B-Bret's," I stammered.

Venna gasped behind me, and Trigger nodded, cool as could be.

"Is there a back way out of here?"

"Yeah, south side by the pool."

"In five minutes, make your way there, and I'll be in a blacked-out Lexus. Find me." Trigger dipped low to eye me one last time before he left.

Venna shoved the knife into my bag along with a few of my belongings and covered my bloody clothes with a clean, plush robe.

"No time to clean." Her hands shook as she turned me around and pushed me out the door and into the hallway.

Instead of going downstairs, she took us through the back way.

"It's okay, we're okay," Venna kept repeating.

Is it? I couldn't help but smirk at the power surge that raced through my core.

"Tess!" Clark's voice boomed through my head, and my veins froze solid.

No. Venna looked like she might pass out.

"Tess, where are you going, and what the shit happened to you?" He reached for me, and I pulled out Big Joe's gun and pointed it at him.

"Tess!" Venna screamed but remained by my side. "What are you doing?"

"Give it to me!" I pictured the smooth steel of the knife slicing through his blue shirt and into his murderous heart. A heart I once loved.

"Give you what?" His hands were in the air.

I pointed the gun to his pocket, and he glared.

Come on, Clark. I know you're in there somewhere.

"No."

There he was. Clark had two personalities. Sweet and pricky.

"Does Mom know?" I tilted my head as I tapped into my new, wonderful state of mind. "Does she know you sleep with the man-whores of the house too?"

He did a double take then it clicked for him—the blood, my mood, us escaping.

"Tess," he started to move, but I raised the gun to his head, "I will give you one chance here to do the right thing." He sounded as though he was talking to a child, and that pissed me off further.

"It was *you* I came for."

"You wouldn't have been able to do it, Tess." He seemed so sure of himself.

"He's dead, isn't he?"

I relished the moment. My moment.

Clark's face changed, and his knees wobbled as though he was about to fall to the floor. He looked over his shoulder for a split second, and I took that moment to crack him over the head with the butt of the gun.

Down he went.

"Jesus Christ!" Venna nearly shouted. She watched as I dug in his pocket and grabbed his keys. "We have to go!" She grabbed my arm and pulled me out the side door to where Trigger was waiting.

As soon as we left the gates, the severity of what happened hit me like a brick.

"Don't check out on me, Tess." She touched my arm carefully in the one place the robe wasn't stained with blood. "I don't know him, and he terrifies me a little."

Her words didn't register. I couldn't stop shaking, my vison faded in and out, and my lungs couldn't get enough air.

I couldn't say how long we drove. Maybe fifteen minutes, just enough time for my head to freak out in loops of excitement, power, and full-blown panic.

When we arrived at the Wynn, Trigger pulled me to my feet. Venna followed with all my stuff. I was rushed into an elevator and felt my stomach roll as the smell of dried blood hit my senses hard.

Before I could say anything to Brick, who looked horrified, Trigger pushed me inside the bedroom and straight to the bathroom.

He ran the water and peeled my blood-soaked clothes off piece by piece.

I couldn't look at him, and he didn't look at me. He just kept himself busy until I was naked.

He ran his huge hands up my legs and around my body, checking to see if any of the blood was mine.

I couldn't help but feel the sick spark that we shared whenever anything like this happened between us, and by the way his hands flexed over my stomach, he felt it too.

"Get in," he grunted and pulled back the curtain.

I did as he told me, but mostly because I wanted Bret off me.

***

Trigger

Her blank expression told me she wasn't all there. The water beat off her face, and she opened and closed her mouth as if she was washing away the taste.

I stripped off my shirt, boots, and socks, and pulled the door open to step in. The water pounded my jeans and plastered them to my legs as I took her by the shoulders and turned her to face me.

"Lean back," I ordered and helped move her sticky hair under the spray. As gently as I could, I lathered the soap, coated her scalp, and massaged her head. "That feeling," I lowered my voice, "you'll get used to it."

She closed her eyes to shut out the hurt. The corners of her mouth lowered, and her chin exposed her true feelings. But she didn't break, which I admired. Tess was strong at times I wouldn't think she'd be.

"Arms." I tapped them once to get her to raise them. I moved the soapy puffy-fucking-thing all over her body to remove any sign of that man-whore that was left on her skin.

"I may have to patch you in," I joked.

Her eyes eased open, and I saw a hint of pride flicker across her lips.

"I'll get you something to wear." I stepped out and let her have a few moments alone.

"What the fuck happened to her?" Brick nearly tripped over his own feet when I came into the common area of the penthouse. His bowl of Cheerios stank like beer. I really wished he'd stick to one or the other.

I spotted Venna standing by the window. Her arms were wrapped around her, and she appeared deep in thought.

No doubt wondering how much shit she was in.

"Drink?" I held up a bottle of whiskey.

"No." She shook her head. "Got any vodka?"

I nodded at Brick to take over while I checked my phone.

"Tell me about Bret?" I asked over my shoulder.

Brick handed Venna a drink, and she took a sip and coughed. "He's…" She coughed again. Brick mixed a strong drink. "He's an asshole, although they all are. He's had it out for Tess forever. He keeps begging her mother for a threesome. If it was anyone but Tess, they'd have done it. Felicia is the freakin' devil stuck on a pair of legs. Well, a pair of freakin' good legs." She giggled darkly. "That's where Tess gets her looks. I think her father was some piece of shit who owned the strip joint her mom worked at…"

I tuned her out. Fuck me, I asked one simple question. I glanced at the bedroom door and waited for Tess to show herself.

"Why do you think Tess killed Bret?" Brick tried to force her back on track.

"She didn't mean to kill him. No," she corrected. "Tess and I ran into Clark on the way downstairs."

That caught my attention.

I whirled around and waited for her to go on. Her eyes widened as she stumbled over her own words.

"Tess made it very clear to Clark that she meant to go for *him.* Now she knows Clark was banging Bret, and she threatened to out him. He got pissed, but when he started to freak out, Tess hit him over the head with the gun." She shook her head. "All gangster style." She stopped herself. "No offense."

"Go on." I waved off her stupid comment.

"That was it. Oh, wait!" She tilted her head like she remembered something "She took the USB that hangs off his keychain. It's some stupid power trip thing he keeps over the employees of the house. I heard a rumor once that it holds a lot of secrets. I don't know, but Clark likes to play the flashy businessman. The dude is from Oklahoma, for God's sake. Just keep it real, ya know?"

The urge to kick her out was strong, but I wouldn't do that to Tess, so I'd keep her here…for now.

"Hey." Brick rose to his feet and greeted Tess with a hug. "You feeling a little better?"

She tugged at my t-shirt she was wearing and sank into the couch. "I'm…yeah, I'm okay."

"Hungry?"

"Very." She held her stomach.

"I got just the thing." Brick grabbed the hotel phone and prattled off an order.

Venna moved to Tess, and they started to chat quietly. Well, Venna did most of the talking.

Fifteen minutes later, there was a feast for six in the dining area. Wings, burgers, ribs, fries, rice, and potatoes sat in front of us. Finally, food I could get on board with. Vegas had a lot of pretentious food. I liked my meat.

I noticed Tess went for a burger and some fries. It was interesting that such a little woman could eat so much and stay that skinny.

"Nice to see you eat." Brick beamed behind a wing.

"Nice to want to eat." She sipped her water then glanced over at me. "What?"

"Venna mentioned you had a gun."

"Yup," was all she offered before she took another bite.

"Where did you get it?"

She swallowed then shrugged. "Big Joe."

What? Brick looked confused too.

"When was this?" He beat me to the punch.

She wiped her fingers then leaned back with a satisfied sigh. "Joe doesn't like Loose, and when Loose took me out for a walk, Joe got pissed and told me to take it just in case."

Joe needed a raise.

"Too bad you didn't use it on him." Brick snickered.

"Perhaps if I had a knife," she said darkly.

"Tess!" Venna gasped as she fought a smile. Her hand clamped down on Tess's, and she turned red from laughing. "Oh, it's too soon for that."

I raised an eyebrow at Brick, who looked shocked as hell. Who was this chick?

Later that afternoon, I settled everything with Eli. He seemed pleased we were leaving. I headed back to the room where I found Venna passed out on the couch, Brick at the TV, and Tess was…somewhere.

"Bedroom." Brick answered my unasked question.

I found her curled up in the center of the bed. I could tell she was awake even though she had pulled the drapes closed.

"You good?"

"Yup."

"We're going to leave soon."

"Yup."

As much as I wanted to sink myself deep inside her, it wasn't the time. She wasn't in the right head space, and now Bret was most likely consuming her. I wouldn't compete with the dead.

***

Allen

"You think you can control yourself?" I pointed my gun at him to show I wasn't fucking around.

"Yeah."

"You sure?" I leaned forward and ran my tongue along my teeth.

He pulled at his jacket then flexed his fingers over his helmet. Little green eyes stared at me, begging me to use him again.

"Like I said, I got this. I really do. Last time, my head got away from me."

"Mmm." I flopped back on my seat. "If you can't get a good enough hold, don't risk it. Death is not an option tonight."

"Understood."

I glanced over at my hungry least weasels and pushed to my feet. They paced about their cages so aggressively that they'd shredded the bottoms of their feet.

"You six are just going to have to wait for your dinner." I turned to look over my shoulder at him to let him know I wasn't fucking around.

"Got it." He slammed his helmet over his head and rushed to join the others.

I smacked the cage and listened to the bloodthirsty screams from inside. I'd seen what these shits could do. You just drizzled a little rabbit blood over a human in a hole and let them feast.

They were the newest members in my army.

"Where do you want him?" Zay asked with his arm draped over a whore from the house.

"Out back."

"You have me confused!" the man screamed. "My name is James. I'm married with kids. Please! Please, Father, have mercy."

I straightened my collar and rubbed the dust from my arm.

"I'm very aware of who you are, Mr. Johnson. I just want to talk."

He knew better.

"Anything you want, but please don't hurt me."

"What do you know about Trigger?"

His gaze snapped up to mine. "Who?"

"Kill him."

CHAPTER NINE

Tess

"You can come with us." I hugged Ven again, but she shook her head.

"Maybe later, but right now I want to go see my brother. Thanks to you, I can."

"You need more?" I was willing to give her every last cent to thank her for all her help.

"No. I'm just happy to be out of there."

"Me too."

"Be careful, okay?" I nodded. "You go enjoy that fine specimen of a man."

I forced a smiled as she stepped up onto the Greyhound and waved when she found her seat in the back. I was going to miss her.

Trigger sat on the hood of the car, happy to give us some space. He didn't do emotion well, and I was sure with what I did, he looked at me differently.

I made my way over to him and ran my hands over my arms. The temperature had dropped, and the insane day was quickly coming to an end.

"Ready?" he asked as he put his phone away.

"Yeah." We really should get out of town.

He glanced at my pocket, and I knew what was coming. He saw the box in my bag, and when I tucked it away when he came into to the hotel earlier.

"What was in the box?"

I licked my lips, and my mouth went dry as I pulled out the engagement ring.

His eyes flickered up to mine then back to the ring.

"My eighteenth birthday, he asked me to marry him. It was one of our many secrets."

It wouldn't have been legal, but Clark wanted me to know he loved me as much as my mother.

Trigger nodded.

"It was a lie, like everything else. It was used as a control tactic that, sadly, I kept falling for."

"Did you go through with it?"

I hung my head, feeling so damn stupid and so hurt all at once.

"Almost."

"What stopped you?"

"Found him in bed with another girl. I threw the ring at him and left for a few days."

"Just a few days?"

"Look, Trigger, there's more to this…" I paused when I heard his phone alert him of a text, and Brick's name popped up.

"We need to leave." His voice almost scared me. I wished I knew what was going through his mind.

He headed for the driver's door, and I was left feeling raw and slightly judged. I knew my past was fucked up, and it was why I didn't get close to people.

Instead of opening the door, I walked over to the edge of the cliff that dropped off into a canyon. I whispered a goodbye to the ring and threw it as far as I could. It glistened as it spun in the air, then it was out of sight.

"Hey," Mags's warm hand landed on mine and she gave it a friendly squeeze, "everything okay here?"

I glanced at my mother. She had her hands on a new client, who was asking for me to be his date for the evening.

No fucking way.

"George, is it?" my mother purred like the whore she was. "I'm sure there are several other ladies who would suit your needs better than Tessa."

My mother couldn't care less if I banged every man in the house, but because I wasn't cooperating, she had to divert the attention away from me and onto her. I'd get my ass handed to me later.

"It's her eyes." He ignored my mother and fixed his gaze on me. "They are a passionate mix of wild and worldly."

"If that's what you must see," she glared at me beneath her fake lashes, and I noticed they had peeled away at the corners, "I will see what Tessa's schedule looks like."

Mags read my terrified expression like an open book. There was no way that was going to happen.

"Hi, there." She stepped around me and offered her slender hand to him. He squinted before he tore his gaze off me and focused on my best friend. "I heard you said something about liking it rough?"

"I did." He held her hand so tight her skin turned white from lack of blood.

Something felt off about this ass even before he opened his mouth and showed his vampire- like teeth.

"Well, you're in luck. So do I." She winked, but I heard the hesitation in her voice. She felt it too. "Shall we discuss this over a drink?"

"What are you drinking?"

"Martini, dirty, hold the olives." She nodded to the bar and held her hand up to let him know she'd just be a moment.

"You don't have to do this, Mags." I pulled her closer to me so we could talk.

"Yes," she eyed my mother, "I do. You helped me keep this job after my little encounter with speed, and now it's time for me to take one for the team. Besides," her voice lowered, and she lovingly tucked a piece of hair behind my ear, "we both know this is not who you are. You're not like the rest of us, Tess. You're one of the good ones."

"So are you."

"I love you for saying that, but we both know who has more experience in this department. Besides, once he," she nodded at Clark, who greeted George at the bar, "gets wind that our new client is interested in you, there will be another dramatic episode between the three of you."

She was right on that one.

"There's something off about him, Mags."

"I know." She let out a shaky breath. "And I do plan on staying very far away from whatever the hell it is."

My mother strolled by with a look that could kill and hurried over to Clark to make sure she got her digs in on me. He may be her husband, but it was me he visited at night.

"Only three hundred and sixty-two more days, and then we'll be free of this place." Mags tried to pull my thoughts away from the

matter at hand.

I grinned at her. It had been our plan since the day we met and realized how much we needed each other's friendship. "We'll live in a villa, a beautiful villa wedged in the side of a mountain. In Italy."

"With all the wine in the world."

"Wine and men," I corrected before she hugged me and left to sit next to the dark villain who would later shatter both our lives.

I shook the painful memory clear, and as far as I was concerned, Clark died along with Bret. He was nothing to me, history or not.

Trigger started the engine. I slipped inside the car and fell quiet with my thoughts.

It wasn't long before my eyes grew heavy, and I let myself drift off to an emotional sleep.

I woke to Trigger shaking my shoulder. It took me a moment to register him. He was back in jeans, black hoodie, and his cut. He smelled like weed and leather.

I had missed that smell.

"I let you sleep for as long as possible, but we need get moving again."

Huh?

"Where are we?"

"State line."

With a groggy head, I stood on shaky legs and saw Brick's smile from his bike.

"Hey, beautiful."

I returned the warmth with a big hug. We were now going to be riding on the bikes. Well, shit. I looked longingly back at the nice, warm, comfy car, but knew I had to get my head back in the game.

"Here." He handed me my jeans.

I shimmied into them as Trigger watched. The man had no shame. Then he held out my leather jacket and threaded my arms through the sleeves like a child. He helped me with my helmet before he fired up the bike.

He waited for me to get on then nodded to Brick.

Guess we're leaving the car here.

The bike jolted forward, and I squeezed my eyes shut as he weaved down the on ramp and picked up speed on I-15. The air was freezing, and the further we drove, the colder it grew. It felt wonderful to press up against his back, my arms around his body and my thighs pressed around his ass. I felt at home on his bike. I rubbed my cold hands together whenever we had to slow down for merging traffic. Trigger unzipped his jacket pockets and urged my hands inside. They instantly thawed in his body warmth.

He might be an ass some of the time, but he could be incredibly thoughtful.

About two hours into the drive, my eyes started to grow heavy. Between the hum of the bike and the setting sun, I wasn't sure I could stay awake. I leaned my forehead on his back and for a moment gave in to the urge.

"Tess." Trigger jolted me awake. "You asleep?"

"No," I lied, fiddling with the button on the helmet.

He reached back and squeezed my thigh. "Don't lie to me. If we need to stop, tell me."

"I'm fine."

He shook his head as he suddenly slipped in between two trucks. I ducked my head but kept my eyes on his patchwork. Anything to keep my eyes open.

We jumped off the I-15 and headed into the San Gabriel Mountains. His chest vibrated as he spoke to someone. I glanced back to Brick, who had pulled out a cell phone.

I began to feel like something was off by the way Trigger's head started to move around. The tenseness in his body gave me a bad feeling in the pit of my stomach. I pushed the button.

"Something wrong?"

"No."

I rolled my eyes. "Now who's lying?"

He didn't answer, so I started mimicking his movements. I wasn't sure what I was looking for, but I wanted to help if I could.

We got to a point where we were surrounded by mountains. Rain had started to fall in a cold drizzle, and it became hard to see very far through the mist.

I grew cold deep in my bones with his uneasiness.

I leaned back to stretch my arms, feeling them snap at the elbows. God, that felt great.

Then I spotted a single light off in the tree line, then another and another.

"Trigger…" My voice trailed off.

"I see them."

Fear licked through me at the word *them*. He placed a gun into my hands. "Point and shoot. Watch out for Brick."

Shit. It was one thing to shoot at a slow-moving target, but to shoot sitting behind someone on a bike that was moving around like crazy was something else.

Zip. Zip.

I yelped as two bullets whipped by my helmet.

So, point and fucking shoot. Got it!

I tried to aim at something and pulled the trigger, hoping like hell I would hit someone. Trigger fired back and swerved the bike around to make us harder targets. I heard Brick's gun as he fired, but all I could see were flashes of light. How could they tell if they were hitting them or not?

Trigger made a hand signal, and Brick disappeared. I wanted to ask where he was going, but now wasn't the time.

A different sounding motor caused a prickle up my spine and into my scalp. Two shots flew by, and one broke our mirror.

Shit! Shit! Shit!

My stomach dropped, and my hand flexed over the cold steel grip of the gun.

Fuck it!

I grabbed Trigger's waist, twisted around hard, and concentrated on my fire. Each shot made my heart speed up. My muscles tightened and filled me with adrenaline.

I could tell by the light and the squeal of brakes that the bike spun out over the slick road. It turned completely around before he went out of sight in the ditch.

Trigger grabbed my hand and shoved it over his erection. His hand covered mine as he stroked it twice.

Jesus, I was wet.

We are seriously two fucked up individuals.

Just when I thought we were in the clear, two more bikes came up behind us. How did we not hear them?

Trigger popped one of them in the shoulder, but he didn't go down. The other tried to reach for me, pulling up alongside.

What the fuck?

I held up my gun and took the shot, but nothing happened. Shit! No bullets. He came up close again and grabbed my arm and tugged hard.

I slipped, but Trigger reached back and slammed me to him. He shot the guy to our right and got him in the thigh. He lost control, and his bike went flying into the trees.

Trigger waited until the guy went for me again. He suddenly turned and shot him under the arm.

Jesus Christ!

Trigger yelled something into his radio and revved the engine. We surged forward, picking up speed.

It was so fast, I had to duck to block the wind because it hurt my neck so badly. I closed my eyes and counted my wild heartbeats until we finally slowed.

Holy shit.

Holy hell.

Holy Mother of Christ.

The words looped around and around in my head. I was trying to absorb what the hell had happened.

The bike hit gravel, and I was finally able to look around. Thick trees lined the road as we started up a big hill. We stopped at a rusty trailer set up on concrete blocks.

Once Trigger stopped, I hopped off, tossed my helmet, and headed into the woods. I had no idea where I was going, but shit, I needed a moment.

***

Trigger

As I tucked the bike away, I watched Tess fade into the darkness. These woods were safe, and I knew them well, so I wasn't worried.

"Heard you ran into some trouble." Gus appeared by my side. "I was about ready to send Rail and Cooper."

"Nothing we couldn't handle." I glanced at the woods again. "Brick make it back?"

"He did." He nodded at the woods. "That Tiger?"

"Yeah."

"You piss her off again?"

I smirked. "Turns out the girl can shoot, along with a few other hidden talents."

"Really?"

"Mmm." I threaded her helmet through the handlebar. "She needs a moment to come down, and so do we." I headed over to his fire pit, grabbed a beer, and set it on the stone. I opened another and eased into the metal contraption he called a chair.

Gus hobbled over and pulled back the tab. He always drank shit beer, even if I brought the good stuff.

"Stripe Backs. They had the advantage, and they could have taken Tess out, but they didn't. They tried to take her."

Gus set his beer down and rubbed his bottom lip as he thought. "She did overhear them in the desert, and they did try to attack her after Tiago. Maybe they just want to shut her up?"

"Maybe they have orders to take her." I played the Devil's advocate.

"You think Allen is behind this?"

"I think a lot of things."

He spat and took another swig. The sound of crickets filled the air, and I strained to hear Tess.

"How was the house?"

I shrugged. "Eye-opening."

"Meaning?"

"A lot of shit there." Gus knew about Tess and Bret, but I would deal with that later.

"Any part of it you can't get past?"

I tossed the beer in the rusty trashcan and grabbed another. "Getting past it would mean I cared."

"Cut the shit, Trigger. I saw your face that night in the trailer when we got her back."

I felt uncomfortable showing emotions, even with Gus.

His chuckle broke down into a nasty cough as he reached for another beer. "If Brick's sister was in trouble, you wouldn't have gone to the extent you did to get her back like you did Tess." He laughed again and nodded at the woods. "You're pissing me off. Just go get her."

"Whatever." I pushed to my feet and headed into the woods. It didn't take me long to find her at Gus's hideout near the brook. She was bent over the railing with her hands to her mouth in an attempt to warm them. She seemed to be restless and struggling over the day.

"Come on up. You're freezing."

"I'm fine."

"I wasn't asking."

"I know."

She just about drove me to the edge with all I had already going on inside me.

"Tess."

"Trigger."

"Why do you have to fight me on everything?" I bit out.

"Why do you have to be so demanding on everything?"

I rubbed my head and cursed.

"Trigger," she sighed, "I just had my ex play mind games with me, found out he killed my best friend, killed *his* lover, said goodbye again to an old friend, shot someone, was nearly yanked off a bike by what I assume was rival gang member, and am here with nothing but a backpack and a few belongings." She stopped to catch her breath. "I think I deserve a moment to stop my head from spinning."

"I get that—"

"No, you don't," she tossed back at me angrily. "You have a home, a family, and a sense of belonging. People would genuinely care if something happened to you. I don't know where the hell I belong. I'm just some girl who walks in and out of people's lives."

I stepped closer, and she held up her hand.

I grabbed it and pulled her to me. She looked pissed and shoved me, but I didn't move. She tried to do it again, and I wrapped my arms around her to pin her and backed her up against the railing.

"You are not just some girl, Tess. You belong with me at my club, and not with that mind fuck of an ex." I freed my hand and held her chin to look at me. Her eyes were wild, but there was a sadness behind it. I hated how it made me feel. I hated that it made me feel at all. "Let that shit go, or I'll make you."

"Try." Her face was flushed, and I saw what she wanted—no, what she needed. I also knew what it felt like to have all that adrenaline inside. We were both still riding the high from what we had experienced.

I unzipped her pants and split her folds to find her hot wetness. When she started to speak, I flipped her around and planted her hands on the rail.

"You might think you're in control, Tess." I shoved up her shirt and undid my pants. My heavy erection twitched with need at her opening. "You might even think you want it." I leaned down and licked the entire length of her spine. "But I can assure you, when you're with me," I lined up and broke her opening with my tip, "you will give in to me." I eased in steadily, determined that this time we would finish.

Her insides squeezed me, and my fingers dug into her hips.

"Do you understand me?" I wanted to drive my point home. "Answer me." I slapped her ass, and she moaned loudly. I pulled out and waited for her to wiggle. When she backed up, I stepped back. I grabbed her neck, knowing she liked it rough, and tilted her head back. "Do-you-understand-me?"

"Fuck me, flip your switch," she snarled. "Make me scream."

I bent her over, plowed back in, and beat myself into her. She bucked, screamed, and begged for more. I didn't care who heard us. I was inside this woman, and I needed it as much as she did. The silence that took over me was bliss in itself. My balls smacked her clit, and she fought to chase the climax that ripped through her. Her skin broke out in a sexy pink, and my handprints on her hips marked my ownership.

Over and over again, I reminded her who was in charge, and with each thrust, I increased the speed. She could do nothing but hang on. Her hair was wild, and she jolted as she screamed my name. I loved that I could be me inside of her. No holding back, just pure, animal sex. We were meant to fuck this way.

I picked up the pace, changed the angle, and let myself coat her insides after weeks of frustration. She started to fall forward, totally done, but I held her to my chest, still inside her. Her breathing slowed, and I bit down on her neck.

"I will ground you next time. Now get dressed. Someone wants to see you."

I slipped out.

We climbed the hill, and I gave her my seat and took an even shittier one. Gus handed her a plate of shredded meat, tortilla, and salsa.

"So good to see you again, Tiger," Gus grunted and urged a beer in her hand.

She looked around for a moment and made the connection. "You live here?"

"My rusty slice of paradise." He grinned, and I huffed out a laugh.

Tess studied my face before she set her beer down and started in on the food.

"You here for good now?"

She paused before she took her next bite. "I'm not really sure of that yet."

My glare should have burned her. She tried everything not to look at me, but she felt it.

"Well," he sighed, "I sure hope you do."

My phone vibrated, and I saw it was Big Joe. I moved to the tree line before I answered it.

"Yeah?"

"There's a letter here for you."

"Open it." I glanced at Gus, who looked to be telling Tess a story. She tossed her head back and laughed. My dick twitched again. Fuck, she turned me on.

"Shit." Big Joe's tone brought me back to our conversation.

"What?"

"It's a flyer for a fight in Las Vegas."

"Toss it."

"Trigger." There was a pause, and before I could remind him how I hated long stories, he spat it out. "Your dad's making his first public appearance and calling you out to fight."

So, I didn't take the bait the first time, and now he's insuring it.

I felt my addiction for the cage surface for the first time in years. It was something I had buried for many reasons, the main one being that it changed me, turned me into an animal. I knew I would lose myself once the scent of blood in the ring freed the demons inside.

"Toss it," I repeated, feeling my body come alive.

When Big Joe didn't respond, I sensed something was off.

"No, brother, I don't think I can."

"Why?"

"If you don't fight, he said he'll come for her."

I glanced at Tess. She watched me, and I lowered my voice before I spoke.

"This stays between you and me."

"Got it."

CHAPTER TEN

Tess

Something was wrong. I could tell by the way Trigger's hands were clenched into fists, and when I added in his murderous expression, I had no doubt something big was up. Gus did everything to keep my attention on him, so I decided to use it to my advantage.

"Gus," I lowered my tone and traced the top of the beer can with my fingertip, "when I first arrived at the club, Brick told me the guys got their nicknames by the way they killed."

He nodded. "Yeah."

"I know Morgan isn't as high up as Brick and Rail, but why hasn't he gotten his nickname yet?"

He laughed. "He has."

"But I thought…" I looked at him, confused. What was I not getting?

"Trigger recruited Morgan from a biker bar in Palm Springs. Morgan smashed a bottle over a guy's head, jammed the jagged glass into his throat. He used the same bottle on a few more. It was a real bloodbath." He waited for me to make the connection.

"A bottle of Captain Morgan." I smiled. "That's kind of funny."

"Yeah, he likes his nickname. Morgan doesn't like too much attention on himself."

"Reminds me of someone else we know."

Gus took a drink from his beer. "Sure does." He winked at me.

"So, if everyone has a nickname, that means they had different names first." I glanced at Trigger and back to Gus. "What's Trigger's real name?"

"You're going to get me in trouble, here, Tiger."

"Not my intent, Gus. Promise."

"I know." He glanced over his shoulder to make sure Trigger was out of earshot. "Nolan was the name his mother gave him at birth."

Nolan. Seemed different enough to suit him. I really couldn't picture a Scott or Eric.

"Why do you say 'at birth?'"

Gus rubbed his weathered eyes. "His father preferred *little shit* until his ability to fight without a conscience kicked in. Then it was Trigger. It was supposed to be a stage name, but as you can see, it fits."

"And now his father is posing as a *Father* of the Church?"

"Sick fucker will stop at nothing to become more powerful than his son. You need to be careful, Tess. Allen being back brings a whole new level of trouble to the club."

"You think he sent the Stripe Backs after us tonight?"

"If you connect the dots, yeah, I think so."

"Dots?" I knew what he meant, but if he could offer some more detail, I'd be happy.

"You overheard a familiar voice in the desert, that night you also got attacked by Tiago."

"But they said he was a Serpent, talking to the mole."

"Yeah, but it was all part of Allen's twisted fuckery. He knew it was a matter of time before Carlos would make a deal with Trigger. He was getting worn down by the Devil's Reach at every turn. I think they sent in a Stripe Back to talk to whoever is the fuckin' mole, and he found out Devil's Reach had a weak link."

He held my gaze a little longer to make his point. I shifted uneasily.

"Before he could make his move, Tiago got to you first. Thus ending the Serpents' contract, and now Trigger has all of Santa Monica. The one town Allen has always wanted."

"Why?"

"It's like this. Every city has a value. Santa Monica is one of the highest, next to Oakland."

"Okay." I tried to follow.

"So, by running the Serpents out of town, more clubs will be chopping at the city limits. Trigger has more ground to cover and will need more men. Meanwhile, Allen will have the Stripe Backs do his dirty work of fucking with the club. One day when Trigger's not looking," he made a Hannibal Lecter chop noise, and my stomach lunged into my throat, "he'll take the one thing that will hurt the club the most."

"Which is…?" My nails bit into my skin.

He leaned forward, and the crow's feet around his eyes deepened as he become serious. "You."

My skin shivered as a gust of wind sent my hair all around me. "I wouldn't hurt the whole club."

"If Trigger's hurting, the club is hurting."

"Why?" I cleared my throat. "Why did he bring me back here if I'm the target? Why not leave me at the house?"

"Because he can't protect you if he can't be near you."

Gus let out an ear-piercing cough, and a moment later, I saw why. Trigger was approaching, and he didn't want him to hear us talking.

"Good?" Gus asked. Trigger looked a million miles away.

"Yeah."

I was so lost in my thoughts, I didn't hear Trigger speak to me. His hand landed on my thigh and gave it a little squeeze.

"We need to leave."

"Stay here if you like," Gus chimed in, and I nodded. I liked that idea better. "The hideout has heat."

"I'd like that." I smiled weakly at Gus and hoped he'd see I wasn't ready to go back to the clubhouse yet.

"Fine." Trigger sent off a quick text and pulled me to my feet.

We said goodnight and walked back down the hill to the little log cabin. He opened the door and started to make a fire while I stood in the doorway, unsure what to think.

"What?" he muttered over his shoulder.

"Just thinking."

"About?" He took out his lighter and lit the paper.

"Just some things."

He stood and scowled at me. "Why did you want to stay here?"

I looked around and covered one arm with the other. "I like it here. Feels safe, I guess."

"You don't feel safe at the club?"

"I do. I guess I just…" I fumbled for my words.

"Just what?"

"I think I'm just tired." I wished I hadn't said anything.

"Well, there's the bed." He pointed to a queen size bed up against a wall under a window. "Bathroom is over there."

I washed my face and brushed my teeth, my reflection showing the past twelve hours. Stress and a murder would do that to you.

I stripped down to my tank top and panties and crawled under the old quilt. It was beautiful, with light and dark blue threading that created pretty little flowers and swirls. Not at all something I would think Gus would own.

Trigger pulled up a seat next to the fire and nursed a glass of something brown. My guess would be more whiskey. There seemed to be an endless supply of it with this guy.

I rolled to my side and watched him study the flames. His profile was that of a man who had seen and done too much, but at the same time, there was this incredibly sexy sense of strength surrounding him.

"Trigger," I whispered, and he looked over at me. One side of his face glowed from the flickering flames, and the other was cloaked in shadow. Funny how true that seemed right now.

"Why did you come back for me?"

I could see he was mulling the answer. His jaw ticked, and his head bowed. I swallowed hard and wished I hadn't asked. I was fishing for some kind of warmth from him. I should've known better.

"You were in a bad place, and we thought it would be better to get you out of there."

I gave a little nod and looked away. I hated that my emotions were so close to the surface. Darkness started to eat away at my thoughts, and I fought back my insecurities, trying to pull on the inner strength I always managed to find.

My eyes grew hot with tears, so I gave up and flipped over and let them tumble down and hide in my pillow.

This was what happened whenever I stepped foot in that goddamned house. My entire body folded inward, and I lost my backbone. My mother had always undermined my confidence, and I still felt the control Clark had over me for so long. I really needed to pull my shit together.

The bed dipped, and Trigger lifted the covers and let in a rush of cold air.

"Tess," he grunted. "Roll over."

Afraid he would see my tears, I pretended I was asleep. He sighed heavily before he shifted and spooned me from behind. His arm slipped under my neck to cradle my head.

"Why are you crying?"

I dried my cheeks and shook my head. He shifted to reach above me, and I caught a whiff of a strong scent.

He reached down and took my hand and fiddled with the cuff, then undid the three snaps to reveal my scar.

My hand slapped down to stop him, but he moved it out of the way.

"Never hide yourself from me," he warned, but there was a softness to it.

I bit back my normal urge to pull away, but it was difficult.

Something wet touched my skin. I jumped, and he grunted, "Stay still."

He skimmed over my scar with a black Sharpie. I watched in fascination as his huge hand drew such delicate lines. He threaded some ivy through the scar and embedded a tiny lily toward the bottom. My eyes blurred when I realized he remembered my story. I wondered if Brick told him who she was. Lily was Mags's daughter, the only piece I had left of my best friend.

When I thought he was done, he started to draw something else. I sniffed, and he leaned over me. His weight felt good, and I relaxed and emptied my head of all but what he was doing. Soon, a skeleton key appeared and became entangled in the ivy, but it was at a strange angle. He continued to draw vines and left the key alone like a hidden secret among it all.

"It's beautiful," I barely whispered. "I didn't know you could draw."

"I have a guy who can do this. I'll make you an appointment."

"The key?" I questioned, curious.

But he didn't say anything else. He went still, and I guessed he drifted off. The more I studied his work, the more I realized it was Trigger's way of comforting me. I pulled his hand to my lips and kissed his fingers softly then wiggled closer to him and closed my eyes.

***

Trigger

I woke with a jolt and noticed something was wrong. Tess wasn't in the hideout. I scrambled to get dressed and did a double take at the time. Ten a.m.

Shit. I'd slept like a rock.

I headed to where Gus was pouring a cup of coffee.

"Where's Tess?"

Gus splashed the coffee as he hobbled over to his chair. "She and I had breakfast, and then she went off for a walk."

"Where?"

He pointed in the opposite direction of the hideout.

"She's fine."

"We need to get back." I headed into the trees and scanned for her. My boots crunched over the sticks and rocks. I wasn't someone who could be quiet. Hunting animals was never my strong suit. Hunting humans was a different game.

Something snapped loudly, and I turned around, but didn't see anything. Then something hit my back, and I whirled in the other direction.

Whack!

A pinecone nailed my thigh, but this time I didn't react.

"Come out." I listened for her footsteps, but all I got was another cone to the stomach. "I'm warning you, Tess."

"Your last warning," she said from above me in an old hunting blind, "landed me some great sex. I wonder what this will land me?"

I wanted to get mad, but all I could think of was my dick straining against my zipper.

"Ah, there's that look."

"Come down," I ordered.

She slowly unzipped her jeans, and I backed up to get a better look.

"I think I'll stay up here." She held up her purple lipstick vibrator. "I'm in good company."

I can play dirty too.

"Okay. You have fifteen minutes before we leave." With that, I left her up there and headed back to the trailer. My dick nearly turned blue, but I would get my way with her soon.

Ten minutes later, she came up the hill, looking flushed and sexually frustrated.

Perfect.

"Gus, you have a double A battery kickin' around?"

He looked at her oddly and pointed to a tool box on the step. She held it up and excused herself.

I blocked her path and snatched the battery from her hand and replaced it with the helmet.

"Time to go."

"Just need five minutes."

I stepped closer, leaned down, and inhaled her smell. "I. Don't. Share."

Her breath caught in her lungs as I grabbed her ass and gave it a hard squeeze.

We said goodbye to Gus, and I rushed her onto the bike before she decided to find another way to get off.

On the drive back into town, I could feel her frustration through the vibrating bike. I couldn't help but smirk when we parked behind the club.

She was in a pissy, wound-up mood, and it was fucking hot. Her cheeks were flushed, and her glare was enough for me to bend her over my bike and remind her who she belonged to.

"Go get changed. Your shift started ten minutes ago."

She rolled her eyes but disappeared into the club as Brick came out with a newspaper held high in the air.

"Shit's gettin' real."

I tossed the keys at Jace to take my bike into the garage then removed the paper from Brick's hand.

Three men found dead this morning in an alley on the lower east side, apparently from an overdose of a tainted strain of cocaine. The local PD is attempting to match the symbol on the baggie to known drug runners. Detective Doyle of SMPD reports they have a few leads but have made no arrests yet. We encourage anyone who knows anything to please call the nearest detachment of the SMPD.

"So glad we stopped distributing those drugs." Brick snickered sarcastically. "I want to kill the mole myself by feeding him some."

"We need to flush him out."

"How?"

"If I knew, he'd be in the slaughter room right now."

The sight of Tess behind the bar in tight black shorts and a red tank top made my pounding headache ease. Morgan looked less stressed and back to his old self. Loose wasted no time and was already on a stool nursing a drink.

Big Joe waited for me to be alone in the back of the bar before he came over with the letter.

"I checked on this, and it's legit. Sounds like Allen was in touch with Charlie himself and is working the angle of a father and son showdown. If you don't show, not sure what that will say about your reputation."

Fuck me.

"Don't give a shit about my reputation."

"But you do about hers." He flicked his head over at the bar. When I didn't respond, he went on. "Not like the old man will have much steam left, anyway."

I nodded. It would be an unfair fight, but a fight, nonetheless.

"There's something else you should know." He checked over his shoulder at the guys. "Cooper and Rail have been in and out the last few days. I followed them, and they've been hanging out at the Flying Arrow."

"Okay." I needed a moment to digest that information. The Flying Arrow was where a lot of the Stripe Backs hung out. "Anything else?"

"You want me to find Loose something to do?"

I shook my head, and he walked back to his post at the door.

"Trigger?" Her voice made my head hurt. "When did you get back?"

Tess had spotted her too, and she made her way toward us with a bottle of whiskey in her hand.

Tammy fiddled with the ties on her dress and gave me the same look she used whenever she wanted me to fuck her.

"I thought your ass was kicked out of here, Tammy." Tess filled my glass like it was an everyday conversation.

"I left."

"But you're back."

"I need to talk to Trigger."

Tess glanced at me and lifted an eyebrow. "I'm sure it's something *really* important."

Tammy rolled her eyes and turned to me. "Can we talk in your office?"

"Regarding?" I didn't have time for her.

"Your father."

I flicked my head toward my office, and she turned and started to walk. Tess closed her eyes as she shook her head.

"Give me a minute," I muttered.

"Whatever, Trigger."

"What does that mean?"

"You do remember what she did, right?"

"Yes."

Her eyebrows pinched together, and she drew her lips in as she thought about something. Then she turned and headed back to the bar.

Women.

Tammy sat on my desk with her dress hiked up to her ass.

"Get off." I pointed to the chair. "You have five minutes to explain why you're here."

"What the hell do you see in that bitch?"

"Careful," I warned. "Four minutes."

"I'm dating Jet now." She waited for a reaction to her dating the rat from the Stripe Backs. Somehow, it didn't shock me. "He drills me for a lot of your club's information."

"That so?"

"Um-hm."

"What do you tell them?"

"Well, that depends." She grabbed the bottom of her dress and peeled it off over her head. She stood naked, in nothing but heels. "You take me back, and I'll let you stick it anywhere you want. If not, I'll tell Jet all your dirty little secrets."

I bolted from where I stood and wrapped my hands around her neck, slamming her to the wall. Her head bounced off the plaster, and her eyes widened.

"You don't know shit about my club!" I felt my switch begin to tick.

"I know more than you think," she spat. "I know your chick of the month is going to destroy everything. I know she took a USB drive from a guy named Clark, and it holds information they want back. Allen will hunt her down and carve out her insides if the Stripe Backs don't get to her first."

"How do the Stripe Backs know Clark?" The words shot off my tongue.

"Dumbasses had a run-in with him and made a shitty deal."

I looked at her, confused. She gave a dramatic sigh, and I let my grip loosen slightly.

"You're not the only club that visits Vegas." She gripped my hands, but I didn't move, and she dropped them again. "I like Jet, but the Stripe Backs are one dumbass bunch of people. They made a shit deal with Clark, and then screwed him over. Clark found out something on them and now has leverage." Tammy nodded toward the door. "Allen wants her. And the USB."

My head spun, and the demons rattled in their cages.

She laughed, and her split lip bled. She touched a finger to her mouth, tasting it, then traced a line of blood down to her erect nipple.

"Not such a dumb bitch now, am I?"

The door swung open, and Big Joe looked stunned. "Shit, I'm sorry. Find me later." Just as he backed up, I saw Tess's face turn white before she darted back to the bar.

Fuck!

"Whatcha going to do, Trigger? Run after her? Don't you want to find out what else I know?"

My chest heaved because she was right. I was cornered. A pawn once again.

"What do you know about my father? Why Tess?"

"Loosen your fucking grip."

I did, a little, and she sucked in a few breaths of air. "He has eyes on you. He's feeding the PD information, and," she laughed, savoring her power, "he's going to kill her right in front of you."

"Where is he?" I slammed her head into the wall again.

"You don't get it." She smirked. "He's everywhere. Right outside your door, listening to your every word."

Fucking mole!

"Who's the mole?"

"Step into the ring, and you'll find out."

I squeezed my eyes shut and pushed aside the urge to fight.

No.

Don't even think it.

She opened her mouth like she wanted to give me head. I opened the door and pushed her out, and she landed on her bare ass. The entire room fell silent as a naked Tammy scrambled to her feet.

"Big fucking mistake, Trigger! I will ruin your club and make sure that blonde bitch gets what she deserves."

Brick looked ready to charge her, and I shook my head. At the sound of squealing tires, my senses went on high alert.

Everything went still, and I felt the chill as everything fit into place. They were here for her.

"Get down!" I yelled as bullets flew through the window.

Glass burst all around us in slow motion. I raced to cover my nephew Fin, who had run out of his mother's hold. My hands covered his head as we raced behind the bar. "Gun!" I shouted at Morgan, and he handed me his extra rifle.

"Stay here!" I ordered Fin as tears streamed down his face. "Don't move, okay, Finny?"

"Where's Tess?" He covered his ears. "I want Tess!"

I scanned the bar, and as far as I could see, where the hell…?

"Morgan?"

He shrugged as more bullets sprayed the room. "She went out back after she saw you guys."

Zip.

Zip.

Zip.

Wood, glass, booze, and screams filled the air all at once. It seemed to linger before it fell all around us. Fin clung to my arm, his little hands white at the knuckles.

The place fell quiet once again as the tires screamed away.

A lot are going to die for this.

"Call out!" I shouted to the guys.

"Yeah," Brick huffed.

"Second that," Rail answered. "I think." He patted down his body. "Yeah, I'm here."

Gus wasn't here, so…

"Good," Cray piped up.

Morgan was good; Fin was too.

"Denton?"

"He's here with me." Vib screamed in a panic, "Where's Fin?"

"He's here too."

More people started to call out. Tammy, on the other hand, had been hit several times. I assumed she was set up for this shit storm.

"Trigg—" She fought for breath as her lungs filled with blood. "Help."

"I'm not the one who can help you." I leaned down to get a closer look at the bullet holes.

"Morgan," I ordered and heard him whirl Fin around so he wouldn't see what I was about to do. I raised my foot and slammed down on the shred of glass sticking out of her jugular.

Crunch.

Her cold, lifeless eyes stared at me. I kicked her torso, and her head flopped to the other side. Fuck, I hated that bitch.

"Trigger?" Fin pulled at my shirt. His snotty nose made his voice sound muffled. "Where's Tess?"

"Brick, Rail," I said calmly, and they spread out. "Get Jace and Loose to clean this shit up."

"Let's not forget," Loose pulled a piece of glass from his arm and tossed it on the floor, "who started all this. You want this cleaned up, you do it."

My head became tight as a drum as I slowly turned to look at the ungrateful little prick who had lived under my roof for far too long.

"You didn't seem to have a problem spending my money, living in my home, drinking my booze up until now."

"Well, now I do."

I sucked in a deep breath and looked down at my frightened nephew. He didn't need to see anyone else die right now. It suddenly hit me that two of my men didn't check in.

"Morgan," I pointed to Loose, and he ripped the cut off the cunt in front of me, "put him on ice."

"Fuck you, Trigger! You know what?" He stepped up to my face, and my men all pulled their weapons and waited for my command. "You don't deserve her." He held up his middle finger as Morgan pointed his gun at Loose's head and dragged him out of the room.

I wanted to kill him. I wanted to rip his throat out and beat him to a pulp, and I would, but right now I needed to find Tess. "Morgan, find the others then check in with me."

***

Allen

"How many?" I leaned back in my chair and lit my cigar while Fox, a member of the Stripe Backs, gave me a play by play on what happened at Trigger's club earlier. Fox was a loose cannon. He almost killed Tess in the desert and could have potentially fucked up all my hard work.

"Three."

"Including the snitch slut?"

"Yeah."

Three wasn't the number I hoped for, but maybe it would convince Trigger to fight.

"The girl?" I squinted and dared him to lie to me.

Fox rubbed the top of his bald head, which made my urge to rip out his throat stronger.

"We didn't think she'd go back to work the first day she came back. I can't confirm if she was hit or not."

I snapped my pen in half and considered what Fox would look like with a piece in each eyeball. Pulling out my phone, I sent a text.

Allen: Come in.

"Who were the other two?"

He sat a little straighter when he realized I wasn't going to kill him right now.

"Moe and Maze."

I dropped my head with annoyance and beat the desk. "Fucking amateurs! The club's runner and a beef-head? That doesn't mean shit. Fucking Christ!"

Fox looked around like we might get struck by lightning because I cursed in a church.

I leaned over and glared at the six-foot-two wannabe thug. "What the fuck? You got religion or something? Do some real damage, or I will." I turned toward the door and yelled out to the others. They were probably dick high in cocaine. "Where the fuck is Zay?"

"He's out trying to see if the girl is alive," one of my prospects answered with powder all over his face.

I dropped my head into my hands. "Waste of human beings. Go away." I waved dramatically at Fox. "Your face makes me want to kill you."

He left a lot quicker than he arrived. I rubbed my temple and wondered if I would need to deal with the girl myself.

"I can't keep meeting you like this." My shitty mood instantly evaporated at the sound of his voice. I couldn't help myself. I felt like a child getting his first look at the pretty puppy in the box.

"You're fast."

He came into the room and sank onto a chair. He hated being here, and I didn't blame him. He shifted in his cut like it was uncomfortable, or maybe he felt his disloyalty burning through the Devil's Reach patch.

"Do I have a choice?"

"No." I grinned. "You really don't." I kicked my feet up and leaned back in the chair. "Now, tell me everything."

CHAPTER ELEVEN

Tess

Wind whipped my hair and blocked my view of the choppy sea. My feet dangled over the edge of the pier as I held on to the rail and watched three surfers decide if they wanted to do battle with Mother Nature tonight.

One man, who looked to be in his forties, raced into the water, duck-dove under the whitecaps, and surfaced a few yards from shore. He looked back at the other two, and they waved him off and headed back up toward the parking lot.

He paddled out farther past the break. His movements were smooth and thought out. Once he got to a certain point, he hiked up to a seated position and watched the waves as if he were counting them. Or maybe he was waiting for just the right one. Either way, he seemed calm and fearless.

His sense of serenity seemed to pass over me as I relaxed into the cool wood.

I brushed my hair out of my face and held it down to the side with one hand. A raindrop hit the tip of my eyelash, then another and another. It didn't matter if it poured. I wanted to watch him.

To be so fearless, faced with such a great force, was hypnotizing. I could almost feel his rush as his body tensed. The wave he was watching began to rise, and it gained height and speed as it plowed toward him, its power building. I stepped up to get a better look, gripping the wooden post between my legs to steady myself.

He turned his board and started to paddle with all his might. Just as he was on the top, about to be toppled over, he stood and effortlessly glided along the inside of the tube. The curve of the wave chased wildly behind him.

Water sprayed with the chaos of the wind. The moon fought to shine brightly through the heavy clouds. Yet another moment I wished my camera was attached to my hip.

My breath was caught in my throat and my hands were white, unsure of how he was going to end his ride.

It was graceful beauty the way he showed respect to the sea, and the sea to him. His hand reached out and skimmed the water as if to say thanks before he jerked and tumbled beneath the surface.

Wow. I stood motionless as the dark water swallowed him up and he disappeared. Their moment was over.

I laughed at how wrapped up I was in it all. Growing up without the coast, you never really understood the draw, but now I did.

My phone rang, and I saw there was a missed call from a Vegas area code.

Hmm.

I tapped the play button and heard my doctor's tired voice telling me I need to come back in, but since she knew I wouldn't, as I'd avoided all her other calls, she would like me to call the office tomorrow for a phone consultation.

Well, shit, that can't be good.

"I hope you can swim."

I turned to find the surfer behind me with his board in hand. He was aged and weathered, but the smile in his eyes left no doubt how young his soul was.

"Well enough."

His eyes crinkled as he came a little closer. "You'd be dealing with a strong current and one hell of an undertow."

"Good thing I didn't fall in, then."

"Yeah, Trigger would open Pandora's box."

I carefully eased off the railing and tugged my shirt back down in place.

"You know Trigger?"

He motioned for me to follow him back down the pier.

"Everyone knows Trigger and his club. They're good people, despite their rep." He flung his wet hair out of his face. "Known him for about ten years now. He's my best client."

I couldn't help but laugh, and he eyed me strangely.

"Can't see Trigger on a surfboard."

"Ha! Like cats and water, they don't mix." He joined in my

laughter. "No, I have a tattoo parlor in the back of my surf shop. I've probably done eighty-five percent of Trigger's tats."

"Really?" I raised an eyebrow, curious what he knew about Trigger.

"Yup." He lifted his huge board into the back of his topless Jeep. "You need a lift back?"

I shook my head. "Honestly, I'm not ready to go back yet."

"You can't stay here."

"Why?" I shrugged. "It's peaceful."

He opened the passenger side door and rested his arm over the top. "Storm is coming in, and this is neutral territory—which really means fair game."

"Serpents are gone," I reminded him.

"Yeah, but the Stripe Backs aren't. Besides, Trigger would have my head on a stick if he knew I saw you and didn't take you back."

"I appreciate it, but I'm good."

He rubbed the water from his face and smirked.

"He certainly didn't sugarcoat your stubbornness." I rolled my eyes. "I could use the company at my shop. You can hang out there until you feel like going back."

I hesitated. Just because he said he knew Trigger didn't mean he did. He must have noticed my mood change, as he pointed to his forearm.

"Under his right arm, he has the words *Forever Damned* written in script. I promise you, I'm the least of your worries."

He came around to his side and started the Jeep. I looked over my shoulder before I hopped inside and closed the door. Trigger wasn't one for letting people get close, and he did have that tattoo, so I felt a little more relaxed.

He held out his freezing hand. "Name's Mud."

"Tess."

"I know." He smiled and backed up and headed down the street.

Mud's shop, housed in his garage, was the ultimate man cave. Pin-up models lined the ceiling and walls, a flat screen hung on a back wall with a chair strategically placed in front of it, and I saw a no doubt fully stocked Coca Cola fridge. Fans shot cool air from all angles. Pot hung in the air, and a heavy metal band could be heard throughout the room. It was oddly comforting.

"You have any clients coming tonight?" I asked as I admired his bonsai tree and the sand swirled around it.

"Nah, my buddy got caught up with his old lady. I was supposed to fix his train wreck of a tattoo he got in Reno." He lit a joint about as thick as a hotdog.

I took in the needles, ink, and blue gloves.

"Come here." He nodded and stared at me strangely. He turned my arm over and examined Trigger's Sharpie work. "You want that done professionally?"

"Maybe." I shrugged, but the more I thought about it, I knew I did. "Yeah, I do."

"First tat?"

I nodded.

"Good way to hide the scar."

My other hand slapped over it as I turned to stare at the photos. I felt naked without something to conceal the evidence of my past.

"Sit here." He pointed to the chair. "Let me outline it before the marker wears off."

"I don't have much money right now."

"Don't recall asking for any."

I didn't like it, but he seemed determined to outline it, so I sank into the plush chair and gave him my arm.

"Here," he handed me his joint, "it will help."

"I think I'm okay."

"I like that you're tough, Tess, but this shit will hurt."

Fine.

I sucked back a few long puffs and soon felt as if I were flying out of my body and around the room. I jolted at the needle, but there was no pain. I felt free.

"Your hotdog of a joint is fantastic. My arm feels independent from me." I giggled.

He smirked. "Who drew this?"

"Trigger." I moved my arm to the left and felt like I was across the room looking at us.

"Why?"

I laughed and then cringed at the sound of the needle. "That's a good question, Mud. He drew it while we were in bed. I think it's his way to speak without having to."

"That key," he pointed, "you know what it's to?"

I rolled my head to look at him. "That would require him to use more than three words at a time."

He laughed and took the joint from me. His hand was incredibly steady, which made me calm.

"Do you know the DR well?"

He nodded and tapped the joint to drop the ash at his feet. "Been doing their tattoos for years."

"You do anyone else besides Trigger?"

"Morgan, Brick, and Rail."

"Impressive."

"Thanks." He nodded in agreement.

"I find it interesting that you've done Trigger's."

"Yeah?"

"You're the only person I know who can touch him."

"Besides you," he corrected.

"True." I shifted my weight to my other hip. "Wait." I tried to catch up with my thoughts. "Do you know what this key unlocks?"

"Yup."

"Well?"

"Well, I'll let you figure it out."

"Where's the fun in that?"

"Oh, trust me, Tess. There's a lot of it."

I closed my eyes and enjoyed the ride of the high. Clearly, Mud wasn't going to spill the truth. I asked a few questions here and there and loved that he would go off on a long story and let me picture it. He mostly shared stories of him and his waves and how a great board makes all the difference.

"You want me to stop?"

My eyes opened, and I saw he had outlined everything. It was dark and gray and fit me so well. Mud expressed what the scar meant to me without even knowing my story. I cleared my emotions from my throat and smiled at him.

"No, keep going, please."

"You want color?"

"Honestly, you do what you think would look the best."

"My favorite kind of client."

***

Trigger

It didn't take long for the smell of blood to fill the room. Tammy was pretty much drained before her naked ass was dragged out to the shed. We'd dispose of her later when there weren't as many eyes on the club. Rich was on his fourth bucket of cleaner before Jace slipped and fell in her juices with a disgusted moan.

Gus was with Vib and Denton in the back. Fin was still glued to my side.

My men's deaths weighed on me, but not Tammy's. She'd brought hers on herself, but Maze was loyal, and Moe had been around for a while. They were good men and shouldn't have gone out that way. They were family, and family didn't come easy.

"Rail," I called out, and he hurried over. "Where's Brick?"

"It's okay. Last I saw, he was with Tess." He rubbed his face. "You think this was—" He glanced down at Fin, who still appeared to be in shock. I stepped away, and he mirrored me like he was a third leg.

I shook my head, unsure what to do with Fin.

"You think it was the Stripe Backs?"

"No, this was an order from above." I looked around again. "Where the fuck are Brick and Tess?" I looked at Rail. "You know anything about this?"

"Why would I know any more than you?"

He looked genuinely shocked at my question. I didn't think Rail would be stupid enough to cross me.

"You want to ask me somethin'?"

I cracked my neck. What the hell was happening to my club?

"You and Cooper have been hanging out at the Flying Arrow."

"Yeah, we have."

"Making friends with the Stripe Backs?"

Rail crossed his arms and held my gaze. "Been by your side for a long-ass time now, worked my way up your ladder, and you stand here accusing me of something?"

"Just asking."

He licked his lips and dropped his arms heavily at his sides. "Not sure who is puttin' shit in your head, Trigger, or if you're just trippin' over Tess, but don't ever question my loyalty to the club. I say that to your face, knowing the consequences of my words right now."

"Careful," I warned but was pleased he had the balls to speak his mind.

His brows pinched together, and he let out a frustrated sigh. I needed to find Tess. My guess was this hit may have included her too.

"Fin, come!" Vib barked from the doorway. She looked like shit. No doubt she'd done a line out back. Such a fucking mess. "I said come here."

Fin didn't move. He just stood there, eyes locked on the floor. When his mother got closer, his hand latched on to mine. I flinched at the sudden contact, but forced myself not to shake him off.

"When I call, you come!" She reached for him, but I pulled him behind me and raised my free hand to stop her.

"Go lay down for a bit, Vib."

Her face twisted. "Give me my son."

"You think he wants to be with you when you're strung out? The boy's just seen some pretty bad shit go down. He doesn't need *your* shit right now."

"My shit?" she yelled when Gus appeared.

"Vib!" he hissed. "Get the hell out of here."

She turned to me and stuck a finger in my face. "He's not yours to make that decision for."

"Maybe he should be."

"Whatever!" She grabbed her jacket, kicked a chair, and marched out the door.

Gus glanced at me then dropped his head, tired of Vib and her crap. I felt for the old man. He helped raise me when I was at my worst, and now he had two little ones and a strung-out junkie wife who'd fuck any pair of legs around.

My phone vibrated in my pocket, and I reached for it, hoping it was Tess.

"Yeah?"

"Just heard. Everyone all right?"

"Lost Maze and Moe."

There was a small pause before he spoke again. "Sorry, man. What happened?" Mike sounded like he was in a helicopter, judging by the constant roar in the background.

"Stripe Backs came to shut up a snitch. My men got in the crossfire."

I reached for the drink Morgan handed me and tried not to trip over Fin. I covered the mic on the phone. "Find Tess."

Morgan nodded and rushed out back, and I grabbed my keys.

"Is Tess okay?"

"Yeah, she had left just before it happened."

"Good. Look, man, I need to meet with you next week. You got some time?"

I downed the glass and pointed for another when Morgan returned with a shake of the head.

"Yeah, when and where?"

"Friday, Courtside Pub. Bring Tess."

"I don't want her involved in anything."

"Should have thought of that before you fell in love, buddy." He laughed while I dismissed his comment. "Be there at nine p.m."

"Yeah." I hung up.

I looked around at the mess that still littered the floor and wanted to kill someone.

"Morgan," I muttered, "find her. Fin," I turned to my nephew, "go to my office where it's quiet." He didn't say anything as he slowly turned and did what I asked.

"Yeah, boss." Morgan whistled at Jace, who was cleaning the glass. "Let's go."

I hurried outside, needing to clear my head before I fucked with any of my own men. Just when I got on my bike, Minnie showed up.

"Where the fuck are Tess and Brick?" I called out as I pulled my helmet back off.

"Brick is with me. He's parking out back. I haven't seen Tess since the shooting."

"Brick told me she's okay. Said she's with Mud," Big Joe called out from his post. "Brick texted her, and she said she was okay."

"You think you can hold me here?" I heard Loose bark at Ryder. "I could break your face like that." He snapped his fingers.

I tossed my helmet and rushed through the back door and plowed Loose football style into the side of my pickup truck.

I didn't have the time for this.

"Ahh!" he shouted as he held his broken ribs. "What the fuck?"

I was so tired of his shit.

I swung and smoked his jaw so hard it tossed him around in a circle.

"You disrespected me." I elbowed him in the nose, and he stepped back a few feet, but I closed the gap. Blood dripped everywhere, and his expression changed to fight mode. "You disrespected my men and the club." I sent a knee to his balls. "You hit on my girl." I stopped walking when I had him where I wanted.

"She doesn't know the real you," he huffed in an attempt to look tough. "If she did, she'd see what I do. A monster."

"Too bad for you."

For a split second, he was confused, and when it finally hit him that I wasn't about to let him live, I punched him in the throat and he flew backward into the pool.

I bent down, grabbed his hair, and shoved him back under. With a throat punch, your body naturally drew in deep breaths, so I held him down while he slowly killed himself. His struggle satisfied my years of hate for the man. Loose was a weasel, and with the way my club was these days, I needed every last piece of shit gone.

I waited an extra minute before I let go. His body drifted away, the reaper's face smiling back at me from his club shirt.

"Morgan," I barked into the phone. "Pool."

"Copy that."

I went back to my bike and turned over my engine and tore off down the street. The air had a nip to it and felt good over my churning head.

How the hell did she get tangled up with Mud?

Why am I not told anything?

Mud was outside when I arrived. He pulled down on the garage door and gave me a wave as I parked.

"Tess here?" I tried not to sound annoyed.

"Yeah, man, inside."

"Why?"

He smiled behind his joint as he locked the door with a padlock. "You think I'd touch something of yours?"

"Mud." The demons started to tempt me for a good fight.

"I called you twice."

I pulled out my phone and saw he did. How did I miss that?

"Why is she here?"

He waved over his head for me to follow. Once inside, I found her asleep on his long leather couch. My body relaxed, and the noise settled inside. I moved closer and checked her over.

"She okay?"

"Yeah."

"How did she end up here?"

"I was out catching the storm, and I noticed a woman watching me from the pier. As I got closer, I saw it was your girl. She seemed off, so I told her I'd bring her back to you, but she wasn't ready. Couldn't leave her there, man. It would only be a matter of time before the Stripes found her."

"Appreciate that."

I bent down and rubbed her shoulder, but she didn't open her eyes.

"Tess," I whispered harshly.

"Might be a bit hard to wake her."

"What'd she take?"

"She had a few puffs off my Dragon Butter."

I couldn't help but smile; she must have felt pretty damn good.

Mud handed me the bottle of whiskey I kept under his work bench. "She'll wake in a few hours. Sounds like you could use a breather. I heard about your men, and I'm sorry."

"Me too."

I sat at her feet and listened to Mud tell me about his day. His stories were short and to the point. I liked that he skipped the mindless details.

By three a.m., the shop was cleaned, and we had finished off more than half the bottle.

"She's good people." Mud nodded at Tess.

"Yeah."

"Brave too."

I chuckled at the sleeping tiger next to me and thought about how much she pushed me and how much I'd let her get away with. I was still trying to understand that one.

"She is."

Tess stirred, and her eyes fluttered open. When she saw me sitting next to her, she moved to sit upright.

"Ohh," she moaned and held her arms out to steady herself. "When did you get here?"

"Few hours."

She licked her lips, no doubt suffering from cotton mouth.

"Here." I handed her a beer. She took a little and closed her eyes, trying to wake up. She tugged on the sleeves of her jacket.

"Where is my phone?" Mud leaned over the table and handed it to her. "Thanks." She glanced at a missed call and went to the voicemail but hesitated when she caught me watching.

"Thanks, Mud." She stood and kept her back to me. "I appreciate what you did for me, and I'll pay you back for the…" She trailed off.

"You won't. Consider it a gift. Just stop by once in a while, okay?"

She nodded and headed for the door. I looked at Mud, confused, but followed her out.

I caught up to her and grabbed her arm.

"Hey, what's with the quick exit, and who called you?"

She rubbed her head. "You jealous, Trigger? Oh, no, wait. That would require feelings."

"Who called?" I hated that she wouldn't tell me.

"You fuck Tammy?"

She hadn't heard yet?

"Hard to fuck the dead." It was a poor joke, but I was pissed she'd implied it.

"What?"

"Stripe Backs hit our club after you left. Killed Tammy, Moe, and Maze."

Her hands flew to her mouth in disbelief.

"Oh, my God! I'm so sorry, Trigger."

I crossed my arms and waited for her to tell me about the phone call.

"And everyone else is fine?"

"Physically, yeah. Mentally, Fin is suffering."

"Poor baby." Her hands moved to her hair, and she turned away from me as she processed it all.

"Tess—"

"It wasn't Clark." She cut me off and stepped closer to my bike. I could tell she was ready to go back to the club. "I wouldn't do that to you."

Good. One less person to kill…right now.

I nodded once before I handed her the helmet.

"Tammy did try to get me to screw her, in exchange for information. I didn't."

She let out an unsteady breath and slipped onto the back of my bike.

I wouldn't do that to you.

CHAPTER TWELVE

Tess

Big Joe held the door for me, and I saw the damage the Stripe Backs had done. Bullet holes dotted the walls, and the bar was only half stocked. Morgan gave me a stressed smile before I headed out back.

"Oh, thank God, you're back!" Minnie wrapped her arms around me and whispered, "He's such an asshole when you're gone. Can you believe what happened?"

I caught Trigger's annoyed expression as he muttered something mean next to us, and Morgan cleared his throat with a warning. Minnie missed the tension and pulled back and looked at me before I could get a word in. "You look thinner. Are you eating? Lord, tell me your secret!"

I shifted in embarrassment. I knew I was thinner. It was what happened when I was at the house. "No sleep."

"Oh." Her gaze fell, and she stroked my arm. "Date night tomorrow? I could use some girl time."

"Sure."

Trigger's hot hand landed on my back, and I knew he was growing restless. I waved goodnight and let him lead me in the direction of his room.

He disappeared into the bathroom, and when I heard the water running, I took that moment to head back to my room and get cleaned up. My tattoo was stuck to my shirt, so I cleaned it and rubbed in the sample lotion Mud gave me and quickly slipped into a silky, long-sleeve nightshirt. The USB was in my night table, and I hesitated as it gnawed at my curiosity. What was on it? Did I want to know? I pushed that aside and grabbed my book instead.

I tucked myself under his cool sheets, happy I chose a long-sleeve shirt, and pulled the comforter up under my chin to will my body to stop shaking. I was frozen. Trigger liked to sleep in a temperature reminiscent of the Arctic. Once I created a warm spot, I rolled over, clicked on the little light that hung over the spine of the book, and felt the rush that came with a second book in a trilogy.

Hello, old friends.

I was so lost in my fictional world that I hadn't heard Trigger come in. The bed dipped, and he lifted the blanket, destroying my hot air bubble.

He missed my glare, and I went back to the words in front of me. I couldn't help but sneak a peek as he lay facing the ceiling, one arm under his head, his muscles flexed as he thought about something.

God, between the story and this man, I'm doomed.

"What's on the USB?"

I hated that he interrupted me, but I was waiting for that conversation.

"All I know is he guards it with his life. I wanted to hurt him, so I took it."

"You haven't watched it yet?"

"No."

He stayed quiet after that, so I went back to reading.

The pages couldn't turn fast enough. I knew it was coming, but when? My eyes and my mind were in a battle as to which could absorb the story faster. My heart was in my throat. Mike was hinting at something, but what?

Suddenly, I gasped and felt my eyes prickle.

"Yes!" I blurted and heard the pillow slap as he turned to look at me. I ignored him and kept one hell of a grip on my book.

I could feel his eyes on me. They made my skin heat up, but so did the scene. He rolled to face me and stared harder.

"Read me what part you're at." His tone was raspy and hit me in the center of the stomach.

"I can't."

"Why?"

I tried to think of a good excuse, but I was fresh out. I licked my lips. Why the hell not? I dropped my tone to a low, raspy whisper.

"Mmm, you were ready for me." He groaned as he pushed his fingers in further, feeling her velvet insides squeeze around him.

"I'm always ready when it comes to you, Cole." She flopped her

head against his chest. "Please, I need you."

I flicked my gaze up to his and was caught off guard by his expression. He looked hungry or pissed. I wasn't sure which.

"What?"

"Does that turn you on?"

I blushed, thankful the moon wasn't overly bright tonight, and the little book light was turned away from me.

"Maybe."

"What exactly about it does? Cole or the sex?"

I wanted to run and hide. Men would never understand the feelings behind a romance book. It wasn't that the men were sexy, so much as the *fantasy* was sexy. They were fictional characters, created to make women feel something amazing, make us feel wanted no matter our flaws, something that barely existed in this world. But, shit, there was always hope.

However, I knew this book was based on a true story, so I decided to tread carefully.

"It's not Cole that turns me on. It's the way he is with her."

"Meaning?"

My book flopped out of my hands when I rolled onto my back. I couldn't look at him. Trigger didn't do deep feelings, so it was hard for me to open up with him, but I was willing to try.

"Meaning he's primal, alpha, protective, but all the while she knows he loves her beyond anything else in this world. It's just so…"

"So…what?"

"Right, I guess. Cole shows romance here and there, but not all the time—"

"You like romance?" He pushed for more answers while I fought to find the right words.

"Not all the time, but yes, sometimes, just to know you matter enough, you know, that they are thinking of you, and you only." I rubbed my face. I wasn't good at this—*we* weren't good at this. "That no matter what, however angry the guy was, or if there was another girl in the room, you know they only have eyes for you."

"And Cole is that way?"

I shrugged and rolled my head to look at him straight on. "I don't know. I've never met him. The author sure paints him that way." I tucked my hands under my cheek so I could see him better. "Can I ask you something?"

"Maybe."

I rolled my eyes dramatically. "When I was gone, did you sleep with anyone?"

"No."

"Kiss anyone?"

He flinched, and I got the answer. I hated that it hurt so much.

"You?"

"Never slept with anyone."

His eyes flickered with anger but paused when I reached out and ran my hand along his tattooed chest.

"Doesn't feel good, does it?" I stopped to make my point. "To know the one you care for had a little kiss with someone else."

He took my hand and held it over his heart. I wasn't sure what he was thinking, but I went with it. Slowly, he reached out and skimmed his finger along my jaw and stopped at my lips. His gaze landed there and narrowed in on them.

"How did your body react when Clark kissed you here?" His thumb brushed over my bottom lip like he was wiping away the memory.

I went with the truth, because the truth was all I had right now.

"It was confusion mixed with comfort." I swallowed hard. "But," his eyes turned up to mine, "it took me a moment to realize what I wanted."

"What do you want, Tess?" he whispered as his hand brushed over my brow.

You.

To myself.

I swallowed past the giant lump that formed in my throat. My mouth felt dry, and I was sure he could see my panic. I was always nervous to show anything remotely romantic with Trigger. He and I had both made it clear we didn't want more from each other. I didn't want to rock the boat. I just got back, and already so much had happened.

"I'm not sure."

His hand stilled, and I knew he felt my lie.

"Try again." The force of his glare dared me.

"Fine." I stared into his eyes and secretly begged his softer side to show itself. "I want what I've never had. I want someone to love me." I thought about Matt and how he'd always loved me, but in a brotherly way. He filled that void, and I, in return, had filled his, but that was different. "Someone who can see past my wall, past all my flaws and mistakes." I thought about my tattoo, hidden from his view under my shirt. I wasn't ready to show it to him yet. I didn't regret it. I was waiting for the right moment. I ducked my head down when I felt my face flush again. "Things like that don't happen to girls like me. We are unlovable, broken pieces of someone we could have been." I stopped when I realized my mouth ran away with me. "And you wonder why I read," I muttered to lighten the mood.

Just when I thought he was going to say something, he grabbed my waist and rolled me over. He pressed against my back and tucked his arm around my midsection.

I let a sad smile creep across my face. I was sure I had just made another wall go up. Trigger wasn't built to understand what I had said. Though he had his moments, I wasn't sure how to get through to him, or even if it was possible. For now, I'd hold on to the fact that I was the one in his arms tonight.

"What's wrong?" I sat next to Clark on the bed.

"I need to tell you something, something that is going to hurt you, but you need to hear me out before you freak out, okay?" I heard him, but his face scared the shit out of me.

"I don't know if I can take any more hurt."

His mouth opened, and the words came out, but I soon felt like I was falling down a black hole. My stomach dropped. How could this happen? He just kept going, and the last words that ripped me apart were...

"I'm still here, just in a different way now."

I shifted to smooth my shirt over my leggings, but it was really so I could buy some time to let the words sink in.

"I don't understand."

Clark reached out and cupped my chin. "I love you, but I also love your mother."

My heart ripped from its anchor and floated around inside, bumping into other organs.

"I want to be with you, Gumdrop, but in order for that to happen, I need to marry your mother."

"Have you slept with her yet?" I didn't want to know the answer, but at the same time, I needed to know.

"Yes."

I stood on shaky legs and leaned against my dresser. "I'm confused. You say you love me, but you sleep with my mother. You say you love me, but you are marrying my mother."

"I know it's confusing."

"No." I laughed because if I didn't I would cry, and that was pointless here. "What's confusing are things like when I had a boy over to help me with a project and you sent him home. I got an F on that project. You act like we're together, but you're marrying my mother." Oh, God, I felt sick.

"I don't expect you to understand. This is a grown-up matter."

I glared at him. We both knew I had grown up entirely too fast.

"No, what I understand is that you want to have your cake and eat it too."

"Gumdrop." He lifted off my bed and tried to hug me, but I stepped out of his reach.

"Answer me one question."

"What?"

"Was this just a game to get to my mother?"

"No." His actions didn't match his words. "Of course not."

Punch to the gut.

I was done.

"Clark!" My mother's voice ripped through the thick tension. "Open the door."

Clark slowly went over and opened the door. "Felicia, I was just telling Tessa the good news."

"Well," she paused to grab our full attention, "we may need to speed the wedding up."

"Why?" Clark looked interested.

My mother's hand rested on her stomach, and she smiled up at him.

No.

"Really?" His face lit up. "How far along?"

I shoved him out of the way and slammed the bathroom door in their faces. I sank to the toilet and covered my eyes. My entire world was crashing down, and there was no way to stop it. Sick. This was all a sick, twisted game they were playing. How could he? He was mine. I saw him first. He was closer to my age than hers.

I pulled at the tissues that stuck out of the drawer, tugging it open. Something caught the light, and my fingers brushed over the sharp edges.

I glanced in the mirror and saw how pathetic I looked.

It had never been clearer. I was unlovable, used up, and disposable now.

I took a deep breath and...

My eyes jolted open, and I jumped in the darkness. My skin had a layer of sweat across it, and my heart raced to play catch up. I was not in the house. I was safe, away from them.

I carefully padded across the icy floor and over to the door where I slipped out, leaving Trigger to sleep.

***

Trigger

I slept like the dead. The demons reminded me that I was never free. My father hovered on the edge of my dreams, taunting me to agree to the fight.

I knew it would be a slippery slope if I stepped into the ring. I had a love-hate relationship with it, but, fuck, I felt alive between the ropes.

Sunlight burned through the gap between the curtains. I could use another few hours, but I knew my head wouldn't allow it.

I flipped the covers off and rubbed my head as I rolled to the side of the bed. I already sensed Tess wasn't there. I went for my gun when I detected movement.

It took me three seconds to register the little shit on my couch, rolled up like a burrito in his beloved green blanket.

He was dead to the world, and I saw a wet spot on the corner of the blanket where he had been crying. His snotty nose was a bit of a put-off, but I felt sorry for the kid.

Fuck. He is too young for this shit.

I scooped Fin up and tucked him in the middle of my bed. Maybe one of us would get some more sleep.

I wondered when Tess had slipped out and where she was. Last night was heavy, and I was still trying to figure out how to take what she said. Why the fuck were women so damn complicated? I figured I was safer to keep my mouth shut because I didn't want to say the wrong thing.

"Hungry?" Peggy asked when I slid into my booth in the back.

"Yeah," I huffed into my hands. "Normal."

"Coming right up." She swung her hips as she walked away. Peggy needed to stop trying. If I hadn't made her my old lady by now, it wasn't going to happen.

Morgan brought me a coffee, and I rubbed my face, fighting the fog in my head. So many things were on my mind, not the least of which was how to get Tess to hand over the USB she had taken from Clark. I had a feeling it wasn't going to be easy to convince her. I was still working on the problem when I heard her voice.

"Want some company?"

Tess was dressed in jeans, a tank top, and an oversized sweater that hung open in the front. Her hair smelled like that stuff I liked when she blew it dry.

"Sure." I signaled Morgan to bring her some coffee. He put the mugs down and left us alone. "You get much sleep?"

She wove her fingers through her hair and let out a long sigh. "Enough."

"What time did you get up?"

"Three something, don't know." She sprinkled some sugar into her mug. "I just went back to my room. I didn't want to wake you."

Peggy slid my bowl of oatmeal and toast in front of me and glared at Tess.

"What do you want?"

Tess shook her head but granted her a genuine smile. "I'm fine, Peggy, but thanks."

"Good. One less thing to do," she snarled and turned, but I caught her arm.

"Bring her what I'm having."

Tess waved her hand. "Really, I'm good."

"No, you're not." I sent Peggy off. "You need to eat more, Tess."

She looked me square in the eyes and then glanced over her shoulder. "I lost my appetite earlier this morning."

"Oh?"

"I decided to open the USB drive."

I dropped the toast from between my fingers. I knew I was on that thing and what it might show, but I also knew there was a lot more there I needed to see.

"Detective Aaron planted coke on some business guy, and then proceeded to smash his head in."

"Really?"

"Yeah." She stirred her coffee, lost in her thoughts. "It was weird, though. He kept looking at the camera on his dash, and when he was finished, he said, 'There, I did as you said.'"

"Hm." I bit into my toast and let my mind wander over that.

"Your coke has the reaper hood stamped on it, right?"

I squinted at her, wondering how the fuck she knew that.

"Why do you ask?" I'd never let her get that close to it. "You been poking around? Old ladies are not allowed in the back room."

Her elbows fell to the table, and she put her head in her hands.

"Having a conversation with you, Trigger, is maddening. Remind me to keep shit to myself."

She stood to leave, and I cursed. "Tess, I didn't mean to—"

"To what? Accuse me? I feel like I've been down this path before, only that time you believed me. What's changed now?"

Peggy, of course, showed up at that moment and tossed Tess's food on the table. The toast flipped off the plate and fell on the bench seat.

"Five second rule." Peggy picked up the bread with her bright orange nails and dropped it on the plate. "All good."

I grabbed her arm and twisted hard, and she yelped. "Get her some new shit, Peggy, now!" I ordered, and the entire room went silent.

"Fine." She left with her hand in the air.

"When?" Tess had her eyes closed, and her tone told me she was close to being finished. "When will you see I'm only looking out for the club?"

"You ask a lot of questions. I'm not used to a woman being this involved in my club. It takes a while for any member to be trusted enough to know as much as you do now."

"Have I ever made you doubt my loyalty?"

I leaned back and crossed my arms after I pushed my breakfast away from me. She hadn't, but that didn't mean I could lower my guard. It just wasn't in my nature.

"Tammy was here a lot longer than you, and she flipped."

The second I mentioned her name, I saw the fire ignite inside her.

"Don't you *ever* compare me to that skank."

I wanted to lash back at her tone, but I could see she was moments from making a scene.

"She wasn't always a skank."

She chuckled, and I could tell I wasn't going to like this next part.

"Now you're defending her." Her head fell backward as she took a moment. "Why did you bring me back here, Trigger?"

"You didn't belong there. It wasn't safe." I hated being asked that question.

"Let me get this straight. You brought me back, for what? An apology to Brick? For lying to me? And here I am trying to help you connect the dots to something so much bigger, and you question me? You want to see some fucking loyalty?" she hissed in a whisper then yanked up her sleeve and showed me the tattoo of the drawing I had traced on her arm.

Holy shit.

"Screw you, Trigger." She turned on her heel and headed for her room.

Holy shit. She actually got the tattoo, and it looked fucking amazing. By far one of the sexiest things Tess had done yet. It was right up there with her ability to shoot a goddamn gun. My dick screamed at me to go after her, but the bar was filled with members waiting to see what my reaction would be. Sure, they only caught some of it, but I sure as hell didn't need to look pussy whipped.

"Fresh toast." Peggy snickered. "Where the fuck is she?"

"Take it back." I flicked my wrist at her and pulled out my phone.

"Un-fucking-believable!"

I waited for as long as I could before I went to her room, and just as I was about to knock on her door, I heard her talking. I pushed open the door a bit and listened.

"Why are you leavin', Tess?" Fin was on her bed, sitting inside her duffle bag. Every time she'd put something in he'd take it out. "Take me with you."

She sighed and sat next to him and folded the shirt that would be going back into her closet in a few minutes.

"I'm just going to visit a friend for a while. Besides, that wouldn't be fair to your mom."

"Like she'd notice."

Tess reached out and ruffled his hair. "What about Gus?"

"He's okay." He shrugged. "But if you leave, Uncle Trig won't be happy."

"Trigger doesn't have any room in this club for someone like me, Fin." She grabbed her stack of shirts and tucked them next to his legs.

"But…" He sniffed, and it took me a moment to see he was panicking. "But what about me?"

She turned and knelt in front of him and tucked a piece of his shaggy hair behind his ear. Her head tilted as a frown broke out across her face.

"You have so many people here who love you so much, Finny. No family is perfect. You have to see past the bad to see the good. Your mom is just a little lost, but she loves you with all her heart."

"But I love you more." He lunged into her arms and buried his head in her neck. She leaned back against the headboard and held him as he cried. "I hate that he's making you leave."

"Who?" She rubbed his back.

"Uncle Trig. He's supposed to be my hero, but he's being an asshole."

For once in my life, I felt like an asshole. Apparently, it was something I was good at.

"He's not an asshole." She started to laugh. "Okay, well, yes, some of the time he is, but under all that crap, he has a huge heart. You two are a lot alike, you know?"

"How?" He wiped his eyes dry.

"You're both strong, smart people. You're both looking for love, just in different ways."

Her words hit hard. Shit, I really was an asshole. It was hard to hear her words, but it was eye-opening.

"Do you love him?"

I held my breath, unsure if I wanted to hear her answer.

"You're a little young to ask such a big question." She stood him on his feet and looked up at him.

"I'm five." He stood a little taller and tried to look strong. I smiled at his feistiness.

"I want to love him." I hardly breathed at her honestly. "But what's the point of loving someone who can never love you back? I've been there before, Fin, and you know where it got me?" He shook his head. "It got me knocking on the reaper's door."

"He loves you too, 'cause you're pretty, and mom says you make his balls hard."

She laughed out loud. "Well, thank you, I think."

"For what?" His brows pinched together.

"For caring about me this much. Feels pretty nice."

"Can I tell you a secret?"

She nodded, and he leaned in and whispered something in her ear. Her smile dropped, and her gaze fluttered to the floor.

"That's…" She fought back tears. "That's the nicest thing anyone has ever said to me, Fin."

"See why you can't leave?"

"Trigger?" Brick called out, and Tess looked over at me. Our eyes met, her back straightened, and she made a point to return to her packing. "Oh, shit, were you creepin'?" Brick waved at Tess, not at all caring that he had outed me. "Sorry, but you need to make a decision."

He handed me the iPad and showed me the email informing me I had to register if this fight was going to happen.

I nodded once before I handed it back to him. "I'll deal with it tonight."

"Deadline is seven p.m."

"Yeah."

I felt a tap on the back, and Fin stared up at me before he sucker punched me in the balls.

"Come here, you little shit." I grabbed the back of his hoodie and hung him in the air in front of me. His eyes were bloodshot, and is nose was still snotty. "What the hell?"

He wiggled before he gave up, knowing there was no use. "Stop her, like you always do, or I'll never talk to you again."

"Fin," Tess shook her head, "it's not up to him."

"The hell it isn't!" we both shot back in unison.

"Jesus Christ, he's your damn Mini You." Brick tossed his hands up. "I'm not sure I'm ready for this."

I dismissed Brick's comment and glared at my nephew. "You wanna toss a punch, at least learn how first. Meet me in the ring in twenty."

His eyes lit up, and I dropped him to his feet and watched him hurry down the hallway. Nice to see the little shit was feeling better.

I turned to deal with Tess. "Where the hell do think you're going?"

Tess packed even faster, shoving her clothes in the bag. "I'm going to go stay with Ven and her brother. Take a break."

I closed the door behind me, then whirled Tess around and grabbed her face so she'd look at me.

Say it.

Fuck me, just say it!

Nolan appeared out of nowhere.

"I do trust you, Tess, more than most here. You've proven your loyalty more than once, but this…" My fingers found her arm and held it up to show her. "This is unbelievable." I leaned my forehead to hers and breathed in her scent. Her body made me feel alive for the first time in…ever. Oh, shit.

Say it.

My entire body vibrated. The truth made me feel weak and vulnerable, but fuck me, she couldn't leave.

"Don't leave."

I felt her shoulders rise and fall before she leaned forward on her toes and kissed my cheek tenderly.

"I'll stay under one condition."

I raised an eyebrow, curious what she was willing to bargain.

"What does the key go to?"

Oh, shit. She already knows, just doesn't remember.

"Pick another one."

She glared at me, but just as I thought she was going to start packing again, I saw a familiar dark expression flicker across her sexy eyes.

"Kiss me here." She pointed to her cheek.

I almost laughed but didn't hesitate. My lips skimmed her cheek.

"Now here." She slid her finger to the side of her jaw. I obeyed, thinking I had the better end of this deal. "Here." She pointed to the spot on her neck. "Here." Her collarbone.

My jeans felt crowded as I licked every spot she wanted.

"Right here." She pointed to her chest. "And here." She tapped right between her breasts.

My body hummed as her flavor sank into my taste buds and drove me wild. I skimmed her spine as I sucked at her neck again. I drew in her skin and grazed it with the tips of my teeth. Lost. I was lost in the moment, wanting to suck on other parts of her, when she stepped out of my hold and pressed my arms to my side.

"I'll unpack."

"That can wait." I grabbed for her, but she stuck a finger in my face with a smirk.

"The deal was you kiss me where I said. I never said a thing about anything else."

I moved to stand in front of her, but her hands fell to my chest.

"I love your alpha-ness, Trigger. That's no secret." She bit her lip as she stared at her hands sprawled across my chest. I was sure she could feel my need for her. My blood was screaming her name.

"But, you need to stop lashing out and assuming things about me. So, from now on, when that happens, you can't touch me until I say otherwise."

Ha!

I reached for her again, but she grabbed my hands.

"And if you care about me at all," she studied me, searching for some trace of my feelings, "you'll respect me enough not to cross that line. If not, then take me." She stepped back and held her arms open.

Fuck me, she plays dirty.

I dropped my arms and held my switch down.

"I need to work." I ran a frustrated hand through my hair. "And I need to be away from you right now."

I stopped at the door and turned.

"Only for you, Tess." Her eyes lit up, and my gaze roamed her body one last time. "Game on."

Her eyes widened as my words hit her.

CHAPTER THIRTEEN

Tess

"What in the ever-loving fuck are you wearing?" Brick scowled at me as I slid behind the bar. "I feel like I'm committing some incest crime just being in the same room as you."

I rolled my eyes and started to turn all the bottles so the labels were facing outward.

"Wowza," Rail yelled from across the room when he saw my tight leather pants and matching leather halter top that stopped a little below my breasts, and as an added bonus, gave me some massive cleavage. I had pulled my hair into a ponytail, which hung down to the middle of my back.

"Hey, Brick, from this angle I can see side boob!"

"Does it look like your mother's?"

"Oh, come on." I smacked Brick's arm.

I was happy about my encounter with Trigger earlier. It was always baby steps with him, but every little step seemed like a milestone to me and made me feel a little more like my old self.

"Hey, Tess!" Minnie came up to the bar and wrapped her arms around Brick. He held her tightly and kissed her hard. "Hey to you too." She beamed at my best friend. It made me unbelievably glad Brick had found someone who truly made him happy. He deserved it.

"So," she leaned over the bar top, "you ready for girls' night?"

Oh, my God, I almost forgot we had plans. Jesus, I almost left. What an asshole I would have looked like.

Morgan chuckled and shook his head. "What's one more night with Peggy?"

"You clear it with him yet?" Brick nodded toward Trigger's office.

"I have to clear it with him first?"

I don't fucking think so.

"Where do you want to go?' I asked over Brick's shocked expression.

"Well, you want to go dancing? Or dinner?"

I handed her a shot, picked up one myself, and raised it to her. "Both?"

She let out a whoop and slammed hers back. Yes! A girls' night that might actually be fun.

"At least tell him," Brick warned then pulled out his cell phone and sighed. "Fucking Jilly."

"Don't, Matt." I reached over and pushed the phone away from his view. "She only wants money."

"What if she's in trouble?"

"When you were in trouble, where was she?" I knew my point hit home. "Take it from me. Don't let life's anchors drag you down from being happy."

"Tess!" Fin screamed from the hallway. "You're still here!" He raced under the bar and slammed into me for a hug.

"Hey, how was the ring?" His body was hot and sticky.

"Cool! Uncle Trig taught me how to throw a punch. Watch." He did a little karate kick.

I laughed at how seriously he took it. "You'll be able to take Den on soon."

"Yeah, he better watch out. Uncle Trig told me if I kept up bein' good, he'll teach me a choke hold and a roundhouse."

"That sounds like a good deal." I handed him a bottle of water. "You hungry?"

"Yes, I want a burger."

I eyed him. He knew better than to ask for that shit from me.

"Um, you pick."

Smart boy.

I headed to kitchen and ordered him a veggie plate, with chicken strips and milk.

When I returned, I grabbed my bag from under the bar, hugged Morgan—though he acted like he didn't love it—and headed for Trigger's office. I knocked and pushed the door open.

He was sitting at his desk, shirtless, sweaty, and staring at his computer screen.

He plays dirty too, I see.

"Hey," I whispered, just in case it was something serious. I didn't want to break his train of thought. "Got a sec?"

He looked up and lifted an eyebrow at my outfit. "I do."

"Morgan's covering my shift. I forgot I had plans tonight with Minnie."

He folded his arms, and I knew it wasn't going to be easy getting out of here, but my stubborn nature was standing right next to me.

"Where?"

"Not sure. Some place Min knows."

"What are you doing?"

"Dinner and dancing."

He tilted his head as he leaned back in his chair and thought about what I was saying.

"You need to change first."

I rolled my eyes. He was something else. "I'll see you later." I began to leave but made a sudden decision. "Um," I stepped closer to his desk, "Trigger, I knew about the logo on the coke because Big Joe explained that each bag was marked with a little symbol so the buyer knew what they were getting." I pulled out the USB stick. "I think you should watch it. I haven't watched a lot of it, but I know there must be stuff on there that's important, or Clark wouldn't have been so upset that I took it. Who knows, maybe you can find some dirt on Detective Aaron on there. A little blackmail never hurt anyone." I winked as I set it on his desk. "I have my own copy, if you want to keep the original. I might get time to look at the whole thing one day."

He leaned forward and examined the little piece of technology that held too many secrets.

"All right." He flicked it through his fingers like he did with his joints, and I waited for more, but there was nothing. *Man of few words* was an understatement. "Take Jace with you."

"No." I held my ground. "Don't even think of it."

He leaned forward, pushed to his feet, and started a slow walk toward me. His chest rose high and fell hard, then his eyes turned dark, and it took all my effort not to run to him.

That's what he wants.

"Trigger, the last time I got a day off I went to the beach, and you had Jace watch me the entire time. Then you showed up and took me home. I'll be with Minnie, and that's it." I raised my chin to look a little taller. He towered over me, and my eyes blazed at him. I hated that his sweat turned me on, and I felt the rush of heat that pounded between my legs.

He leaned his head down and brushed his lips over my ear.

"If I want to protect what's mine, I have the goddamn right to," he growled but backed off. "Text me when you change locations. Do you understand me?"

"Fine. We're in agreement, then." I could handle that. He slid a hand into my hair and kissed me hard—to make a point, I was sure. But as fast as he swooped in and stole my breath, he was gone behind his desk, buried in whatever he was doing.

I didn't question it and left.

***

"Where the hell did you take me, Min?" I laughed as she took the menu from me and prattled off something to the waiter.

We were in the basement of a clothing store in Venice. There was red velvet wallpaper glued to every inch of the walls, gold chandeliers dangled above us, and round leather tables with matching half cup seats were scattered as far as the stage. I felt like I was stuck on the set of *Moulin Rouge* where the sinful atmosphere was laced with dark and dirty promises.

"We, my friend," she removed a glass of champagne from the waiter's tray and handed it to me, "are having a true girls' night." She tapped the delicate rim of her glass to mine. "To *finally* having a girl around I don't want to smash in the teeth with a shovel."

I tossed my head back and laughed. That was possibility the best toast I'd heard in a long time.

"To us." I took a long sip of the crisp, bubbly drink then relaxed in my seat and pulled out my phone.

Tess: At the Rusty Diamond

Trigger: What the hell is that?

I laughed at his reaction. Minnie questioned my sudden outburst.

"Trigger wants to know where we are."

"Tell him to Google it."

We both waited a beat and burst out laughing together. Trigger didn't Google.

"Give me your phone."

I hesitated but thought why not. He'd be less apt to kill her than me.

One eyebrow slowly rose as her fingers tapped on the screen. I could only imagine the things she'd write, but before I could ask, the lights flickered out, and a spotlight illuminated a man standing at center stage. He was dressed in a black suit, his hair hung a little shaggy, and there was an intriguing grin on his face.

"Min—?" I began, but he beat me to the punch.

"Ladies and, well, dirty gentlemen," he flashed a wicked grin, "you all know the drill, and if you don't, here is a quick rundown." He swaggered across the stage. "Keep your arms and legs outside your seat at all times. If you need assistance, kindly slap the nearest ass you can find, and if you need to use the restroom, good luck, because I cannot help what may happen to you along the way. Now," he slapped his hands loudly by his head mic, "are you ready?"

The crowd screamed so loud my ears rang.

"I said, are you *ready*?"

I shook my head, and Minnie mouthed, "Girls' night, baby!"

Smoke rose from under our feet, and an under-glow of color engulfed us. Then a roar started from the corner of the room, and a man was slowly lowered from the roof and landed like a panther about five feet from me.

Drums beat to a familiar tune, and it took me a moment to recognize it. The man closest to me pointed in my direction just as a spotlight lit him up. He started to lip sync to "Comin' to Your City" by Big & Rich.

I grinned at Minnie. She had the best expression on her face, like a kid in a candy shop. She had taken me to a country drag queen show! Holy shit, it was perfect.

My train of thought was interrupted when a man started to come toward me. I closed my eyes. Fuck me. If Trigger showed up, there would be a bloodbath in here. Although I had to say Trigger was surprisingly good with Shantee.

A finger lifted my chin, and by the thick scent of the cocoa butter, I knew it was the dancer.

"Smile, darling!" he yelled over the music with a dramatic wink. I laughed at his totally over the top gorgeous eyelashes.

Three songs went by, and I had never seen so much glitter, feathers, and sequins in my life, and that was saying something. The men were incredible, and I hadn't laughed so hard in a very long time. Who would have thought this was under Venice?

The song changed to "Fake ID" by Big & Rich, and the place went wild. I looked around, puzzled at what was I missing.

Minnie hopped up on her seat and waved her arms. The guys started pulling people up on stage and dressing them in costumes.

I grabbed my friend and pulled her down into her seat while I signaled for another round of drinks. Oh, my God. This place was beyond fun, but my ass was not about to go on stage. I didn't dare risk a photo that would set Trigger's switch off for damn sure.

"You have got to be fucking kidding me!" I yelled, and anger licked at my insides. "He's impossible!"

"What?"

I leaned over and carefully pointed at the man back by the door.

"No way." She started to get up, but I stopped her.

"Wait. I have a better idea."

I hurried toward the stage and grabbed one of the men and whispered my idea to him. I handed him a twenty. He refused it, saying it was "all his pleasure."

"What did you do?" Minnie shouted, her champagne breath in my face.

"Just get your phone ready."

I waited for the song to switch, but it took all my power not to look in his direction.

My entire body jumped when I heard the beat. I scrambled to grab my phone as the man dressed like a horse raced toward him.

"Save a Horse" burst through the speakers, and the moment Rail caught sight of the man coming toward him, his horrified expression shot over to me.

I gave a little wave and held up my phone.

Three men circled Rail and rushed him up to the stage. They stuck a brown cowboy hat on him and looped a pair of reins around his waist. He tried everything to fight them, but they were too fast. Clearly, they'd dealt with people like him before.

When the song got to the chorus, the entire place went wild with the words, and guys pretended to ride him.

The look on his face when he locked eyes with me was that of man who was going to spend the rest of his life making sure mine was miserable.

Oh, Matt, this one is for you.

As soon as the song ended, they stripped him of his get-up and made him bow with the rest of them.

Rail pointed at me, but all I could do was laugh so hard tears streamed down my face. Minnie buried her face in her hands, but I could see her shoulders shaking.

"I will never forgive you for that." He pulled out a chair and downed the rest of both our drinks then grabbed a waiter. "Whiskey on *her* tab." He pointed to me.

Five more songs, some bubbles, and a lot more mist, and the show ended. We were finally served dinner, and I was starved.

I was surprised to see a lobster tail smothered in garlic sauce, and scallops paired with baby potatoes.

"You wouldn't think one of the best seafood chefs around worked here, would you?" Minnie bit into the scallop.

Rail ordered a steak and cringed when the man brought him his food wearing ass-less chaps. The music was turned down, and we were able to talk a little easier.

"I have never wanted to kill so many half naked men in my life." Rail dumped a half a bottle of A-1 sauce on his meat.

"Serves you right." Minnie stuck her fork at him. "We don't need an escort."

"I wasn't really sent *here*." He madly cut into the overdone cow. "I just got back to the club, and Trigger told me to check in on you. I wasn't going to stay. You weren't even supposed to see me."

"Well," I lifted my hands dramatically, "that makes it even better, doesn't it?"

***

Trigger

The cursor flashed over the *submit* button. I knew it was a bad idea, but what choice did I have? I either said no and this shit storm stayed, or I ended it once and for all.

My phone rang, and I quickly scooped it up.

"Yeah?"

"Boss, there's someone here who wants to speak to Tess." Morgan cleared his throat as I leaned forward in my chair. "You got a minute?"

Who the hell was here?

"Yeah." I hung up and clicked the button. The demons went wild and stirred up my hot blood to a dangerous level. My hands formed into fists. Who the hell would come here looking for Tess?

Blood could be shed, and the reaper might be rewarded tonight. I could almost taste it. I needed it.

I swung open the door, disappointed to find a medium-sized man dressed in black at my bar, a beer held between battered hands. Hands I recognized had seen a fight or two.

He felt me come up and slowly turned and took a moment to let my appearance sink in. I knew I was big, and I knew I fit the biker look. I'd let my beard grow, my hair was shaved on either side, and the rest hung in a messy, long mohawk that flopped to the right. Tattoos inked my skin, and my past was as evident as his was across my knuckles.

"He's clear," Joe chimed in and held up the gun he had taken from him. "Offered it at the door."

"Got no beef with you, man. Always carry it like my wallet." He stood and offered me a hand.

Morgan slid over a bottle of whiskey and two glasses. I ignored his hand and folded my arms, not wanting to touch him. The demons were so loud I could barely hear, and I knew he had better have a good explanation why he wanted to see Tess.

"Why do I know you?" I couldn't place him.

"I, ah…" He stumbled at my coldness. "I live in Vegas and know some friends of Tess's. I overheard some shit I thought she might want to know about."

"Like?"

He sank back onto the stool and looked around. "No offense, but I'd rather speak directly to Tess."

It wasn't lost on me that he called her Tess and not Tessa. He either did know her, or he'd heard about her recently.

"If you want to talk to Tess, you talk to me first." Just as the last word came out, Big Joe backed up and let someone in.

"Honey, I'm home!" Minnie called out as she and Tess stumbled into the bar, looking more than half in the bag. Rail was behind them and seemed relieved to be back.

Shit.

"Oh, look, Tess! We have company." Minnie giggled, and Tess grinned, but it was obvious she tried with her all might not to join in.

"Shh, you'll make him mad," Tess whispered loudly. "Although I kinda like Trigger angry. It's real exciting." Her expression turned devilish.

"You had fun tonight, Tiger?" Morgan broke through her dirty thoughts to try to make her see our unknown visitor.

"You know what Min and I did?" She pointed. "Railey wouldn't let us dance, so we came here to get the party started."

"She's all yours, man." Rail raised his hands. "Please don't ever ask me to check on them again. This one," he pointed at Tess, "thought it was cute to slip out of the club to make a phone call alone, then went back and did endless shots."

Tess broke out in a loud laugh. "Three men made Rail their bitch!" Minnie had to hold onto the stool to stop from falling over, she was in such a fit of laugher. "I will never forget his face when they bent him over and rode him with reins."

Morgan glanced at me and waved over Brick as he came in from out back.

"Hey, ladies, how was—" He stopped when he saw how piss-eyed drunk they were. "Damn, I really missed a fun night, hey?"

"Oh, Matt, you have no idea." I glanced back to her. I hated that she had used his real name in front of the unknown guy. They had their names for protection and honor, and their old names had no place here in the club. "I have an early birthday gift for you. Or maybe it's mine. Whatever. We can share."

"Die. All of you, die." Rail grabbed a beer from behind the bar. "Who the fuck is this?" He nodded to the guy who was staring at Tess like he was way too friendly with her.

"Brick, take Minnie to bed," I ordered. He caught my tone and scooped Minnie up and whisked her out of the room. "Morgan, coffee for Tess."

"Sure thing, boss."

Tess stood straight and gave me a salute, giggled, and stumbled as she peeled off her coat. I caught her arm before she fell.

"I would love to snap my fingers and have everyone jump to my command." She finally seemed to notice the guy next to me and dramatically offered her hand. "You look kinda familiar. How are ya?"

His face relaxed, and he broke out in a smile, taking her hand in his a little longer than I would have liked.

"I'm a friend of your mother's."

Tess yanked her hand free, and she immediately lost all sense of fun. "My past just keeps comin' to knock me down, and all I wanted was one night to have a little fun."

My attention moved to her face, and I saw something flicker across it. What did she mean? And what the hell? The guy never said anything about her mother.

"I'm not here on her behalf. I'm really not. I'm here to warn you about something."

She glanced at me, her eyes heavy with sadness. Or was it fear? Slowly, she leaned into the side of the bar in front of me and took the coffee Morgan handed her along with three Advil.

"No disrespect, but I really don't give a shit what happened to those people."

He nodded but then looked over at me and downed his beer. "Can we talk somewhere private?"

I considered his words and looked around the bar, which was littered with my men and a few random women, then back to Tess.

"This is my family, so my business is their business," she said.

I felt a sense of pride at her words. My hand slipped around her waist, and I pressed her against my side. She sagged into my hold.

"Okay." He cleared his throat. "You took a USB from Clark?"

"And if I did?"

"Have you watched it yet?"

"Only a little of it. Why?"

"So, you haven't gotten to file thirty-three?"

She shook her head.

He purposefully glanced down and then back to her eyes again. It only took her a moment before her entire body went stiff. She pulled herself free of me and stood off to one side, holding his gaze.

"Trigger, could you please get me the USB drive I gave you?"

"Rail, third drawer, left side."

Rail returned a moment later and handed it to Tess. She tossed it on the floor and jammed the heel of her shoe on it, crushing it into pieces.

"Shit!" Her hand covered her mouth. "How do you know—I mean, is that what you're here to warn me about, or is there…Jesus!" She grabbed the bar top and looked like she might pass out.

"Tess?" I reached out for her, and she gripped my arm. Her hands were ice. "What is in file thirty-three?"

"Not my place, man." He shook his head. "I'm here to let you know Clark won't give up. He's already headed this way."

"What? Tell him I destroyed it. I want nothing to do with all that crap. It's just a stupid stick full of lies. I only took it so he would know how serious I was about being done with him and the whole house."

"Do you have a copy?"

"No." She didn't miss a beat. I knew she had another copy, but I didn't know where.

"But it's not just about the USB, Tess. He wants you."

My blood thickened at the thought of Clark touching what was mine. He had his chance, and she choose the club—she chose me.

"I hate him! I've made that very clear. I loved him once. Well, actually, I'm not sure I ever really did. Not the way I love—the club." She whirled around. "Trigger? Can we borrow your office for a minute, please?"

No. No way in hell.

Her expression stopped me. I gave a nod, and she motioned for him to follow.

"Wait." She turned to him. "I never got your name."

He smiled. "Name's Zay."

I was pissed with this whole thing, and when the door closed, I turned to face Morgan. He stared at the barrier that separated us from them.

"Something feels off, man." He turned back to me and started wiping off the counter. "You think Clark is really coming?"

"No fucking clue."

"And what the hell is file thirty-three?"

I looked down to the broken USB. "Something bad, I assume."

"I hate that she can't have one night of fun."

"Mmm," I agreed. I couldn't help myself. Her phone was face-down on the bar, and I flipped it over and swiped the screen open. I tapped the phone log and saw a couple of Vegas area numbers had repeatedly called her.

Who the hell was that? Just as I went to call the number, a text came through from another number.

Clark: I'm sorry, Gumdrop. I don't blame you for what happened, and I took care of it. You were upset, that's all. I can't go another day without touching you or hearing the sounds you make when you're turned on. I NEED to see you NOW. I know where you're staying now. If you won't come to me, I'll come to you.

Oh, hell no! So many ways of killing that bastard flashed through my head.

"Dude has texted her three times tonight." Rail broke through my murderous state. "Look." He held up his phone and showed me a picture he took of the text messages. "I deleted them so she wouldn't see them. Look what good that did." He snickered.

Clark: I need you.

Clark: I'm tired of your damn voicemail! PICK UP, DAMMIT!

Clark: I miss me inside you.

The door to my office opened, and Zay came out, followed by Tess. She looked totally done.

"Sorry for the nature of my visit, Trigger. I meant no disrespect to you or your club. I just needed to warn Tess of what was happening."

I nodded at him but kept my eyes on Tess as she moved to the bar and leaned against it.

"You seem good here, Tess. I'm glad to see that. I'll do my best to keep Clark away."

"Thank you, Zay," she whispered.

"Take care."

Big Joe handed him his gun at the door, and he disappeared into the night.

"You okay, Tiger?"

I glanced at her.

"Not even a little."

I needed to get a look at her copy of that damn USB.

CHAPTER FOURTEEN

Tess

My breathing was heavy by the time I got to Trigger's room. I knew better than to go to my room; he'd only insist. I had no fight left in me.

I never used his bath before, but it looked inviting, so I ran the water and stripped off my clothes. I almost giggled when I found bubble soap under the sink. I decided I wouldn't go there, then I helped myself to some.

I eased into the hot water and tuned in to the soothing sounds around me. Rain pelted off the window, and I stared at the glass as the wind drove the drops in random patterns on the panes. Even the weather matched my mood. Cold, dark, and chaotic.

My eyelids grew heavy from my pounding head, so I let them lower and rest. I must have passed out for a bit because when I opened them, I was surrounded by candles and a glass of red wine.

"Trigger?" I whispered, hoping to hell it was him and not Brick.

He appeared in the doorway in only his jeans.

"Did you do this for me?"

He nodded, and his hair flopped forward in a sweet, messy way.

"Thank you." I felt the pesky tears brew in my lower lids.

"I do listen." His voice was low. "I may not be good at it, but I hear you."

My lips turned up, but my burning eyes held the truth. I was hurting from a very old wound.

"It's a big tub." I tried to focus on something else.

He smirked. "Never sat in one before. You enjoy it."

"You just ruined this for me."

"Why?"

"You had this bubble bath under your sink. Am I to assume you had other women in here?"

He sat on the bench next to the shower. His muscles looked even sexier against the flickering flames that highlighted his lean, toned body and cast yummy shadows in all the right places.

"Fin likes to pretend he's a shark." He shrugged, but I noticed his eyes crinkled when he spoke about his nephew. He cared about both the boys, although he pretended he didn't. They were part of his family. I understood that, and they really were pretty sweet when you considered the life they were being brought up in. "I never let anyone in here but me, and, well, maybe the kid."

"What makes me different?"

His lips sucked inward as he thought. "I'll make you a deal. You answer a question for me, and I'll answer one for you."

"No vetoes," I added. For once, I wanted some answers, and I was ready to share some truths.

"All right." He waited for me to start. "You don't want to go first?"

"Truthfully, you need to hear about my past in order to answer the question I'm going to ask."

He flipped his hair out of his eyes before he pulled a joint free from his pocket. "What's on file thirty-three?"

"It's my biggest regret." I pushed the bubbles around, unable to look at him. "My mother faked a pregnancy to trap Clark into rushing the wedding date. Everyone thinks I cut myself because of their wedding, but it was really because they would be forever tied together. I knew that baby would be loved the way I never was. Selfish, I know, but I was eleven and mentally warped." I wiped a tear that rested on my cheek. "When I was twenty-six, I had been living on the streets with Brick for some time. One night, he met a girl and left me to go spend the night with her in a motel. I ran into a pack of guys who were always causing trouble, and they tried to attack me. Before I knew what I was doing, I raced back to the house, which I said I would never do, and that night, I ended up in bed with Clark."

I tried to speed past the dirty details. I didn't need to make this any worse than it was. "I took off again the very next morning and met up with Brick, but I couldn't bear to confess what I had done. I couldn't admit to him that I had gone to see Clark after I got away from those guys. Brick would never forgive himself." I let out a long sigh, trying to gather enough strength to go on. "Three weeks later, I knew something was off with me. It didn't take long to figure out what had happened. I was so ashamed." The tears fell harder. "Brick risked so much for me to stay away from that house, and the one time he left me alone, I got into trouble and ran back there. I couldn't face him. He would never have understood. I don't deserve his forgiveness. So," I sniffed, "I packed my shit and went back to the house. Left him a note saying where I went and that I needed to work some stuff out. I left him all the money I had on me and thought I could live without my best friend."

Trigger's phone rang, but he turned it off and tossed it on the counter. He waited for me to continue.

"My mother was livid and tried to figure out why I'd come home. One night, she overheard me crying to Venna about how awful I felt." My voice trailed off, nervous of his reaction. "I was about a month pregnant and terrified." I glanced up, only to find his face like stone. "I didn't want children. I knew I'd be a horrible mother. What kind of role model would I be, sleeping with my stepfather?" I stopped to let the hurt rip across my chest.

"My mother grabbed my hair, dragged me upstairs to Clark's office, and shoved me to my knees. She screamed at him, called me a whore, and all Clark did was stare at me. He never protected me. He just looked at me like I was someone else, not someone he had made love to a few weeks before." Heavy, hot tears raced down my face, running away from me like everyone else in my life.

I shook off my emotions and pushed on. "A few nights later, three men who worked at the house woke me up and forced me downstairs into one of the back rooms." I swallowed hard, as the next part was a haunting blur of pain. "Venna said they could hear me screaming for hours. She tried to help, but they had the room guarded. Clark paced the room but didn't even try to intervene." Trigger's throat contracted, but the rest of him was still.

"I couldn't believe what they were doing to me, my own mother and the man I thought loved me. They stood there and watched while I was held down and my baby ripped out of me by some cold-faced stranger. They killed my child. Whether I wanted it or not, they took a life. I checked out, and it took me a long time to find the will to even bother to leave that place. I fell into a bad crowd. Sex and alcohol were all I cared about for four years. Funny how quickly time passed when you've been stuck between two lives." I took a moment to remember. "It felt good, helped me cope. That was where I learned how to turn *it* off. Just stop caring. I guess we all have a switch somewhere." I shrugged. "I just didn't give a damn what happened to me. Until one day I reached out to the only person who had ever loved me."

"Tess," Trigger started, but I wasn't done.

"The number that keeps calling me is my doctor. I had some liquid courage tonight and finally called her back. I saw her when I was at the house for the pain in my side. The Serpents really did a number on my stomach. It really took a long time to heal. Turns out my doctor had more *great* news. What happened to me at the house years ago…well, that rent-a-doctor didn't do the procedure right and did a lot of damage. Since I never dealt with the old injury, my new one flared up the scarring, and…I guess my loving mother took yet another thing from me."

I laughed darkly and dried my cheeks. I was a mess, but at least he now knew the whole truth.

"Tess—"

"I'm fine, Trigger, really. I just wanted you to know, so you can decide what to do."

He huffed loudly. "Do with what?"

"With me. I can leave tonight if Clark is really coming. You don't need this shit right—"

"You're not going anywhere."

"Trigger—"

"That's three times now, Tess. You interrupt me again, and I'll tie you up and gag you myself to make you listen."

The anger in his voice shook me to the core, but it also awakened a foreign feeling. He still cared. I wasn't expecting that.

"I don't want kids. Never have. I'm sorry you went through that, but fuck me, I'm damn happy you never had his kid. As for your mother, I will deal with her myself. If Clark shows…I hope he does because I can't wait to give him the full clubhouse tour."

Ah, yes, the slaughter room.

"As for you," he twisted to sit on the side of the tub, his eyes dark in the dim light, "you're not going anywhere. I can't protect you if you run off again." His finger curled around a fallen strand of hair that was stuck to my chest. He peeled it free, running the back of his finger down my hot skin.

"I don't want to be a problem."

His hand disappeared into the water and gently urged my legs open. He found my opening and circled my clit. My stomach tightened as I bowed upward and tried to direct them inside.

My eyes closed when the delicious warmth tingled up my skin, preparing me for what was to come. I snapped my hand around his wrist and pushed him to where I needed it.

He suddenly stood, leaving my feverish body to fend for itself. He kicked off his pants and briefs and stepped into the tub in front of me. I grabbed his hips and swallowed his erection before he could stop me.

"Jesus, Tess!" My name vibrated from deep inside his throat, and he grabbed a handful of hair and held me in place as he set the pace. His tip rolled over my taste buds, so I curled my tongue to cup and caress the velvet slit.

I took him deeper, and he hissed loudly.

"Enough." He pulled out and eased me backward into the water. He hovered over me, legs on either side of mine, and pinched my nipples. His expression was one I hadn't seen before, like he was contemplating something. His brows drew together, and his eyes widened. Before I discovered what it was, he broke his hold on me.

"Turn over," he commanded. I wasted no time and flipped around. He took hold of my waist and pulled me onto his lap as he sat on his knees. "Lift." His voice was tight. "Now down." He slammed up as I dropped down.

I screamed at the sudden fullness. He hit the end of me with a force that took my words away.

"Again." He nipped at my neck, and I obeyed.

And again, I rose, completely at his mercy. His hands started to roam as I repeated the action. The water splashed onto the floor with each thrust. I'd never had sex in a tub before, and as awkward as it seemed, Trigger made it easy. Maybe because the space was so large, or because it was exactly what I needed at that moment. I needed so much to feel something other than shame and disappointment.

"Stop." He turned my chin to look at him. "When you're with me, you're with me. Nowhere else. Ever."

I nodded and tried to let the ugly thoughts go. Easier said than done, and I knew he felt my struggle.

When I rose to slam back down, he pushed me to my knees and placed my hands on the side of the tub. He slid in fast and took me from behind. I could barely think at the pace. My vision blurred, and I struggled to catch my breath. He slapped my ass and pulled my attention back to him.

"Give it to me!" He was close to losing it. "Now!"

I leaped off the edge and burst into a hundred million pieces. Colors of every shade sparkled behind my eyelids and pricked at my sensitive skin. My heartbeat strummed a wicked melody as I floated back to reality. Sex with Trigger was like unwrapping a present. The outcome was always wanted, but it was seriously unpredictable.

He nibbled my neck to see if I was back with him.

“Mmm,” I moaned because it was all I had in me.

“I will kill anyone who touches you.”

***

Trigger

I couldn’t stop touching her. Her skin was like silk, and each time I inhaled her scent, she calmed the raging storm inside my head. It wasn’t lost on me that I was becoming addicted to Tess. So much of me wanted to push her away, send her back to Clark. Go back to my familiar hell. But the other part told me I deserved her. I’d put in my time to the reaper. I did his dirty work, and I had the savages in their cages to remind me that I wasn’t free.

My father popped into my head, and I flinched at his image. I’d need to start training soon. I knew I had this, but I needed my head in the game.

I reached for my phone and sent a text.

Trigger: Call me.

It rang three seconds later.

“Been awhile,” I whispered as I rose off the bed and moved out to the hallway.

“Am I to assume you contacted me because you’re heading back into the ring?”

I waited for the door to click shut behind me before I answered him.

“Yeah.”

Langley paused, and I knew what was rolling through his mind.

“Spare me the whole ‘you go to the dark side in the ring,’ Lang.” I pushed my anger aside. “I need your help.”

“I’ve taught you everything you need to know. Not sure why you’d call on me now.”

I rubbed my head and thought about getting a drink, but my liver needed the break, and my body needed to be in the best shape it could be.

"What's really going on?"

I licked my lips. "My father is back."

"Impossible."

"I would say the same thing if I hadn't seen him myself."

Langley let out a puff of air, and I heard a chair scrape along the floor.

"But you—"

"I know. I'm out of ideas on that score. I know I have a mole. I'm just not sure how long he's been around or who the fuck he is. He's tied to my father, I know that much, and they screwed with my drug route and killed some of my men. Now he's got…" I glanced at the bedroom door and pictured Tess so small in my bed.

"Got what?"

"He's got leverage over me."

"What, a video or something?"

"Something," I repeated, unsure how to describe Tess.

"Oh," he chuckled, "well, now I really need to come."

I closed my eyes and wished to hell people would stop making comments about the situation. They all saw something that wasn't there. I cared for Tess, I needed her, but I wasn't in love with her. That was something I simply wasn't capable of. Neither was she.

"You got room for me there? I don't do motels."

"Yeah."

"I'll be there tonight."

"Morgan will be here. I have something to handle tonight."

"See you soon, son."

I lowered the phone and watched as the call disconnected. No turning back now.

Tess worked the bar with Peggy in the morning. Morgan had to help Cooper with a family problem. Peggy was a raging bitch, but Tess ignored her and did her own thing.

Rail and Brick worked out the details for the fight in my office away from anyone who might want to listen.

Jace hovered around the bar, trying not to trip over Maze's cousin, who came by to collect his shit. She was a cute little one but was barely twenty-two and clearly had hang-ups of her own.

Cray: Last shipment has been collected. You are no longer walking with the white witch.

Trigger: Now I walk with the monsters.

Cray: Not that long now, my friend.

My head pounded. I was about to signal Tess when she appeared at my table with a double whiskey. She set it in front of me then stepped up and ran her hands through my long hair. I hooked my arm around her waist and pulled her closer. She studied my face, and her hands slid down and ran along my brow to my temples.

"Do you always carry such heavy shadows with you?"

"I could ask you the same."

The corner of her mouth twitched before it faded away.

"I guess it makes it easier to spot them, then." She touched her lips to mine then sighed. "You can talk to me, you know. I know I'm not one of the guys, but—"

"No, you're not." I forced a smile, but I knew she saw through it.

"Okay." She tried to step back, but I locked my arms.

"We have plans tonight."

"We do?" She looked confused, then her face fell. "What kind of plans? I will not hide out, if that's what you're thinking."

"As tempting as that sounds, no, you have been requested at my meeting tonight."

"With who?"

I grinned at her sudden interest. She made the little things fun again.

There was a loud crash, and I jumped to my feet and shoved Tess behind my back.

"Slippery little fuckers!" Peggy cursed at the pile of glass in front of her.

"Karma's a bitch when you're a bitch," Gus muttered at his empty glass, which made Tess laugh, and Peggy glared at her.

"You gonna just watch me or actually be useful around here?" She raised an eyebrow at Tess.

"I just figured you spend so much time on your knees it would be like you were home down there."

"Screw you, bitch!"

"Not if you paid me."

Peggy picked up a bottle of vodka by the neck like she was going to throw it.

"Peggy!" I barked as Gus began to get up. "Get this shit cleaned up and get the fuck out."

Her hands went to her hips. “You’re seriously pussy whipped, Trigger.”

“Enough!” I felt my switch tremble. “I don’t need this shit right now.”

Tess ran her hand up my back, and I swung around to grab it. I held it tightly in mine, wanting to crush the bones, but my head stopped me.

I brought her hand to my mouth and kissed it. The urge to hurt someone was right below the surface. As much as Tess calmed me, I couldn’t always control my temper. Yet another reason we shouldn’t be together.

“When should I be ready?” Her voice was low. I wondered if I scared her.

Fuck.

“Eight.” She looked about to leave as I hooked her waist and pulled her to my chest. I leaned down and whispered a warning in her ear. “Don’t wear anything sexy.”

Her devilish stare made me hard. I slapped her ass as she sauntered away.

I scanned the room and spotted Rail. “Rail, suit up.”

His eyes widened, and he cursed. “Why me?”

Three hours in the ring with Rail, and he was done. He heaved over the ropes to catch his breath and held his side in pain.

I was jacked up on adrenaline. My body had at least five more hours left in it, and all I could get Rail to do was stand there while I did circles.

“Come on, Uncle Trig. Nail him in the sack!” Fin squealed from the corner of the room.

“Shut up!” Rail huffed. “Don’t you need to be in school or something, shit?”

“Not my fault you hit like a girl.”

Rail straightened. “Seriously, why the fuck is he here?”

“School’s closed.” I tossed a punch at his shoulder, which did dick for my mood. I had to wear gloves with the guys or I’d kill them.

“Nipple twist him!” Fin screamed again.

“No, don’t,” Brick laughed from the doorway. “He likes that.”

My arms fell when Rail glared at Brick. “So does your momma.”

“Yeah, and so does yours.” Brick gave him the finger then licked the tip.

“Fuck me,” I hissed and knew another pissing match was on the way.

"Can I play?" They fell silent as I whirled around and saw Maze's cousin in a little pair of tight shorts and a sports bra.

She ducked under the ropes and smiled up at me. "You think you can take me?"

"No chicks in the ring," I muttered, brushing past her. My head wasn't in the mood for another child right now.

"Is he always so friendly?" she whispered as I tossed off my gloves and slicked my hair back.

"No," Brick and Rail said in unison.

She appeared at my side, her oversized blue eyes blinked up at me. She was pretty, but in an annoying way. You could tell she'd be high maintenance once she roped you in.

Ignoring her, I grabbed my towel and headed to the front of the club. I didn't have much time before I needed to get ready.

"So, I, ah…" She rushed to match my strides. "I was wondering if I could stay here for a while."

"Why?" I didn't care for the answer, but I wanted her to know this wasn't a hangout for strays.

"Maze paid for my apartment, but now that he's gone, I'm being evicted. Got nowhere else to go."

I snatched a water bottle from the fridge behind the bar and caught Tess serving Cooper and a few of his friends.

She didn't spot me right away; the bar was in full swing.

"So?" I vaguely heard the girl as I moved around the bar. Just as I was about to approach Tess, a hot hand clamped around my forearm.

The entire place went quiet when I stopped and whirled around, feeling the demons flip the fuck out inside. Acidic rage coursed through my bloodstream, rushing to the surface and scarring the inside of me.

I dropped my gaze to her hand then backed up. She was confused but didn't let go.

Morgan whistled from behind the bar and glanced at her hand with a warning. Finally, she got the hint, and her arm fell with a thud.

"So, you don't like to be touched?" she asked in disbelief. "The great, almighty fighter can kill with his bare hands, but he can't be touched by a woman?" She nearly laughed, and I saw her death flash in front of me. A quick snap to her neck to shut her up would be ideal.

"How do you screw?"

"Bitches with mouths don't last long here," Morgan warned again.

My switch vibrated, and the maddening screams became ear-piercing.

"First rule in a club is respect, little girl." I stepped closer, and she cowered away from me. I almost smirked. Tess would have given me lip. "Maze's blood or not, you don't belong here."

"I'll vouch for her," Jace said, and I flicked my gaze over to him.

"Quit thinkin' with your dick."

"She's got nowhere to go." He shrugged.

"Yeah, man." Tat, one of Cooper's cocky friends, said and rose out of his chair. "She got no one since you got her cousin killed." He smirked at the girl, and I glared at Cooper. He knew better than to let a non-club member hear club information.

"Tat, shut the fuck up." Cooper punched his buddy in the arm. I knew that shithead used Cooper for free booze and tried to join the club a few years back, but I refused him. He never got over the fact I didn't let him in.

"That's the problem with this club. Everyone is expendable. Just takin' this one a little longer to see it." Tat draped his arm over Tess, and she sidestepped out of his reach with a hiss.

Red. I saw nothing but red.

I rubbed my mouth to take a moment to calm down, but it didn't work. I snatched the hunting knife Rail carried, held it by the tip, and whipped it with all my might into Tat's shoulder.

His eyes popped while he grabbed at the blade. Blood lined the wound and soaked into his shirt.

The girl screamed as Tat struggled to comprehend what had happened. I eased into the chair and took the drink Morgan set in front of me.

Tat shot up behind me, white as a sheet, and stuck a gun to the back of my head.

"No," Tess whispered. "Tat, don't." She started to move, but Brick stopped her. "Tat, look at me," she tried again as my patience fizzed away.

"How can you love such a monster, Tess?" Tat shouted, foaming at the mouth. I guessed I underestimated his interest in Tess. Tat's body was rejecting the sudden intrusion.

"Because," her voice shook, "I'm one too." She pushed Brick's hand away when he tried to stop her again. "So, point that at me, not him."

I sipped the amber liquid and watched as he tried to push the blinding pain away. If he so much as twitched in her direction, he was dead. Well, he was dead anyway.

Tess moved closer, and I tried not to reach for her. She was insane. What the fuck was she doing?

Tat blinked a few times before he focused back on me.

"I hope she watches you die by your father's hand," he whispered.

Flip.

CHAPTER FIFTEEN

Tess

Trigger flipped his hair out of his face and turned to the screaming chick in Jace's arms. The broken whiskey bottle was tossed to the ground a few feet away.

"Remove her, or I will."

"How can you kill someone like that?" she screamed. "Sick son of a bitch!"

"Now! Or she's next."

"Come on." Jace literally had to yank her along by the arm to get her to leave.

Trigger turned to me then closed his eyes. He was trying hard to get himself back under control, and it wasn't easy for him. "Everyone out!"

Within seconds, the room had emptied except Tat on the floor in a puddle of blood, myself, and Trigger. Trigger reached out and held onto the bar. I had never seen him like that. He seemed to be struggling with something.

"Trigger?" I whispered, unsure what the hell was running through his head. "You okay?"

"No," he hissed and glared at me, and his pupils searched mine before he spoke. "Are you fucking insane?"

"You sure you want to pull at that thread?" I attempted to joke.

"I'm not fucking kidding!" His voice echoed throughout the room. I was thankful the music was still on, but I was sure some may have heard him.

"He had a gun to your head. What was I supposed to—"

"You let me deal with it, Tess! Not get him to point a gun at *your* fucking face!" He kicked Tat hard and covered his mouth and muttered something.

"I knew he wouldn't hurt me."

"How?" His bark made me jump. "How the fuck do you know what was going through that fucker's head?"

I felt my back go up.

"He asked me to leave you for him. He told me he wanted me, and that he could make me happier."

It was true. He had pulled me aside while Trigger was in the ring that afternoon. I laughed at first, thinking he was drunk, but when he leaned in to kiss me, I shoved him aside.

"And?"

Oh, please!

"We're planning our marriage right now." I dripped with sarcasm, and my fury burned through my eyes. Shit, when would he ever get that I wanted him?

"Be careful, Tess. I just killed a man. You push me too far, and I'll kill again."

I stepped closer and pushed my chest into his. His heat smoldered around me, holding me tight.

"You saying you'd hurt me?"

"I'm saying I'd kill for you." He grabbed my face between his huge hands and pressed his forehead to mine. I clutched his shoulders and held him just as hard. He needed an anchor. "Don't ever do that to me again. Promise me. If anything happens to you, I…" He stopped himself.

"You'd what?"

"Promise me, Tess." His voice was strained, and I needed to stop pushing. It was enough for now.

"I'm sorry." I pressed my lips to his and let him devour my mouth. Right as I was about to grab his belt, he pulled away.

"We need to leave."

Just like that, the moment was gone, and just like that, Tat was forgotten. The MC world had no room for screw-ups or mourning, and if I was going to allow myself to fully fall for this man, I needed to learn that now.

***

"Who are we meeting up with?" I walked through the door he held open for me.

"Mike."

I grinned with delight. I liked Mike and was curious why I was brought along for the ride.

"Really?"

"Don't be too excited," he grunted, but I saw the humor in his smile.

Trigger's playful moods didn't happen often, so when they did, I relished them.

"Can't blame me. He has all the goods on the books…" I trailed off when I caught sight of a table full of beautiful people. "Oh, my sweet non-fictional heaven, what have you done?"

There sat the cast of the *Broken* trilogy. I knew because I Googled the shit out of them when I finished the first book.

Savannah was dressed in a pair of blue jeans and an oversized sweater. She wrapped me in her arms. "It is such a pleasure to meet you, Tess!" She smelled like heaven in a jar. "I'm Savannah, but please call me Savi."

All I could do was freak the fuck out inside while I played it cool on the outside.

"Please, the pleasure is all mine."

Her smile made me blush. She had a whimsical way of moving that reminded me of a ballet dancer. She had such grace and poise.

Then there was me.

Trigger and Mike stepped off to the side to speak while Savi introduced me to everyone else.

Mark was cute as hell. He was clearly a boy in men's clothes. Keith was the silent, broody type, and then there was Cole. Holy hell, there were no words to describe that kind of sexy. Not entirely *my* type, but I sure wouldn't kick him out of bed for any reason, ever.

Savannah handed me a glass of champagne when the waiter returned. I raised an eyebrow and wondered how she knew what I liked.

"Trigger filled us in."

"That so?" I laughed softly. "What else did he say?"

"Actually, a lot," Mark said with a wink. "Like how he wanted us to meet you for your birthday."

"What?"

Shit just got interesting.

"Yup, but something happened, and our last trip got canceled. So, when Mike said he was coming here for a meeting, we all tagged along."

"Wait." I flipped my hair out of my face, more to cool off my warm cheeks than anything. "Trigger planned for you all to meet me for my birthday?"

"That's right." Mike flashed me a killer smile. "First time I have ever heard him speak about a girl."

"Hmm." I tried to hide my smile, but Savi mirrored my mood.

"Feels pretty good, doesn't it?"

I tapped my glass to hers. "Kind of does."

I loved how Cole found some way to touch Savannah, or how he watched her tell a story. He was obviously captivated by her. Part of me was envious of how he didn't mind showing his affection for Savannah in public. His finger twisted a lock of her hair, which made her lean in and press her cheek to his chest. They were beautiful together.

They grilled me about Trigger. It was odd to think they were interested in us when I had a thousand and one questions to ask about them, but I went along with it. Truth be told, I rather liked it. I felt like I was in a normal relationship, or something like it, anyway.

Keith caught my attention though. He kept glancing at his phone, and his mood seemed edgy. Finally, Cole picked up on it, or maybe he was just as curious as I was.

"Everything—" Cole started when Keith answered his phone.

We all went quiet when he spoke, obviously agitated. "No, you can't do that," he said then paused to listen. "I will not bail you out again!" He paused. "No, no way. I won't do it. I told you that the last time."

Mark tried to hold back his smirk. I guessed he knew who was on the other end of the line.

Keith leaned forward and tried to muffle his voice. "The boy is twenty-two. You cannot pinch his ass in the checkout line! I will not be a part of this—" He stopped mid-sentence. "No! I will not." He stopped again. "Dammit, Nan! Fine, but I'm callin' Mom." His eyes widened. "Watch me."

"He won't." Mark shook his head.

"Find your own way to bingo."

"Such a lie." Mark sighed, and I tried not to laugh while Savi pressed her lips together to hide her smile.

Just when I thought Keith was going to hang up, he lowered his voice. "See you Thursday."

"For bingo." Mark leaned out of the way of Keith's swat. "Nan puts a seventeen-year-old boy on prom night to shame."

"Not gonna lie, I kinda want to meet the woman." I made the table laugh, Keith included.

Trigger glanced over at me from the bar. He didn't smile, but he held my gaze. My lungs contracted and trapped the air, and I felt a rush of lust hit the center of my belly.

"I know that look," Mark stole my attention, "and I don't mean yours."

Savi beamed at me. "So, we have something for you."

"Me?" I shook off my moment with Trigger and sat a little straighter, intrigued by what was in the silver box in front of her.

She slid it over. I pulled on the ribbon and opened the top. There sat a paperback with the whole *Broken* trilogy.

"The author signed it, and we all did too." She laughed.

Holy...

"You did this for me?"

"Not entirely." Cole nodded at Trigger. "It was his idea too."

I gently pulled the cover back and flipped the pages in disbelief. "Can I ask some questions?"

"Of course." Savannah pulled her hair to one side and leaned in like she was ready to go.

Where to begin…?

"Keith." He broke out in a smile. I guessed he didn't think I would start with him. "I haven't gotten to your book yet, but I have to know. Why did you leave Shadows?"

"It wasn't easy." He glanced at Cole, who gave a slight nod. I assumed it was his way of asking how much he could talk about. "At first, it was so I could be closer to my family and to keep Lexi close."

"But now?"

"All I can say is Mike and I are getting things set up the way we want them, and it takes a while to get a house to run smoothly. Will we stay there forever? Probably not."

Mark broke out in a boyish grin. "They're training some guys to run the house. Only a matter of time."

"Really?" I liked that idea. "I mean, I get it. You can't really have a safe house with kids running around."

"Well, that was the problem at first," Cole chimed in. "But after they left, the house hasn't been the same, so Savi came up with the idea of building some homes on the property. We are a family first, and special ops second."

"Life's too short to be without the ones you love," Savannah added with a laugh.

Keith reached over and squeezed her hand. Jesus, they were all such good friends. I had to admit I was a little jealous, but we had our *club love,* maybe just a little warped and sharp around the edges.

"Okay," Mike shook them off, "what else you wanna know?"

"Well, I have one for you." I leaned forward so he could hear me better. "Are you dating anyone?"

Everyone looked at him with smiles.

"Yeah, Mikey." Mark spat soda out of his mouth. "You datin' anyone?"

"Nah." He glance down at his colorful hands. "I'm not exactly the boy you bring home to meet the parents."

I thought I heard my heart break.

"I disagree."

"That's 'cause you're dating him." He nodded at Trigger. "You, Tess, are a rare breed, and I appreciate that a lot."

Warmth spread through me; I understood being an outcast.

"Savi," I grabbed her attention from Mike, "you play any more paintball?"

Cole's face dropped but lit up when Savannah smiled at him. "Not that I can openly admit to."

"Pardon me?"

"Bah!" Mark jammed at Cole's shoulder. "Great question, Tess!"

"So help me God, Lopez."

Mark held up his hands in defense, and it gave me an opener for my next topic.

"Okay, okay, one more, and I promise I'm done." I couldn't help but smirk. "Is Doc Roberts still dating Abigail?"

"*No*!" Mark yelled, but the entire table broke out in a loud laughter, and I was thrown a million and one *yesses*.

***

Trigger

"I don't know, man. Listening to all this sounds like you got a real shit pile going on." Mike rubbed his head while he nursed his beer.

"Aaron and Doyle been joined at the hip lately. Those two are sure as hell on someone's payroll." He tapped the photos he brought of the two cops having coffee. "Clark has some USB drive with a bunch of secret shit on it, you have a mole, Tammy says there's more to this than you know, and now you've agreed to a fight."

"Yeah." I nodded slowly.

"You seem unfazed, my friend."

"Shit's coming. Just gotta be ready."

Mike nodded and asked for another drink. "Now that the coke contract is done, what will you do?"

"Between the garage, strip club, and debts owed to me, the club will be fine."

"If you ever need anything, you know we could use you at the house."

I smiled at his offer. "Appreciate that, but I think it's better for me to stay down here and you up there." I knew he got my reference. Too many skeletons kept me rooted in the dirt.

"The offer doesn't expire."

"Good to know. Oh," I pulled out my phone and brought up a still shot from the club's outside cameras, "know who this is?"

Mike took it from my hand an examined the image. "No, but if you send it to me, I can look into it."

"Yeah, okay. He said his name was Zay. Said he knew Tess's mother, and we both know him from somewhere." I sent it to his phone.

"I'll see what I can dig up."

I offered my hand—not something I did. He blinked before he took it. Mike had been a loyal friend to me for years and had helped me out even when he shouldn't have.

"Can I ask you something?"

I glanced over at Tess, her face lit up with excitement as she talked with her book friends, and nodded.

"Does your sixty-some-year-old father really want to fight you publicly?"

"Apparently."

"You don't think he's planning on bringing anyone else in?"

"Despite his huge ego, I'm sure there's someone or something else coming."

"Why not grab him right before?"

"My father is all about the attention, the performance, and the win.

To bring him to his knees and prove I'm better is the victory I want. Whether it's with him or some jacked-up asshole he brings in."

"Then what?"

I allowed myself a moment to relish the darkness inside, my mood shifted, and I felt the old urge to hurt him fill me. "Then I kill him."

"What about everyone else?"

"My father has something on Doyle. He made that clear at the station. I just need to know what it is, so I can swing the power to my side. As for Detective Aaron, he was working for Clark to get Tess back. They have something on me, but I'm working on that."

"Any idea what it is?"

"Yeah, I might. You remember when that strip joint Billy owned went up in flames a few years back? There was a huge explosion, and they lost millions in their meth lab."

Mike thought for a moment. "Ah, yeah, bunch of guys were killed when it exploded, but quite a few more were trapped down below. Burned to death or something? Santa Barbara?"

"Yeah, well, I was in town that week for something else. A friend asked me to pay Billy a visit to discuss something. Things went south, but I left before anything went down. Billy was a piece of shit and not worth my time. I just did it for a favor."

"Any witnesses?"

"Just one, but she went MIA, and no one else would talk. It was ruled an accident, but my guess would be they have photos of me that day."

"Shit, seriously?"

"Look," I leaned in closer, "we both know I don't kill sloppy. When I do, I do it right. I walked into that one. Bad timing."

"You trust that friend who asked you for the favor?"

For a split second, I hesitated, but shook off the feeling. "I do. But it's no secret many people want to see me dead. If the info was brought to the cops and put the right way, it could look bad."

Mike dropped his head and squeezed his eyes shut and sighed.

"And Doyle? Any ideas what he has on him?"

"Doyle is a power trippin' little asshole who hides behind his badge. He's just lookin' to make my life shit. He's the least of my problems."

Mike grabbed some peanuts from the bowl on the bar and peered over at me.

"Say it."

He half smiled. "And for the elephant in the room? You think she's safe?"

"Nope."

"Your father knows how you feel about her. You don't keep women around, and you've never done something like this." He full-out smiled and waved at his friends.

I ran my hand down my beard and wished she'd never come to the church that day. Maybe the devil wouldn't have seen my fear.

"She can always come back with us, you know."

"I've thought about that."

"Where can I go?" Tess asked. Shit, the girl moved fast. She shouldn't be eavesdropping or butting in my conversations. She needed to know her place.

"You don't listen or interrupt me when I'm in a meeting." I grew angry fast. "You need to learn your role, dammit, Tess."

"And what is that, exactly?" Her hands flew to hips, and her eyes shot fire.

"You're the girl I'm fucking. Not an old lady or—" I stopped myself when I heard my own words echo back at me. Fuck my father. My own temper was going to kill me.

"Well, the girl you're just *fucking*," her eyes seemed to change, "wants to thank you for your thoughtful gift."

I took a moment to calm myself. I knew I needed to back off here, but the grin on Mike's face pissed me off.

"Mike," I controlled the urge to punch something, "offered his safe house for you until this shit with my father ends."

Tess's face softened, and her posture relaxed. She smiled sweetly over at Mike. He was enjoying this way too much.

"I deeply appreciate the offer, Mike, more than you know, but for now, I'm fine at the club."

"Not your choice to make, sweetheart." I ground my teeth.

Her eyes flickered over to mine. "Funny how I just made it, *honey*."

"Tess," I warned.

"Trigger." She matched my tone.

Mike snorted a laugh as she walked back to the table. "You're fucked, Trig!"

We ordered another round and joined the others at the table. Tess was in the middle of a story Mark found hysterically funny. Cole had his arm around Savannah, and they both laughed, engulfed in her story as well. I felt Mike's eyes on me and squinted at him, wondering what the hell he was thinking.

Once Tess was finished, she looked back at me and smiled. Her eyes raked across my face.

"Tess," Mike called, "can I ask you something?"

"Of course."

"There's something to your story at the church that confused me."

Tess stood straight. I knew it wasn't a topic she liked to talk about.

She cleared her throat. "Okay."

"You got to the church by hiding in the ammo truck, right?"

"Yes."

Mike nodded. "You slipped out and raced into the church, where you found Trigger and Allen talking?"

"Yes, that's right."

"But then you went to the bus station."

She shook her head. "No, I went to the trailer to grab my stuff, and then went to the bus station."

"But how did you get there?"

Her slim fingers skimmed down the long stem of the champagne glass as she considered her answer. "When I raced down the driveway, I ran into Tristan. He freaked out that I was there and took me back to the trailer."

"Really?" First I'd heard about this.

She nodded at me before she turned back to Mike. "I grabbed all my stuff, and when I went to find Gus, Big Joe said he'd give me a lift."

The table went quiet, and I could hear my heartbeat in my ears.

"Wonder why that was never shared?" Mike glanced at me.

"That's Joe for you. He's loyal where loyalty needs to be. He did nothing wrong," Tess said. "He wanted to stop me, but I told him I was leaving with either his help or with Loose." She peeked at me over her shoulder. "I'm sorry, Trigger, but I played dirty, and even he said you'd kill him if he took me. I promised I'd never tell, but to get me out of there."

My mouth went dry. Big Joe had always been loyal, but I knew he did bend the rules at times. I knew the club always came first with him, but the fact that he knew where she was when I was flipping out fucking bothered me. I wasn't done with him.

"If you're going to be mad at someone, it should be me. He saw the situation for what it was and did what he thought you'd want him to do."

"Well," Savannah broke the tension, "I don't know about you guys, but I could use some food."

"Music to my ears." Mark snatched up the menu and started to prattle off the appetizers.

Tess leaned back in her chair and looked up at me. I knew she was worried, and in a way, it showed me how much she had protected my club by protecting one of the family.

"I'm sorry."

"He should've told me."

Her eyes closed, and I saw how much it bothered her. Without thinking, I rested my heavy hand on hers. She glanced down at the contact and slowly laced her fingers through mine. I tensed but didn't pull away.

I tuned back to Mark speaking with the waiter. "Mozza sticks—no, wait—sweet potato fries. No, you know what? Just bring one of everything."

"Watch your fingers when you place it in front of him," Keith joked. "He has sharp teeth."

"I have a healthy appetite." Mark shrugged. "Don't project your negativity on me just because I can eat whatever I want and look this fabulous."

Keith stuck a finger in his face. "What did I tell you about using the word 'fabulous' outside the house?"

Jesus Christ, you'd think they were married.

"Yeah," Cole laughed, "I really need to second that shit."

Mark rolled his eyes but rubbed his stomach when the plates arrived.

Tess appeared right at home with everyone, and she and Savannah seemed to like each other. They were all good guys, and I could understand why Mike fit in. He was lot more outgoing than I would ever be. My bike and bar were my comfort zone. I liked space and didn't have much to say in a group. Never did.

The girls went to the bathroom, and Keith and Mike were talking. I finally relaxed and got out my phone.

CHAPTER SIXTEEN

Tess

Trigger was alone at the table when I returned. Savi took a call from Abigail, who was watching Olivia, and needed a few minutes.

"How are you doing?" I shifted into my seat next to him.

He tucked his phone away and leaned his arms on his knees to rub his face. "Fine."

I wondered if he was still angry that I hadn't told him about Joe. As always, he was hard to read. I decided to probe a bit. "You and Mike have a good chat?"

"Yup."

I took a sip of my drink, but decided to keep at it, even though I risked poking the beast.

"I know you don't like crowds."

"Nope."

"So, why did you do this?" I wanted him to say it was for me. Just once, I'd love him to say he was thinking about me out loud.

His attention was glued to the door. "Mike wanted a meeting, and he thought you should come along."

"So, it was all his idea to bring Savannah and Cole and the guys."

Throw me some kind of bone here, dude, just a little shred of emotion.

"You got something you wanna ask, Tess, just ask it." He stunned me for a moment. *Shit, let's dance!*

"I want to know why you did all this." I slapped my hand on the table to make him look at me. His eyes flickered with anger. I knew he hated when I took control. "Give me the truth."

"Why?"

"Why not?" I challenged.

"Jesus, Tess, not here." He glanced around.

I was never the girl who made a scene in public, or even remotely liked drama, but I really wanted him to say he had done something nice for me. It seemed important for him to say it out loud.

"Sorry, guys." Cole was suddenly at the far end of the table. "Don't meant to cut the evening short, but we need to go."

Savannah grabbed her purse and waited for me to stand. "Story of my life, but I wouldn't change a moment of it." She hugged me like she really meant it. "I'll call you. Happy late birthday, Tess. It was really nice getting to know you."

"You too, Savi." I really did mean it. "Thanks for everything."

The guys all wrapped me in bear hugs before they disappeared, and I was left with the memory of the nicest gift anyone had ever given me and the moody gift-giver.

I grabbed my stuff and pushed my chair in. "I think I'll walk back." Before he could speak, I headed for the door. I didn't get far before I heard him behind me. His arm swiped around my waist and pulled me hard against a wall. Trigger trapped my arms and pressed them back against the cold concrete.

"I don't do drama. I don't do public fights—"

"I'm not asking for a high school relationship, Trigger!" I snapped, knowing it pissed him off. "I just want *you* to know that *I* know I'm more to you than just a fuck buddy. You know my history, and you still care about me. I need to know I count for something in this fucked up world! I know you get that, Trigger, because you just proved it to me by what you did back there."

He grabbed my chin and held my head in place. His eyes burned into mine. He struggled for words then dropped his hands. Just as I thought he would walk away, he spoke with his back turned to me.

"You know I'm not good at all this feeling shit. I've never had to explain myself to anyone before. I feel this way, I feel that way. Fuck. You are my woman. That's enough." He shook his head.

Suddenly, it dawned on me. "I get a question that you can't veto, and you have to answer."

His mouth opened to say something, but he quickly shut it.

"I told you my deepest, darkest secret. That took me out of *my* comfort zone, and you promised me a question back."

He cursed then shook his head for me to go on.

I couldn't help but feel the power, but there was still a part of me that was frightened to hell.

"Tell me why you came back for me."

He didn't move. Said nothing.

"Never mind, Trigger. Just drop it. I guess I just wanted more." I knew I wouldn't get any farther, and now we were both pissed off. I wished I had let it go.

I started back toward the club. I struggled with the fact I let myself feel something, only to get rejected. We both agreed we wanted nothing from each other. So, what the hell was I doing?

I needed to stop pushing him or I would be seen as another Peggy, and that would be the end of us—no, the end of me.

I had to accept him for what he was. I had to get over my pity party and learn my place with him. I had the club and Brick. They were all family now.

When I got back, I noticed I was alone. I was so consumed with my thoughts I assumed he was behind me.

When I walked in, Big Joe's forehead creased as he pushed off from his post and looked around.

"You by yourself?"

"Just needed the quiet."

He turned back around to me, his head slightly tilted like he was listening to something. "Where's Trigger?"

"I think he went to visit Mud or something."

His puffy eyebrow rose to question my lie.

I pointed over my shoulder. "Brick inside?"

"Yeah." He nodded, but when I attempted to move, he blocked my path. "Everything good? Trigger seem okay to you tonight?"

"Same as normal. Why?"

"He didn't mention anything to you?"

"Like?"

"Like…" He shook his head. "Never mind." He opened the door, and I moved inside. I was too mentally fried to ask what the hell he meant. "Watch your step."

My foot stepped down into something tacky, and then my eyes took in the mess.

"Oh, my God."

The place was trashed. Beer bottles were everywhere, not a table was clean, and all the guys were piss loaded drunk.

"Tess!" Rail called out from beneath a chick who looked half his age. "Girl, you missed out on one hell of a night."

"I can," I paused to kick a pink bra out of my way, "see that."

"Please tell me you got my text!" Brick said from the booth. Minnie was passed out next to him.

"No." I shook my head but froze when I saw Fin under the pool table with his blanket and book, looking at pictures.

It was past midnight. Why was he here? Where the hell was Vib?

"We had a party." Rail laughed from somewhere.

No shit.

I headed for my room, ignoring the others who wanted me to join them. I changed into yoga pants, a tank top, and a big, comfy sweater. I grabbed a blanket and pillow and set the box of books on my shelf for later.

My phone buzzed with an incoming message.

Savannah: Hey, I'll be in town next week. We should meet up.

Oh, that would be fun.

Tess: Sure, call me with the details.

Savannah: Will do!

I went back out and reached for Fin under the table. "Fin, come with me."

I wondered where his brother was and headed outside where it was quiet and clean.

"Where's Denton?"

"He's with Aunt Jaqueline. Mom is sick." I wiped the snot from his nasty little nose.

"Why didn't you go with them?"

"I don't like to go with her. I like to be with Uncle Trig."

I lifted him up on the back of Trigger's pickup then hopped in and covered us both with the fuzzy blanket. The pillow was tucked behind us, and I took the book from his hands.

"What are you reading?"

He shrugged. "Don't know, but I like the pictures. This one," he flipped a few pages, "is my favorite. I like the red rocket ship."

"It is pretty cool." I couldn't help but ask. "Fin, were you in there the whole night?"

He nodded with a small yawn. "I couldn't find Dad or you, so I just waited."

"You were in the bar with all those people?"

He nodded, unfazed by my horror. It was bad enough he saw what he did in the run of a day, but it sounded like a whore-fest tonight.

"Tess?"

"Mmm." I tucked the blanket around my sides. The air was cold tonight, and the temperature was on its way down. I heard a small meow from underneath us and wondered who else was camping out here tonight.

"Can you read this to me?" His eyes were so hopeful I wondered if anyone ever read to him.

"Sure." I pulled the book from between his grubby fingers and opened the page.

We went on the journey of the choo-train that got each of its freight cars full by all the circus animals. Halfway through, Fin lifted my arm and curled to fit against my side. He rested his head on my chest and asked a few questions. At first, I wasn't sure how Vib would feel if she saw us cuddled, but the way he seemed at ease made me relax too. Clearly, he was starved for affection, and I guessed I was too.

***

Trigger

"Where have you been?" Brick handed me a coffee when I returned from a night of punching a hole in my Everlast bag. My hands were worn out, and my muscles finally stopped twitching from the workout.

"Out."

"I see that." He slipped into the booth across from me. "I'll take it last night didn't go as planned?"

We were out of sugar, so I whistled for Jace to bring me more. "Tess got pissed."

He chuckled with a knowing look. "What did you do this time?"

I needed to shed some anger before I blew up and killed another member of my own club.

"She wants too much."

Brick lowered his mug, and his humorous expression faded. He glanced over his shoulder then lowered his voice. "Too much in what way?"

"Too much from me, I guess." I rubbed my beard, unsure how to navigate the conversation.

"She said that?"

"More or less."

"What did she say, exactly?"

"She wants me to tell her she matters and how I feel about this and that. I don't do feelings. Why can't women leave well enough alone?"

Brick's eyes bulged, and I could tell he was thrown by this. He leaned back and let out a long breath of air. "You sure she said that?"

"Yeah."

"I find that odd."

"Why?"

"Just, wow."

"Wow, what?" I started to grow annoyed. He needed to spit it out.

"Look," he leaned a little closer to me in case anyone was listening, "Tess doesn't normally do feelings. Clark robbed her of that. He broke her in two then broke her some more. I've only heard her say she loved two people in her life, and Clark never counted because he brainwashed her. Seriously, that house fucks her up something bad, but if she's lookin' for more from you…" He shook his head. "I don't…I don't know what to say to that. I mean, fuck, you must have really gotten to her."

I leaned back and let out a heavy breath. My head swirled with all the words she had said last night, and then her face before I left her.

"Trigger, I think it's pretty obvious…" Brick started to say before my face made him stumble. "I mean, we've been friends for a long time, man, and I'm going to step over a line here." He paused to see if I'd argue. "You owe me this, okay?" I glared but gave a nod. He was right; I did toss him under the bus before. "When you came out of the church, I have never seen you like that before. Man, I think there's a pretty good chance you might love that girl."

My first reaction was no, but I couldn't say the words. I cared for her a lot. She calmed the voices and the chaos and blew me away sexually. Her touch was something else, but was that love? I wasn't sure.

"Trig," he stopped my internal dialog, "you can at least start with saying you do care for her. Tess isn't some chick who the moment you say it is going to be lookin' for a proposal. She just needs to know she matters."

He moved to slide off the bench, but I reached out to stop him.

"Who did she say she loved?"

Brick grinned big like I'd handed him a gun to kill a Stripe Back. "Lily, Mags's daughter, and me. One of the best days of my life."

"Should I be jealous?" I half joked.

"Only if you love her like a sister." He chuckled before he turned.

"Where is she now?"

He whirled around but kept walking. "Pickup truck."

I pushed open the back door and took note of the heavy clouds rolling in. They did say we were getting a storm, but I didn't think it was supposed to start until the afternoon. My coffee was hot and felt good on my sore hands. I was careful not to spill it as I made my way over to my pickup. As I got close, I saw her lying under a blanket, and I nearly spilled my coffee when I noticed she wasn't alone. Black hair stuck out from underneath the blanket. I reached over and pulled it back. There was Fin curled into a ball, his hand over top of Tess's. I felt a moment of jealousy looking at the kid lying there with my woman. Shit, he was just a little kid, snotty nose and all.

A small part of me felt a pinch of warmth. For someone who never wanted kids, she sure took to Fin.

As I pulled the blanket back up, movement caught my eye, and a little pink nose and dark eyes stared up at me. Carefully, I lifted the kitten, rubbed her back, and placed her inside the wheel well.

Tess's phone lit up, and I reached for it.

Unknown Number: I'm here in the city. I need to see you, Gumdrop. Please tell me where to meet you. Give me twenty minutes, that's all I ask.

I expected to see red. I expected to want to murder someone, but instead, I was calm. Maybe it was because of my conversation with Brick. I knew she was warped by Clark, but I also knew she didn't love him. It was me she wanted more from, and that felt pretty good.

Tess: 5627 Dustin Street, Helmond's Bar. Noon.

A moment later, I saw him typing.

Unknown Number: Will Trigger be there?

Tess: Yes.

Unknown Number: Can we meet somewhere he won't be?

Tess: No.

Unknown Number: How do I know you aren't setting me up?

Tess: I never asked you to come. Take it or leave it.

Unknown Number: Fine, I'll be there. Just hear me out.

I tucked the phone back where it was and shook her shoulder.

"Tess," I whispered.

Her eyes opened, and it took her a moment to see where she was.

"Oh." She held her neck like it was sore. "Oh, my God, what time is it?"

"Nine."

"Shit." She looked down at Fin. "Is Vib freaking out?"

"No." I leaned my arms over the side of the truck, and the steam from my coffee swirled. "Doubt she's even noticed he's gone."

"I'm sorry." She tried to sit up straight.

"Why?"

"I didn't mean for this to happen. He spent the night in the bar waiting for you, and I felt horrible for what he saw. I started to read to him, and I guess we both fell asleep. I—"

"Why are you sorry?"

She looked at me strangely, her mouth pulled into a straight line. "He's not my kid, and I don't want to cross a line with Vib."

"Vib's done nothing more than give up an egg and a warm stomach to grow in. She has zero maternal instincts. That boy is looking for someone to cling to." I sipped my coffee and watched her absorb my words. "You're good for him, Tess. You're good for a lot of us."

She studied me for a moment before she looked over my shoulder with tired eyes. "About last night, just forget what I said. I was wrapped up in Cole and Savannah's happiness—" She paused, and her gaze dropped. "I appreciate what you did for me. Nicest thing anyone's done in a long time."

"Tess—" I had no idea what I was going to say, but she interrupted me.

"Is there any coffee left inside?"

I handed her mine, and she hesitated but took it anyway.

“Thanks.” She closed her eyes and sighed at the taste. “At least I know this isn’t laced with anything. Fucking Peggy,” she muttered.

She handed it back and woke Fin, who yawned and batted her hand away.

Her smile was one I hadn’t seen before. I knew she was growing attached to him too.

Suddenly, she froze. “Shit.” She scrambled to stand. I caught her waist and lowered her to the ground.

“Thanks.” She stepped back and ran her fingers through her hair. “I need to get to work. Morgan needed the morning off.”

With that, she was gone, and I was left with a grumpy Fin.

“Trigger?” Gus called from the door. “You’re needed.”

“So are you.” I pointed down at Fin.

He squinted and limped over. “What’s he doing there? Vib said her sister took them.”

“The junkie lied. Fin and Tess had a sleepover.”

“Would anyone notice if I buried that bitch under the pool house?” He snickered as he tried to wake Fin.

“Notice? No. Give a fuck? Hell, no. You need a shovel, I have plenty.” I reached over and pulled the blanket by the sides and lifted the grump out like he was in a bag.

“Hey,” he stopped me, “why is Langley here? You didn’t agree, did you?”

“Submitted the forms the other day.”

“Trigger, you think that’s wise? You know how you get.”

I glanced down at Fin. “You should get him to bed. Looks like the rain will start early.”

I needed to train and get ready for our company.

“Trigger!” Rail popped his head out the door. “There’s a fire, my garage.”

I hurried to follow him next door.

CHAPTER SEVENTEEN

Tess

"You seem different." Peggy blocked my path when I went to wash down the tables.

"Go away, Peggy." I pushed her aside, but she followed me.

"You do." She stood beside me and stared. "But what is it?"

I closed my eyes and calmed my temper. The bar had a few stragglers, and I really didn't need her shit right now.

She sucked in a breath. "Oh, my God." She beamed with excitement. "Did Trigger dump you?"

"Fuck off, Peggy." I tried to ignore her, but my grip on the rag was tight.

"Oh, this is great! Don't feel bad, Tess. It was bound to happen. He gets bored. He's a fuck and chuck kinda guy."

"Good to know." I moved on to the next table.

She kept going. "You *love* him, don't you?"

It was too early for this shit.

I stopped and pinched the bridge of my nose. "Peggy, he's all yours."

She glared at me for a moment then one eyebrow rose with amusement. She pulled out some gloss and ran it over her fake lips. "Time to lube up the runway."

"What a bumpy runway that is," Rail chimed in as he whisked by.

"I've never blown you!"

"Yeah, 'cause I like my dick clean."

"I'm clean, you jackass."

Rail stuck his head around the corner. "Peggy, your vag is about as clean as a dirty hotdog in an alley."

"Please, some of us are trying to eat!" Cooper dropped his fork and pushed his food away. "Fuck me, I'm getting a visual. I'm gonna be sick."

"Are you fantasizing?" She licked her lips at Cooper, and he pretended to stab himself.

Jesus, what a crew.

I turned back to the table but froze. My stomach jolted, and vomit crept up the back of my throat.

"Wow, Gumdrop." Clark's gaze dragged down from my mouth to my thighs.

I was squeezed into a pair of tight jeans with a red corset-style top and heels. My hair was wavy because I didn't have time to dry it. How I wished I was in sweats and a sweater like this morning. My mind was in a tailspin. I looked around, desperate to find a way out, and at the same time was terrified Trigger would come in.

"Well, now." Peggy slithered into view like the slippery snake she was. "And who might you be?"

"Clark." He extended his hand, and she took it with a giggle.

"How do you know Tess?"

"Peggy, leave," I warned, but of course she didn't listen.

"I'm an…" Clark smirked at me with that smile he used to get me into bed. "An old friend."

I couldn't move. I was stuck in this fuck hole of a situation.

How? How did he know where I was?

"Everything okay?" Big Joe asked, and I shot him a dirty look. Why did he let him in?

"He was cleared, Tess."

What? Cleared by who?

Clark tossed a file on the table before he stepped forward and ran a hand down my arm. It burned like acid against my skin. "Damn, I've missed you." He leaned down to kiss my lips, and I shoved him away. He was ready for it and hooked an arm around my waist to hold me in place. He leaned down again, but instead he brushed his lips by my ear. "I forgive you."

"Get the fuck off me."

"Keep talkin' dirty to me, Tessa. I know how feisty you can get."

This was a dream, a horrible dream that had sunk its claw deep and rattled my bones. I desperately needed to wake up. Clark here in

Trigger's club. It just couldn't be happening.

I wiggled to get free, but he was too strong. Cooper suddenly appeared at my side.

"She said get off her. Respect the lady."

"Respect." Clark laughed. "Right, when did the MC world ever respect their women?"

"We respect family, asshole, and if you want to keep that hand, you better get it the fuck off her." Cooper raised his voice. "Tess, you want me to get—"

"That won't be necessary." Clark cut him off and pulled his hand back. "I'm not staying long."

If that was true, I'd rather deal with Clark myself than involve Trigger. He didn't need to fight for me.

"Thanks, Cooper, but I'm okay."

He thought for a moment then headed out back, I was sure to find Trigger.

I needed to be quick.

"Ouch," I whimpered as he grabbed my wrist again and squeezed.

"You fuck him too?" Clark hissed at me. He was classic for mood swings, a sign that he was on steroids again.

"No." I glared at him. "Not yet, at least." I couldn't help myself. Clark was a jealous asshole when it came to me and men. He hated Brick but had never met him.

"Bet you're spreading for all these men." His tone was nasty.

"Most." I chuckled, and he lifted on his toes to use his body weight to squeeze me harder. I yelped, and he smirked. "How's your wife?" The words were like acid on my tongue, but it was my slap in his face that he fucked me over by fucking my mother.

He let go, and I stepped back and rubbed at the sudden rush of pain when the blood returned to its normal path.

"I hate that you get me that crazy." He switched back to calm, loving Clark.

"I hate that you hurt me. I hate a lot of things about you."

"I don't want to hurt you, Gumdrop."

"But yet you have, many times. Let's start with you killing my best friend." Anger corroded my insides.

"You should never have seen that video."

"God!" I huffed in disbelief. "You're insane! You can't even see it. You killed her, and that very night, you came to my room. Have you no soul? No heart?"

He scratched his chin and turned away. "We've always had a unique relationship, haven't we?"

Wow.

"You call it unique. Others call it abusive." I glared at him and felt the surge of anger flow and take over the shock and fear his showing up had brought. The club was my home, and it gave me a sense of power. He was on my turf.

"Abusive? When have I ever truly hurt you?"

"Do you even hear me?"

His stare burned into mine, and I felt my power slowly being sucked away. I needed to move before Trigger got wind he was here. I was shocked he hadn't stormed in yet.

"Why are you here?"

His eyes flickered with a darkness I had only seen a few times in the past.

Shit.

"You told me I could come."

What? He was mad.

"When?"

"This morning. You sent me the address." He held up his phone and showed me his messages.

"I never texted you that."

"Someone did." He shrugged, and I felt sick when I realized Trigger had done it.

Oh, my God. So, where the hell was Trigger, since he set up this fucking meeting?

"Whatever. Look, I wanted to give you an eyeopener about the man you think you know."

I folded my arms and tried to control my temper.

"Such as?"

"Here?" He glanced around.

Perfect. Just the moment I was waiting for.

I waited a beat, rolled my eyes dramatically, and waved for him to follow me.

"Don't touch me," I snapped when his hand fell on my back.

"I need to touch you," he grunted, but in a pathetic way. Funny how I was seeing things so clearly now. The tables had finally turned.

"You lost that privilege years ago."

"And yet you keep coming back."

I turned and faced him dead on. "*Children* who are mentally abused don't see their abuser as the monster. It takes time, but I see you now."

Before he could snap back at me, I changed our destination and skipped my bedroom. If we were going to do this, we were going to do it right.

I opened the door and waved him inside. His face dropped, and he choked on the smell.

"What is that?"

"Bleach." I fought back my own cough. I needed to be strong. I could not afford to look scared. "Sit." I pointed at a steel table with two metal chairs across from one another.

"Seriously? I feel like we're on the set of *Saw*."

"You wanted to talk alone, so talk." I eased into the chair.

He flipped the file open.

"I'm guessing I have about ten minutes before your boyfriend shows up." He pointed to the photo. "I thought you might like to know who you're sleeping with."

I slid the photo over and tried not to react at the image of Trigger doing a girl from behind at some party.

"Okay."

He tossed over another of a different girl and Trigger. One by one, he piled the photos on top of each other until there were about eight different girls. It stung, but I had no right to Trigger before now, and he had none to me. I only hoped these were all before me.

"Hope he wears a rubber." He snickered then pulled out another photo. "I'm guessing you're curious if these were all before you?"

"I don't really care." That was a lie.

"You should, Tess." He tossed another photo at me. "This was when you were with me. Check out his haircut."

Ouch. The girl was on her knees giving him a blow job, or at least it looked that way. Trigger said he cut his hair right before he came to get me. He said he needed a change.

"How did you even get this shit?

"Please," he sighed. "We both know Aaron is working for me. You give someone enough money, and they'll be your bitch. Plus, it doesn't hurt that I have something on him too."

"Which is?"

"Let's just say he's a dirty cop, but we're not here to talk about Aaron. We're here for you, Tessa."

"Shit, is that it? That's all you got? Him fucking a bunch of women?"

He picked up another picture. “Your twisted little biker family can go up in flames with one phone call from me, Tessa.” He handed me the picture, and I blinked a few times to register what I was seeing.

Trigger had blood on his hands and seemed to be surrounded by dead bodies. Brick was next to him, standing over a man, a rope dangled from his fingertips. Morgan and Cray were off in the background, and Rail was on the phone.

Sweat broke out along the back of my neck, my ears rang, and my heart pounded.

“It’s not proof they did it,” I whispered, terrified that my voice was gone. I was right. It outed me for being beyond terrified that the club could go down for murder.

“Does it matter? Dead bodies, weapons, right place at the right time. They never called it in. They just checked the men for something and left. Stellar MC family you got here, Gumdrop.”

His nickname made my stomach roll.

“So, now what? What now?” I could barely breathe as I eyed the door. Where the hell was Trigger?

He waited until I looked up at him. His face was serious, and his jaw was locked in place.

“I want you to come home for good. No more running. You will not date anyone else, and you will dance for the house, but nothing more. You will give yourself to me whenever I want. If not, I will hand-deliver these to the police tonight.”

I laughed out of shock at what I was hearing.

“You’re mad.”

“I’m in love.”

My anger burst through, and I knew my own fucking switch was about to be flipped.

“You had me! But you chose greed over love. You screwed my mother while you screwed me!” I dug deep for strength. “I have proof it was you.” My words came out like a hiss. “Proof you killed Mags. You’d be lucky to become someone’s bitch and not be sliced up under a bed sheet.” My lungs nearly popped at how hard I was drawing in air. His face snapped up to meet mine. “Don’t you get it? I came to kill *you*, not him.”

“Tessa!”

“No! You listen!” I rose out of my seat. I couldn’t feel my body as I pounded my fist on the table. “You knocked me up and let them butcher me! Forever scarring me, preventing me from ever having children. Now you're here threatening my chance at being happy with these pictures of sex and violence."

"Yes, I do!" he boomed as he jumped out of his chair and around the table. He walked me back a few steps and let his temper go. "I've loved you since I met in you in the common room of the house."

"I was ten, you sick bastard! Ten and alone with no one to love me. You took advantage of a little girl and warped her so much that she will always second guess anything and anyone. How can you think that's okay?" I hated him so much it was painful. I turned off my rational side and let my mouth go.

"Took advantage?" He came closer, and I held my ground. "You baited me, Tessa," he gritted through his teeth.

"You're insane, Clark. How I ever thought you were my savior, I will never know."

He narrowed his eyes and hovered over me. "You know the best part of all this?" He pronounced the words perfectly, and my stomach dropped. "At least I know you can never have a child with Trigger. No chance at a family."

Done.

I reached for whatever was on the wall and swung. The steel pipe smoked him across the side of the knees, and he fell to the ground with a shout. He reached for me, and I swung again and pounded his wrist with all my might.

"You fucking bitch!" he screamed and rolled around holding his hands to his chest. "You want to know why I let them carve that baby out of you?"

I froze.

"I saved it. You would have been a shitty mother. A mother who tried to kill herself over a man? Pathetic, weak, unlovable Tessa."

I dropped the pipe and stepped back while he laughed like he thought he had gotten to me.

"I rest my case," he cried. "Worthless."

"I may be all those things, Clark, but you know what?" I waited for him to look at me. "You could have had one more blow to the head, but instead, I think I'll return what you've given me."

His eyes bulged as I slammed the pipe hard at his stomach.

Whack.

Whack.

Whack.

I pulled my phone free.

Karma really is a wonderful bitch.

***

Trigger

"Where is she?" I could barely see straight. The fire at the garage was small, but nonetheless a fire. We checked the cameras, and it wasn't arson. Seemed like a faulty line in the office. Once it was under control and the fire department left, I raced back.

I slammed the door to the bar, and Peggy jumped and almost dropped a tray full of beer.

"Peggy, where the hell is Tess?"

"Last I saw her, the guy's lips were on hers and they headed for her room." She swayed her hips, making sucky sounds as she handed the guys their drinks. "Seems to me she was excited to get her freak on."

"Was that before or after he grabbed her arms and made her scream?" Cooper barked. "She went out back."

"We all know Tess likes it rough," Peggy purred, and I wanted to slam her head into the beam next to her. "You can see where I got confused."

"Peggy, shut the fuck up or you're out of here," I warned, which made her blink. "Where is she?"

My phone rang,

"Where are you?" My heart pounded so loud I had to focus on her voice.

"Slaughter room."

"Brick." He dropped his beer and hurried over.

We headed to the slaughter room. My fists pumped with excitement, but I also needed to know she was okay.

"Watch the door."

Brick stood in place, and I tore open the door to hear Clark's cries. Tess was holding a pipe. She looked fuckin' sexy. She was breathing hard through her flared nose. Her eyes were shiny and wide.

"You okay?"

"Thought you should know your guest arrived." Her voice sounded husky.

I deserved that.

"Thought this whole little situation should end now. Revenge doesn't always end badly. It can be closure."

She walked around Clark, and the pipe made an eerie sound as it bounced over the grooves in the tile floor. The sound echoed off the walls, and Clark's breathing picked up. He was sweating and bleeding and wasn't able to get up.

Tess suddenly swung and crushed his ribs with a hard blow.

"Ah!" He shook and tried to turn himself to see her. She dropped her arm and dragged the bar as she continued to circle him.

When she got to me, she reached in my pocket and removed my phone. I watched as she fumbled through my music and tapped on a song. It took a second, and then I heard Weezer's "Say It Ain't So." Interesting choice of music.

Clark's head flicked over to her, and something passed between them.

Tess started to circle again, and I popped my neck, wanting a piece of him. He hurt her, therefore, he hurt me.

Once the chorus came on, Tess screamed and slammed the pipe right next to his head.

"Fuck, Tess!" He shook and curled into a ball. "I didn't know you were watching us!"

"She did! She saw me watching you guys screw like rabbits while this fucking song looped over and over." She dropped the pipe, crawled onto his stomach, and punched his face. He grabbed her shoulders and shoved her off. She went flying to the floor, and I couldn't hold back anymore. I lunged and fisted his collar to haul him backward. He couldn't stand. His knees were broken, but he could still hurt her.

Once he was far enough away, I stepped on his leg and rolled my shoe to rotate the broken bone. He bellowed and clawed at the floor. His nails broke away, and he foamed at the mouth.

He started to laugh hysterically.

"She tell you I made it so she can't have kids? You can never have kids with her, Trigger!" He spat out blood.

I swallowed past my need to kill. I needed her to give me the green light. This was her kill, not mine.

She stood and walked over to the sink. I thought she was going to be sick, but to my surprise, she pulled the bleach down and poured it into a spray bottle.

As she drew closer, he started up again.

"I can still hear your screams for help as that doctor tore it from you. Sometimes it gets me off."

She grabbed a handful of hair and sprayed the bleach into his wild eyes. He bucked, twisted, and screamed.

"Bitch!"

I let her go until she exhausted herself, then I stepped in, hauled back my fist, and slammed it down on top of his head. He dropped like a stone.

Quickly, I checked his pulse. He was still alive. Good.

Tess dropped the spray bottle, looking fuckin' amazing. It took everything I had in me not to take her there. She looked at Clark, then at me, then turned and walked out.

A deep ache still burned in my chest. I dragged him to the center of the room, tied his hands and feet together to the hook above the drain, and flipped off the light.

"She's outside." Gus limped into the bar and saw my expression. "Although I say that loosely, as I'm not really sure Tess is home." He pointed to his head. "Tried talking to her, but she didn't answer me. She's just sitting there.

I walked past him and out the door to where she was sitting by the pool. I wasn't sure what to expect from her, so I approached her slowly.

When I got closer, I saw her cheeks were puffy and her eyes were bloodshot. Evidence she had come down off the high I knew only too well. This was one of those moments where I didn't know if she wanted me to say something.

I reached over and gently stroked her arm.

"What can I do?" I whispered as quietly as possible.

She didn't answer me.

Shit, I'm really tryin', here.

"Tess, are you okay?" I changed the pitch of my voice to take a new approach. She turned to me, and I knew that look. Her mind was racing.

Her head rose ever so slowly, and her eyes were a dark gray that showed the wicked battle that held her mind hostage.

"He deserves to die."

"He does. What did he say to you, Tess?"

"He told me something that will haunt me for the rest of my life, and I don't know if I'm okay." She fought the tears. I could see she was deeply wounded, and I knew the depth of that pain.

"Brick," I glanced over to where he hovered a few feet away, "the cameras are on in the slaughter room. Have Jace monitor them."

"Is she okay?"

I lifted my shoulders, unsure, and he walked over, stopped in front of Tess, bent down on his heels, and slowly traced a square on the back of her hand. She gave a tiny nod, and he turned and raced off to the house.

Once we were alone, I leaned toward her. "What all did he say to you?"

She smiled. "Where to begin?"

"How 'bout the start?"

"After you took my phone and invited him to come visit," she glared at me for a second but broke eye contact before she went on, "he showed me a bunch of pornographic pictures of you and a bunch of women, then a photo of you and Brick, Rail, Morgan, and Cray standing around about eight dead guys."

"What?" My hands went cold, and my mind raced. "I wonder who else has copies of the pictures. They can't be the only ones."

Her head snapped up, and the feisty tiger was back. "I don't have any idea," she huffed, "but I think they're the originals."

"But you're not sure." I needed a clear answer.

"No, I'm not." She pointed to the house. "Why the hell do you think his knees were smashed and his hands were broken before you came in?"

I wanted to grin with pride, but now wasn't the time.

"I'll be back, okay?"

"I expect nothing less," she muttered, and I felt a ping to the chest.

What the shit was that? I rubbed my chest over my heart and hoped I wasn't about to have a heart attack. What fucking luck that would be. At least let me know I had put my father *down there* first.

Three hours later, I cleaned Clark off me and felt pretty sure Detective Aaron had the original photos. I had Brick and Rail on their phones, so we would be ready when the shit hit the fan.

"Still alive?" Morgan slid a beer at me from the bar and handed me my lunch.

"Just." I bit into the burger and eyed Langley as he rounded the corner. "Don't want to rush his leavin'."

"Good morning, Mr. Morgan." Langley gave a polite nod.

"Morgan," he corrected. He hated being called Mister. It reminded him of his father. It was one of the many things Morgan and I had in common.

"Of course, Mr. Morgan." He stopped in front of me. "You've been fighting."

"Just dealing with something."

"That will mess with your head. Deal with it now, or regret it later."

"I'm not worried."

"I am." He pointed to a power drink in the mini fridge and thanked Morgan for it. "Oh," he smiled warmly, "you must be Tess."

I looked over my shoulder and saw Tess coming in from a run. When the hell did she start running, and when did she get those tight-ass leggings?

"Um…" She glanced at me, and I saw the weight still on her shoulders. "I am."

He took her hand. "It's lovely to meet you. I'm Trigger's ring trainer, Langley."

"Ring trainer?" Her eyebrows pinched.

"Yes, I'm here to get him back into shape for the fight."

Her face dropped, and the little color she had faded from her cheeks. "I wasn't aware he was training for a fight."

"No?" Langley glanced at me disapprovingly.

She glared at me. "I should go. It was nice to meet you, Langley."

"You too." He smacked my arm once she was out of earshot. "You're an asshole."

"I get that a lot."

Guess I forgot to bring it up.

***

Three more nights to the fight, and I could barely sleep. Tess seemed to spend every free minute when she wasn't working the bar on her newfound love of running, which in turn left Jace exhausted. I'd given him strict instructions to follow her to keep her away from the ring. I was almost disappointed she didn't put up a fight when she found out about her escort. It was like she simply stopped caring in general.

I fucking hated it, and I needed to blow off the tension.

I felt around the wall and switched on the light that hung above him. His battered face tilted in the direction of my footsteps.

"Tessa?" Clark's eyebrows rose over the black blindfold. "That you?"

I snapped my knuckles, ready to end this fight once and for all.

His face fell when he heard it was me, and he muttered something before he cleared his throat.

"I have money."

Pathetic.

"Don't want your money."

"I can get you any woman you want. I have connections."

"I have what I want." I peeled off my cut and shirt and hung them away from potential spray.

His chest heaved, and his neck contracted. He was scared, as he should be.

"Please." Saliva pooled at the corners of his mouth. "Please, there's got to be some—" He stopped himself and sat a little straighter. "I can share what I have on you."

My hand twitched as I pulled up a chair and settled in front of him. I was interested in what he thought he had on me, but at the same time, I did have a copy of the USB.

"It won't help." I grew annoyed with him, and my fingers ached for a good fight.

"I know you slept with Doyle's sister."

"Who doesn't?" I tossed my phone onto the table behind me.

"Y-you killed those men in that New York bar after your fight at fifteen."

I stood and kicked my chair away. "I've killed many."

"Wait!" he screamed with a jolt, and the chains slapped the wall, filling the air with an ear-piercing sound. "Does Brick know you've located his brother?"

With my fist drawn back and my body weight behind it, I froze.

How the fuck did he know that?

"Ahh." His demeanor relaxed. "So, he doesn't know…"

"Time's up!" I slammed my fist on the top of his head and caved it in. His neck snapped loudly, and he flopped to the ground.

Clark may have known more, but when you were faced with a life and death situation, most would spill their deepest secrets…or mine, and mine were hidden for a reason.

I nodded at the reaper who waited in the corner for me. His dark presence engulfed the room.

My part was finished.

***

"Coffee?" Morgan set the mug in front of me and eyed my swollen knuckles. "Are we down a guy?"

I started to speak when Tess came through the doors and over to the bar for a water. Jace tumbled in behind her and held onto a chair for support.

"Lookin' good." Brick laughed with me.

"Fuck off," he wheezed, unable to speak.

"Tess," I called as she went to leave, "come here."

She hesitated. "I need a shower."

"This will just take a minute."

"Yeah?" She stood a few feet away, holding my gaze.

"Clark is dead."

No emotion surfaced on her face. "Okay."

Not what I wanted or expected.

Even Brick was stunned and cleared his throat. "You okay, Tess?"

She shrugged. "Why? I was part of it. I'm glad. Wish I'd finished him myself."

"Tess," Brick tried to get her to open up, "come on."

"What do you want me to say?" She checked her phone. "One down, one to go?"

Her phone vibrated, and her eyes scanned side to side as she read it.

"I gotta go."

Brick watched her leave before he turned around. "Christ, she's turning into you."

Lucky me.

CHAPTER EIGHTEEN

Tess

"Tess," Minnie stuck her head in the door and looked around my room, "are you ready for this trip?"

I sank onto the side of the bed. I used to love Vegas, but I couldn't get my head into this trip.

"Clothes-wise, yes. Nerves-wise? I have no clue."

She glanced over her shoulder before she shut the door. "Girl, you need to let whatever the hell is bothering you go."

I attempted a smile, and she narrowed her eyes.

"When was the last time you and Trigger bumped fuzzies?"

"Wow." I pulled up the handle of my suitcase. "Where my head just went was not okay."

"That long, hey?"

"I don't know. I have mixed feelings on the whole Tess and Trigger thing."

She thought for a moment. "Whenever Brick and I are out of sync, I just need to get laid. I really think you need it, girl."

I glanced at the time. "You know he brought Clark here by texting him from my phone."

"Yeah, but you got what you wanted, right?"

I shrugged. She was right, and I didn't know why it bothered me.

Brick appeared at the door. "Ready?"

"Yeah." Minnie stopped me from following him. "Do you trust me?"

She waved me off and dug out a silver tube. "Stick out your

tongue." She tapped a little white pill into her palm.

"What is it?"

"Trust me, it will make the four-hour bike ride a whole lot more comfortable." She held it out and waited for my mouth to open.

I opened, and she stuck the pill on the center of my tongue. She did the same to herself, which made me feel a little better.

"Now," she stepped back and examined my outfit, "leather pants are perfect. I love the skull top, just change out of heels to boots. Your heels will go numb from the vibration." She was right. I remembered I had that problem on the last long drive to the desert.

Threading my arms through my leather jacket, I fixed my hair and held up my arms. "Well?"

"I'd do you."

"Good to know." I winked, happy Minnie got me out of my funk, if only for a moment.

With my suitcase in hand, I followed her out to the van where Jace was loading our luggage.

"Jesus." He smirked at me. "Whoa, sexy outfit."

"Leaves nothing to the imagination, and that's the point." Minnie grinned at me and slammed her suitcase in the van. She grabbed my hand and pulled me close as we walked over to the guys standing by their bikes. "If it becomes too much, there's a few rest stops."

"If what becomes too much? Minnie…" I tried to grab her hand, but she veered off toward Brick. "I thought it was just an edible, as in pot."

"Hello again, leather pants." Rail appeared at my side. "I was wondering when we were going to meet you again."

Trigger rolled up on his bike. He was in a black t-shirt that hugged his biceps and chest, and dark jeans and boots. His cut seemed a bit tight, a sign he had been working out a lot.

He didn't remove his sunglasses, but his stare nearly made me trip as I walked over and took the helmet he handed me.

"You look good," he muttered. "You've been missing for the past week."

"Just dealing with some stuff."

"I don't like it."

"I know." I flipped my hair back and pulled the helmet on. "Me either." I swung my leg over the bike and rested my hands on his hips, and he pulled me so I hugged him. He flicked the engine over and backed us out.

An hour later, we hit a wall of traffic and came to a complete stop.

That was when I began to notice the leather cut that wrapped Trigger's midsection was as smooth as lamb skin. As I moved my sensitive fingertips over it, I felt a ball of warmth grow in my belly.

My thighs flexed as Trigger shifted his weight. I didn't mean to ball his shirt in my hands, but fuck me, everything felt amazing.

"You okay?" His raspy voice caught me off guard, and I jolted on the seat, and oh-my-God, it was amazing. "Tess?"

"Please stop moving," was all that shot out of my mouth. He flipped up his visor and turned to look at me. I shook my head and moaned as his ass rubbed my front. My jaw clenched, and I started to grind my teeth.

"Put your visor up."

Oh, shit, don't get alpha on me. I may lose it right here on the freeway.

I quickly shoved it up and stared into his confused eyes.

"What are you on?"

"Nothing." I almost moaned when he moved again.

He stared a beat longer before he snapped his visor down and turned back around.

Ohhh, yes. I wanted to tap his shoulder to get him to do that again, but the traffic started to move.

Sweet, horny Lucifer. I'd broken out in a light layer of sweat, and my thighs burned from the grip on the seat. Three hours on the bike, and its vibrations had built me up to a pleasure-painful level. I'd finish myself off if I weren't surrounded by the crew.

Thankfully, Trigger signaled we were stopping for a break at the next rest stop. We took the exit and rolled up at the light before the small park.

When Trigger kicked his foot out to stabilize us, I grabbed the side of his leg and begged my body to let go.

His hand landed on mine, and I wanted to cry. His touch, his smell, his everything made my world tilt on its axis. I didn't know how much longer I could hold on.

I was either going to kill someone or have the most mind-blowing orgasm known to woman in public.

The bike slowed to a stop, and he proceeded to wiggle around then slid the length of his leg across me. I tossed my helmet, and my palms dug deep into the hot leather. I felt like I was balancing on the loose rocks that lined edge of my orgasm. I had never not-wanted to come so badly in my life.

My mind shifted to images of Trigger touching me.

Oh, no.

Oh, yes.

Oh, please.

"That's one major fuck-me face." Rail burst my steamy moment.

I glared at him, but it did nothing for my problem. "What?"

"Just makin' an observation."

"*Observate* somewhere else."

"Yeah, you probably need to finish that off." He wiggled his fingers and winked.

I closed my eyes and managed to channel my thoughts back to being underneath Trigger. His hands on my skin, his lips on my neck, his…

A shadow crossed my face and blocked my warmth. "What did you take?"

A deep jolt tore through me as my mind decided if it he was real or not.

"Please," I nearly panted. "Don't talk." I rubbed my hands down my pants. The leather was warm and sent goosebumps through me.

"What?"

"I'm not entirely sure, as this is the first time I ever took ecstasy, but I *think* I took ecstasy."

He blinked "Where did you get E?"

"A fr—"

"What the hell were you thinkin', taking drugs before you got on the bike?"

I reached out and wrapped my fingers around his arm to get him to pull back from the angry path he was about to go down.

Once my sense of touch got hold of what I was doing, I got a head rush. A strange prickle shot through my arms, up my chest, wrapped around my neck, and burst through my mind.

Trigger's warm hand landed just above my elbow and tugged me toward him.

"Look at me." His jaw flexed as my eyes climbed. "Tell me what you're feeling."

When I tried to break eye contact, his finger lifted my chin back in place.

I unlocked the doors to my mind and let the words flow out.

"I'm wishing we weren't standing in a parking lot because I've discovered ecstasy and a vibrating bike is the way for a woman to experience blue balls."

He ran his fingers down to the center of my collarbone with a little chuckle. *Kill me now!*

"Tell me what else is going through you head."

My mouth opened, and more words flew out. "It scares me that my mother will come looking for Clark. So much, in fact, I've had nightmares the last few nights."

His eyes burned into mine before he leaned down to brush his lips across my temple. "And?"

"And if you don't—" His fingers danced along my cleavage, and he palmed my breast. "Trigger." I couldn't think straight…his touch, his hot breath, his raspy voice.

"How ya doing, Tess?" Minnie shouted from Brick's bike as they pulled up next to us.

"Thanks for the heads up." I referenced the bike and the last three hours of pleasure-pain.

She laughed. "Where would the fun be in that?" She glanced at Trigger. "Wanna join in?"

"No! No way," Langley snapped from beside me. Christ, he was like a damn ninja. He made no noise; he just appeared. "And none of that." He pointed at me. "Not until after."

"What?" I nearly choked. "Don't make me go elsewhere."

Where the hell was my filter?

"Tess, don't give Trigger a stroke." Cray shook his head. "We need him focused."

"What the hell did I do?" How did I get sucked into this shit? And why did his arm feel like butter? My mind momentary slipped.

"You and your *fuck-me face*."

"Thank you!" Rail fist bumped Cray.

"It's written all over you." Cray circled his face with his hands.

"Unbelievable."

"Go on ahead." Trigger waved the guys off, and I was thankful to go back to what I was doing. He pulled my hair back and rolled his fist to the root.

"Everything feels good, doesn't it?" His knowing smile almost made me mad. He knew he had the upper hand. "Open." Two of his fingers pushed past my lips and stroked my tongue gently.

"Mmhm." I sucked and swirled them around like I would his erection.

He drew in a breath before he pulled them free. His lips smashed into mine as his hand lowered into my pants and broke the slick opening.

I couldn't care less if the entire crew watched. I needed this.

"You're dripping, Tess," he purred.

My toes were on the edge. All I needed was a little push. He was content to hold still, so I unlocked my knees and dropped down a few inches, and all four delicious fingers made their way inside and rubbed all the right spots.

But before I could utilize them, they were gone.

***

Trigger

"Where do you want these?" Jace had our bags.

"Last door at the end of the hall."

"Both?" he asked, and I folded my arms. "Sure thing."

Apparently, even the guys had noticed the distance between me and Tess. The truck stop was the first time in a week I had touched her. Something changed with her after the dinner with Mike, but I'd been so preoccupied with the fight, I let it go.

"Checked the perimeter." Big Joe nursed a beer, and I studied him for a moment. I never got the chance to talk to him about the desert.

"Good." I nodded, still deep in thought.

"Something up?"

"Why didn't you tell me you helped Tess in the desert?"

He looked around then hung his head. Joe had never crossed me, so I was sure this weighed on him. "She was leaving, regardless. I couldn't just leave her there on the side of the road. I should've told you, but she asked me not to."

I didn't say anything more to make my point, but I wasn't happy about it.

"Sorry, man, but you know I watch over that girl. She's family now."

I shook my head and tried to understand. His loyalty should be to me first, but since I knew Tess was all right, I'd let it go this time.

"We've got steaks, we've got sausage, we've got ribs," Cooper yelled as he walked by me with a huge box from Costco. "Who's hungry?"

"Me!" Rail shouted from the doorway.

"What do you want?"

"Sausage!"

"Shocker." Brick punched him in the arm.

"Tess?" I asked.

"Pool, I think." Brick grabbed the beer from Jace and raced off.

Jace cursed as he opened another one. "I hate being the bitch."

"And I hate carrying my own shit." Rail dropped his bags at Jace's feet. "Third room on the right." He snatched Jace's newly opened beer and roamed over my way.

Jace wanted to be a prospect, and this was all part of it. The faster he got that, the better.

"So," Rail glanced around, "this was where you stayed when you fought?"

My face scrunched with disgust. "No, that was a Motel 6."

"Oh, so why the huge house?"

"I don't like people."

He huffed. "Of course." He downed the neck of his beer. "Heads up, Tess is like a cat in heat. You can smell her mile away. You might want to go piss on her, you know, mark your territory. We have a lot of company." He nodded to the Vegas and Arizona crews. A hot blonde walked by in a towel, and Rail beamed at me. "That's my cue."

Most of the guys were huddled by the barbecue when I came out. Some were in the heated pool, and others were drinking by the fire pits. The property the house was on was massive. It belonged to a friend I made a deal with many years ago. He had made some fast cash, and in return, I got to use this place whenever I wanted.

The less attention I had in this town, the better.

"Trigger," Gus huddled over to me, "I know I've said it before, but I have a bad feeling about this fight. Something still feels off."

"We've been over this already, Gus."

"I know, but something just isn't sitting right in my gut."

I rubbed my beard. Gus never liked me fighting, always said it fucked with my head. It was true. I did get sucked into it, but I always found my way out.

"You know I don't have a choice here, Gus. Gotta play it through. I'm feelin' good."

He closed his eyes for a moment, "Where's Tess? I've been wanting to talk to her all day."

"Not sure," I lied. "Did Vib end up coming?"

He nodded. "Free booze, coke, and cock. She wouldn't miss it.

Denton is with his aunt, and Fin is around here somewhere. Little shit ran off earlier, talkin' about your new fightin' ring."

I couldn't help but smile. That kid really did have the fighting gene.

Waving off Gus, I headed down the hill to the hot tub built into the side of a cliff. It had private rooms with streamed music to help drown out nearby noise.

I nodded my thanks to Cooper as he pointed out the room Tess went into. I stepped into the hot water and ditched my t-shirt. My trunks stuck to me in the freezing cold air.

I dove in and stayed under the water until I swam up to the turn in the walkway. Flipping my hair out of my face, I blinked my eyes dry and spotted Tess on the ledge.

Her arms skimmed the surface of the water before she brought them up and let the water run down her skin. I moved closer until she sensed me.

"How are you feeling?" I came closer.

"Better now." She glared. "Nothing my vibrator couldn't fix."

The way she broke eye contact led me to believe she was lying.

I didn't break stride as I came up to her, and she backed up to the rock wall.

"What are you doing?" Her hot chest pressed into mine, and her hands landed on my arms. She might be coming down from her high, but the drug was still very much in her system.

"Fucking you."

"You think so?" Her head tilted, and I ripped her scrap of bikini bottoms off. She yelped but couldn't hold back a moan. Everything in her body was heightened, and I wasn't about to miss an opportunity to make her feel amazing.

"Yeah." I bent down and hiked her up on the rock ledge. "You've been pissed at me, and I'm not sure why, but right now I am going to fuck you senseless."

"You really don't know why?" she started, and I pushed her legs open, and my mouth landed on her swollen mound. Her head dropped back with a moan. I licked, sucked, groaned—I did everything I could to bring her to the edge before I pulled back. She tried to hold my head in place, but I grabbed her hands and held them down as I dove deeper. Her hips bucked, and her chest heaved.

"Trigger, I hate you! Make me come, or I'll—"

"What?" I teased as I came up for air. "What will you do at this very moment, Tess?"

"Something." She covered her face. "If you care about me at all, you'll make me come a million times—Oh!"

I took that moment she had her face covered to sink myself deep into her hot, slick walls. She ate me to the root, and I had to stabilize myself before I could thrust again.

"Yes!" she screamed in bliss. "More!"

I reached around and brought her body to mine. Her legs wrapped around my waist and squeezed.

Slowly, I licked the drops that trickled between her breasts then gently took her nipple between my teeth and tugged. Her forehead landed on my shoulder with a long-annoyed sigh as her nails dug into my back.

I nipped at her neck and massaged her ass. Her body felt amazing against mine. I could literally feel my demons close their cage doors and lie down for the night.

"Hey," she took my head with both hands, "you need to flip your switch, or I will." The look of dark promise nearly kicked me in the gut.

When I didn't react fast enough, she tried to shove me away, but I slammed her to me. I grabbed her neck and bit her skin to show her who was in control.

When she tried to pull away, I swung her around and slammed into her. She fought to hold herself out of the water, so I walked her over to the carved-out seat and laid her front on the smooth stone.

With my hands on her hips, I took her savagely from behind. Water lapped the walls, and her screams echoed around us. It was like a goddamn fucking porno just for me.

"Trigger," she fought to catch her breath, "harder!"

Fuck me, I loved this chick's sex drive.

I smacked her ass and pumped harder, my fingers entwined in her hair, and I found myself groaning out loud.

"Shit, Tess!" I blurted. "I don't want to come."

"I need more!" She flinched but reached around and grabbed my balls.

Flip.

I didn't remember changing positions, or grabbing her around the throat and kissing her with all I had inside me, but I did remember coming so hard I lost my vision.

She was the only woman I would ever lose control with.

***

After a shower, I joined everyone downstairs. I lost Tess once she returned to the house. Something about Minnie needing her. She was totally out of it when I peeled her off the rock and sat her upright. She had scurried out of the cave the first free moment she had.

"You looked fucked out." Brick laughed as he came to my side with a plate full of ribs. My stomach growled, and I stole one off his plate. "Tess come off her high yet?"

"Think so." The flavor smothered my tongue and reminded me of where it was just an hour ago. My pants grew tight, and the thought of doing another round with Tess started to overcome my hunger.

Jace walked by, and I snatched his plate from his hands. I needed to fuel up quick.

"Seriously?" he growled but left before I could remind him he shouldn't even be eating yet.

Gus hurried by like he was looking for someone. He had been off lately too. Fin zipped by, nearly knocking him over, and the three slices of pizza he carried almost slid off the plate. I was sure the little shit would go find a quiet spot and eat it all himself. I'd never seen a kid with such an appetite.

"You find out why she's pissed at you?" Brick asked with a rib sticking out of his mouth. "The only time she works out is when she's mad. So, what did you do?"

I shrugged.

"I bet it's over the whole 'she wants more' thing. Women dwell."

Her words, *"I want more!"* suddenly smacked me across the face.

"Trigger!" Langley popped up by the doorway like he appeared out of nowhere. "Time to train."

Brick jumped. "Jesus. Has he always done that?"

"Yeah."

"Langley," he yelled, "feel free to announce yourself instead of fucking jumping out of shadows."

"Maybe you shouldn't be so jumpy, Mr. Brick."

"Man, I've been shot at more times than I can count and been stabbed in the gut. I'm gonna be jumpy."

Langley shrugged. "Maybe you should be more observant so you can see what's coming." He ignored Brick's pissed look and checked his watch. "We are late."

I tossed the rib bone on Brick's plate and rubbed my hands on my jeans.

"Watch the guys."

"Seriously?" Brick snickered at the bone. "Ew."

"You'll live."

"Let's go!" Langley shouted, and Brick dropped his plate, sending hot sauce across the stones. "Heads up, Mr. Brick."

"Shit! That's fucked up, man."

CHAPTER NINETEEN

Tess

Morning broke through the thin curtains of the sunroom where I had fallen asleep the night before with the third book in my hands.

My eyes were still puffy from crying. Thank God no one saw me last night. My heart broke when I got to the part where Keith brought Savannah the fish because she kept pushing people away.

Gawd, I'm a sucker for angsty books!

I ran my hands through my hair and tugged my clothes back into place as I heard voices outside the door.

"Morning." Gus's raspy voice broke through my fog, and I smiled when I saw he had two mugs of coffee in his hands. I stood to take them from him as he struggled to walk without splashing. "Thanks."

"How'd you find me?"

His smile quickly changed into a squint as he dropped into the overstuffed chair across from me. I hated that he was always in so much pain and had two little boys to raise.

"You think Trigger goes to bed without knowing you're okay first?"

"Oh." I almost blushed. I liked how he cared enough to look for me. "I'm shocked he didn't wake me."

"He wanted to." He coughed loudly and fought to catch his breath. "But he thought you probably wanted to be left alone. Do you?"

His blunt question threw me, and when I didn't answer right away, he remained quiet.

"You're different since you came back. Clark's death botherin' you?"

I played with a piece of my hair for something to do and shifted uncomfortably. "I'm not bothered by his death, just by the things he said." I shrugged. I realized I really didn't give a shit. I tried to kill him before, and now it had been done. "I think I struggle with the fact it wasn't my mother lying limp and pathetic on the slaughter room floor."

"Just say the word, sweetheart, and Trigger will make that happen."

"I know. I also know her time will come." I knew Trigger would take her out, but, "I guess it's not time yet. I want her to feel his loss the way I did when she took him away from me. Then I'll make my move."

"There's the fire I love about you."

I nodded. "Trust me, Gus, the fire is right at the surface, but I'm feeling…"

"What?"

"Like I'm a floater, like I'm not really sure what to think about things."

"Things like Trigger?"

"Yeah." I went with the truth. I never thought of Gus as my person to talk to, but he really was the only one who had any insight into Trigger.

"What's he doing?"

I sipped my coffee and nearly moaned at the flavor. It was a strong brew with hazelnut woven through it. "Nothing, really. It's me." My mind spun with the right words.

"I'm confused."

I laughed and set my mug on a triangle-shaped coaster. "Welcome to my head." I crossed my legs and took a deep breath. "Look, Gus, I was always the girl who was in love with someone I couldn't have. Clark strung me along for years, took my innocence, took my choices from me, but even through it all, I did know he truly cared for me. But Trigger…" A lump grew in the center of my throat. "His walls are so high, he won't allow himself to admit how he feels, and when I think I've made progress with him, I'm wrong. I never thought I wanted to fall in love again, but now that I have, I'm not sure how to navigate it…" I trailed off when his face froze.

What?

Oh-my-fresh-hell, what did I just say?

A cold sweat broke out along my neck, and my head started to pound.

"You love my boy?"

"No," I blurted. "My mouth just ran away with me."

"Oh." His smile showed such unconditional pride for his nephew that it made me want to retract that last comment.

"Even…" I cleared my throat and lowered my voice. "Even if I did, that's not what he wants. He's made that very clear…and so have I. Gus, I didn't mean to fall for him. Truly, I didn't. We had an understanding, but before the whole church thing happened, we had a few days there where I saw behind his walls, and I hate that I fell. Hard." I stood abruptly, unable to stay still, so I paced the room. "I thought about dating someone else just to prove these feelings aren't real. I mean, this isn't me. I never wanted this. I'm the ice queen. But…" I held my head, feeling dizzy. "Help, help me fix this! I can't run and leave Brick again. I owe him the world."

"Tess." Gus stopped my madness. "Sit."

I did as he said but still felt like I was on a hamster wheel with no end in sight.

"Trigger has had women fall at his feet his entire life, but never once have they been able to touch him, sleep in the same bed with him, none of them was kept around this long. And this is a big one—never, ever would he have gone after them. He's shit at communicating his feelings, but let me tell you, he feels something for you. And I know you know that."

"I do, but anytime I let him know I can see he cares about me, he shuts down. It's not like I want marriage." I shuddered at the thought. "But I need to hear from him that I matter."

Gus leaned back, his lips pressed together in thought. I took the moment to down some more coffee. "I came in here to talk to you about something else, but now I'm wondering if I can use your confession as a tool to help me."

"I don't know what you mean."

"Hear me out." He rubbed his face then leaned forward, resting his arms on his thighs. One shoulder rose higher than the other. His body was in such bad shape.

"Look, Tess," he massaged his knee, yet another sign how much his body hurt, "you have Trigger's ear more than anyone right now, and that's sayin' a lot. I need you to do something for me."

"I'm listening."

"I need you to convince Trigger not to fight."

"Why?" The conversation had taken a strange turn.

My senses went on overdrive. I knew something was up, something more than just Trigger going back into the ring. Gus looked straight at me, and his jaw bulged as if he was gritting his teeth.

"You think you've seen Trigger at his worst in the slaughter room. Well, you haven't. The ring is what makes Trigger go into beast mode. It messes up his head, and it takes him over. They talk about how he has a switch, but you really haven't seen his switch fully flipped until you've seen him after that bell has rung."

"So what? He flips it, fights, wins, and we're done."

"No," he shook his head, "it's not that simple. He'll probably win, yes. Allen is sixty-something, but it's the after that scares me. He might go back to the old Trigger. I'm afraid he'll get lost in his hell again, and he won't want to get back out. I've seen it before, firsthand, and I don't ever want to again."

"I'm not sure what I'm supposed to do, Gus. We all know Trigger does what he wants, when he wants to."

He nodded then rolled my arm over and pushed up the sleeve of my cashmere sweater. The corners of his mouth went up and he chuckled quietly.

"What?"

"Nothing."

I glanced at the black and gray tattoo key that was hidden in the thick ivy of ink. I loved how my scar was now hidden so well. The only way you'd know it was there was if you touched it.

His hand fell on top of mine, and I looked over. He seemed to be struggling with words.

"Spit it out, Gus."

"Tess, promise me you'll try anything you can to keep him out of that ring." He swallowed hard before he looked deep in my eyes. "Give him a reason not to."

His words echoed around my head, and then it hit me.

"You want me to ask him not to fight if he truly does love me?" I felt sick. What a way to ask someone to prove they love you. With a threat.

"I get how this sounds, Tess, but there's more to it than Trigger getting lost back in his own hell." He shifted and hesitated. "I have a shitty feeling there's a lot more going on with this fight."

"Like what?"

"I don't know, but Allen hates his son more than anything, and he never does anything without a damn good reason, and he always has a backup plan."

And his backup plan could be death…

***

My shoes pounded the pavement, my arms pumped at my sides, and the cool, crisp air lined my lungs with a thin layer of frost. Light mist hung in the morning air, and dark rain clouds promised another wet afternoon.

I missed my usual running companion who left me alone with my thoughts. Instead, I had a wheezy Rail who had stopped twice now for a smoke break. Jace disappeared this morning to run an errand for Big Joe. Really, I thought he'd offered himself up so he could avoid running with me.

I glanced over my shoulder to see Rail heaved over, hands on his knees. A guy in tight shorts and a headband ran by him in perfect form and slowed.

"Slap my ass and call me jazzed. Beautiful morning for a run, hey, man?"

I fought my laughter at Rail being hit on.

"Yeah, we get it." Rail snickered as he drew closer to him. "You work out, and we're all *so* impressed."

"What?" The cute guy looked confused but kept moving.

"You about done?" I folded my arms once again, annoyed I wasn't able to go out for a run on my own.

"I just need—" He coughed and pulled out another smoke, lit the tip, and closed his eyes as the poison smothered his insides. "Sweet," he purred. "Tastes like sex in the dirt."

"Oh, for fuck's sake." I covered my face and groaned. "Can we just get this done?"

"Why can't we quit now? What are…" He sucked in another breath, and something crossed his mind and his eyes widened. "What are you running *from,* anyway?"

"I'm not running from anything." We both stopped, and he walked over to a railing. He rolled his head and blew a white cloud at my face.

Sexy.

But was it that noticeable?

"Ugh," I huffed and flopped down next to him on the railing. My muscles screamed for a break, and I could really use some food. "Myself. Trigger. I don't know."

"Wow, I was just grasping for an excuse, here. I didn't know there really was something going on," he joked, but when he caught my unimpressed expression, he tried to get serious. "Okay, let me get in the headspace." He squeezed his eyes shut and chanted. "Chick talk, chick talk, chick talk. Ass, tits, scissoring, and wet bits. Okay," he sighed dramatically, "I'm ready."

"Aren't I lucky?" I rolled my eyes at his views on women. "I've been asked to do something, and I don't know where to begin."

"Ah," he nodded, "Gus got to you about Trigger and the fight."

"How did—" I stopped myself. I wasn't sure how much he really knew.

"Not like we all aren't thinking the same thing. Trigger goes rogue after he fights. I've seen the tail end of it, and it wasn't pretty. Ever since he told Gus, the old man has been stressed out."

"Oh." My mind slapped me around a little. *Gus needed your help and what did you do? You decided to go for a run. Talk about ungrateful.*

"Trigger listens to no one but himself. Of course, there's the whole 'is Allen really the one fighting Trigger, and if not, who is he bringing in' thing."

"Yeah, there's that too." Who would be good enough to fight Trigger?

Rail pushed himself up. I joined him and looked around at the clouds closing in. It suddenly felt like it was a race to tell Trigger before the storm hit.

"Gus thinks you might have an in."

"Do I?"

"Don't you?" he countered.

"Fuck me."

"That's the spirit." He slapped my shoulder. "Now, are we done here, or do I have to choke on this fresh fucking air some more?"

"No, let's go."

"Good." He raised his hand. "Taxi!"

After we returned to the house, Rail went directly to the bar and yelled for a beer while he dramatically clutched his chest as if in pain.

I showered and headed downstairs for something to eat. I was almost lightheaded with hunger.

Just as I rounded the corner, I heard voices and slowed my pace. Trigger and Brick were at the island discussing something, and the way they were hunched over and speaking in low voices, I assumed it wasn't something they wanted me to hear.

"You kill him?" Brick quickly switched topics and kissed my cheek.

"Yeah, about that." I rested my hands on my hips. "Why the hell would you send Smokey Joe to run with me when he has the lung capacity of a five-year-old?"

"Jace was busy." Brick shrugged.

"That so?" Trigger checked his phone. "I just saw him."

"He's avoiding the workout." I hoped Trigger was in a chatty mood.

"Won't hurt Rail." Trigger grunted as he texted someone. "Next time, take Cooper."

"Or *you* could run with me."

Brick laughed as he left the room, and Trigger looked up at me. "You couldn't keep up."

"Wanna bet?" I bit into an apple.

The corners of his mouth went up into that oh-so-sexy look he gave me when the promise of sex was in the air.

"And when I win?" He set his phone down and stood like a panther, excited at the challenge.

"Me, anywhere you want." I lifted my head as he came closer. "And if I win," I held my ground, "I want to speak to you about something without you shutting down on me."

His brows drew together, and I could see he was interested. His curiosity would get the best of him.

"What's wrong?"

Seriously? Here?

"Can we talk alone?"

"No." Rail leaned over the back of the couch. When did he get here? "If you leave, I can't eavesdrop."

"Fuck off, Rail." Trigger took my hand and pulled me outside. He led me to a pathway partially covered with palm trees so we could have some privacy. He didn't seem to mind the cold weather, whereas I held onto his arm with both hands to steal his warmth.

"So," Trigger glanced down at me, "we're alone now."

I tucked a piece of hair behind my ear and thought about my words. I wanted to make sure I made my point without scaring the hell out of him. "Promise you won't shut down."

"Okay."

"Okay." I mirrored his tone. "Who am I to you?"

I felt him hesitate, but he shook it off. "We've been down this road, Tess."

Okay…

Here comes a classic female moment.

"Am I your girlfriend?"

His expression changed, and he turned to block my path. "What is this all about?"

My face heated, and I wanted to break eye contact, but I also wanted to hold my ground. "Why did you come back for me?"

"I like having you around."

"Is that the only reason?"

"Tess," he rubbed his head like I stressed him out, "you know I don't do this stuff well. Either say what you want to, or don't."

"Okay. Never once have you asked *me* why I let you take me back to the club."

He shook his head as if he never thought about it that way. "Okay. Why, then?"

"I asked you first."

"And I answered you."

"Did you?" I wanted some answers, and I was going to get them if I was going to put myself out there.

"Fuck! I…" He paused. "I have never wanted to have a woman around me. No one gets me. I used the chicks around the club for a release, but that's it. Until you…"

Holy shit, we're making progress.

"Like I've said before, you turn off the shit inside me. You bring me silence, and you flip my switch during sex, and that's never happened before."

I nodded but was nervous to speak. I didn't want him to close up. When he seemed like he was, I tried a different angle. "What if I told you I met someone else?"

His face dropped, and his jaw twitched. "Who?" The tone sent a shiver through me. "Is that what you're doing here, telling me you're interested in someone else?"

"If I was?"

"I'd murder him."

"Why?"

"'Cause you're my woman."

"But I'm not your girlfriend," I reminded him.

"Tess," he warned, and I got pissed.

"Trigger, I get it. We always said we wanted nothing more than to just be fuck buddies, but I—" My mouth slammed shut.

He stepped closer and slid his warm hand around the back of my neck. My eyes fluttered, and I was once again consumed by his simple touch. "You, what?" he whispered as he leaned down and licked my lobe. "Tell me."

"I've fallen in love with you."

His muscles locked, and his head drew back slightly to read my face. "I'm unlovable, Tess. It's just lust."

I saw red.

I wiggled out of his hold and jammed my finger in his face. "Don't you ever tell me how I feel," I hissed. "I don't want to be—I don't want to be feeling this way when the other person doesn't. I've been here my whole life!" Raw, empty feelings started to surface, feelings I'd buried deep down inside, and anchored themselves to my soul.

"Hey!" he snapped and reached for my arm, but I was too fast and jumped out of his way.

"Jesus Christ!" I covered my forehead with my hands as I thought about what I just admitted. "Fucking Gus and Rail all inside my head."

"Gus?" he asked, clearly confused what I was rambling about. "What the fuck does Gus have to do with this?"

"Nothing. Just forget all of this." I turned to walk away when he hooked my waist and pushed me up against the trunk of a palm tree.

"Stop running. Just give me a fucking second to process this."

"There's nothing to process. One of your dumb chicks opened her mouth."

"Don't *ever* compare yourself to those women," he barked. "No one has ever told me they loved me and meant it for the right reasons."

"I have no desire for your money, Trigger. There's no hidden motive here."

He shot me a look like he knew that already.

I figured since I was doing a stellar job of fucking this moment up, I might as well say it all.

"If you have any feelings for me whatsoever, please hear me when I say this. Please don't fight your father."

He cocked his head, confused. "So, Gus has been talking to you."

"Yes."

"Fucking Gus."

"It's not just Gus, Trigger. Your whole club is worried. I'm worried."

His body seemed to relax, and he closed his eyes as he thought. I reached up and ran my fingertips along his cheek.

"You and I are a lot alike, Trigger. I never meant to mess up what we had. I was content with it, but there was a point where it hit me. When Clark kissed me, everything inside suddenly became clear, and I knew. When I saw you in the house, dressed in a suit and tie, I almost died. You did that for me, and I thought maybe, just maybe, you felt it too, but—"

"What does it feel like?" He towered over me, and I couldn't help but slide my hands up his arms. He was stunning in a dark way that made my mouth water. He was everything Clark wasn't, and that called to me.

"I'm dizzy around you," I murmured as the first few drops of the storm fell. "My body heats and reacts when you enter or leave a room." His throat contracted, and his eyes looked hungry. "I think about you all the time, and I get…" I stopped, feeling exposed, "jealous when you're around other women."

"Jealousy can be a bitch." He smiled, and I felt the lust burst through me, like a bubble deep down in my belly that picked up speed as it rose. "I feel that way with you."

His confession caught me off guard, and I matched his smile.

"Go on." He kissed the corners of my mouth.

"Your touch," I nearly moaned, "calls my body to attention. It's not just pure lust, but pure need."

"Mmm." His breath shot across my collarbone. "Why do you think I spend so much time here," he kissed his way up my neck, "and here?" He sucked at his spot. "I can't get enough of your body."

He pressed his massive erection into my stomach, so I reached down and wrapped my hand around it and gave a good tug.

"Jesus, Tess!" His head dove into my neck as he panted. "I need to be inside of you." He grabbed my waist and held me over his shoulder.

"What the hell?"

"Shh." He slapped my ass and hurried to the garage. Once inside, he sat me down on the lawnmower then left to lock the door. I noticed he looked around first.

"You see something?"

"Don't need Langley interrupting."

"You're not allowed to have sex, are you?"

He grabbed my jeans and hauled them down, and his hand was between my legs before I could even think.

"I love that you're so wet for me."

"Should we be doing this?" I wasn't about to stop, but I didn't want to fuck up his fight if I couldn't convince him not to go through with it.

"Come here." He lifted me onto the workbench, which had a fairly smooth surface, and undid his pants. His gorgeous erection bowed under its weight and leaked from anticipation.

He lined up and pushed just the tip in before he held my head in his hands and stared into my eyes.

"You came into my life and showed me that I am worthy of something, maybe even love. Countless times you have proven you're loyal. Any man who can't see what you are is a fool."

I am speechless.

"I'm not good at this, but I will try for *you*. I might struggle with the words, but I can always show you my feelings." He nudged further in.

My head spun, and my heart opened wide.

"You can't miss something you've never known before." He held my gaze. "But, shit, when you left, it felt like my insides were bein' ripped out. I couldn't think straight and couldn't do anything but kill. Never do I want to go through that again."

When I tried to speak, he shook his head like he didn't want me to break in on his train of thought.

"You're so fucking pretty, Tess."

Tears fought their way to the surface, and I rubbed the back of his neck while I let his words sink in. It was the most he ever said to me at once about anything so personal.

"Thank you," flew out of my mouth. The corners of his mouth rose, and I saw a real, genuine smile.

Jesus.

His hands slowly descended my back and curled around my ass. He pulled me to him and dove deep inside of me.

I jolted, and he nuzzled my hair. "I laid out all my feelings for you, but I will never change the way I fuck you."

Good!

***

Trigger

"He's been sitting like that since he won the fight." Langley eyed me from behind the asshole who lost his bet and was now trying to get his money back. "What's wrong with you?"

"He's fine." My father smacked my shoulder hard, but even that couldn't shake me from the alternate world I was caught in. I hated it

there, but it was the only way I could handle the demons that ran free whenever I fought. It was as if I needed to be still and stay quiet so they'd retreat to their cages.

I could feel their nails. They seemed to click against my bones and drag me back to each swing, each blood spray, each moment I punched my opponent. The reaper loomed a little closer, and his cold, dark presence cloaked my world as I had fought like hell through their heavy shadow to get back. Sometimes I wondered what it would be like to stay there and just give in to the madness.

"Hey, boy!" The loser kicked my leg. "Show some respect when I'm talking to you." He went to kick me again, but I latched onto his wrist, yanked him down, and smashed his face into my knee, and the blood sprayed. Next, I rammed the heel of my boot into his mouth, and his teeth broke off and fell from his tongue as he screamed. I covered his lips and watched as he struggled to breathe and not swallow little chips of bone.

My father caught my attention, and he smiled and shook his head at someone who was about to intervene. He held up a hand to stop him.

"The boy's a natural killer. Let him finish."

A chill pricked at my skin. He *was here, ready to take my next offering. I leaned back and gave him some room.*

"Again," Langley shouted from the corner of the ring. "Arms up!"

The boxing opponent Langley had brought in had a hard time standing, and I could see he had a concussion. Five hours in a ring and multiple blows to the temple would do that.

"Tap out or fight," I spat and waited. He blinked, but he wasn't there.

He stepped forward but collapsed, nearly taking my shoulder off in the process.

"Jace!" Langley pointed at him, and Rich, my newest prospect, grabbed both arms and pulled him out of the ring.

Another man took his place and got into position.

Once the word was out I was in town, there were lots of men willing to help me train. There was a time when the underground world was my life. I ate, slept, and breathed the ring. Everyone knew my name and placed their bets in my favor.

The excitement sent a feverish rush through my veins, and I twisted and sent a kick straight into his neck. His eyes bulged, and when he went to grab his neck, I punched his shoulder, knocking it out of its socket.

He yelped but stayed standing. I smirked, happy with his decision.

"Name?"

"Hugo."

I nodded and waited for Langley to reset his shoulder, then we started back up again.

Back and forth we went. No helmets, no gloves, just skin to skin, bones to bones.

Every punch I took made my demons scream. Their nails clawed the floor, and their teeth gnawed at the bars. They wanted out, they wanted to be free, but it wasn't time yet. Tomorrow they could feed.

Hugo's gaze flicked over my shoulder, and I saw a change in his face. I didn't need to see who it was. I felt her.

Rail looked uneasy as he dropped the screwdriver and headed over. I tried to stay focused. I didn't need Langley up my ass with Tess. Three more punches and a few more glances from Hugo, and I finally called a break.

"Like what you see?"

His eyes took another detour to Tess, then snapped back to mine, and he shook his head. "No."

Tess caught the attention of both males and females. She held herself with confidence, and dressed fucking hot. Having her in the same room as guys like Hugo made me want to take on every one of them.

I knew I'd kill anyone who went near her if I wasn't careful.

"Where's your head, Trig?" Langley's voice broke through my murderous thoughts.

I jumped and kicked Hugo in the chest, and he flew back into the ropes. His knees hit the floor first, then his hands.

He didn't speak as he peeled himself off the mat and stood on shaky legs.

"Take a break," Langley shouted and tossed me a cold Gatorade.

"Hey." She hopped up and stood on the other side of the ropes. Her breasts were squeezed into a black tank, and her ass was in a pair of tight jeans.

I leaned over and kissed her and grabbed a large handful of her ass, giving it a grope. She started to protest but soon gave in. Her body sagged into mine. She didn't seem to care I was covered in sweat.

"Territorial much?" She rolled her eyes, but she couldn't hide the fact she was horny.

"Get used to it."

She looked over at Langley then smiled and nodded at the ring.

"Can I try?"

A sudden flash went off in my head, and it nearly froze me. Tess crossing over into my past scared the shit out of me.

"No."

She completely ignored me and ducked under the ropes.

"Hey," she waved at Hugo, "I'm Tess."

"Hi, Tess." He stepped to the side of the ring with Langley, who shot me an unimpressed glare. He muttered something and handed Hugo a bottle of water.

"So, like this?" She put her hands up like she wanted to fight.

A cold rush broke over me, and I almost felt sick. She needed to get out of here now.

"Tess, get out."

"Why?" She moved around the ring with a wink. "Think you can't handle me?"

I shook my head and fought my switch. I wanted to yell and tear a strip off her, but I also didn't want to hurt her. I had done that enough already.

Instead, I lunged at her, wrapped myself around her arms, and pinned her back to my front.

My mouth rested above her ear, and I tried to speak very calmly. Each word came out slow. "I need you *out* of the ring."

"Why?"

She wiggled her ass, and I wanted to fuck her into submission.

Calm yourself.

"Tess."

She turned and looked up at me. "Okay." Gently, she pulled away, but when she started to duck back under the ropes, I caught her worried face.

"Hey." I grabbed her arm to turn her around. "What?"

Her eyebrow rose, and she shrugged. "Have you thought about what your father really has in store for you? Or are you overshadowed by the need to fight again?"

"I have."

"And?"

"And nothing. We're prepared for everything."

She let out a long sigh. "I heard a saying once. Just because you can't see evil, doesn't mean it can't see you."

"Oh, trust me, sweetheart, I can see evil." *By looking in the damn mirror.*

She played with the necklace that hung between her breasts, and my hungry gazed followed her fingertips as they descended into her cleavage.

"If you won't listen to me in the ring, maybe you will in bed tonight?" Her sexy mouth curved up, and her gaze dropped to my lips. "Or will you be too tired?"

"Never too tired for that." I hooked her waist and slammed her tight little body to mine.

I shook my head, and as I was about to devour her mouth, I heard a voice.

"Tess, you need to leave." Langley appeared at my side. "You're a distraction."

She tried to hide her smile as she ducked under the ropes.

"We wouldn't want that."

"Your timing is flawless." I snickered at my coach.

"Your mind is elsewhere."

True.

***

I didn't stop training until nine o'clock that night. Everything burned and started to feel stiff. I had a massage and a cortisone shot to help with my back. It was acting up, and Langley thought it was necessary. I disagreed, but I trusted his opinion. He had never steered me wrong.

I set the whiskey bottle on the night table and flopped into bed. Took me a moment to realize the smell that drifted from the bathroom.

"You're interrupting my date." Tess came into view with a thick joint between her slim fingers. She took a drag as I took in her outfit. Heels, purple silk nightgown, matching robe, and her hair was curled.

"Am I?"

"Mmhm," she purred before she sat on the couch across from the bed.

"Who do I need to kill?" I shifted the pillow under me so I could see her better.

"You're hurt."

"Sore," I corrected.

"You fight tomorrow. You think it was wise to train that much on the day before?"

"Are you questioning my methods?"

She blew out a long trail of smoke while she thought. She fished around in her purse and pulled out her lipstick vibrator.

My brows rose, and so did my erection.

Slowly, her legs spread, and one hand inched its way to her opening. I licked my lips, hungry to see more. Her eyes fluttered closed, and she shifted down the couch a little. Her movements were mesmerizing, and the way her fingers eased in and out in the slick coating had me unzipping my pants.

The click of the vibrator made my stomach knot and my head swim.

She set the joint on the rim of her wine glass and pushed the tip of the lipstick into her mouth to moisten it.

I groaned with primal need. Everything inside of me ached and begged to be released. Heat burned its way to the surface to the point of pain.

She slipped the vibrator between her folds, and her head flopped back with a huff. Her free hand pulled at her nipple, and her chest rose and fell heavily.

"Mmm," she moaned, and I joined her with a few pumps to my erection.

"Come here," I ordered, but even my voice seemed strained.

She ignored me and kept going. She pushed, twisted, and pumped that little shit into her hole, and I started to get frustrated. She wasn't listening, and I needed her to.

"Tess," I warned when she got dangerously close to coming.

A layer of sweat glistened on her forehead, her cheeks were pink, and her breathing told me she was close.

"So close," she hissed.

"Fuck that!" I jumped out of bed and grabbed her waist and tossed her on the mattress face down. I crawled over top of her ass and hiked up her nightgown. Holding her down with my body weight, I spread her legs and thrust.

She was so tight, so ready that she took me to the root. She was flat on the bed, and when she turned her head to the side to gasp for air, I saw the need in her eyes. Sex was our drug, one that we shared. She consumed me in every way, and that scared the shit out of me. But I was addicted and willing to fight to the end to keep her.

Grabbing both hands, I pulled them forward and held them as I molded to her curves. We were both slick, and I slid around easily to change direction.

I used my free hand to hold some of my weight. Using only my hips, I fucked her hard. Occasionally, I slowed and ran my fingers down the curve of her spine. Her skin heated under my touch, and she wiggled when I hit a sweet spot.

I allowed myself to smile, feel, and be raw in these moments. When we were together, nothing mattered.

"Trigger," her knuckles were white as the anticipation built, "please."

With my knees on either side of her hips and my hands on the headboard, I flicked my hips upward, and she jolted forward with a sexy cry.

She clawed helplessly at the tangled sheets. Her lungs fought for air. Her eyes squeezed shut.

My favorite part was when she first let go. Her insides clamped around me, and her back bowed as her orgasm ripped through her center and slingshotted me into mine.

I dropped down, and my head hit her back. I wrapped my arms around her midsection as I hung on. It was the only moment I was completely defenseless. Completely at her mercy.

***

Allen

"What, exactly, do you mean?" His forehead had broken out in a heavy sweat, and he squinted as he absorbed my words.

"I mean it's time."

"I don't think I can do this."

I slapped my hands together and smirked. "I don't recall asking you."

"He'll kill me."

"Him or me. Really, I think you're getting the better end of the deal if he does." I glanced back at my hungry weasels. "I'm done with you now."

He slowly rose and looked out the window at the other guys.

"Time to go." Zay popped his head in the door, holding my bag. He turned to my visitor. "You better not fuck this up."

"Don't have a choice, do I?"

"No," we said in unison.

He muttered as he went for the door. Zay stepped in his path momentarily before he let him go.

"She's pretty." Zay turned his phone around so I could see. Tess was at the market looking through the wine section. Her hair was long, and her ass was stuck in the air.

"Yes, she'll be a fine match for you."

I tapped on my laptop and checked in. "Shall we?"

Zay hopped to his feet with my bag in hand. "You worried?"

"Scared of my own son? No."

"Of him." He nodded out the door.

"He knows what will come if he doesn't do his part."

CHAPTER TWENTY

Tess

"Thanks." I nodded at the doorman who handed me an all-access pass to hang around my neck. Trigger, Langley, Brick, and Rail all came to the event before the rest of us.

I was told to wait for the all-clear back at the house with Gus. He seemed to hover around me the entire morning. *I have never seen him this way.* He kept asking if I needed anything or if I wanted a drink. It didn't take me long to see he was the one who needed one.

Even on the car ride there, he checked his phone a million times, and his fucked-up knee bounced out of control.

"Shit, Gus." Big Joe shook his head across the limo from us. "If I didn't know better, I'd think you were the fucking mole."

The entire car went silent.

"Poor taste," Gus muttered as he stared out the window. He was right, though. It wasn't the time to go there. We needed to get through today.

Jace covered his face and sighed. "I don't think I have ever been this nervous over someone else fighting."

"Trigger will win." Cooper poured himself another brandy.

The dude was feeling no pain today. I guessed we all coped differently.

The guys hopped out, but when I reached for the door handle, Gus hauled me back in and locked the doors.

"What the hell?" I whirled around and looked for an exit plan.

Cooper looked panicked and called to the other guys.

"Tess!" He grabbed my hands so I would make eye contact. "I did something. Something bad."

"Gus, if you're the mole, you're about to break my heart. You're like a dad to Trigger and to me." Why on earth I admitted that now was beyond me.

"Are you fucking kidding me? I love Trigger like he's my kid, and you too." He rubbed his face like he was weighing his decision. "I found her." He paused so I could connect the dots.

"Who?"

"His mother."

Oh, shit. I looked over my shoulder at the guys waiting by the door. Cooper was the only one who wouldn't take his eyes off the car. I motioned to him that everything was okay.

"Why were you looking for her?"

"No one can get through to Trigger. She was my last try."

"Gus," I fought for the right words, "do you really think it's smart to bring her in at this time to fuck with his head?"

"What choice do I have? The fight starts in an hour."

I leaned forward and took his hands. "Why are you really so nervous about this fight? What are you not telling me?"

"You wouldn't understand."

"Try me." I squared my shoulders to show I was ready.

"I watched that boy become something big, and never once did he get cocky. He fought, he won, he lived that life. But every punch, every blow, every victory pushed him into a dark place. He fucks with fate, doesn't feel the fear, just rides full speed ahead. He'll look at you differently, Tess, and it will hurt. That something you have between you two will fizzle out. He'll flip off his humanity switch, and you'll grow tired of waiting for him to return. That's what you'll feel."

I could tell by his tone he had more to say.

"What about you? What will you feel?"

"I will lose my nephew, the club will have a ruthless leader, and my sons will lose their father."

My head snapped back at that last statement.

"Come on, Tess." He shrugged one shoulder. "He's been more of a father to my boys than I have. They weren't planned. Vib just needed an anchor to the club, and I'm weak when it comes to her. They need him. I need him, and I cannot believe I found my sister."

"Hold on." I felt twenty different things fire off at once. "I thought you were Allen's brother?"

"Nope." He raised his head a little higher. "She is my sister. I hung out at the strip joint where she worked."

"Ahh." I couldn't help but be freaked out by that.

"No," he made a disgusted face, "it's not like that at all, but she is only a half-sister."

"Doesn't make it better."

He huffed, but the humor quickly faded. "I watched over her. I knew Allen was shitty from the moment he walked in, but my sister saw what you saw in Trigger. Tall, hot, brooding." He rolled his eyes. "He pursued her until she gave in. He was relentless. I warned her he would fuck and chuck, and that's exactly what happened. She really thought he'd come back after she told him she was pregnant. Instead, he ran, and that's when she started to go down the rabbit hole. She was always on coke, but it was the speed that did her in. She couldn't handle the baby. I was useless when it came to the kid. All I did was worry about her, and one day she came home without him. She packed up her stuff and left. I never saw her again."

His eyes saddened, and he looked down at the floor, lost in his thoughts. "Took me a year to find him. Trigger was about one and half by then. Fucking cute little thing, big dark eyes and a mop of hair to match. Allen didn't want me around at first. Took me a long time to show him I only wanted to be a part of the boy's life. I was in and out of prison for a while, doing stupid shit. But I came back," he whispered more to himself. "I always came back."

I shook my head to try to shake the visions clear. "I had…wow. How did you find her? I mean, does she even want to see him?"

"Anyone can be found eventually. You just need to know who to ask." He massaged his knee and winced. "She's clean, at least she seems to be. I know I'm playin' with fire here, but this whole thing…" He pointed to the windowless building. "I know it's going to be something bad. Allen's planning something. Nothing is ever what it seems with him."

Fuck. I didn't know what to think. His mother could throw him over the edge. What if Allen saw her? What would he do?

"Where is she?"

"She's inside."

"Does Brick know about this?"

"Brick knows some things about it, but he thinks she's a friend of mine. That's all. I might need you to run interference. Will you help me?"

Fuck!

"Ycs."

"Good." He leaned forward, unlocked the door, and motioned for me to get out.

"This way." Gus pointed down the hallway. As we got closer, the sound of the crowd grew louder, and my anxiety kicked in bigtime. It was a cocktail of nerves, fear, excitement, sadness, and, I couldn't deny it, a little hope.

"Hey," Gus stopped me at the door, "if anything happens tonight, please remind Trigger of Mr. Rabbit."

"Huh?"

Gus pushed the door open, and there stood a woman with long black hair, dark eyes, and prefect teeth. There were signs of drug use, but she was extremely pretty, and she was the spitting image of Trigger.

"Hi." She extended her hand and waited for me to do the same. "I'm Elizabeth Wise."

"Tess." I glanced at Rail, who was devouring a chocolate bar like it was a one-night stand. He stood there completely oblivious to what was happening around him.

Men.

"She's a friend of Gus's," Brick chimed in from across the room. "Guess she was in town or something."

Finally! I knew I could count on my best friend to feel the strangeness of the situation. He gave me a worried look as he pushed off the wall and headed for the door. "Tess, you should see if Trigger needs anything."

"Oh." Elizabeth eyed me a little more closely, and the corners of her mouth raised. "Are you and my son dating?"

Gus flinched bedside me, and Brick nearly tripped into Rail, who was still busy with the wrapper of the bar.

"What the fuck?" Brick blurted. "What the fuck did you guys do?"

"I didn't," I started, but stopped. I didn't want to toss Gus under the bus, not when he was legitimately trying to help.

"Brick," Langley stuck his head in the door, "I need more tape."

"Get some Gatorade," Trigger ordered behind him.

Oh, shit. It was like a snowball gaining speed as it came toward us. Just as I turned to get the hell out of its path, Trigger walked in, and I froze to the spot.

"Hey." He started to give me his lazy smile but stopped when he felt the mood. His eyes flickered over to his mother, and his brows pinched together. It would be impossible for him to remember her, but not impossible to see they were related. He was looking in a damn mirror, for shit's sake.

"Do you know who I am?" she said softly.

"I do."

"Good." She let out a small breath.

"Is it?" he challenged.

"I get it, you're mad at me—"

"Are you fucking kidding me? Why now? Why here?" She started to speak, but he squeezed my hip and urged me out the door before she could convince him to stay. "I will not feed more to *those*..." he hit the side of his head hard, "savages!"

Once outside, he pulled out his phone and headed in the opposite direction.

"Don't go back in there."

"I won't," I assured him and waited for him to leave before I went to find Brick to see just how bad this shit storm had become.

***

Trigger

The bottle called my name. It dangled from my fingers, but I knew better. I didn't abuse drugs, but right now I could use a hit of something. I needed my head clear, but my mother showing up threw me off center in a major way.

Shit.

I snatched up my phone and texted Tess.

Trigger: Where are you?

Nothing.

I switched screens and called her.

Nothing.

Fuck.

I tried calling two more times before I turned and caught my cold, dark reflection in the mirror. My tortured soul stared back at me from the glass, and a dark aura hovered around me like a shadow. Was there ever going to be an end to all of this?

With all my might, I swung back and smashed the bottle into the mirror and watched as bits of clear and green glass sprayed into the air like blood.

My temper rose as I lunged at the door. I could not believe my mother was really here right now.

"Where is Tess?" I barked at Langley while he tried desperately to look over my shoulder at the mystery guest who had just flipped my world upside down fifteen minutes before my fucking fight.

Wrong room, Langley.

"Trigger, I didn't mean to—"

I whirled around and jammed a finger in my uncle's face. I wanted to snap his neck for what he did. For the second time in my life, he flinched at my reaction. My arm dropped, and I covered my face to calm myself. The first time was when he saw me covered in bruises after my first fight. I guessed he thought he had failed me as a protector, and to be truthful, he did. I never blamed him. I wasn't his problem. He wasn't the one who gave birth to me then tossed me aside, and he wasn't the one who left the scars on my body. He was an uncle who dropped by to check on me occasionally. He was the one, however, who had become more of a father to me than my own ever had. He was the one who was there when he saw I was heading down an even darker path, and the one, after all, who suggested I kill my father.

"I had to do something," he whispered and stepped back into line with the guys.

"We need to talk. Just give me a second." I couldn't do this here.

"What the hell is going on?" Langley snapped, clearly annoyed. "You disappear minutes before the fight, there's some chick in there with you, and now you'll be going in cold! Are you trying to kill me?"

I turned. "Where's Tess?"

"And now you're thinking about pussy?"

"You mean that blonde with the great rack?" the little shit who carried our stuff chimed in. "She's talking to some guy by your room."

I did a quick sweep of my guys and saw they were all here. Pushing past Rail, I raced down the hallway. People pressed into the wall to get out of my way.

"Trigger, wait," Jace called out, a bunch of girls surrounding him. "These ladies want to meet you."

Turning the corner, I came to a stop and saw her reading something on her phone. She must have sensed me, because she looked up.

I grabbed her by the waist and hauled her into the empty room, slamming the door in Langley's pissed off face.

"Are you okay?" She touched my face as I stood over her, trapping her against the wall.

I squeezed my eyes tightly shut and fought my way through the darkness, using her scent to guide me.

"You're scaring me a little, here," she whispered. "Speak to me."

I opened my eyes, and for the first time in my life, I felt something other than pain and emptiness.

"I love you, Tess." I shook my head in disbelief that I could finally see it so clearly. "I love you so much that the idea of anyone hurting you, or even flirting with you, makes me want to snap every limb on their body very slowly. I'm sorry I didn't see it before, but I need you to know I'm here now, and I want all of you."

She blinked, and I was sure I threw her off course, but I didn't care.

"You've already had me." She kissed me in the dirty way she did. When we came up for air, I pressed my forehead to hers to catch my breath.

"But," I paused, knowing this would set her back, "I need to fight now."

She tensed, and I pulled back so she could see my face.

"I need you to trust me on this."

"I do trust you, Trigger, but I'm with Gus. Something is not right here. Do you really think he's going to just fight and be done?"

"No, I don't. But I need to do this."

"Tell me," she blurted, and I knew exactly what she was referring to.

I held my arm next to hers, so her key lined up with my skeleton wrapped in chains. The angle allowed the key to fit the padlock.

"You free me."

Her lips parted as her fingers slowly drew over my arm.

"I can't believe I never made the connection."

I held her head in my hands. "Give me tonight, and I'll give you the rest."

I didn't wait for her answer before I peeled away and out the door. If she had said no, I didn't think I could fight.

"Ready?" Langley mouthed through the sea of people shouting behind the main doors.

I nodded but looked back to see Tess standing next to Gus. Both looked very unhappy. Gus leaned over and whispered something to her, and she nodded with her eyes on the ground.

When she looked over, I gave her a wink. Her eyes lit up, but I knew the trouble that still stormed inside her, and it wouldn't take a lot for it to brew to the surface.

I reached out to grab her hand and tugged her to my side once more.

"No," Langley shouted. "Your fans don't want to see her. They want you. Bad marketing move, Trigger."

"Don't care," I grunted and pushed the steel doors open. Cameras flashed from all directions, and fluorescent lights beat down on my shoulders. I felt my shoes squish on the rubber mat, and my hearing tuned in and out of the insane crowd ahead of me. Tess flexed her grip and stepped closer as I urged her forward down the ramp to the ring.

Eighty percent of the crowd were my old fans, and the rest were new. I recognized the black t-shirts my father had made up many years ago when I was at the top.

"Flip your switch" ran across the front in red letters, and "Trigger" was underneath.

The buildup started in the pit of my stomach. The warmth invaded my veins and sent a steroid shot to my system.

I was back.

I pointed to a chair and leaned in next to her ear. "Stay here."

She nodded and took the chair next to Brick, and he wrapped his arm around her for comfort.

She mouthed, "Good luck."

I locked eyes with her once more then broke away. I could feel the fear radiating off her. I was aware of my habit after a fight, that I'd disappear into another dimension, but now I knew I had a reason to come back.

I needed to get my head in this now, one hundred percent, before I stepped up the stairs.

Langley lifted the ropes, and I ducked under and did a turn for the crowd. I was never an attention seeker, nor was I now, but I felt they deserved a little attention considering it had been nearly two decades since I stepped foot in the ring.

The vibrations of the crowd traveled up the length of my body, powering everything to the max. It was like when you started a carnival ride. The lights flickered on, and you could hear the beast of the engine start with a roar.

I have been awakened.

The announcer spoke, but only his mouth moved. I whirled around, waiting for the devil to show its ugly head.

It was time.

I saw Jace and Rail lean over and say something to Tess. She looked unsure but stood. I didn't have time to think as the crowd went crazy. The energy in the room swirled around like a wild dirt devil, and there he was. The man I feared as a boy, killed as a teenager, and hunted as an adult.

He stood just shy of a foot away from me. He wasn't as built, but he was lean. I never underestimated Allen and what he brought to the table, and I wasn't about to now.

"Son," he greeted me, and I felt the same rush of hate I got when I was younger. Instead of letting it fester into fear, I channeled it into fuel.

He made sure to glance over at the ropes like he always did, when he'd lean over them and wait like the reaper. He was referring to my tattoo. *Death is never far.*

The announcer, dressed in a flashy suit, stepped into the center of the ring, lifted his hand, and waited for the mic to lower from the ceiling.

"Ladies and gentlemen, welcome!" I was momentarily deafened by the roar of the thirsty crowd.

His mouth started to move again, but I had my eyes on my father, who wore an evil smirk. If I concentrated, I could snap back to twenty years ago when he loomed over me with the same expression.

Suddenly, my father raised his hand and stepped over to the announcer. The man bowed and got out of the way.

"Damn, it's good to be back!" He egged on the crowd, and they went wild for this sideshow act. "Now, let's be honest, here." He did a spin, making sure to show his respect. "This," he waved between us, "isn't a fair fight. I'm sixty-three, and he's thirty-six. That's a twenty-seven-year difference." The crowd booed, but he held his hand up, and a cold feeling washed over me. "So, I thought to myself, who would be wild enough to go up against my son? The boy who killed his own father? Well," he patted himself down, "almost."

I looked around to connect the dots, but I didn't see anyone come in from his door, and no one was waiting around the ring.

"Son?" My father's voice snapped my attention back to him. His arms were stretched out, his hands raised like some kind of prophet.

Just when I thought I couldn't be any more betrayed, I saw my childhood anchor whip off his t-shirt and pants and his raise his fists to start.

"Why?" was all that came out.

"Money can make you do a lot of things, son." Langley shrugged and nodded at my father, who slipped between the ropes and whispered something to the announcer.

"Place your new bets now!" screamed over the mic.

I gave in to the dark hole that opened at my feet. I had been betrayed before, but this cut to the core. Langley was the only one I thought ever cared. He had tried to protect me from my father. What the fuck had changed?

"You gonna fight me or stand there?"

I vaguely noticed the bell ringing, and my arms shot up to block my face.

Langley moved in to throw a punch, but I leaned back, and it fell short. I counterpunched with my right. I moved toward him, but he expected that and threw a kick to my ribcage and followed through with a left. Fuck, he knew all my moves. He was the one who trained me.

I threw a left, a right, an uppercut, and Langley moved back out of the way to the corner. I grabbed him around the chest and held him, throwing my knee toward his stomach. Langley blocked my knee with his arms.

I had to come up with a move he wouldn't expect. I had to slow the fight down to think. I pushed off him and threw my elbow desperately into his face, cutting him above the right eye, then stepped back and turned with a three-hundred-sixty-degree roundhouse swing. Langley anticipated me by ducking and countered with another kick to my ribs, then threw a left, right, left, opening a cut above my eye. He followed that with a kick to my thigh, buckling my knee, and as I fell forward, he kneed me in the face, busting my nose. Blood streamed down my face. Shit, he was all over me. I fell into the ropes, and Langley stepped back, knowing if he grabbed me, I would be able to overpower him. So, he switched up and threw another kick to my thigh. I knew I had to get into the game fast. My head was ringing.

Langley threw a couple of left jabs, followed with a right that rocked me backward, and sent a kick to my ribs, but this time I grabbed his leg and knocked him off balance to the canvas. I jumped on him and threw a couple of punches. He grabbed me and pulled himself up close to my chest, so I couldn't get a swing at him. I dropped an elbow hard into his already bloody face.

Suddenly, I heard hands slamming against the canvas and Brick roaring, "Trigger, end this shit. They got Tess!"

"What the fuck?" Langley escaped from the hold when I lost my concentration to scan the crowd for Tess. Her seat was empty. Langley threw a kick at my face, spraying blood over the spectators.

Punch, punch, punch. I turned into a robot. Kick, kick, kick.

One of my punches hit air, and I shook my head, confused. The darkness faded into grays, and I saw Langley on the ground, unconscious.

The announcer raced over and checked his neck while I searched the ring's perimeter for my father.

He was gone, but what caught my eye was Zay. He was climbing the steps to go outside. What the fuck was he doing here?

I felt a stab to the gut and whirled as Brick's words hit me like a wall. Tess was gone. I vaguely heard the results. "Our victor! Trigger!"

CHAPTER TWENTY-ONE

Tess

Fifteen minutes earlier…

"Okay, okay!" Jace wiggled his way through the seats and repeated our order to himself.

"Don't fuck it up, prospect, or the next round is on you."

"Hysterical." He flipped Rail the finger, and I shifted at the nerves eating away at my core. Trigger was on the bench in a zone, while Langley yelled a bunch of things that couldn't be heard over the roaring crowd.

"Oh." Jace's hand landed on the back of my seat. His eyes closed, and he looked almost sick by the way he swayed on his feet.

"You good, Jace?"

"Yeah." He took a deep breath through his nose then started up the ramp we came down. The doorman glanced at his ID badge and let him out. The door swung wider as someone came in with a cart, and I saw Jace double over on the floor.

"Oh, my God!" I leaped from my seat and raced out the door before it closed. My knees hit the floor hard as I pushed someone out of the way.

"Jace!" I shook his shoulders. "You okay?"

His eyes fluttered open, and he looked at me strangely. "Oh," his hand landed on his head, "I feel like shit."

"Well, you look like it, so that would make sense," I joked, but I looked around for a place to prop him up. I scrambled to my feet and tried to help him up. I wasn't strong enough, and he fell back down.

"Shit, let me grab Brick."

"No." He grabbed my hand again and tried to rise, and just as his legs began to give out, someone caught him under the arms.

"Damn, dude, what'd you drink?"

"Nothing yet," I replied for Jace. "I think he may have eaten something."

Jace shook the man's hands off him and glanced around. "I just need the noise to stop." He grabbed my shoulders and sagged into me. "Help to the manager's office. He knows me. He'll let me crash for a second."

"Okay." I tried to smile at the man. "Thank you."

"Yup." He stepped away and shook his head like he was annoyed.

He's not drunk, dude.

I pushed the door open and found a room littered with trophies and medals, a rusty desk, no windows, a small door in the far wall with pictures framing it, and a leather couch. I nearly dropped Jace onto it and rolled my shoulder to relieve the muscle strain from his weight.

"Fuck, that's better." He rolled to his side and pulled his knees up to his chest. "What the hell was in that burrito?"

"If you insist on eating street meat, you get what you deserve."

"Stop parenting me."

I chuckled. "Stop acting like a child, and I wouldn't have to."

He rolled his head to look at me but didn't move his body. "This won't count for much later, but thank you."

"Why won't it count later?" That was a strange comment, but I couldn't focus on Jace anymore. The noise of the crowd told me the fight had started, and I needed to get back to the arena.

"I'm sorry, Tess."

"You're losing it, Jace." I stood and gave a little wave. "I'm going to grab Brick, okay?"

"Tess…"

Just as he said my name, I turned to find Zay standing in the doorway.

Huh? No!

I mentally kicked myself for believing the piece of shit in front of me knew my family. He was that prickle up my spine sometimes when I was out in public. He was the one who watched me from across the street or at the pier. How did I not remember his face? *Stay calm, Tess.*

"Jace, go get Trigger."

"I can't. I'm sorry." His tone made my heart drop into my stomach as it all clicked together.

"No, not you, Jace?" I wanted to cry. Not my friend, not the mole. Please, no.

"Now," Zay pulled on a pair of leather gloves, and I almost laughed out of pure fear, "we need to leave before they arrive."

"Who?" I jumped when Jace grabbed my arm, looking much better than before, and pulled me toward the door. I couldn't look at him, I was so hurt. I had been there for Jace after Ty was killed. We had formed a bond, and this was where it got me. "Don't fucking touch me!"

"She runs," Zay checked his gun clip, "shoot her."

"Shut up, Tess," Jace warned as I tried to wiggle out of his hold, but he latched on tighter and pushed me out the exit door to the outside. "Just do as they say."

Fucking cliché line, Jace.

"Help!" I screamed at the top of my lungs. "Someone help me!" Zay flipped around and slammed the butt of his gun into my stomach and knocked the wind right out of me. Before I could think, I was shoved into a limo, and as the door shut, I heard Gus's voice. I scrambled to my knees and tried the doors and windows.

"Take me too." He waved his arms. "Two for one. We are all he cares about, Zay. You know that. Why not hit him where it hurts the most? Family."

Holy shit, what was he doing?

"Gus! No!" I hardly recognized my tone, it was laced with such terror. He wouldn't be able to handle this.

A thick dose of panic rippled through me like an earthquake. What were they going to do?

"Just fucking grab him, man!" Jace screamed. He seemed amped up, unlike the Jace I knew and became friends with.

Zay put a radio up to his ear and looked all around. I went for the handle of the door when it clicked open, but Jace beat me to it. He shoved me back hard as he sat next to me.

"Don't make me hurt you, Tess, please." He covered his face and whispered, "Shit, this is so fucked up."

"Jace," I reached over, but he jumped at my touch, "please, please don't do this."

"You think I want this? You think I had a choice?" he nearly screamed. "I'm a goddamn prospect. I do as I'm fucking told."

"Wait." I tried to understand. "Trigger asked you to take me?"

"No!" He shook his head. "Him." He nodded, and for the third time in my life, I had the devil in my sights. Trigger's father.

Zay pointed his gun at Gus, and I snapped back to what was happening. I screamed and clawed at the window for him to stop. Not Gus, not someone as sweet and harmless as Gus. The boys popped into my head, and I wanted to cry and take his place. No kid should go through life without parents. They needed him. Shit, I needed him. He filled a void I hadn't even known I had.

"If that's her reaction, imagine Trigger's." Zay snickered. "Get in, old man." He grabbed Gus by the shirt and tossed him inside.

"Jesus Christ, be careful," I snapped at Zay. He tried to elbow me in the throat, but I ducked out of the way. He slammed the door, and I helped Gus to the seat and held his hand.

"You okay?"

"Yeah." He squinted and held his knee. "You?"

"Why would you make them take you? What about the boys?"

He rolled his head to face me. "I'm your only hope of getting through this." He lowered his voice. "And that ain't saying much."

He snapped his gaze over to Jace, who looked to have lost three shades of color. They exchanged some kind of look, almost an understanding that we were royally fucked.

My phone vibrated against my leg, and I shifted to pull it free.

Oh, my God!

Gus bumped my knee to get my attention and mouthed, "One, two, three."

"Savi!" I screamed in a desperate plea, and Jace's head whipped around in confusion. "Savi! Allen took us. Gus and I are in—"

Jace lunged for the phone, but Gus tossed his body weight at him.

"Tess! Where are you right now?"

"Vegas! Outside the fight. Trigger is still inside!"

"You stupid bitch!" Jace grabbed my leg and tried to pull himself upright. "Give me that!"

"Savi, you need to tell Trigger that Jace is the mole and—"

"Listen to me," she said to stop my mad chatter. "Where are they taking you? Did they say?"

Just as I was about to answer, Jace knocked the phone from my hands and scooped it up.

Gus huffed with his arm wrapped around his stomach and struggled to get back into the seat.

"You're fucking insane, Tess!" Jace quickly turned it off, but I noticed he didn't toss it away. He just tucked it in his pocket. "You're going to get me into trouble."

"Yes, and we wouldn't want that." My voice dripped with sarcasm as my heart dropped into my stomach again. Did I fuck everything up by showing I had my phone? Did I just lose our one lifeline? Gus was still holding his side. One eye opened, and I saw him peel back his fingers to show me he had his phone on, and it was on a map.

Sneaky old man.

Jace was staring out the window, and when he suddenly sat up straight, I knew things were about to get a whole lot worse.

He rolled down the window. "They're here."

Blue and red flashing lights filled the inside of the limo and flooded the main parking lot.

Zay waited as a blue car rolled up, and out stepped an officer I hadn't seen before. I squinted to read his patches. Why wasn't I surprised to find a Santa Monica cop here? A flashlight skimmed his name tag, and I caught the first few letters. DOY.

"Who's that?" I whispered to Gus, who looked like he'd seen a ghost. The engine started, and we peeled out of the driveway and onto the street. I turned to see the lights of the building slowly trickle away like so many fireflies.

Gus shook his head at Jace. "What the fuck did you guys do?"

***

Trigger

"Where is she?" I screamed over the crowd as people tried to grab at me from every direction.

I was wild and drunk for his kill. I needed to smell his blood, to watch as it drained from his body and circled my feet. I wanted to remove his eyes, teeth, and burn off his fingerprints so he didn't exist anymore. I wanted so much more, but he was gone, like so much fucking smoke and mirrors.

I tore myself away from the darkness, but it felt like I had left a layer of my skin behind.

Focus.

"Find him," I barked at Rail, who had fought his way over to me.

"On it." He ducked under the sea of people and disappeared.

I had my father inches from the reaper's grip. He was there in the flesh, ready to be taken out, but I lost my focus, once again trapped by betrayal. I yanked the door back and screamed with frustration.

"Where is she?" I boomed at Cray, and he put his hands up so I wouldn't hit him. I heard my men come up behind me, but nothing mattered.

"Hang on!" He tried to stop me, but I was five strides ahead. "Trigger, before you flip out, you need to hear this!"

I ignored him and tore open my door and saw the room was empty. I went on to the next, and the next, and every empty room elevated my anger.

"Nolan!" my mother squealed. "I saw what happened."

That stopped me.

"I saw them take—"

My hands snapped around her neck and pushed her into the wall. Brick appeared on one side of me and started to shout, but nothing made it through the demons' cries for more. They were savages and slowly taking over.

Cray and Cooper came up with their weapons drawn, ready to do what was necessary.

Her fingers clawed at my arms while her face turned bright red.

"Allen. He took…her."

My grip tightened as I fought to stay in the present, but Nolan was fading fast, and so was Tess.

No. This wasn't happening.

"His fucking assholes jumped me!" Rail held his broken nose and limped as he came into view. "I'm sorry, man. Allen's gone."

What the hell?

"You did this, didn't you? You played me! You know I love her, and you took her from me!"

If I couldn't kill my father, my mother was the next best thing.

"No." Tears streamed down her terrified face. "I don't even know her. But I can help you find her."

"Trigger!" The familiar voice cut through my rage, and a small body slammed into mine. I didn't move. I was stone, but I broke the hold on my mother, my fist still raised, about to pound.

"Listen to me!" Fin's face was bright red, and tears pooled around his cape Tess had helped him make to support the fight. So much terror was held in such a tiny face. "Stop fighting and find her!" He started to sob, and I broke. I scooped him up and buried my face in his neck. He shook as he sobbed and held onto me tight. I knew that fear. It was that of a boy who just lost his mother.

A feeling I knew and held onto for many years.

"I'm sorry," I whispered. "We'll get her back, I promise."

"Oh, my God." Brick covered his face as he turned around, looking about ready to puke. I reached out and grabbed his shoulder. Anchor to anchor.

"Where's Gus?" I barely heard Cray ask.

I glanced at Minnie and handed Fin to her. I started to scan the hallway. He was slower than the rest of us.

"Watch her." I jammed a finger at my mother but directed my words to Minnie. "She moves, shoot her."

"Yeah, okay." I noticed Brick as he tucked a gun into the waist of her pants, careful not to show Fin.

"Trigger?" Morgan nearly ran into me and turned his phone to face me.

Mike: Jace is your mole! Get Trigger to call me now!

What? That sucked the breath right out of me.

"Jace." He shook his head, the betrayal deepening the creases around his eyes. "He took her. He's the goddamn mole!"

Motherfucker! I clenched my fist, and my muscles quivered with the need to kill something. I should have known. Jace and Tess became close quickly. He burrowed his way into her trust, only to rip it away.

He betrayed me—no, us—his fucking family that fed and housed him.

I am done.

My head tried to keep ahead of the demons. I wanted so much to give in and let them take over, so I could get through this without the terrible ache that held my body prisoner.

"Trigger!" Big Joe burst around the corner. His face was broken out in a sweat. "You need to see this."

"Joe, if this has something to do with Tess, you need to—" Brick couldn't finish the sentence, and I didn't want him to.

"No." Big Joe motioned for us to follow him. We raced down two hallways, through the lobby, and down another hall. He held open the door, and we rushed in and our boots were covered in…blood?

"Holy shit." Brick glanced around at the five twisted bodies. One's neck had been snapped, an ear looked like it had been ripped off another, and the smell of bleach almost took our breath away. "Who?"

"Stripe Backs." I pointed to the lime green eyes staring back at me as the rest of the guys joined us. Minnie covered Fin's eyes and hurried back out with my mother on her heels. "Trigger." Brick turned with a haunted look, and I nodded. It looked like one of my kills.

"Get Rich to call Sam," I quickly instructed Rail. I had a sinking feeling we'd need our lawyer. He went to pull out his phone but stopped when we felt someone come in.

"You mean your prospect?" One of the men who carried our bags in before the fight suddenly appeared next to Cooper. "Yeah, man, he left, like, ten minutes ago with that girl Trigger had on his arm."

What the fuck?

"With who?"

"Shit!" Big Joe jumped back, and a team of police held their weapons on me.

"Oh, my God!" My mother snagged my attention as she stared at her phone, not the police.

"Everyone freeze!" one cop shouted, clearly taken over by fear.

I raised my arms, ready to fight. The sound of their weapons filled the room as most of the guns pointed in my direction.

"Stop." My mother stepped forward, almost as if to shield me. "Let me say goodbye to my son."

I couldn't help but feel a strange ripple run through me at the word *son*. Before anyone could say anything, she wrapped her arms around me and whispered, "They have Gus. He has his tracker on." She slipped the phone into my hand. She stepped back and blocked the SWAT team's view of the phone. I watched as the little blue dot moved farther and farther away from me. I couldn't believe it.

"Nolan Vineyard, Matthew Montgomery, and…" Officer Doyle stepped into the room with a rag over his nose, and my blood went wild. He turned to Rail. "Silas Hunter, you're under arrest."

No.

Morgan sidestepped behind me and pulled the phone from my grip as Doyle went on.

"For the mass murder at the Final Temptations Strip Club in Santa Barbara four years ago, and," he paused, and I saw him smile behind the rag, "the murder of these five Stripe Backs."

My blood ran cold as I made the connection that I had indeed been played by one of my own. But it wasn't only Jace who'd betrayed me. I slowly shifted and locked eyes with my second mole.

Nolan disappeared into dust as the cold steel clamped down around my wrists.

The End

Too strong to run,
Too proud to hide.
For this I'll pay…
For this I'll die.

My soul is black,
The demons are worse.

Pain was spread,
Love has burst.
Won't move forward,
Can't go back.

The reaper is circling,
Can't fight back.
The world has gone black.

She is gone,
Time will pass.
Evil has spread,
Will we last?

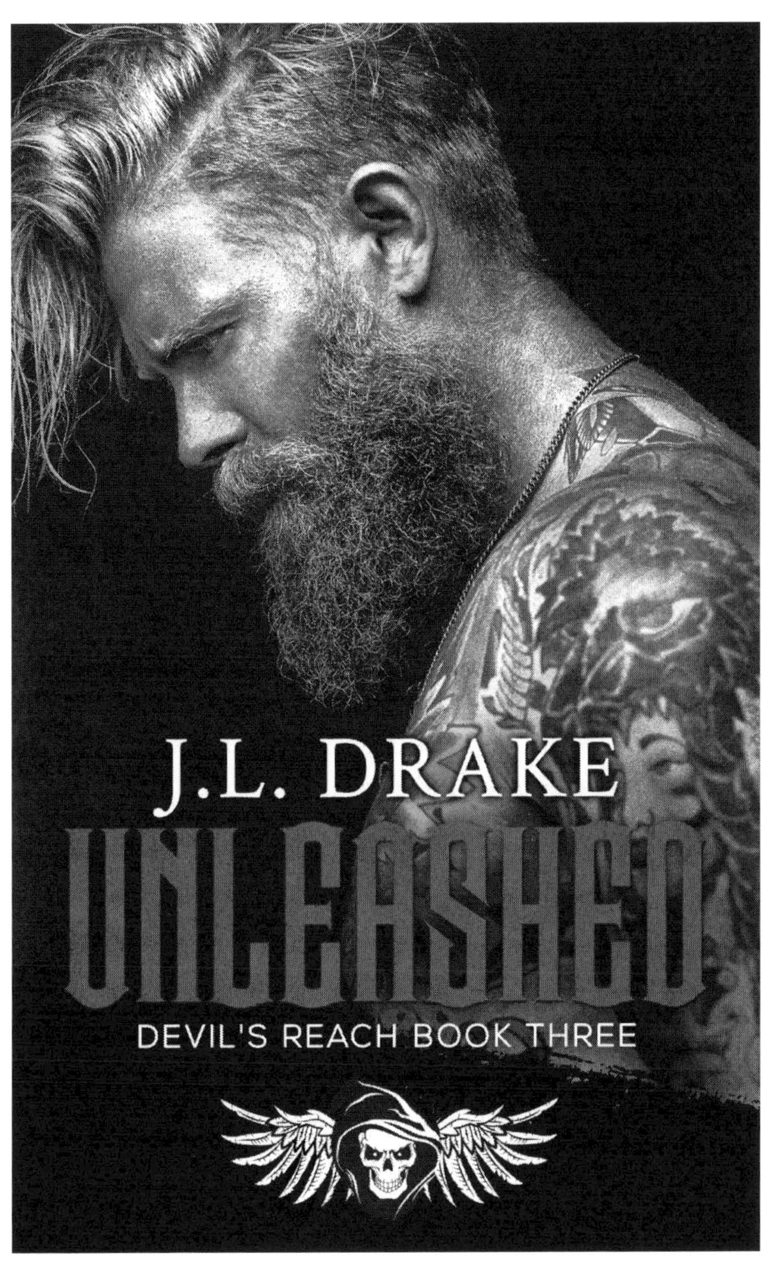
J.L. DRAKE
UNLEASHED
DEVIL'S REACH BOOK THREE

PROLOGUE

My fists beat at my temples, my head screamed at me to kill, and the room spun like someone had ripped open the door to Pandora's box. I clawed at the walls, ignoring the pain of my torn nails. I smashed the chair against the table and yanked the camera from the wall then gathered up the wire. Quickly, I wrapped it around my hands, ready to take on Doyle.

I shook my head to clear the screams, and the demons swung from bone to bone like an army of apes about to swarm their prey.

No windows, no air, nothing.

Pure, untamed adrenaline coated my insides, destroying any trace of good left in me.

I popped my neck and felt the blood rush away from my palms. Back and forth I shifted my weight, ready to fight. Ready to get the fuck out of here.

"Ahhhhh!" I couldn't keep in the madness. Chaos gnawed at my nerves.

The smell of blood lingered in the air, a promise I intended to keep for myself once he showed his face.

I rubbed my head vigorously in an attempt to keep it together.

I didn't lose control; this wasn't me.

What was happening?

What was the holdup?

Where the fuck was Sam?

Suddenly, as if someone snapped on a light, the door opened, and Officer Doyle stepped in. He glanced up at me from the file in his hand.

The window behind him shook, and I allowed it to draw my attention for a moment.

There I sat, cool, calm, relaxed in my chair.
If only he knew the storm that raged inside me.

CHAPTER ONE

Trigger

"I told you not to fight this, Trigger." Sam tugged at his tie. The skin around it was red. In all the years he'd been our lawyer, I had never seen him this stressed. "You're up for multiple murder charges, and you have a rottweiler named Rothweiler for a judge. Biggest dick on the west coast."

"The proof will show itself," I muttered, still lost in the dark thoughts that simmered with the need to tell my men who the mole was. It was too risky a move. They'd more than likely kill him before I could. Just knowing he was walking around freely in my club without a fuck made me wild with the urge to break out of here and rip his throat out.

Then there was *her*.

"Will it?" Brick rubbed his face, his tone hopeless. He'd completely worn through the pad of his thumb from rubbing the top of the screw on the chair leg. He pointed to the camera on the wall. "They clearly have some people in their pockets to have made this happen. That's some high-up power."

I know people too. I just need to wait for the right moment to play my cards.

The acidic ache in my chest alerted me that I was about to be hit with an image of her.

I jolted at the tear in my armor and pushed it away, back into its place, away from *them*. I felt their claws scrape at my insides as if they smelled my weakness.

"Trigger," Sam broke my focus, "this is bad. My hands are tied. No one is listening. All they want is to see you gone. I had no idea Doyle was working as a U.S. Marshals Liaison."

"I *can't* be someone's bitch." Rail's high-pitched voice piped in from the corner. "I have limits."

"Come on, Rail, you nailed that cougar from the gym in a Goodwill parking lot last month." Brick shook his head. "You have no limits."

"Ah, yeah, that's right." Rail chuckled. "She was a freak."

As jacked as they were inside, neither of them could keep their mouths shut.

"Fuck." Sam pressed his hands against his forehead. "You're all going to prison. I'll be the one left here on the other side of the wall."

"Why are you worried?" Rail dropped his feet from the table, his shoes smacking the floor. "Not like you're the one who's going to be showering with company."

"I'd rather that than what awaits me if I can't get you out." He glanced at me but quickly turned away. *That's right, you little fuck. You better be scared to shit.* I would kill his entire family if he didn't get us out, and he knew that, hence why he was freaking out.

The dusty, caged-in clock on the wall ticked loudly above Sam. Each second that passed seemed to toss another bucket of dirt on my grave…or hers. I knew Morgan had been monitoring Gus's location, but that was a few days ago, and I hadn't heard anything in a while. Sam chose to know nothing, so it couldn't be beaten out of him later. He was right to be paranoid. With me behind bars, he would be a target for sure, and not just for Allen, but for me too.

I dropped my head in my hands to soothe my achy eyes. I couldn't sleep, and it fucked with my mind. I'd woken to the sound of her voice, only to realize it was Rail in the bunk above me.

I followed the chains of the skeleton on my forearm and stopped at the lock. A heaviness settled in the pit of my tortured soul. I needed to get out of there, but I also knew I needed to play my cards right.

The door swung open, and in walked my parole officer, Chamness, shaking his head in his normal disapproving way. I rolled my eyes. The man was tired of working with me, and the feeling was mutual.

"Congratulations, Trigger, you're royally fucked."

"Please don't sugar coat it, Chamness," Rail hissed.

"Oh, trust me, I don't plan to." He dropped a file on the table and pinched the bridge of his nose. "You don't listen to me, your lawyer, or the law. You made your bed, now lay in the shit that awaits you, because I have no more tricks up my sleeve."

"Meaning?" I met his exhausted stare.

"Meaning they," he pointed at the window, "are finished with you and the revolving prison door you've had since you were sixteen. They've moved up your trial, given the number of deaths, and are prepared to get the ball rolling *now*."

"But it's been a week." Brick stood and pounded his fist on the table. "This shit should take months!"

"Yup," he nodded, "but you've pissed on them so many times, they want to make their point, and they're willing to pull out every judiciary trick in the book to do it."

"And their point is?" I was about to go on when the door opened. Three officers stepped in and quickly ushered us back into the courtroom.

"For fuck's sake, Trigger, keep your mouth shut," Chamness warned before we entered the courtroom.

I didn't recall much of what was said because I immediately locked eyes with Morgan, who shook his head, indicating they hadn't found her or Gus.

The wild things inside me went nuts when they felt my mood shift south.

Shit.

Sam elbowed me hard in the arm when I didn't give the judge the attention he demanded.

"Matthew Montgomery and Silas Hunter, you boys are looking at forty-five years, and by God, I aim to make sure you serve every second of it."

Brick huffed out a heavy breath, and Rail muttered something about how he'd rather die.

Judge Rottweiler—*Rothweiler*—narrowed his blue eyes partially hidden behind his bushy eyebrows on me. "Nolan Vineyard." He struggled to keep the corners of his mouth down. I stood a little straighter and waited for my fate.

"I guarantee, Vineyard, you can look forward to three life terms." I blinked at his words. "And if I had it my way, I'd give you the death penalty."

Rail reached out for the table while I bent to whisper to Sam.

"Links." He quickly pulled out his phone. Links was the guy who made things happen. As soon as we were arrested, Morgan pulled some strings, and he got to work. Now I knew we just had to wait.

I scanned the faces in the benches and stopped at my mother. She gave me a slight nod. I wasn't sure if she was telling me it was all right, or that she was giving me her support. Either way, I didn't want it. Why the fuck was she even there?

An officer came up behind me and pulled my wrists, indicating for me to follow.

"Sam," I yanked back and stepped closer, "she comes before us."

"I know." His answer sounded distant; the judge's malice had thrown him.

"Play dirty. I pay you enough to do so."

"You have my word."

"I better." I stopped myself from reminding him I knew his family well.

"Let's go." The officer grabbed my arm and pulled me away. I followed quietly to make my point to Sam. I'd do my part if he did his.

***

Tess

I tossed the paper plate in the trash and glanced out the window at the driveway and wondered how long it actually was. Three, maybe four miles? I knew it took it four minutes from the time I heard the engine until I could actually see the truck. Gus said six, but I thought his timing was off.

His smell hit me before I could react. My muscles locked in place as he stepped up behind me and whispered over my shoulder.

"You doing okay?" Zay trapped me at the counter with his arms. "Can I get you anything? Your skin looks so pretty in the sun. Like diamonds." Fox walked through the kitchen, stuffing his mouth full of potato chips.

"Yuck," I muttered. "You really know nothing about me, Zay."

"I know more than you think I do."

I wanted to elbow him in the ribs, but the last time I did that, Allen took it out on Gus.

"Really?" I couldn't help myself. Zay pissed me the hell off. "Then you should know making a *Twilight* reference is far from sexy, and seriously, I hate romance."

"Where the fuck are my shoes?" Allen snapped from behind us.

"Fine." Zay's tone changed, and he yanked one arm behind me and undid his belt. I started to panic. There was no way he was doing that. "I tried to be nice, tried to control myself around you, but you consistently push me away. So, we'll do it your way."

Allen sniggered, and I tried to whirl around, but Zay held my hips in place while his other hand fought to undo my pants. He was doing a shitty job. His hands kept slipping off my button, so I used that to my advantage.

"You sick fuck!" I drove my heel into his foot and drew back to punch him, but he caught my arms and bent me over the counter.

"I love that you fight, Tess, but you also need to know who you belong to now."

"Bitch needs to learn." Allen grinned with excitement as he raced upstairs.

"You mean a sicko who gets off by raping women?" I yelled at him because that was all I could do. He was too strong and completely overpowered me.

"It's not rape if the other wants it, and I can tell you do. You just don't know it yet."

Holy shit, he was insane! My shirt was pulled up and ripped a little at the neck, though I was thankful he gave up on my pants.

Suddenly, I heard a loud crack and Zay's full weight fell on top of me then slid to the floor.

"Fuck, Tess, you okay?" Gus pulled me to my feet while I scrambled to haul my shirt down.

"Yeah," I huffed, wiping tears of fury from my face.

I hauled off and kicked the son of a bitch in the ribs as hard as I could and was about to do more, but Gus put his arm on me and held a finger to his lips.

Footsteps sounded coming down the stairs. We looked at one another, knowing what was about to happen.

"It's gotta be tomorrow, Tess."

I wanted to be sick, but I knew he was right.

"Okay."

We braced ourselves for what would happen in the next few minutes.

The beating made me ill; it always did. All I could do was watch in horror as Zay held me back. He'd whisper for me to be calm and to stay quiet, but I would tune him out. He was a monster, just like the rest of them.

Gus had a fat lip, and blood oozed from a cut on his head. All things considered, he looked okay, but I knew with all the kicks and hits he'd taken, the damage on the inside would be a lot worse.

I inched closer to him. The grass was thin around the trunk of the tree where it was fighting for space with the thick roots, providing us a little sitting area.

I reached out and gently tapped his head with a rag. "You okay?"

He laughed, which turned into a nasty cough. "I haven't been okay since 1997, sweetheart."

I fumbled with my emotions. Gus and I had grown closer since we arrived here. It was funny how a horrible situation could draw people together.

I glanced over at the miles of cornfields. "I don't think I can do it."

Gus closed his eyes and struggled to sit straighter against the tree trunk. "You can, and you will."

"What if I can't?"

"You know what, sweetheart? That's just not an option." He reached out and covered my hand. "They need you."

"We need *you,*" I countered. "You'll die here."

His smile showed he had already made peace with his decision, and it nearly brought me to tears.

"Tess, I've been battling for my life for as long as I can remember. I've had three different types of cancer, but this one," he covered his chest with one hand, "this one refuses to let up."

"Breast cancer?" I wanted to be sure.

He nodded. "Stage three for some time now. I only have a matter of months."

A tear slipped down my cheek. "I didn't know."

"No one needs to."

"Does Trigger?"

"He knows enough. He can connect the dots."

"The boys?"

"Nah." He reached down and pulled his leg up with a wince. "I would be dead weight for you out there." His gaze moved to the fields. "We should get some sleep."

I helped him to his feet and walked him inside. As I was leaving his room, he cleared his throat.

"You're the best thing to ever walk into my sons' lives." He reached up and clicked the light off, leaving me in the dark to mull over his words.

A heavy weight hit my chest hard as I took one last glance at him. "Second best," I closed the door behind me and avoided Zay, who stared at me from the doorway of his room. I sure hoped he didn't know what the hell we were up to.

Goodnight, you creepy fucker.

I'd been preparing for this since we got here, but I still didn't feel ready. I glanced out the window and saw the heavy, dark clouds headed our way.

Great.

***

I opened the door slowly and cursed at the loud sound of the old hinges. With a mental kick to the head, I made my way downstairs and out the kitchen door.

My feet beat the cold earth, and it flung up behind me and pricked the back of my calves. The thick cornstalks were maddening, as they only allowed me to have a few inches of view. I was a runner and could normally go for miles without a thought, but this was completely different. This was like something designed by an Army boot camp.

My lungs screamed for a break, but I knew better than to stop. Rain formed paths down my body, and the wet corn slapped against me as I ran, dragging their cold, wet tassels across my face and chest.

"No." I came to a stop and strained to listen. "Shit!" The low-pitched buzz sent a shiver across my skin. I bolted forward desperately on some deep-dredged hidden energy for a few more yards. I wasn't sure what kind of range the camera on the drone had, but I knew I had to try.

"Ah!" I fell without warning. My hands caught me, preventing my face from meeting another skull, and I shifted back and swallowed my screams. Two bodies were shoved into a hole. I pulled back to look at them and noticed they both had their stomachs torn away, victims of Allen's weasels. The hum grew stronger, and I still hadn't found any sign of a lake.

Frantically, I searched for any possible place to hide, and then it hit me. I nearly vomited with the mere of idea of it, but if I wanted to help Gus, it was my only choice.

"Eww." I cried inside and gagged as I pulled the bodies to the side and tucked myself into a ball beneath them then dragged them back over me. They were heavyset men, so it took a lot of effort to move them, and the rain didn't help either. Their clothes felt like paste. I squeezed my eyes shut, turned off my nose, and prayed to anyone who could hear me for help.

It didn't take long for the drone to find me, or at least I thought it did. It hovered above for what seemed like ten minutes before it moved away and began to run systematic paths to hunt me down. The sound of its blades cutting through the storm was eerie and sent a triple dose of fear through me.

"You can do this," I whispered to myself over and over. I needed something to hold on to.

Maybe it was the stress of the past two weeks or the emotional roller coaster I had been on, but somehow, I managed to fall asleep.

I peeled my eyes open at the vibration of a closing door. The last twenty-four hours came rushing back, and I shot straight up in...bed?

What the hell? I tried to process where I was.

The room was small, and there was a thin layer of dust covering everything. The bed and a two-drawer dresser were the only items in the room. There was a bathroom in the corner and a closet on one wall.

Call me crazy, but I thought I'd be in some basement chained to a wall, not waking up in a bedroom that smelled like—I sniffed deeply and placed the scent—pancakes.

I flipped the covers off and looked down at my clothes. Nothing had been removed but my shoes. I quietly moved around the room checking things out. I leaned down and pulled open the top drawer of the dresser to find a set of clean clothes.

Weird. They were my size.

I couldn't help but think this was much like Savannah's moment when she awoke in the safe house, only she was actually safe. I was not.

Or was I? It was a giant mind-fuckery of an event.

I raced to pull on the fresh clothes and hopped on one foot to the window and tried to push it open. Two nails stuck out on the sides, keeping it locked it in place.

I tried the window in the bathroom, and it was the same. Locked.

Shadows moved under the door, alerting me I was about to have company.

I looked around for something to use as a weapon, but all I came across was a bottle of water on the dresser.

Slowly, the door handle turned, and there stood Allen in his church collar.

"Holy Lucifer," shot from my trembling lips as I fell captive to his

stare. Part of me wanted to cry. Allen was like an older version of Trigger, but just as you felt remotely comfortable, the devil would flicker across his pupils and remind you of the darkness that filled his soul.

"No, not Lucifer, but if you care to bare your soul, I'm listening, Tessa."

"Tess," I corrected him.

He tugged on his collar before he stepped into the room. He looked around like he was approving how nice it was.

"Look," he bent down and sat on the arm of the chair, "I'm not in the business of kidnapping. Never really cared for it, so most were dead by hour four." He shrugged. "But what I do care about is taking back what's mine."

"Which is?" I folded my arms to hide the shakes.

"Devil's Reach and to return the favor my son so lovingly did for me." He raised his head, and a smug smile played across his dry lips.

"So, how do Gus and I fit into this?"

"Gus doesn't. He was just being Gussy. Always had a moral probe stuck up his ass for the ones he cared about. He's like a tick that burrows into your skin and attaches itself to your veins and never leaves unless you either cut off its head or force it from your body."

"And me?"

His eyes widened. "You, Tessa," he slowed my name down, "you're my son's weakness, my ace in this game. You," he pointed to me, "will be mine."

"Ha!" burst out of my mouth before I could stop it. "Not a chance. I don't do seniors."

He licked his lips, annoyed at my comment. "As flattered as I am you thought I would consider you, I don't do hand-me-downs." He brushed the arm of his jacket free from dust. "When I say mine, I actually mean..." He paused and glanced at the door. I followed his line of sight to Zay standing there in jeans and a fisherman's knit sweater, wearing the same blank expression he always did when he was around me.

What?

"Now that we have that cleared up..." He stood, and I saw the blood on his cuff. He noticed and raised his cuff to get a better look. "Rick was a fighter."

Nice.

"Tessa," he purred out my name, "don't bother running. You have

no shoes, and the cornfield will slice your feet to pieces." He smacked Zay on the shoulder as he left. "All yours."

Not a chance.

"Hungry?" Zay asked quietly.

"No."

"Can I get you anything?"

"A lift to town." I dripped with sarcasm.

He gave an amused smile. "We'll grow on you."

"Like a tapeworm, maybe, or a tick."

He unfolded his arms and dropped them heavily to his sides. He stepped into the room and stopped a few feet from me. "He'll only take so much lip, Tess, and me too."

"Good to know." I folded my arms.

"Trigger might like it—" I slapped him across the face with my open palm. Trigger's name was too hard to hear right now. I sucked in a sharp breath, anticipating his reaction. He closed his eyes for a moment, waiting for the sting to pass. I knew because my hand hurt like a bitch.

"I won't sleep with you, Zay," I muttered to fill the silence.

He stepped back and stood in the doorway. "Like I said, we'll grow on you. Now, let's go."

"Where?"

"Gus."

The feeling of cold earth stuck to my face, and the stink jolted me fully awake. I tried to shift back from the bodies on top of me.

Panic rippled through my bones, and my mind spun out of control. I forced myself to count to ten so as not to move too quickly then wiggled my way out from under the human remains. I looked around and stood on shaky legs.

"That's so fucked up," I hissed to help loosen my nerves. I paced the little clearing in the corn and tried to focus. "That's some dark shit right there." I took some deep breaths and thought of Gus.

"You can make that," Gus whispered from across the picnic table. He angled his head so I could see the reflection of the truck leaving the driveway through his sunglasses. "Truck goes out and swings left every time."

"Which means the main road must be just over there." I didn't point. He knew I understood.

"Follow the path straight down, and it should dump you on the road. Tonight."

"What?" Panic rippled through me. "Your knee isn't any better. How would you keep up?"

His lips formed a hard line, and I knew what he was about to say.

"No, Gus. What about the—"

"The only way I'll get back to my boys is through you." He lowered his voice and started to use a rock to dig into the soft wood. "Here's what you're going to do."

A tear slipped down my face. I needed to keep moving. I would never forget the look on Gus's face when I returned with my hands tied, being pulled out of the cornfield by Fox the first time I tried to escape. They made me watch them take a piece of wood to Gus's knees.

Monsters.

CHAPTER TWO

Trigger

"Vineyard," a guard barked at me, "this is you."

I glanced at Brick, who was being ushered into the cell next to me with Rail.

"You get one hour to freshen up, then lights out." He laughed.

The door slammed behind me as I chucked my sheets on the nasty cot. Easing onto the mattress, I rubbed my face and looked over at my bunkmate. He had his eyes glued to a book. I knew he felt me staring because his leg shifted uneasily.

"We gonna have trouble?" I grunted.

The kid peeled his eyes over to me and slowly twisted to a sitting position. "No, sir, we will not." His thick southern accent rolled off his tongue.

I eyed him curiously. "What's your name?"

He extended his hand, but I didn't move to shake it. "Wes."

"Trigger."

"I know." He gave a tight nod before he went back to his book.

It didn't shock me that he knew my name; most did in prison. I've been in and out of them my whole life. Besides, my club was international, so we owned many chapters. I was proud I had grown the club from just Santa Monica and LA to stretch as far as New Zealand.

I pushed the sheets into a thicker pillow and focused on where else I could send my men to look for Tess.

"Nolan Vineyard, I sentence you to three life terms in Terre Haute State Prison," broke through my thoughts and made the creatures inside beat at the bars of their own cages.

Links better come through.

"I can hear them." Rail's tired voice filled the dark, damp cell from next door. We were all a bit wired from the kitchen duty we were assigned today. "They can smell me out."

Fuck me, he was always so dramatic. Rail was smaller, his body a little slimmer than the rest of us. Prison was hard on him, but he always made it.

"I miss the garage, the smell of the steel and oil." The mattress squeaked as he flopped to his side. "These shit sheets feel like sandpaper." He paused. "You're awake," I heard him say.

"No," Brick grunted.

"How you can sleep on the first night is beyond me."

"Shut up."

The first night was always the longest. It weeded the weak from the strong. I was no stranger to inmate life, but I never stayed long enough to make it my own, and I sure as shit wasn't about to now. I closed my eyes to tune them out and thought about the mole in my clubhouse, eating my food, drinking my whiskey. Fire licked the hairs on my arms as I felt the need to snap. I somehow willed my head to clear and fell into a restless sleep.

The morning came too quickly. I blinked my eyes to focus and swung my feet to sit up. Once the doors scraped open on the tracks, I made my way downstairs, signaling to my men I was skipping breakfast and headed in the opposite direction.

The line for the phone wrapped around the corner and down the hall, but one look at me, and most scattered. My reputation in prison had traveled far.

I caught the eye of a Stripe Back I sent here last year. Kale had murdered a gas attendant for his initiation and tried to pin it on Morgan, who happened to be there at the same time. With a little pressure, I got the proof I needed to clear Morgan's name and sent Kale away for life.

It didn't help that I spread some rumors so he would become someone's bitch in a matter of days.

"Nice limp." Rail nodded. "Rough night under the sheets?"

Kale shot him a death look but was more focused on me.

"Tell me something." He rubbed his crew cut and leaned against the wall. "How is it that you're in here while your old lady is shackin' up with your old man out there?"

Rail shifted and blocked the view of the guards while Brick appeared from the cafeteria and stood on the other side. I stepped up closer so we were nose to nose, and slapped my hand down on his pencil dick.

"I will be out of here before your next date with your cellmate," I twisted him tighter in my grip as he struggled to keep his composure, "peeling the clothes off your sister, just like I did the night you were sentenced."

He tried to lunge, but I squeezed with all my might. He stifled a scream as his veins bulged. He couldn't afford to get put in the hole again, and he knew I knew that.

"Vineyard!" a guard yelled. "Do we have a problem here?"

I raised my hands and stepped back. "Just getting reacquainted with an old friend."

The guard gave a red-faced Kale a questioning look. "That true?"

"Yeah," he muttered.

"Good. Move on, then." He waved us off as I stood back in line for the phone.

Three rings after I stated my name to the stupid recording, someone finally answered.

"Helmond's Bar, Peggy speaking. Trigger, is that you?"

Why is she questioning me?

"Peggy, get me Morgan."

"Oh, my God, Trigger! I thought maybe it was Brick or Rail. It's been so jacked up without you here—"

"Peggy," I snapped, "where's Morgan?"

"No clue. I figured you had him dealing with somethin'."

"Find me Cooper."

"Do you know how hard it is to run this bar myself? The till doesn't add up right. I don't know what I'm doing wrong. Morgan keeps throwing Tess in my face. He really can be an asshole—"

"Peggy!" I shouted, and a guard glared at me. "Cooper."

"Fine!" she huffed and screamed for Cooper, who must have been in the bar, as he yelled back at her. "Trigger is on the phone."

There was bickering before he tore the phone away from her.

"Hey, man, you okay in there?"

"Where is Morgan?" I didn't have much more time.

"I don't know. He left the day before yesterday, said he'd be back tomorrow. Maybe his dad is back?"

Morgan wouldn't leave unless something came up, but why not tell Cooper or Cray?

"You heard from Links yet?" he asked. The bar must have picked up, because he started yelling over the noise.

"No. You?"

"He was here poking around yesterday, but he wouldn't share anything."

Really?

"Find Morgan."

"Yeah, boss."

I hung up and went to find Brick. Something didn't sit right.

***

"Stop!" the guard shouted, clearly new and nervous. Sweat rode across his lip and down along his sideburns. His day didn't seem to be going very well. The pits of his shirt were damp, and he smelled like a jock strap.

His hands shook as he removed my handcuffs. I stepped too close as I passed him and heard the air get sucked from his lungs. He was the guard I would target when I needed something.

Three chairs over, I located Sam and went to sit across from him. He was as white as a ghost.

Tess.

I brought the receiver to my ear and watched as he mirrored me through the glass.

"What?"

His lips parted, and he let out a small sigh. "Links won't talk to me, only Morgan."

"And?"

"And Morgan is gone, won't answer his phone."

Now Morgan wasn't answering Sam's calls? *What the fuck?*

"And?"

"And I can't find him. Cooper is a mess trying to run everything. Cray is coming to help. That stupid blonde behind the bar can't count to ten, and Links wouldn't even give me a moment of his time when he was at the club yesterday." Sam tugged at his red tie. "Fuck forbid he answers his phone today. He won't even text me."

My thumb rubbed over my ring finger as I thought about what the fuck was going down at my club. A bright red head caught my attention. I glanced over and saw Brick ease in two seats down from me. He gave me a questioning look when he caught my grim expression.

The guard smacked his shoulder so he'd focus on Minnie. He picked up the receiver, and his jaw locked in place when Minnie slowly shook her head.

No sign of Tess yet.

"Sam," I grunted, darkness escaping from my tongue, "find Links, or I will find another lawyer."

I heard him call out my name as I slammed the receiver down and yelled for a guard.

We were done here.

I saw the stress that hung heavily in Minnie's eyes when her gaze moved up to mine. She looked drained. She forced a weak smile, and I waited a beat before Brick and I stepped through the door.

None of this was supposed to happen. I always had a plan, and this wasn't it.

"Inmate number 909576, Vineyard." The young guard tried to sound scary, but his voice cracked when he met my gaze. "You have, um, yard duty."

I stared blankly and waited for him to lead the way. Fuck, I needed to kill someone.

The yard was mainly hard-packed dirt. The few little sprigs of grass that tried desperately to survive were slowly being choked to death under the boots of hundreds of inmates. It seemed like random groups at first glance, but each cluster was in a specific spot divided by race.

I glanced at Rail as he rolled a cigarette like it was the fifties, and Brick eyed the Koreans, who felt we didn't belong here.

A guard with shiny black boots stepped into the yard and walked the inside perimeter. He didn't carry a gun or a baton, and his unmarked hands were a dead giveaway that he wasn't a fighter. Once he completed his rounds, he eased down onto a bucket and started to drum a song. It was Otis Redding's "Sittin' on the Dock of the Bay." I noticed the leaders of each gang tuned in to him and stopped what they were doing.

A dark chill filled the yard, and the scruffy hair on the backs of the wild beasts inside me stood to attention as they started to hiss.

A big Hispanic man cast a shadow over my face and cracked his knuckles like he was about to fight. "Heard you take out some of my men." His English was broken, but I understood enough.

I nodded and blew a puff of smoke toward him.

He snapped his fingers, and the rest of his gang joined him.

"You die now."

Flip.

***

Tess

I woke to a tightness in my lungs. My body was nearly frozen, but what caught my attention were the little drops of rain that tapped my face. A storm was coming; the clouds were low and heavy. When I moved, I felt it, a thick, heavy chain wrapped snugly around my neck. I was attached to the trunk of a tree.

Seriously? I fought to keep back the panic. What the fuck was this, Black Snake Moan? *Oh, my God, it was terrifying!*

"Are you enjoying the show?"

I screamed inside my head. The house was black, and I wondered what time it was.

Suddenly, the air was trapped in my lungs as something dark raced by. I was limited in my head movement, so I strained to move my eyes.

Shit, shit, shit. The little hairs on my neck stood to attention, like a wolf aware of immediate danger.

"Tess," Jace hissed from behind me.

Oh, fuck, no!

I tried to pull away, but I didn't have much wiggle room.

"Stop!" His lips touched my ear, and I wanted to claw his eyes out. "I get it you hate me. Whatever. But you will listen to me if you want to get the hell out of here." I felt him jiggle the chain.

"Don't want your help," I hissed.

He let out a dark chuckle. "Yeah, you seem to be in good shape."

I bit my tongue as he fiddled some more with the chains. I hated that I felt a heavy sadness inside over him.

"I'm sorry," he whispered. "I made a bad decision, but he promised to help find my sister." Jace had mentioned his sister to me once before, that they were separated when she was sixteen, and he'd always wanted to know where she was. I knew he just wanted family, but that was the club, and he'd pissed all over it.

Although a part of me wanted to hug him, the other part wanted to stab him in the gut, just once, to make my point.

"What was the information for?"

I felt the chain give way. Its tension went lax, and I sucked in a deep breath of relief.

"You."

"So, you led them right to me. The night Trigger took me home, we got ambushed in the mountains. That was you?"

My stomach twisted into knots. So much could have gone wrong, and it all would have been his doing.

He carefully moved us to stay in the shadows.

"I'm sorry, Tess. I know it doesn't count for much to you, but it does to me. Now…" His voice turned sharper, and I knew the talk was over. We were out of time. "There is a river four miles from here, which leads to a lake. You have to reach it, or the drone will find you."

"How? I can't seem to outrun it."

"You won't, unless you hit the river. It reads body heat. Get in the water and hold your damn breath. Gimme your hand."

I pulled away, annoyed.

"Give it to me," he nearly shouted. I did, and he sliced my palm and squeezed the blood over the grass. "You never go down easy, so we need to play that up."

My head swarmed with a million questions, but most of all, my heart broke. Jace was young, like a child in a grown-up's body. He just wanted to get to his family.

I started to panic, and I wasn't sure if I was more scared to be alone out there or of the beating Gus would get once they realized I was gone.

"Jace," I grabbed his shoulders, "come with me! We can tell Trigger the truth. That it was a mistake."

"They're going to kill Gus." I froze in place as the rain pelted all around us. "I'm the only one who can stop that from happening."

I couldn't argue with that. Gus was too important to me.

"Here." He handed me a flip phone. "I don't know if it will work, but it's from Fox's room."

"Fox?" I tried to gain as much information as I could. The look on Jace's face made me more curious.

"Does the name Green Bend mean anything to you?"

"Ahh…" I searched my spinning head. "No, I don't know."

I could tell he knew more than what he was offering.

"Spit it out, Jace," I glanced at the house and wondered how long it would be before they realized I was missing.

"When you get home, alone, check the USB drive for a file called Skeleton Key."

"What does all that mean?"

"Tess, you need to leave now. Two miles to the river, one more to the road. Stay off the road, follow the tree line. Once in town, call a cab." He handed me a roll of money, and I quickly tucked it into my soaking wet jean shorts.

"Jace!" I started to panic again with the thought of leaving Gus here on his own. Lightning flashed across the sky, and Jace seemed to match my internal fear.

"Run, Tess!"

I turned and disappeared into the corn maze.

"Fuck." I stopped to lean forward against my thighs and clear the memory from my head. I had been walking for hours, the sun was starting to set, and I couldn't for the life of me find the damn river. What screwed with my head even more was the fact the drone hadn't been around. Why?

My stomach grumbled to remind me that I hadn't eaten. I had been drinking the water that ran off the leaves in the field. That wouldn't last much longer, and I wasn't sure how much more I could take of being surrounded by nothing but corn. I was becoming claustrophobic.

Thud.

I once again tripped over a dead body with a missing stomach. My own stomach took a turn as I put two and two together. I remembered I'd been fed corn for a week at the house. Human bodies fertilized the corn field. Sweet Jesus, I was Hannibal Lecter.

As I peeled myself up, I spotted a little flashlight tucked into a case on the corpse's belt. I wiggled it free, and the light flickered on. It must have been waterproof. I would like to say I'd never stolen off a dead person before, but that would be lying. I had, and it probably wouldn't be the last time. It wasn't like they were going to need it.

I held my sore foot up to his shoes and saw they were about a size too big, but I didn't care. With a pull, I freed the boat-looking shoes and jammed both feet in. The backs folded inward, which created a slip-on shoe, but anything was better than bare feet.

I wanted his shirt too, as the temperature had dropped again. The sun was quickly fading from between the leaves, and I didn't want to take the time to get it off him. I should keep moving.

The drum of my heartbeat sped up as I saw a light a few yards away. My arms pumped, and I picked up my knees.

So close.

At the edge of the field, I froze. There was Zay with a flashlight, running it along the perimeter of the corn, and beyond him was the river. I quickly stepped back into the corn and waited for the light to pass.

Dammit!

This can't be it.

Not now, not when I've come this far.

They'll kill me or Gus.

Crouching, I grabbed a few rocks and tossed them over into the water behind him. The light whirled around, and he came close to the water's edge.

I tossed another small one a few feet away.

"You see something?" Fox the meathead Stripe Back grunted from his four-wheeler. It was a suitable ride for him.

"Fish jumping," Zay muttered, annoyed.

"She can't escape."

Zay shook his head. "Allen will lose his shit."

"We could just say we found her dead."

"We have to find her first." Zay pulled out his cell phone and answered it. "Any luck?"

As soon as he turned his back and Fox took a seat on the back of Zay's truck, I slid my body into the water. I was careful not to cause many ripples, and I took in a deep breath then fully submerged into the black water.

It was murky and hard to see, but I felt around the edge of the river and tried to pull myself along. It was a slow pace, and my air was running out, but I held it longer than I thought I could. Finally, I allowed myself up to breathe through my nose. I ducked back down when the light skimmed above me. Once it moved, I slowly rose and took another deep breath.

"What's that?" Fox hopped up and strained to see.

"I'm looking! For fuck's sake, shut up." Zay turned and tossed the flashlight in the pickup and lit a cigarette. "She'll show up. No one ever makes it past the river."

I couldn't help but feel a sense of pride that I was beating them at their own game.

"Hey!" Allen yelled from somewhere. "What the fuck?"

I didn't wait around. I sucked in a deep breath and slid back under and swam hard toward the opposite bank.

I felt something sharp wrap around my leg. The pain was terrible, and a silent cry ripped through me. I tasted copper in my mouth and realized I had bitten my tongue. I wondered how bad it was, and fear flooded me as I wondered if I would still be able to walk.

With a hard tug, I freed myself and carefully continued to suck air and swim underwater until I reached the edge of the river on the opposite side.

Oh, my God, I could barely think straight. The pain throbbed from mid-thigh down to my ankle.

A quick glance with the flashlight, and I saw a deep, angry scratch, but it hurt a lot worse than it really was.

The flashlight suddenly gave me an idea. As much as I didn't want to give it up, I thought this would benefit me more.

I dropped the flashlight into the water and ripped a part of my shirt, balled it up, and tossed it on top. My hope was they would think I drowned, or at the very least would spend some more time here looking for me.

Getting back into that water wasn't an option. I was terrified to think of what I could catch from that death-infected water. I wouldn't have put it past Allen to sink some of his dead bodies in the river too.

I was exhausted, and my leg throbbed, but I had to crouch and head away from the water's edge to put as much distance as I could between them and me.

"Ouch." I clung to a tree trunk to catch my breath. My skin felt sticky from the mist. It made it so hard to see, and every direction looked the same. The early morning light made it just bright enough that I could see a few feet in front of me.

A flash of color made my stomach drop. I ducked down and waited. *Snap*! I drew my legs up to my chest to make myself smaller and tried not to move. I searched for a possible weapon. There were a few big rocks and some weak-looking sticks, but that was about it. Or…

I balanced my foot on the stump and hauled myself up with all my might, my leg burning with the effort. It was just high enough that I could reach the next branch and hike myself up. The bark chafed my legs, but I ignored the pain and shimmied upward.

I froze when I caught sight of the orange t-shirt. I flattened my body and held my breath while he came into view. Shit. I recognized one of Allen's men. He had picked up my trail and followed me from the water's edge. A slow prickle of fear traveled across my skin, and I knew it was a fight or die situation if he spotted me. He had about thirty-five pounds on me, so I needed to be smart about my next move.

"Did you lose her?" His radio crackled.

"Nah, the bitch is nearby. I can feel her. She'll show herself soon."

My fingers started to sweat as he stood directly under me. I was about six feet above him, and all he had to do was look up.

I felt the blood drop before it fell. I tried to roll my leg against the bark so it could absorb it, but I wasn't fast enough.

Drip.

Drip.

Shit.

He reached up and swiped the back of his neck then held his hand up to his face and looked at the blood. Just as he did, I dropped from the branch, twisted in the air, and fell directly on top of his head. We both landed hard, but he was quicker to his feet than I was. He scrambled to catch my foot. He yanked me toward him, and I flipped over and clawed at the ground.

"You stupid bitch!" he screamed, and I managed to kick hard and catch him right in the windpipe. That shut him up momentarily.

I started to run, but I only got about two yards before he pushed me from behind and sent me flying down a slope. I hit a tree trunk and knocked the wind out of me. He came into view above me with a rock high over his head, and his crazy eyes and heaving chest told me he was going to do it.

I rolled to my side with a scream just as the rock slammed down. I hopped to my feet, using pure adrenaline to channel my next move. I kicked his ankle and shoved him back with all my strength, and he fell back against a tree. His feet made a funny twitch, and his body jerked. I looked at his face with disbelief as blood trickled from his mouth. He looked as surprised as I felt. We both looked down at the dead branch that stuck out of his stomach.

"Bitch," he sputtered.

"Says the guy with wood stuck through him." I couldn't help but smile as the life slowly drained out of him. The skin around his eyes went lax, and his locked jaw slipped out of its hold. He was gone.

It was gross, but shit. "Ooo-rah, baby!"

It was daylight by the time I got to the road. I wanted to cry with excitement at finding it at all. I stopped and looked down at my leg. Blood seeped out of my knee and from several places down my leg, my calf was red and swollen, and my ankle was sore, but nothing mattered right now except finding my way out of this hellhole.

Later, I sat on a rock and took a breather. I was frozen, tired, and hungry, but none of that mattered when I thought about Trigger behind bars wondering where the hell I was.

An engine in the distance brought me to my feet but also made me nervous that it could be them. I waited to let it get a little closer, and I could read the letters on the side.

Clifton's Farm Eggs.

I stepped onto the road and waved my arms like mad.

"Help!" I mouthed, as I was scared to yell too loudly. I didn't know how far away they might be.

The driver jammed on the brakes and came to a stop. I hobbled over to the driver's side window and almost cried when I saw it was a female.

"Jesus, Mary, and Joseph, where the hell did you come from?" she asked in a southern accent.

***

Allen

"Wait for it." I paused when Zay licked his lips with anticipation. "Wait for it." The men started their engines, they roared to life, and a ripple of excitement went through me.

I raised my hand as the man crossed the gully and into the field.

"Now!" The six of us tore off toward him. A dust cloud formed behind us, and the smell of a kill lingered in the air.

The man looked over his shoulder as his arms pumped hard to try to keep up with his legs. I knew he would be terrified. He should be. He had taken an oath to stay and become part of my army. I demanded loyalty, and the pathetic little shit wanted to go home.

We gained ground quickly. I shouted like the wild beast I was as I approached my prey. I imagined myself a dragon as I swooped. Mud splashed up on my face as Zay changed positions in front of me. I rubbed my finger to make lines under my eyes and around my mouth. I breathed fire.

"Close in on your left," Zay screamed at our men. We started to form into a horseshoe, so he couldn't disappear into the cornfields.

"He's mine," I screamed, and Zay motioned to the others. I reached back and grabbed my rope, rose out of my seat, and used my knees to hold me in place as the beast of a machine hummed beneath me.

The rope swung in a circle over my head before I flipped it forward and let it wrap around his neck.

His body jerked, and his hands tried frantically to loosen the hold I had on him. A moment later, I twisted the handlebars and swerved to the side, yanking him down to the ground where his body flopped and bounced from the speed.

There were no screams. He had no air and more than likely a snapped neck, but just in case, I turned back to the house and let him drag the mile and a half through the rocks and thorns.

I loved a good hunt.

Now I stepped up to the house ready to deal with Gus.

CHAPTER THREE

Trigger

"Shit," I muttered as Sam held a photo to the glass. His face had its usual pallor, and he looked ill.

We were fucked, or least we were for now.

"A shot to the back of the head from about ten feet away."

Coward.

Sam tugged on his ancient brown tie. "Someone didn't want Links to help you. Any idea who that would be?"

I shook my head, but all I could picture was the mole's face. He would die for this, but he would be a long time doing it.

"Nope," I lied and bit back the deep urge to flip.

"What now?"

I leaned back and popped my neck to relieve some tension. He needed to get me out, but fuck me, I needed to know Tess was safe. "Stop worrying about me for now and find her."

"Trigger," he began to argue, but I didn't want to hear it.

"I'll figure out me, you figure out her."

With that, I stood and hung up. There was nothing left to discuss. I was buzzed back through three sets of doors before we came to a narrow hallway. It was the one spot all the guards complained about. You nearly had to rub shoulders with the inmates as you came and went, and it made the guards uneasy. So, when an opportunity arose, I took it. I stuck my foot out to trip an inmate coming toward us. He doubled over and headed straight for the guard with his hands stretched out. He looked like he was about to attack him. I grabbed the guard and twisted his body so the inmate would fall, and the guard was left standing.

"Jesus," the young guard yelped as he fought to catch his breath. He eyed me for a moment, but I slowly raised my arms and turned to flatten my palms to the wall. The alarm screamed, and all the doors of that section slammed shut.

"Up against the wall!" they yelled at us. I stayed where I was but felt the corners of my mouth turn up. False trust was easy to gain here.

The sun shone brightly, and I squinted as I made my way through the sea of inmates, each watching me in their peripheral vision. I was on high alert at all times.

"Wait." Brick rubbed the back of his neck when I met him and Rail by the fence. "Links, our only way out of here, was killed last night?"

I nodded while watching a group of inmates work out across the yard. Of course, they weren't just working out. I knew they were planning their next hit, who happened to be Brick's bunkmate.

I hadn't shared that information since Rail was already so strung out with fear.

"So, now what?" Rail tossed a rock into a soup can. "If only the mole would show himself."

Both men went silent, and it took me a moment to realize they were staring at me.

"You know, don't you?" Brick leaned forward and rested his arms on his knees.

Rail took a long drag from his cigarette before he looked down at the ground.

"Just tell me if it's Morgan."

The club was our fucked-up family, but it was our family, so the idea of someone betraying us weighed heavily on all our shoulders.

"Vineyard!" A guard shouted. "Step up to the fence."

Shit, what now?

Somehow, I avoided the hole and was allowed back in with the general population after three days of isolation. I lost my shit after Sam notified me that Felicia had put out a missing persons report for Tess. Her bitch of a mother just wanted to get her hands on what was mine. Sam assured me that Cray was handling it, but it still didn't help with the rage inside. If Felicia got to Tess first, who knew what could happen to her. She had killed before, and I was sure the thought had crossed the bitch's mind countless times. She probably thought Clark was with Tess, and that would make her fucking wild.

***

Tess

With shaky hands, I ripped open the sugar packet and dumped it in the hot coffee.

"Anything else?" The young waitress looked worried as she shifted her weight onto her other hip.

I shook my head and stared out the window. The last three days had been hell, and I wasn't sure where to go from here.

"Where you headed?" the toothless driver asked.

"Anywhere but here."

She brushed her greasy hair out of her face. "I'm heading northeast. You wanna go that way, I could use the company."

It was hard to describe her unnerving smile, but what choice did I have? And when was the next person going to come by, and how did I know they weren't connected to Allen?

I felt them closing in on me, so I jumped up and pulled on the handle of the rig door. The truck bed was littered with Jack in the Box bags and AM/PM coffee cups.

"Be careful with that one." She pointed to the bag next to my feet. "Might be some chicken nuggets left. I like 'em cold and chewy."

I tried to hide my disgust—not that I was better than she was. Shit, I'd eaten worse food before, but Jack in the Box turned into mystery meat the next day.

"You want some?" She nodded down at the open container of Fluff. A fly buzzed around the lid and landed on the rim.

"I'm good."

She extended her hand, and I saw two of her fingers were missing. "Name's Dela, as in Delaware. It's where my momma birthed me."

I shook her hand. "Tess."

Dela took the corners of the winding roads with great speed, and a few times I had to reach out and grab the "holy shit" handles.

"You wanna tell me why you look like Julie James?"

My brows rose in confusion as I slid across the seat like a passenger on a fishing boat.

"I Know What You Did Last Summer*, the 1997 thriller flick."*

"Never seen it." I glanced down at my ripped jean shorts and the tank top that was slicked to my skin.

"I love them thrillers. Gets my blood pumpin'. So?"

"So?"

"You in the woods, shoes that ain't yours, no purse, no nothin'. You in some kinda trouble?"

I leaned my head against the seat and took a deep breath. Where the fuck to begin? "You have a phone I could use?"

She spit her chew into a paper cup before she pulled a cell phone from the visor.

Eagerly, I plucked it from her fingers, only to draw a blank on anyone's number.

Shit.

"Who you tryin to call?"

"Helmond's bar."

"Where's that?"

"Santa Monica."

She cackled. "I don't have long distance."

I stopped to take in my surroundings—lush green forest, cold crisp air, clouds moving in.

"Where are we?"

"St. Louis."

What?

"What can I get you?" The waitress pulled me from my thoughts. She tried not to stare, but who wouldn't? "Tony out back makes a mean pie."

I eyed the few dollars I had left and contemplated.

"You know," she lowered her voice, "I just so happen to have an order of eggs and toast goin' to waste back there. Tony added cheese, and I can't eat cheese. I was gonna toss it, but if you'd like it..."

I smiled and pushed away my pride.

"That would be nice, thank you."

"Let me go grab it."

I sank back into a daze.

Everything blurred as her words sank in. How the hell did I not know I was being taken across country? Was I drugged?

I could feel my body starting to shut down, the magnitude of what happened settling in.

"Here." Dela handed me an old blanket. "Next stop, Nashville."

What Dela failed to mention was she liked to stop a lot and meet up with old friends. Since she was an independent trucker, she adjusted her timelines and marched to her own drum. However, by the end of day two, I'd had enough of sitting in her truck waiting for her to finish. I hadn't showered in God knew how many days, and my leg was surely infected, as it was angry-looking and hurt like hell. I needed to find a phone ASAP. Plus, if I had to smell any more Jack in the Box, I thought I'd turn vegan.

My head was killing me, and I was beyond stressed about the club, Trigger, and Gus.

I climbed back over the seat and opened the little door to Dela's cabin. I had slept in the front seat the night before.

The smell of pot hit me like a brick wall. I even coughed at the strength. Shifting to sit on the bed, I started to open the cabinets, hoping to find some painkillers.

"What the..." I blinked at the naked photos of her and random men. She had an AK47 pointed at one of them, with a collar hanging off her neck. In another, she had a sheet of plastic over someone's face. She was smiling and had a crazy look in her eye.

Fuck that.

I shoved a bag of pot in my pocket, took the spare cash from her center console, and snagged the phone. As I was about to leave, I turned back and grabbed her flip flops and sweater.

I wanted to feel bad for what I did, but I didn't. The streets had already shown me it was all about survival, and survival was about taking opportunities when you saw them.

That night, I walked to a nearby gas station and locked myself in their outside bathroom. Other than the glory hole, it wasn't in that bad of shape.

I hitchhiked my way to the nearest diner, where I finally was able to find some warm coffee.

"Here." The waitress placed a plate of heavenly-smelling eggs in front of me. "I had him warm it up."

"Thank you." I was starving. "Oh, hey." Bacon rolled around my tongue, and I thought I might moan. "You happen to have a computer I could look up a number?"

She looked over her shoulder toward the kitchen before she reached for an iPhone from the counter.

Where in the hell did I start? I frantically searched my brain but came up empty. So instead, I Googled "US Army" and started there. Forty minutes and four frustrating phone calls later, I was passed off to some guy named Frank.

"Frank." His tone was clipped and slightly annoyed. At least I knew we were on the same page.

I stumbled. "Hi, I…ah, I'm not sure how to start this."

"Feel free to start at any time."

My back went up. "Oh, sarcasm. Now you're speaking my language." I took a breath. "I need to get in touch with Savannah Logan."

Silence.

"Why?"

"I need her help."

I heard something close. "I didn't catch your name."

"I didn't give it to you."

"Will you now?"

I glanced around the empty diner. "Will you help me if I do?"

"You have my attention, so my guess would be yes."

Please be the right move.

"Tess," was all I offered.

Silence again.

"As in Tessa Marin?"

Shit.

"How do you know my last name?"

"You would be surprised what I know. Give me a moment. Don't hang up."

***

Allen

Gus was in the corner of the kitchen, propped up on a bench. He could barely lift his hand to eat. If he hadn't attempted to intervene last night, he might still be up and walking. But no, he had tried to throw us off Tess's scent by pulling his own little stunt. I couldn't believe the little bitch escaped. The storm had knocked out my cameras, and it wasn't until later that I got the alerts she was gone. I had an idea of who might have helped her, and I eyed the young prospect, but I couldn't be sure, as I also knew his sister was more important than Trigger's little fuck.

The sound of a baby crying had me whirling toward the TV, haunted by the last time I heard a scream like that.

I was slumped in the orange and blue chair. I ran my finger along the stains that dotted the pattern, proof of my numerous fucks. The Everlast punching bag dangled from the living room ceiling. It was the only thing I remotely cared about.

I crushed the beer can and tossed it on top of the pile on the couch then stuck my hand into my pants for some relief. My eyes started to close, and I felt myself drift off once again into a buzzed stupor when a loud knock woke me.

"Go away!" I growled.

The knock came louder and longer.

I swung my feet up to help me rock out of the chair, but I tipped over the bottle of whiskey in the process. Amber liquid flowed across the carpet.

"Shit!" I snatched the bottle and took a swig. The dog could clean up the spill. The knock came again, and I swung open the door to find a woman holding a baby.

"What?" I squinted at the bright sun. "You know what time it is?"

She looked over her shoulder and back at me. Her skin was pocked, her arms lined with track marks.

"You 'member me?" She shifted the infant in her arms.

"Depends. You go down on me or did we fuck?" I took another swig from the bottle.

"Sadly, we fucked, and I told you about him." She dropped a bag at my feet. "I can't do this anymore. All his info is in the bag. I don't have the money to feed him or a place to keep him."

"What?" I couldn't keep up with her words as she spoke so fast, and she started to cry, which pissed me off. The booze made me fuzzy and clouded my head.

"I'm sorry, Nolan." She kissed his head and pressed his cheek to hers. "I didn't want to do this, but I have no choice." She wrapped the blanket tight around him and shoved him in my arms, knocking my whiskey bottle to the floor. It shattered, drawing my attention to it, and when I looked back up, she was halfway down the street, and I was left with a fucking baby.

"Well, find it!" I heard Zay shout from the other room. He was pissed at the IT nerds we had hired to try to break past the firewall the Devil's Reach had in place. Trigger had blocked me years ago, but there was always a way in. I needed a copy of the Serpents' contract, and those fuckers had run out of town and scattered, so it was hard to locate them. If I couldn't find out how Trigger was shipping his coke, I was screwed.

I needed coke badly. The guns were proving to be too hard to move. My debt with the cartel was growing by the day, and my deadline was getting uncomfortably close. Once Trigger knew I was back and was responsible for the zig-zag on his coke orders, I assumed he was just getting rid of what he had been sitting on. Shit, that ended any opportunity I might have had to score in that direction.

Fuck me, I had clients with a shit-load of money but no goddamn blow!

"You can't type faster?" Zay hissed.

Enough.

I grabbed my glasses, raced into the room, and jabbed their plastic arms into both eyes of the lead IT kid. He screamed and flopped to the floor as his hands flew to his ruined eyeballs. I turned to the other three IT nerds and pointed at each one of them slowly.

"If you can't break into that firewall by the end of the week, I will make sure you never see again either."

I glanced at Zay, who rubbed his head. He wasn't one for how I dealt with shit, but he'd get over it. He always did.

"She's been spotted at the clubhouse," Fox huffed as he tried to catch his breath. He was sweaty, and he badly needed to lose weight, but Fox wasn't going to last very much longer anyway.

"If you didn't swallow everything in sight," I muttered, "you might have been able to finish your damn job on her in the desert."

He flinched. "I improvised and told her to make sure Trigger kept the drugs moving. Anyways, it was dark, and I wasn't able to hear Tiago coming until it was too late."

"Too busy feelin' up something that wasn't yours." Zay snickered.

"Don't see you stickin' it to her either." Fox spat at his feet, and Zay tossed a right hook. Fox was flung back into the computers, sending shit everywhere.

"Zay," I kicked the now blind IT kid who had fallen into shock, "get rid of him. Fox," I blocked his way when he went to leave, "get your fat ass to California and get rid of that fucker Links."

CHAPTER FOUR

Trigger

"I always wanted to know what it would be like to fight the unstoppable cocaine king," Inmate number 5768048 said quietly before he turned and spat in my face. I never cared enough to learn his name. I just knew he went after Rail. Therefore, a point must be made.

My jumpsuit was folded down over my hips so my torso was exposed. The rain pelted off the tops of my shoulders and raced across my chest, creating a slick surface for when the fucker grabbed at my waist. He was predictable; they all were.

He reached to stab me in the gut, but I knocked the four-inch blade from his grip. He twisted, grabbed my middle, and slammed me back into the cement wall. The impact felt great, exactly what I needed to awaken the starving demons.

Before I went for his thigh to crush the muscle, I tilted my head and made eye contact with the guard whose trust I'd gained the other day. He monitored the yard that week. With a slight nod, he assured me with his fingers I had six minutes.

Perks of the weak.

The asshole yelped and buckled under the pressure, and once he was down, I bent at the knee and slowly sank my shin into his windpipe using my body weight. His eyes bulged, and his hands clawed at me, but he couldn't get a grip, and he couldn't push me off.

I scanned the perimeter. The inmates in Block C watched, and their hands waved from the bars in the windows. My gaze went along the gutter that was unable to keep up with the rainfall, followed it to the corner, and stopped twenty feet from the ground.

I pulled him to his knees and dragged his nearly unconscious body across the yard to the heavy flow of rain that poured from the gutter. He started to wave his arms around when I pinned his head face-up between my knees. He bucked and choked on the water as it filled him to the brim. His rapid heartbeat slowed beneath the pads of my fingers, and his struggles weakened.

The light from his soul started to dim, so I leaned forward over him and blocked the rain so it poured around us like a curtain, cutting us off from the world.

I slapped his face and saw the light shine slightly brighter. He was still there. I just needed him to hear me.

"I'm untouchable, behind bars or not." I grabbed his throat and shook him back to me again. I held his gaze for a moment longer. "Never go after one of my men again." Then I let him drop and raced around the corner and through the kitchen where a dry jumpsuit waited for me.

"We good?" Brick asked under his breath as he slapped mashed potatoes on a plate. He tossed it at Rail, who gagged over the green beans he was in charge of.

"Yeah."

The siren blasted through the speakers, and the guards started to yell.

Here we go.

***

"You play with fire, you're gonna get burned." Sam glanced out of the corner of his eye and nodded at the guard who was listening to us.

"So, I get burned."

"Trigger, the judge is leaning toward three life sentences. Stop playing with your life here."

"Sounds to me I may not have a life to care about."

Sam shook his head. He looked beat, but he wasn't in here, so I couldn't have cared less. He had one job to do and he fucking sucked at it.

"Tess?" I changed the subject. I didn't get caught, and I wouldn't. Just like I didn't go to the hole. I had power here.

Sam pushed his chair back and waved at someone. A strange feeling crept over me as my trust in him was suddenly shaken. Sam had never brought anyone to the jail before because that was my rule.

My gaze shot to the man standing in front of me. He waited for me to give him permission to sit. I gave a tight nod.

Sam handed him the receiver, and I waited to hear what he had to say.

"Good?" he rasped.

I didn't respond.

"Okay." He pulled out a file and held it up for the guard to see as he pressed a small piece of paper up against the glass. In black Sharpie was a single word. *Tennessee.*

My fingers twitched with mixed emotion.

Morgan's face dropped, and the stress lines embedded around his eyes deepened. "I had to try."

I rubbed my beard and tugged it a few times while I allowed the shadow of betrayal to fall from my shoulders. He had done what I asked and got a goddamn answer.

"And?"

He shook his head. "Someone said they heard a trucker picked up a girl on the side of the road. Said she wouldn't talk, just wanted a ride and to use the phone. When the trucker went to use the bathroom, she robbed her and took off." Morgan matched my grin. That'd be Tess. "Seems even the devil can't hold that little tiger down."

I opened my mouth to speak when the lines between his eyes suddenly deepened.

"I swear to God, Trigger, I saw your mother in the parking lot when I went to pick up Tess from the hotel."

What? I pushed that thought out of my head. I couldn't handle *ifs* right now.

"Leave tonight, use the safe in my office, and keep Sam in the loop." I paused. "If you see her again, approach her."

I stood to leave, but Morgan remained seated. I pulled the receiver back to my ear.

"What?"

The crackle over the shitty speaker of the phone was all I heard for a second, and I knew I wasn't going like what I was about to hear.

"I know who the second mole is."

My stomach tightened. I didn't want anyone to get to him before I did.

"I saw him shoot Links."

"Okay," I grunted.

"Took everything I had not to return the favor."

"He still alive?"

"Yeah, only 'cause I heard him mention he needed to ride to Tennessee, and it had me curious. I left that night and started diggin'. Took a bit of time, but the truckers know all." He was right. When shit went down, we went to the truckers first. "I wanna follow him."

More than anything, I wanted Morgan at the club, but if the mole could lead us to Tess or Gus, I needed to know.

"Fine, but check in."

"I will." He put his fist to the window as a sign of our brotherhood then left.

Sam dropped down in his chair and started to speak. "Trig—"

"I need to get the fuck out of here, and I don't care how." I slammed the phone down.

I stalked through the common room and up to the library to have a moment alone with my demons.

I wove through the aisle of books. It was the only room the guards didn't seem to linger in. The smell of old pages and musty leather hung thick in the air. I tapped the bottom of the spine, so the book fell into my hands, and I opened it to the middle and pretended to read as I scanned the room with my peripheral vision. Rail and Brick were over by the office. When they looked up, their eyes showed me someone was approaching me from behind.

Something slammed onto the top of my head and stunned me. I nearly lost my footing. The flash of a knife caught my eye, aimed at my neck. As I reacted and grabbed the hand that held it, I saw Wes, my cellmate, crack a lunch tray in half over his thigh and jam it into the fucker's side.

"Damn," Rail leaned over and inspected the guy's side, "that's gotta hurt."

The man tried to swipe at him, but Wes kicked the tray in further, ending it.

I half smiled, impressed to see the kid had quick reflexes and a strong stomach.

"You good?" Wes looked over my shoulder.

"Yeah."

The sound of boots had us all looking for an exit. Wes waved for us to follow him in the back and into a second office. "In here." He pointed to a small book cupboard with barely enough room to hold us. We jammed ourselves in just in time.

"Inmate Wesley!" the guard yelled out. "Where are you?"

Wes shut the door quickly, but there was still a small crack visible. I could see the guard as he came in.

"Hey," Wes responded with a friendly voice. "What can I help you with, sir?"

"What the fuck happened out there?"

My skin tightened at the thought he could out us. It would be suicide, but it happened…

"Shit, I have no idea." He rubbed his head like he was worried. "Is he dead?" He walked out with the guard, leading him away from us.

"I did hear that Kale guy talkin' about a hit on the Latinos." Wes looked around and sighed. "Shit, *he* was the mark."

"No one else is in here?" the guard asked as he peered around the room.

"No, sir. I've been back there all day, but I never heard anyone come in."

He pulled his Taser out and held it to Wes's head. "You know why you work here, right?" Wes nodded. "Because you don't cause any trouble. Don't make me doubt my decision."

"Why would I risk it?"

"Smart kid." He tapped his temple before he turned and walked back to the dead body then raised his radio to call it in.

Huh. I was impressed.

On a nod from Wes, we slipped quietly out of the office and retreated down the opposite hall while the guard was occupied with his radio.

***

The cold air drifted in through the open window of our cell. Night blooming jasmine was a welcome change, since my bed was two feet from the shitter.

"Why did you help us tonight?" I asked, knowing Wes was awake.

"I took an oath."

"I don't follow."

He waited a beat before he answered. "If you don't ride with me, you'll never be free."

I smirked, beyond impressed he hadn't told me right off the bat.

"Kansas chapter, until I took a fall for the VP."

I was surprised I hadn't heard about Wes before.

"What went down?"

Wes hooked an arm under his head. "Same old prospect shit. They killed someone they shouldn't have and needed someone to take the fall."

"How long?"

"I have three months left." He went silent for a moment. "Haven't seen freedom since I was sixteen." He cleared his throat. "The day they say I'll be released will be my twenty-fifth birthday." I heard him chuckle. "I have no idea what I'm supposed to do."

"You won't go back to Kansas?"

"Nah," he muttered. "Nothing there for me. Hell, there's nothing for me anywhere."

I understood that comment all too well. I often felt like a nomad when I was younger too.

"I heard about your old lady." A burn shot up my throat, but I held my tongue. "Any word on her whereabouts?"

Don't flip.

Don't flip.

Don't flip.

Once my blood pressure lowered and the stretch of silence got too long for comfort, I spoke.

"We have a lead."

"Good. I have—"

"No, I won't!" Rail suddenly yelled from the next cell.

"What I wouldn't do to have a solid wall between us," Brick hissed.

"Like you're a peach to live with."

"I know I am," Brick barked back.

"Fuck me." I covered my sore eyes and willed something bad to happen to that fucking cell.

"Are *Brail* always like this?" Wes half laughed at the bickering dicks next door.

"The jury is still out," I joked darkly.

***

Tess

"You know, Savannah said you were badass, and this proves it." Keith slid in across the table from me. Mike gave me a wave from the door. I could tell we weren't sticking around for long.

The waitress came over, but he waved her off kindly before he redirected himself to me.

"Are you okay?"

"Banged up my leg, but all things considered…" I started to move my leg, but he stopped me.

"Stay sitting." His eyes did a quick sweep behind me. "I know you're quick, Tess, so I'm not going to play the victim game with you."

"Good." I sat a little straighter, happy to be classified as strong rather than weak.

"After I'm done talking, I want you to smile at me then leave. Head outside to the black SUV with the light blue plates and go to the back passenger door and slip inside. Do not look back, do not talk to anyone, but most of all, act natural. Nerves will show."

My hand immediately reached down to my wrist to fiddle with my bracelets, but they weren't there.

Shit.

"Are they here?" My palms became sweaty.

"Don't know, so we assume they are." He dropped some cash on the table. "Time to go, Tess."

My knees shook as I planted a fake smile and headed down the row of tables, past Mike, and out into the daylight. I felt way too exposed, but I bit down on my fear and did what I was told. I heard the doors unlock just as I reached for the handle and pulled it open. The male in the seat next to me continued to look straight ahead. It wasn't until the door was shut that the two looked at me.

"Hi, Tess. I'm Corporal Davie." A young man offered his hand.

"Hey." I fumbled with my seatbelt.

"That's Corporal Quinn." He pointed to the driver as Mike jumped in the back and Keith got in the front.

"Go," Keith ordered.

And just like in the movies, we took off, leaving the tiny diner to wonder what the hell just happened.

Keith set an iPad on his lap and pulled a stylus from his pocket. Tilting the visor to look at me through the mirror, he started to talk.

"This might seem too fast, but I don't want to wait until we get to our next stop."

I knew what he was referring to. I'd been around enough of this shit to get it.

"We were in Vegas for Trigger's fight." He started to type on the keyboard, and I tried to focus on the details. I knew I had to be as brief and to the point as I could. "Jace lured me away from my seat, away from the guys. He faked being sick." I licked my bottom lip and tried to hold back the lash of anger that came with his name. "Zay, who is Allen's right-hand man, took me to a limo where he kept me until Jace joined us."

"How did Jace seem?"

"At that point, he was frustrated and annoyed." Keith nodded. "He made it clear he didn't have a choice in what he had done."

"Okay, what happened next?"

I spent the next thirty minutes going over all the details. Keith asked many questions about the house where I was kept, but I didn't have any clue where we were. It was incredibly maddening to have no idea how you got from point A to point B. All I knew was I was on foot, and I ran for about four-ish hours after the lake before I hit the road.

Tears threatened my eyes, but I held them off, although my voice cracked on Keith's last question.

"How was Gus before you left?"

I pressed my tongue to the roof of my mouth and fought like hell not to cry. "Needing *me* to get home for the boys."

"He has two, right?"

"I wasn't just referring to them, but, yes, Fin and Denton."

He turned around and removed his sunglasses. I could see the sympathy in his eyes—not the kind that made you uncomfortable, but the kind that showed he understood you.

"We'll do what we can for him."

"Thanks."

"Tess?" Mike bumped my shoulder. He handed me his phone, and it was calling someone. "Thought he'd be your choice, after Brick."

"Hello." Morgan's husky voice broke through the signal.

My stomach clenched at his tone. "Morgan." My voice quivered, as I felt that much closer to Trigger. I slapped my hand down on Mike's and gave it a squeeze. "It's Tess."

"Holy shit! Where are you?"

"I'm with Keith and Mike. It's a long story, but I'm okay."

"Jesus, Tess, it's good to hear that."

"Yeah, is um…?" I shook my head, trying to say his name.

"He's in a lot of trouble, Tess, so the sooner I get to you, the better."

"Will you tell him I'm okay?"

"No," he said without emotion. "If something happens between now and when I get to you, I'll be the one to take the blame. Just because he's in jail doesn't mean he won't flip."

I froze for a moment. To see Trigger in jail would be hard to swallow. He was so big and carried such authority that to see him behind bars, following orders from others, would be a trip, and not a good one.

"Okay, I understand." I glanced at Mike. "I'm going to hand you over to Mike so he can fill you in."

"Yeah."

I settled in my seat, leaned my head back, and let my mind drift to Mike's husky voice.

You're safe, Tess. Sleep.

***

"Not too bad for the Army," I joked when Mike set a bag of clean clothes on the hotel bed.

"You haven't even seen the best part yet." He grinned when he opened the mini bar. "Tiny peanuts and tiny whiskeys."

"So, that would make them micro-mini for you." I tried to play along, but a giant ball of anxiety was corroding my insides.

"Mmm." He steadied the bottle for a moment before he set it back in place. "It's barely even a drink."

"So," I eased down into the leather chair, "tell me what we do now."

"First, we have a good look at that leg. I can tell it's nasty. And then," he folded his arms with a sigh, "we wait for Morgan, and you decide if you want to go back with him or to our safe house."

"I need to get back to the club." I stumbled. "Not that I'm not grateful, but this isn't a case like Savannah's."

"It's not." He pulled a bottle of water out of the bag and handed it to me, along with a couple of tablets. "Take these every four hours, and make sure you watch that leg. It doesn't look infected, at least not yet, and the cut isn't deep enough for stitches, but it'll still leave a scar." He clucked his tongue as he wrapped my leg then considered his next words. "Sometimes the hard part is at the beginning. You know who took you and why. That makes you lucky."

"I'm not sure if I would use the word lucky."

"Trust me," he kept his eyes down, "you're lucky."

Two loud knocks sounded at the door, and Mike's hand flew to his ear.

"Keith?" He jumped to his feet, checked the peephole, slid his gun free, and slowly opened the door. The hairs on my arms rose, alerting me it wasn't Morgan.

"Room service."

"I didn't—"

"I texted you." Dell came around the corner and tipped the man, who had his gaze locked on Mike's 9 mm.

"Text? Seriously?" Mike shook his head and pointed to his ear. "Use this."

"You would have said no, and the girl needs to eat."

"I really do," I said through a bite of chocolate éclair then mouthed a "thank you" at Dell. He was a cutie.

It wasn't until that evening that Mike started to relax a little. He and Keith were pretty serious people, which I found comforting. *I can't imagine why.* But nonetheless, when Mike smiled, he was surprisingly charming.

As nice as it was that they were trying, I couldn't focus on anything but getting back to California. My head was stuck in a loop, wondering if those bastards had taken my escape out on Gus. How would Fin and Denton be when I came back without their father? How could we get Trigger out?

"Stop," I whispered to myself before I became dizzy.

"You got another call." Mike handed me the phone, and they all left the room and went into the kitchenette.

Please let it be Trigger!

"Hello?"

"Tess, hi, it's Savi."

Oh!

"Hey." I let out the breath I was holding.

"That constant loop you're stuck in is totally normal."

I gave a little smile; Mike must have sensed my spiral.

"Well, I've never liked normal."

"It's overrated," she murmured. "Do me a favor and grab a pen and paper. The hotel should have some on the desk."

I whirled around and started to search. The paper had been used, and the pen was out of ink. I must have taken too long, because she started back up.

"You see Keith's black book bag? It's on the suitcase stand."

I hurried over. "How did you know that?"

"He's a creature of habit." She huffed. "In the big section, you'll find his iPad. Grab it."

"I can't do that."

"Trust me. Do it."

I looked over to where the guys were deep in conversation and pulled the black tablet free from its sleeve.

"Code is 4-5-4-5." I chuckled at the number, and she joined me. "I know. Okay, now go to maps and use the overlay. Try to map the route you traveled."

"That's the problem. I don't remember."

"You do, you just can't grab at the memory. That's why I'm here. I work with Doc Roberts now, and he's taught me a lot. Most memories are stored behind a wall or doors, and they're opened when triggered." I closed my eyes at her wording. God, I missed him. "So, let's get you open."

We spoke until the battery was low and the phone was hot. Once I hung up, I dove even further into my memories and drew a diagram of the house, somewhat of a map, listed the names of the men who were at the house, and my conversation with Jace. No detail was left out in case it could help.

"What's that?" Keith asked over my shoulder. I felt my face go red. I had used something that wasn't mine. "What is that?" He pointed to the half-moon shapes in the cornfields.

"Allen has holes dug all around the field to dispose of his dead bodies. Most of them are barely even covered."

Keith nodded as he squinted at the rest of my stuff. "That's pretty impressive."

"You can thank Savi. She helped me do this."

He grinned with pride. "She's our little hero—" He stood mid-sentence, glanced at Mike, then moved to open the door.

"Didn't mean to take so long, but I needed to shake a tail." Morgan caught my gaze and shook his head in disbelief. "We should go."

***

Allen

I slammed the door on Fox. My head hurt, and nothing seemed to touch it. The mattress was crap, but I needed to sleep this shit off or I might kill someone. The small amount of light that peeked in burned a hole through my lids. I batted the curtain shut with my foot, which caused the heap of clothes to fall to the floor. My computer clicked on, and I saw the flash drive sticking out of the side. My blood boiled and sent a hammer to my brain.

That fucker wouldn't share his copy after mine was destroyed. I should have killed him when I had the chance.

We pulled into the strip joint just past midnight. I tossed a ten at the driver, and he muttered about the cheap tip. He should be thankful I didn't slice his head in two when he lit that cigar.

The Show Girls Strip Joint wasn't classy, but I figured I was safe from running into anyone I knew.

"Can I get you anything?" She eyed the white collar that showed at my neck. "Ahh...Father."

"Rum and Coke, no ice."

"Sure." She hesitated and continued to stare until I cleared my throat, and her cheeks flushed with embarrassment. "Coming right up."

I eased into the chair at the back of the room so I could watch who was around me. I pulled out what little cash I had and counted enough to cover the drink. One drink, that was all I could buy. I hated to be broke, but the money would come in soon if all went the way I hoped.

"Hey, there." A woman with giant tits pushed into my view. "I was told you might like to do a little roleplaying." She tugged at my collar, plopped on my lap, and began to massage my crotch.

I glanced at the waitress as she set my drink down, tossed the change on her tray, and waved her off.

"Listen, sweetheart, you want a good night, you come home with me, but I ain't paying you shit to rub me off in public."

Her mouth twisted as she rocked herself upward. "I don't do freebees."

"Well, aren't you classy." I snickered. "Run along to your pimp, then."

"Asshole."

"Yup." I downed a quarter of the cheap drink. I hated rum, but I didn't have enough for my whiskey.

A younger man in a flashy suit sat at the table next to me, which pissed me off because the place was dead. He could move somewhere else.

"Whiskey, neat." He handed the waitress a fifty, and she hurried off. He brushed his hair back before he removed his jacket and began to get comfortable.

The side door swung open, and I noticed the alleyway in the back. I could lure this fucker out, snap his neck, and take his wallet. That way, I could sleep on an actual comfortable bed instead of the church shit where I was holed up.

Yes, that was what I would do.

"Long day?" If I wanted to lure him outside, he would need to trust me.

"Long month."

"Woman problems?" I took a stab in the dark.

"Ha, yeah!" He thanked the waitress for the drink and waited for her to leave. "What about you?" He pointed to his neck. "You seem to be in the wrong house."

"Nah," I smirked inwardly, "I'm exactly where I should be."

The man smiled with a slight nod and raised his drink to me. "Cheers to that."

I tapped his glass with mine and swallowed it back in one sip.

The man waved at the waitress and pointed to his glass and stuck two fingers in the air to indicate he wanted two more. "So, tell me, what is it you do, besides the obvious?"

"This is all an illusion." I decided to play a little; I couldn't help myself. "I'm actually hunting for the perfect time to kill my son."

To my utter shock, the man nodded. "I'll take it he did you wrong?"

"Yes." My senses were on high alert. I was prepared to laugh it off and pretend I was only kidding, but this just got a lot more interesting. "Took my club."

"What are you planning on doing about that?"

I figured there was no harm in sharing with the man. He only had minutes to live, anyway.

"I need to come into some money and hire an army to take him out."

"Sure, you could do it that way." He leaned over the table to get a little closer. "Or you could gather some dirt and save your money."

Now, that got my attention.

"How would I go about doing that?"

"You just have to know the right people and have the right get-up." He pulled back my jacket and eyed my suit to make his point. "Everyone has a skeleton tucked away somewhere. Whether it's big or small, they don't want it exposed."

"Just that easy, hey?"

His phone went off, so he rose and finished his drink. He tossed a few twenties on the table and handed me his card. "I think you and I could have a lot of fun together. We both have assets the other could use. If you ever want to play dirty, you have my number."

He left the bar, and I grabbed the money and slipped out into the back alleyway.

I flipped the collar of my jacket further around my neck and hurried down to the parking lot. I saw a scuffle on the other side of the fence and ran over. The light from a neon sign advertising the show girls lit the scene well. A few men had a young girl on the ground, and they looked like they were about to attack her.

I was sure the bitch deserved what was about to happen.

I hailed a cab and prattled off the address. Once on the way, I pulled the matte card from my pocket and twisted it so the grooves on the card caught the light of the street lamp.

Dirty Promises Strip Club, Owner—Clark Anderson.

CHAPTER FIVE

Trigger

"Rail," I pointed my head in the direction of the door, "he here?"

He dropped his feet from the container and leaned the chair back to see. "Nope, it's Brick's hot friend."

The camera outside caused an alert to pop up on my phone.

"He's here," I warned Rail.

He clapped his hands together. "Let's deal with this weasel."

The shit in front of me was in a puddle of his own filth, he was so terrified.

"Say the words," I hissed inches from his face.

"I sk-skimmed."

I licked the inside of my bottom lip as I sucked in a deep breath through my nose. I started to lean back then quickly switched it up instead and slammed the side of his face into my knee. The pain shot up to my hip as I stood and felt the rush prickle through my veins.

"Why?" I grabbed his shoulder, forcing him to look at me.

He held back his scream and tried to appear hard. "Because I could."

Rail opened the door, and I tossed my fist into his stomach, and he toppled backward into the club.

"Wait." Rail stopped me from going out. "We could watch him, see where he goes?"

"Find out how much he took and get it back."

"Will d—" was all I heard before I tuned in to that fucking little skimming bastard yelling at someone.

"Little cunt-face. You want to know what it feels like to get a fist to the—"

My hand slammed down into his face, and I hissed, "Get the fuck out."

I needed to kill someone.

I curled my fingers around the leather of his cut, then lifted him in the air and slammed him heavily on the floor.

The demons squealed with hunger, and I fought like hell to force them back. Rail was right, we should find out where he went. My veins were forced to widen so the adrenaline could pump me up further.

Somehow, something next to me was able to break my murderous mindset. I looked over to find a little blonde woman looking scrappy as hell, eyes wide on my tattooed hands. Her gaze wandered up my body, and everything went silent until I heard her gasp when she met my eyes. My dick twitched at her reaction. She wasn't scared; she was fucking turned on. I watched her breasts rise. She rubbed her arm, and I noticed the bright red spot. I saw what the fucker had done. It wasn't lost on me that my demons went still.

"He's out," I barked, not leaving her gaze. "Take care of it."

"Will do." Brick acknowledged my command. His fingers brushed over her shoulder. "You all right, Tess?"

"Yeah." She nodded.

"Trigger, this is Tessa." Brick cleared his throat. "She's the one I was tellin' you about."

I could see her connecting the dots on who I was, and her eyes widened.

"Tess," she corrected him.

I didn't say a word but held her gaze until she looked down my front and back up again. I tugged on the bottom of my beard because my urge to taste her was fierce. Her skin pinked across her chest, a chest I wanted shoved in my face as I sank deep inside.

Suddenly, she looked away, almost annoyed that I had an effect on her. Reality kicked in, and so did the demons. She might have a little fight in her, but my club was ruthless. She didn't belong.

I leaned forward to reach behind the bar, and my eyes locked with hers again. I removed the whiskey bottle and tossed the cap next to her. She flinched, and I saw her weakness—strong men. She was a topper, and I hated those. I downed about a quarter of it then finally broke my hold to focus on Brick.

"They're gonna eat her alive."

Tess stood a little straighter, and I could nearly hear her cursing me inside.

"Gotta love the encouragement here, boys." She snickered, to my surprise. Brick sucked in a sharp breath and waited for me to blow. Instead, I turned and smirked. She was entertaining and hot, and that would do until she quit.

"I am your master," Rail muttered loudly in his sleep, drawing my mind back to my bunk and my drafty cement hell. "And you're mine."

My mattress squeaked when I rolled over. Fucking Rail always repeated lines from whatever shit show he was watching.

"Mmm, yeah, right there…"

I made a fist and punched the bars to jolt Rail awake.

"What?" he barked at Brick instead of me.

"Shut the fuck up."

His huff was muffed by his hands. "You need to start watching *Outlander*, Trig."

I squeezed my eyes shut and welcomed the chaos silence brought me.

***

The sun beat down on my shoulders. I was in my spot against the far wall—the one spot no one could approach me from behind. I didn't count the days in prison. I didn't have a set time. Regardless of the sentence, it didn't meant dick when it came to my club. There was always a way out. You just needed to find it.

Brick sat next to me and flopped his head back with a sigh. I knew he was worried about everyone. Too much time could be deadly on the head.

"Sam?" he asked.

"Said we should hear the final ruling in a month. Until then, we sit tight."

"Lucky us." He cursed under his breath, but I knew that wasn't what was bothering him.

"How long did my old man work for you?"

"Long enough."

"How long have I?"

"Long enough."

"So, where's the trust?"

I shifted, uneasy with the conversation. We didn't do this. "You never lost it."

"I get not telling Rail. The chances of him becoming someone's bitch is high, but why not tell me who the fucking mole is?"

I wanted to shut him up, but Brick and I had had enough shit lately, and I needed him to be on, so I could focus on getting us the hell out of this shithole.

"Because the fucker will know, and I need him to sweat it out and reveal the magnitude of what he's done."

Brick cracked his knuckles before he nodded. "Okay, fine. I get that. Just remember, I earned my seat here because I'm loyal to you and the club. Don't fucking hold back shit that I need to know."

I eyed him with a warning, but I heard him, and he knew that.

It was fucked up to keep the mole to myself, and it was bad enough that Morgan knew, but at least he'd gone searching for Tess and Gus and wouldn't slip up.

Brick traced a square over his hand. Tess shared with me what that meant, so I attempted to put myself in his shoes. It wasn't easy.

I split a blade of grass between my thumbnail and separated the pieces while I dug deep inside my head.

"My fifteenth birthday, my father came home with an escort." I cleared my throat free of hate. I'd never shared this with anyone. "Birthdays always made me want to hide inside my head. It was a day my father chose to teach me a lesson on manhood."

Brick kept quiet while he listened to me bitch about my past.

"He swung open my door and tossed a chick at me." I kept my head straight. No need to see his reaction. "She stayed on her knees and smiled at me with a mouthful of silver teeth. Her hair was all fucked up from her gig before mine. I was pissed and glared at my father, because there was no way I was stickin' anything inside that sack of mixed juices."

"Sick," Brick whispered.

"He hauled me out of bed, tossed me at her, and told me to fuck her, or else."

I half laughed to myself. Maybe there was some advantage to the fact I got to kill my father again.

"What happened?"

I waited a moment to push the memory back in its spot. "I took the *else*, got beat so bad my left eye wouldn't open for weeks. I had to watch him get his money's worth, watch how a real man would have fucked her. I couldn't fight, so that made things worse for both of us."

Another piece of grass rolled around my fingers.

"That's fucked up."

"Yeah, well, I'm fucked up."

"Hard not to be." He seemed to settle and become Brick again.

It wasn't the only attempt my father made to ensure I was a man. There were many times I'd woken up to find some random chick in my bedroom or my living room. After a while, I just gave in. It was easier.

We both sat for a bit to let the details of my jacked-up childhood sink in. I knew Brick's was anything but perfect, but it was far from my nightmare.

"You think Tess is all right?"

Her name did odd things to my head. My sense of control was lost when she wasn't near. It seriously fucked with my demons.

Brick ran a hand through his hair and dropped his head as reality came crashing down around us. He stayed silent, both of us mulling through our thoughts, wondering if she and Gus were alive.

"Did Tess tell you why she disappeared on me for those six years?"

I didn't answer, which gave him all he needed to know.

"Did it involve Clark?"

Again, I remained quiet, it wasn't my secret to tell.

"I knew I should have killed him years ago."

I agreed with that one. "She didn't want you to know." I rolled my head to look at him, and his jaw ticked as he processed the little bit he knew. "I don't share what I want to handle myself, but you are the one I trust."

Brick gave a quick nod, careful to hold back his emotion, which I was thankful for.

After about five minutes, he dropped his head. "I need to get out of here."

"We will. Just need to find another angle."

***

Tess

"What happened?" Morgan pointed at my bandaged leg but kept his eyes on the road. We were in a huge pickup truck he'd borrowed. He explained a bike wasn't smart, as we needed to blend with the rest of the traffic. Really, I knew Trigger would flip if I rode on another man's bike, regardless of the situation.

"When I was swimming, something snagged my leg." I shrugged.

"Nothing that won't heal in time."

"Anything else?"

"Not really, nothin' physical, anyway." I really didn't want any sort of pity that should be saved for Gus. "Is Trigger okay in jail?"

Morgan smirked. "Trigger pretty much runs that prison at this point. Motorcycle clubs have a lot of pull in there. Once he dealt with Rail's problem, they let him be."

"What happened to Rail?"

"Ha!" Morgan covered his mouth with his arm. "Rail is prime meat in jail, which is why he got to bunk with Brick." He laughed again. "I feel for Trig. Rail can be a handful in those situations."

"You've been in jail with Rail?" Now I was curious.

"A few times. He's the worst to share a cell with. He's a sleep talker. We did as little time as we could, and obviously, we always got out."

"How did you?" My stomach twisted with hope.

"There's always someone who will take the fall. You just need to figure out who. However, we don't have much time. Once the judge pronounces sentence, it could take months to get things overturned."

My nose scrunched at the thought, and the word *months* sent a chill through me. I pushed it aside and focused on the other part that kind of bothered me. "So, you'd put away innocent people?"

"None of us are innocent, Tess. The sooner you see that, the better off you'll be."

I shifted so my head rested against the glass. "I think we can find another way."

Morgan glanced at me sideways. "If you can, I'll buy you a bike myself."

I smiled a little. "Is that a challenge, Captain?" I couldn't help but let him know I knew the truth about his name.

"I believe it is, Tiger." He dismissed my acknowledgment.

We stayed quiet for the rest of the ride, both of us running through multiple options to get the guys out. It wasn't until we hit the driveway of the club that I felt safe again. I was home. I hopped out of the truck and hurried inside.

"Holy shit!" Minnie squealed from behind the bar as she raced over and nearly picked me right up off the floor. "How? Oh, my God! How are you here?"

"Gus," I whispered. When I heard Fin race into the room, I didn't have time to think before…

"Tess!" His little voice jumped to a high pitch as he ran as fast as he could and leapt into my arms. "Yes!" His head buried into my neck. "You're here!"

"Oh, Fin!" I ate up every moment that little boy gave me. I hugged him for me, and I triple hugged him for Gus. "I missed you so much!"

He sniffed and tightened his grip around my neck. "Never leave me again!"

"I'm sorry, little guy. I won't." I was hit from behind, and a pair of small arms wrapped around my stomach.

"You're back!"

"Hey, Denton," I purred as I held onto his hands. "You okay?"

"Yeah," he said, squeezing me a little tighter. "You bring Dad home?"

I wanted to cry, sob like a child and scream at the world that it wasn't fair for me to be here and not him.

"He, ah…" I cleared the emotion that clogged my throat. The last thing these boys needed was to see me break down. "He had to stay back and handle a few things for Uncle Trigger. But he sends me with hugs!"

They didn't say anything. I thought they knew the truth, but they didn't show their fear. Instead, they told me they were hungry. Good, something I could actually do for them.

"Nice to see you back, Tess." Big Joe gave me a friendly slap on the shoulder as I whisked through the bar. "You all good?"

"I feel like I need an *I'm good* sign," I joked as I walked backward.

"It would help." He winked. "Happy, though."

"Thanks."

After I got the boys fed and had a much-needed shower, I pulled my laptop free and blew the dust off the top. The curser blinked at me as my head spun with a million different what-ifs. The big one was "what if Trigger doesn't get released?" Could I really be me without him? I pushed that dark thought out of my head and clicked on the USB drive I had saved in my Drop Box.

"Please work." I clicked on the Skeleton Key file, and a million different numbers came up.

0111

0112

0113

"Shit." I didn't know what they meant. The others I had viewed earlier had been videos, but this was the only one that had only numbers.

"What do you mean?" I muttered to myself as I started to copy and paste it into a Word document to show Morgan later. Then a box popped up for a password.

I stopped and thought. Click by click I tried to recall what Jace had said.

Green Bay

Green Day

Green Way

Each time, it turned red, indicating I was incorrect. Shit. I closed my eyes and tried to recall what he'd said by using Savi's technique.

I'm there in the rain, Jace is a foot away from my face. His lips are moving, but I can't hear him.

Stop. Back up. What could I pull from that memory? The smell of rain, the wind battering my hair into knots, and Jace speaking.

Come on!

Jace's lips are moving, but where's the sound? Come on, dammit!

Bend.

That's it!

Green Bend!

It took me two tries to type the words in the tiny box, but the moment I hit enter, everything came to a standstill.

"Holy shit." I slammed the laptop closed and raced out of my room.

"Do you need anything, Tess?" Cooper called out from the pool table.

"No, thanks!" I waved him off as I went down the hallway and stopped at the door at the end.

I carefully knocked twice before I heard Morgan say, "What?"

I pushed open the door and held up my laptop. "I found something."

At the excitement in my voice, his feet hit the floor with a thud. "What?"

"The night Jace helped me escape, he talked to me about a file called Skeleton Key. I had seen it before, but it was just a series of numbers that didn't seem to mean anything. But watch." I opened my laptop and swiveled it in front of him. "When you try to view anything, this password protection box pops up. I thought it was just so no one could change the numbers, but when you type in the password he gave me," I slowly typed the words *Green Bend,* "the whole screen flickered to video links."

"Videos of what?"

I clicked on the third one down, and Morgan shifted to sit closer to me on the bed.

"Well, I'll be the devil's bitch. Officer Doyle?"

"Him and the city councilman's seventeen-year-old daughter."

"Wow." He rubbed his head and watched me exit the nasty video. He pointed to one that was highlighted in red. "What's that one?"

"The ace in our pocket, even without the rest." I clicked on the link and waited for his reaction. Judge Rothweiler in bed with another man.

"Fuck me, that's…" He stood and paced the room. "Well, that explains why they were all after you. You hold the skeleton key to the whole fucking city's secrets." He shook his head and whispered more to himself. "How were you not killed?"

"Because I had no clue! If Jace hadn't told me about this, I wouldn't have known. I think they saw that after a while. Plus, look," I tapped another file, "I don't know much about the law, but I would think a video of the prosecuting attorney visiting his nanny at home for a few hours a week between ten p.m. and one a.m. would help us out some. No?"

"Holy fuck, Tess!" He blew out the breath he was holding. "This is huge."

He suddenly took both hands and clamped down on my shoulders, "Tess, we need to play this carefully." He stood and quietly closed his door. "You want Trigger to get out, right?"

"Of course."

"Then you can't mention a lick of this to anyone."

"I promise."

"You can't just go in with this and demand their freedom. We will be squashed or killed before we could ever use it."

"Okay, so how?"

"We use our assets."

"Which are?"

"Your friends."

Okay…

Morgan's eyes flashed with something dark, but before I could ask what it was, he grabbed his phone and started to scroll through his contacts. "Shit, okay, let's do this." He pressed dial.

***

We were in the corner of Bubba Gump's restaurant. Morgan wanted a place to meet where we wouldn't stand out. I failed to mention that Morgan alone stood out *loudly* most anywhere, but whatever. We needed to focus.

"He's late." Morgan strangled the neck of his beer. "Is he normally late?"

"I trust him, and most of all, Trigger trusts him, therefore you should." My voice failed to match my words. Truth be told, I was scared shitless if this backfired. What if we poked the devil from behind a little too hard? And I didn't mean just Allen. I meant all the shit we could unleash on the high and mighty of West LA.

"Light post, by the door," I quietly said to Morgan as I nodded with my chin at Mike, who had a phone to his ear. He was in jeans and an Under Armour shirt with a hat pulled down to hide his eyes. At first glance, he appeared to be like any other man, perhaps here to have dinner with his family, but he was really here to help us deliver the first blow.

"Jesus Christ," Mike rubbed his bottom lip, "the magnitude of information embedded on this flash drive is unbelievable." He leaned back and covered his face with his hand.

"I know this is a lot to ask, Mike, but I have no one else to turn to." I glanced at Morgan before I took a seat across the table from him. I really needed to make my case here.

"You protect the good from the bad, and this is what we're doing here. Well, in a way, we are. Things are not only black and white, but black and white and gray. We're dealing with high-placed political people, here, people who are well-respected in the community, but they are the ones in the wrong. I know there will be consequences." I reached out and rested my hand on his arm. "We both know if Trigger committed those murders he would've owned up to it, but we know he didn't do it. I know he doesn't have the best track record, but he does not deserve to be in prison for life for murders he didn't commit. Nor do Brick or Rail. Please, Mike, please help me get them back."

"It's not safe, Tess. This is seriously dangerous shit."

I gave him a dark smirk. "Do I look like I play it safe?"

He chuckled softly. "I think you need to meet Lexi."

"I've heard great things about her." I grinned and knew he was in.

"Okay, tell me what to do, and I'll do it."

The door to Bubba Gump's opened, and in walked an overweight, badly dressed Judge Rothweiler.

"Fuck me, I hate that man. He's put me away twice." A gleam in Morgan's eye told me he was more than ready to do this. "Now, this is gonna' be fun."

"Judge Rothweiler." I waved him over and kicked out a chair as a way of telling him to sit the fuck down.

"I was told my wife was here." He looked around, confused, then eyed Morgan. "Why do I know you?"

"That's not important right now." I opened the laptop and pointed it toward the wall. "But this is."

The judged leaned around to get a better view. I wished we had recorded his expression. His neck turned bright red, the corners of his mouth dropped, and the veins in his neck bulged.

"Where did you get this?"

"I rather like this movie," I muttered.

"Agreed. Although that just looks painful," Morgan grunted.

The judge pounded his fist on the table, which made the silverware clink loudly. "Where the hell did you get this?"

"Hush, Judge, you don't want to draw attention to yourself right now. Do you want your wife and kids to see this?" Morgan sipped his beer. "How is Becky these days?"

Judge Rothweiler jammed a finger in his face. "You even breathe a word about this to her, and I will make sure you are behind bars for the rest of your life."

"Empty promises," he sighed.

"What do you want?" The judge glared at me. "You're a stupid little girl, thinking you can take me down. You are in for a major reality check—"

"Am I?" I clicked on another link of him and his secretary, Greg. He slammed the laptop closed and took a deep breath. His skin had turned a pasty color. "We have a lot more on here, Judge, including the district attorney and her obsession with the chief of police." I glanced at Morgan. "I'm sure the chief's wife would *love* to know who was over for dinner while she was at cards with her girlfriends."

"Shit," the Judge rubbed the sweat from above his lip. "If this gets unleashed to the media, it would bring total chaos to this city. I was supposed to be meeting my wife for an early dinner." He seemed a million miles away.

"And I just want my family back."

He shook his head as if to clear it. "Family?" He let out a belly laugh. "You mean those tattooed monsters."

I stood and leaned over the table so I was inches from his sweaty, fat face. "We're *all* monsters inside, now, aren't we, Judge?"

"You can't blackmail me. I don't work that way!"

Morgan chuckled, which turned into a cough. We knew the judge had done many favors for many people, so he was living yet another lie. I started to grow impatient.

"Release the following three men, and I'll shelve this. You don't, and the messenger outside your wife's office will hand deliver it to her for us. Your Greg is kind of handsome at that angle, don't you think?" I enlarged the picture a little. "I think your wife might disagree, though." I showed him a photo on my phone of Dell holding a package outside her office. "Your choice, Judge."

"No," he whispered.

"Once that is done, we will move on to Greg's wife and teenaged kids."

"You'd be ruining whole families," he sputtered.

"That's rich, coming from you."

"You *are* a monster!"

I grinned proudly. "You have no idea." I handed him a paper with the list of the guys' names and the name of the prison. "You have until six o'clock tonight to release them."

"I can't pull that off." He opened the paperwork. "Oh, no way! No one would ever let that happen."

"No?" I questioned then turned to Morgan. "Jessica gets out of school soon, doesn't she? That private school in Vegas?"

"Yes, and she usually leaves by the east side gate."

"Okay!" He held out his arms to make us stop. "Okay! Don't do anything to her. I'll handle it."

"Wise choice." I slid my laptop off the table. "Oh, Judge?" I waited for his pale face to turn to me. "This better be handled quietly."

Morgan and I walked out, leaving him to come to terms with the enormity of what we had on him. Mike gave me a nod to make sure I was okay, so I smiled and waved that everything was fine. He would stay and make sure the judge didn't make any unnecessary calls.

Morgan jumped in the driver's seat and drum-rolled the steering wheel.

"Whoo!" he shouted. "Fuck me, I wish Trigger was here to see you! Damn, girl, you are all kinds of badass!"

"Thanks." I swallowed hard, as I was just realizing the extent of the power we held. Badass or not, it was fucking scary as hell.

"Chick or not, you should be patched in!"

***

Allen

Ring!

Ring!

Ring!

"Who the hell is calling me?" I felt around my bed and under the sheets, until I couldn't take it anymore and ripped the charger from the wall and finally felt the weight of the ringing contraption.

"What?"

"Mr. Vineyard," his voice purred through the phone like a lion circling its prey, "is that any way to answer your phone?

Shit.

"Been a rough night, Mac. What can I do for you?" I flipped on the light above my bed.

"We've been more than fair to you. Now it's time for you to do the same."

I fingered the trigger of my gun and pointed it at the phone. He had worn thin with me lately.

"Like I mentioned last month, I will, but I don't have it yet."

"Tick tock, Mr. Vineyard."

Click, the call ended.

"Tic tock boom, you fucker."

I tossed my phone into the wall and pulled the blankets over my head. As soon as my eyes closed, I slipped back into a memory.

Allen: I told you to meet me at the club. Where are you?

Clark: And I reminded you we had an agreement. We each had our own copy. If you lost yours, it's not my problem.

Allen: That's bullshit.

Clark: Perhaps, but I still have my copy.

Allen: Do you know what I'm capable of?

A few moments passed, and a recording popped up.

Clark: Audio attachment. Press play to listen.

"This is all an illusion. I actually am hunting for the perfect time to kill my son."

Clark: One can never be too careful. Don't contact me again.

Son of a bitch!

Allen: This isn't over!

Clark: It just ended.

I kicked the blankets off and felt my body temperature rise to an uncomfortable level. I spun the top of the bottle and downed a few cups of the amber. Clark was one shady asshole.

CHAPTER SIX

Trigger

"I wish we hadn't taken kitchen duty." Brick pushed his bowl of split pea soup away from him. "Now I know what's in this shit."

"Leftovers." Rail slurped back the last of his. He flicked a fly off his toast and chowed it down.

I left mine untouched. I had some Power Bars at my bunk I would eat. They served garbage here, scraps of unwanted meat to make up a soup and then call it something normal. I eyed the floating brown lump in the center of my bowl. Last I checked, there wasn't beef in that recipe.

"Where are you going?" Brick stood when I did.

"Work out," I muttered at his question. I did the same thing three times a day. If I didn't, I would be in the hole for multiple murders. I needed an outlet to calm the dark thoughts the wild things stirred up to test my sanity. They'd love nothing more than to see me switch and never come back. If things went south, there was a part of me that would want to give in. Everything was black and white on the other side, no room for gray. It was cold, unremorseful darkness that coated me like a thick glue. It filled every little crack and smoothed over reality, and it sharpened things and made it very clear what needed to be done.

It wasn't until my shoulders burned to the point of blinding pain that I sensed someone was approaching me. I hooked the bar back in place and swiveled up to a seated position. Sweat dripped down my spine and continued to soak my waistband.

The warden stood with the sun above him. He shifted to block the light from my eyes. He looked pissed, with a file tucked under his arm.

"Nolan Vineyard."

I nodded once. He looked over at my guys.

"Matthew Montgomery and Silas Hunter?"

"Yes, sir," Brick confirmed for both of them.

The warden scratched his cheek, annoyed. "You have ten minutes to grab your bunk shit and meet me in my office." He waved at three armed guards to escort us to our cells.

I did what I was told, more out of curiosity than anything else. The entire yard stopped and watched as we were moved quickly from the general population to our corridor.

"How the hell did you pull off this one?" the guard I befriended whispered under his breath.

"Feel like sharing what you know?" I kept my head straight as we passed a series of cameras.

"Just that you pissed off a lot of high-powered people."

"That so?" I wondered what the fuck Sam was up to now.

"Someone came to visit the warden about you three."

"Who?

"No clue, some fat guy with a red face and gray hair."

"Sounds like our judge." Rail snickered.

"Japson!" the guard up ahead snapped at the officer who was speaking to me. "Keep your fucking pie hole closed. They're convicts, not friends at a bar."

I didn't push for more information. Instead, I gathered my few belongings and waited for the guys to do the same.

"You leaving?" Wes returned with another book stuck in the homemade pocket of his jumpsuit.

"No clue," was all I offered, and his face dropped. I took the pencil from his desk and scribbled down the bar's address. "You'll be out before long. Go there and ask for Morgan."

"Sure." He nodded, but he wasn't listening.

"Wes." I fought the urge to shut him out. I despised feelings. "You took a hit for one of my men. It's a place to go when you're out."

"Okay." He extended a hand. "Thank you."

Shortly after we walked through three buildings and several flights of stairs, we got to the warden's office.

"Anyone else feel like they're on the set for *Shawshank*?" Rail muttered, amused at the early 1940s wooden office with old steel filing cabinets.

"Shut up, Rail," Brick said uneasily. "We could be getting moved or separated."

The door swung open, and in walked the warden.

"Everyone out," he ordered the officers.

Once they left, the door I assumed was a restroom opened, and in walked the governor of the state. Brick glanced at me, and I kept my head forward, but I gave it a small shake. I had no clue what was about to happen. I'd seen the governor around before, but never actually inside the prison walls. Something told me this was a first for him too.

His gaze locked onto mine, and his jaw moved back and forth as he ground his teeth.

"I don't know how the hell you did it, but trust me when I say this, Nolan, if I ever see your face again, I will personally handle you myself." He took a step forward. "And there'll be no witness to account for your whereabouts."

The warden huffed under his breath as the governor stepped back and gave him a wave. The warden didn't waste any time and handed us three sealed envelopes before he moved around his desk and slammed open his top drawer. With one hand, he flipped open all three of our files and slammed down a huge stamp that read RELEASED.

Boom.

Boom.

Boom.

That was all the paperwork it took before we were told to get the fuck out.

I'd never seen anything like it.

"Mr. Vineyard," the warden hissed, and I turned to face him. "You are playing a dangerous game here. Don't fuck with the devil. He will always win."

I smirked. "I don't always win." His eyes widened at my reference to myself. I was raised by the devil, after all, and some of him was bound to stick.

Rail started to speak, but I shot him a glare. I needed to focus. Something was up. I didn't trust this. Were we about to be handed off to another warden? Which prison? We hadn't even heard our fate, the verdict hadn't been announced yet, and never before had it been that easy to leave. What the fuck had happened?

We kept our mouths shut as we were escorted back through the stairs and hallways, three officers in front and three in the back. The man behind the heavy bars shoved the clothes at me through a slot. "Sign here." He pointed to the paperwork.

"I feel like we're missing something," Brick whispered as we walked out the door and through the caged-in walkway to the parking lot.

"Yeah, like our one phone call for a ride." Rail searched his pockets for a lighter. We were miles from a phone, and we had, what, eighty bucks between the three of us? "How far can we get on that?"

"What the hell?" Rail nearly slammed into Brick, who had suddenly slowed his pace. "Ryan?"

There was Ryan from our Nashville chapter flipping the keys to a blue pickup.

"Thought you boys might need a ride" He shook Brick's hand first, then mine. "I couldn't believe it when I heard you were gettin' out, Trigger!" He waved at us to hop in, and I took the front, and the guys took the back bench.

Once we hit the road and the prison was out of sight in my mirror, I let out a long breath. It was the first time I questioned my ability to get out of prison. It was also the first time I came out with someone waiting for me. A heavy weight landed in the pit of my stomach. That was a fucking lie. She wasn't waiting for me; she was still with my father.

Tess.

I needed to know everything Morgan and Sam knew.

"What do you know?" Rail beat me to the punch.

Ryan checked his mirrors before he switched lanes. "I got a call from Morgan, who told me to meet you here and hand you these." He pointed under their seats. Brick hauled out a black duffle bag for each of us.

"Fuck, yes!" Rail cheered over my shoulder. "Clean clothes, soap, and smokes. It's been a long while since I've been excited about a shower." He shuddered.

"What else?" I took over the conversation.

"Just that someone knew someone who you got out."

"How?" I hated that I didn't have the answers.

"All I know," he raised his hand, "is it has something to do with some guy named Mike and a judge."

Mike?

"No idea, man, sorry. I was told to get to you to the airstrip before sundown."

"Please tell me it's not that prop plane we use to transport our shit."

Ryan fought back a smile as Rail complained about how shitty the seats were and how the plane was designed to carry packages, not people.

"No one needs a rod up the ass. Fucking seats." He tossed up his hands. "Like I'm not scarred enough."

I settled into the seat and tuned out Rail. Fuck me, I needed to soak myself in Tess. How I missed her. It drove me crazy that I didn't know where she was. Even to think about her made my chest burn.

It bothered the hell out of me that Mike was involved in this somehow. He would have cashed in a lot of favors to get me cleared, and I wasn't sure how I felt about that. He was the one who had chosen to fight on the good side.

According to my heartrate, I should be to the first checkpoint at 03:45, which would land me at checkpoint two at 4:57. Made sense. I shouldn't need to stop. My lungs were clear. I was pot-free for the past eleven months, and I had extreme self-discipline. I picked up the pace when I felt good to save seconds when I wasn't. I understood the structure the Army offered, and I liked how you were a family, a working unit. It was appealing.

Just as I rounded the cliff, I saw Mike heeled over but still keeping a good stride. He was a goddamn ox, and I fucking respected that.

"Does your stomach hurt?"

He shook his head and wavered in his fast step. "Right side."

Fuck.

I lunged toward him and made him stop.

"Dude, what the—"

I somehow dropped the tight guard I had on myself when I recognized the situation for what it was. The test wasn't for three more days, and he needed help. This wasn't something that came easily to me, but there was something about this guy that I could relate to.

"Fuck me, dude." I glared to make my point. "I know a lot of fucked-up people who do a lot of fucked-up things. If you ever repeat what I'm about to do, your family will never know what happened to you."

"Fine." He was beyond caring at this point, anyway, and he just stared at me.

I glared at him not to say a word as I held my arms up above my head and blew out my mouth like a horse. I repeated it two more times, and he couldn't hold in his damn smirk.

"Do it or I'll punch you in the throat." I pulled back my arm, and

he held up a hand and mimicked my stupid-ass dance, and he soon was able to breathe more comfortably. Three minutes later, he was back to normal.

He sat and rubbed his chest, looking at me in amazement. "How did you know to do that?"

"Old boxing move."

"You mentioned that before. When did you start?"

I hated that question, but somehow when he asked, I knew it wouldn't go anywhere.

"My father would say seven, but I say three."

"Why is that?"

"Hard to answer, but I guess he slugged me around a lot from a young age." I allowed some water to go down the back of my throat before I went on. "Not every boxer understands what's happening to them, especially when they start young. Some of the blows take you somewhere else, where time stands still. Even though you're only there for a few seconds, it's kind of better than what you face when it's over and you go home." Shit where had that come from?

He held up his arms before he rested his elbows on his knees. I glanced at his tattoos. I forgot one night he briefly had told me why he got them.

I pushed to my feet and nodded for him to join me. "If you do that at the start and at checkpoints seven, fourteen, and eighteen, you'll be fine."

"Just that many?" He dripped with sarcasm but fist bumped my shoulder in thanks.

By Friday, Mike came second in track and passed over all. I, however, was asked to go to the office and was told there were only a few spots open, and I hadn't made it in. I knew they had probably reviewed my rap sheet. I'd wondered if they would overlook it. They probably figured I'd never make it through the training.

It was what it was. The fact that I wasn't overly disappointed said a lot.

Mike was blown away and said I should take his spot. He was relentless. By the second day, I was just honest.

"Fuck off and go join the Army, because I'll probably need some help one day, and I'll be cashing in that fucking favor."

"Fair enough." He offered me his hand.

We all knew he was a better soldier than I'd ever be. I didn't do well with authority.

***

"Sweet hell in my ass!" Rail white-knuckled the seat in front of him, a cigarette hanging from his lips. "The reaper is pissed, Trigger!" He laughed like a nut job when the plane shook and jolted as we took on some turbulence. "You think he's tryin' to make a point?"

"And what would that be?" I glanced out the window. We should be landing within the next fifteen minutes.

"I think we need a good kill to settle the fucker down."

I had a few in mind…

Mike's tone was different, something was off.

"Didn't mean to dodge your calls, just been dealing with something."

"Didn't take it personally," I assured him and leaned forward to let the ash from my joint fall on my boot. "You good?"

He laughed, but it was heavy. "Sometimes I wonder." I heard a door close quietly. "My sister's ex is becoming a problem, and our good old justice system won't do shit about it."

"Has he met you yet?" I joked. Mike's physique alone would scare off an unwanted boyfriend.

"Yeah, he has, but his father has a ton of money, and he thinks he's above the law."

I cracked my neck. "You talkin' about that shit Trevor Collins?" I remembered hearing about his father and how he owned some casino and hotel in New York.

"Yeah. As soon as she met his family, she backed off. They weren't her kind of people. Besides, he…ah, well, she's saying he scares her. I don't know the details, and I don't want to, but fuck, Trigger, I'm questioning if I can hold myself back."

"I get that."

"I need to keep my head clear. I have a chance to join an elite team, and if I fuck up, I'm done, back at my father's business choppin' wood."

"Mike?" his mother called from somewhere far away.

"Shit. Sorry, man, I gotta go."

"Yeah, no worries. We'll talk again soon." I hung up.

It took me three days to track that fucker down, beat the shit out of him, and send a message. Mike never questioned me, but I did get a text message with his sister smiling a few weeks later. That was the first and only time I crossed that line.

"Wait," Brick's tone cut through Rail's meltdown, "I think we have company."

I leaned closer to the window and saw a trail of dust in the distance. I watched as it grew closer, and I nearly saw red when I realized someone was driving *my* bike. That broke every club rule known to the MC world. If they had wanted to bring my goddamn bike, they would have put it on a trailer.

I cracked my neck, but it didn't help. I could feel my switch quiver with fury as the wheels lowered, ready for the touchdown.

"Shit," Brick felt around his back, "I really miss my nine mil."

Once we hit the ground, Rail did a sign of the cross over his chest before he kissed the reaper that hung from one of his rope bracelets.

"What the hell was that?" Brick laughed.

"Might as well play nice with both."

I grabbed my bag of shit and ducked to step out onto the stairs. Morgan removed his helmet and started to walk toward me.

"Nice to have you back." Morgan held out his hand as he ignored the fact that I was glaring over his shoulder toward my bike.

"Any word from Tess?" I managed to choke out.

"Yeah."

I looked at him and wanted to kick him in the throat for not spitting it out. Morgan turned and nodded at the fucker on my bike. It took me a moment, but when the rider stood, leaned forward, and removed the helmet, blonde hair spilled in every direction.

Fuck…Tess.

She bit her lip as she tossed her helmet and raced toward me in her leather pants and jacket. I found myself moving toward her, and she leapt into my arms and wrapped her legs around my waist as she buried her face into my neck.

I slammed her to me and held on tight.

"Shit, Trigger!" she cried.

Everything went silent.

Everything went calm.

I stroked her head once before I lowered her to her feet and held onto her shoulders to look her over.

"You okay?"

"Yeah." She smiled up at me, and I wanted to take her right there in the middle of the fucking chaos.

"You?"

"Better," slipped from my mouth.

She leaned up for a kiss, and I devoured her mouth. I was incredibly pent-up, and having her tongue inside my mouth was dangerous. I peeled her away in spite of her confused face.

"What?"

I leaned my forehead to hers then rested my lips by her ear.

"I've been in a cage with men for almost a month." I slapped my hand on her ass and gave it a hard squeeze. "My mind has been in some dark places, and I need to control myself around you."

She turned to me and licked my jaw bone. "When have I ever liked control?"

"Tess," I warned, but even I could hear the moan in my tone.

"Just promise me you'll flip later," she whispered as she ran her tongue over her lip.

"Get on the bike, Tess."

She stepped back with a sigh but turned and swaggered back to my bike.

"We need to talk before we hit the clubhouse." Morgan walked with me. "Strokes?"

"Yeah," I agreed. As much as I wanted to be alone with Tess, he was right. We couldn't be around the mole until we were prepared.

Just as I was about to pull my helmet on, Tess ran her hand along my thigh, using her nails to outline my insane erection.

I pulled her hand to my mouth and bit down on a finger and sucked it into my mouth, swirling my tongue along the edges.

Enough.

I started to lose my control.

I'd never felt more split down the middle in my head. My brain couldn't seem to settle.

With a flick of my wrist, I started the bike and waited for her to hang on. Her hands wrapped my waist, and I felt a sense of normalcy wash over me.

We took our formation and headed down Lincoln Boulevard. Tess stroked my leg and rested her head on my back.

Everything came alive inside me. My erection was beyond painful, and I didn't know how much more I could take. Weeks of men was hell, and I needed my woman.

***

Tess

I could barely control my hands. I felt like I was on E again. Everything about this man spoke to me, and it didn't help that he was at least a size bigger in the arms. My dark navy-blue nails matched his ink beautifully. It was almost mesmerizing watching my fingers skim his art. I wanted him so much.

Guilt swept through me then, and pain quickly spread through my body.

Gus.

I fought the tears that chased my desire to be happy. How could I be happy when Gus might now be in that cornfield himself?

Stop.

Just stop.

"Where did you learn to ride?" Trigger broke through my thoughts.

"Morgan gave me some pointers…from the sidewalk," I assured him and waited a beat. "You mad?"

"No." He stroked my leg while I grinned like a fool.

Twenty minutes later, we pulled into Strokes, the words "Enter with a soul, Leave with a task" etched into the glass. I'd normally question the meaning, but honestly, I couldn't care less. I was just relieved Trigger was Trigger and not someone else.

"Oh, good, you made it back okay!" Minnie cheered and hugged me from behind. "I wasn't sure how you would do with that beast of a bike between your legs."

"Hey." I reached behind me and hugged her the best I could. "Not my first time with a beast between my legs," I joked.

"Seriously?" Brick scowled at Minnie before he grabbed a handful of her hair and made out with her with like he was seventeen.

Yeah, that's what I needed to see.

"Um, hello?" Rail hissed but granted me a big bear hug when I took pity on him. "You really okay, Tess?"

I shrugged. "Sure."

He lit a cigarette and sucked back a long breath as I glared at him, then he lifted his hands. "You'd be proud." The cig bounced around his lips, sending ash everywhere. "I lifted weights." He held up his arm and flexed. "Yup, those fifteens really make the blood burn."

"I can see that."

He winked as he stood from his seat at the table. I excused myself and headed to the bathroom. I didn't get the stall door closed before a huge hand stopped it.

"Jesus, Trigger." My stomach flip-flopped. "Feel free to remember what I've been through."

He pushed me further into the stall and cupped my head so I'd look at him.

"I'm horny as hell too, Trigger, but I've waited a long-ass time, and I know I'm not classy, but a public bathroom is—"

"Shut up, Tess," he grunted as he studied my face then closed his eyes. He was obviously struggling with something.

"What?" I stroked his forearms; I needed his touch.

"I want to know everything." He cleared his throat, and something fucking scary flashed across both pupils. "Did he hurt you?"

It was instinct to lie, but I found myself stuck in a parallel moment where I wanted to spare him the details, yet I couldn't. Instead, I sucked in my bottom lip and hoped to someone they'd steer him in a different direction.

His head almost did a tick, like a glitch in a robot, before his system powered down and he kissed my lips.

"Trigger," was all I could muster.

"I'm sorry my demons collided with you."

I froze. He had never said anything that deep before. Come to think of it, I didn't think anyone had ever spoken to me like that before.

I wasn't entirely sure how to respond. "Sometimes it's okay to let me help you fight them."

His hand clasped my chin and tilted my head higher. He smiled oddly before he stepped back and closed the stall door, leaving me stunned.

Sweet hell, he was a man of few words, and to come out with something like that left me reeling.

"Fuck this!" The door swung open and banged loudly against the stall wall. I shrieked as he grabbed my waist and pushed me back, locking the door.

His hand was down my pants and inside me before I could even think.

"I've been stuck with men for too long." He pumped his fingers while I let the cloud of lust build. He licked the length of my neck, then he pulled down my pants and kicked them aside, and he dropped his, leaving them at his ankles.

I turned and leaned over the toilet. He didn't waste any time and drove himself inside me. His hands held my shoulders as he fought to slow his pace. He'd pull almost all the way out then furiously shoot back in.

I screamed at the sensation. It was exactly what I needed after our time apart. Rough sex with Trigger always grounded me. It was fucked up, but it made me feel beautiful inside.

His hand moved to stroke my spine. He inched his way up each vertebra then slid his hands around my neck with a slight squeeze.

My blood rushed around my body with excitement. I loved the way he fucked. Like a wild animal, and I was the only one who could tame him.

He pinched my nipple, and I felt him shift. He was about to come but needed me to first.

"Come." He slapped my ass hard, and I let go. My nerves shot off in all directions as he pounded out a few more thrusts and joined me in my bliss.

"Shit," he panted as he pulled me up and sucked his spot on my neck.

"Yeah." I smiled, my hair stuck to my sweaty forehead.

The door swung open, and I heard someone yell at the band. A flash of red hair could be seen through the crack in the door. I heard a giggle as Trigger grabbed the top of the stall and thrust one last time.

"I smell sex and candy," she sang.

We hurried to dress and let ourselves out of the stall and headed toward the door. I heard her chuckle again and call out something that sounded like, "Lucky girl."

"Double Oban with a dropper for my water." I plopped down on a bar stool, and the bartender reached under the counter and pulled out a wooden box. He removed a glass from its red velvet casing.

"Rough day?" He poured the dark amber slowly to let the liquid open. He was clearly impressed with my drink of choice.

"Fancy." My fingers explored the grooves etched in the glass.

"Fancy glass for a fancy drink."

"Rough *week*." Huh. I held the glass up and twisted it in my palm to watch the light play over its curves.

"Citadel."

I looked over to question him.

"That's the pattern name." He pointed to the other glass in the box. "It's made in Nova Scotia, Canada."

I held it up to my eye. "You're long away from home."

"I am." He tapped a sign that read, "Once a Maritimer, always a

Maritimer."

"What the hell does that mean?"

He laughed and poured me another. "It means the glasses come from a humble place."

My back hit the chair, and I relaxed a little. "I like that."

"Me too." He smiled warmly as he went back to polishing his glasses.

Bartenders. We all had a way of letting the other know we got this.

"A double Fireball, please." The redhead from the bathroom slipped into the chair next to me, and I tried to hide my smile. She pulled out a lipstick and lined her bottom lip before she looked over. "You here to see the band?"

I looked over at the stage and saw three men doing a sound check. "The guitarist is hot."

She grinned. "That's Ben Carey. He used to be the guitarist for Lifehouse, and that's," she pointed at a guy with a sleek mohawk, "the lead singer, Bryan Hopkins. He used to be with Paperback Hero."

"You know your music."

"I do."

"So, who are they? Country?" I guessed by their boots.

"Elvis Monro. Thcy play country rock."

Huh. I hadn't heard of them before, but I was interested. I loved all music.

"Nice tat." She pointed at Trigger's artwork on my forearm then hauled up her shirt and showed me her angel tat. It wrapped around her midsection and up to the halo that incorporated her breasts.

"Wow." Impressive.

"Yeah, I got it right after my divorce. Ex hated them."

"Why the angel?"

"My favorite song of theirs." She nodded to the band. "Plus, they call me their little angel since I'm anything but."

I laughed. She did look like trouble. She carried an excitement about her, and that fiery red hair of hers seemed to vibrate with energy. She reminded me of someone else. I turned to look for Minnie and caught Trigger fixated on me.

"Name's Rose." She offered her hand, so I peeled my eyes from his. "I take it you're with them?" She nodded toward the guys.

"Tess." I ordered another drink and examined the glass again. It was almost hypnotic. "Yeah, motorcycle club."

"I know who they are. I saw one of the members in here the other day."

I glanced over my shoulder to find Trigger's eyes still locked on me. Damn, his gaze made my knees go weak.

"Oh, yeah? Was it that man over there with the long beard?" I motioned to Morgan.

She swiveled in her seat and focused on Morgan then looked around. "Nah, none of them. I'd remember him. He was all pissed off because couldn't find someone."

"Huh. No clue." It was probably Cooper diggin' dirt on Allen to help Trigger and the guys get out.

"I'll be back." I held up a finger and answered my phone but ducked next to the stage to get some privacy.

"Hey, Tess." Savi's voice seemed a little worried. "You make it to Trigger okay?"

"Yeah, we're here together now."

"Good, good…" She trailed off. "Look, Tess, I should have mentioned this to you earlier, but I know you had to do what you needed to do, and of all people, I understand that. However, I'm safe on a mountaintop, and you're exposed in the city."

I shook my head and tried to follow.

"I just wanted to extend an invitation to come and stay here for a bit, you know, until the dust settles. You've been through a lot, and I thought maybe you could use a breather."

I loved that she cared enough to invite me. We weren't exactly from the same world, but the truth was you couldn't pay me enough to leave right now. I had just gotten Trigger back, and I was going to fight like hell right by his side until Allen was taken down.

"Thanks, Savi. That really means a lot, probably more than you know, but right now I really need to be here."

She chuckled a little. "I figured, but just know there's no expiration on the invite."

"I'll remember that."

"Call me once you get settled, and maybe we can set up a visit."

"I'd like that."

I slipped the phone back in my pocket and caught Trigger's eyes on me again. I liked that he always watched me. I decided to join him instead of heading back to the bar.

CHAPTER SEVEN

Trigger

"She was found in this area." Morgan pulled my attention from Tess as he placed an iPad in front of me. "She thinks she walked for about four hours." He pulled his finger across the screen, which created a red line. "So, if we were to map her route, we're thinking the house would be somewhere in this area."

"I'm sure they're gone by now," Rail huffed while he watched Tess at the bar. "Wish I'd seen the look on that devil's face when Tess got away."

"Mm," I muttered, curious as to what Allen might do next.

"Oh, Tess," Morgan said over my shoulder, "you think you can fill the guys in on what—" He paused. "You okay?"

She slipped onto the chair next to me and smiled at the chick at the bar. I didn't even need to speak to that redhead. She had "wild" written all over her.

"Yeah." She sounded tired, but she shook her shoulders and focused on what he had asked her. "Um, okay."

She told her version of what happened at the fight, and how they drew her out, and why Gus got tangled up with it.

"They kept us separated for a few days. Allen told me that I now belonged to Zay." She glanced at me, uneasy. "He wore that stupid fake priest collar the entire time and made us call him Father. The whole thing was just one big mind fuck."

"How was Gus when you last saw him?" Brick jumped in.

She looked down at her hands and fiddled with a ring. "Bad. He took some beatings but handled it okay. At least he was still okay before I left. I hate to think what they did to him after they realized I was gone."

"You get a chance to talk to Jace?" Brick leaned forward on the table.

"Yeah." Her eyes moved to Morgan, who gave her a nod. "Um, turned out he has a sister, and Allen found out where she was and promised to tell Jace, but only if he helped them get to me. I know he feels bad for it—"

"Club rules," I interrupted to set her straight.

"Yeah, but he—"

"Doesn't matter, he—"

"He was the one who helped me to get you out of jail. Does that not count for anything?"

"No," we all said at once.

"That's fucked up."

It wasn't, but I wasn't about to fight with her.

"He knew the rules, Tess." Brick tried a softer approach. "And he chose not to follow them."

"He was thinking of his family."

"And so am I." I held her wildfire glare. I loved the fight in her, but she also needed to know an MC is black and white. There is no room for gray.

"Then what?" Rail tried to move the conversation along.

She waited a beat before she spoke. "They always fed us corn, and I realized it was because we were surrounded by acres of it. I also realized the fields were fertilized with dead bodies. I was able to escape because I hid under them, so the drone couldn't find me."

"God damn, girl," Rail hooted, impressed. "Fucking fearless."

"Damn straight." She looked me in the eye. *Shit, I could take her right here and now.*

Morgan helped her along with her story. There were still some spots I was unsure about, but I could address them later.

"How was Mike involved in all of this?"

She looked away from me and hesitated, and I wondered why.

"Ah, I didn't know what else to do. I didn't have my phone, so I couldn't remember anyone's damn number. All I could think of was who helped Savannah, and you were in pri…I mean, you couldn't come." She looked at me. "When Mike realized the extent of what was on the flash drive, he flew down with Dell and Quinn to make sure it didn't go south." She rubbed her hands together uneasily. "I know it was a big risk involving him, and I tried to protest, but he insisted.

Later, he gave me his card and told me that since I was yours, I would always have his help."

"Good."

I will return the favor.

Not long afterward, we headed for home. I needed to get back to my club.

"Honey, I'm home! Double whiskey, Peggy!" Rail hollered as he burst through the doors of the club.

The entire place roared, and the music was cranked up high.

"Peggy, baby," Rail grabbed his crotch, "it's been weeks since I got any. Help me out."

Peggy rolled her eyes and smiled at me. "You need some help?"

Tess held her hand up to look at it, then right hooked Peggy, sending her backward.

"Oh, fuck, I have wanted to do that for so long!" Tess laughed. "Stand up, Peggy. I wanna try it again."

"Bitch!" She spat blood on the bar top. "What the fuck, Trigger? Do something."

I reached over and grabbed Tess by the hair and slammed my lips to hers.

Tess was reckless, impulsive, and gnarly, which was motherfucking sexy.

I sucked on her bottom lip before I pulled away and squeezed her ass.

I was hungry for her.

"The fuck!" I felt something hit my arm.

"'Bout time you're home!" Fin punched my arm again; his little fist was red just like his glossy eyes. I could see he was hurt I didn't come find him, but truth be told, I was so wrapped up in Tess I forgot.

"Why aren't you in your jammies?" Tess went from sexy to sexy mother in two seconds.

"Vib didn't wash our clothes, so I got nothing to wear."

It was the first time I ever heard him call his mother that. I wondered how she was dealing with Gus being gone.

Tess moved from my hold and disappeared out back.

"Glad Tess is back." Fin sniffed away his tears.

"Not me?" I half smirked.

"Like you care." He folded his arms and turned away.

Something inside of me shifted, and I was able to feel something for the little runt. I always liked the kid, but he clearly was upset I didn't go see him.

Fuck. This wasn't something I was used to. I blamed Tess for this shit feeling.

"I care, Fin," I muttered uncomfortably. "I'm just not good at showing shit like that."

"Yeah," he sniffed. "That's nothin' new."

"Then why are you givin' me shit?"

"Because he wants you to try." Tess hit my shoulder. "Come here, rug rat, you need to be in bed."

"Where's your mom?" I asked, curious where the junkie was tonight.

"Asleep in bed, since yesterday."

Tess snapped me a look.

"Cooper," I grunted, "what's up with Vib?"

He rolled his eyes, annoyed. "Gus is away, so Vib will play."

Fucking cokehead.

I watched Tess take Fin to bed and chuckled at Peggy, who was headed my way with her bloody nose.

"Any other chick would have been thrown out on her ass for that shit she pulled."

"Yeah," I agreed with a smirk.

"What makes her different?"

I hated personal talk, but something made me speak to it. Peggy had been a hangaround for a lot of years.

"She ain't going anywhere, Peggy."

She went silent. She better not cry. I hated when they cried.

"Fuck, I fuckin' hate you. I been trying hard to show you I want you for a long time, and you want that little piece."

I finished my drink, not wanting to give her an inch.

I held her gaze; I wasn't going any further with the conversation.

"You know what?" She dropped her annoying act and took a moment to think about her words. "Tess is a dime a dozen. When you're done being blinded by her hot ass and teeny tits, you know where to find me, and you can get some of this." She grabbed her big boobs and held them up.

"Can I cash in on that?" Rail tapped his beer to her glass.

I pushed off my seat and headed for my room. I was fucking tired of talk. I glanced in the boys' room and saw they were already asleep. I couldn't help but scowl at Vib's naked body, her fake tits pointed at the ceiling.

Fucking train wreck.

My room was empty. I went to hunt for the one person I needed to sink nine inches of myself into.

"Where is she?" I found Brick with Minnie, heading to their room.

"Pool." Minnie giggled.

I tossed my wallet and keys in my room before I headed out that way. The wind was warm tonight, which had drawn more of the guys outdoors than usual.

"So, you just left?" Cooper was sitting on a lounge chair next to the pool while Tess floated near the edge.

"It's not so cut and dried, but yes, I got away."

"Have you considered they'll come for you?"

She shifted and drew her leg up to her chin, and the double air mattress bounced up and down. She was in a black bikini, lying on her back, and her hair was spread out around her. The water on her skin make her tits glisten in the low light from the pool house.

"Be truthful," he said as I tossed a blanket in the back of my pickup.

She sighed before she answered. "I would be lying if I said I wasn't scared, but I would trade places with Gus in a heartbeat."

"Why didn't he leave with you?"

"They did a number on his knees."

"Cooper." I flicked my head at him so he'd leave.

He stood and waved at Tess. "Good to have you back, Trigger."

I nodded and waited for him to leave, then I pulled off my pants and slid into the water, moving silently toward her.

She lit a fat joint as she watched me approach and sucked back a long puff before she let it go into the dark sky above.

"What are you thinking?" she whispered.

I smirked as I dove and overturned the air mattress, pulling her into me.

***

Allen

Blood dripped down my fingers as I glanced dispassionately down at the mess on the floor. I pressed my head hard into my fists up against the wall.

This can't be happening. How in hell did he get released?

"Boss," Zay whispered cautiously behind me.

"No," I hissed. "Leave."

He sighed heavily, but he didn't leave. "Fox thinks he has an idea to lure her out. Give me fifteen minutes, and we might be able to convince her."

A low chuckle came from the across the room. I turned my head and saw the sly grin on Gus's face.

The man had a death wish.

"You think she's ever going to betray Trigger?" He squinted through his two black eyes. "You clearly don't know her at all."

I tapped my fingers on the bloody wall while I mulled over his comment.

"Perhaps she won't betray Trigger, but how far would she go to save you?"

The eyes gave nothing away, and he held his irritating, smug face.

"I'm nothing but a fuckin' weathered old man. She's tougher than you think an' won't risk the club for me."

I smirked. "Yes. You are a weak old man, not worth shit, I agree, but those two boys of yours might be worth exploring. She will do what I want because of them."

His tongue darted out to lick his lips. I'd hit home.

"Ah, yes," I purred, pleased to have hit the nail on the head. "The moment you set eyes on your nephew years ago, I knew I had you. You have a weakness for kids, like so many people do. It's interesting to me that people get so emotional over sniveling, snot-nosed little brats. I'll never understand the allure."

With that, I left and headed upstairs to shower the techy nerd's blood off me. My green eyes stared back at me from the mirror. I knew my reflection was just a mask, and as I stared, I opened my mind to reveal my real self. I stuck out my tongue. Oh, yes, there it was.

The devil's fork.

"Allen," Gus banged on the window, "stop fucking around and let me in. I have a right to see my nephew."

"Did I say you could touch that?" I screamed at the little shit who held a piece of bread he'd stolen from the bag on the counter. "You already ate."

His gaze dropped to the ground, but he didn't put it back.

"What are you, stupid? Put that shit back. You think I'm made of money?"

He shook his head and rested the bread on the counter. His hands fell to his sides as I marched over and tossed the bread in the trash.

"That was your fault I had to throw it out. Now you don't get dinner."

He stood still like he always did when he was in trouble. It was frustrating when he didn't answer me.

I gave him a smack to the head, but he didn't react. He was a tough little son of a bitch.

"Answer me," I commanded.

He cleared his throat, lifted his head, and held my gaze. "Sorry, sir."

I could swear I saw a tiny smirk before he lowered his head again.

"Get the fuck in your room before I give you the belt again."

Suddenly, the door flew open, and Gus blew in. The little shit took that moment to run to his bedroom. Gus, of course, followed, and I plopped in my chair.

"So, you're out of prison again, Gussy?" I shouted before I tuned into the TV, annoyed.

"Hey, kid," Gus whispered loudly, "sorry it's been a while. What do you have there?"

Silence.

"Ha," he chuckled lightly, "it looks well used." I heard the squeak of the mattress. He must have sat down. Please, make yourself at home, Gus. *I rolled my eyes. How pathetic. I listened for the kid to answer him.*

"Do you know who gave you that?"

I turned my head toward his room, curious about what the kid had.

"No," the kid answered.

"Someone special, that's who." There was a scuffle of feet, and then the bed squeaked again. "Is that where you keep it?" Pause. "That's a good spot." The kid's grunt seemed to agree.

I started to push up from the chair to go see what the fuck the little shit had been hiding from me, when I noticed a flyer on the coffee table. My buddy Nick had dropped it off the other day, but I hadn't looked at it.

Underground fight taken to a new level.
Come see Mad Mike, the untouchable eleven-year-old!

My blood ran hot as excitement raced through me. I needed to make some quick cash, and Nick had said that Mad Mike kid was insane.

"What do you call him?" Gus's voice pushed through my thoughts as I hurried to the phone to let Nick know I was in for tonight.

"Mr. Rabbit."

"Father!" Zay raced into my room. He held his hands in the air so I wouldn't snap his fucking head off. "She still has it! The chick has some balls because she used it to blackmail the fuckin' judge to get them released."

"You said you saw her destroy—"

"I know," he interrupted me, and I glared at him with a twitch in my neck. "But I had no idea she had a second copy. It wasn't like I could look around the club, and Trigger was there, and that stupid fucking bartender had eyes in the back of his head." He stumbled over his words.

My hands covered my mouth as I thought about my plan. The bitch had a second copy, or maybe even more.

I almost felt the power surging through my body. All was not lost.

***

Tess

"Ah!" I yelped. "Trigger, it's cold!"

"Mm," he moaned in my ear. "I've tried to play the understanding role, but you're out here in this," he fingered my swimsuit and twisted my nipple, "talkin' to Cooper while I'm dealing with my own problems." He grabbed my hand and pushed it to his giant erection. I gave it a squeeze before I nipped at his chin. He picked me up and plunked me back on the mattress then crawled up and lay beside me. He paddled us over to the side to snag a joint out of the bag on the pool deck and pushed us off again.

He sucked back a large puff before he twisted and blew it slowly in my face.

What was it about Trigger when he smoked pot? It was as if he was mind fucking me in all the right places. His eyes would darken, his breath smelled sweet like the drug, and the feeling I'd get when he drew the smoke into his lungs made me clench internally.

"I can help you with that problem." I panted and dragged my tongue up his neck to his jaw. "I'm here. Do what you want."

He leaned up and flexed his strong muscles and looked down at me through hooded eyes.

"Too many people."

"Never stopped you before." I couldn't help but say it. Trigger was known for fucking women wherever, whenever.

"No." He hopped off and pulled the mattress over to the edge and hauled me off. He hiked me up over his shoulder and walked to the back of his pickup.

"It's cold," I yelped as my back hit…a blanket? "Oh."

His fingers clawed at my bottoms and tossed them over his head, and before I had a moment to think, his mouth covered my opening, his tongue deep inside me.

"Shit," I cried as I strained to keep up.

He lifted my hips high to plunge his tongue even deeper. My nails combed his hair blindly, and I pressed hard against his head. My body was wound up so tight, I needed this so much, but my inner coil fought the release he offered me.

He dove, sucked, and nipped, but my head was stuck. Guilt wouldn't let go, and I didn't blame it. What right did I have to feel such bliss when Gus was stuck in that hell wondering if I made it back?

"Tess," Trigger grunted, which brought me out of my inner loop, "where the fuck are you?"

"I'm here." I was confused and, honestly, pretty jacked up inside.

He studied me for a moment before he rubbed his lips dry.

"Are you?"

Fuck, this was not how this was supposed to go.

"I'm sorry." I inched back from him.

"Don't." He caught my leg before I could move any more. "Don't pull away like that."

"Trigger," I moved to my knees and took his hand, "I feel so guilty."

I could swear tears were on cue when it came to the situation with Gus.

"I know," I waved him off, "it was the only way out, but it doesn't make it any easier to know he's there and I'm here."

Trigger moved to sit on the truck bed. "What did he say to you before you left the last time?"

"Just that it was the only way to get out of there, and I was to find the blue folder that was in the top of his closet and use it if he didn't return." I shook my head. "I haven't found it yet. I don't want to."

"Mm."

His reaction made me wonder if he knew what it was. "What is the blue folder?"

Trigger pulled me to his chest and kissed my head. "Gus gave me custody of the boys when Fin turned one. I'm their legal guardian, but Vib doesn't know. He got her to sign the agreement when she was wasted."

I moved to face him. "*You're* the boys' legal guardian?" Holy shit. Wow. "Why didn't you ever step in when Vib was spiraling?"

"I did." He tucked my hair behind my ear. I wondered if he knew the tenderness he was showing. "I just don't let the others know."

"That's pretty cool." I grinned boldly. I loved this new insight I had into Trigger. I knew Vib had disappeared into drugs more than once, and the fact that Gus had done that for his boys didn't surprise me.

I turned and tugged at his waist. "You started something a moment ago."

"I did." He pulled at the strings of my top and popped it forward. "Fuck, I missed these." He bit my nipple, and when I moaned, he lifted me over his lap so I straddled him.

His was everywhere. His hands roamed freely, not leaving one place untouched. We were starved for each other.

I felt as if I were flying in and out of a hurricane. My vision would blur as he nudged me toward the edge of my climax then quickly dragged me backward into clarity.

My back bowed in an arch off the flat bed to get him deeper. I dug my heels into the strong muscles over his shoulder blades.

"Yes," I moaned when he tipped my opening. One hand grabbed his hair, and I pushed him further inside me. "Harder!" I forgot how much I needed his wildness to come out when I was exposed like this. I needed to know it was okay to let go.

He pulled back and stared down at me with hooded eyes. "Shift down." He offered me a hand before he pulled his jeans off. His erection flopped down heavily, and a little excitement dripped from the tip.

His hands slid slowly up my inner thighs then came together at my opening. His thumb rubbed a small circle as his other hand gave himself a few pumps.

I dripped with need, my stomach clenched, and my breathing was hot and heavy. I was two seconds to losing my shit in the clubhouse's back yard.

A fever broke across my tender skin as he pushed inside me to the base.

Trigger released a low growl, and both hands palmed my breasts as he twitched inside me and drove my clit crazy. My body ached with need. I needed a goddamn release now!

Just as I started to move, he pulled out. "Flip over."

I didn't waste any time. I waited eagerly for another good thrust. Instead, I jumped when I felt his tongue drag up the length of my spine.

My nipples grew hard and pointed. It was such an intimate act that I had to shake my head clear of emotion. I didn't want to spoil the moment.

"Tess," he groaned in my ear and twisted one of my greedy nipples.

"Damn it, fuck me, Trigger," I wanted to get in a fight just to have him flip his switch.

I barely got the last word out before he slammed into me. One hand held my shoulder and the other my hip. His thrusts knocked the air out of me as I clung with sweaty hands to the edge of the steel frame.

Yes.

Over and over and over again he took what was his and left me feeling wanted and loved in our twisted, fucked-up way.

I barely felt him lift me as he swung me around and put my back against a tree.

"Open your eyes," he grunted. "I fucked you up against a tree the first time, and it won't be the last." He dropped me onto his erection and found his spot on my neck and started to suck away. I clawed at his back, wanting more, but wanting less. It was wonderfully painful in all the right places.

Trigger let out a roar as he came. His stomach flexed and quivered, which tipped me over.

Fuck me.

I couldn't care less at who was around. It was our moment, and we so desperately needed it.

***

After my shower, I pulled on my clothes and headed out to the bar.

My phone lit up the space under the bar. I waited until I served my last customer before I finally checked it.

Shantee: Girl, I'm in town tonight. We need to go out!

An hour later…

Shantee: Don't make me hunt you down, Tess.

I laughed to myself. She was such a trip. I quickly wrote her back.

Tess: Meet me at Duke's in twenty.

Shantee: On the way.

I grabbed my bag, let Morgan know where I was going, and headed down the road.

I was halfway before I turned and waited for Ryder to catch up.

"For a short chick, you walk fast."

"For a prospect, you suck at following someone."

He rolled his eyes. "Trust me, this is the last thing I want to be doing tonight."

"I'll be with my friend, Shantee. You don't need to spend the entire time there. I can call you when I'm leaving."

He shrugged, and I could tell he left out the part where Trigger forbid him to leave.

"Remind me who she is again?"

"Shan was born in a man's body, so when she was eleven, she started the change."

"Right." He shook his head, and I shot him a dirty look.

"Imagine if you were someone different on the inside than you were on the out." He shut up, which I was thankful for. "Wouldn't be fun." I sighed.

Ryder stayed downstairs, and I met Shantee up on the balcony.

"Holy shit." She held open her long arms and smashed my face into her double D boobs. "Girl, you look amazing!"

"Thanks." I gasped for air. "Is that a new perfume?"

"Yes, it's called Summer Nights." She missed my point of why I said it.

We sat and ordered some food and sipped our drinks while we waited.

"How's the house?"

Her face fell, and one of her drawn-on eyebrows rose. "It's rough there right now. Your mother has lost her shit. I even caught her ripping apart Clark's office, muttering like a madwoman. Whatever she was looking for, she couldn't have found it," she gave me a knowing look, "because every inch of that place was ransacked."

"She's nuts." I downed the rest of my drink.

"She is, but it's my home. Makes me sad to see it go downhill so quickly."

I looked over her shoulder when I remembered something.

I watched as Cooper left, then turned my eyes back to Clark, who had something in his hand.

"You want proof that it was always you I loved, well, here." He handed me a card.

"What's this?"

"My gift to you for all the shit I've ever put you through."

"Whatever." I shoved it in my pocket, annoyed he wouldn't even share what the fuck it was. Classic Clark and his mind games.

After I killed him, I shoved it in my drawer and forgot about it, but now I was curious.

"Ladies," two men pulled my attention away from my thoughts, "can we buy you a drink?"

Shantee glanced at me, concerned, but she forced a friendly smile and said, "No, thanks, guys. We're just having a girls' night."

"Come on," one wrapped an arm playfully around me as he whistled for the waitress to bring us another, "what's the harm in one drink?"

I searched the faces for Ryder, but he seemed to be missing. Maybe he did leave.

When our food arrived, the men pulled up seats to join us. We tried to be polite, but my patience was wearing thin. The guy wrapped his arm around me, and it pissed me off. I pulled away from his grip and struggled to hold my temper.

"Look, man," I pushed his hand off my thigh, "I'll say it one more time. I'm not interested. I have someone."

"Sorry." He held up his hands, but they soon returned. The idea of a throat punch was looking real good.

"Maybe it's time to go?" I eyed Shantee, who had been groped at least three times already.

When she stood, he grabbed her boob, and her voice suddenly dropped several octaves.

"I said no."

The man stepped back and looked disgusted that she wasn't what he thought she was.

"What the fuck?" He wiped his hands on his jeans. "That's fucking wrong! You should wear a goddamn sign that says you have a dick."

"Why do men like you feel embarrassed when they realize I'm trans? I'm beautiful, aren't I? You shouldn't feel badly about it."

His drunk buddies started to laugh and poke fun at their friend. His face grew red, and he looked like he might punch Shantee.

"Time to go." I grabbed her arm and started to walk quickly down the stairs.

"Men are such assholes."

"It's 2018, grow the fuck up," I yelled over my shoulder.

We got about two blocks before they showed up behind us, shouting that they were going to show us what real men could do. I quickly pulled out my phone and sent a text.

Tess: Need your help. On PCH and Pine. Two drunk guys.

Trigger: Keep walking toward the club. I'll meet you.

A sense of relief spread over me until they started to gain ground on us. They were moving faster than I'd realized.

"Shit," I hissed and pushed Shantee, their main target, out of the way.

One laughed. "I could blow, and you'd fall over. Save yourself and move. Let us get to your he-she."

I saw red and punched him straight in the nose. He fell but jumped forward and pushed me into the brick wall.

"You stupid bitch!" He started to throw a punch when he was suddenly flung backward and tossed straight into traffic. Car horns and curses blasted.

Trigger pulled me behind him, and I heard the snap of a switchblade being released from its handle.

They took one look and ran like the bitches they were.

I turned to Shantee, who was fixing her shirt.

"Always an adventure with you, Tess."

I laughed as Trigger put his arm around my shoulder. We walked her back to her car and made sure she got off okay. She was rattled but played it off all right.

Ryder appeared, out of breath and spluttering apologies.

"I was talking with someone and missed you coming out."

Ryder hooked my arm to turn me toward him. "Tess, I'm really sorry, but just so you know, I saw those guys running from Trig. I grabbed one of them and got in a good kick to his nuts."

Trigger cursed under his breath. "Strike one."

CHAPTER EIGHT

Trigger

There wasn't enough whiskey in the world to ease the pain of betrayal. I'd been through many things in my life, but to live in my house, act like my family, live off our money, then turn your back and put my woman into the arms of that devil tore open my scars. I spun a red-tipped bullet between my fingers and wondered where the best place would be to jam it.

Neck.

Heart.

Ribs.

Or all three?

I shook my head. I needed to be more creative. The smells of the slaughter room came into my consciousness and pulled at my memory, and my head filled with more possibilities. The idea hit me across the face.

Wicked adrenaline smoked my veins and called my demons to the surface.

Yes, that would do.

It wasn't until the sun started to set and the temperature dropped that I really felt my body relax and the hold of the prison finally released me.

The wind whipped my face and blew my hair around. It was tradition for me to wear my cap helmet whenever I rode after jail time. Normally, I didn't like the idea of exposing my face at all. It wasn't wise, but tonight, I didn't give a fuck.

I took my favorite route through the mountains and hugged the corners. Speed and weed pumped through me, and I finally felt free.

At the next corner, I dropped the gears and skidded into the dugout. I hopped off my bike and followed the path through the long grass to the beach. The moon was extra bright, which helped guide me to my favorite spot. A bottle of whiskey sat beside me as I watched the ocean crash against the cliff. White noise was my music; it calmed my insides.

I needed this.

In my world, you tended to get a sixth sense for the sound of chopper bikes. The Devil's Reach rode only three different kinds, that was it. So, when I heard a Classic Bobber off in the distance, it brought me to my feet. I hopped up on a rock and looked down at the winding road. Sure as shit, a bike was making its way in my direction.

Call me paranoid, but I knew something was up.

I tossed my joint and slowly made my way back to the road. It was a few yards away when I heard the engine slow.

I had just reached my bike when I heard the first bullet leave the chamber.

Shit!

A giant dirt cloud shot from my wheels as I skidded out of the dugout and up the hill. It wasn't the direction I wanted to go, but I needed to be in front of him rather than head on. Again, I was thankful the light from the moon acted like a lamp above us.

I pulled my gun free from my saddlebag and pointed behind me. When I had a moment of straight road, I twisted in my seat and fired.

Sparks flew from his wheel guard, and he swerved to keep his balance. He glanced behind him then sped up, decreasing the space between us. Two trucks appeared up ahead. They had to see me coming. One pulled out into the other lane so I was trapped behind them, unable to pass.

I knew the road well enough to know the shoulders ran out to shit on the outside, and a truck could run me into the rock wall on the other. I wouldn't put it past them. I knew truck drivers had been warned about biker clubs trying to steal their cargo, so they would attempt to control the road with their big-ass vehicles to keep from being stopped. Couldn't say I blamed them, but right now I needed to get the hell past them.

My speedometer dropped to fifty miles an hour, and I needed to make a decision fast.

I heard the bullet fly by me and saw the damage it spread over my side mirror as it hit. Glass flew, and I swerved the bike to make myself less of a target.

Again, I twisted and sent more fire. He weaved and ducked but still managed to keep his seat. He was good, but I was better.

The road flattened out up ahead, and I took the opportunity to make my move. I sped up and acted like I was going to split the trucks, but at the last second, I swerved and shot out his passenger side mirror. The truck pulled away from the impact and over the center line, a natural human reaction, and I gunned my bike up the space he made on the inside along the gravel shoulder and just managed to slip in front of the truck by a hair. He blasted his horn and tried to speed up, but I was lighter and quickly leapt a good distance ahead.

Pop!

Pop!

What the fuck! Using my good mirror, I tilted it and saw that the other biker must have used my own idea against me with the trucks. Fuck!

I hugged the corners and kept myself swerving in and out in short turns as the bullets nicked at the sides of my bike.

His engine made a strange noise, and he suddenly shot up right next to me.

"Jesus Christ!" I dropped my speed and fell in behind him. His head whipped around, and he tried to do the same to me. I aimed my gun and fired again, but it clicked empty.

Fuck me!

I shoved it back into my bag and decided this shit needed to end, with or without bullets.

The top of the peak was only a few yards away, and I knew what lay up ahead.

I threw back my head laughed out loud. This was it. This was what I lived for, to play chicken with the reaper.

"One," I switched the gear into fifth, "two," I lined up my wheels with his, "three." I jolted forward and raced up the side of his tread. Both bikes twisted around and sent us flying down the steep hill. At such speed, all I could do was protect my head and neck. My bike hit a rock hard and jumped to a stop. His bike flew off the cliff up ahead, while we were sent into the bushes. Weeds and rocks scraped at my clothing as I tumbled through the shrubs. At the very last second, when I felt my body leave the ground, I was ready. I knew what was coming. I twisted and grabbed a narrow tree trunk and felt myself snap back into the side of the cliff.

He came flying down next to me. His hands desperately scrambled for a hold, but I kicked out, and he fell over the cliff backward. I heard a sound then all was quiet.

Carefully, I pulled myself forward arm over arm and was able to shimmy over to the ledge. I peered over. He had gotten wedged between a tree and a rock just below the edge and hung like a bent pretzel. I tried to get closer, and dirt and rock suddenly let go from beneath me and tumbled down the eighty-foot cliff into the angry water below. I pulled back and rested for a bit, thinking the sound I had heard was probably his spine snapping in half, confirmation that the reaper and I had a tie.

I went for it and leaned lower and just managed to snag his jacket. After a bit of sweaty cursing, I managed to finger his cell phone loose and grab his wallet. I drew back for a breather to have a look inside the wallet, but it was empty. I expected nothing less. I needed one more thing, and his obviously dislocated shoulder made it easier. I yanked up his arm, grabbed his hand, and used his thumb to unlock the phone.

I scrolled through the settings and changed his passcode to the club's address before I tucked it in my jeans. I grabbed a shrub with both hands as I kicked the branch he was wedged against and watched him fall into the water below. I knew the sheriffs combed through these back roads, and I didn't need any more problems on my hands. I looked up the hill and squinted at the idea of the seventy-foot climb back up to the top. It was dark, so I would have to watch my footing. Fuck, I really, really hoped my bike would work when I got there.

To my surprise, the beast of a bike roared to life. I swung it around, sending gravel everywhere, and headed for home.

"What the hell happened to you?" Brick jumped from his stool, which caused Tess to race from out behind the bar. It had taken me all night to get my bike going and back into the city. It was now mid-morning, and I was irritated as shit that the entire thing had happened at all.

"Had some company tonight."

"Who?" Tess handed me a bottle of water.

"Don't know, but," I reached into my jeans and held up the phone, "last text he got gave my location, so he was obviously after me." I tossed it to Morgan.

"I'll see what I can find."

"Do you think it was your father?" Brick trailed me into my office, followed by Tess.

"Wouldn't be surprised." I pulled off my filthy t-shirt and tossed it on the couch and tugged on a fresh one. "Get me something stronger than this." I tossed the water on my desk and turned to Tess as she partially closed the door behind Brick.

"What really happened?"

"What I said," I grunted.

She folded her arms and stared at me, and her look gave me what I needed to back her up and hover over her small frame. My body was hot, and I needed release. She was so good at pushing all my buttons to the limit.

"Don't keep things from me," she whispered and sent her hot breath across my cheek.

"Why do you fight me?"

She stepped up on her toes, pressed her chest into mine, and licked the rim of my ear.

"Because you let me."

My hand clamped down on her waist to hold her in place. I was dangerously close to tossing her cute little ass out the door, but I had so much to concentrate on, and I couldn't take the distraction.

"Anything I can help you with?" Her hand slipped down my front and fisted my pulsing erection. I closed my eyes and tried to force the images of the many ways I planned to fuck her from my mind.

"Umm…" Rail appeared at the door then quickly turned around when he saw us.

I didn't care. I was trapped between perfume and a fistful of me.

"Trigger, you need to come out right now."

"Busy." My voice was hoarse. Tess started to pull away, but I slammed her hand back down. "Don't even think of leaving."

"Trig—"

"If it's not a Stripe Back, Gus, or Allen, go away."

"It's Melissa."

I stilled just long enough for Tess to sense something was up. Her hand slowly slipped away, and I didn't stop her.

Fuck.

"Who's Melissa?" She straightened her shoulders and pulled her top back into place.

"Come on, Tess, I could use a drink." Rail reached for her, but she stepped back.

"What's going on?"

"Go," I bit out and watched her face as it twisted in confusion. My blue balls had made me lash out at her. I didn't need this shit right now.

Tess muttered something and left for the bar.

I rubbed my face and tried to get my head on straight.

"He'll be out in a minute," I heard Rail mutter to her. We all wanted nothing to do with Melissa. Her brother was a pain in our ass, and she wanted more than I was willing to give. She was a good lay and was available for a good fuck whenever, but that was all.

I tossed the last of my drink back and slammed the glass on the desk.

When I stepped into the bar, her back was to me as she talked to Brick, who glanced over with a jacked-up face. He rubbed his head and nodded for her to see me.

My stomach shot upward and squeezed my guts into a rock.

***

Tess

"Why are you doing this?" I glared at Cray, who was trying to pull me out back to show me something. "You all are shit at creating a distraction."

"Not trying to play you, Tess, promise. But," he shrugged, "you shouldn't be in there right now."

"Why? And who the hell is Melissa?" I rested my hands on my hips to prove I wasn't about to back down.

"Melissa is Doyle's sister. Trigger and her have history."

"Like Tammy history?"

He nodded, and I instantly wanted to claw her eyes out.

"Why is she here?"

"My guess is she heard he got out and wanted to finish what they started."

"Which was?"

He lit a joint and offered it to me first. I took it and sucked back a rather large hit. My nerves were on high, and I needed to settle before I did something I'd either regret or enjoy. The little dark angel on my shoulder wanted to play, and I wanted to see how wild she could be.

"You gonna stop me if I go in?"

He shook his head and smirked around the edge of the joint.

"Then why take me out here?"

"Had to do what the boss said."

Whatever. I turned on my heel and headed inside.

Morgan caught my eye when I entered the bar and shook his head as a warning to leave. I ignored him, which I was sure he predicted. Rail stiffened and cleared his throat at Trigger, Brick stepped back, and I saw a chick with a little boy who looked an awful lot like…

The lines deepened across his forehead. He didn't have to say anything; I knew it was bad. It hit me like a punch to the gut. Sure, I never really wanted kids, but I would have liked the option to decide. There was a fucked-up part of me that thought I might have kept Clark's baby, but that was all before I met Trigger.

"Tess!" Denton blurted, and I felt a tug on my sleeve that broke my gaze with Trigger. "Mom passed out again. I ate most of my food and—" He caught the mood of the bar and whirled around when he heard the baby squeal.

"Why is that here?"

My hands landed on his shoulders to ground myself.

"Oh," Melissa cooed, directing her attention to us, "aren't you a cute little thing?"

Denton looked up at me, unimpressed, before he directed his gaze back to her. "Your fuckin' baby has a big head."

Melissa's focus jumped up to me. "Wow, sweet kid."

"Tess," he ignored her and turned in my arms, "if I eat all my carrots, can I have my iPad for twenty minutes before bed?"

"Yeah." I barely heard him.

"Yes! You hear that, Uncle Trig?" He cheered, but when everyone stared at him, he dropped his arms. "Who is she, anyway?"

"I'm your uncle's friend, and this is your Uncle Trigger's child."

I nearly fell forward at her words.

"No, she's," he pointed to me, "Uncle Trig's old lady. Not you."

"I know it's confusing."

"Tess?" His little face held so much confusion that I almost wanted to cry for him.

"Why don't you ask Cray to grab your iPad? He's out by the pool." I ruffled his hair and gently pushed him out back.

Once he was out of sight, I glared back at the bitch who had just stirred up that little boy's mind to a shitty place.

"You came, you made your point, now it's time for you to go." I couldn't hide the clip in my tone.

"Um…" She glanced back at Trigger, who was still stuck in some parallel place where he was rendered useless. Big Joe stepped forward and held out his hand as if to help her through the door. "Maybe I overstayed my welcome." She reached for her bag and pulled out a card. "I'm not asking for anything but the opportunity for you to get to know your son." She waited for him to say something, and he took the card and ran a hand through his hair.

"Go home, Melissa. I need time to think about this shit storm." He pushed her out the door.

Acid flowed around the inside of my cheeks and nipped at my tongue. What the hell just happened?

"Tess, we'll talk in a moment." He hurried to his office.

Oh, is that so?

The door slammed shut, and I was left with a bar full of eyes all on me.

Morgan slid a bottle of whiskey in front of me, and instead of pouring a glass, I grabbed the bottle by the neck and left.

I didn't give two shits that I took Trigger's bike. I was getting pretty good at riding the beast. Plus, it meant he wouldn't be able to come find me right away.

"Hey," Big Joe stopped me at the road, "just tell me where you're going."

"For a ride." I inched out to the curb.

"But where?"

"I don't know."

"Tess." He removed his sunglasses, and I saw he was genuinely nervous for me.

Dammit!

"Pier, I think. Not far. I just need a moment to think."

"No pier, okay, it's—"

"Neutral ground, I know. Trust me, it's been beat into my head."

"Then why go?"

I dropped my head, not wanting this conversation. "Makes me remember an easier time."

"He's gonna kill you."

"Nothing left to kill." I slammed down the visor and shot onto the road.

I watched as Morgan joined him and yelled something. I flipped the mirror up and ran a red. I was still too chicken to split traffic, so I eased in with the flow and tried to settle my nerves.

Once the pier came into view, I felt right about my choice to come here. I pulled into Trigger's spot and headed down to the shoreline.

The sand was warm, but once the sun went down, the air grew cool. I wrapped the black and red plaid blanket Trigger kept in his saddlebag tightly around my shoulders and balanced the bottle of whiskey between my legs. Orange and red reflected off the calm sea and made for a quiet sunset.

My body was tingly, and my belly felt full, so I was happy to numb the pain in my chest.

"I thought about sending Minnie, but," Brick shrugged and took a seat next to me, "you got me."

"All I ever wanted, anyway." I flipped the side of the blanket over his leg as he pulled out a fat joint. He took a long drag and handed it to me, so I handed him the whiskey.

He smirked at the bottle. "He's rubbed off on you."

"Don't," I warned. I wanted more than anything to be with Trig tonight, but the image of the baby and him carrying the bag into his office cut too close to the core.

"She's a bitch," he huffed between sips.

"She had every right to do what she did today, but she fucked up telling Denton." I felt my anger rise. "Those boys have been through enough shit. A fucked-up mom, a missing father, and now an uncle who knocked up some chick." I felt my throat stick, and my words fumbled on their way out.

"No one blames you for leaving Gus, Tess."

"I do." I thumped my chest. "I blame myself. He was so weak and tired, and Allen beat him over and over for my mistakes." I felt tears prick my eyes, so I chased them back. Crying got you nowhere. I hated it. "All I got was being given to Zay. What the fuck was the point of taking me?"

"You know the answer to that."

"It didn't even work!" I snatched the bottle back and downed a few more sips.

Brick smiled, but it was followed by a dark expression. "Yeah, it did."

I waved my hands in the air to tell him I was listening.

"Tess, settle down and listen. That man sat in a prison for weeks with multiple people working to track you down. He put your rescue before anything else. That's something that has never happened before. The club has always come first, and the guys have always come after that. You've changed him, Tess. Allen may not have won this round by taking you, but never underestimate him. He is the devil incarnate, and he'll be back and play dirtier than ever. I know Allen from years of being at the club, and I'm telling you to watch your back. He got to you once, and he won't stop until he gets you again. He wants whatever will hurt Trigger the most, and that's you."

"Well, he won't get me. I won't let him." I turned away and took another deep drag of the joint.

CHAPTER NINE

Trigger

Gus always warned me that my dick would get me into trouble. I just never saw that coming. I leaned back in my seat and rubbed my head. *Gus.* I had my guys scouring every corner looking for where they might be holding him. Fuck Allen. My guys had plenty of kills to show for it but hadn't turned up much info. I knew he wouldn't give up and wished to hell I had an idea of what he was planning.

"Whiskey?" Minnie slammed a shot glass down in front of me. "Or a condom?"

The fuck!

I opened my mouth to tell her off, but she held up her hand.

"Yell at me all you want, but I am the one friend who's willing to give you some free advice, even if you don't want it." She pressed her hands flat on the bar top as she leaned down to get in my face.

Fucking hell, don't kill her.

"You've sunk your dick in every hole known to man. Whatever, that's your thing, but with that comes major consequences. One being that if you don't handle this correctly, the *one* and *only* person who can handle your bullshit will walk out of your life again," she tossed back my drink, "and that's on you."

"Done?" I felt my temper rise.

"Nope." She narrowed her bright green eyes at me. "Fuck what that chick is saying, you get a DNA test now. Are you even sure the timelines fit? I mean, you were mostly with Tammy at that point." She took my joint and held it up in my face. "Quit this shit until you can remember, or kiss Tess goodbye." She gave me a dramatic pause. "Or she'll meet someone else, someone who didn't get some random broad knocked up."

A strange ache in my stomach came on quickly. I fought it back, but it burrowed its way through.

"Here, boss." Morgan handed me a clean glass. "Are you fucking insane?" he hissed at Minnie, who hadn't broken her eye contact with me.

"I'm being honest." She turned to look at him. "Can't say the same for you."

"Enough," I mumbled. She'd made her point and was lucky I didn't kill her for it.

She started to speak but stopped herself. "Look." She closed her eyes for a moment.

I snapped my neck because if I didn't, it would be hers.

"I'm half the person Tess is. She's hot, smart, and a damn good friend. I would be crushed to see her go because this blows up in your face."

"No more, Minnie," Morgan warned.

She got smart and nodded once with her hands in the air and left. Morgan went back to cleaning the beer taps.

"Wait." Peggy stopped short when she saw me. "How are you here and your bitch isn't?"

"What?" I glanced at Morgan as he tried to slip out. "Morgan," I shouted, and he whirled around.

"She left," Minnie called from the hallway.

"Where?" The place rattled like thunder.

"Don't know, but Brick is with her. She's fine."

I rolled my eyes at Minnie's choice of words. She wasn't fine!

"Trigger," Cray called from my office with his phone in the air, "they're ready for you."

I had to shove all the bullshit aside and get my head in the game.

"Morgan and Rail." I signaled for them to follow me.

"Hey, boss." Morgan stopped me before we went in and held up the phone I had taken off the dead biker. "Name's Eddie Red. He's some hit man from North Carolina, long-ass rap sheet, worked a bit for the cartel and some indie jobs. No direct link to your father that I can see, but there was a string of texts between him and someone else. Interesting that three times he was at your exact location. He even was at…" he turned the phone around and showed me the Google map that tracked where he had been in the last month, "the prison."

What the fuck? He was there twice?

"Can't imagine where he got all that information." Morgan gave me a knowing look.

I handed him a list. "I'll need that by the end of today." His grin grew wicked when he saw it was supplies for the slaughter room.

The map was stretched out on the meeting room wall, the conference phone was in the center of the table, and fifty-nine VPs waited to hear what their next move would be.

"Two of our own were taken." I didn't waste words. "One's back, but the other's still out there."

"Your Uncle Gus," Cameron, my Nova Scotia VP, confirmed.

"Right. Last we knew, he was in Tennessee." I paused to make sure they listened and spoke slowly and clearly. I needed them to understand how important the next part was.

"I want every single chapter to comb through their territory with a fuckin' fine-toothed comb. Round up every Serpent and Stripe Back and beat every detail out of them you can. I want anything they have on Allen. Once they tell you all they've got, if they don't give you anything, slaughter them. The word will spread, so you'll need to act fast. I don't care if you think it's the smallest piece of shit, it's information, and you will report it back to me or Morgan. I will decide if it's worth our time or not. The one who brings me some valuable info gets a new bike, on me." The mic started to buzz with chatter, which meant I had their attention.

"Now, go!"

Morgan pushed the button to hang up and glanced around the room at me and Cray.

"Let the bloodshed begin."

My phone rang, and I saw it was Melissa. I stepped out of the room and into the bar to get away from the excitement.

"What?" I snapped.

"Oh, um, sorry," she stuttered. "I left in such a hurry. I wondered if you'd have a coffee with me and, you know, work out the details and whatnot."

So, I don't get time to think about this? Pushy bitch.

My gaze snapped over to Minnie chatting with Big Joe at the pool table, her words finding their way inside. *"Kiss Tess goodbye."*

"Where?" I needed this shit over with.

"Rusty's Surf?"

"Fine, be there in fifteen." I hung up and reached for my keys then cursed. "Where the hell are they?"

"Here," Morgan tossed me his but failed to answer my question.

I raced out the door and kicked the bike in gear. I despised riding another man's bike, but I didn't have time to find out if Rail was working on my clutch or not. My luck, it was hoisted up on the lift anyway.

Traffic was light, and I made it there in record time, arriving before Melissa.

"You're late." I kicked out her chair when she walked in.

"Sorry, Brad wouldn't go down for his nap." She flipped her long bangs out of her face. "Thanks for meeting me. I'm sure you're busy."

"I am." I took in the restaurant. It was bright, with lots of windows. I hated windows.

She reached forward and leaned on her tangled fingers. She knew better than to touch me. "You look really good."

"How do I know he's mine?"

She half laughed. "You don't waste any time, do you?"

"Nope."

"Well, then," she pulled some papers from her purse, "here."

I quickly read the first paragraph, but all that stuck out was the word *match.*

Wait.

"How did you get my DNA?"

Her brows pinched together, and I saw guilt race across her face. "Doyle."

My blood grew thick and struggled to circulate.

"Who gave you the right to do that?"

Breathe. Fuck me, breathe!

"I had to know." She held her hands up. "It was between you and one other."

"So, how do I know you're not making all this shit up?"

"Right there." She hit the paper in my hands. "Trust me, Trigger, I prayed it was the other guy."

I stood and tossed the papers at her. "I don't trust you or your brother. We go down to the doctor together and get this shit done."

"Fine, but it can't be until next week. I have work that's taking me out of town."

"Whatever." I walked out.

She ran up behind me and out to the empty parking lot. "I'm sorry, Trigger. I know this isn't what you wanted, but it's not like I wanted this either!"

I whirled around and jammed my finger in her face. "It was, Melissa, it was always your plan."

"It's no secret I love you, Trigger." She knocked the keys out of my hand and grabbed my arm so I'd look at her. I was fucking thankful no one was around to witness this freak show.

Flip!

I grabbed her around the waist and slammed her into the wall, careful not to hurt her, but my temper was at full throttle.

The demons screamed at me for a fight.

No.

"Trigger," she pressed her breasts into my chest, "I know how you like it. Why won't you just give in?"

I panted, not with need, but with hatred. Everything was crashing down.

Suddenly, her lips were on mine. I shoved her backward, but she used the momentum to shoot back at me. Her tongue plunged into my mouth and tried to take control.

"No," I hissed and held her shoulders back. "Fucking desperate chick."

"Just take me," she cried, ripping open her shirt. Buttons flew all around us like some cheesy soap show Cooper watched.

"Go the fuck home, Melissa."

Wait. I squinted to see better. It was my fuckin' bike.

"Go home!"

I pounded my way to the edge of the parking lot and looked down the beach, and sure as shit, there were Tess and Brick hanging out with some locals.

My head was so jacked up, I wasn't sure what I was capable of.

Tess had a large black sweater wrapped around her shoulders, and she was laughing at something Mud was saying.

"What up, brother?" Mud smiled at me through his joint. "Here for the party?"

He was drunk, like he normally was on nights like this. A good ride on the waves meant a party.

"Lookin' for her." I nodded at Tess cuddled up by the firepit. I swallowed hard to try to calm myself.

Brick gave me a nod as a greeting. "Forgot my phone."

Tess suddenly stood, and Brick grabbed her arm and gestured over my shoulder.

Fuck!

Melissa had followed me and was closing in on us fast.

"Who is this?" Mud squinted. "She's got crazy written all over her face." He dusted off his hands as he stood.

"Trigger, baby," she whined, "let's finish what we started!"

Tess's face fell, but when she looked back up her expression had hardened.

"Nothing will ever happen between us. Go the fuck home."

She came a little closer and eyed Tess. "He's a good kisser, huh? But you already know that."

She smirked at the rest of the guys as she moved closer to Tess.

"I spent years obsessing over him." She put her hands through her hair, fucking up her 'do. "The way he fucks like he's really into you."

"Stop," Brick warned. "Your brother know you're here?"

"Be careful. You'll think he's yours, then one day, poof, it's all over. He's out back hittin' another pair of legs, and you'll be left with a hole in the center of your chest."

"Enough," I hissed.

She kept walking until Brick was between them. "I just want a moment alone with the girl who won over Trigger…for now."

Tess pressed her hand against Brick's arm to let her pass. "I'm game."

Fuck.

***

Tess

Melissa may have had three inches on me, but I was scrappy and knew how to fight dirty. I pointed my head in the opposite direction for her to start walking.

"No, Tess," Trigger ordered.

"Don't remember asking for permission." I hated that he had a son with this bitch. It tore at my inner woman, the part that knew I would never give him one.

We walked a few feet away, and I angled her so I could see the guys.

"What?"

She eyed me up and down then reached out and touched my hair.

"I don't get it." She shook her head. "You're such a plain little thing."

I stayed strong. "But yet he loves *me*."

She smiled darkly, her eyes in a slit. "But I've given him a son, the one thing you can't ever do."

It took me a half a second to absorb her fucking words before everything clicked, and I fisted a handful of her hair and yanked hard. My other hand swung around and smashed into her cheekbone.

Rage could be an ugly bitch, and this chick deserved it all. I grabbed her hair again and yanked her up, then put my face up to hers as I shook her like a rat. She just looked at me in disbelief as she screamed.

When I prepared to swing again, Trigger wrapped his arms around my midsection and hauled me back. I kicked at him, trying to get away.

"You stupid bitch!" Melissa yelled as she held her hand to her face. "You're fucking crazy!"

"Me?" I wiggled out of his grip, but he caught me again. "Tell him the truth!"

"What?" Her eyes darted around for help.

"How do you know I can't have kids?" I spat at her. Trigger's grip loosened a little, and Brick stepped up with a confused look. "The only way you could is if your rat of a brother opened his mouth. Well, guess what, you little shit, I know some things about precious Officer Doyle that will bury his ass."

"Melissa," Trigger's ribcage rattled against mine, "go the fuck home."

"This isn't over." She spat at my feet, and I thrashed against Trigger's grip to go after her, but he held fast. "Trigger, that kiss will hold me for now."

Once she was out of sight, I pushed out of his arms and took a few steps away from him. I burned with the need to hit someone. I couldn't look at him right now. I was so mad he hadn't let me finish off that Easy-Bake Oven. I needed a moment to catch my breath and let the sting of her words taper off.

Just when you finally believe you've shed something from your past, it finds a way to come back and poke at your armor.

Trigger handed Brick a set of keys. "Take Morgan's bike back to the club. I need your eyes there."

"Yeah, okay." Brick glanced at me.

What was I missing? Eyes on what? If Allen returned?

"You okay, Tess?"

I shrugged, unable to lie to my best friend, but I was sure as hell going to ask what the fuck all that was about.

A loud crack boomed all around us, and the sky lit up the black sea with a flash of lightning. It suited my mood perfectly. I hadn't noticed the wind had changed or the heavy clouds that had rolled in. As we stood there, the heavens opened and poured down what I was feeling inside. I couldn't help but sigh at the irony of the situation. Mother Nature was able to show what I couldn't.

Brick hurried up to the parking lot, and Mud and his hippy friends started to dance around, embracing the flash storm.

Trigger's hair stuck to the side of his head as we continued to stand there. Neither of us had moved. I hated how drawn to him I was. But the moment our eyes met, I wanted to cry. I knew it was for all the wrong reasons, but I was selfish and wanted every part of him to be mine.

"You wanna hit me?" he growled through the wind.

"Yeah." It was the truth.

He held open his arms as if to say *go for it*.

I shook my head, unable to move. It wasn't going to fix anything.

He took a step toward me, and I took one back.

"You said once you weren't scared of me."

"I'm not."

He moved closer, and I matched to keep our distance even.

"You fight me at every corner. Where is that now?"

"With your son," I blurted, and my body betrayed me as tears flooded my eyes.

He wavered in his step but continued to back me up until I was against the lifeguard hut.

"That bothers you?" His face flinched as he asked. "Bothers you that I screwed her in the parking lot of the club?"

I pulled back my arm and threw my fist as hard as I could into his cheek.

His face shot to the side, but he snapped it back with a dark smirk.

"She kissed *me* tonight." He leaned in without touching me and drew in a deep breath through his nose as if to test my scent.

I hit him again, only this time I nailed him in the neck, a full throat punch. God, I hated him so much at that moment.

"Had her tongue in my mouth." He seemed unfazed by my hit, which pissed me further.

"Stop." I drew back for another punch, but he scooped me up and forced my legs around his waist. He took my chin in his hands, so I'd have to look at him straight on. He flexed his neck, and I felt the vertebrae pop as he relieved some tension.

"I don't know what the fuck is going on, but I will find out."

I was glad my wounds had opened and my tears flowed freely along with the rain. I could put up with a lot, but that one tore deep.

"Their games are getting worse." I felt emotionally drained. "Makes me wonder what's next."

"Me too." He shook his hair back off his face. "Let me take you home."

I nodded.

The ride home was cold, and I was annoyed to see the bar was full of more club members. As soon as Brick caught sight of us, he rushed over and hugged me.

"Pack your bag. We're heading out for the night." He looked at Trig, who nodded.

I wanted to protest, but I was too tired to say no. Besides, I could use a little family time.

I welcomed his hug. "That sounds nice."

"Good." He turned me around and pushed me toward my room. "We leave in ten."

The water ran into the marble sink in the bathroom. I stared blankly at it. My head thumped, and my stomach turned as I let my mind drift off.

"Please!" My scream tore at my throat as Allen punched another dent into Gus's battered body. "I'm sorry. Please stop." I tried to pull away from Zay's tight grip.

"Actions have consequences, Tessa," he purred and flexed his hand with a sick, sadistic smile. "Your body is young, and his is old. Where's the fun in taking you on?"

"This is fun for you?" I hissed like a snake, disgusted with the man in front of me. "You want to hurt Trigger, you hurt me."

"Stop, Tess," Gus moaned from the ground. His face was barely recognizable, and blood lined his teeth.

I thought this might break me. I'd been through many things, but this nearly tore me in half. I knew I couldn't let Allen see how much it hurt me to watch Gus being beaten.

"Hmm." He stepped toward me and waved off Zay. He grabbed my chin and stared into my eyes. "Maybe I can see the appeal." He leaned in and drank in my scent. I shuddered but didn't back down. I was stronger than this. I had to be stronger. If the attention was on me, it

wasn't on Gus.

Zay made a noise like a protest but grabbed my arms, and Allen's lips were suddenly on mine. I bucked and tried to fight him off, but he was much stronger than I was. As soon as he pulled away, I spat in his face and heaved as my stomach turned in a violent roll.

Crack!

My face was hit with such force my ears rang.

"You ever deny me again," he shouted, but he sounded a million miles away, "you'll meet my weasels." He smacked their cage and made them scream with a high-pitched squeal. "Or maybe dear old Gus should warm them up for you?"

I held in the flinch when I saw Gus's expression. It was pure horror.

That brought me back to the present. I let out a weighted sigh.

A movement behind me caused me to look up. There was Trigger in the doorway, gaze locked on me, and the lines between his eyes were deep.

He pushed off the doorframe and stood directly behind me, his chest to my back.

His hand slid into my shirt and rested over my heart, and then he leaned in and kissed my neck.

"Stop worrying."

I understood that he wanted to make me feel better, but it had the opposite effect. Instead, I just squeezed his hand and slid out from under his hold. I grabbed my bag from the bed and walked out of the room.

He wouldn't get it. He wasn't there.

Outside, I handed Brick my bag, and he strapped it on the back of his bike.

"Ready?"

"Where are we going?"

"Not far." He grinned and waited for me to climb on. I hesitated, but I knew Trigger would be okay with me riding with Brick. After all, he was my brother. I tapped his side to let him know I was good to go, and we pulled into the quiet street.

Soon, our feet dangled from the rooftop as the city buzzed below us, unaware of our presence. I dipped a chip in the guacamole and popped it in my mouth. Brick hummed as he finished off his beer and opened another. He checked mine and replaced it as well.

"Never thought we'd be here," he muttered from behind the lip of the beer.

"On top of an old movie theater, with beer and chips?" I joked darkly because a part of that was true. We had spent many a night hungry, looking for a safe place to sleep, but we always managed. There had been the odd rooftop.

"No." He looked over at me. "Never thought we'd have secrets between us."

I squeezed my eyes shut as I felt the guilt. "Secret. Not plural."

"Maybe not in the beginning, but they grow, like a snowball, whether you mean for them to or not."

"I just didn't want you to take the blame."

"If I did, would that be so terrible?" He looked hurt. I always thought I was protecting him, but now I realized he needed to be needed.

"I relapsed, went back to Clark, and got pregnant," I blurted before he could respond. I knew if he stopped me, I wouldn't have the courage to go on. Brick's face smoothed into stone, but he remained silent. "I couldn't stand to see your disappointment, so I stayed." I felt like I might be sick. "Then, mommy dearest and Clark found out, and one night they tore it from me." His expression turned horrified, so I rushed on. "They did damage, and now I can't have kids."

"Tess—"

"No." I took his hand and gave it a squeeze. "Honestly, there's nothing to say anymore. It's over. I told you I never really wanted kids, so it's not like it was a big loss for me. It's just…" I fumbled to find the right words. My whole body seemed to need to shed some of the heaviness inside.

Brick leaned over and wrapped his arm around my shoulders and tugged me over to his side.

"It's just what?" he encouraged me.

"It just would have been nice to have had the option, you know?"

"I know." He kissed my head, and we stayed like that for a while, watching the lights twinkle.

"Trigger never told you?"

"No."

I couldn't help but be happy about that. He had kept his word.

"See that garbage can down there?" He pointed.

"Yeah."

"You ever keep secrets from me again, I stuff you in there and frame Rail."

I laughed and kissed his cheek.
“I love you, Matt.”
“I know.”

CHAPTER TEN

Trigger

"You stare at her like you're mind-fucking her from across the room." Peggy snatched my plate from in front of me. "It's pathetic."

"What's pathetic," Rail lit his cigarette with a smile, "is you've done everyone in here and you're still single."

Brick waited for her to leave before he leaned across the table. "It's been a week. Where the hell is she?"

"Doyle set the whole thing up." Rail flicked the ash off the table. "He's protecting the little slut."

"I wonder if Allen ever saw what was on the USB," Brick said, deep in thought, "or if he helped Clark get the videos."

"I think he's seen them…" I trailed off, remembering what Zay said. He knew about File 33. I hadn't shared that knowledge with the guys, as I promised Tess I wouldn't. "Which means Allen has the same leverage we do."

"It would explain why he was after it." Brick nodded. "He wants it because he's not on it. He wants it because he wants the power."

I rested my hand on the table to stop the conversation when Cooper came in and went directly to the bar. Both Rail and Brick stared at me, and I shook my head. No questions.

"More?" Tess asked Rail with a bottle of whiskey in her hand.

She had been slightly off ever since the beach. Brick never mentioned how their night went, but I assumed he knew everything now. She was still here and hadn't run off back to old habits, so that was a good sign. I hoped.

"Trigger." Big Joe handed me an envelope. It read *To the parents of Denton March*. "It's the third one this week. Thought I'd give this one to you instead of the junkie."

"Why do you have it?" I asked while I eyed the school's seal.

"Den tossed it in the trash when he got home yesterday."

I gave a tight nod, and he went back to his post. I ripped the seal and plucked out the paperwork.

Fuck.

"Everything okay?" Tess stood next to me.

"Where's Denton?"

"In his room," Morgan called from behind the bar. "Been in there since school."

"Have him meet me in the ring."

"Yup." Morgan rushed off, and Tess stepped back as I stood.

"Trigger, what's going on?"

I leaned down and kissed her lips roughly before I left to go deal with my nephew. I stormed down the hallway, stripped down to my shorts and sneakers, and started to warm up. Denton arrived shortly after, and I pointed for him to join me.

He knew he was in some kind of shit.

After an hour of sparring, I held up my arms and watched Denton squint through the sweat that poured down his face. "Again." He jabbed my hand, but I moved, and he missed. He shook off his exhaustion and took another swing but missed and tripped forward.

"My arms hurt." He winced.

"That's not pain. That's your body working out. Fight through it."

"Why?"

I hooked my right arm and clipped his shoulder. His face shifted and showed me his next move, so I jumped out of the way.

"I'm done." He tossed his gloves off and started to step out of the ring, but I shoved his shoulder and punched him square in the nose.

He looked startled and began to cry. He looked at me, all hurt.

"That didn't feel good, did it? We got a meeting with your principal tomorrow at ten a.m. Now get yourself cleaned up."

I dropped my gloves and left my nephew to deal with the impact of what had just happened.

Kid had to learn sometime.

***

"Move it." I shoved Denton's shoulder as he walked into Principal Barrett's office. She looked up from her desk, and her mouth fell open like a trout when she caught sight of Denton's black and blue swollen face. I noticed she didn't close the door all the way, and it wasn't lost on me that the security guard stayed in the outer office.

"Good heavens!" Her eyes shifted to mine, and I saw her shoulders tighten. She cleared her throat and motioned for us to sit. I was entirely too big for the chair, but I somehow managed to stuff my body into it. What was it about schools that they always had the same smell? Fuck.

"Mr. Vineyard," her voice was meek, a major turn-off, "we have a total hands-off policy here at Santa Monica Elementary. Denton cannot be using his fists on other children. Just last week he punched Tommy Daloca right in the eye, and the week before that, Paul Perry received a punch in his tummy. I'm not sure what is happening at home, but I need…"

She stopped and glanced down at Denton's file, and I saw what she saw. My name on the form. She pulled her yellow sweater closed over her blouse and pressed her hand to her chest.

"I've done all I can do with Denton. I know there is a 'delicate,'" she finger-quoted at me, "situation regarding his mother, but this behavior must stop. I hesitate to say our only recourse will be expulsion." She swallowed hard as I stared at her.

Fuck me. I rubbed my head and took a moment to think.

"Has the kid shown you any disrespect?" She shook her head. "Has he disrespected any of his teachers?"

"No. He hasn't." She glanced at Denton and shook her head again.

There was a long stretch of silence as I mulled over her answer. I turned to Denton. "Look at me, kid." He did as he was told. "Do you think any of my guys would disrespect me?"

Den gulped and shook his head emphatically.

"Why do you think that is?"

"Because you'd kill them."

The principal gasped.

"Did you think you deserved that punch I gave you yesterday?"

Principal Barrett's eyes bulged, and she put a hand to her face to cover her expression.

"No," Den shook his head, "I wasn't ready for it."

"Right. Felt pretty bad, didn't it?" Den teared up, but I didn't care. He needed to learn. "You want respect, you gotta earn it, kid. You don't throw your weight around, and you don't hit people unless they deserve it."

"Yes, sir."

I stood and turned to the principal, who didn't get up.

"He won't do it again." I pulled the kid out of his chair by the back of the shirt and urged him out of the office. Fucking school rules. I hated them, but I didn't want what I went through at school for Denton. It sucked being the odd one out. Being weird wasn't cool, but he didn't need to be throwing his weight around.

"Welcome to parenthood," the security guard muttered under her breath. I let the door slam behind me.

The walk home was quiet. It wasn't often I was alone with the boy. I wasn't sure how to connect, other than when we were in the ring. Fighting was my connection, so walking along the sidewalk like normal people was strange.

He finally spoke as we waited for the light to change. "Gus isn't coming home, is he?" He kicked a rock and watched it bounce.

"Don't know." I figured it was best to be blunt.

He shoulders sagged. "Those kids, they deserved what they got, Uncle Trig. They're fuckin' assholes."

I gave him a sideways glance.

"They said me and Fin were orphans living in a warehouse."

I tried to hide my annoyance. Kids were assholes.

"It's not blood that makes family. It's about loyalty and respect." His hopeful eyes blinked up at me, and I could see he needed more. Fuck. "You got more family than all those kids combined."

"Still assholes, though."

My hand clamped down on Den's shoulder when I caught sight of someone's head as it jerked back between two buildings. I should have known he'd be here. His partner's family owned the coffee shop he was next to.

"What?"

I shook my head and kept moving forward, placing him on the other side of me. Just as we came up on the alleyway, I swung out and slammed the man to the brick wall.

"Jesus, Trigger!" Officer Doyle screamed in my face, fear widening his eyes. "What are you doing here?"

Was he hiding from me? Normally, Doyle pranced around all puffed up and shit. Usually hid behind his badge.

Everything clicked.

"Whose kid is it?"

He tried to shove my hand away, but my grip only tightened.

"You thought sending your slutty sister with a kid to my club was going to rock me?" I managed a dark smile and showed the devil's damage in my eyes. "I crawled my way out of a triple life sentence with no chance of parole." I leaned in and lowered my voice. "Let's remember how I managed that."

"It wasn't my idea—"

My fist met his stomach, but I kept him upright, so the pain was more intense.

"You touch my family, I'll touch yours."

"I have to do as he asks!"

"Who?" I twisted my fingers into his bruised muscles.

"Your father! Your fucking father!"

What?

"Where is he?" He tried to answer, but I shook him hard.

"Last I heard," he struggled to think straight, "he was back in Vegas."

"If I find out you know more, I'll start to leak the information about you and the sergeant's daughter."

His face fell, and I knew I had him.

"It's not your kid."

"Keep your sister away from my family, or you'll find her at the bottom of the pier."

I slugged him again and dropped him to the ground then pushed Denton back out on the street. I heard him giggle, and I shook my head.

"That was different."

"Sure thing, Uncle Trig."

***

Tess

My skin was covered in a thin layer of sweat, and it made my shirt grab and hold as I stretched to reach the glasses. The storm system that was coming in brought rain, which meant high humidity and an all-around sticky feel.

I felt him come up behind me and trap me in place. His hands landed on my hips, and his lips found my neck. I loved the solid feel of his muscled body.

"The kid isn't mine."

I froze for a half a second before I sagged with relief.

"How are you sure?"

"I ran into Doyle."

I didn't want to know what that meant, so I happily shook off that particular stress as I grabbed a wedge of lemon and started to chop it into little pieces.

"Anything else I should know about?" I twisted in his hold to look at him face to face. His eyes were dark pools of pissed-off-ness. Of course, my chest tightened, and my nipples hardened. "I don't share, so don't stray."

His thumb stroked down the side of my neck, and I heard Morgan whistle at the others to get out.

Trigger reached behind me and grabbed something, then his hand slipped into the front of my bikini bottoms under my skirt and pushed something up inside me.

I yelped when I felt the cold and realized it was an ice cube. He lowered his head and slowly drank me in. Fuck, that alone nearly tipped me over the edge.

I heard the release of his belt, but I was lost in the delicious smell of his shaving cream. The ice was starting to melt, and it was a pain-pleasure thing.

He reached down and swung me out from behind the bar and onto the pool table. I didn't have a moment to think before he glided into me. He sucked in a sharp breath at the chill, but he didn't stop until he was all the way in.

Trigger grabbed my hips and hauled me up so he was still in me, but I had to strain to look into his eyes.

"Choose your words carefully, Tess." He gave a hard flick of his hips that made my mouth open. "You are embedded deeply into this club now, and there's no getting out." He smiled at his choice of words.

I nearly licked my lips with need—need for him to lose it. My back bowed, and every part of me screamed for him to flip.

"Don't ever give me a reason to leave." I barely registered the words coming out of my mouth, but I was hanging on by a thread.

"We got to stop meeting like this," a familiar voice broke through my bubble of lust. Trigger jerked back, grabbed his gun, and pointed it at the man standing by the bar with a smug smile.

I wiggled back and pulled my skirt down, not that there was a reason to. He'd seen all of me before.

"Who the fuck are you?" Trigger barked and eyed the door for Big

Joe.

"Your bouncer is a little distracted with my friend outside. I'm here to see her." He smiled at me, and I wanted to coil up like a snake and strike. His eyes flickered over my shoulder, and I saw his demeanor change. "Matt, it's been a while."

Brick came to my side, his gun held up like Trigger's. "Not long enough."

"Agreed." He stepped a little closer but held his hands up to show us he wasn't carrying. "Tessa, can I have a moment alone with you?"

"No," both Trigger and Brick answered for me.

"Brick?" Trigger's tone changed.

"Leon Davis, old client before Felicia made him her errand boy." Leon nodded like he was impressed. "Clark never liked him."

"Why?"

Brick glanced over at Trigger and gave him a look. "The same reason you hated Clark." I watched him as he absorbed that one.

"Guys." I rounded the pool table and pushed Leon to the front of the bar and into a chair. "You have five minutes."

"Only need two." He pulled out a wrinkled envelope. "Tess, Lilly's mom needs your help."

I snatched the envelope and fished out the letter. I quickly scanned the words, a mother's desperate plea for help. Lilly was sick, and the bills were becoming too much for her.

I held the paper up with a laugh. "Seriously? This is just pathetic, Leon."

"What?" He glanced at Trigger, who had gotten a phone call.

"Oh, come on, I really expected a little more from you—" In a heartbeat, he whipped out of his chair, pressed a gun to my head, and wrapped his other arm around my neck.

What? My head fought to catch up.

"And I expected a little more from you, Tess." He half laughed but stopped when Trigger and Brick both raised their guns. "You went from luxury to frat house."

"Screw you, Leon. You don't know jack shit about my life."

"I know more than you think." His sweaty fingers dragged across my scar, and I wanted to head butt him.

"Hey!" Trigger drew our attention. "You come into my club and point a gun at my family?" Trigger's voice was deep and haunting. "That's suicide." I noticed he kept his phone to his ear.

Leon yanked me back against him and leaned to look out the door.

"You think I'd come here alone?" He breathed in deeply through his nose. "You still smell how I remember."

"Sadly, so do you." I tried to wiggle free, but he pressed the tip of the steel harder into my temple, and my pulse beat wildly against it.

Think, Tess.

"You know what happened to the last guy who did this?" I bit out. "I slaughtered him in his lover's bed."

He chuckled in my ear and fixed his grip around my neck. "I know. I watched the video of you leaving. Nothing sexier than a dangerous woman. Turns me on." He pressed his erection into my back, and I wanted nothing more than to cut it off at the root.

"Tess," Trigger began but stopped as at least fifteen other men I had never seen before came in with long rifles.

My body temperature plummeted, and I locked eyes with Trigger. I could tell he was counting how many of them there were.

"Like I said," Leon stood a little straighter and visibly relaxed, "I didn't come alone."

"Here, take this." He shoved me into the arms of some other sweaty guy who reeked of BO. "Now," Leon rubbed his gun against his brow, "all this can go away, if you just give me the flash drive."

"What?" flew out of my mouth. "That's why you're here?"

"Why are you so surprised? Oh!" He laughed wickedly. "You thought I was here to find dear old Clark. Why would I do that when I can make a quick eighty grand for delivering the flash drive?"

Huh?

Leon traveled over to the bar and examined a bottle of whiskey on the shelf. He rolled it along the palm of his hand. "Now, hand over the flash drive or your club will be blown to shit."

As soon as I saw Morgan and Big Joe peek around the corner, something came over me.

"Fine," I said, and Trigger hissed at me to shut up. "It's not worth the club, Trigger."

"Oh, Tessa," Leon dropped the bottle on the floor with a smash and rounded the bar toward me, "you think after all these years I would trust anything that comes out of that pretty little mouth of yours?"

I shrugged. "Yeah, I guess you're right." I bent down and shot backward to use the fucker who was holding me as a brace to kick Leon straight in the chest. He was bigger than I was, but for that one second, he lost his focus, and I was freed.

Bullets flew in all directions. I quickly dropped to the floor and crawled under a table. The shit-ass that held me fell with his head turned toward me, half his face missing.

I reached out and grabbed the handgun from his holster. I checked the clip, and there was a full round. I popped up and popped right back down again.

Holy shit.

I gave myself a mini pep talk in the middle of a freakin' shootout. I pushed aside my fear and peeked out to find one of Leon's guys firing off a huge rifle. The sound nearly burst my eardrums. I pointed at him and squeezed the trigger. Nothing. His pissed expression turned toward me, and he smiled. The gun swung at me as my finger flipped over the safety.

Pop!

Pop!

Two shots to the neck, not my best work, but it would fucking do. I swiveled around to find my next victim, then Rail flung his body over the table I was under and landed nearly on top of me.

"Thought you could use this." He held up a gun, all excited about the fight.

Pop!

I shot the man who came up behind Rail.

"Already got one."

"I think I just came."

I was able to take out four more men before the silence took over. Trigger's massive hand reached down and hauled me to my feet.

"You good?"

"Think so."

"Everyone else?" Everyone checked in, and I let my breath go when I saw Brick step out from behind the door in one piece.

Trigger tucked me against him while he looked around the room.

"I'm thinking we need to stop using glass behind the bar," Rail muttered as he sidestepped one of the dead guys. "Joe's hit."

"I'm fine." Joe pulled his shirt down to look at the bullet graze. "Nothing a Band-Aid and some rum can't fix."

"What the hell was this?" Morgan tossed his gun on the bar, pissed. "We're just letting anyone in now?"

Trigger grabbed Big Joe by the shirt and shoved his gun in his face. "Why did you let him in?"

"Some chick distracted me." Joe's eyes bulged. "I didn't even see the others."

“She could have been killed!” he boomed. “We all could have been killed. You’re telling me you didn’t see twenty men hanging outside the clubhouse with long guns?”

“No,” he answered calmly, “I didn’t. I’m sorry, but I didn’t.”

Trigger waited a beat before he let him go and reached for me and tugged me forward.

“Is anyone going to point out the big, fat elephant in the room?” Rail lit a joint and squinted. He always looked so relaxed after anything insane happened.

Brick tipped a stool to clear the glass and eased onto it. “Dear old Felicia, always about money, never about love.”

“Was it ever about love, or just about the competition with her daughter?” Rail snickered.

“She’s twisted.” Trigger spoke like he was a million miles from us.

“And people wonder why I am the way I am.”

“I’m fucking sick of this shit.” Trigger looked around the bar at all the dead bodies that littered the floor.

“Clean this shit up and hire a second doorman.”

CHAPTER ELEVEN

Trigger

"Where is he?" I parked my bike, slammed down the kickstand, and headed toward the bar.

"Back window." Park, my Oregon VP, pointed. "Doorman's got itchy fingers. Last time, I lost my prospect. Don't want to lose another."

I nodded and moved in front of him, and they followed.

"Nah, man." The sweaty guy with cheap sunglasses stepped in my way. "No DRs in this club." I didn't break stride. My fingers curled into a heavy fist, and in a blur, I plowed it into the side of the doorman's head. He crumpled to the ground, and I kicked the door in.

The place went silent. Some scattered, and I could hear the scrape of several guns as they were snatched up and pointed at me. I cracked my neck slowly and stood there to let my eyes adjust. My cut said a lot, and no one wanted to be the one to draw attention. I pointed at the shit in the corner.

"I'm here for him."

The bartender nodded, and they lowered their weapons. The shit in question looked everywhere at once to find an escape route and started to run, but someone tripped him. I walked over and stood above him then reached down and hauled him up. I nodded my thanks toward the room; I wanted no interference. Then I threw the piece of shit up against the wall.

"Tell me what you know."

"I don't know shit."

"I hate repeating myself." I reached back for a stool and snapped off one of the legs over my knee.

"You're insane." He held up his hands and closed his eyes. "All I know is they were traveling back to the west coast."

"What else?"

"Nothing! I swear, nothing."

I snapped my fingers, and Park handed me his phone. I turned it around and watched his face fall.

"You know nothing, yet you were seen with Zay?"

"They just wanted me to find your girl. They did mention your uncle was still alive."

"Did you find my girl?"

"No, I haven't! Fuck, man, I hardly looked." He sputtered in fear as spit flew from his mouth, and his eyes were wild. "Look, man, I mean nothin' to them, really."

"Lucky for you, you mean nothing to me either."

I tossed the broken wood in the air, caught the bottom, turned, and jammed it through his neck. He cried out as I stepped forward and pulled out the stick, and blood shot from his neck all over me and my crew. I kicked his feet out from under him and pushed him backward.

"Anyone have any information for me? Now is the time to speak up." The entire bar went still; they knew I meant what I said. "I know you've heard Devil's Reach is on a hunt for any Stripe Back and Serpent who has hooked up with my father. If you hear anything, find me, and I will compensate you. If I hear you have helped him in any way, I will find you, and I will fuckin' kill you slow." I tossed the dripping stick on the ground, turned, and left the bar.

Before I got on my bike, I swiped at the blood that dripped from my hoodie with sticky fingers, then pushed it back and ran my hands through my hair to clean them. I kicked it into gear and signaled my men to fall into formation. I wasted no time heading back to the city. I needed to know how the rest of the chapters were doing.

"Where were you?" Cooper met me in the hallway with a handful of vodka bottles.

"Oregon is handled."

"Stripe Backs?"

"Yeah."

"Long-ass drive for you."

I shrugged. "Worth it to make a point."

"Looks like it." He grinned and headed down the hallway.

My shower was stained red when I was finished. I tossed out my clothes and hung up my cut. I didn't like not wearing it, but it needed to dry. I tugged on a t-shirt and headed outside to clear my head.

I rubbed the cat under her chin and listened to her whine. It had been weeks since I'd seen her. After all the shit that went down, I wouldn't have been surprised if she was gone.

"I kept her company." Morgan came up behind me and rested his arms on the back of the truck. "I found her eating in the trash. I tried to catch her, but she bolted to your truck. I figured you allowed it, so I fed her 'til you came back."

I nodded my thanks. Morgan was good at keepin' shit quiet.

"He's heading out," he said quietly as he lit a smoke. "Was hopin' to tail him."

My forearms rested on the side of the truck bed as we both faced away from the clubhouse.

"Where's he off to?"

"Death Valley Junction."

Slowly, I turned, and we mirrored the same expression.

"That so?"

"Hmm. Could be a trap?"

"Yeah, could be."

I ran through all the scenarios that might come from tailing him, but none ended with all my guys returning in one piece.

"Looks like we need to do a road trip of our own." I rubbed the kitty's ear. "Call Cray, tell him to set up a meeting. *He* wouldn't question that."

"Will do."

Trigger: Will you track someone for me?

Mike: What's the number?

I snapped a photo of the serial number on the back of the tracking device and attached it to my text.

Trigger: I'll turn it on within the next twenty.

Mike: I'll be in touch.

Trigger: My debt is getting large.

Mike: Repayment's a bitch.

The bar was quiet when I left my office. Tess was chatting with Minnie, and Peggy was making a show of scraping shit off a table but really was hitting on a friend of Cooper's.

"Peggy." I waved her over, and she dropped the knife she was using and hurried like she was about to get laid.

"Come to your senses yet?"

"Do me a favor."

"What do I get in return?" She glanced down at her boobs.

"Advice."

Her face twisted in confusion. "Advice?"

"Take this," I handed her the black device that looked like a cell phone, "give it to Rail."

"Why can't you?"

I glared at her. The fucking nerve of this woman.

"Fine!" She tossed up her hands. "Whatever."

"Brick and Morgan, pack your bags. We leave for Cray's in an hour."

The two men didn't miss a beat as they headed to their rooms to pack up.

Tess was watching me. She told Minnie to hold on while she made her way in my direction.

"Where are we going?"

"You need to stay here."

She looked doubtful as she folded her arms.

"Is it Gus?"

"It's a lead." I scanned the room to see who was in earshot. "Stay here and don't leave the club. I'll be back tomorrow night."

"Trigger," she pulled my attention down to her worried face, "you're going to come back to me, right?"

"Tess—"

"Don't lie to me, Trigger." I saw the fire lick her insides. It was one of the things I loved about her. No bullshit, she wanted it straight. "I will cut you in your sleep."

I couldn't help but smirk, but it quickly faded when I realized she was serious.

"Just ask Bret. Oh, wait, you can't," she joked darkly, but I could see a part of her was bothered by it.

"I will." I wrapped my arms around her shoulders and kissed her hard. "Don't leave."

"Fine." She nodded then went back to where Minnie was waiting for Brick to come out.

"Ryder." My voice boomed through the room as he raced by with a bag of trash. He fit in well as a prospect, kept his head down and listened. I guided him away from the others. "You watch Tess. She stays at the club. You hear me?"

He nodded, but I could tell he was worried. "You, ah…you know she doesn't really listen, right?"

I handed him a different cell, ignoring the fact that he was right. "Use this to call me. Don't use yours. I want updates every few hours."

"Okay. Everything okay, boss?"

"No one comes in the club unless they're a member."

He nodded again. "Are we expecting company?"

"I sure fucking hope not."

I answered my phone and headed out, giving Tess one last look. "Mike, tell me you have it."

***

Tess

"I really can't tell if you're flirting." I laughed, and Rail gave me a wink from behind the cigarette that flopped around between his lips.

"Well," he eyed the man sitting next to him, "that's just depressing."

"It's your approach." I finished drying the cutting board and leaned my hip into the bar as I gave him the once-over. "You come in hard and fast like some seventeen-year-old pimple puss, all hyped up and round-eyed with the prospect of sex."

"And that's a bad thing, I'm excited?"

"Yes." I swatted his arm. "I'm not a woman who wants romance, but," I held up my hand, "I'm still a woman, and we still have a built-in little swoon factor. You need to be smooth but not sleazy."

"I'm not sleazy." His head pulled back like he was genuinely shocked by this idea.

"Oh, Rail," I cupped his cheek, "you are the sleaziest."

"That hurts, you know." He lit another joint then openly ogled a woman who walked by. When his eyes met mine again, his eyebrows rose with guilt. "That was different."

"Hopeless." I started to turn, but he grabbed my arm to stop me.

"Please don't give up on me, Tess. I have a problem."

"We all know that already," Peggy huffed then glared at me. "There's a package for you in Trigger's room."

"Hey, Peggy," Rail leaned over and fingered a piece of her hair, "your eyes are like little drops of heaven. If I'm not careful, I might get lost in them."

Of course, a sleazy line like that would get Peggy to grin. Only thing was, her lipstick had stained her teeth red, and it definitely broke the moment.

"I can't." Rail stood with his hands in the air. "Nope. Not happening."

"Don't blame you." I laughed and locked the bar cash box.

"What?" Peggy whined and looked around to try to understand what we were talking about. "What did I do?"

"You need a mirror in your life," Brick muttered from the front door.

"Tess!" Cooper slumped at the bar. "I thought you were meeting me for breakfast by the pier?"

"Oh, my God." I smacked my forehead, irritated that I'd stood him up. "I'm sorry, Coop. Fin needed a walk to school, and halfway there I noticed Vib hadn't packed him a lunch, so I swung by the store to get some stuff to make him one." I leaned forward to smile at him. "I'm really sorry." I didn't mention the hardest part was convincing Ryder it was okay for me to leave the club to walk the kid the short distance to school.

"Meh, you can make it up to me somehow."

"Absolutely." I gave him a quick squeeze before I stepped away from the bar.

I glanced at Ryder, who watched me like a hawk. Clearly, he had strict instructions to keep an eye on me. "I'll be right back. I just need to take him his lunch."

He nodded but looked pathetic. I thought he should feel a little better because I had returned after walking Fin the first time. "It's hot, and I need a quick change before I go. Do you want to come watch?" I couldn't help but tease him. He was such a mess, and I could almost see the sweat as it stained his armpits. He shook his head and stepped aside to let me pass. He really needed to relax a little. Freaking out about my every move wasn't going to help anyone.

Once I was down the hallway and away from the others, I pulled out my phone, hoping Trigger had texted me.

Nothing.

With my head down, I rounded the corner and into our room. I set my Netflix to *The Fall* and headed into the bathroom where I kicked off my shoes, peeled off my clothes, and shimmed on a cotton shirt and jean shorts.

The box caught my attention. Oh, yeah, my package. I wondered who it was from. It was bulky and looked damp, and the sides bowed out a bit.

Why would they set it on the bed? Why not on the floor or the table?

With a pocketknife, I tore back the clear tape and pried the flaps open. My knees balanced on the mattress as I peeled the plastic back.

What the hell?

It took about four seconds for my head to catch up with my eyes, and about six for my voice to find itself and tear through my vocal cords in a throat-ripping scream.

I hopped back, which made the bed jerk and the box jump. The severed head was stuffed into the box so it stared straight up into my eyes.

"Ahhh!" I couldn't do anything but scream. The smell hit my nose, and my stomach tried everything not to bring up my breakfast.

Holy shit! I squeezed my eyes shut and tried to erase the memory that was now burned into my retinas.

From somewhere, the screams became louder. I fisted my chin and locked my elbows together as my chest shook with fear.

There were moments when shock could be so damaging that your brain turns off. The impact of what you have witnessed plowed through to your core, like a punch to the soul. Everything stopped, and you were left a fragile, empty casing.

That was me, right here, in this very moment.

"Sweet hell!" Rail, gun drawn, burst through the door with Ryder right behind him. Big Joe was tight on their heels. Both circled my room, all sense of fun from the earlier banter lost.

"Tess?" Big Joe stood in front of me and shook my shoulders gently. "What happened?"

"The box." I pulled myself together enough to point with a shaky hand. "Jace is inside." Once the words slipped past my lips, I slapped my hand over my mouth to stop what was coming next. I couldn't break down, not yet.

"Oh, shit." Rail gagged dramatically, which was shit. Rail loved anything disturbing. "That's just nasty."

Big Joe positioned himself in front of me to block my view, and his arm landed over my shoulders to give me a side hug.

"I'm sorry you had to see that, Tess. People are animals." Most people would have thought Big Joe didn't have feelings. He just worked the door and remained in the background most of the time. Really, he was a huge softy who had been nothing but good to me since I arrived. He never questioned my loyalty to the club either, unlike some others. I hugged him back.

"They couldn't have left his arms on? I have nothing to grab onto. Gross." Rail snickered. "Ears it is, man." He pulled out his cigarette and put it out on the side of Jace's face. My mouth dropped open, and Joe made a sick sound.

"What?" Rail shrugged. "Not like he can feel it."

"Come on," Joe pulled me out of the room, "let Rail deal with it."

Big Joe sat me at a table, and Ryder joined us.

"Shit, Tess, I'm so sorry. Are you okay?"

"Somebody sent her Jace's head in a box." Big Joe had his phone out. "What do you think? I need to call Trigger."

"No, don't," I pleaded. "He's got enough on his plate. Give me the night to deal with it. I'll be all right."

"Sorry, chicky, we have rules." He tried two times, but Trigger wasn't picking up.

"I have—" Ryder started to say but stopped short.

"You have what?" Joe asked.

"I thought I had something, but I remember it broke." He eyed me for a moment before he left the room.

"Strange kid." Joe took the seat across from me and gave me a sad smile. "You okay?"

I shrugged. "Yeah. I think I'm still in shock."

"Good." He nodded. "It's a numb feeling like a car idling. Live in that moment for as long as you can."

Super.

***

Allen

DR: Change in plans. Meet me in the other spot.

"Fuck."

Allen: On the way.

"Fox, Zay, change in plans. We're meeting at the shop." I grabbed the keys and headed out to the car.

"Father Allen, is that you? Are you back in town?" One of the most annoying chicks in the church stopped me at the door.

Gawd. I forced my annoyance down.

"Ms. Terrance, how are you this fine day?" I flashed a million-dollar smile at her but secretly hoped she'd get hit by the next car that drove by.

"I'm well, thank you. I'm thankful for our Grace that I'm able to stand without any help."

It took all my power not to roll my eyes as her long story continued about her painful gout condition. She should stop eating, for fuck's sake. Fat old cow.

She reached out and touched my arm and left her hand there. "I can feel him, you know, every time I touch you."

That's the Devil reaching out to say if you don't leave, he will send the reaper to deal with your gout. But think what you will, you old bat.

I kind of liked the idea that she could feel the power inside me.

"How kind." I covered her hand with mine and gave it a squeeze. It took everything inside me not to break her fingers. Fuck me, what was it with people needing to touch me to feel complete?

"I'm sorry, Ms. Terrance," I removed her hand from my arm, "but I'm in desperate need of supplies for our church, so if you don't mind—"

"Oh, dear, do you need help? Perhaps a donation? I'd love to help our church."

That stopped me.

"My, Ms. Terrance, I think that would be a lovely gesture. Your generosity will be rewarded by the Lord, I'm sure."

She pulled out a sizable wad of cash and started to count the hundreds. "Will this do?" She showed me six hundred.

I took the wrist that held the rest of the money and closed my eyes, "Dear Lord, will you please steer the dear, sweet Ms. Terrance on just how much money we need?"

I peeked out from under my lashes and saw she was beaming at the opportunity.

"Oh," I jerked excitedly, "he says this will do." I gently pulled the stack of cash from one hand and the six hundred from the other. "Bless your kind heart." I turned and walked back to the car.

"I feel him!" she shouted, still stuck in her trance. "I feel the Lord."

I nodded at her with a smile and started the car.

"Nice." Fox reached through the seat and started to count the money while Zay remained quiet. "Six, eight, a thousand. Damn, boss, we have about fifteen hundred."

"Not bad for the Lord's work."

"That was messed up," Zay muttered and avoided my glare.

"You can't be a killer and harp about my methods."

"You speak about the devil, so I know you believe. What will you do when you meet the man above?"

I laughed, which pissed him off. Zay was no saint, but he had become fucked up in the head after setting eyes on Tess.

"I'll be saying the same thing you will be, Zay. Where's the down elevator?"

I laughed and slammed the car into reverse but not before I gave Ms. Terrence an overly dramatic wave goodbye.

The parking lot was empty, so it was easy to spot his bike parked a bit away in the bushes. I noticed his overnight bag was not in evidence, which made me curious.

"You're not staying?" I asked as he stepped out of the side door.

"Not this time. Something feels off."

"Hence the new meeting place. Stop worrying. Everything is going to go smoothly. Are we still on for Friday?"

His gaze followed a truck behind me. "Let's do it tonight. Trigger has his chapters combing for information on you. It's only a matter of time."

I took a moment to think it through. Yeah, that was doable. "All right." I nodded at Fox to make it happen.

"How's Gus?"

I shrugged. "Still alive, if that's what you're asking."

"Won't be able to walk right anymore." Fox jabbed him in the arm, missing the social cues that he wasn't in the mood to play around.

"Did he ever?" Zay snickered from behind me. He was a moody son of a bitch sometimes.

I checked my phone while I rubbed my chin, thinking. "You have anything to tell me?"

"No, they're still chasing a lead up north. They have no clue you're so close."

I tugged on my stiff collar, about ready to knife his balls. He must have caught my mood, as he cleared his throat and tried again.

"You just need to say when and where, and I'll have her there."

"Tomorrow morning," Zay cut in.

I made a hissing sound in the back of my throat as a warning to Zay to shut the fuck up.

"You want tomorrow, boss, I'll have her there."

My head started to pound, not with pain but with excitement. To have that little bitch back in my custody would really send Trigger off the deep end.

"Tomorrow, nine a.m., surf shop by the pier." I stepped up and removed his glasses, handing them to Zay. I studied his eyes, searching for any signs of betrayal, but all I got was a tired, burned-out soul staring back at me.

"I've kept your secret for well over a decade, Allen," he muttered. "Think by now I've earned a little trust."

"Can't blame a man for lack of trust after his own son tried to kill him."

He snatched his Ray-Bans back from Zay and slipped them over his eyes to give them the cover they needed. The shades couldn't hide the deeply etched crow's feet at the corners.

"And who saved your life when no one else did?"

"Case in point, and you will soon have your promised reward." I offered my hand, and he gave it a good shake before he settled in on his bike and left.

CHAPTER TWELVE

Trigger

"How many?" I whispered to Morgan when he poked his head inside the garage. We had chased Fox to this location, and even though it was a trap, I didn't care. We were that much closer to Gus.

Morgan closed his eyes and cursed. "At least twelve."

"Which really means fifteen." No one accounted for the men at the doors and the men who stayed on high ground.

"What now?" Brick crawled over and leaned against the cool wall.

I checked my ammo and flexed my neck. "Now we go in."

"Oh, fuck," Morgan hissed. "Your father is here."

Really?

My phone buzzed, but I didn't have the mind space to check it.

"Now we let them know we took the bait."

I grabbed my radio. "You ready?"

"Yup, ten-four," Cray responded. "Waitin' on your word to move."

I nodded to the guys, and we hopped to our feet, kicked in the door, and started to spray bullets.

I got almost a clip off when I saw Gus in the corner of the room. He looked close to dead.

"Morgan." I pointed to my uncle. He raced over while I covered him.

Brick took out two men who came up behind me, and three more when they raced through the door. My gun became useless, so I tossed it and started to cage fight the men who kept coming. I punched, kicked, snapped, and popped any bone that swung my direction. Screams filled the air, and I only hoped my men were coming out on top.

"Ah." I got the wind knocked out of me by a two-by-four. The man who held it had a chain around his neck like a dog. I grinned and waited for him to make his move. Classic beef-head went to punch me in my gut. I jumped so he'd miss and followed through with a blow right under the arm. He twisted and exposed his other side, and I kicked and ground my heel into his ribs. Once he felt the impact, I put an elbow to his nose and rammed his head into the concrete floor.

I stood and cracked my neck then caught sight of *him* way up high in the rafters, watching the bloodshed.

A long, powerful grin spread across his lips before he stepped back into the shadows.

"Brick!" I pointed to the stairs, and he followed me. I took three at a time, sometimes four, and made it to the top in a matter of seconds.

Back and forth I searched the rafters but found no sign of anyone.

"Shit!" My shout shook the old windows.

"We got Gus." That was something.

I leaned over the railing, drew in a deep breath, and tried to calm myself. My hands shook in front of me. He was so close I could barely handle the rage.

"I got you." Morgan helped Gus to his feet. He wobbled, but he was able to carry most of his own weight.

I pushed off the rail and hurried past Brick.

"Hey," he stepped in front of me, "we came to get Gus, and we got him. That's something positive."

I smiled.

"He wanted us to find Gus."

I raced down the steps and out to the van. I yanked open the door and sat next to Gus, who was propped up against the back of the driver's seat. I placed my hand on his shoulder until he opened his eyes and focused on me.

"Should've left me there."

"Don't tempt me." I gave him a light swat before I let him close his eyes. He looked like shit, but he could talk, so that meant something.

"Hey," he stopped me as I turned to leave, "it's getting worse, anyway." He patted his chest, and I knew what he meant. Gus had stage three breast cancer. He had been through all the treatments before, and if it was back, I knew this time around he probably wasn't going to beat it. Although the bastard would never admit it, I knew he would be scared. After all he'd been through in his life, what a shit-assed way to go.

I hit the side of the van to let them know to leave, and to let off some of my residual pressure.

My phone vibrated, and I fished it out of my pocket and saw three missed calls and five texts.

6:02 p.m.
Ryder: Problem at the club. Call me.

6:20 p.m.
Ryder: Something doesn't feel right.

10:00 p.m.
Ryder: Tess is fine. She's in bed.

10:30 p.m.
Big Joe: Call me.

11:00 p.m.
Big Joe: Tess had a hard night.

I tried Tess's phone three times, but she wasn't picking up. What the fuck was going on? I tried Ryder, but his phone went right to voicemail. I rubbed my head and tried the other phone I'd given him, but still no answer. Frustrated as hell, I punched in another number.

"Hey, man." Rail sounded tired.

"What the fuck happened?"

"Your father thought Tess would like a souvenir of her friend."

"Meaning?" I grew annoyed.

"Allen sent her Jace's head in a box."

What?

"It was all juicy and soaked right through the cardboard. Whoever dropped it off put it on your bed."

That made my blood burn. Who the fuck would do that, and how would they get into my room? Then it hit me—the mole.

"How is she?"

"Freaked out, but she looks calm. She spent most of the night with the boys. I think she's nervous to sleep in the room. You know Tess. She won't show much emotion when it comes to this stuff."

"I'm an hour away. Get the medic there in time for us."

"You mean you found him?"

"Get a medic."

"Yeah, boss."

A text came through, and I yanked the phone away to look at the screen.

Cameron: 8 Stripe Backs dead, zero info. On to the next hit.

I didn't have the head space or the desire to send the word out that Gus was found. For now, they could continue killing as many rats as they could find.

I tried Tess one more time but had no luck. Instead, I leaned my head back and closed my eyes.

"Here." Gus handed me a shiny baseball bat. "Ever played before?"

I shook my head, but I knew from TV what to do. Gus grinned and started to walk backward.

"You ready?" He drew his hand back, lifted his knee, and threw the ball right to me. I waited to see its angle then swung with all my might. The ball hit the bat and soared well over Gus's head and into the woods.

"Shit, boy!" He pulled his hat off and wiped his forehead free of sweat. "You can hit!"

I had no clue I was good at any sport. I had never been given the opportunity to try.

Gus raced over. "Nolan, that was...wow! I've never seen anyone hit like that!" He raised his hands to show me what he was going to do. They landed on my shoulders, and his face beamed down at me.

"I'm proud of you."

Okay.

"Do you know what that means?"

I shrugged.

"It means you can do so much more than just toss a punch or a powerhouse kick. You have real talent."

Someone was proud of me? That felt odd, but strangely, I was all right with it. I mustered up a tiny smile, and I knew he caught it.

"Proud," he repeated then pulled out another ball from his pocket. "Let's see what else you can do."

The van stopped, and my eyes popped open. I turned to see out the window. We were home.

I opened the doors and jumped out. Brick and Morgan helped Gus out and into the bar.

The place went wild. Within minutes, the music was amped, the whiskey was passed around, and the celebration of one of our family being returned was in full swing.

Once the doctor took Gus out back to check him over, I rushed to my room, only to find it empty. I thought a moment then checked the boys' room, and sure as shit, she was there tucked in between them.

"Mother of shit!" I yelped in a loud whisper. A Lego gun had fired and shot something with prongs at my leg.

Suddenly, Tess sat straight up and pointed a handgun at me. Her eyes were wild, and her hair was everywhere, but she looked gorgeous. She was there protecting the last piece of Gus she could. My woman.

"Babe, lower the gun."

It took her a moment to register my voice, but she slowly lowered the weapon then covered her face with one hand.

"Hey," I sat on the edge of the bed and pulled a piece of her hair over her shoulder, "you all right?"

"Yeah," she whispered, sounding completely exhausted.

"I have something to show you."

She sniffed, and I leaned over the bed and scooped her up from between the boys. I put her on the floor and lifted her face and studied it. Her eyes were dull, and I wanted to completely check her over, but it could wait.

"You sure you're okay?"

She nodded, but I could tell what happened had really shaken her up. Jace and Tess had been friends, and what Allen pulled was fucked up.

"Come on." I tugged her hand for her to follow.

As soon as she felt the atmosphere of the bar, she picked up the pace.

"Oh, my God!" she cried in disbelief. "Oh, my God. *Gus!*"

Gus gave her a smile and tried to get up, but she ran over and forced him back into the chair. Her arms wrapped around him, and they took a moment to reconnect.

"You want me to get the boys?" she finally asked him as she eased carefully into the seat next to him, her arm still wrapped around him.

"Nah, let them sleep." He smiled warmly. "I'm tired, anyway. I'll just climb into bed and let them find me in the morning."

"Yikes. Look at you," Rail blurted but shrugged when everyone looked over. "Sorry, but he looks like a giant bruise." He pointed his beer at Gus. "That's where kids get nightmares."

"What?" Tess sighed dramatically. "I have so many questions about your upbringing, but no clue where to start."

"He's the perfect example why cousins shouldn't mate." Brick laughed, which sent the club into full party mode.

I sat back with my drink in my hand and watched my club begin to mend itself. Tonight, we could party and celebrate the return of our own, but tomorrow, the hunt continued.

Most partied well into the morning. I didn't think I could feel my hands at one point, we drank so much. Most of my men passed out in the chairs, but somehow, I peeled myself off the bar stool and made it to my bed.

The smell of peanut butter brought me out of my sleep. A strange sound found my ears, and then my eye was being pried open by sticky fingers.

"You in there?" Fin leaned right down and nearly touched his eye to mine. "Uncle T!" He shouted a little louder. "Hello."

"He's going to swat you," Denton muttered from somewhere else in the room.

My eyelid was released, and I snapped it closed. I wasn't ready to get up yet. The last time I looked at the clock, it was three, and Tess had come to bed naked, so I hadn't shut my eyes until five. It was now seven, and someone was about to be killed.

"I know what will work." I heard Fin run out of the room and race back in a few moments later. "Shhh," he whispered loudly. "He's like a lion. One wrong move, and whack!"

More footsteps came and went.

"I wouldn't do that," Denton warned, and I wanted to roll over to see what the fuck was going on, but I was too tired to bother, and I still hoped they would bugger off. I heard someone leave and relaxed a bit.

A warm, small hand slid over my shoulder. I froze momentarily but shook off the instant wave of hate that being touched brought as she moved to my chest. Slowly, she shifted onto the bed, and her hand found my erection. Every morning should be this way.

I rolled onto my back and let her lips travel down my chest to the waistband of my briefs. I lifted so she could pull them down. Again, her lips were on me, making their way down. My hands found her hair, and my eyes snapped open.

"What the fuck, Peggy?" I glared at Fin, who was in the doorway with Tess. They both looked confused, and Tess looked like she might murder both of us.

"What?" She smiled with wet lips and stared back at me. "You didn't seem to mind." She grabbed my erection and made me jump.

"You're a ho, Peggy!" Fin screamed before he ran down the hallway and slammed the door.

Tess crossed her arms and shook her head as she kicked the door shut behind her. Peggy stayed on her knees on the bed while I fought to get up.

"First Tammy, now Peggy." Fire blazed across her eyes. "She leaves, or I do."

"The fuck you say, bitch." Peggy wiggled to her feet and made her way over to Tess. "Who the fuck do you think you are?"

I should have seen it coming. Tess had on her look.

She hauled back and drove the palm of her hand hard upward into Peggy's nose and broke it.

The impact was powerful, and Peggy flew backward.

I allowed Tess to get a few kicks in, but when she grabbed a fistful of hair and pulled Peggy's head back, I grabbed her around the waist and turned her away.

"Enough," I hissed in her ear. "No more."

"Let me go!" She bucked out of my arms and stuck a finger in my face. "I told you I don't share."

"Tess," I sighed, annoyed at the situation, "I thought it was you."

"If you can't tell that tramp's kiss from mine—"

"Excuse me?" Peggy stood, blood pouring from her nose. "I've been here for a shit longer than you, and you need to watch your back, little girl. No one does this to me and gets away with it."

Tess went for her in a full-on charge. I held up a hand, but Tess ignored it. "Leave, Peggy." I grabbed Tess before she could do more damage. "That's enough, Tess."

"Like you wouldn't shoot someone if you found us in bed and someone was going down on me?"

It was like someone slugged me right in the center of my chest. I had to focus hard to keep a lid on my anger.

"Maybe we should test that theory." Her eyes blazed.

"I'll flip, and you won't like it this time." My chest heaved with the effort I was making to hold myself in.

She rushed toward me and shoved my shoulder, and it hit the wall.

Her hand clamped down on my erection, and she glared into my eyes.

"Open your goddamn eyes, Trigger. It's not like this was the first time."

My head jolted back. I wasn't aware she knew about the other times Peggy broke into my room.

"Yeah," she paused, "there's a lot I know." She squeezed me harder, and I fucking liked it. "I will not be one of your fuck and chucks. If I find you in bed with another chick, I'm done. Last warning."

I couldn't help but grin as I grabbed her hand, twisted her arm, and pushed her up against the wall, pinning her with my hips. I cupped her neck, and my thumbs held her chin in place to look at me.

"You think I would let you leave?" I lowered my head and drank in her scent. My dick begged for a dip, but I knew I needed her to see she wasn't like one of them.

"Then don't give me a reason to."

Something shifted inside. I dropped my hands and stepped back, confused by the feeling.

Her brows drew together, confused as well, then she looked down at herself and pretended to brush something off her shirt.

"I need to see Fin," she muttered and headed for the door.

"Tess." I struggled to find the right words.

"Don't bother, Trigger."

***

Tess

"As ordered." Big Joe set a box on the bar top with a huff. "Shit's heavy."

"Tess," Morgan tossed me his pocketknife, "stock the shelf."

I felt sick. The knife slipped around my sweaty palm, and my mouth felt dry.

"You okay, Tiger?" Morgan came into my view.

"Yeah, sorry." I shook off the haunted feeling.

Morgan waited a beat before he ripped the box open for me. "Just whiskey."

I nodded and let out long breath as the thought of the rest of Jace's body, possibly squashed into the box, faded from my head.

"You'll get past that feeling," Morgan muttered quietly.

"That's what I hear."

Trigger appeared, looking a little uneasy. His hands were at his sides, and his gaze shifted around the room.

"Morgan," his head was down, looking at his phone, "let the guys know about Gus, but that they have the green light to keep killing."

"Yeah, boss."

"Tess," he glanced up, "let's go."

"Where?" I pulled a bottle free and placed it on the top shelf, label out.

"I didn't say."

"Why not?" I pulled another from the box.

"Tess," he warned, and I knew not to push. I shrugged at Morgan, who nodded for me to go.

To my surprise, we drove to the pier, parked in the normal spot with the bike hidden from view, and like once before, he took my shoes and tucked them into his saddlebag.

"Come," he ordered and threaded a leather messenger bag over his shoulder. His huge hand engulfed mine, and I had to hurry to keep up with his strides.

I loved this place, especially at night when the sky was riddled with stars. Countless little flickers of light twinkled down on us, and the ocean reflected the moon's bright belly. It wasn't this clear very often, especially since we'd had so many storms lately. The clouds normally ruled the sky at night.

My eyes lit up when I saw the Ferris wheel was working again. I kind of hoped we were headed there, but he tugged me along underneath the pier and continued walking. The cool sand wedged its way between my toes and brushed over my ankles. I was enjoying the sensation when we came to a stop.

The lifeguard hut.

"What are we doing here?"

He tossed the bag then climbed up and reached down for me. He pulled me up effortlessly. My hands landed on his broad shoulders to stabilize my balance when he set me on my feet. I hopped up on the ledge to sit comfortably.

"This was where I knew."

"Knew what?" I shifted back when he hopped up and joined me on the ledge. For someone so massive, he was shockingly agile.

He reached into his bag, lit a joint, and offered it to me to take the first hit. It hit hard, but it was more of a body high versus a head high.

My muscles soon turned into goo, and I felt completely at ease.

"New?" I pointed to the tip that was held between his fingers.

"Nope, just wanted something a little different tonight."

"Why?"

He glanced over at me with his bright green eyes. I could see the moon reflected in them.

"This isn't something I thought I could do."

"What, sit here with me in silence?" I joked.

"Fall in love this hard."

My lungs felt sucked dry. Trigger didn't share emotion. I almost didn't know what to say. I shook off the discomfort of sharing our feelings because this was, after all, what I wanted. I needed to know I mattered more to him than anyone, and I wasn't just an easy lay. Trigger made me want even more.

"Peggy's out," he continued.

"I've heard that before, you know, about Tammy, but she still came back like a damn alley cat in heat."

He half smiled before he ghosted the dark sky with white smoke.

"And look where she ended up."

"True." I snagged the joint, needing something to do with my hands. "Is she really gone?"

"Yeah," he nodded, "Ryder packed her shit up and left it on the back step this morning."

"How was she?"

He shrugged. "You care?"

"Yeah, I kinda do."

"She was pissed, but that was because Rail chose some interesting words about her leaving."

"I totally missed all the good shit." I laughed, relieved the nasty tramp was finally gone.

We sat in silence for a while longer, our bodies molded to the side of the hut. The sea breeze kissed my cheeks with salty spray, and it left a sticky coating over my skin. Some people hated that feeling, but I loved it. For me, there was nothing like the ocean to calm my head.

"Why do you put those sticky markers all through the books you read?"

I pulled my mind away from the waves and repeated what he said to myself.

"Ah, you mean Savi's story?"

He nodded.

"Reasons." I was glad it was dark. I felt my cheeks heat.

"Which are?"

I knew he wasn't going to let it go. Trigger liked to know why I did things, especially if they were odd or unusual to him.

I tried to think about how to explain in a way he'd understand.

"Reading is personal, and certain scenes will make you feel a certain way. I like the way I feel when I read them, so I mark them. When I feel down or just want to feel something in general, I go back and read them again. To me, it's like reuniting with an old friend."

"Huh." He moved to sit a little straighter. "I read some of them."

That completely blew me away. "Why?"

"I wanted to know."

"Okay." I felt my neck join in on the blushing. "What did you feel when you read it?"

"It was a romance thing."

"Yeah." I sat up to see him better through the darkness. "But how did it make you feel?"

"I didn't feel much. I hardly do. But I maybe understand Cole a little."

Wow, I never thought I'd be here having this conversation with Trigger.

"How so?"

"He loved Savannah when he knew he shouldn't."

I wondered how much he had read to get that. Maybe more than he would ever say. I couldn't help but like that he said that, that he even picked up on it. I swung my legs over the edge to let them dangle and let my hair fall forward to act as a barrier between us.

"Are you saying you shouldn't love me?"

"Yes," he said roughly.

"Fuck me, Trigger, if you took me here to tell me that, then you really will give me a complex about Peggy."

He moved so one leg was behind my back while the other joined my legs that hung off the edge.

"I'm also saying I'm not someone you should love, but like Cole, I don't care. Call it selfish." He leaned in close and brushed his lips against my bare shoulder. "You make me see Nolan."

I turned my head to look at him. His face was inches from mine.

"Do you feel him?" I pressed my hand over his chest.

"Yeah," he whispered.

"You like that?"

"Yeah." He held still.

"How does it make you feel?" I sounded like a fucking therapist, but I wanted to know.

"Makes me feel human."

I felt the corners of my mouth rise. "I make you feel human?"

"Yeah."

I huffed with happiness from deep down in my throat. "That's a really nice thing to say."

He leaned in and gently kissed my cheek.

"You mentioned earlier that this was the place where you knew. What did you mean?"

He shifted closer. His body was wrapped around mine now.

"Remember when we hid in here from the Serpents?" I nodded and wiggled in closer to steal his warmth. "The next morning, when I sank the last body, I turned around and caught you flipping over the bloody rocks."

"Ha! Yeah."

"Most chicks would have freaked and run, or stood and watched. You helped."

"Equally fucked up, remember?" I grinned, and he let out a huff of amusement. I waited a beat and went with the truth. "I helped to protect you." I thought I should clear that up.

"Why?"

"Maybe I knew too," I whispered.

He shifted back, but then his chest returned to warm up the cool spot he made.

"The MC rules are if you're with us, you're with us for life."

"Okay." I wasn't sure what he was getting at.

"Are you with us?"

I hesitated for a moment, but when he opened his hand, I nearly fell forward. A huge black stone rested in the center of a black band lined with miniature black diamonds.

"I've got a jacked-up life and a seriously dysfunctional family, but you came in and made your mark, not just with me, but with everyone."

I couldn't find the right words, or maybe I was in shock, but he kept going, so I stayed quiet.

"You and I are different. We've learned to turn off and not feel, but you sparked something that was dead in me." He paused when he took my left hand in his. "You got no choice but to marry me, Tess." I pushed my finger through the ring then turned to grab his neck and pulled his lips to mine.

I twisted without breaking our kiss and straddled his lap. My mind fired off a hundred different emotions, but the one that stood out the most was that Trigger just confessed he needed me as much as I needed him.

"Say it, Tess," Trigger muttered between our kiss.

I grinned when I recognized a moment I couldn't resist.

"Not until you flip."

His eyes flickered with need, and in a blink, I was tossed on my back, and he was tearing off my clothes.

"Yes!" I screamed when he plunged inside me.

***

Allen

"She what?" I backhanded him across the face. "Don't lie to me."

"I'm not." He stood with his head down. "Happened three days ago."

I glanced at Zay, who looked like he was about to murder someone. He had his black gloves on as he screwed the silencer onto the end of his gun. He just needed me to say the word, but I wanted to be the one to kill my son, not him. He had lust, but I had rage. Rage always won.

"And Gus?"

"Better. He's up walking around. Things seem back to the way it was."

"Good." I rubbed my forehead and thought about my next move.

"When does school get out?"

His face fell, but he cleared his throat when I glared at him.

"You know the boys are my next move." I grabbed his Devil's Reach cut and held him to my face. "When does the youngest get off school?"

"One fifteen."

I smiled and roughly tapped his cheek, "Kids are never off limits."

"I thought you wanted the girl?"

"I did, but since you failed to deliver, I have now changed targets." I rubbed the jagged scar Gus had given me before I beat his ass to a bloody pulp and left him for Trigger. "The boy will be painful for Tessa, and that will be her payback for leaving."

"He's just a kid."

"And I'm just a man trying to gain back what was rightfully mine."

"Fucking sick. Am I done here?" he muttered.

"For now."

He glanced over at Zay with a grim look before he left.

"Zay," I watched my mole slam the door behind him, "make sure he doesn't get soft and tip anyone off."

"Gladly."

"Zay."

"Yeah?"

"Just the boy for now."

"Sure, for now."

CHAPTER THIRTEEN

Trigger

"I appreciate you meeting me here." I pulled the chair out and took a swig of the cold beer he had ordered me.

"Interesting location." Mike looked around at the restaurant I had chosen. It was a dive, but it was lowkey, and I knew most who of those who came and went.

I shrugged. "I know the owner, so we won't have any surprise visitors." Plus, I knew Mike didn't like being seen at my club. Cole had a hard enough time with it, so I didn't need to cause more shit for him.

"Why do you seem different?" He squinted at me. "You seem less stressed or some shit."

I wasn't about to share what happened with Tess and me. That was private. But what I did want to share was a long time coming. I never wanted the Devil's Reach to follow in my father's footsteps because that would mean the boys would have to follow after me. Nothing good came from dirty deals, so the fact this shit was over meant one less chain strapped around my chest. I pulled out a stack of papers and tossed them in front of him.

"What's this?" He studied the top sheet then looked up at me. "A coke deal?"

"A voided cocaine deal," I corrected. "As of last week, the Devil's Reach will no longer be under the Serpents' hold." There was a sense of pride to my tone. I hated that I had been tied to the Serpents, but hated even more that it had been my father's deal.

"Wait," he leaned back with a smile, "you're not running drugs anymore?"

"I'm not saying that. I'm saying the deal is over."

"I can't say that was the answer I was hoping for, but it's progress."

"Next deal will be my way, none of this middleman shit. The product goes in and out clean."

"There's nothing clean about running drugs, Trig."

I couldn't help but smirk. He was right, but this was who I was, and he knew it.

"Well, fuck. That's great, man."

I downed more than half of my beer and felt the noose release a bit.

"Feels like I regained some control."

"I bet." He smiled and hit his bottle to mine. Mike always accepted me, and I always appreciated it. "Happy to hear it."

Mike stayed for another hour and filled me in on his family. I could tell he needed to shoot the shit, so I let him have at it before I headed home.

"Stop," I warned Rail, who had worn a stupid-ass grin for the past few days.

"Stop what?"

"I'll snap your fuckin' neck."

"Nah, you won't." He laughed as he downed his third beer. "You lost your balls slappin' that ring on her finger."

"I assure you, he still has balls." Tess winked and let her gaze float down to my crotch.

"Tess, you're like that chick," he snapped his fingers trying to recall the name, "you know, that rich dude with the," he closed his eyes, "gray tie on the front."

"*Fifty Shades*?" She laughed.

"Yeah, you're like Ana, and you snagged the billionaire." Her mouth dropped open. "Only you snagged a MC pres and get to deal with crazy-ass fuckers trying to kill us."

I was lost. "What the fuck are you talking about?"

"*Fifty Shades of Grey*," they both said.

Tess held up a hand to stop my next question. "Rail, at what point were you going to tell me you read romance?"

He grinned proudly. "You never asked."

"How…" She paused. "How would I know to ask you that?"

"Meh." He shrugged.

"Rail, we could be reading together."

"Is that what's in the locked trunk at the end of your bed?" Brick asked as he sat next to Tess and gave her a kiss on the cheek. His Cheerios sloshed onto the table, and I had to resist the urge to look away. His obsession with beer and cereal was disgusting.

"That and many other things." He winked at Tess, and I gave him a kick in the shin.

"Yeah, and a fuckin' blow-up doll," Gus huffed behind me and squinted at his watch.

"Her name is Misty, and you didn't mind her last night."

"I wouldn't waste my time with a blow-up doll when I have my own version high as a kite on my fucking bathroom floor right now." He glanced at the door. "Anyone see Fin?"

"Ryder should be back soon," I assured him, but he was right. They were twenty minutes late.

"All right, boys," Tess stood, "I need to run to the store as soon as Ryder comes back."

"Tess," Big Joe came rushing over, "if you're heading to the store, can I put in an order?"

"Sure." She made a face when Cray came in with his newest prospect, Bruce. "Does he ever run his own club?" She laughed, and Brick pulled her back into the seat.

"Trigger," Cray offered a nod, "I need to speak with you."

"Yeah." I stopped when his prospect eyed me strangely.

"Nice to meet the famous Trigger." He offered his hand, and I just stared at him.

"Is it true that you don't try your own coke?"

What the fuck kind of question was that?

"No." Big Joe stepped in.

"Why not?"

"He only has one interest." Joe cut Brick off. "The blonde."

Tess knocked over Brick's Cheerios, and she just looked down at it as the slop poured over her lap.

"Tess, shit." Brick pulled her stunned body up from the chair. "You're soaked."

She turned toward me. All the color had drained from her cheeks.

She eyed me, and I moved toward her to make a show of helping her out. "Come on, Tess." I tugged her toward the bedroom. "Let's get you undressed." I laughed as we headed down the hall.

"Look at me." I forced her to look into my eyes. "What the hell is it? I know something shocked you back there."

"It's him."

"Him, who?"

"The mole! The fucking mole!"

I covered her mouth and leaned in. "I know." Her eyes jumped around as she tried to follow me.

"How do you know?" Her words were muffled under my hand, so I dropped it away and let her sag against me.

"You know when I was charged for that mass murder at the Final Temptations Strip Club in Santa Barbara?" She nodded. "He asked me to go there as a favor to help out a buddy. I was set up, I know it, but I haven't done anything about it. I had to get my head around how to deal with it. It won't be long now."

"Holy shit," she huffed. "I can't believe it was Joe!"

"Morgan saw him kill Links too."

"The guy you had working to get you out of jail?" I nodded. "Seriously?" Her hands drew into fists as she thought. "How is he not dead? Trigger, you don't let anyone do anything, but Joe's still here with a fucking heartbeat."

"I needed to find Gus."

"Well, now we have him!"

"I know, but I also need to find my father. I need that traitor bastard alive right now. He's our frickin' ace in the hole. The fact that my father trusts him will be the key to hunting him down."

She shook her head and rubbed her arms. "I trusted him. He looked after me when you weren't around. I just can't believe it."

"I know." I felt her pain and knew it was really personal, but sometimes things had to play out differently than you wanted.

"He gave me a gun. I should have used it on *him*." Her head snapped up. "Does he have any idea you two know?"

"No. He'd be gone if he did."

"So, now what?"

"Now," I pulled her off the bed and urged her toward the door, "you get cleaned up and act the same as you did before you made the connection."

Both hands slammed down on my chest. "Trigger, it was Joe. Joe! It was his voice I heard in the desert before I got attacked. I knew it was familiar, but—Oh, it was him *and* someone else."

I licked my dry mouth and tried like hell to channel my anger. I'd never wanted to kill someone as much as I did in that very moment. The demons screamed and shook their cages at the betrayal.

"Go get changed, Tess. Take a few to get yourself under control. You have to do this for me, for all of us."

***

Tess

"Seventy-six even." The salesclerk bagged up the rest of the food while I swiped the card. He eyed me a couple of times before he handed me my last bag. I was sure he knew who I was. The Devil's Reach wasn't exactly a lowkey club. "Receipt?"

"No, thanks."

"Have a nice day."

I waited an extra beat before I shot him a kind smile. "You too."

See? I'm nice.

"Here, let me help you with that."

I didn't have to turn to know who it was. I froze, a surge of adrenaline raced up my spine, and my blood ran cold.

"I don't need your help, Zay."

"You all right, miss?" The clerk stepped away from his register and came around to the front.

Zay turned and gave him a look. "She's fine."

"Are you?" he asked me, and I tried to muster up another friendly smile. I didn't want him to get hurt, but I knew he could tell I wasn't.

Zay stood in front of me to block the clerk's view and pulled up my left hand to look at my ring.

"You really going to marry him?"

I snapped my hand away. "What, you think I was going to marry you? I don't even know you!"

"No. I'm just shocked, that's all."

"Wow." I shook my head in disbelief and tried to walk around him. I wondered what the fuck he was here for. I scanned the room, looking for some kind of nasty-ass weapon to use on him.

"Tess," he came up behind me and spoke quietly, "can we talk for a moment?"

"Seriously, the last time I saw you, I was told I no longer had my freedom. Why in hell would I give you a moment of my time?" I tried to see if he was alone or if Allen was nearby. I picked up my pace and hoped to hell the light would change so I could walk straight across.

"Tess." He grabbed my arm and tugged me between two buildings.

"Don't touch me!" I tried to wiggle, but he was too strong, and my arms were already weighted down with what I had bought.

"I don't want to hurt you, but I will if I have to."

"Oh, trust me, I remember." Sarcasm dripped from my lip as the memory of his fist to my face came rushing back.

"I suppose I deserved that."

"You think?" I spat. "What the hell are we doing here?" Curiosity soon pushed the fear of being recaptured aside. Memories of all the times he'd watched Allen beat Gus flickered all around me. I knew this man was a dangerous killer. I wasn't stupid, but something was off here.

He grabbed my wrist and twisted until I stopped trying to fight him, and my groceries fell all over the ground.

"Let me go!" I screamed in his face, but he twisted harder until I cried out and he had my attention.

"Will you fuckin' listen? I'm trying to stop you from being a part of something bigger."

"You trying to protect me?" I snarled. "Are you nuts?" I kneed him in the dick, but he only grabbed my neck and slammed my head against the wall. He shut his eyes like he was trying to calm himself while I fought to clear the ringing in my ears. *Ouch!*

"He has the boy."

That stopped my fight dead in its tracks, and my body went slack.

"What! Which one?" I choked through the small airway he left me.

"The littlest."

Fin!

My heart sped up, and my emotions started to ping pong through my rib cage.

"Take me, Zay, trade me for him. He's just a baby."

Zay squeezed his eyes shut and muttered, "What I wouldn't do for that to happen." He was so close to my face, and his breath smelled gross, like a bad combo of booze and cigarettes.

"Where is he, Zay?" I clawed at his grip, but it tightened as his face grew red. "Please, don't take Fin."

"It's not just about him," he whispered. "He's just the decoy."

"What?" He suddenly let me go, and I had to lock my knees to stand upright.

"A decoy," he repeated.

I sucked in as many gasps of air as I could muster. My lungs felt like sandpaper, and my head felt light. This was no time for weakness. "Where is Fin?"

"This has gone way too far." He madly rubbed his face. "He's out of control." His phone rang, and he stared down at the screen with a blank look on his face. “The park by the pier.”

He didn’t get to finish. I dropped everything and raced down the street. I wove between cars and used the bike lane when the lights were red.

“What the hell, lady?” a man screamed at me when I cut him off at the corner of an intersection. Horns blew, tires squealed, and every curse word imaginable found my ears, but nothing mattered except to get there. I jumped in front of a truck and felt no fear as my feet pounded the pavement. My arms pumped at my sides, and my hair whipped all around me as my lungs labored to keep up.

“Fin!” I screamed when I saw his small body standing near a tree. His shoulders were slumped over, and his hoodie looked ripped. “Fin! Come to me!”

Somehow, I picked up the pace, but when I was just moments from reaching him, someone stepped out from behind the slide.

I came to a complete stop as fear once again tightened around my chest and held me hostage.

“I didn’t expect you, Tess.” Fox gave me a grin before he shoved Fin’s shoulder. His head rose, and I saw his busted lip and swollen cheek. I could tell he had been crying.

“You’re looking good, Tess.” His sleazy gaze dragged down my front. “I take it someone tipped you off?”

“Fox,” dropped off my tongue in a whisper, “just give me the boy.”

“I can’t do that.” He pulled out a gun and rested it on Fin’s shoulder, the tip pressed into his neck. “I have my instructions.”

I wanted to puke. It was something I would never be able to un-see. Fin’s mouth opened as he cried, his eyes locked on mine.

“What is it you want?”

“The flash drive.”

“Okay.” I nodded a few more times than I needed to. Damn, Zay had been right. I guessed this was their next move—an innocent child. “Give me the boy, and I’ll take you to the flash drive.”

He laughed. “I didn’t say I wanted *you* to do it.”

The word decoy echoed through my memory.

Shit.

I glanced over my shoulder in the direction of the club. What the hell was going on?

“You have a choice, Tess. Run back to the club to warn whoever’s left that we’re here, or stay here with me and the boy.”

Fin’s bloodshot eyes shifted wildly in a secret plea for me to stay.

I'd never had a maternal instinct, not even with Lilly. I loved her. She was Mags's little girl, and I would always be there for her, but she had grandparents and didn't need me. But Fin and Denton were different. They had a father figure, but they needed a strong, stable female. The little beasts had burrowed their way into my life and into my heart. They needed me, and as much as I had trouble admitting it, I needed them. My need to protect the boys like they were my own coursed through me, and I made my decision. Truth be told, I loved them.

"Fine, I'll stay here." I straightened my spine. "Just remove the gun from his neck."

He shifted it, but only slightly, and fifteen painful minutes ticked by. Fin's eyes were enormous, and he seemed to be in a daze. I stood and stared at Fox, who in turn stared at his phone.

"Are you going to give me the 'you don't have to do this' speech?" He half laughed before he drew his eyes up to mine.

When I moved my weight to my other foot, I caught a glint of something shiny by the sandbox. A shovel someone had left behind, and a decent sized one, at that.

"No, you're a weak piece of shit. You will do whatever Allen tells you, even to the point of hurting an innocent child."

"She says to the man holding a gun to the kid's head." He laughed.

I dropped my arms and started to step toward the shovel. He made a hissing sound for me to stop, but I pushed my limit and kept moving. I knew he wouldn't hesitate to hurt Fin.

"You know," I took a step, "I always wanted to see the Pacific."

"Stop moving," he warned.

"Always wanted to dip my toes in every ocean there is." I moved another three steps and hoped he didn't see what I was after.

"I said hold still." He started to approach me slowly, Fin still in his hold.

"I never thought all of this," I waved at him, "would come with my bucket list." I was a foot away from the shovel.

"So, my warning wasn't enough for you." He gave me a grin, one that I felt hit the center of my core as it triggered a memory I had buried.

"You?" I stepped back, then everything fell into place, and I connected the murky dots and put it all straight in my memory. "It was *you,* wasn't it? In the desert. You attacked me up on the ledge!"

"You smelled so good, your skin was like butter. I just wanted a taste of you."

Something inside me snapped. One moment I was standing there, and the next I had the shovel and swung it straight at his neck. I saw arterial spray and had the satisfaction of knowing I had put him down.

His eyes bulged, and his gun wobbled, but he didn't let it go. He was still a threat.

"No!" I grabbed Fin and tackled him to the ground. Then I flew at Fox and kicked the gun from his hand, then jabbed my foot down hard into his throat. I stood and watched the man who had once tried to rape me leak onto the ground. He tried to say something but only gurgled, and then his eyes glazed over.

"Shit." I looked around wildly. What if someone saw? I thought I heard sirens. My fucking fingerprints were all over the shovel handle. "Ah…" I dropped to my knees and fished around Fin's backpack. "Sorry, Fin, I just need," I pulled out his water bottle, "this."

I dumped it over the handle, grabbed a fistful of sand, and with the sleeve of my jacket, rubbed it into the wood in hopes it would scrub my prints clean. Fox's glazed stare and still-jerking body lay nearby as I tried to hide the evidence of what I had done.

I tried not to think of how Fin would react to all this. I did what had to be done. I tucked the bottle back in his bag, tossed it over my arm, grabbed Fin's hand, and quickly walked out of the park and onto the road.

"It's okay, it's okay," I kept repeating to Fin as we walked at a normal pace. I wiped at the blood to help blend it into my clothes. Thank God I had on something dark. I didn't need to draw any more attention to us. Anger flooded my brain, and I fought like hell to keep it under control.

"You're okay, sweetie," I reassured him once we turned the corner. "You're going to be fine."

I wasn't sure if anything was okay right now. Something was happening, and I needed to know what was going down. I did know that no matter what got in my way, I was going to make sure he was safe.

"One more block, and then we're back at the club." I finally saw the rusty sign and knew I just needed to make it inside. Savannah always said "baby steps." I could really use her right now.

"Here we go." I opened the door and should have known by the fact Joe wasn't at his post something was very wrong.

Fin's drawn-out scream stopped my entire body from working, and all that was left was the word decoy.

Decoy.

***

Allen

"Should I be worried?" I turned to Zay. I knew he had tipped off Tess about the kid.

"No."

I clucked my tongue on the roof of my mouth. "We had a plan."

"*My* plan never included hurting the kid, only to use him to draw her out."

"So, now you care?"

"No, not at all. I've killed and will kill again, but I don't hurt kids." He raised his hand like he had something else to say. "I'm beyond confused why you wouldn't have taken out Trigger. You had the perfect moment when he walked out of his office. Silver platter, Trigger," he made the motion with his hands, "right there for the taking!"

I shrugged. "I enjoy toying with my food."

"We don't have the time, and we're running out of money. At what point will you put a bullet in his head? Because, apparently, you won't fight him in the ring."

I shot him a nasty look and waited for him to realize he was too far over the fucking line.

"I thought you were one of us." I shook my head in disappointment. "Is this because your dick is jealous because she's marrying my son?"

"No," he hissed and changed his angle. "It's because you hit a five-year-old kid across the face, and when he cried, you punched him. He's an innocent fuckin' little kid, for Christ's sake. You didn't need to do that."

"Oh, what *is* it about people and kids? I hit Trigger all the time when he was a kid, and he was fine." I fixed my collar in the rearview mirror and smiled at the memory.

Police, fire trucks, and an ambulance roared by with their sirens screaming.

"You didn't need to kill him, and you didn't need to do it in front of his oldest."

"I don't *need* to kill anyone, but that has never stopped me before.

The boy will move on. Kids are resilient." I pinched my eyebrows and shot him a disgusted look. "Are you next to be killed? Because of all people, I never thought you'd be the one to get soft on me."

He opened his mouth to speak but then held up a hand as if to stop himself again.

"Wise choice." I rolled my eyes as I went back to the mirror to make sure I looked just right.

His head dropped to his phone, and his mouth twisted into a thin line.

"What?" I snapped over my shoulder.

"Fox was found dead, shovel to the neck."

"Well, fuck me, that chick has bigger balls than you."

Zay closed his phone and bent to get out of the car.

"Hey," I barked, annoyed that he left before I had given him permission. "Let's always remember who helped you when you got sloppy with that Italian hit."

"That was nine years ago."

"Yeah, and one picture to the police, and you'll be in jail for life."

"So, now you're blackmailing me?"

"You expected anything less?"

"No." He paused with his hand on the door handle, eyebrows raised, and waited for me to dismiss him.

I flicked my wrist and eyed my bloody jacket in the back seat. The splatter had stained my clerical collar. Luckily, I had a backup for times like this. It was a hazard of the job, I supposed. A strong surge of pure joy moved through me, and my spine tingled. I could almost feel the energy from his soul entwine with mine and meld with the many others who joined us.

I hummed with my palms downward.

"One down, a few to go."

CHAPTER FOURTEEN

Trigger

Fin's mouth was open, and his chest heaved, but there was no sound. Denton was stone next to Cray, who still had his backpack in his hands.

Brick ran in, but he was in slow motion. He shouted at Rail, but there was no sound.

Morgan had his gun drawn, and his wild eyes scanned the room along with Cray and Bruce.

Again, no sound.

The muscles in my arms were locked solid, my jaw was clenched so tight I thought my teeth would crack, but above all, the demons within wailed in high-pitched shrieks that made my head pound to their wild beat.

What the fuck just happened?

Where the hell did they come from?

Why the living fuck is the fucking mole staring at the body?

Flashing lights poured through the windows, and the sound of sirens filled the air while the vibration in the floor drew my attention to the guys. They were grabbing the last few bricks of coke from my office as fast as they could, then they slipped out back to hide it under the floor of the pool house. I knew all this, but I stood still. I observed, but I did nothing.

To my surprise, the lights and sirens seemed to move away toward the park.

I locked eyes with Fin. I took in his beaten face. Tears made a path down his dirty cheeks, and my eyes moved to the blood spatter across his white shirt. Fin's white shirt? Blood on Finny's white shirt.

Suddenly, something inside me broke.

It felt as if someone had turned off the lights, turned off the sound, and I was left in the bottom of a cold, dark cave. The demons were free, and they were hungry. Their claws ripped at the flesh on my bones. They were wild, excited I had finally returned home.

I'd never taken speed, but the way my rage burned through my blood, I felt amped up and racing.

I needed to kill someone, and at this point, anyone would do.

"Trigger?" Tess sounded like she was a million miles away. "Oh, my God, Trigger," she sobbed with Fin's face tucked against her stomach. "What happened?"

Her horrified face turned to look over my shoulder, and I barely heard her scream Denton's name.

Tess started to run to me, but Brick stopped her.

He eyed me carefully before he held up a hand and shook his head.

She looked confused as she sobbed and held the boy, and I felt nothing. Just emptiness. Lost.

I let my gaze fall to my uncle's lifeless body.

"When was the last time you saw him?" Gus was pissed, but he was good at keeping his voice calm when he spoke to the school. Unlike me. "So, he did meet up with Ryder?" He paused. "Okay, I'll wait." He slammed the phone down and eased into the seat with a hiss. He was still in a lot of pain, but he tried to ignore it.

I set a bottle of Coors Light beside him—a shitty beer, but his favorite—and pulled out my phone.

"Ryder," I said when he answered on the first ring. "Put Fin on the phone." Gus leaned over the table with his hand stretched out. There was a pause before he spoke.

"I, ah, I can't do that, boss."

"Why?"

"Because he's not with me."

My eyes shot up to Gus, who was now by the door, ready to leave. "Explain."

"I met him as usual, and we were walking along the street. The next thing I remember, I'm getting up from the sidewalk. I must have been knocked unconscious, and Fin's gone. I was just reaching for my phone to call you."

"When?"

"I just came to. Couldn't have been out long."

Shit!

"Morgan!" I shouted, and the entire club went silent. "Get the guys and get out there, find Fin fast." I could hear their bikes as they fired them up and roared out onto the street. What the fuck was happening here?

Denton came in with Cray, looking confused at the commotion.

"Why are you not in school? Gus shouted.

"I got in trouble, and the school called and got Cray." Cray came in behind with his book bag.

"Where is Tess?" Gus looked at me, worried. "Where is my youngest? I have a bad feeling."

Boom!

We were knocked off our feet, momentarily stunned, and the place quickly filled with smoke. I was hit in the back and dropped to my knees. I managed to catch my weight with my hands before my face hit the floor. Black boots came into view, and my head was pulled back by my hair. A rifle butt was shoved in my face, and then I saw him.

"Hello, son." Allen smiled down at me. "We thought we'd stop by and finish what we started. I've been so looking forward to this."

There was no warning as he let my hair go and stepped toward Gus, and there was no warning as he plunged a knife into my uncle's chest and ripped it downward, blood spraying everywhere.

Gus's eyes locked onto mine as his soul was brutally torn from his body.

The only man who meant anything to me, the only person I looked to as a father figure, the only man who truly loved me, was just murdered in front of my eyes.

"You took my life from me, so I plan on removing every last piece of yours. Then I will kill you."

Just as quickly as they arrived, they disappeared, leaving me with the aftermath. I could barely comprehend what had happened. Where were my men? I could've prevented this. I should've killed Allen the first time.

This was my fault.

"How the fuck did they get in!" Brick's booming voice pulled me back.

"Three men dead at the door," Morgan barked from the doorway.

"Where was Joe?"

Morgan swiped the sweat from his forehead and avoided looking at

Gus's body. "He was watching the back gate tonight."

The screams became too much. I needed to get out of there.

My foot kicked the bike to life, and I pointed it north. I split traffic and watched as the speedometer climbed along with my adrenaline.

***

Tess

The water beat against my face. I wished it would clear the fog that had wrapped itself tightly around my brain. Every time I thought I couldn't cry any more, more tears came, which turned into sobs, and then more fog enveloped me. It was a horrible loop, one I knew all too well with Mags's death. Gus and I had become so close. I thought I had lost him once, and when he was returned to us, I realized how important he had become to me. He made me feel like I was family, even though we weren't blood related. He filled a hole I never knew I craved—a parent figure.

I pressed my back against the cool wall and let my knees give out until my butt hit the tile. I drew my legs up and tucked myself into a ball and let my soul have its way.

I needed few minutes to be weak, so I could be stronger.

"Where are the boys?" Morgan handed me a glass of whiskey, but I took the bottle instead.

"My bed," I whispered and ran a hand through my damp hair.

"How are they?"

"Denton has shut down, and Fin cried himself to sleep."

"And you?"

I shrugged. "I have no idea."

"Tess, how are the bo—"

Big Joe stopped when I turned and glared at him. I couldn't help but pour every venomous emotion I had been holding back in that one look. It was all directed toward the man in front of me.

"Their father was murdered in their home. How would you be, Joe?"

"Sorry," he quickly stepped back, "I should be a little more sympathetic." He turned away, and I fisted the neck of the bottle.

Morgan pinched his brows together before he leaned over the bar top and stared right into my eyes.

"You know."

"And so do you." I downed the glass in front of me, hugged the bottle, and walked out back. Instead of going to the pool, I turned and went down the long hallway and into the slaughter room.

The door was locked, but I had seen Trigger use a key before. I rocked up on my toes and reached into the lampshade that was attached to the wall and fished around the bottom of the bowl. I hooked the ring and pulled it free. A long skeleton key hung from a chain with a tag that read "Devil's Playground." It was a fitting saying for the use of the room.

Carefully, I turned the lock and headed inside.

It was always so clean, and the smell of bleach burned the lining of my throat. It was oddly comforting.

I flipped on the light above the industrial drain. It was a small light, so the rest of the room remained dark. With the remote in hand, I flicked on the Apple TV and searched for one of Gus's favorites, "The Sky Is Crying" by Stevie Ray Vaughan and Double Trouble. I turned it up, tossed the remote, and made my way over to the weapons hanging on the wall. The whiskey dangled from my fingers, and the amber sloshed around in the body of the bottle.

I ran my hand along the bat I had used to kill Clark. My fingers dipped along the grooves, and my eyes shut at the memory.

"The only reason he's even paying attention to you, sweetheart, is because he's trying to get my attention." My mother gave me a smirk when she saw the damage her words did to me. "You're nothing but a steppingstone."

I shook my head clear and moved on to the ball on the end of a leather tether.

"No one will ever love you, Tessa." My mother found me again. "How can you love a thorn in the side?"

My hand slammed the wall, and I saw something move by the sink. I repeated the action and saw part of the wall move again. There was a door there I hadn't noticed before. It must not have been shut properly. I suspected Trigger wouldn't like me to pry.

I pulled the door open and found where the *real* weapons were—car cables, a club with nails, ropes, small benches, pulleys, a crossbow, a double-bladed axe, and various swords. A computer sat on a metal table, and I tapped the keyboard. The light flickered on, and I studied the screen.

Rows and rows of files filled the background, all named for the slaughter room's "guests." I tapped one and realized they were videos. I tapped Clark's name. I was tempted to watch it, but now wasn't the time. I would save that for the one-year anniversary of his death, a personal treat.

I pressed another key, and when a live video popped up, I realized it was the slaughter room. I clicked on the little picture of the feed of the front bar. Trigger was home.

I brought my face closer to the screen as I caught the mood in the room, and I watched, fascinated. Trigger's arms were tense, and anger flowed from him. He pulled himself up to his full height, then his ear went down to his shoulder on one side then the other. His hands were fisted at his side.

"Trigger," Morgan had his back to the camera when he spoke, "Joe wanted you to—"

Crash!

The back of the bar, freshly re-stocked, blew up like a grenade. Trigger had thrown one of the bar tables straight into it.

"Holy shit." Morgan covered his head as he jumped out of the way. I jumped myself as the noise sent shock waves through the room.

Big Joe had stepped into view, and I felt my body drain of blood.

Trigger grabbed a whiskey bottle, flipped it around, caught it by its neck, and chucked it straight at Joe's head.

"Shit!" I yelped with my hands over my mouth.

Joe went down hard and hit the floor, knocking over a chair. Trigger threw another chair out of the way and grabbed of one of Joe's arms and started to drag him out of the room.

I stood frozen and wondered what would happen next, torn as to whether I wanted to run to see it in person or stay with the screen. I watched Morgan for some kind of guidance. He called out to someone, and moments later, Brick and Rail came running in.

"What the fuck happened?" Rail had his hands over his head. "Whose blood is that?"

"Where is he?" Brick's tone was completely different, almost eerie.

Oh, no.

I fumbled with the keys to switch the camera feed back to the slaughter room. I realized Trigger was headed to this room with Joe, and my mind imagined the blood trail behind him.

Fuck.

I wasn't ready to show myself in case I was sent away. I searched the small room for somewhere to hide, but there really wasn't much choice. I tucked myself behind a heavy jacket that hung on the wall and waited.

The door flung open, and the room echoed with angry jeers. I peeked out from behind the jacket to the screen and saw Brick, Rail, Morgan, Cooper, Cray, Bruce, Ryder, Tristen, and a few others I didn't know. They stood along the perimeter as Trigger ordered Ryder to tie Joe's torso to the wall and his arms and legs to the chair.

He waved something under his nose, and Joe woke slowly with a groan.

"Whoop!" one of Tristen's crew yelled, and he hit the fight bell next to the door.

Ring!

Trigger turned. Every muscle in his body stood out as he twisted, and then I caught sight of his face and saw the demons glaring from his pupils.

Oh, shit.

"Morgan," Trigger grunted as he peeled his t-shirt over his head, "rope."

Damn. The screen had gone black. I was not missing this. I stepped out and tapped the computer to wake it up and waited to see what they would do to a mole. A traitor. I couldn't even think his name. The anger and betrayal were too raw.

A thrill went through me. A part of me was twisted with excitement to watch this without them knowing I was there. Trigger seemed so different, so magnificent.

Morgan put a rope and a bucket with some liquid in it at Trigger's feet and stepped back.

Trigger cracked his knuckles then his neck before he ran both hands through his hair and tied it back. Some escaped the tie and fell over his face, but he ignored it. He walked up to Joe's chair and kicked it to bring him to attention. I studied the mole. His cut was gone, and his shoes had been removed.

"Look at me," he grunted again, and this time Joe's eyes flickered open, and his face twisted in terror.

"Shit." He squinted and groaned as blood ran down his face from the gash on his head. "I wondered when this day would come."

I tapped the key to turn it up. Trigger's back was to me, and I didn't want to miss a thing.

"How long did you know?" he asked.

"No," Trigger shook his head, "you don't get to ask the questions." He stepped back and tossed the rope in the bucket. Morgan handed him latex gloves while the rest watched like it was a live fight.

Joe sniffed at something, and his eyes went wide. That seemed to wake him up.

"Jesus Christ!"

"Will not save you now," Brick muttered without missing a beat.

After the rope soaked for a minute, Trigger held one end and ran his other hand down the fibers to drain off the excess liquid. He then tied a rag that was dipped in the same liquid around Joe's head to cover his eyes.

He stepped back and held out his hand. Brick handed him a paddle with nails through the end. Trigger didn't hesitate and swung the wicked-looking beast into Joe's kneecap. His scream was so loud, it made the speakers on the laptop crackle.

"Holy shit!" He spat and foamed at the mouth. His neck veins popped, and his teeth bit down. "Mother of shit! I'm sorry, I'm sorry!"

"Fuck that. It's too late. I want to know what happened that day," Trigger shouted over his suffering.

"Fuck you, Trigger!"

Whack!

The other knee was driven in by the ruthless nails. His body jolted forward with a heave as he screamed and sobbed.

"You, of all people, should know I don't like to repeat myself." He took a third swing to the thigh.

"Ahh!" Joe shook his head as if the pain was too much. "I had to go back, to get Allen's fuckin' wallet. The assholes just dumped him and didn't strip him down. Fuck, Trigger, I was loyal to Allen before you even took over."

"Loyal! That's rich." Morgan took a sip of a drink.

"Fuck you, Morgan. What do you know about it?" He panted. "He said you were never fit to run the club," he blurted between sobs. "Said you would have run the DR into the ground if you took over. He promised to make me VP."

Trigger popped his neck and snapped his fingers at Brick, who handed him something.

What the hell?

"If you had let that fucker die, Gus would still be here. You lied to me." The bright yellow flame from the lighter grazed his cheek before…

Holy shit!

The rag must have been dipped in gasoline, because it shot fire straight across the cloth, and the sound that came out of Joe was indescribable. The image of his eyeballs burning while he was still alive would haunt my dreams.

They watched until he begged for it to stop. The smell of burned flesh made it under the door of my hiding place, and I almost lost my stomach contents.

Trigger hooked the still-burning rag away from Joe's eyes and tossed it on the floor.

Joe's head flipped from side to side as the flesh around his eyes continued to burn. Saliva dripped from his lips as he fought to breathe.

Trigger paced the room like a caged lion, and I lost sight of him. *Shit.* I leapt behind the jacket and froze as he suddenly pulled the door open. He seemed not to see me as his eyes roamed over the wall. He selected a weapon and left as quickly as he had entered.

I took a deep breath and turned my attention back to the screen.

Brick tossed a bucket of ice water over Joe's head to jolt him back. "Shit! Trigger, let me live," he begged. "I promise I'll tell you where he is. I'll help you get him." He fought to breathe, his muscles twitched, and his head rolled in agony. I was sure the mixture of different pain was quite a trip for him. I felt no sympathy as I watched.

Brick looked over at Trigger for a moment then stepped up to Joe.

"You lived with us like family. You betrayed us…your family."

Joe jerked, and his burned eye sockets stared toward Brick. "All the years I worked for the club, you never saw me. All I ever was to you was a doorman." Saliva dripped from his white lips. "I just wanted to be somebody."

Trigger's laugh sent a chill across my skin as he stepped up to the mole again. "He saw what I always saw, your fucking weakness."

Joe made a noise then spat in Trigger's face. A movement in the top left screen drew my eye. Trigger's mother stood in the hallway listening to what was happening.

The entire slaughter room went silent and drew back my focus.

The mole's face went red. He knew he was done. "Now every single one of the people you care about will be taken from you," he screamed. "You think she's safe." He grinned darkly through the pain. "How wrong you are. As long as Allen is alive, that girl will be hunted like the wild animal she is. Then those kids and everyone in this room will die. Then he'll kill you."

No one saw me approach. The weapon in my hand seemed to have a life of its own as I swung it toward him with all my strength. The blade caught him across the upper arm, and blood sprayed as it fell to the floor. Trigger spun around, and his wild eyes turned to mine as Brick grabbed the weapon from my hand.

"Enough!" Trigger shouted as he seized the weapon from Brick, swivelled, and drove the battle-axe straight down the middle of the mole's head.

My chest heaved at the strength it must have taken to slice a skull nearly in two.

Blood poured down his lips, into his open mouth, and around his neck.

It was fucking sick.

Trigger grabbed the bucket and poured it over the mole. Then with a flick of his hand, flames jumped, and the mole burned.

"Feed," he ordered as his eyes stayed on mine.

Where the fuck was Trigger? Because that man wasn't him.

***

Allen

I sank into the dingy comforter in room 605 of the Holiday Inn in Santa Monica. Normally, I'd find some church to camp out in, but I needed to focus after the shit hit the fan with Gus. I grinned up at the stained ceiling. The feel of the knife slicing through his flesh was riveting. Like a rare steak from Ruth's Chris, a slight touch of the blade, and you slid right down to the bone.

"Come on!" Zay hissed at his phone. "Where the fuck are you?"

"Your negative aura is ruining my moment."

"What are the chances Joe flipped on us?"

That brought me up to a sitting position. "Why would you ask that?"

"You killed Gus, and now Joe isn't answering his fuckin' phone."

"'Cause you're the one calling."

"No," he held up my phone, "I'm not."

Shit.

I scrambled off the bed, snatched my phone, and tried it again. We had rules, and that was number one. Always answer my calls. Joe always picked up.

I licked my dry lips and pressed my forehead to the murky window. "On to the next plan."

I watched Zay's reflection in the window. I knew he didn't like this plan, but I didn't give a rat's ass what he thought. He just better watch himself. He was on thin ice with me as it was. If I didn't need him, I would have gutted him like Gus.

"Now!"

I waited for him to leave before I closed my eyes and tried to clear my head.

"Where is he?" I pumped my arms wildly as I hurried into my office. My fucking son was on the phone. The meeting had blown up in my face all because of my own goddamn son!

Without a thought, I pulled back my hand and slashed him across the back as deep as I could, not once, but twice.

He jolted upward, which dragged the blade deeper the second time. He whirled around with angry, dark eyes, and I saw his expression as he realized I was the one who had done it.

"What the fuck?" His voice boomed throughout the room.

Trigger was anything but a president. He had tried to ruin my deal with the Serpents, the one deal that would have allowed us to stay in Santa Monica and own our own turf. The piece of shit thought he knew best and that he was too good to sell drugs. He was about to ruin all my hard work. He needed to die.

"You aren't worthy to run such an empire. You're weak and worthless!"

The door opened, and I let my defenses down for half a second. I felt a knife rip into my stomach. I froze as the pain tore through me. My fingers tingled, and I knew this was it. I went down hard.

"Joe," Trigger barked from somewhere far away, "get the prospects to deal with this shit."

"Yes, boss. You need some help?" He nodded to the blood that ran from my son's back.

"No, just get him out of here."

"Yeah, boss."

The word boss *made me want to vomit. My son was going to fucking pay for this. I tried to move, but the pain was awful, and I decided otherwise. My lungs started to hurt, and my breathing became shallow.*

Oh, shit, everything hurt.

Brent, the prospect, grabbed my arm and hauled me over his shoulder like a sack of potatoes. I tried to mask my groan, but it was hard.

Blood dripped down my face, and my vision blurred as I was tossed into the back of a pickup. Next thing I remembered, I saw clouds racing by above me, and the wind had dried the blood on my cheeks. Blinding pain shot down my legs, but I was thankful I could wiggle my toes.

I wasn't sure how long we drove, but at one point, the truck stopped, and I found Brent above me. He kicked my shoulder, and my head flopped in his direction.

"Looks fucking dead to me." He bent down and checked my pulse. He sucked at it, because I knew I still had a fucking heartbeat. "He smells like shit."

Fuck you!

"Grab his shoulders," someone said.

I flopped on the ground, and it took everything not to yell out. My pants dragged down to my hips as they pulled me across the forest floor and rolled me under some bushes.

"Do we bury him?"

"The ground's hard. It would take hours." Brent sighed.

"We can just say we did. It's not like he's coming out here any time soon."

Some branches were thrown on top of me, but I could still see their feet moving about in front of me.

"That's good enough." Brent tossed the rest of the brush next to me and pulled out his phone. "Let's get out of here. This place is fucking creepy."

I knew I was done. What a way to go. Fuck, layin' here under a bush with my guts cut open, waiting for the animals to get a whiff of me. Hate filled me, but it couldn't sustain me. I knew I was about to pass out.

I must have been out for a bit because it was almost dark when I came to. I felt my pants being tugged at. I panicked. I knew it was the animals here to feast on me, and I screamed inside my head when my body refused to move.

"Come on," a voice said as a pair of boots appeared in front of my face. He rolled me onto my back, dug into my pocket, and pulled my wallet free.

"Stupid assholes, can't do anything fuckin' right."

I reached deep down for the strength to grab his wrist and managed a feeble hand flop.

"You," I huffed when I saw who it was.

"Oh, shit!" He hopped back in disbelief. "You're still alive?" He pulled his gun and pointed it at my head. I could tell he was confused as to what he should do. I took that valuable moment and used it to my advantage.

"Wait," I wheezed so he'd lean down and I wouldn't have to speak as loudly. "You help me, and I promise to make you vice president of the club as soon that contract is done. I'll give you all the money you could ever want."

"Allen," he rubbed his head with his free hand, "I don't know—"

"My son will run my club into the ground if he tries to break that contract. Where will you be then, Joe? You need the club as much as I do."

He mulled over my words. His jaw twitched, and the corners of his mouth lifted upward.

"You want to be a doorman forever?" I could see that got through. I coughed. Shit, everything hurt.

He stood and started to pace, but the fact that he didn't kill me right away was a good sign. Joe was stupid, and I was sure he didn't get the respect he felt he deserved, so I knew he'd be an easy target. I just had to say the right things.

"I don't know, Allen. Trigger knows a lot of people, and if this ever got out, I'd be killed on the spot."

I closed my eyes. Maybe I was wrong to think I could flip him.

After what seemed like an eternity, he reached down and grabbed me by the armpits and dragged me over to the truck. He tossed me in, and I hit the bed of the truck hard.

Fuck me, he was going to return me to the club!

The engine started, and I thought of the many different ways I could roll my body off the truck and into the bushes. Anything would be better than being returned to the hands of my son.

The night sky raced by, and the stars started to blur together. What was in store for me next?

When the truck came to a stop and I heard the water hit the dock, I knew where we were.

I smiled through the pain with the realization.

He had turned.

CHAPTER FIFTEEN

Trigger

Nolan appeared through the heavy fog. He stayed far enough away so as not to draw the attention of the wild things, but I felt his presence. He always fought his way to the surface whenever she was around.

I stayed on the edge. Chains wrapped my wrists and torso, rooting me in place—a reminder I belonged to them when I was here.

"Where the fuck did you come from, Tiger?" Morgan's disbelief jolted me back from my head.

Her wide eyes were locked onto mine, and I could tell she had heard what Joe said. Oddly enough, I knew I should care, but I didn't, really.

I turned my gaze away and focused my attention where it belonged, on the burned pile of shit that lay in front of me.

"Tess," I heard Brick warn from behind me.

She looked up at me, her head cocked to the side.

"I've been surrounded by liars my entire life." Her voice barely made it through the madness inside. "I trusted him too. How stupid I must have been."

"He never got it, what it's like to have family."

She didn't look back as she walked out the door and muttered to someone in the hallway.

I continued to look down at what was left of Joe. I had relished his screams and was happy both moles were now taken care of.

Only Brick and I stayed until the last flame flickered out. Brick swallowed at the smell, but I didn't register it, or maybe I was just filled with the scent of victory.

"What now?"

"Now we find Allen."

"Trigger?"

I turned to look at Brick. He had a rag over his mouth and nose, but his eyes were visible, his brows drawn together. He seemed worried. Why? We just took down a decade-long mole.

"Never mind."

"You got something to say, say it."

He shook his head then stepped back so I could leave.

I kicked the door open and headed to my room.

***

In typical club fashion, they held a huge party whenever we had a victory. The pool was full of women, and the bar was busy, the booze flowing freely. As word got out, my other crews started to arrive in droves, ready to join in the celebration. Money flowed along with the liquor. It was a good night.

My body was jacked up. The demons were on speed, and I felt restless and edgy. I still needed more.

"Trigger!" Tristen shouted with one girl under each arm. "I have a treat for you." He pushed one of the blondes in my direction. She tripped over her heels and fell toward my chest. I quickly grabbed her wrists and stood her on her feet before her body reached me. "She's a gymnast." He mouthed the word, "flexible."

"Hey," she blinked up at me, "I'm Jessica."

I smiled down at her and felt the erection as it strained against my pants. She had plump lips, which could be used in my favor.

"Who are you?" Tess snapped from behind her. "I don't fucking think so."

"Who are you?" The girl squared her shoulders then wrapped her arm around my waist with a smile.

Tess shot me a nasty look, then that crazed expression of hers flashed across her eyes.

She grabbed my erection forcefully. It was sexy as fuck until I felt her nails dig in.

"This," she stuck up her finger, indicating her ring, "belongs to me."

"Whooo, Trigger," Tristen laughed, "your bitch needs a leash."

Tess whirled around, and to my surprise, she slapped Tristen right across his face. "Just because you're a manwhore doesn't mean you need to spread your STD sluts on him."

Tristen pushed the girl he was with away and drew back a fist to hit

Tess. I blocked his swing and slammed him back into the pool house.

Tess prepared to charge him, but Rail snagged her around the waist.

"Don't," I warned with another shove to Tristen. He raised his hands in surrender.

I flicked my fingers at Rail, and he released Tess, who shoved his shoulder and scowled at me.

"You're a feisty little one, aren't you?" Tristen egged her on.

"Was the first hit not hard enough?"

"Beginner's luck."

"Ha!" She shoved her middle finger in the air. "Wanna test that theory?"

"Fuck." Morgan tossed his bottle in the trash and glanced at me. "You gonna step in?"

I shrugged and squinted. I had a headache. Something was off inside me. The darkness that held me captive was only more dense.

"Here." Gus sat beside me and tried to hand me a white cup with a blue straw. "It's lemonade, Nolan."

It was strange when he used my other name, but he always insisted on it, so I went along. My eyebrows pinched together as I examined the cup. There was a silhouette of two lemon slices squeezed in between blocks of ice on the side. It was really hot out, and lemonade wasn't something I had often. Gently, he pushed it into my hand then went back to watching the game.

"What's the score?"

"Bottom of the fifth, Angels up seven to three."

"Nice." He shoved more than half a hotdog down his throat in the first bite. I couldn't help but smirk as his head tilted and he tried to swallow. "Yum."

I liked Gus. He was fun and kept things light. He never hit or even touched me. He just liked to spend a few hours with me on Sunday. It helped me get through my week or my next fight.

"You want one?" Gus moved the box to my lap, and I saw he had bought at least eight hotdogs.

I picked the one on the end and inhaled the dog in one bite.

"What?" Gus laughed, mouth wide open, and half a wiener fell from his mouth. "I'm so proud."

I laughed and went back to the game. Who knew I could laugh like that?

"Shit!" Brick's shout brought me back, and it took me a moment to catch up with the situation. Tristen's chick had Tess by the neck. She was three times her size, and it showed in her powerful grip.

I hopped over the table and tossed the chick in the pool with one arm. Tess fell but batted my arm away when I tried to help her up.

"Don't touch me!" Her hands felt for the wall.

"You okay?" Brick came up to her and wrapped his arm around her waist. Which, of course, she allowed.

"I'm fine," she huffed.

"Why are you so scrappy?"

She held her neck and shook her head. "This place," she heaved. "I need a drink." She pushed by Brick and headed inside.

"What the hell was that all about?" Brick held his hands up then looked back at me. "What happened?"

"Little bitch has a set of balls," Tristen called out, clearly drunk as shit.

"Enough," I barked, which sent the entire back yard into a sudden silence.

I headed inside, and the crowd parted as I stormed through. So many sounds in my head fought to break my train of thought. The demons screamed and insisted I go in another direction. A direction that was away from Tess.

***

Tess

"Get inside." Vib pushed Fin into the bar. He tripped on his book bag and fell to his knees with a small cry. "Christ, Fin, get your ass up and out of my face." She dropped her cheap, flashy purse on the stool and pushed her wild hair out of her face. "I need a goddamn break!" She lit a match and touched it to the tip of a cigarette.

"Ouch." Tears filled Fin's big eyes. "It hurts." There was a pretty nasty cut on his knee.

"Shut up!" She smacked the side of his head, and I'd had enough.

I bent down on one knee and took Fin's leg and looked up at him. "That looks like it hurts. You want me to get a Band-Aid?" He gave me a little nod but eyed his mother behind me.

"Hey," Vib slurred. I assumed whatever she took was starting to kick in. When I didn't look up at her, she rose on her five-inch porn heels and cocked out her bony hip. "I said, hey, you!"

I knew I had overstepped, but frankly, I didn't give a shit. These boys had been through enough, and now this junkie was only adding to their list of problems.

"Are you hungry?" I ignored her.

"Yup, a lot hungry."

I used the back of my hand to dry the tears from his dirty face. I bit my tongue and wondered in silence when he last had a bath.

"I can feed my own son." Vib came up next to me.

"Like you can bathe him too?" *Oh, shit, Tess, shut your mouth.*

"What did you say? You're a little bitch."

When I started to stand, she grabbed my hair and shoved me, and I fell back and smacked the side of my head against a chair.

"Don't touch her!" Fin screamed and pushed his mother's hip with all his strength, causing her to lose her balance and tumble into the bar stool. "I hate you. I hate that you touched her."

"Shut up, you little shit."

"You're a shit. At least dad didn't hit me."

"Well, your dad's dead…"

Fin froze and his nostrils flared. I'd swear I could hear his heart break from across the room. His face went red, and his fists slammed down at his sides. "I wish it was you being eaten by worms!"

Vib struggled to stand, and her knees bent inward as she tried to find her balance in her stupid shoes. She looked around for something, and I tried to clear my head from the hit to the side of my skull. Dammit, that hurt.

I wished I could keep my temper better, but I saw red when Fin screamed in pain. That fuckin' junkie had pressed the hot end of her cigarette into his upper arm. He bucked and cried. I don't know when I jumped to my feet, but I yanked his arm out of her grip and started on her ugly face.

"What the hell!" I screamed, beyond finished with this tramp. "He's your son, Vib! How can you do that to your own child?" Fin buried his head in my back and sobbed while I still had a grip on her. "Gus would beat your ass to the grave if he knew you did that to his boy."

She pulled herself from my grip. Her lipstick was smeared all over her mouth, and tears from my blows had run tracks through her thick makeup. She tossed back a half-finished drink someone had left on the bar then smirked as she wiped her mouth dry.

"Can't beat my ass now, can he?"

"He can't, but I obviously still can."

She swung and missed, only to tumble to the floor with a huff.

"Get out." I stood above her.

"You can't do that."

"Can't I?" I held up my engagement ring and watched her eyes connect the dots. Yup. I was about to marry the president of the club.

"You can't make a decision like that. You're only a whore on Trigger's arm until he tires of you. It's always the same with him. Fuck and chuck. We're just waiting you out."

"Well," I rubbed my chin like I was deep in thought, "I guess until I get chucked, you're out of here."

"The boys are coming too!"

"No!" Fin yelped.

"Guess that's your answer."

She once again made it to her feet and towered over me and Fin. "You can't take them from me. They're mine," she leaned in, "and I'll take them to hell with me if only because *you* want them."

"Vib!" Trigger barked from his office. "You don't have custody of the boys. I do." He held up a blue folder, the one Gus had mentioned before. "I have the right to step in when I choose. You have one hour to get your shit out of my club. The boys stay."

Her mouth fell open as she took in what he said. "Trigger," she whined, turning all girly, "it was just a misunderstanding. Tess saw something and thought I was hurting Fin. You know I wouldn't hurt my babies. You know I love them."

"One hour," he repeated.

Her body language changed instantly, and she ran a hand over her fake chest. "You're getting rid of all the chicks in the club to make this waste of space happy? You don't love her. She just puts up with all your shit, so you're blind to her. Your uncle would roll over in his grave if he saw you now."

Trigger glanced over to me before he muttered, "Maybe, but now you only have fifty minutes. Get out fast. You're making my head hurt."

Maybe? What was "maybe?" The part where he didn't love me, or that Gus would roll over?

Vib glared at me before she snatched her purse and headed to her room. I lifted Fin up on the bar top and examined his burn.

"You okay?"

He shrugged and whimpered as I bandaged his arm. What kind of a monster would hurt a child like Fin? The little guy might talk like a sailor and hit like a fighter, but deep down inside, all he and his brother wanted was to be loved by their mother.

Vib appeared again and walked out of the club, but not before she glanced at me. Her eyes looked wild and unsure. What the hell was she up to?

"Okay," I changed my focus back to Fin, "I'll order you some food. Why don't you lay down and wait for the pain pill to kick in, and I'll have Morgan bring it in to you, okay?"

He sniffed. "'Kay."

I lifted him down off the bar and turned to clean up my mess when he hugged me from behind.

"Can you be my mom?"

A million emotions ran through me, but what hit the hardest was that he looked at me as a mother. Never once in my life did I think I could or even would want to be a parent. I was fine with handing off Lilly. I knew she would have a better life without me raising her. But now, years later, things were different, and when I looked down at the little boy in front of me, who had lost so much in such a short period of time, all I wanted to do was hold him and promise him the world.

What the hell happened to me?

I brushed his cheek and down his jaw to his chin. "Fin, I can be whatever you want me to be."

He gave me a small smile, which I was sure was hard to muster, given what just happened, and headed down to my room.

I sagged against the bar. Between the fight out by the pool and then Vib, I was spent, physically and emotionally.

I needed something to do, so I went to clean the soda machines.

When I was almost finished, I checked the clock. Three a.m. I was impressed with my progress and looked forward to showing Morgan in the morning. I knew it was the one job he hated to do.

The office door opened, and Trigger leaned his weight on the doorframe. I tossed my rag down and locked the cash box.

"You about done causing trouble tonight?"

"You ready to come back from the dark side tonight?"

He grinned, but not the sexy smirk he gave me when I'd entertained him. It was something colder.

It sent a chill up my spine. He took split personality to a whole new level.

"You coming to bed?"

I shook my head.

"Why?" His tone was different, and it matched his grin. Gus had warned me that Trigger could flip and not come back. A part of me had been thrilled by the idea, but now I saw what they did. He wasn't Trigger anymore. He was someone else, someone I wasn't sure of.

I decided to be honest. I wouldn't sugarcoat my feelings, and I wouldn't make him think I liked this version of him.

"Because I want to sleep with Trigger, not his demons."

I flipped the light off and left him alone in the dark.

***

Allen

"Father." Zay hurried over to me in the hardware store. I pricked the tip of the pitchfork and imagined it severing Trigger's jugular. I rather liked the weight of the farm tool, so I stuck it in the cart.

"What?" I snapped as I moved on to the next aisle.

"They're coming back. They got my message and agreed to come back."

That stopped me.

"When?"

"One week from Tuesday."

I grabbed a box of garbage bags. I knew I had to get Zay to clean up the mess I made earlier with the maid. She had decided to clean my room after I specifically requested her not to. Some people just didn't know how to listen.

"Excellent. Tell them to meet us at the hotel bar at nine p.m. next Tuesday."

"Should be interesting."

"Indeed, it shall."

I caught my smirk in the surveillance monitor and saw a flicker of black race across my pupils.

CHAPTER SIXTEEN

Trigger

It had been eight days since Gus was killed. We had just returned from the funeral, and everyone was in a shit mood. I didn't blame them. I was feeling extra low myself.

"She didn't deserve to be there," Morgan snarled as he sank into a chair.

"She did," Cooper chimed in. "Just not with another man on her arm."

"I still think you should have let Tess have a run at her." Rail winked at Tess, who had remained quiet most of the day. Gus meant a lot to Tess, and she was even more closed off than she had been lately.

Rail hit Tess with his elbow. "You need a drink, Tiger?"

She peeled her gaze from her lap, and I saw the flash of her phone.

"Hmm?" She squinted while she thought about what Rail said. "No, I'm not hungry."

Rail's chin pulled back, but before he could repeat the question, Brick touched her shoulder.

"All good?"

"Sure." She left the bar and headed out back.

What the hell was up with her? I started to follow her when Cray skipped through the front door like a kid in a candy store.

"Whoop! Boys, do I have a treat for you!"

Brick looked at me, confused.

"Trigger," he went to grab my shoulders but stopped himself, "Christmas came early for you!" He leaned back and rang the bell at the bar.

"Meaning?"

"Meaning," he turned his phone around and let me see the text and photo, "wanna go play?"

Fuck me, Christmas had come early this year.

We headed out, and soon the six of us waited in the shadows beneath the red rotating sign. The Snake's Den was off the 15 freeway, a hidden biker bar only the locals knew about. It was not a bar where the Devil's Reach was welcomed. I couldn't imagine why.

A single strand of circle lights wove through the high-rise above us. It looked like a string of Christmas lights. Cray gave me a wink as if to say, "See? Christmas."

"No one move unless I say otherwise." My skin prickled when I heard the sound of steel being pulled from leather.

"How many, Morgan?"

"At least eighteen."

"And?"

"You have about a minute and ten seconds."

I signed to Cooper across the street to toss the spikes out. The light on the bikes wouldn't see it until it was too late. He waved his hand when he was done.

I shifted to the center of the road and aimed my gun at the lead biker.

"Boom," I whispered then counted out loud, and at the last second slipped back into the shadows.

It was like time stood still just to sweeten the moment.

The first bike hit the spikes straight on and flipped into the air like a carnival trick. The two after him reacted too slowly and landed on top of the first. The rest squealed their tires to a dead stop and dismounted. I shot around them to force them in the direction I wanted, away from the bar.

"Hold fire!" I shouted.

Flickers of light lit up the sky, outing where they were.

"Move out!"

We raced across the road and onto flat ground that ran for miles. I stopped at their downed president and let the rest run. I'd catch up with them later. I stared down and listened to his groans. The pavement had eaten away some of his leather and burned his flesh a few layers deep.

"I don't like to repeat myself. I told you once, and now look where we are."

"How did you know he sent for us?" he spat.

Who? "My father?"

What a sweet victory this turned out to be.

I barely heard him. My hunger for a good kill took over. Resting my gun in my waistband, I removed my jagged knife and carved his stomach. It was only a matter of minutes before he checked out.

"Jesus, Trig." Cooper covered his mouth, but he didn't question my action.

"Remove his cut and put it in my saddlebag."

"Yeah, all right."

"Cooper, document this."

"Yeah, boss."

A bullet grazed my shoulder and sent my demons into a frenzy. Cooper ducked but finished what I asked him to do.

I raced to catch up with the others. My feet beat against the dusty ground, and my shoulder oozed with blood.

I never felt more alive than when I was on this side of my head.

"Trigger!" Morgan waved from up ahead. "All but three are inside."

The moment I reached them, I kicked the top of the crate and grabbed one of the bottles and lit the rag that hung out.

The guys followed my action but waited for my command. I whistled, and everything went silent.

"You didn't bend to my club, you didn't listen when I warned you to stay away, and you've plotted against me with the devil. Well, now you can all go to hell!" My voice bounced off the mountains. A few bullets pierced the silence. I stood where I was as the others took cover and waited. "You should have realized his son would be worse."

I flung my arm back and threw the gasoline bottle at the side of the small trailer the owner of the bar used to sleep in during the weekends. My men mimicked me. Screams and wails tore through the night air. Some tried to run, but they were met with bullets and fists.

We didn't leave until every last one of them was either burned or splattered across the desert floor.

Just as the sun started to show, I ordered Cooper and Cray to take a couple of guys to clean up anything visible from the road and to ditch their bikes.

"Boss," Morgan came up behind me and handed me another cut, "I had no clue Jimmy Lawful was with them."

I rested the joint between my lips and grinned at the lettering. Holy shit.

"Stripe Backs hooking up with Satan's Serpents?" Brick asked, confused. "Fuck, they must be feeling the pressure!"

Morgan laughed. "Not bad wiping out both presidents either."

"This will be a blow to my father."

"What does Allen have to do with this?" Brick's eyebrows pinched together.

"He sent for them."

"How do you know that?" All my men's focus was on me now.

"He told me," I nodded at the Stripe Back president's disemboweled body jammed up against a bush, "before I removed his insides."

We sat in silence, happy with the outcome. I noticed Brick's mood but ignored him.

I got up and walked over to my bike then jumped on and started it up. Just as I was about to slam it into drive, he stood in my way.

I flipped up my visor. "What?"

"You didn't tell me."

"And?" I was annoyed at his questioning.

"And you promised you wouldn't keep silent on shit I needed to know."

"You didn't need to know that."

He smiled and shook his head, then waited a beat before he stepped out of my way, and I slammed my bike into gear and rode free with my demons.

***

Tess

I woke to an empty bar, with the exception of Ryder, who was propped up against the door with a rifle in his hand.

The door was chained shut, the music was off, and the till hadn't been opened since I closed down last night.

The only noise was my phone, which was lit up under the bar top. Seventeen missed text messages and three phone calls.

Shit. What the hell happened?

I lowered my phone as I hit call back and carefully slipped out back to the pool.

"Where have you been?" Venna hissed desperately. We hadn't spoken much since she helped me escape from the house after I killed Bret. We both agreed to lay low.

My skin prickled with terror. Something was up, and I was sure I wasn't going to like it.

"Sorry. We had a funeral yesterday. Things are heavy around here, and I misplaced my phone—"

"Tess," her voice changed, "you should come back to the house."

Ha! "I don't think you could pay me enough to do that." *Wait.* "Why are you back?"

There was a stretch of silence. "My old man has a new wife who doesn't seem to like me." Her voice dripped sarcasm. "I needed money, and she wanted me out. I didn't want to put my dad in a difficult position, so I left."

"I'm sorry, Ven, but you know you can come here, right?"

"I may someday, but right now I'm hearing shit that directly affects you, and you need to hear this."

"Okay, I'm listening."

"With Clark missing, your mother has lost her shit. She thinks you and him are living in Santa Monica, and she's planning to send her *A team* after you, which means the club is about to get hit with some real dark shit."

"Fuck," I whispered and sank into a lawn chair. "That's the last thing the club needs right now." Given Trigger's current state of mind, he might lose his shit altogether. He was incredibly unpredictable.

"Look, I only know what I know, but if I were you, I would deal with this right now, right here, and maybe stop it before they go after everybody there."

I dropped my head and cursed a long stream of hatred toward my mother.

"Let me see if I can find a way there. I don't feel comfortable driving a bike that far." The memory of the last time I was in Vegas came crashing down.

"Can they help?"

I heard a loud noise as the front door opened and the guys spilled in with loud cheers. Bottles crashed, leaving no doubt that they were happy with whatever they'd been up to.

"Sorry, they just got back. Honestly, I don't think so. I'll be in touch, and thanks, Ven." I hung up and made my way inside.

"Check it out, Tess!" Rail help up a bloody cut. "We scored a double hit. Stripes and Serpents no longer exist!"

"What?" I let the cut Rail shoved into my arms dangle from my fingertips. A stranger's blood wasn't something I needed on me at the moment. If it wasn't my kill, I didn't want it. "I thought they were rivals too?"

"Allen rounded them up," Brick added as he leaned in for kiss and hit my cheek. "That's all I know." He glanced back at Trigger, who had already downed half a glass of whiskey.

"Everything okay?" I always knew when Brick was bothered by something. He seemed quieter and uneasy in his own skin.

"Just waiting for him to come back." Brick's lips pulled into a thin line before he mouthed, "Be careful."

"Um, Brick, I wanted to ask—"

"Brick," Cooper popped his head through the door, "Minnie needs you."

"Shit." He rubbed his head. "Can you hang on a second? I agreed to take her to Santa Barbara this weekend."

"Fun! Yeah, go." I waved him off. Minnie needed to come first in his life. I knew where I stood with my friend, but I also knew Minnie meant a whole lot to him, and I refused to be that friend who got in the middle.

Ven: Not sure if you can survive a four-hour drive with her, but Shantee is in town. Maybe she can drive you here?

Tess: I'll think about it. Thanks.

I would consider it, but right now, I could feel Trigger's eyes on me.

"Well?" He leaned back in his seat. "What do you think?"

"I don't know." I shrugged. "I wasn't aware you were heading out to kill them."

I heard Tristen's laugh from behind me. He and I apparently had a problem.

"You need to get something straight, chicky." His arm wrapped around my shoulders, and I wanted to push him off but tried not to start another fight. "Pussies don't get a say in a man's world. They don't get a say in anything at all. Other than what's for dinner."

Trigger licked his lips and slammed his glass down.

"Get the fuck off my girl."

His arm dropped away, and I felt a bubble of warmth brew in my chest at Trigger's words. It had been almost two weeks since he showed much of anything toward me, and frankly, I was tired of it.

"I'm just playing around." He grinned at me. "Right, Tess?"

I matched his grin with a glare and straightened out my top. Trigger headed into his office and slammed the door behind him.

"What's his problem?" Tristen laughed. "Trigger didn't seem to mind the long pair of legs that found him last night."

I rubbed my arms for a second before I turned to leave.

"He's just startin' shit," Morgan said after me. "He's not used to Trigger being with one woman, let alone one he's gonna tie the knot with."

"What the fuck?" Tristen shouted over my head. "No fucking way! He did not." He grabbed my hand and studied my ring. "That's just messed up. What the hell did you do to our pres?"

I yanked my hand away and pushed by Morgan.

"Tess, where you going?" he called.

"I have some things to do."

I was seriously over men right now.

***

"What are you doing?" Trigger made me jump right out of my skin. He was propped up in the doorway, his jaw locked in place, and the rest of his body was tense. He was so different. I really missed my Trigger.

I hated to lie, but I wasn't sure how he would handle this one.

"Brick and Minnie are going up to Santa Barbara for the weekend to visit a friend. They asked me along."

"I never heard about this."

I shrugged and totally acted like Brick was supposed to have told him. Some friend I was.

"You shouldn't go."

I went back to packing my stuff. I had made my decision to end this feud with my mother. I wasn't going to allow her shit to blow back on the club.

"It's just for the weekend."

He cleared his throat and snapped his neck.

"Maybe you didn't hear me correctly. You're not going."

My movements slowed, but I kept talking. "Seems I won't be missed."

"Meaning?"

"Trigger…" I whirled around but knew Tristen was lying. He had to be. "Never mind."

He cursed and flexed his arms like he was at war inside. I knew he was struggling, but how the fuck did I get him back? I was trying to handle so much here, with Gus's death, the boys, avoiding a kidnapping by Allen, Zay's sick obsession with me, and the list just kept growing. I was a strong person, but there were chips in my armor too.

"I don't want you to leave," he muttered.

I hooked my bag over my shoulder and stepped up to face him. His eyes flickered, but the darkness behind them made me feel disconnected from the man I loved.

"Which one of you doesn't want me to leave?"

His eyes closed, and I felt the mood shift back to the demons.

"That's an order, Tess."

My heart dropped into my belly at his tone, and I knew he wasn't there.

I leaned up on my toes and softly kissed his cheek then stepped around him and headed to meet Shantee.

What hurt the most was he let me leave.

***

Allen

"Is the podium in the center of the stage?"

"It's in the center of the room, yes." Zay tried to hide his sarcasm.

I knew he thought I had a flare for the dramatic, but I was very particular and liked to control my environment. I chuckled to myself because I had to admit I did like to add in a little drama for the fun of it.

"Father, I need to tell you something."

"Not now, Zay." I tugged at my shirt cuff. "I need to get my head space just right."

"Seriously, you really need to hear this."

I opened the door. "Everything can wait until I'm prepared." He started to speak, and I glared. "Now," I clapped my hands together with a hop in my step, "let's do this."

"This can't wait." He followed me down the hallway and tried to pull my arm as I burst through the doors of the rec center.

"Hellooo." The word dragged out as I glanced around a "crowd" of only seven people.

What the hell?

"I tried to warn you," Zay hissed behind me.

"Where the fuck are my Stripe Backs and Serpents?"

"Your son." He stepped back as I felt my face flush with anger. I didn't even have a moment to lose my shit before one of the men came up to me and removed his hat.

"I'm sorry, Father." He fisted his hat between his hands. "I'd like nothing more than to see Trigger epically fall, but after what they did to the others last night…" He paused. "I just can't join you. I have kids, and my brother is sick, and his family needs my help. It is too risky for me."

My mouth nearly fell open as each man I had recruited to be part of my army quit because they were afraid of my fucking son. So, he had intercepted the last eighteen or so I had contacted. We would have succeeded in taking him down together if they weren't such cowardly shits. I seemed to be made of stone and just stood there.

When the last one started to speak and the place was almost empty, I snapped. All my hard work was down the drain.

I reached for my gun and popped two in the man's head. The three stragglers who raced for the door got bullets in their backs. They died like the cowards they were.

"Fine, leave! See if I care! Zay, get the names of all of those fuckers and leak them to Trigger. Let them die at the hands of the man they seem to fear most and show them who they *really* should be afraid of!"

I whirled around and sank into the chair. The podium stared at me—no, it mocked me.

"I wanted a goddamn army. I have so much to accomplish. Why am I being denied this? Why?"

"I can't begin to come up with an answer." Zay snickered.

"How the hell did my son even know they were coming?"

Zay unbuttoned his jacket and hopped up on the stage. "He has contacts everywhere."

"Everything he has is mine, damn him to hell! I will find a way to bring him down, with or without them. He is an abomination!" I raged. I jumped to my feet and threw my arms to the ceiling.

"He's *your* son."

How dare he talk to me that way? I hated this man and hated that he didn't understand my suffering. He just sat there and enjoyed my failure. I knew I needed him, so I had to calm myself and swallow my desire to kill him.

"What would you do?" I waited to see what *Zay the great* would do.

"All our cards have been used up. We did do some damage, but they seem to always come out on top."

"I asked what you would do, not a fucking recap."

"Fine," he tossed his hands in the air, "I would ditch the army idea. It's obviously dead in the water anyway, they have the ace in the hole—the flash drive. I would take the guys we have left and come in hard and fast when they least expect it and open fire. Just take him out. It's what I'd do."

"What about your precious Tess? Wouldn't *she* be caught in the crossfire?" I knew she was his weakness and couldn't help the jab.

He hesitated. "No, I would make sure she wasn't there."

"What makes you think you could get her out of there? She hates you." I waited for him to let that sink in.

"She would do anything to protect those kids. It worked before. I can use them again to lure her out."

"I thought you didn't hurt kids." I couldn't help but sneer at him. He was so damn high and mighty, sure of himself in everything.

"I didn't say I would hurt them. I just don't mind using them."

"So, now you don't mind playing dirty." I cocked an eyebrow at him.

"I didn't say I never play dirty, *Father*. I'm just not blinded by my own fantasy."

CHAPTER SEVENTEEN

Trigger

I was in an unusually shitty mood by midnight. Most of the men scattered whenever I walked into a room, and Rail seemed uneasy about something. I knew he had tried a few times to bring it up to me.

"Fucking spit it out or leave," I grunted when Rail buzzed by my door again.

"Just wanted to ask if you didn't find it odd that your father went so quiet after we took out all those men. I wanted your thoughts on what you think he might be up to."

I rubbed my head and tried to push the freshly stirred rage out of the way. "If I knew the answer to that, wouldn't I have brought it to your attention by now?"

"I don't know, would you?"

I snapped my head up and glared. "What did you say?"

He raised his hands in apology. "You're not yourself right now, Trig. I wasn't sure if maybe you forgot to share something with us."

Careful...

His phone rang, and he pulled it from his jeans. He quickly responded while I waited in obvious impatience.

"Whenever you're done."

"It's Brick."

"And?" I grew even more annoyed.

"He's dropping off the grid with Minnie tonight."

"Where's Tess?"

His gaze moved to mine, and he squinted his question. "What do you mean?"

"Where is Tess?" I repeated each word slowly.

"I thought you had her somewhere with the boys?"

I dropped the phone from my hand, and in two strides snatched his phone to read the text.

Brick: Headin' out with Minnie tonight, no cell service where we'll be. I'll be back tomorrow a.m. to check in.

"You want to call Brick, see if he can get hold of her?"

"No. Don't say a word to anyone."

I'll deal with her myself.

"You sure?"

I tossed his phone at him, grabbed mine, and left.

"Morgan," I barked and heard Cooper scratch the pool table with a yelp.

"Yeah, boss," he called from down the hallway. "I'm in the storage closest."

I picked up my keys on the way over to him. "Have you heard from Mike yet about the boys?"

"Yeah, he called about an hour ago. They're settled in at the safe house, Savannah has 'em making cookies and shit."

Good.

"Why the hell do I have to go?" Denton snapped from his bed.

"Get your shit packed."

"What if Tess needs me?" Fin joined in and made my head spin. "You don't do a good enough job."

"I never asked for your opinion."

"Maybe you should."

I glared at the little shit, and his face changed from pissed to nervous. Fuck me.

"Here." I reached into his closet and pulled a box from the shelf. I knocked off the top and dug to the bottom then shoved the gangly stuffed animal in his hands.

"A bunny?"

"A rabbit." I corrected without thinking.

"Was it yours?" Why did kids have to ask so many questions?

"Get packed, Fin." I walked out.

I shook my head clear. "You see Tess tonight?"

He set the box he was about to put on the shelf on the table and looked at me. "She left a little while ago with Brick and Minnie."

What the fuck was she pulling here?

"She say anything else to you?"

"Tess hasn't been herself since Gus, really. She's still messed up over it." He stopped himself. "She was on the phone with someone earlier, and she did seem pissed off."

"You got a name?"

"No, but Cray was there. I'll give him a call, see if he remembers. Anything I should be doing to help you out right now?"

Morgan's way of asking was a lot less fucking annoying than Rail's.

"Watch the club for me."

"Yeah, if you need anything…"

"Yeah."

I headed for my room and packed my bag, grabbed my weapons, and headed out to my bike.

Trigger: Did Tess call Savannah tonight?

Mike: Not sure, let me see what I can find out.

"Trigger?" I heard a female's meek voice behind me. The soft tone of it made it through my crazy head. "Can I speak with you for a moment?"

No.

"Not now."

She took a cautious step forward and tucked her purse under her arm. Her tense shoulders and rigid movement gave away her nervousness. She appeared slimmer than the last time I saw her in the courtroom, and her face was pale against her dark hair.

"When would be a better time, then?"

I pulled the strap and fastened the buckle on my bag. "Thirty-seven years ago."

"I deserved that."

I flipped my hair out of my face and tugged on my helmet.

"I truly thought I was doing the right thing."

"I'm sure you did," I said, not wanting this conversation right now…or ever.

"Oh, hey, there." Rail tossed the trash and joined us. "Where are you staying?"

"Motel 6 down the road."

I didn't wait to listen; I peeled off. I needed space to think.

***

Punch.

Punch.

Punch.

Sweat dripped down my face and coated my skin in a thin layer. My knuckles screamed at me to stop, but the demons had other plans. The moment I'd take a break, they flipped out and screamed in their high-pitched chant. I was slipping further and further away from the surface, and the energy it took to stay something close to normal was dwindling fast.

I saw my phone screen light up, so I dropped my gloves on the ground and snatched it up.

"Hello," I panted before my head took over.

"Hey."

Her voice drew me up from somewhere deep, and I knew I wanted to play this carefully. Something was up, and I needed to hear what she had to say. I twisted to sit on the ledge and took in the early city lights that stretched along the PCH for miles.

"How's it going?"

"Good."

"Where's Brick?"

There was a pause before she cleared her throat. "Off with Minnie somewhere."

I closed my eyes and fought against the urge to lash out.

"When will you be back?"

"Um, Monday, I hope."

Hope?

"Anything you want to tell me?"

"No…" Her voice trailed off. "I just wanted to call and see how the boys settled in and to say goodnight and hear your voice."

"They're fine."

"Good. Okay, well, goodnight."

I glanced at the time. It was 3:30 a.m.

"Night."

As soon as the call disconnected, the wild things went into savage mode.

***

Tess

"Troubles in paradise?" Shantee hummed over my shoulder. She loved that I had decided to come back with her. Although what she thought I was going to do once I was there was very far from my actual purpose. *Some things are best left unsaid.*

"You okay?"

"Yup."

She fiddled with the air conditioning before she set it back to where it was. "Damn hot flashes."

I smiled. She was a trip. She loved her transformation, but her hormone shots were a little intense, especially if you did them as often as she did. Shantee was determined to be as female as possible.

"You know, it's been pretty damn great not having Clark around." She paused as she changed lanes, totally cutting off someone, and they gave her the finger. "Sure hope he doesn't return home anytime soon."

I felt my neck heat, but I pushed it aside. I didn't feel bad for killing Clark. He deserved it. He had taken too many people from me in this life for me to care a damn about taking his.

"A few years ago, I had a problem with one of my brother's friends." Her tone changed. "He didn't like me, didn't agree with my decision to change over, and he became a real problem. I couldn't even go out to the store without him causing a scene. Night clubs became scary, then one night he took it too far, and him and his friends jumped me in a parking lot." She pulled into the Arizona Charlie's hotel and parked near the front door. "Broke two teeth, fractured a few ribs, broke my nose. I was in rough shape."

"I'm sorry." I turned to face her. She deserved my attention. She'd never shared anything like this before.

"I was too, at first." She blinked her long, fake eyelashes, but I caught the hurt that flashed across her face. "But three years later, after he was released from jail, I saw him in a club, and all the hate and fear came rushing back." She pulled her huge Louis Vuitton bag onto her lap. "Some go to a therapist, and others," she pulled out a bottle, "take matters into their own hands." She handed it to me but wrapped her fingers around my wrist when I took it. “I don’t know what’s running through that pretty little head of yours, but know if you ever need anything, I’m a phone call away.”

I leaned forward and hugged her, then I grabbed my bag and went inside without a word. She understood.

I didn’t like sleeping alone. I missed Trigger’s warm body and his smell of whiskey and smoke. I set my bag on the bed and slumped down next to it. I hated to be alone at all now.

By morning, I didn’t think I slept for even a moment, but as it turned out, staring at the wallpaper for six hours was really quite relaxing. I showered twice for something to do and made an attempt to text Trigger as I had at least million times during the night, but I didn’t know what to say. I was convinced he knew I wasn’t with Brick, but he hadn’t let on. That was odd in itself. Surely by now Brick had checked in, and Trigger would have asked about me, but things were different now. Trigger was different. I hated it, but I had no idea how to get him back. However, it was good timing. He would never have let me do this alone, and I needed to handle this for myself. It was time.

I dried my hands free of sweat and dialed her number.

“He better not be with you, Tessa.” My mother’s voice cut through the silence.

“Hello, Mother.” My tone was clipped. “If Clark was with me, you’d know already. I’m sure you have plenty of people watching me.”

“Where is he, Tessa?”

“Meet me for lunch, and I’ll explain.”

“Come to the house at twelve-thirty.”

“No.” I cut her off. “I will not walk into the snake’s pit. If I’m going to tell you about Clark, it will be on my terms.”

There was a long stretch of silence before she huffed in her usual annoyed way.

“Fine. Where, then?”

I pulled the brochure from my purse. “Mary’s Tea Garden.”

“Tessa, that’s almost an hour from me. Why there?”

“You took me there for my tenth birthday. Guess it meant something to me, but obviously not to you.”

“I don’t remember that, but whatever. I’ll see you there at noon.”

I hung up, grabbed my keys, and rushed out of the hotel room. The cabby was too chatty for my liking, so I tuned him out and counted the seconds until we arrived.

The tea room was just as I remembered, old fashioned chairs in big flower prints, mini throw pillows everywhere, and finger-sized pastries that would melt in your mouth.

"How many today?" the receptionist asked.

"Actually, there will be two of us. It's a special occasion, and we'd like somewhere private, if at all possible."

The woman dragged her finger down the iPad and chose a table.

"Ah, yes." She picked up two menus and pointed over her shoulder. "Right this way."

I followed her down a long path and ducked under lush ivy. The entire place was an overgrown garden with every color rose imaginable. Nothing was left undone. It was a treat for the eye, and a heavenly scent floated in the air, depending on which room you were in. I loved this place, but after today, I would not be returning.

"Here you go, your own private terrace." I made sure I sat to face the door, so I could see her when she arrived.

"Can I get you anything?"

"Yes, I'll order the tea for us both now. La Cour Tisane iced, please, one blueberry and one orange caprice."

Her smile spread across her lips. "Lovely choice. So, you know our teas."

"Yes, you could say that."

The drinks arrived in attractive iced glasses decorated with fruit, just as I remembered. I sat and relaxed as I waited for my mother, who I knew always had to be fashionably late. Sure enough, about ten minutes later, she strolled in with two men. Her security. I smirked to myself. Of course she thought this was a trap. Little did she know it was just me here with her.

I rolled my eyes at her light pink skirt and matching blouse. She was a poser, and because of the venue I had chosen, she couldn't wear what she normally would. That was my point. I wanted to take her out of her comfort zone. I enjoyed her obvious discomfort in the surroundings. It seemed fitting, under the circumstances.

"Hello, dear." Her greeting was formal as she handed the hostess her jacket. "You come alone?" She looked over her shoulder then down the other hallway.

"Unlike you, yes, I did."

She shot me a glare before she eased into her seat and folded her napkin over her lap in a very conscious, ladylike manner. "Don't start, Tessa."

I dropped my head back with a throaty laugh. "That's rich, coming from you."

"What does that mean?"

"It means you've sent how many of your guard dogs to see if Clark was with me?"

She glanced around carefully again, and she lowered her voice. "Was he?"

Oh, how I wanted to lie through my teeth, but I thought the truth would be the best of all.

"I left because I found my happiness."

"Oh, please, with your outlaw biker?"

"Yes." I sipped my tea and savored the moment. "But Clark did come and visit me."

Her head shot up, and her eyes widened.

"And?"

"And he wanted me back."

Her throat contracted. "I suppose he was confused. He was thrown by Bret's sudden death."

I held my composure as I studied her reaction. Leon had promised me Felicia had never seen the tape, so she had no idea what really happened.

"You ladies ready to order?" The waitress broke our moment.

"Cheesecake for me, please." I gave her a warm smile, but I let it drop as I saw my mother rub her stomach like she might get fat just from the damn air around her.

"Angel food cake and no whipped cream."

Sounds yummy.

"Confused or not, Mother, there was still a part of Clark that wanted me over you." I felt a sense of victory skip up my spine. "Yes, he came to visit me." I couldn't help but continue with my story. "It was so pathetic to watch a grown man grovel at my feet."

"Enough."

"He wanted *me,* Mother, not you."

Her fists banged down on the table, rattling our glasses. A few people on the other terrace looked in our direction, but they couldn't see us that well through all the flowers.

"I said enough, Tessa. You say that again, and I'll—"

"You'll what?" I leaned back in my chair and studied the pretty glass in my hand.

"I'll..." She stumbled on her words and reached for her glass, took a sip, and swallowed. "I'll have my men take you back to the house."

"Well, you were the one who wanted to know about Clark, Mother."

I dabbed the corners of my mouth and thought about my next play.

"After I killed Bret, I met Clark in the hallway and stole the flash drive."

Her head snapped over to me, and some color drained from her face.

"What?"

"I found something rather interesting."

She downed the rest of her tea and slammed the glass down. She drew in a long breath and went to say something, but I held up my hand to stop her.

"Seems *our* Clark had the skeleton key to the city. Well, not just our city, but a few others as well." I reached for the paperwork in my purse and shifted gear. "You will be happy to know, Mother, that he signed over his share of the club to me a while back. Love can be a real bitch at times, hey?" I winked.

"Naturally. We are married, after all. I already knew that." She tried to smile but seemed to know I had more.

"Well, did you also know that if anything happened to you, your share of the house and The Dirty Demons Club goes into my name?"

Her eyes bugged out, and I was pleased to see how much my news affected her.

I spread the paperwork out on her placemat. "The terms clearly state that if anything happens to you, or if you so graciously sign over your shares, I get the house, the club, and the cars."

"What makes you think I would," she cleared her throat again, "hand my hard-earned business over to you?"

"What choice do you have?"

"Over my dead body will you ever own—" She grabbed my water and tried to drink it. I smiled at her.

I sat perfectly still and watched her world crumble all around her.

"What did you do?" Her eyes were wild, and her hands flew to her chest.

"I had many fantasies of how I wanted you to die, Mother. A shot to the head, or perhaps a pair of weasels to feast on your stomach, a baseball bat." I smirked almost more to myself than to her. "But I realized having the last word and forcing you to hear me without interruption would be the best way of all."

Her pupils dilated, and the vein in her neck ticked.

"It's not that hard to get. You just need to know the right people." She started to turn blue, and her body was slowly becoming paralyzed. "It's called belladonna." My mother's face looked waxy. I could see she realized she could no longer move. "In Latin, it means beautiful woman, which I found to be pretty ironic. It is also called the Devil's Berry. See how the names are so perfectly suited to the situation?"

One of her men, who stood a little way from us, took a step closer, so I reached over and covered her hand with mine and gave her a smile as I talked. He seemed to buy it and went back to his post. I felt a little movement in her fingers underneath mine.

"Belladonna is poisonous if eaten. The root is the deadliest, then the leaves, then the flower." My voice sounded eerie and calm; I rather liked this me. "It takes fifteen to twenty berries to kill an adult, but," I held up my hand then rooted through my purse and held up the small vial, "if you ingest it in liquid form, you only need the tiniest drop. I gave you three." I winked.

A sound came from her throat. "What was that, Mother? I can't make you out. Yes, your own daughter has finally outmatched you."

I moved to the seat next to her, took her hand, and scribbled her familiar signature on the paper. It wasn't great, but it would do. I tucked it away back in my purse and leaned in to brush her hair that had fallen in her face.

"You stole a life from me once, so it's only fitting I do the same to you." I rubbed her arm to make sure her head was still with me. "Say hi to Clark for me."

My mother's jaw twitched as I held her hand, but she was too far gone. She had only minutes before her heart would stop, and I would finally be free.

I threaded my purse through my arm and set a tiny bottle of charcoal on the windowsill just out of her reach. It was too late to save her, but it satisfied something in me to let her see that one thing that could have saved her life was just slightly out of reach.

"Bye, Felicia."

CHAPTER EIGHTEEN

Trigger

Mike: She didn't speak to Savi, but you're right, she's in Vegas.

Trigger: Where?

Mike: 6 miles from you. 740 S. Decatur Blvd.

I dropped my joint on the ground, kicked my bike into gear, and turned north on the Strip. Lights shot by me in a blurred line of color. Traffic was light, so I made good time.

The hotel was attached to the casino, and I immediately spotted four bikes in the driveway, but they were crotch rockets and clearly nothing to do with a biker club.

The hotel was a giant rectangle inside. Each room had its own patio and front porch window.

I rang the bell, and a middle-aged man stepped out from behind the wall.

"How can I help you tonight?"

"Lookin' for a girl, blonde, tattoo on her arm." I held up my phone and showed a picture of Tess. "What room is she in?" I wasn't in the mood to play games.

"I'm sorry, sir, I can't give out that kind of information."

"Holy shit," I heard someone whisper behind me. "That's Trigger. He's the president of Devil's Reach."

I rolled my eyes and shoved the phone further in the guy's face.

"Her name is Tess Marin."

"Like I said—"

"I won't repeat myself again." I fought the urge to pull my gun.

"Hey, man." A guy came up to the counter. I could tell by the racing colors on his jacket he owned one of the bikes out front. "You looking for that smokin' hot blonde with a long tat on the arm?"

"Yeah."

"We saw her. She throat-punched my buddy when he grabbed her ass in the elevator."

I half smirked.

"I swear he meant no harm. Just had too many beers."

"What room is she in?"

He whistled to his friends that he was heading upstairs. They seemed uneasy about me but let him go.

"Last I saw, she was heading up there with a couple of guys." He pointed to a door by the elevator. "She was pissed about something but seemed fine."

I handed him a fifty and started to walk away. "Thanks."

"Yeah, sure, anytime. Hey, I'm a huge fan. I've wanted to be in your club for as long as I can remember. So, do you have, like, a card or something, so I can look you up?"

Something came over me. Maybe it was because he reminded me of Denton, I wasn't sure, but I turned and headed back to him.

"You ever kill a man with your bare hands, feel the life get sucked from his lungs, not stop until his soul had completely left his body?" The kid swallowed hard. "Have you ever stood in front of a judge and heard you're facing three life counts, with no chance of parole?" He shook his head, and I leaned in close to drive my point home. "It's not a life anyone would want once you're in it, kid. If you need to be a part of something, pick anything else, because this shit will jack you up in ways you can't even imagine."

"Yes, sir." He pulled back from me as he said it and hurried back the way we had come.

With that, I went up the stairs to the second floor. The moment I turned the corner, I heard Tess scream. I pulled my gun and rushed to the door. She screamed again, and everything went red.

I stood back and kicked the door with all my weight. It shot inward, and both men scrambled for their weapons. The last thing I wanted were spectators, so I slammed the door behind me and glanced at Tess. She had tears streaming down her face, but her eyes were like fire. She gathered the sheet in her hands and tied it around her, but not before I saw the scratch marks on her thighs.

Rage tore through every single fiber of my being.

They touched what's mine. They hurt what's mine.

"Tess, come to me." I motioned for her to join me, but just as she moved, the guy closest to her grabbed her around the waist and stuck a gun in her mouth.

The wild things who were normally dormant when she was around began to scream. Their voices were so shrill they nearly split my head in two. My muscles twitched with hunger, and my focus clouded.

Right here, this is my hell.

I felt as though I was falling from a ledge, and the small hold I had on Nolan let go as the dark hole swallowed me up. My head pounded, and my vision shook with each heartbeat.

One moment I was by the door, and the next I was covered in their blood in the middle of the room.

What?

I whirled around to find the two men nearly ripped to shreds near the bathroom doorway, and Tess was huddled in a ball in the corner. My chest beat hard, my body shook, and I couldn't pull what the hell just happened from my memory.

Shit!

"Tess." I scooped her up and placed her on the bed. Madly, I grabbed her Chucks and slipped them on her feet. "Where's your bag?"

She blinked a few times and snapped back to the present with me, but then I saw the blood on the sheet.

"Not mine," she said before she pulled herself together and hurried to the bathroom, saying she had to change. A couple of minutes later, she came out and followed me back downstairs. I did the best I could to hide the bodies in the closet, but there was a lot of blood, and they were big guys. I knew no one should have reason to go into the room for a while, but I couldn't chance it and didn't want to waste time.

I grabbed her hand, closed the door softly, and we walked down the hall, just two people headed out for the night.

"Glad you found her," the kid called from his table. I gave a slight nod and pushed open the main door and urged Tess along.

Instead of heading down the street toward home, I turned right. Tess didn't say a word the whole drive, but I did notice her shake out her hands every few minutes.

"What's wrong?" I asked through the mic.

"Hands are numb."

"What from?"

"Adrenaline."

She needed a break, and a drive of about four hours to home wasn't the answer. After one phone call, I pulled into the Wynn parking lot, and we were soon escorted up to the penthouse where we were finally safe and out of the public eye.

"We'll stay for the night and leave in the morning." I set her bag down and tried to hold back my questions.

"I need a shower," she said, her voice heavy.

"I need to know what happened."

"I know, but just give me a few." She headed for the bathroom with a slight waver in her step.

I poured myself a drink and texted Mike.

Trigger: Found her. Appreciate your help.

Mike: Happy to hear it. Anytime.

I cracked my neck and changed chats.

Trigger: I need you to take care of a situation.

Two minutes later, my phone rang, and I stepped up to the window and explained to Cray where to go and what he needed to do to clear things up back at the hotel. I also needed him on standby for whatever other mess Tess might have created while she was here.

I glanced over at her bag and saw some documents sticking out. I pulled them out and scanned the wording.

What the fuck? She went back to the house to get these signed? What the hell was she thinking? The words "ownership" and "Tessa Marin" hit me hard. Was she planning on running the house here in Vegas?

Anger fueled me once again. I jammed the paperwork back into her bag and burst through the bathroom doors, only to find her standing in a towel as though in a trance in front of the mirror.

Her bloodshot eyes slowly dragged up to mine. Her chin quivered, and then she broke.

***

Tess

My knees gave out as Trigger's hard body slammed into mine just in time. His arms wrapped around me, and he supported my weight when I couldn't. It had been too long since I really felt him hold me the way he used to.

"I got you," he whispered into my hair, and for a moment, I felt Nolan was there. I sobbed. I needed to release the heaviness from the last twenty-four hours. I knew my mother's death wouldn't bother me. She totally deserved everything she got, but I was human, and Trigger arriving precisely at the right time turned my world completely upside down.

Once I shed the emotional crap, I pulled away and dried my cheeks. Trigger stepped back but didn't leave. He just watched as I slowly pulled on a tank top that barely covered my ass.

"Did they hurt you?" he asked. Anger still simmered. I could hear it in the timbre of his voice.

"Just a little sore, but nothing some Advil couldn't fix. My mother always picks the lowest of assholes to protect her."

He disappeared and returned with a bottle of water and some pills. I swallowed them down, and when I looked in the glass, he was directly behind me. His chest pressed into my back, and his hands clamped down on either side of the counter. His dark green eyes smoldered and held mine captive in the mirror as he pushed his erection through his jeans and against my opening.

I bit my bottom lip and let the prickle of lust race across my nerve endings.

His fingers started low at my thighs and traveled up under my shirt and flipped it over my bare ass before they brushed over my wetness.

I heard his jeans hit the floor and felt his hand pump his erection a few times.

I needed this.

Just as the tip broke my seal, I jerked forward with a tiny whimper.

My heart won the battle.

His hands fell away, his eyes darkened, and I could feel his internal conflict. A confused expression raced across his face, deepening the creases of his eyes.

"Who are you right now?"

His face softened, and he slid his hands up the curve of my spine.

"Does it matter?"

"It matters to me." I held my ground, and he closed his eyes and took a breath. "I want you to come back." I turned around to face him. "Fight for us, if not for yourself. I can't handle the distance and uncertainty anymore." I knew this next comment was going to sting. "Gus is dead, but you aren't. Please don't push me away and let them win." I gently touched his temple to reference his demons. "You asked me to marry you, but…" His eyes opened wide, and I could see he was finally hearing me.

"But what?"

"But do you still even want to?"

Trigger's face fell, and a grim line traced across his lips.

What just happened?

He backed up and left as I stood there and wondered if I was still engaged to the only man I truly loved.

I paced the bathroom, unsure what to do. We were always so up and down in our relationship. Just once I wished I knew where we stood.

Finally, I headed out through the living room and into the kitchen where I plucked a bottle of tequila from the bar, three limes, a knife, some salt, and my phone. I noticed the spare room door was closed and figured he needed a moment alone.

I lined the cut limes on the wooden railing next to the bottle and snapped a picture and attached it to a text message.

Tess: To freedom.

I waited and saw the little bubbles appear before her text came through.

Ven: I can't believe it! Now what?

I couldn't help but smile. We both had been under my mother's thumb for years.

Tess: Now I need to see you. Can you slip away for a bit? Meet me at the Wynn. I'll leave your name at the desk.

Ven: Sure, the boss is gone, so I'm free as a bird. Be there in fifteen.

I laughed at our sick, twisted humor and took three shots to ease the discomfort the empty penthouse brought on.

The front desk assured me she could come straight up, and in only ten minutes, she arrived at the door and nearly knocked me over in greeting.

"Come," I took her hand and pulled her out to the patio, "we have so much to talk about."

"I really hope karma was watching when you did it." Ven giggled as she took another shot after hearing my story.

"Why do you think I got away?" I raised an eyebrow and clicked my cup to hers. "Shc knew what we went through and knew what had to come."

"I can't believe her men followed you back to the hotel and tried to…"

The spare room door opened, and in came Trigger. He stopped short when he saw Venna sitting on the floor of the penthouse. I guessed he didn't hear us. I noticed he had a tight grip on his phone.

"Hi," she squeaked.

"Nice to see you again," he greeted her kindly, which was almost a little scary.

He came over and eyed the paperwork that lay between us. "What are you doing?"

"You asked me before what happened and why I came here." I pointed to the couch, and again to my surprise, he sat.

Ven looked at me for guidance, clearly wondering if she should leave. I shook my head. I wanted her to stay. She was a part of this now.

"So?" He leaned forward and eyed my outfit. I was still wearing the tank top and nothing else.

I reached for my purse and handed him the tiny vial of belladonna and let his eyes skim over the label.

"Deadly stuff. How did you get it?"

"A friend."

His eyebrows rose, and he waited for me to explain further.

"Ven warned me that my mother was going to send some men to the club to get answers about Clark. I couldn't let that happen again, so I hatched a plan to tell you that I was going to stay with Brick, when really I hitched a ride to Vegas." He tilted his head to pop his neck.

Trigger eyed Venna, and she looked at me and swallowed hard.

"With who?"

Shit.

"Shantee."

"Who?"

"She was the transsexual you helped save at the bar the other day when the men tried to hurt us."

"Right. I first met her at the house, when you went back." He licked his lips and rubbed his hands together. That was a hard memory for both of us.

"Then what?"

"I lured my mother to a spot where I knew I could carry out my plan." I folded my legs under me and leaned my weight on one hand. "She showed, I said what I wanted, confessed to killing Clark, and that I knew about this." I tossed him the ownership paperwork for the house and club. "Turns out Clark signed his shares of the house over to me a few years ago, to show his love for me or some shit. He had it worked out with the lawyer that if my mother died before he did, and he is legally still alive right now, or signed over the rest of the rights to me, that I would be the full owner of the house. Of course, that would never normally happen, but given some tasteless poison, I got her John Hancock. It was rather satisfying to watch her sign away her beloved career to the one person she loathed. I wasn't about to wait for the paperwork to come through over her death. The signature will be faster."

I smiled. Maybe Trigger could get the footage and I could bask in that moment over and over again.

"So, you're working there now?" I could almost hear the hurt in his voice.

"Look," I slowed the pace of the conversation so he would hear me out instead of jumping to conclusions, "normally, you couldn't pay me enough to step foot in that house, but what I will do is appoint Venna the manager, and we run the place ourselves." His eyes narrowed. "That place will forever haunt me, but it brings in a ton of money. The DR doesn't have the Serpents contract anymore, so this will be a great source of income to hold us over until the drug deal comes through."

Venna pulled out a folder and showed Trigger the annual income. "The house has made at least three hundred and sixty thousand consistently the past six years." She moved her finger along a chart. "And as you can see, it's growing."

"You have my attention."

"Dirty Demons could be Dirty Promises's sister company, but," I raised my hand, "I want to put twenty percent of the house yearly income into a fund for Lilly." I lowered my voice. "My family killed her mother. It's the least I can do."

When I looked up, he was staring at me with an unreadable expression.

"What?"

"Every time I think I have you figured out, I don't."

"Is that a bad thing?"

"Not…at all." He shook his head in amazement, and I cleared my throat.

"Okay, kids," Ven scooped the paperwork off the floor and stood. "I have a lot to prepare for, so I should be going." She reached down and gave me a hug. "I can't wait for the girls to hear about the new changes."

I lifted my hand to stop her, but she beat me to it.

"I promise I won't say a word until you give me the green light. But the first to go are those friggin' house uniforms."

"Agreed!"

She turned. "Bye, Trigger."

He gave her a tight nod while he stared at me.

He waited for the door to close before he spoke. "What happened after you left the Tea House?"

"The cabby took me back to my hotel, but before I even got to the elevator, her two men joined me and stuck a gun in my side. They didn't care what I had done to my mother. They're nothing but hired muscle with no loyalty. They were just happy to get me alone, so they could have a piece of me. They forced me into my room, stripped me down, and…" I couldn't go on; there was no point. "I fought hard, but there were two of them. Anyway, you came in just as they were about to…"

"We have a problem here, Tess."

"Which is?"

He rubbed his beard as he thought. "You have to stop lying to me. What if I wasn't there to stop them?"

"I would have been able to handle it." That was a lie.

Trigger glared at me. "Sure looked like you had the upper hand as they stripped your pants off." He stopped himself and let out a heavy sigh. "No more lying."

"Would you have let me leave?"

"No."

"Well—"

"I would have, just not by yourself."

I dropped my head forward and bit my tongue. He was right. Everything could have gone to shit very quickly.

"Okay, I'll work on that." I picked a piece of lint off my shirt. "But you have to work on your own demons too."

He stood and pulled me to my feet. He didn't say a word as he pulled me down on the bed and lay next to me. We both stared at the ceiling. The lights from the fireworks danced along the walls, and Frank Sinatra crooned off in the distance.

Ever so slowly, Trigger's fingers inched over to entwine with mine, his grip becoming tighter. I held on, needing a lifeline of my own.

"Help me find my way back," he whispered.

***

Allen

"What do you mean, the boys aren't there?" I tossed my glass of gin across the room where it shattered into the flames of the fireplace. "That's horse shit! Where could they be?"

"I don't know, Father. A lot of the club members seem to be out this weekend, even Trigger."

"Zay," I rubbed my head with frustration, "I don't know how much longer I can play this game."

"At the risk of sending you over the edge, Joe isn't at the door. He hasn't been around all weekend either. I have a bad feeling."

I ripped my collar from my neck and tossed it into the fire. It took a moment to catch, but when it did, it burned hard and fast.

"I can't take another setback. We move in this week."

"You sure?"

I grabbed the bottle of gin and hung up.

Just as I was about to go into the bedroom, I heard a loud knock at the door.

"What?"

"Open the goddamn door."

You have got to be shittin' me.

I swung open the door, and there was the fuckin' woman who had hosted my sperm for nine months and stuck me with that demon offspring.

"How the living fuck did you find me, Elizabeth?"

Her hand pulled back and slapped me straight across the face. “How could you kill him?” she screamed and went in for another hit, but I caught her arms and yanked them down and pushed her on the floor.

“He was dying of tit cancer, anyway. I just sped up the processes.”

She licked her bottom lip and pulled back her anger. Her legs were shaky, but she managed to hold herself with poise.

“Now,” I thumbed my sore cheek, “how the fuck did you find me?”

“You think like crap, you’ll eventually step in it.” She pushed by me and whirled around with a finger stuck in my face. “My brother told me what you did to our son, you sick son of a bitch. I know I don’t have much ground to stand on, but shit, Allen, what the hell are you up to now?”

I laughed and poured myself another glass. “I love that you think you can question me.”

“Don’t screw with me, Allen. Enough is enough.”

I sipped my drink and lazily flopped into my chair and flipped on the TV. “You’re, ah, blockin’ my view.”

She hit the TV button and it switched off.

“All it would take is one call, and our son would take you out.”

“He tried once and failed, remember?”

“He’s your blood!” Her hands went in the air, and her face grew red. She really was sexy when she got mad.

“Not by choice.”

“I should have killed you when I had the chance.”

I rose out of my seat and walked her backward toward the door.

“And I could kill you, but what’s the point when you already have one foot in the grave?”

Her face fell, and tears rimmed her eyes. “What does that mean?”

“It means I know.”

“Know what?” She tried to stand a little straighter.

“Tick tock, Elizabeth.”

She hauled back her hand and slapped me in the face again. I saw it coming, but I loved a woman who liked to get rough.

“Have a good night, sweetheart.” I opened the door and watched her hurry to her car.

You can run, but the reaper is only one step behind.

CHAPTER NINETEEN

Trigger

I inched my fingers out for her, but the sheets were cool, confirming she was not within my reach. I blinked to clear the blur of the clock. 5:30 a.m.

My body hummed for hers. Sleep wasn't in my future…in fact…I sat up and waited.

Nothing.

No demons screamed in my head or gnawed at my bones. I had actually slept a solid four hours. I closed my eyes for a moment to enjoy the quiet and realized no headache pounded behind my eyes.

Well, shit, even the fog was gone.

My phone buzzed next to me, and I groaned while I checked the text.

Rail: Your mother is back and wants to talk.

Trigger: Send her home.

Rail: Can't do it, boss.

I rubbed my head out of habit.

Trigger: Why is that?

Rail: She scares me. She's the female version of you.

Trigger: That was an order.

Rail: Ahh, she's mastered that look of yours and she makes my skin crawl. She wins.

Fuck me.

I answered the door and was greeted with two fresh cups of coffee. I tipped the man and headed out to the living room where I found it empty, then the sound of water caught my attention. I sat the coffees down and headed over. The glass doors slid open without a sound, and I saw her.

Her spine was perfectly straight, and her hair was pulled up into a messy bun as she leaned against the infinity wall. The lights of the city created a massive backdrop behind her. Slowly, her head turned as if she sensed me. I eased into the water and up behind her.

"Morning."

She leaned her head back on my shoulder. "Not a bad view to wake up to."

I kissed her neck and lightly drew her skin into my mouth.

"Sure is." I felt her body react to mine. "Why are you wearing a suit when this is a private pool?"

"Gotta make you work for it," she teased.

I kissed her shoulder, along her neck, and up to her jaw. My hand sprawled low across her stomach, and I felt it tighten when my finger dipped into her suit.

"Trigger?"

"Mm," was all I offered. I was starved for her taste.

"What were you doing in the spare room last night?"

"Priest."

She stilled. "What?"

I didn't stop. My free hand flexed on her hip while I ground against her perky, tight ass.

"You wanted to know if I still wanted you," I answered as I continued to devour her neck.

"You were going to marry me last night?"

Both thumbs hooked under the sides of her bikini bottoms and ripped the seam apart. I tore the scraps away and freed myself.

I need to be in her.

"Yes," I whispered as I slid inside her slowly so I could savor every inch of her snug hold on me.

Her back bowed as she sucked in a sharp breath.

"Don't ever question my desire for you, Tess." My arms wrapped around her midsection as she took the last two inches of me. My knees bent, and I circled my hips to hit her in all the right spots.

She reached over her head and fisted my hair. I pulled the tie with my teeth, and her top fell down to expose her breasts.

Fuck me, she was beautiful.

I moved in and out, painfully slow, to get her feisty side to show itself. I circled her nipple with my thumb and nipped at her neck with a growl.

"Trigger," she huffed, "you play dirty."

"Says the sexy woman dressed in the pool."

She laughed. "It was a bathing suit."

"I hated it."

"Clearly." She shot forward when I flicked my hips. "More." She tried to pull away, but I slammed her to me. "Trigger!"

"Tess," I growled. "Flip."

She suddenly twisted, wrapped herself around my waist, and grabbed my head in her hands. Her eyes searched mine before she pulled my hair back. "Fuck me." She pronounced each word carefully. A wild need flashed deep within her eyes, and I wanted every single drop of it. I slammed her mouth to mine, and my hands palmed her ass. Her sleek skin felt like silk against mine. It was maddening to keep control.

She pulled back, leaned on the ledge, and lifted her legs to hike over my shoulders. I didn't waste any time and grabbed her hips to slam back in. Back where I belonged.

"Yes!" She dropped her arms over her head and held onto the bar to arch her back in that sexy, mouth-watering curve.

The water lapped around us. Her breasts matched the rhythm, and I swore I grew harder just before she squeezed and bucked through her orgasm. Nothing sexier than when Tess gave in. Her cheeks got pink, her breasts swelled, and her screams took me to a place that was pure bliss. I never thought such a place existed until I met her.

As much as I wanted to keep going, I couldn't control myself. I dove off and joined in the wild ride.

If I could have stopped time and lived in the high of my orgasm with Tess, Nolan would never leave.

"I need a shower." Tess kissed my cheek and hurried into the bathroom, and I headed out to the living room with my phone to my ear and waited for him to answer.

"Who was that?" Tess came out in leather pants and heels just as I ended the call. I handed the warm coffee to her. "Thanks."

"Cray. He was confirming everything was cleaned up."

"How do you do that?"

"Money." I sent off a quick text. "And expendables if we need them."

"That's kinda messed up, isn't it?"

I shrugged. It was part of the MC world. The men knew all this shit before they joined.

Tess stood to remove her phone from her back pocket.

"Oh," she glanced over at me, "I need to take this." She slipped into the bedroom, and I followed but waited by the door to see who it was.

She sat on the bed and answered. Denton's face popped up on the screen.

"Hi, Tess!" He waved.

"Hey, buddy, how's it going there?"

"Good, lots of places to hide, although the grass is itchy, but I saw a goat yesterday, and it chased Fin down to the house. Oh, my God, Tess, you should have seen it. It was so fuckin' funny." He burst out laughing, and Tess joined in. "Mike had to pick him up because it was going to climb him like a tree."

"I'm sorry I missed that." She smiled, and I felt her warmth from where I stood. "How's everyone else?"

"Good." He lowered his voice. "I think Fin has a crush on Olivia."

"She's three, isn't she?" Tess asked, amused.

He shrugged. "Age is just a number, baby."

I fought back a smirk.

"Mark's boys fuckin' bite." He glanced over his shoulder. "Oh, ah, I mean Mark's boys bite. Savannah says I have to watch my language, especially around the boys." His face scrunched up. "I wish Uncle Trig was here to give them his scary face."

"It's all an act," she said playfully. "Just nail one in the shoulder when their dad's back is turned. A little fear never hurt anyone."

Ha!

"I might do that."

"Don't tell Trigger I said that, though."

"Too late." He pointed at me in the doorway.

Tess laughed when she saw me. "Oops."

"Uncle Trig," he called out, and I moved closer, "when can we come home?"

A ping of sadness hit my gut. Gus's death played on all of us, and the past few months had been pretty rough.

"Not yet, but soon."

Denton's face fell, but he shrugged. "At least I get to play paintball here. You know who's just as scary as you?"

"Who?" I was curious about his answer.

"Cole, but Savannah gives him shit like you do Tess, and it makes me feel better, but I wish I was back at the club."

"See?" Tess bumped my arm. "My defiance entertains everyone."

"Oh! Gotta go, guys!" The phone went black.

"I miss them." Tess stood and headed back out of the room.

"I don't miss their random punches to the balls," I muttered.

Tess laughed and followed me out the door. "Fin only did that because you don't give him enough attention."

"There's plenty of others to do that."

"But he wants yours."

"Mm."

"Trigger," she turned to face me in the elevator, "they love you and look at you like a father now. You, of all people, know how hard it is growing up without a father. Well, one who actually loved you, so have a little empathy." I grabbed her by the waist and pulled her into me. "I'm serious."

"I know." I kissed the side of her neck and got drunk off her smell.

"Don't get me all horny before a four-hour bike ride."

"Wouldn't dream of it." I sucked in her skin and felt her knees sag.

She reached down and stroked my erection before she dropped to her knees. She looked up with bright green eyes, unzipped my pants, and swallowed me whole.

"Jesus," I hissed and leaned against the wall. She was like a goddamn Hoover. Over and over she took me to the root, her tongue curved to guide me where she wanted. Tess was a drug, one I wanted to be addicted to forever.

Just as I felt like I could come, she pulled away with a wicked grin.

"What?"

She rose to her feet and wiped her mouth dry. "I can play dirty too."

The doors opened, and she walked out with a spring in her step.

Game on.

***

Tess

"What's your problem?" Brick stepped in my way. "You look annoyed or something."

"I'm not."

"Hey," he took my arm to stop me, "what's up?"

"You don't want to know."

"Yeah, I do."

Oh, really? Okay.

"I'm sexually frustrated." I smiled as his hand fell away like a deadweight.

"Oh, come on, Tess, no."

"Yeah, a game we had going got a little out of hand near Ventura. Nearly creamed my pants right there on the bike."

He cringed at my wording, and I smacked his arm cheerfully.

"Aren't you glad you asked?"

"I think I need to go lay down." He felt his forehead in a sickly way. "I'm feeling flushed."

"Feel free to spend less time with Rail."

He glared and walked away muttering.

I saw Elizabeth nursing a cup of tea in the corner of the bar. I set my bag down in the hallway and headed in her direction.

"Hi, Tess," she greeted me kindly. "Would you like to sit?"

"Sure." I noticed her knuckles were white around the handle of the cup. "You all right?"

She smiled, but it didn't reach her eyes. "Not really. Do you think you could get Trigger to talk to me?"

Probably not, but the worry that was written across her face made me say, "I can try." I walked to the office and knocked on the open door. "Trig?"

"Can't take it anymore?" He smirked.

"I have a date with Pace, so I'm good." I loved that he hated my toys.

He shot me a warning not to do it, but he knew I never listen, so he could use that glare all he wanted.

"So, you know how you love me, right?"

He dropped his pen and leaned back in his chair. I closed the door behind me and moved to lean over his desk just enough for my shirt to hang open. On cue, his eyes moved down to my cleavage.

"Will you do me a favor?"

"Depends."

I moved around the desk and rolled his chair back enough for me to sit on his desk. He immediately ran his hands up my thighs and kissed my neck. "You have my attention."

I pushed my fingers through his hair and gave it a tug at the root. He groaned with a yummy hiss. "Talk to your mother."

He stilled.

"Please. She's right outside."

"Tess," he sighed and leaned back.

"She's been hanging around a lot lately, and I'm assuming it's because she wants to talk but didn't know how to approach you."

"Don't get involved."

"Too late." I held up my finger to show him the ring. "I won't pretend like I understand what you're going through with her, and if you want to send her away, I won't say another word about it, but," I leaned forward and gently brushed my lips over his, "she came back for a reason. At least hear her out before you show her the door."

He growled deep in his throat and yanked me onto his lap. He roughly kissed me, and his hands held me down by my waist while he pushed his erection into my hip.

"I want you, Tess."

"You can have me," I peeled myself off his lap, "after you speak with Elizabeth."

I gave him a wink and hurried out the door before he decided to lock it.

I couldn't help but try to eavesdrop from behind the counter. Several guys strolled in and out of the bar, ordered, and hung around, but I couldn't tell you one person's name.

Brick suddenly popped into view, his hands on his hips and one brow cocked.

"You're back for more detail?" I grinned, but he didn't. "What?"

"What?" he repeated, and I knew he was really mad. "Imagine my surprise when Cray checked in to tell me the body left in Mary's Tea House was handled."

"Did I fail to mention that?"

"Tess Marin, I swear to God, I will remove your eyelids and feed them to the rats if you lie to me."

"That's a tad specific."

"Tess!"

"Brick, it's fine, I'm fine. I had a plan, and everything worked out fucking flawlessly."

Well, kinda.

He leaned his hands on the bar and stepped back to lower his head. "Christ, woman."

"Hey." I rested my hand on his. He was struggling, and his eyes were squeezed shut. "Spit it out."

When he finally looked up at me, he seemed so young, like the first day we met.

"You're all I have for family that I can count on, and I feel like you keep the most shit from me."

That hit me right in the center of the chest. He was right. I did.

"Truth?" I hopped up on the counter, swiveling so I was directly in front of him. "You're right, I do, but it's not for the reason you think. It was always you and me—"

"And Clark," he added bitterly.

"No, it was always you and me. Clark was on the side."

"Fine."

"You spent how many nights protecting me when you could have been out with girls and shit?" He started to speak, but I covered his mouth. "You sacrificed a lot for me. I guess I'm trying to do the same for you."

He batted my hand away. "I'm lost."

"Hey!" Cooper looked like he might be sick. "Have you seen my cut?"

"No," we both said, and he flew out of the bar and down the hallway.

"Check the boys' room!" I called after him.

I rested my hands on Brick's shoulders. "I really like Minnie. She's a feisty little shit, kinda reminds me of myself." I winked. "I don't bother you with all my problems 'cause you should be focusing on her."

"You don't—"

"You might not see it, Matt, but a wedge could form between you two because of me. It's now your turn to focus your energy on protecting Minnie, because shit knows I have enough versions of Trigger protecting me."

He sighed and rubbed his head. "When did you get so smart?"

"It comes in waves."

***

Allen

My bloodstained boots dripped on the hot steps of the Catholic church. I hated Texas with a passion. It was always hot, and they had the most asshole gunslingin' cowboys known to man.

"Where should I put him?" Zay dragged the body of the priest who used to run the church.

"Stuff him in the tire swing." I waved him off and sipped my warm sweet tea.

I grumbled as I saw a woman and her son approach me.

"Good morning." The lady looked past me. "I'm looking for Father Parie. Is he around?"

"Sorry, he's not in this morning. He called me to fill in while he dealt with a flat tire." I laughed inside at my choice of words.

"Perhaps we can come by tomorrow."

"Absolutely." I flashed my smile and watched them leave. The little boy looked over his shoulder, and I gave him a wink. His eyebrows rose in surprise. I was sure the devil spoke to him through my grin.

An alarm went off inside the church, and I jumped to my feet with my binoculars.

"Zay," I called out and pointed, "we have a runner."

He pulled on a rope, and a huge white flag fell from the roof with a huge blue cross on it. Christ, it was like a beacon waving down the illegals.

"Please," a man dressed in dirty clothes pleaded as he ran toward us. He dropped at my feet with his hands in the air. "Please, Father," he fought to catch his breath, "I need you to protect me. They're coming for me."

"Who?" I glanced at the horizon.

"The coyotes." His accent was thick, but he spoke English well. "We are not allowed to break off, but they took my kids, and I can't find them."

Perfect.

"The Lord will help you." I reached down and lifted him to his feet. "Let's get you some water."

"Thank you, thank you," he sobbed.

He ate, showered, and was given new shoes, thanks to the dead man hanging in the yard. We sat inside the church while he prayed, and I grew bored.

After half an hour, I'd had enough and pulled his attention to me.

"Jer, I need to understand what happened out there in order for us," I pointed to the Jesus statue, "to protect you. What did you see?"

"Five men took us across the border. We had to carry bricks of cocaine on our backs, and there was barely any room for water. When we started, there were thirty of us. When we arrived, there were only seven." Tears dripped down his face.

"Where are the drugs now?"

He rubbed his eyes dry like he was frustrated. "We spent last night in the woods, about five miles from here. When they told us to drop the cocaine, we knew something bad was about to happen. That's when they took my girls, told me I had to return to Mexico and bring over one more load before they would release them. You don't understand these men. They are bad men. They don't keep their word. They—"

"Yeah, yeah, yeah." I waved him off to shut him up and opened the Bible to where I had a map. "Show me where the drugs are."

He eyed me in fear but slowly took the map and studied it. "Here."

"You sure?"

"Yes."

I shot him in the face.

"Whoop!" I held up the map to Zay. "Go get your customs outfit on. It's time to go play."

Zay fired up the quad and raced into the desert with two men I had recently recruited.

I watched until the dust trail disappeared then headed back inside the church. I could really use a nap.

CHAPTER TWENTY

Trigger

"I'm not proud of my choices, Nolan. If I could go back, I would, but I'm here now. I'm not expecting you to forgive me or to even see me again after this. I just wanted the chance for you to hear me out."

I glanced at Tess, who was with Brick at the bar, and then back to my mother. A lot of shit had happened lately, and my curiosity about who my mother really was had always gnawed at my gut.

"Fine. You have two minutes."

"First," she handed me a Post-it with an address on it, "I'm sure he's gone, but Allen was staying there last night."

"Brick," I called. He looked up and headed over as I held up the Post-it. "Allen's last location."

"On it." He grabbed Rail by the cut and pulled him away from some chick.

"How did *you* find him?" My men couldn't seem to track him, but she could? What was I missing?

She looked away for a moment and studied the club. "Well, that's part of the reason I'm here."

I glanced at my phone, annoyed. I didn't have time for mind games.

"The truth is, Nolan, I'm sick." She waited for a reaction, but I didn't have one I cared to share. "Turns out I have bad kidneys." She leaned back in her chair with a sigh. "Serves me right, all those years treating my body like a garbage can. Stripping wasn't something I wanted to do, but one wrong move can define your life. I know that now, and I want to fix it. I made many mistakes, but the biggest was leaving you behind."

"I won't argue with you there."

"I'm sorry." I could tell by the way her body slumped forward she meant it. "I've been seeing a doctor here in town, and he's one of the best. When I left the office, I saw Zay. I know he's Allen's hired killer. I followed him back to that hotel, and that's where I found Allen. I knew he would still be after you. I wanted to talk to him."

"Did you find out anything that would tell you what he's up to?"

She licked her lips like she wanted to say something but stopped herself. "No," she paused. "But my guess would be that he won't go far from wherever you are. He's a horrible man. I know that now."

"Horrible wouldn't be the word I'd use."

"True, but I'm here now and can help."

"I am not interested in your help."

"I get it." She held up her hand and didn't push it any further.

"Okay." I grabbed my phone and stood. I had waited three decades to know and understand my mother, and now she was here and sick, and all I really cared about was killing my father. How fucked up was that? I turned and headed for the door, but Nolan suddenly appeared and stopped me in my tracks.

Fucking head.

I turned to look over my shoulder. "Get your shit from your motel and come stay here. The rest can be handled later."

"I wasn't asking to stay here. I just wanted you to—"

"I know."

The club door swung open, and Mud held up his arms. "I'm here with a package." He twisted and pointed to Wes, my former cellmate, who squinted at the change in light. "Found him hitchhiking up on the 210 freeway. Never thought I'd ever hear your name as a drop-off location."

"Thanks." I nodded and signaled for Tess to bring us two beers. "Sit."

He sat and dropped his bag at his feet. I noticed Mud had found his way over to my mother.

"How are ya, Wes?"

"Confused." He laughed at me. "And now, by your lack of surprise at seeing me, I think I may have my answer to why I was released early."

"I've come into some leverage." I ran my hand up Tess's leg when she set the drinks on the table. "Tess, this is Tray." I gave him a look, and he knew what the nickname meant. He earned a place at the club. "He's from the Tennessee chapter, but he'll be joining ours now."

She held out her hand, and he respectfully shook it.

"Nice to put a face to the name, Tess. You're pretty famous, you know?"

"Am I, now?" She grinned at me, knowing that most of the men still couldn't believe I gave her a ring. Rail spread that shit like a crack in the ice. "Well, I'll leave you two be, and I'll find you later." She gave me a sexy smile as she walked away.

"Can't thank you enough for what you did. I am in your debt."

"No," I corrected him, "now we're even."

We finished our beers, and I brought him up to speed on what I expected from him. For now, he would stay with Rail until we got Gus's room cleaned out. I hated that it still made my neck tick thinking of my uncle.

"Trigger!" Morgan shouted from the back room and stormed into the bar with his phone to his ear. "We may have a problem."

I heard a noise at the door before it flew open. One of my doormen looked shook up and pointed over his shoulder.

"Trigger, there's some men here to see you."

I pulled out my phone and checked the cameras.

"Let 'em in."

"You sure, boss?" He waited a beat before he hurried back out.

In walked five Hispanic men with their guns at their sides.

"Trigger," the man with all the flashy rings pointed at me, "I thought maybe I should come and kill you, but I hesitate. Given our history, I thought a chat might be in order first."

"After years of working together, I'm pleased you chose that route," I muttered sarcastically.

"Who's that?" I heard Tess whisper to Rail.

"That would be the cartel."

"Holy shit."

"Yeah…" He trailed off. "So, curb your inner tiger around these guys."

"Where can we talk?" He glanced around and spotted Tess. "She will serve us drinks."

It was the one and only time I wished fuckin' Peggy was back. Her fake tits would have been more his speed.

I nodded at Tess, and for once, she didn't argue. She just headed back to the bar and started to load up her tray with booze.

"This way." I waved him to head into the meeting room. I glanced at Morgan, who tucked an extra gun into the back of his pants before he hurried inside and joined Brick and Rail. “Hey,” I met Tess at the bar, “don’t linger within their reach, don’t speak to them, and don’t get lippy. Serve and get the hell out.”

She nodded. “Why are they here?”

“No clue.”

I waited for her to enter the room before I shut the doors and sat at the head of the table.

Bruno’s men formed a horseshoe around him. They carried at least four guns each, and their eyes scanned the room carefully. Not guys to mess with.

“Let’s skip the shit and jump right in,” I started. “Why are you here?”

“I want my coke back.”

My face twisted in confusion. “Everything I had from you sold. Your cut was signed off by your own men. I have nothing left of yours.”

“Ah, my friend, but what about the one-point-one million you took last night from my coyotes?”

What? I tried to calm myself. I had never stolen from the cartel, not once. I wouldn’t be that stupid.

“We’ve worked together long enough for you to know I would never touch another man’s product. I believe I’ve earned that respect.”

He leaned back and looked up Tess’s skirt as she leaned to put a drink on the table. I knew what he was doing, and I tried hard not to let it bother me. She set a shot of tequila in front of him and stepped back next to Brick.

At least she listened.

“Pictures don’t lie, Mr. Vineyard.” He signed for one of his men to drop a photo in front of me.

I snatched up the photo of a man on a quad. The back was piled high with bricks of cocaine, and there was my fucking reaper staring back at me. What the fuck? I held it closer and studied the face. I handed it to Brick, and his face went hard. Tess leaned forward and looked at the photo Brick held, then she cupped her mouth when she saw who it was.

“That’s not my man. The cut is mine, but that man is Zay. He works for my father.”

“Interesting you let the *chica* in your business.” He tilted his head at Tess.

I hated that he even paid attention to what was mine. It felt like

Serpents were back in the room.

"Are we here to talk about pussy or the fact that I was set up?"

His face snapped over to mine. "Why not both?" When I didn't budge, he unfolded his fingers and held them up. "Fine, educate me. Who is this Zay in the photo?"

"He's some hit man my father hired to help him kill me. I'm sure you've heard that my father holds no love for me."

His eyes darkened when he made the connection. "Yes, I have heard many things lately, and I wondered about the timing of this unfortunate theft. Your father owes me a lot of money. I have been very generous with him, even loaned him guns. I have been very patient. Now he steals over one million in drugs from me as well?"

"Looks that way."

I wasn't aware my father owed money to the cartel. It was a game changer. I couldn't help but wonder why he would take such a risk.

"Interesting." He rubbed his chin and eased back into his seat. "What to do now," he said, more to himself than anyone in the room.

My mind mulled over all the possibilities, and after a few moments, I knew what the best move might be for me and my club.

"I have an idea that I think will work for both of us."

"I'm listening."

***

Tess

"Holy shit, Tess." Minnie rose from her chair. "I've never seen a more badass wedding dress in my life."

"I'd do you," Rail sputtered.

"Huh, like you'd ever get a chance," Minnie scoffed. "Why on earth Trigger would send him to watch over us is beyond me."

I stepped out of the tiny dressing room and stood in front of the mirror. There was zero way I was going to wear white, so any traditional wedding shop was out of the question. No, I wanted something that was me, and this—I turned around and admired my ass—was me. A tight black leather dress hugged my body. It looped around my neck, low in the front, and sexy lace held the two pieces together. The back was my favorite. It dipped dangerously low and settled right above my ass.

"I can't wait to see how Trigger will react!" Minnie squealed with joy.

"That's her wedding dress?" a lady whispered to her friend. "What are her bridesmaids wearing, pasties?" They laughed and rolled their eyes.

"Hey, Tess," Rail leaned over the back of the seat to see me better, "remember how you stabbed that asshole over twelve times because he hit on you? That should be in your vows." He winked at me as the nasty women grabbed their bags and ran out of the store.

"Not a bad idea, Rail." I laughed. "Okay, this is it, I'm done. Ring it up."

"What else do you need to do?" Minnie slurped back a rum and Coke in a Big Gulp cup.

"Nothin', really. Just needed my dress and shoes." I patted my bag. "The rest will fall into place. It's just a party in the back yard. That's all we want."

"I love that you love simple." She grinned. "Because there's no room for a white wedding in the MC world."

"Amen to that shit," Rail piped in and draped his arm over my shoulders. "I'm still waiting for Trigger to change his mind so I can swoop in and steal ya." He grinned playfully.

"Did you feel that way before or after you thought I was the mole?"

"No, I got my hard-on *after* you slapped me."

"Thanks for the visual."

I should have known something was up when we were on our way back. Rail had spent most of our walk home on the phone, texting like mad, and not at all paying attention to the people around us.

"Want to play a little?" I nodded at the parade up ahead that was just about to start.

"Oh, God, you make life so much fun." She laughed, and we continued our lazy walk past our street and into the sea of half-naked men. We dove behind a float, and I pulled my phone out and hit record.

A chick with giant tits stuck them in Rail's face and waited for him to glance up. When he did, his eyes bulged out, and he grinned, clearly interested.

Poor Rail didn't have a chance in hell to understand what was happening before she grabbed his neck and plunged her tongue in his mouth.

"Holy shit." Minnie nearly pissed herself. "It's like a train wreck. I can't look away."

I could barely hold the phone upright, I was laughing so hard. He was going to kill us dead.

The chick let him go, and he looked up, dazed, until she spoke, and he noticed the Adam's apple.

"Wait." He backed up and looked around. "What the hell?" He immediately spotted us, and to my utter shock, he smiled and muttered something to her.

"Come here!" he shouted, and we bolted for the clubhouse.

"Run!" Minnie grabbed my arm, and we dodged traffic as we whisked across the street and flew into the clubhouse.

"Brick!" I shouted as he came out of Trigger's office. "Catch!" I tossed him my phone as Rail's body slammed me to the ground.

I rolled around, trying to catch my breath while I laughed. With all the heaviness the club had been through the last few months, it felt amazing to laugh all the stress free from my insides.

"Wait," Brick's face broke out into a confused smile, "isn't that a fuckin'…"

"Man? Yup." I shoved Rail's shoulder when he went to cover my mouth. "Tongue and all."

"It explains so much." He glanced at Rail, who was sweating but made one last attempt to grab the phone from Brick.

"Fuck you, Brick."

A set of boots stopped near my head, and Trigger stared down at me. "Having fun?"

"The best." I kept my composure.

"Rail, get ready. We leave in twenty."

He hopped to his feet, but not before he glared at me.

"Oh, wait," I sat up, "you've got a little something right there." I pointed to the corner of my mouth, pretending he had lipstick on his lip.

"I hope you trip and fall in that dress."

"I bet you do." I winked and took Trigger's hand to help me the rest of the way up.

***

Allen

"Two, four, six." I counted the bundles as the three men and Zay piled them into the back of the van. We had a buyer who was willing to take it all, but at a discounted price. I didn't give a shit. My plan was to fire one in his head and rob him blind, anyway.

I just needed to have enough money to give the green light to the men I hired to blow up the Devil's Reach. Everything came with a cost.

The sun beat down on my shoulders. I wanted to remove my jacket, but we'd had some unexpected guests twice today already. People really needed to find a hobby. I still took pleasure in their adoration and wondered if I wasn't meant to be a prophet in another life.

When the last brick was packed, and my dear weasels were safely tucked in, I tossed them a little treat and enjoyed their squeals as they fought over the tidbit. I threw my bag inside and slammed the doors shut.

Zay drove, and the three other men I had recruited to grab the cocaine squeezed in the back while I took the front.

"This will be a life changer for us, boys!" I slapped Zay on the shoulder as he pulled out of the dusty driveway. Well, for me, but they didn't need to know that.

I leaned my head against the headrest and closed my eyes.

"I won't lie, you're the last person I thought would call on a Tuesday morning." I settled in at the back of the bar. I was pleased with the location, but I had two men outside, and Zay was in view if I needed someone to step in. One could never be too careful.

"It seems you and I have similar interests." She jumped right in and fiddled with the light blue scarf that hung loosely around her neck.

"Oh?"

"Yes, we're both after the same thing."

"I'm afraid you're going to have to be a bit more specific, here."

She leaned forward and gave me a familiar glare. "Look, I don't want to screw around here and waste anyone's time, so I'm going to cut to the facts."

"You have my attention."

"I want the flash drive, and so do you. I have some unfinished business that needs to be taken care of, and by the looks of things, so do you. I know your copy got destroyed, and I know she *has a copy.*

"And you know this, how?"

"I know a lot more than most think."

"So, what do you believe is on it?"

She closed her eyes and sank back in her chair. "Look, Allen, I might look like a billionaire's wife, but I built my business from the ground up, and I removed more than a few who got in my way. If you want to ignore me, that's fine, or we can work out some kind of deal and get back what's rightfully ours."

"Interesting use of the word 'ours.'"

"Who do you think gave him the idea to start blackmailing high-profile people? He sure as hell wouldn't have come up with it on his own."

"Okay, so, what's the deal?"

She leaned in, and her eyes flashed with rage. "Kill anyone who gets in our way."

"What about..."

"Anyone," she reiterated.

I thought about it for a moment and let myself get excited. Oh, how the plot thickened.

"You want to team up with me and get it back?"

"Yes."

I rose from my chair and thought for a moment. It could be a trap, or she could be an asset. Life was like Russian roulette sometimes. You just needed to be in or out.

"You have a deal, Felicia."

My eyes opened once we hit the dirt road. The afternoon sun was low on the horizon, and the excitement for what was to come bubbled through my core.

Zay flipped the sun visor down and squinted ahead at the airplane hangar in the distance. I hit the back of the seat to get the men behind us to wake the fuck up.

"Ready, boys?" I tugged on my collar to make sure it sat perfectly straight. There was nothing better than these high-tension deals. I liked to watch their expressions when I'd step out of the van. I loved that moment of discomfort and uncertainty. I would always act quickly to twist it in my favor by taking charge of the situation first. Once you established who was in control, the rest typically fell into place. I couldn't help a small smile. Soon my son would feel my wrath.

"One, two, three," Zay counted the men he could see. "Five on the left, and one on the tip of the wing."

"They're not going to come alone." I sighed. I really wished he'd relax. This was going to be easy. We were in the middle of nowhere and had the upper hand. We had the drugs they wanted and enough ammo to take out a small community, not to mention three expendables in the back seat.

"I don't like this."

I rolled my eyes and reached for the bottle of Jack I had in my bag, "As soon as this is over, we can buy three women who look exactly like that bitch you seem to care about so much."

He shot me a look then shifted his eyes back to the road, and I rubbed my hands together as the power started to prickle the tips of my fingers. Once Zay slammed the van into park, I felt almost giddy.

Showtime!

I kicked open the door, tugged my jacket into place, and slapped on one hell of a grin.

"Gentlemen," I raised my hands in greeting, "shall we do some business?"

The hangar had a layer of dust over everything except the silver bullet Eclipse 550 aircraft.

Shit, she was beautiful. The plane was just under three million and worth every penny. They had good taste.

The man dressed in a suit and tie checked his watch before he stood and stepped behind a steel table. I assumed this was the man I had been dealing with over the phone.

"Mr. Bellium?" I held out my hand, but he didn't make a move toward it. I slowly dropped it and stood still. It was a battle of the alphas.

"Check them," he ordered, and two men hurried over, stuck rifles in my men's faces, and told them to raise their arms while they removed their weapons. One stepped in front of me and tapped my arms so I'd do the same. I glared at him, but I wanted to show I would cooperate. He removed both of my guns, dropped the clips, and tossed the rest on the table in front of Bellium.

Once they went back to their posts, I smirked. "Now it's your turn." I nodded at his gun sticking out of his waistband.

"No," he simply said.

I sucked in my bottom lip and tried not to lash out. If I wanted this deal to happen my way, I knew I would have to let him think he had the power.

"Can we get started, or do we need to draw blood next?" I dripped with sarcasm.

A long smirk raced across his mouth from one corner to the other.

"Interesting choice of words, Mr. Vineyard."

I cocked my head to the side. *How did he know my real name?*

"You did your homework, I see."

"Indeed." He undid the buttons on the front of his suit and shrugged off his jacket to hand to one of his men. The man waited a beat and huffed something I couldn't make out, then he hung it over the back of his chair.

If one of my men hesitated and disrespected me in front of a client like that, I would have shot him straight between the eyes.

"All right, then, let's do business." I snapped my fingers and heard the double doors open on the van. Brick by brick, the cocaine was carried to the table and stacked in rows.

After the last one was placed, I stepped back and waited for him to take a sample.

To my surprised, he didn't. He just stood there.

"Are you one of the few men who trusts the word of another?" I tried to see what the hell was going through his head.

"I'd never trust a man who portrays the Lord by day and the devil by night."

I smiled my confusion at how well he knew me. "Have we met before?"

"No, but he has." He nodded over my shoulder, and a slow chill raced up the back of my neck and over my skull as I turned and met the eyes of my son.

Fuck me.

CHAPTER TWENTY-ONE

Trigger

I stood tall while I lit my joint and squinted as the smoke consumed my lungs then broke free past my lips. I'd waited a lifetime to do this the right way, and now, standing fifteen feet away was the man who had carved me into the monster I was today.

His eyes searched mine before he swallowed and rubbed his fingers together.

"I wondered when I'd see you again, son." He tried to smile, but his confusion got the better of him.

Morgan stepped into the light with his rifle over his shoulder. Tristen followed, and Brick joined my other side.

My father looked around and back to me. "Seems I'm at a disadvantage here. Shall we make it an even playing field?" He went for his weapon on the table, but Rail pointed a gun to his head.

"Okay, okay." He raised his hands.

I held his gaze for another beat before I switched my sight over to the "buyer."

"Cray?"

"Every last brick is accounted for, boss."

My father's face dropped as he made the connection that the buyer was one of my men.

"You're not the only one who can mislead people." I stepped forward and tossed my gun on the table. "Rail, go get them," I ordered, and he walked by me and out to the back of Allen's truck.

"Okay, now, guys," his face twisted into a look I knew all too well, "let's take a moment and discuss this." I moved to stand directly in front of him, and he puffed up his chest like he used to when he wanted to intimidate me. "I have money now. Think of the possibilities."

I slammed my fist into his face and knocked him straight off his feet. He fell to the ground hard but quickly scrambled to his feet.

My father was a dirty fighter, but a fighter nonetheless. He could take a few good cracks to the head before he'd stay down.

"Still have a killer right hook."

"That was my left," I corrected and seethed with anger. "Is that how you bribed Joe?" I snarled.

"Not hard to flip a simple-minded doorman." He smiled and wiped his lip clear of blood. "Maybe you should treat your men better, and you wouldn't have so many holes in your club."

"Must have missed that lesson in my upbringing."

He rolled his eyes but tilted his head when something caught his attention.

"My, my, my." His tone changed. "Well, isn't that Clark's beautiful Tessa."

My blood pumped through my neck and vibrated the demon's cages, an alert that my switch could still be flipped at any moment.

Tess stepped to my side, and I shot a look at Ryder. He was supposed to have kept her out of sight, and now he wouldn't make eye contact. *Strike two.*

"Tess," I warned.

"I just wanted to see him one last time." She kept her eyes on my father as she took a step toward him. I reached out and took her arm to hold her back. She turned to me, and I saw her expression. Her jaw was locked in place, and her eyes burned fire. *Tigress.* I let my fingers relax and released her.

She headed for the table and ran fingertips over the grooves of a gun. Her shoulders were relaxed, and her movements fluid and slow. I could almost hear the dark thoughts that raced through her head. I carried that same look whenever someone needed to die.

Slowly, she stopped and seemed to have made a decision. She snatched up a wrench, whirled around, and smoked Allen on the outside of his kneecap. He jolted sideways as he screamed in pain while he tried unsuccessfully to remain on his feet. He dragged himself to the table and held on for balance.

"Son of bitch!" he screamed as foam flew from his mouth.

Tess dropped the wrench on a fuel barrel and stood in front of him.

"That was for Gus." With that, she came and stood behind me.

I looked over at Zay. He had remained quiet while this was all going down, watching Tess from his post near the door. When he caught my gaze, he stood a little straighter and raised his head.

A challenge?

"You like what you see?" I asked and walked over. Morgan followed a few feet behind.

I licked the inside of my mouth to ease the rage that consumed me. This piece of shit needed to be put in his place. I knew he wanted Tess.

"It's not what you think." He squared his shoulders, but his words didn't match his posture.

"I don't really care." I reached over, took his head between my hands, and to my surprise, he allowed it.

But just as I was about to snap his neck, he spoke. "That's very Cain and Abel of you."

"What?"

"Stop!" a familiar voice said sharply, and a moment later, she showed herself.

My fingers dug hard into Zay's head. What the fuck was going on?

"Lovely," Allen muttered. "I didn't know we were having a family reunion. Zay, feel free to handle this."

"What are you doing here?" I glared at my mother. She seemed to be a little less weak than she had been before.

"I failed you years ago, Nolan. I wasn't about to do it again." She glanced over at Allen while I tried to connect the dots. "You've been nothing but a monster, Allen, and when I heard what you were up to, I played you at your own game."

"Meaning?" I grew annoyed. I hated surprises at the best of times, and right now it interfered with me killing my father.

"Meaning," she turned to face me, "Nolan, meet your brother." She pointed at Zay, but I didn't follow her line of sight. Instead, I saw Tess shake her head like she was as lost as I was.

"Half-brother," Zay clarified. "You can let go now." He pushed my hands away. "I've been the eyes and ears for our mother, feeding her information to help stay ahead of Allen."

My head felt like it might spin right off. I stepped back as my mother joined my side.

"I'll fill in the blanks later, but right now, you have something more pressing to deal with."

Allen let out a hiss and tried to stand without the help of the table as

I moved my attention over to him again. The demons screamed, and the rage came roaring back.

"You traitorous shit!" Allen hissed at Zay. "I should have known better. I should have let you become someone's bitch in the shower. "

"You mean that fake proof you had?" Zay fixed his jacket. "Like I'd be stupid enough to let someone film me."

Allan fell as he tried to take a step toward Zay.

Enough! This was my fight!

"For years, I feared you," I said loud enough for all to hear. "For years, I feared I'd be like you. Until the day I got a knife to the back and found you at the other end of it. You turned my fear into fuel, and without hesitation, I returned your kindness." I frowned slightly and remembered my disappointment when his limp body was carried away last time. "I was almost sad it had ended so quickly. I really didn't feel like I got my revenge."

"Well, here we are." He held open his arms and hobbled a couple of steps.

"Yes, and here we are." I waited a beat to savor the moment.

"So, kill me!"

I kicked his feet out from under him and drove my fist into his gut. He shot up against the van and heaved to catch his breath. His eyes watered, and his hands raced around his midsection to find a way to ease the pain.

I lowered myself to just above his eye level and whispered for only him to hear. "The difference between then and now is I saw an opportunity and took it. Sometimes the best revenge is the one you never see coming."

"What?" He gasped as two sets of boots appeared on either side of me. I stood and stepped back while three more cartel men took my place.

"We seem to have a problem here, Mr. Vineyard." Bruno dropped the picture of Zay wearing a DR cut on Allen's lap.

I grabbed Tess by the arm and turned her around while the hungry weasels squealed as they awaited their next victim. Like my father, the weasels had no loyalty.

Just before we hit the cool night air, I heard the screams and felt my own demons race across the desert floor and join in on the kill.

"I can't believe you didn't kill him yourself," Tess huffed as I helped her onto my bike. "He was right there for the taking."

"A year ago, I would have dragged his sorry body to the slaughter room, but now they owe me." I nodded to the cartel outside guarding the hanger. "I gained a debt, and that's more valuable."

"Ah," she gave me a knowing smile, "growth."

I supposed so.

She leaned up and kissed me hard. I started my bike, waited for her arms to wrap around me, and we took off toward home.

I never once looked back. I was finally free.

***

It had been a long time since the club had enjoyed a real party free of worry. A level of lightness was felt by all as the endless bottles of whiskey and rum where passed around. Ryder had recruited three more prospects who seemed to fit in well. It was good to see my club numbers grow again.

"Congrats, you old bastard." Brick slapped Morgan on the shoulder.

"I wear it with honor." He gave me a tight nod. It had been hard to convince Morgan to take over the position of Sergeant at Arms. I assured him Gus wouldn't have wanted it any other way.

Rail bumped into Morgan as he made out with some redheaded chick. She threw me a cocky grin and made me laugh. She looked familiar, then I remembered it was that wild little number from Strokes.

"Have you seen the women here?" His words were slurred. "We're outnumbered."

I grabbed his bottle of whiskey and downed the rest. I searched the sea of bodies and spotted her by my pickup.

Fuck me.

"You sure Tess didn't send that one?" Brick laughed.

"Fuck you." Rail punched his arm. "She got me so messed up I always check the throat. That one sure doesn't have a lump. Believe me, any she's got are all in the right places."

"I don't know, Rail." Morgan joined in. "You never can tell."

"Chicks with dicks, man. Stay away." Brick ducked the fist that came at his head.

"Trigger?" My mother stepped out of the crowd. "Can we speak?"

I noticed Zay was back against the door, looking as uneasy as shit. I nodded at her to follow me. We headed into my office, and he followed suit.

"I'm sorry I didn't tell you what I was up to. Truthfully, I didn't think you'd allow it."

"Nope."

She sighed. "Just let me explain, then you can kick us to the curb, so to speak."

I waved for her to continue.

"I'll keep it short. I had Zay six years after I had you. I was in a better position then." She rubbed her neck uneasily. "He's not a saint, Lord knows that, but when he answered a call one night to do a hit, I heard the voice on the other end of the phone, and it chilled my soul. I knew it was him, and I told Zay. He met up with him. He was all dressed to impress and wanting to do a hit on a member of the cartel. We kept an eye on him, following him, and soon learned what his real motives were."

"Gus was poking around a long time ago," Zay spoke up, "lookin' for her." He nodded at my mother. "Word spread quickly that Allen was back from the dead and looking to build an army to take down Devil's Reach. So, one thing led to another, and we embedded me into his life."

"Why?" I found this all very hard to believe.

"We'll call it an opportunity."

"Meaning?" I folded my arms.

"Meaning," my mother stepped closer, "I had one last chance to do right by you, Nolan. Zay agreed to do this. All he wants in return is a place at your table."

I shook my head and ran my hand down my beard.

"How nice of you to let him think I'd ever consider that." I dripped with sarcasm.

"Look," her tone sharpened, "you can be pissed off all you want, but I'm a fighter too, and I don't have a lot of time. If this is what it takes to bring you two together before I'm six feet under, then so fucking be it."

I glanced at Zay, who smirked with a shrug. "She's a lot feistier than she lets on."

I pushed off my desk and thought for a moment. I never saw this coming, but it was shoved in my face, and I needed to sort it out. The party was getting louder and drew my attention to the fact that devil was finally gone, and I apparently had gained not only a mother but a brother.

I looked at him intently; his face was unreadable.

Fuck.

"I'll find a room for you tomorrow. We'll hash out the rest of the shit another time." I put Rail's bottle on the desk before I chucked it at someone and moved toward the door. I needed to get the hell out of there before I changed my mind.

I pushed through the back doors and let that shit stay inside. It was time to party. Fuck knew I deserved that much.

Rail was already back on the hunt for his little redhead. I moved past them and over to Tess. She had on a tight black leather dress, and when she turned to let someone pass, I saw the back, and my dick stood to attention. Crisscrossed down her back was a thin biker chain that held the fabric in place.

She had never looked sexier.

She pivoted on her studded heel when she saw Minnie point over her shoulder. A big smile spread across her lips and lit up her eyes.

"Hi. You like?" She bit her lip, and my erection twitched.

"Tray!" I shouted above the music.

He was next to me in three beats.

"Now."

He whistled for everyone to shut the fuck up before he looked down and thought for a moment.

"Nothing traditional, Tray," Morgan yelled. "We keep it short and sweet."

Tray nodded and stepped up to us. "I had the privilege to get ordained in prison, and now I have the privilege of standing here in front of you two to tie you together forever."

"I said short," Morgan joked.

Tray held up a hand like he got it. "Nolan Vineyard, do you take Tess Marin to be yours today, tomorrow, and forever?"

"Yeah."

"Tess, the same shit goes for you?"

"Yes." She gave me a wink.

"With the power of some dusty church in prison, I can now say…you're married."

The entire place blew up with cheers, bottles breaking, and gunshots into the air.

I grabbed Tess by the waist and slammed her against me and kissed her with every single part of me.

The party lasted well into the night. Tess toyed with my patience because she wanted to stay, and all I wanted to do was have her naked beneath me. She assured me she was mine to do whatever with as soon as the place died down.

"Brick." I signaled for him to step away from the group.

"What do you need, boss?"

I handed him a piece of paper with an address scribbled on it. "I don't know much, because it's not my shit to know, but he's alive and working in Washington. He goes by a different last name now, Wilson."

Brick studied the paperwork for a few beats before he glanced at me with a complex expression. His eyebrows were pinched together, and his mouth twisted as he thought.

"Follow the lead or don't, just couldn't sit on it any longer."

"Right, thanks."

"Yeah." I slapped his shoulder before he wove through the crowd and disappeared. I understood that feeling all too well, and I wasn't sure if I liked that I was the one who just dropped my VP in some unwanted shit, but it was something he deserved to know. I knew Brick had never met his father, but he was a good man. So, if he decided to find his brother, I'd back him.

Some guy body-slammed me. His face fell when he saw who I was. I pushed him into the wall, and he bounced off and into the pool. Jackass.

Mike: Congrats, man. Well deserved.

I tucked my phone away and found Tess and Minnie doing shots with Morgan. I knew she would have liked to have had Savannah and Mike here, but there was a line we didn't cross. We might be acquaintances—friends, even—but our worlds operated very differently.

The chatter got to be too much for me, so I moved away.

I sat on the seat of my pickup, door open and feet on the ground, arms resting on my knees. The little purr that came from behind me soon showed herself. Now that she was bigger, she had moved into the cab of the truck. She squeezed under my arm and onto my lap.

"Too loud for ya?" I rubbed her ear, and she yawned and settled in. I wasn't an animal person, but this little shit had grown on me.

"Hey! What the fuck do you think you're doing?" I heard Rail shout behind the gate. I set the cat down on the passenger seat and started to make my way over to him.

I swung open the gate to find Rail and Denton kicking the shit out of a Stripe Back. I reached over and hauled Denton back as he pulled his boot back and was about to kick the man's face in.

"What the—" Denton went to swing but stopped short when he saw it was me. "This dick was about to crash the party!"

"Get rid of him," I ordered Rail.

Denton tried to wiggle out of my hold. "Come on, Uncle T. Let me have one last swing at him." His face was red and sweaty, and his eyes held a familiar gleam.

"Not yet." I waited for him to calm down before I released his arm. He fought to fix his shirt and wiped his forehead on his shirtsleeve. Denton was scrappy, and I admired that. "Your time will come."

We watched as Rail stuffed the man into the back of the weapons van. He'd be dumped later.

Denton slowly lifted his head to look at me, and the dark promise that raced through his expression and lit his eyes proved my opinion was right about him.

He would take my seat at the head of the table someday, after I made this club something he could be proud of.

***

Tess

"Come on." I hopped off the bike and motioned for him to follow.

"You promised me a night of you beneath me," he muttered darkly.

I took his hand and pulled him to follow me. "Trigger, you can have as many nights as you want, but on this one night, this is important to me, so shut up and come."

"I would love to," he grunted, and I laughed.

With my bag over my shoulder, I hit the button, and the elevator rose. When the doors opened, we were met with the cool night air and a sky full of stars.

It was exactly what I hoped for, and as I looked around, I saw Minnie had done a great job.

A few candles were lit along the edge of the stone rail, a bed was set up across from us in the corner, and my favorite part was right where it needed to be.

"Night's looking up." He smiled at the bed.

I twisted and removed his shirt then pulled back his hair and studied his face.

"Will you do something for me? Don't say anything until I've finished my story."

He nodded.

"Okay, well, when I moved here, Brick got me the place right over there." I pointed, but he didn't look. He kept his intense gaze on me. "I was reading my book and heard this noise over and over again. I went to my window and saw a man. He seemed almost to be dancing. He was punching a bag—in perfect form, I might add. I grabbed my camera and snapped this photo." I held it up for him to see. "I called you my rooftop boxer. I was intrigued by you, and when I met *Trigger* at the bar, I almost felt conflicted on who I wanted to know more. It wasn't until Minnie and I were in the desert that I shared this story, and she told me it was you."

He kept looking intently at me as I rushed on. I wanted him to hear it all. "My point to this story is you have many different sides to you, Trigger, the good, the bad, *and* the flip, and no matter where you are inside this head of yours, know I will always be there to bring you back." He smiled, but a real smile—one I hadn't seen in a very long time, if ever.

"I love you," I whispered through the unwanted emotion that flooded me.

He kept his eyes on me as his chest rose and fell. I wondered if I had gone a little too far with my story, but as I went to step back, he grabbed my arms and closed his eyes.

His fingers inched down and found mine, and something cold and smooth slipped over my ring finger.

"I hate traditional shit, but you deserve one."

I swallowed the lump that formed in my throat. A simple black band that matched my engagement ring shone in the low light.

"You're better with words than I am, but I heard every single damn word you said." He pressed his lips to my forehead. "I never thought a woman could free me from my hell." His arm pressed into mine to reference the tattoo.

"Okay." I waved off the sappy moment that became too much for me. "Now…" I grabbed a bottle of champagne, popped the cork, and hopped up on the ledge. "Go!"

He chuckled and stood in front of the bag and started to punch the leather.

Christ, he was sexy.

***

"You're married," Minnie repeated for the third time as we left the store, and I balanced the brown paper bag in my arms. "I mean, shit, Trigger is married." She laughed. "I think this will take me a little time to get used to. What I wouldn't have done to see Peggy's lipstick-stained teeth as she sobbed at your wedding."

"I sent her an invite," I confessed.

"You had invites?" Her face twisted in disgust.

"No, just for her."

"Oh, shit, that's great!" She hit me on the shoulder, and I bumped into someone.

"Sorry!" I fumbled with my bags so they wouldn't spill. A hand came up and steadied my arm, and I was greeted with a friendly smile.

"It was my fault. I was on my phone." He took his hand from my arm, as my bags were now safe, and I saw his uniform. "Don't tell, okay?" He winked and patted his police badge. His name tag read "O'Brian."

"I won't, Officer O'Brian, but here comes your friend."

"Garrett!" a cop in the same color uniform called from across the street and waved. "We gotta go."

"Have a nice day, ladies." Hc gave a smile before he quickly jaywalked across the road.

"Don't tell Brick, but shit, I love a man in uniform."

I nodded in appreciation and watched him meet up with his friend. "You're not alone in that thought, Minnie."

"Whatcha lookin' at?" Fin broke our moment.

"Nothing," we said in unison.

"Where's Rail?" I looked around and wondered where the hell he was.

"I waited for him to have a smoke, then I ran off." He laughed. "Old shit can't keep up."

I pushed him forward, and we made our way into the club. I heard Trigger's bike start up out back, and I dropped my stuff off at bar and sent Fin to help Minnie then hurried outside.

"Where were you?" One of his hands fell on his lap where my eyes were drawn to his erection. His gaze was hungry.

"Out for groceries."

"Where you headed?"

"Gonna go for a ride, check out some new bikers in town."

I felt the rush of excitement. Nothing like the possibility of trouble to fuel the fire inside.

He smirked as if he could read my mind. "Come on." He tossed my helmet and jacket at me.

I flipped my hair back and pulled the helmet on. He tugged me forward and ran his hand down my hip.

"Damn, you look good in leather." He nodded for me to hop on then revved the engine to alert the guys we were leaving.

They hit their bikes, and we headed out and quickly moved into formation. I loved the way we looked, everyone in their spot by rank. We might be ruthless, but we were a family, and respect was strong throughout the club.

Once we were on the Pacific Coast Highway and the sun was at our backs, I clicked on the mic.

"So, now what?" I squirmed with excitement and flexed my fingers on his erection.

"Now we sit back and enjoy the power."

Ah, yes, the beauty of owning the key to the skeletons in the closet and owning two strip joints and a brothel.

"Whatever will we do with all the free time?" I teased.

He reached back and squeezed my thigh. "I can only think of one thing."

I laughed, hugged my legs to his, and leaned back as far as I could go. The hot sun beat down on my shoulders, and I felt the wind flow up through the bottom of the helmet.

Trigger checked his mirror before he hit his mic. "We're finally free, baby."

The End

Trigger

Won't break, whatever the cost
Time is moving, feeling lost
Can't go on, can't stay behind
In you, rest I find
Silence the demons, you hold them back
Calm the chaos and ease the storm
Even the ones that run and swarm
Once was dark, now is bright
You hold the key to my light

I want you, you want me
Give up and let this shit be
Time to move on, struggle past
Spark the fire, burns so fast

Silence the demons, you hold them back
Calm the chaos and ease the storm
Even the ones that run and swarm
Once was dark, now is bright
You hold the key to my light

Hop on and hold on tight
Ride away our worries into the night
Dark I'll always be
But you'll be my light for eternity

Silence the demons, you hold them back
Calm the chaos and ease the storm
Even the ones that run and swarm
Once was dark, now is bright
You hold the key to my light

About the Author

J. L. Drake was born and raised in Nova Scotia, Canada, later moving to Southern California where she now lives with her husband and two children.

When she is not writing she loves to spend time with her family, travelling or just enjoying a night at home. One thing you might notice in her books is her love of the four seasons. Growing up on the east coast of Canada the change in the seasons is in her blood and is often mentioned in her writing.

An avid reader of James Patterson, J.L. Drake has often found herself inspired by his many stories of mystery and intrigue. She hopes you will enjoy her books as much as she has enjoyed writing them.

Facebook:
https://www.facebook.com/JLDrakeauthor

Twitter:
https://twitter.com/jodildrake_j

Website:
http://www.authorjldrake.com/

Goodreads:
http://www.goodreads.com/author/show/8300313.J_L_Drake

25737606R00421

Printed in Great Britain
by Amazon